THE OFFI

ZINA ROHAN worked for
writing fiction in her spare time....
lives in London. Her two previous novels are *The Book of Wishes and Complaints* which won the Authors' Club First Novel Award and was shortlisted for the David Higham Prize for Fiction, and *The Sandbeetle*.

From the reviews of *The Officer's Daughter*

'This big, boisterous adventure novel is a spirited coming-of-age story and an irresistible romantic epic.' **Saga Magazine**

'*The Officer's Daughter* is a gem... a haunting quality saturates the story, a rawness reminiscent of *A Thousand Splendid Suns*, and like Khaled Hosseini's novel, it leaves you with a deeply felt sense of the powerlessness and arbitrariness of life adrift on the detritus of war. Part of this is due no doubt to the fact that at its core is a story wrapped around real people, which lends it a rare power and authenticity that lingers after the last page.' **Bookseller**

'This good, old-fashioned tale cries out for a screen adaptation.' **The Tablet**

'Rohan's work is quite simply fascinating, wholly gripping and a delight to read. We award Zina ten Bookmunch points.' **Bookmunch**

'An involving and sweeping novel... epic.' **The Lady**

From the reviews of *The Book of Wishes and Complaints*

'Zina Rohan's first novel is clever and warm – a convincing portrayal of human hopes and dreams... A beautifully portrayed comedy of everyday human failure... Rohan shares Kundera's piercing sense of irony but adds her own brand of warmth and humanity… From start to finish *The Book of Wishes and Complaints* is a novel of admirable wit and clarity.' **Times Literary Supplement**

'Rohan has a wonderful, often comic instinct for the everyday, the kind of domestic detail that tells us everything.' **Independent on Sunday**

'Zina Rohan writes with style and wit. This is an amusing first novel, where west tries to go east and east west, and both get hopelessly lost on the way.' **The Times**

'The emotions are all described with unnerving clarity and you become totally involved with Hana's dilemmas… Cleverly, Rohan denies us the Hollywood happy ending, offering us a question mark instead. A compelling first novel.' **Time Out**

'Zina Rohan's quiet understatement says more about ordinary, unheroic lives than many more overtly political books.' **Sunday Times**

From the reviews of *The Sandbeetle*

'Rohan handles her material well, without sensationalism or sentimentality. Her clear, clean prose packs a cumulative punch… It is a good story well told.' **Guardian**

'Rohan is a teller of tales able to span years with one sharply etched scene, to hold her reader to events even while she is lifting them across the arc of a fable about pain and the heartless necessities of living.' **Independent on Sunday**

'There is a quiet, trenchant elegance to Zina Rohan's prose which, together with a lurking sense of irony, strikes a rich, dynamic balance between coolness and warmth, darkness and light, comedy and outrage… Her astute compassion, her refusal either to judge or offer pat solutions, combine with a consummate storytelling skill to produce a novel which rewards you more the further you read.' **Scotsman**

THE OFFICER'S DAUGHTER

Zina Rohan

Portobello
BOOKS

First published by Portobello Books Ltd 2007
This paperback edition published 2008

Portobello Books Ltd
Eardley House
4 Uxbridge Street
Notting Hill Gate
London W8 7SY, UK

A CIP catalogue record is available from the British Library

2 4 6 8 9 7 5 3 1

ISBN 978 1 84627 068 0

www.portobellobooks.com

Text designed by Patty Rennie
Map designed by Andrew Farmer
Typeset in Columbus by Avon DataSet Ltd, Bidford on Avon, Warwickshire

Printed in the UK by CPI Bookmarque, Croydon, CR0 4TD

For Dula with love, and thanks for the inspiration,
and for Shahpoor, who never asked.

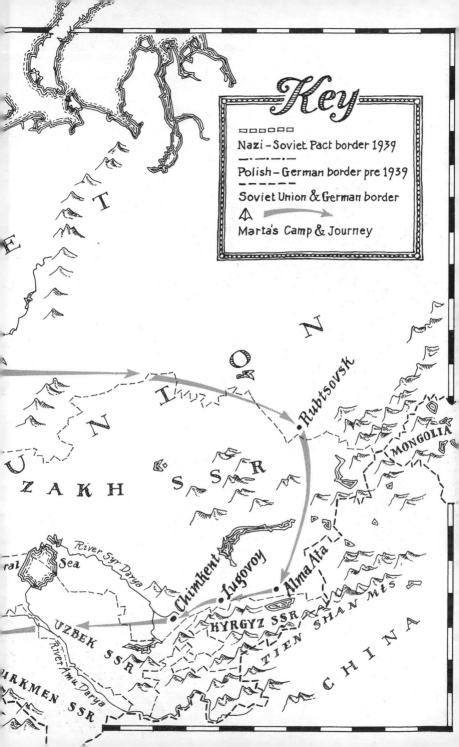

1

1 September 1939 some time before dawn

'Get out there now. Round those girls up and bring them back!'

The young second lieutenant has never been ordered to ride through the night before, and never so fast. It was a matter of luck, his colonel said, that anyone knew there were youngsters out there at all – Girl Guides, on their own and probably unaware. Obviously they've got to be escorted out of harm's way, but in the scheme of things it's a distraction and a nuisance. Almost comical, though. A war begins and your first active duty is galloping down a country track looking for a band of girls who are camping at the frontier as some sort of patriotic gesture. Everybody's a patriot, but if only young women would keep to where they're most useful.

Ahead he picks out the line of the river and, blocking it, the dark humps that must be their tents. The ground is damp under the horse's hooves from yesterday evening's sudden rainstorm and there are still clouds intermittently blanking the moon. People are about, shapes moving between the tents. The nearest pair look like an adult and a child. Can that be right? But as he gets nearer he sees that both are girls, one very much taller than the other. Talk to the taller one: she's probably older, and in charge. For a second he has the impression she saluted him, in full military style.

'Miss!' he snaps. 'You young ladies must pack up and get to the station right away. There's going to be trouble and you'll have heard the planes. They weren't ours. Tell your friends to get going. Leave everything except what you can carry, leave the tents, everything, do you

1

hear, and follow me quickly. You're to get out, you're to get the train. The Germans are coming. They're on their way.'

'But if we leave the tents the Germans will take them and use them,' says this girl, arguing, answering back.

If you waste any time they're more likely to take and use you, he thinks, but dubs it crude and holds his tongue. There's always one awkward character who quibbles when they should be obeying. She's a big girl, this one, all the ins and outs in the right places, and in the light of his torch her eyes are like great green lanterns. But she's looking at him as if she's read his mind, and he flushes. Then he has work to do. As he swings his horse away he hears the other girl giggle: 'Oh, Marta. Shush!'

The day before

'Marta, we can't. That's not what they said to do.'

'Maybe not. But they didn't know what we do. They didn't see what we can.'

Best friends, Marta Dolniak and Ania Dorosz, both sixteen, both Girl Guides. Along with eighteen others they've spent the past fortnight in the most western region of their country, pitching their tents in the afternoon, striking them again the following morning, hiking from one Polish village to the next, all to give backbone to the local peasants. Germany is just across the way, a Germany poised for war, as everyone knows, and the peasants, the parent generation, are scared witless because all the burly sons are away on exercises.

Until this afternoon it was all going to plan. But then the Guides' marching column – with Marta in the lead, where you will always find her – rounds a bend of the tiny river that traces the German–Polish frontier. To their left is a meadow where the hay has been set to dry over small wooden frames, and further back they can pick out the low roofs of the village houses. To their right, beyond the opposite bank, is a similar meadow, identical you'd say, except that over there a dozen adolescent boys from the Hitler Youth have already set up a camp of their own. To Marta those tightly erected German tents are a gauntlet thrown at her feet. She turns on her heel and addresses her companions. They are going to sing, she announces, not to ginger up the peasantry. They are going to sing those cowardly Germans into the ground. But first they must set up camp.

Today, as never before, they're lucky that Marta is as assured as a soldier in manipulating tents. They are grateful to her for that, and for the fact that she can distinguish grass snakes from venomous ones and is always the first to wade into a stream to gauge its depth. Every group needs a leader, and they really don't mind she's decided it's to be her. She is the tallest, after all, and the loudest.

They can all hear the jeering and whistling coming from the opposite bank. Whether it's because they are girls, or Poles, or both, isn't clear, but what these Hitler Youth don't understand is that the more they hoot the greater is Marta's determination to face them off. Her companions know this. In particular Ania knows this, and only hopes that the Guides' singing, when it comes, will not provoke those boys to wade across and start throwing punches. Not everyone is like Marta, wishing she'd been born a boy so that she could join the army like her brother Gienek. Not everyone has a father who is a professional soldier.

Colonel Marek Dolniak looks round the mess hall at the barracks where he and his regiment have been stationed for the past few weeks. He has an uneasy feeling in the pit of his stomach, like the butterflies of youthful expectation, or perhaps like the premonitory sense animals and birds are said to have before an earthquake. It could be any day now. Any minute now. Like the rest of his countrymen he's known for three years that war is coming, ever since Hitler reoccupied the Rhineland. What has baffled him is how others can fail to see its inevitability. Austria was annexed; Hitler seized Czechoslovakia's Sudetenland, then sauntered into the rest of the country. But Britain and France made the Czechs stand their armies down because the British and the French didn't want another war so soon after the last one. Peace at any price, they kept saying. Colonel Dolniak had listened to the contemptuous response of his country's Foreign

Minister, Colonel Jozef Beck, and approved it. 'We in Poland do not recognize the conception of peace at any price!' he'd said. 'There is only one thing in the life of men, nations and states which is beyond price, and that is honour.' Why can't others see that?

But at least Britain has promised to help Poland, with a formal pact of mutual assistance. And at least the British generals have promised that any German air raids over Poland will be matched by raids from the Royal Air Force over Germany, while the French generals have pledged the full weight of their armies across the Maginot Line if Poland is attacked. So perhaps, when it begins, which it must, it won't all go the Germans' way. It's not that Colonel Dolniak wants a war. He's been through two already: the first began in 1914, and he was in one of the legions that Pilsudski put under Austrian command, at a time when Poland wasn't on any map but partitioned between three ailing empires; the second – at last – for the reborn Polish republic, against the Soviet Union in 1920. But after 150 years of occupation twenty years of independence isn't enough for any nation: certainly not for his.

The only thing is, if the attack does come as soon as he fears, he won't have had a chance to say goodbye to his family. Jola, thank God, is a confirmed optimist. He'll worry for her safety, of course, but not for her state of mind. Some of his colleagues have wives who are so prone to panic it makes their work well-nigh impossible. No, it's the children who'll trouble him the most. Now here's a fine piece of hypocrisy. Surely, if he appreciates Jola's ability to keep calm when he's at the front, then he should be able to do the same. But, as he knows himself, it won't be so easy. This time Gienek will be fighting as well, and, although Colonel Dolniak anticipates the danger he himself must face with the normal trepidation, where Gienek is concerned he wonders if he can bear it. Perhaps Jola is so phlegmatic because she hasn't directly experienced battle, and lacks imagination. But that's unkind. He dismisses the thought. Perhaps, though, she's been pretending all these years: such a good actress that he doesn't know her. He dismisses that thought too.

And the girls? What about his girls? Little Sonia, so quiet and studious bending over her homework, but sucking on the end of her plait in a way that drives Jola mad. So affectionate, Sonia his youngest. And quick to notice other people's distress. So kind. But kindness is not at a premium when bombs are dropping and enemy tanks trundle the doors down. The people who come through best are the ones with a flinty sense of self-preservation – precisely the quality that a good upbringing in a good family carefully disciplines young ladies not to have. Has Sonia got what it takes? Never mind. Marta will see to her.

Thinking about his elder daughter, Colonel Dolniak finds himself laughing and shaking his head. She'll throw herself at this war as if it had been laid on for her benefit, just so that she can show her mettle. If ever nature set out to undermine a person's aspirations, his beloved Marta is the example. Someone else might call it malice. He can still remember the tantrums, the shrieks when they finally told her – aged... what was it?... six? seven? – that she could never be a soldier, for all God had given her a soldier's soul. 'But he's put that soul into a girl's body, sweetheart,' he had tried to explain, 'and girls can't be soldiers. I know it's an unfair world but you just have to learn to put up with it.' As if to make things worse, her girl's body turned out more womanly than any of her friends'. A beautiful, curvaceous feminine vessel for the steely-eyed corporal who despised everything to do with womanhood. How she clashed with her mother! How she deliberately drove away first her music teacher, then the dancing teacher! How she contrived to make leaden pastries that even the most doting parent couldn't bring himself to swallow. How she managed to pretend she wasn't afraid of spiders simply in order to be the one to rescue her friends. And what good had it done her, with her growing breasts and the hips that nothing could disguise?

Yes. Tomorrow Marta will be home from the summer camping, and she will take care of Sonia. If he were at home he'd say to her, *Now you'll have to be the man of the family.* She might bridle at that, suspecting him of irony. And of course she'd be right.

*

Marta sniffs at the overcast August air. She can smell *their* wood smoke and *their* coffee quite separately from the dank willow leaves the trees dangle in the stream. She thinks, *You can smell the Germans sweating if you try.* Their uniforms won't help them; their marching and singing won't help them; and, for all his hoarse speeches and glittery eyes, their Hitler won't be able to help them either.

The Girl Guides eye their self-proclaimed conductor currently wearing her most ferocious face. She can be such a bossy-boots sometimes, and thank God there aren't too many people like her. But tonight, their last night, her pressed lips and clenched fists fill them with affection. Even if she's got the most awful voice at least she always knows all the words.

Marta calls her singers to order, raising hooped arms, as a bandsman drummer might, and they push out their chests, shoulders drawn back, and turn to face Germany. They inhale: two, three, four…

'Forward we go to serve you,
Oh Fatherland whom we adore.
The young and the old will guard you
From traitors at the door.'

For their efforts the villagers on this side of the stream, elderly peasant women in scarves and bulky skirts, have ambled out ahead of their men and brought bread and hardboiled eggs wrapped in washed cloths, lumps of sweating cheese and pink sausage. Behind them stumps one of the farmers with a samovar on his back and a bucket for water. He's lit the fire and waited to hear the water boil, keeping time with a spoon chinking on the samovar, his head bobbing to the words everyone knows, grinning to himself in the firelight. You have to hand it to these lassies, for all their city voices and elegant hands, they do make you feel a bit better. Not much, though. A sudden volley from the opposite bank turns his knees to water.

'Auf, hebt unsre Fahnen
In den frischen Morgenwind,
Lasst sie weh'n und mahnen
Die, die müssig sind!
Wo Mauern fallen
Bau'n sich andre vor uns auf
Doch sie weichen alle
Unserem Siegeslauf.'

The Girl Guides surge forward, two, three…

'Let's keep in step together,
Be vigilant, one and all.
May Poland live for ever!
Will be our clarion call.'

On the further bank the Hitler Youth reply with ululating war whoops like Indians circling a wagon train. Marta pictures them, shoulder to shoulder in the dark, jutting out their chins and patting their hands over their mouths. Under cover of the gloom she makes the most obscene gesture she knows, which once got Gienek into trouble and must therefore have value. She wishes the Germans could see her. She wishes her friends could see her, and be shocked and proud all at once. No one sees but the peasant at her elbow, who is now astonished at what city girls have been taught. If it was *his* daughter…

There's a gust of wind. Willow branches crack against one another in belated applause, and it's raining; raining to send both choirs dashing back to their tents. In Germany the young men punch one another in self-congratulation, as well they might, since only last week Germany and the Soviet Union signed a Pact of Non-Aggression, and they know that across the Atlantic the United States Congress has once again said America wants no part of what's to come. So the field will be theirs. They roar and laugh, newly deepened voices still in training.

In Poland, the girls hug each other and hold their faces up to the summer rain, licking the drops that stream onto their lips. The peasant has scorched his hands to bring the samovar under cover of a tent, but he fills the girls' proffered glasses and eyes Marta, who notices that in this enclosed space he stinks.

It must be well after midnight when Marta is woken by something howling like a dog run over by a tram. But it disappears into a thunderclap unlike any she has ever heard. It slams over her tent on and on, shaking the tent, shaking the ground, and even when she covers her ears she can't shut it out. Next to her Ania has rolled herself like a caterpillar into her sleeping-bag and closed the top over her head. Marta can feel the body so close to hers vibrating, shaking. Then the storm passes and the thunder tails away. She waits for the lightning that always comes before, ready to count the kilometres. No lightning. Maybe the freak storm is over.

'I'm going out to see.'

'Marta, don't.'

'Don't be silly. It'll be all right.'

'Wait, then. I'm coming too.'

One by one, Marta first, they crawl out and squint round at their campsite. In the dark everything looks normal. No tents blown away, points of vermilion nesting deep in the ashes of the evening fire. Silence.

The girls shiver.

Then they hear horse's hooves, coming their way at a gallop. Whose horse? Do they stand their ground or make for the tents that only offer protection against the weather? They stand their ground, largely because the rider arrives with such speed. One glance at his uniform, even in the moonlight, tells Marta he is a Polish officer, albeit a junior one.

'Miss!' he gasps. 'You young ladies must pack up and get to the station right away. There's going to be trouble and you'll have heard the planes. They weren't ours. Tell your friends to get going. Leave everything except what you can carry, leave the tents, everything, do you hear, and follow me quickly. You're to get out, you're to get the train. The Germans are coming. They're on their way.'

Horseback gives you height, and height lends authority. From atop his nervy bay the second lieutenant bawls his orders as if to the cavalry, but all around the girls, scrambling from their tents, have been well drilled in their Guide units, and all of them respect the military. The camp is cleared in minutes and suddenly the girls are trotting, two by two, behind the trotting horse, keeping pace with its left–right, following blinded by the dark in its soundtracks. As they reach the road, Marta looks back to the campsite and sees flames burst abruptly from the tents and thinks the Germans are on their heels. Then she recognizes the firelit figure of the peasant moving between the tents with a flaming branch, torching them one by one. *We sang to raise his spirits, and now we're running away.*

2

The column of Girl Guides has found a rhythm, like conscripts with three months' training behind them, leaning left and right, rigid feet click-clacking with their solid-soled shoes on the road that leads to the station. A week ago they bounced from that station in the back of a lorry, bundled together with their laughter and their furled tents, primed with songs to perturb the enemy. But, now that the moment has come, the songs have had to be scrolled away with the sleeping-bags.

Marta trots and seethes. She is not fit. Her fault. Her excuse has been, *If I can't be a soldier why should I run about on route marches like a soldier?* Her breasts are heavy and uncomfortable, not her fault, and her breathing begins to struggle. Yet she will not be the first to plead the need to pause. Through the discomfort she sees a slice of moon sidle from behind the clouds, then, as the clouds amble away, she sees the sweet chestnuts heavy with fruit outlined by moonlight, and the shadows the trotting column casts on the road. She sees ahead of them the low roof of the station building, where a waiting steam-engine coughs acrid breaths into the sky.

But no one is expecting them and the platform is full of soldiers. They seem somehow taller and noisier than the ones Marta has seen on exercises. Where can they have come from, so many and so rapidly, to this unimportant countryside halt? Suddenly she feels she has become a little girl again, playing a game that has turned out not to be a game. Instinctively she reaches out with her hand but when it brushes against Ania's shoulder, and Ania turns with a 'What is it?', she realizes that what she wanted was her mother.

The doors of the Poznan train are open and the soldiers pile in, no room for Girl Guides needing to go home. Then it departs and the Guides are left standing, still in their two-by-twos on the platform. The phone begins a burble in the stationmaster's hut but is answered immediately. They can hear the stationmaster hissing frantically into the instrument. They hold their collective breath to hear him better.

'I don't care what sort of train it is but I need it now... Don't you know how close we are to the frontier here? Don't you know your geography, man?...Well, it's too late for that now. I've got twenty girls here. Twenty young girls, and I'm telling you... yes... no... all right, but now do you hear me?'

The stationmaster bangs down his phone and comes out onto the platform rubbing his face. His stationmaster's hat has slipped to one side but at least he has remembered to put it on.

'There'll be another train in about an hour, my dears. You'd better sit yourselves down while you wait. I'm sorry I don't have any chairs or anything.'

'We're Guides,' says Marta, squaring her shoulders in her uniform. 'We don't need chairs.'

They do, but now cannot admit to it. The platform hardens under their buttocks as the minutes pass. It occurs to Marta that perhaps they might sing again to pass the time but she thinks better of it.

The stationmaster's phone burbles again, and he comes running from somewhere, cursing. He hadn't expected another call and wasn't on hand.

'Yes?... How d'you mean?... Don't be ridiculous... Yes, of course I know it is...Very well. Very well. I'll do what I can.'

This time when he emerges and looks down at the Guides looking up at him, he is covering the bottom of his face with his hands as if there is some blemish there. He speaks through his fingers. Gruffly.

'Change of plan. Problem along the line. You're to go to Wilice straight away. It's not far. It's just not on this line. A few kilometres, that's all. If you set off now you should get there in no time. Anyway, like you said, you're Guides. You'll be used to trekking and the rest of it. Down the road – there, you see?'

By the dim light of the moon he scans the seated forms and picks out the largest. Perhaps she's the oldest, the most responsible. Taking Marta by the arm he raises her to her feet, then, hands on her shoulders, swivels her in the direction he means them to go.

'You get to a little shrine on the left, need to keep your eyes skinned, mind. And just after that there's a turning off to your right. Just keep along that track, you can't miss it. You just keep going till you get there. It's bigger than this, Wilice, so you'll see it well in time.'

They would complain. In other circumstances they would complain, but they have to do their bit, because somewhere their fathers and their brothers are doing theirs. Marta isn't sorry they left their belongings behind in the torched tents. The less they have to carry the better, as far as she's concerned. It's her feet she's worried about.

'Come on, then.'

She grabs Ania and they set off, walking not trotting, and two by two the others fall in behind. Marta pumps her arms as if she's drilling on the parade ground because she knows it keeps you going. It'd help if they could sing now but they mustn't alert the enemy, who could be anywhere in the fields they're passing. Actually, their footsteps are so loud, and so obviously marching, that the German soldiers camouflaged in the farmland may take them for Polish soldiers, and won't know that they have no guns and wouldn't know how to use them anyway. Then what? What will the Germans do then? Will the girls all be arrested and beaten, or tortured, even? People are tortured to make them give information but Marta has no information to give. If she had, she would give it. Now that the reality is so close, she knows she would not be able to hold out. If only she were at home and… But that's no way to think. She must remember what she's here for.

'Look, that's the shrine.'

Thank God for Ania. Every commander needs an adjutant with sharp eyes. Right turn it is, then. She wheels to the right and her men swing after her, Ania beside her almost running because her legs are so short. What a pair they make, tall womanly Marta and little Ania, who looks like someone's baby sister and is flat-chested, lucky thing. The troll and the pixie, the others call them.

'You all right?' she growls to her friend.

'Fine. You?'

'Yes. Well, could be better.'

'But under the circumstances…'

'Oh, under the circumstances, absolutely.'

'Look!'

Ania has spotted the station roof beyond the next field where the track winds round. Marta raises an arm and jabs her hand vigorously ahead to galvanize flagging feet. There's a low cheer in response and she winces.

This time they are expected. A couple of soldiers on the lookout come running down the track to meet them, bouncing with vigour. Another train, so long this time that it extends beyond the length of the platform at both ends. It looks as if it, too, is full but the soldiers bundle them on like so many pieces of luggage, and even hand in bags of bread and cheese. But they are not hungry yet, only glad to be resting, and excited as well as apprehensive. They have never before been allowed out on the roads in the dead of night without a supervising adult. Tonight it was essential. But why should they be given provisions when it's no more than an hour's journey to Poznan, and their beds? Alerted mothers will be up and waiting, making tea, heating soup. They'll have been pulling the eiderdowns off the balconies from their summer airing and stuffing them into their ironed covers, fluffing the pillows to make their brave girls comfy again. Somewhere else, though, their fathers are twitching their jackets into place and pulling on their boots.

As she gets her breath back, Marta thinks of her own father at his unknown posting and a lump of dread scorches her throat as if she has swallowed a potato dumpling straight from the tureen. Then she thinks how odd it is that this fear has only overtaken her now that she can breathe again, that when she was lumbering in file along the road, panting and holding her side, she wasn't thinking about her father at all, or about the danger he might be about to face. How disappointed he would be if he knew! She can picture him so clearly: upright but not stiff, so effortlessly in command. When she was little, she used to dabble her fingertips over the smile-lines at the corners of his eyes, so that he would laugh and the lines would deepen. But if he is disappointed in someone his eyes wander and he fixes his gaze on the top of the doorframe, and smiles slightly but only with his lips. It's a terrible expression, and Marta quails at the memory of it.

The last time wasn't so long ago. Her great-aunt was about to visit, a great-aunt she knew neither of her parents liked, and her mother had announced that Marta must give up her room to the interloper and sleep instead on the sofa. It would mean spring-cleaning her room in preparation, and Marta balked, disdaining housework. So she got up early, left her bed tousled, padded along the corridor and slipped out into the town, telling herself she would pretend she had forgotten today was the day the great-aunt was due and say she had gone to the library to return some books. But while she was sitting in the square in the spring sunshine Gienek came by with a group of his friends. 'You'd better get back on the double,' he whispered, 'or you'll be for it. Mama's tearing her hair. She'll be weeping next.' So Marta had to hurry home, and she found her father, on his hands and knees, cleaning the floor round her bed. 'Oh, Tata!' she cried. 'I'm so sorry. I forgot it was today. Let me do that.' But her father glanced up, looked past her to the doorframe, smiled his awful smile and said quietly, 'I wouldn't dream of having you do what is clearly beneath you.' And he pushed her gently out of her own room, closed the door in her face, locked it, and didn't open it again until the room was in perfect order.

Remembering it, Marta flushes hot and her hands feel as clammy as they had that day as she stood with her face pressed against her bedroom door, chastened and powerless, and sensing the rest of her family scurrying about their business, trying not to look in her direction. By the time her father emerged, his sleeves rolled up like a janitor's, broom and bucket in one hand, dirty bedlinen tucked under the other arm, Marta was crouched on the floor, her forehead on her knees. 'Up you get,' he said, 'and put some flowers in there for Her Highness.' And he winked. She flung her arms round him and the bedlinen and the broom. 'I promise I'll never do that again.' But then the humour left his face. 'Be careful what you promise, Marta. Don't make promises you can't be sure to keep.'

The train is in darkness, for security they've been told, trundling steadily through the darkness outside. Impossible to see the villages they are passing, impossible to see the faces of her friends, although she can distinguish the outlines of their motionless bodies, fallen into their separate silences.

Will her father have the chance to visit them at home one more time before he has to go again? She wonders whether her mother has got the gas masks out, laid ready for her and her younger sister Sonia, because everyone has been saying this is going to be a gas war, like the last one. That rubbery smell nauseates her whenever she's locked into her mask, but it's your duty to get used to it.

Next to her, Ania has curled with relief against Marta's shoulder, tired from the marching and from having been wrenched out of sleep. 'Wake me when we get there,' she said, snuggled closer, and was immediately asleep. How does she do that? The jerking of the engine does not disturb her, nor its whistle. And, when they arrive, Marta will have to shake and shake her, and shout into her little pink ear. Whereas Marta herself, big and untidy in comparison, never seems to sleep so deeply that she doesn't hear, just above the surface, the doings of the world, like the whispered conversations of her parents. But now the repetitive *one-two-three-fouuur, one-two-three-fouuur* of the train is as lulling as the murmured exchanges of her childhood and she is aware she is falling asleep, aware while she sleeps of the rumbling wheels, of the pressure of her friend's head heavy on her upper arm, aware that the train has stopped, that doors are banging, male voices on the platform are calling out instructions to which she tries to pay attention but cannot, aware that the train is rumbling on its way again.

Daylight wakes her and at first she takes in only the jumbled bodies of the Girl Guides, helpless in their sleeping, eyes rolled up under the lids. Heavy-headed, she can't understand what they are all doing here, in a railway carriage. Her arm is numb and she looks down onto Ania's head with its glossy chestnut hair. She recalls her saying, 'Wake me when we get there.' But it's light and they are still in motion. They should have arrived hours ago.

She lifts Ania from her arm and eases her away. Gingerly, careful of the tangled feet of the sleepers, she climbs to the door and out into the corridor. A soldier is smoking at one of the doors at the end of the wagon, leaning at the open window. Marta has been brought up not to initiate conversations with men to whom she has not been introduced, but there is no one to make the introduction and she thinks, *This is war now. It's different rules now.* All the same, she stops a window's distance away and coughs.

'Good morning.'

The soldier, who is at that moment dragging on his cigarette, turns to her in surprise and then swears as the wind blows smoke into his eyes.

'Good morning. Sorry, miss. Sorry.' He rubs his smarting eyes.

Embarrassed for him, Marta looks away and out of the window instead, at the passing landscape, flat fields, a tree here, there another, women in the fields bending. The way the shadows are lying tells her it must be late morning.

'Aren't we going to Poznan?'

'Poznan!' The soldier lets out a honking laugh that reminds her of a donkey and picks a fragment of tobacco from his tongue. 'Poznan would have been hours ago if it had been on this line. Where were you?'

'Asleep, I suppose. I thought we were going home.'

'Poznan, eh?' He nods to her nodding. 'Don't reckon anyone's going to be going home for a while.'

'Where are we going, then?'

'Well.' He leans out of his open window and points ahead. 'End of the line's Wilno. That's all I know.'

'Wilno! But that's so far! We have to go…'

What's happened at home that they can't go there? And if it's not

16

safe for them then surely it's not safe for anyone. But her father will have heard, and he'll come with his units and drive the enemy out. Just as he did before, in Wilno. A name to conjure with. Marta can see the region in the top right-hand corner of her country, leaching out like an oblong inkblot. Her father went to war for it before she was born, twice fighting the Bolsheviks and beating them, making the city and its surroundings safe for Poland. But then the Lithuanians, once their allies, had laid claim to it, saying that according to their new constitution it was to be their capital city – which was plainly silly, since there were hardly any Lithuanians in it. So Marta's father, Colonel Dolniak, and his commanding officer, General Lucjan Zeligowski, had ignored the order from the Allied Powers and the League of Nations to turn aside, and had taken Wilno back in a surprise attack.

'Pure insubordination, of course,' her father had whispered with satisfaction. 'But the only patriotic thing to do. When your country has all but disappeared from the atlas it is every soldier's duty to redefine the borders, no matter how much time has passed.'

There were a lot of Jews in Wilno, he said, so he'd kept himself to himself. But the forests were wonderful. So deep, once you were in, you could forget man had ever built cities anywhere; so silent you'd never believe there were noisy streets with trams and traffic. So dark, there were places in it that made you think it was night-time at noon.

And now, finally, she is going too. Through her feet she can feel the solidity of the wheels on the track, unhurried but unstoppable, pounding on, for a reason.

'I don't know anyone in Wilno,' she says.

'Nor me neither.'

'But why are we going there? Why particularly there?'

'I don't know, do I? Look, miss. It's a mess. With the Germans coming, I expect they thought it was best not to go to Poznan, it being so close to the border, and you all being young ladies, if you see what I mean.'

'No. What do you mean?'

But as soon as she's said it she knows, and flushes, angry with him for the implication, and with herself for having begun the conversation.

He's looking at her with a tiny smile. 'Well, I have to get along or I'll be for it. Good morning, miss.' He salutes ironically. 'Pleasant journey.'

3

'We're not going to Poznan, Marta. Did you know?'

All Polish sixteen-year-olds have been well schooled in geography, but no one has a head for detail to match Stefa's. Tapping the window, she lists villages they have passed through that lie well to the east of their home town.

'We must be going somewhere miles on,' she concludes.

'I know,' says Marta. 'A soldier's just told me. We're going to Wilno!'

'Wilno?'

'But that's –'

'Why?'

'But my mother... I haven't told my mother!'

Nobody has told her mother, and all fall to thinking about that.

'She'll be frantic.'

In their pairs and trios of friendship the Guides discuss the degrees of panic that must have set in at home when morning came and no girls arrived. Marta thinks, *I'd rather be the person on the train than the person at home.*

'Ania.' She decides to whisper. 'When I asked that soldier, he said we were going to Wilno because they had to clear us out of the way of the Germans.'

'Yes. Well. They rape everyone, don't they, Germans.'

Why does Ania always know these things? And then articulates them so directly, without shame? She learns it from her mother, thinks Marta, with envy. Marta's parents aren't sure about Ania's mother.

They think Mrs Dorosz odd. They refer to her as 'that crazy Krystyna' because she doesn't observe the proprieties. You might drop in on her one day and find her with a smudge of paint on her nose, so engrossed at her easel that she doesn't even offer you a cup of tea. You might actually be invited round, but the room hasn't been put in order. The cushions are flat, and all the painting paraphernalia has been scrambled into a corner. If only Marta's own mother were more like Ania's, she muses as she stares out of the window, she'd have grown up learning what Ania has. Mrs Dorosz is such fun.

'But what about the people left behind? Will our mothers get raped?'

'Oh, not mothers. Mothers are too old.'

'Sonia, then.'

'Yes. Maybe Sonia.'

Then Marta sees her demure and studious sister with her plait tousled, flailing and thrashing under the weight of a booted German.

'For God's sake, Ania!'

'Well, you asked.'

Ania waits to allow the flush of anger to fade from her friend's face. It won't take long because that's what she's like – red with fury one minute and laughing the next. It's all right now, look. She's calmed down.

Ania says, 'My granny lives just outside Wilno.'

Of course she does! Marta remembers now, and they call her something strange, not granny... but... but... Mrs Benka. That's it. What a name to give your grandmother!

'You haven't seen her for ages, have you?'

'Not since I was little. About ten, or something. I wonder if she's really old now and can't walk or something. Wonder if she remembers me.'

'She's bound to. Grandmothers always do, don't they? Doting on their grandchildren with nothing else to think about.'

'Mrs Benka isn't that kind of granny. You'll see. We'll go out and visit her and you'll see. She had a farm and there was an old fellow working there who'd been there for ever, except I can't remember his name. P'raps he's dead now, though. He was ancient then.'

'Everybody seems ancient when you're little, so maybe he wasn't really that old.'

'No, he was. Anyway, we'll soon find out.'

Now both girls have a reason to look forward to their destination and they sit back and watch the countryside lope by. There are trees beyond the window, the tall pines under which nothing grows. Just looking at them, you can smell the summer resin.

'D'you suppose there are people there who know we're coming? In Wilno?'

'They'll have telegraphed, won't they?'

'Who will?'

'Whoever decided we couldn't go home.'

A man behind a large desk with a telephone on it would have been sipping lemon tea and putting pieces of poppy seed cake into his mouth, chewing while he barked into the receiver. 'And by the way, those Girl Guides from Poznan. I want them in Wilno, understood?' Icing sugar on his lips. Epaulettes with tassels on his shoulders. There'd be gold inlay in the green leather of the desktop. 'You know Germans as well as I do. Remember the last war?'

Different rules for sons and daughters in an unfair world. Gienek will be drafted, but Marta is being sent east. She could have been a nurse, at least. They could have let her be a nurse on the front. If not, what was the purpose of making all the girls spend some of their summer holidays learning first aid while their brothers were taught to march, and wheel, and strip guns?

'I need a pee.'

The corridor is empty. No smoking soldier. Marta walks down the train against its direction until she comes to the small lavatory, but it is locked. She stands by the door waiting. From the wagon beyond a soldier comes and stands behind her. Is it the same soldier? She didn't look carefully at his face, and in uniform everyone looks the same.

The lavatory door opens and a soldier comes out. Now there is a soldier in front of her and a soldier behind her, and both of them know she wants the lavatory, otherwise why is she standing there?

The emerging soldier tries to make way for her and hold open the door at the same time, while Marta tries to push past him, but the space is too small, and for an instant the two are wedged together, and then she is in and the door closed, but the soldiers, she is sure, are sniggering on the other side. Can they hear her peeing? Are they trying to? There is water on the floor – if it is water. And no paper. So many people must have used this lavatory through the night. Her knickers will be damp at the crotch, and she hates that feeling. She stands up wondering if the soldiers are still there, waiting for her. Holding her breath, Marta flings open the door onto an empty corridor, and the train stops.

All along the train, doors are opening. By the time Marta gets back to her compartment the other Guides are already on the platform. The whole world is on the platform. At one end there are soldiers, hundreds it looks like, all together, regrouping the way they've been trained, each one knowing exactly what he is supposed to do. There are children and some mothers with the children, but too many children for the mothers, and there are nuns. Still on the train, Marta looks down and spies Ania's bright head in the turmoil, and fixing on her she can hear her friend's voice clear among the others: 'Let me go. I'm not a child.' A nun in a grey habit has hold of Ania's hand in her own and is patting it, somewhat frantically, there, there, while Ania tugs and tugs. Marta must leap to her aid.

'Oh, there you are, Ania.'

It's said casually, to indicate that these are equals. Marta towers over the grey nun, who looks up at her and down at Ania.

'Is this your little sister? Because if she is, I must say…'

'No, she's not. She's my best friend. She's my classmate.'

'Oh.' The nun releases her captive.

'Thanks,' hisses Ania furiously.

The nun climbs onto a packing case for the height that lends authority. 'Now, children. Young ladies. Guides. When I call out your name I want you to shout out "Here!" loud and clear.' She reads all their names in alphabetical order from a large notebook, so it's like being back at school, but in the circumstances more interesting. 'Now,

22

girls. My name is Sister Irena, and you'll be glad to know we've been expecting you all since yesterday, and everything's ready. Follow me.'

Sister Irena slithers to the level of the massed Guides, swings about in a triangle of grey, and makes off towards the exit as if she too is more accustomed to route-marching than to prayer. Behind her, the column trots again, left right left right; behind the column, the soldiers in formation assess the departing buttocks.

4

The Guides' hard-soled shoes sound like hooves on the cobbles. In the narrow streets, canyons between the high-walled houses, you'd think it was the cavalry come to town, and above them windows open, women pulling their children in front of them to allow them the better view. Some of the names on the shops are unfamiliar, Jewish names perhaps, or Lithuanian ones. This was once Lithuania, as they all know, long, long ago during the union between the two countries. Now, thank the Lord, it is Poland again. 'Wilno, second capital of Poland, home of civilization and the cradle of Mickiewicz, our great national poet.' Marta's knapsack jiggles on her back and her brain jiggles in her skull. There must be better ways to move about than this.

All at once they arrive. Sister Irena spins round, her habit a split second after. Behind her a pair of wrought-iron gates are propped open at the welcome, leading into a courtyard of what may once have been some great family's mansion. A pageant of giant lime trees stands sentinel against the iron fence, so many that in summer the air must be sticky with their scent. The walls of the mansion are a pale milky green and the windows, spaced precisely, flash the sun, evidence of frequent cleaning. Two wide but shallow steps lead to large double doors, also held open. In front stands another nun in grey, like Sister Irena, wearing a small round black cap with a white band rimming her face. She waits for the perspiring column to achieve complete standstill; then, with the unhurried gesture of one who never doubts the attention of her audience, spreads her arms almost as wide as they will go and says, 'My children.'

As if they have been waiting for the signal, younger nuns flap down in a flurry of grey from the depths of the building, swoop on the Guides, one nun to each pair of girls, grasp a girl by each hand, and set off without a word into the interior. Off they go, along corridors, the girls' feet noisy, the nuns' inaudible, up the broad stairway. Like the soldiers on the station platform, they have been trained and know exactly what to do.

It is an upstairs hall, once many rooms, now stretching the length of the building. Both casements of eleven square windows are wide open because the air is still warm. Between the windows are beds, all with coverlets blue as the Virgin's purity, and by each one is a low, narrow cupboard. The first nun leads her pair of charges to the top two beds, deposits them there and backs out of the way to allow entry to the next consignment. So precise are their movements that there is no turmoil, no collision. It is like a dance, and not a word spoken.

When each girl stands with her knapsack clasped to her chest at the foot of her allotted bed, the nuns regroup in the doorway and one of them speaks. She is round, dimpled, cuddly.

'Girls. You're welcome with us on this terrible day. We're sorry for you having to leave your families but we hope you may find safety among us. We're trying to get you ordinary clothes from the townspeople, who welcome you too. Of course, you're all such different sizes...' She looks from Marta to Ania. 'So it may be difficult at first. Please don't be angry.'

Her face under its black cap wears an expression of such doleful appeal that anger would be absurd. Marta starts giggling but thinking at the same time what an inappropriate noise she is making, given her surroundings. She puts her hands over her mouth, blocking one exit, so the giggles seek another, and emerge from her nose in a juicy, agricultural snort. Now all the Guides are convulsed and therefore, after the slightest of pauses, the young nuns are as well. Within minutes, the laughter has become tears and the room resounds with both the helpless sobbing of twenty sixteen-year-olds, terrified lest they never set eyes on their parents again, and the sympathetic sobbing of the nuns who have been alerted to fear the same.

Then, two by two – they must get accustomed to two by two – they are led through the unfamiliar corridors to the bathhouse to sluice away the residues of their journey. Marta begins putting on the clothes the townspeople have donated. They are the sort her mother's cleaner, Pani Malgosia, might wear. Next to her Ania is like a doll in the clothes someone's child has outgrown. The girls turn to each other, hands on hips, and shriek.

Instantly there is a pounding on their cubicle door. Marta yanks it open and bathhouse steam clouds into the corridor like a sudden cough on a cold night to settle on the face of the Mother Superior.

Her features are clear-cut – no dimples here – and her voice is manly and ferociously even. She does not tolerate sudden high-pitched noises within the walls of her convent. It is a place of refuge from the clamour of the world not only now but at all times – a place of holy contemplation in which shrieking has no business. She looks them over and her lips twitch. Then she re-squares her shoulders and strides down the corridor, booted feet jabbing into the flagstones, to the chapel, where neat nuns and assorted girls are already seated. A curt flick of her hand directs them towards their pew and simultaneously informs them how long the others have been kept waiting.

'It is our duty before God to offer charity,' she announces, 'but it is not your duty before God to accept it too easily. You will observe our rules. You will eat all of, but only, what is put on your plates. You will attend both morning and evening Mass. It has been arranged for you to begin the new school term tomorrow at the local *gymnasium* but I would point out to you that you are guests in this city, a fact which you must recall every day. We shall hold a special service tonight for your families, and pray that each and every one of them may be kept safe from the enemy. To this end, please write down in the book I will circulate your names, followed by the names of all your relatives. Precision is indispensable, even in prayer.'

That evening's service lasts over two hours because among them twenty Polish girls are able to account for a sizeable number of relatives. And although by this time the girls are weary and wanting their supper they pronounce each prayer with equal fervour to ensure success, convinced that an apathetic recitation for someone else's grandfather might induce God to overlook their own.

When at last they are filing out, sniffing into the hankies that a far-sighted citizen has included in her hand-me-downs, the Mother Superior thinks, with gloomy satisfaction, *Maybe weeping together will help them now. Poor little things, there's going to be a lot more of that to come.* But when Marta reaches the door and turns by some instinct to cast a backward glance, the Mother Superior is stony-faced.

The tears do not last long because the Guides are young and hungry. As always Marta and Ania swap bits of their supper: Ania scoops Marta's beetroot from her soup but cedes her own dumplings. If the Mother Superior sees she doesn't comment. After all, in the totality of the arrangement, nothing has been left on the plates, in accordance with her commands, and nothing more has been asked for.

In the morning Sister Irena sets such a pace up the hill that Ania has to skip at Marta's side to keep up, and once again Marta finds her breath drawing ragged in her chest. Ever since the war began, she thinks, they have been made to march, always faster than was comfortable. But she mustn't complain because, if she were a soldier after all, she would be marching non-stop, probably all night, no bath-house, no pork and dumplings, no bed with its blue coverlet. No Ania by her side. She gives her friend's arm a sudden tight squeeze.

'What's that for?' pants Ania but returns the squeeze.

'Nothing,' says Marta gruffly. 'Just glad you're here.'

'And you. But I wish Sister Irena would slow down.'

'Me too.'

'I feel so stupid dressed like this.'

'You look about seven.'

'Well, and thank you too. I always knew you were my best friend. And you look like –'

'I know. I know what I look like.'

'And Stefa looks like a librarian.'

'And Agata's a fishmonger.'

'So is Klara.'

'Who needs two fishmongers?'

'Specially when there aren't any fish.'

'How d'you know there aren't any fish?'

'Well, we're so far from the sea.'

'But there are rivers.'

'So there are.'

'And carp ponds, surely.'

'Must be.'

'Good morning, young ladies. My name is Mrs Zubrowska. Welcome to your new school.'

Mrs Zubrowska in her tailored brown suit is one of those contained women who wear their stature with conviction. Her voice is smooth and surprisingly deep, and, as she speaks, her hands dance about her midriff like a pair of courting songbirds; when she falls silent they fold their wings upon each other and lie clasped in soft white silence. Someone has curled her hair and, where the sun touches it, it gleams. Like her shoes, which are high-heeled, polished, elegant.

'Come along in.'

Such white teeth. You'd think she never drank tea. You'd think she wasn't really a teacher at all. Mesmerized, the two fishmongers, the librarian, Mrs Dolniak's cleaner, little girl Ania and the others break away from Sister Irena and tag after Mrs Zubrowska, taking her measured steps across the playground and into the shadows of her realm.

So it comes to be that the Guides are handed back and forth between their queen of the night and their queen of the day. The Mother Superior and Mrs Zubrowska are both absolute monarchs. You would no more contravene Mrs Zubrowska's flashing teeth than you would the two lines between the Mother Superior's eyebrows. But the smiling teacher's dictatorship seems at least benevolent. And when she stands on her raised dais each morning to encourage her pupils, especially her newest arrivals, to treat their studies seriously for the sake of their country, even Marta takes her exhortations to heart. If Sonia could see her now!

Sonia with her tight plait, which will not brook escaping strands of light-brown hair that is so like Marta's. Is she missing her older sister? Is she lonely now that Marta has disappeared and Gienek presumably gone to join the army? Thinking of Sonia at home alone with their mother, Marta shivers. She could not bear that. She doesn't have the patience, the forbearance. Her mother's treble sets her teeth on edge; her cheerful domesticity provokes in Marta a visceral longing to bring the polished glass-fronted cabinet, which contains the Dolniaks' best crockery, tumbling to the parquet. Wedgwood blue and white, brought gingerly over from England years ago by her father as an anniversary present for his wife. None of them has ever eaten off it. Each item was delicately removed from its protective tissue to be immediately displayed in the cabinet. 'What is the point of crockery you don't use?' Marta invariably demanded when it was her weekend chore to rub the smudges she couldn't see from the glass doors. No one ever answered because they seemed not to think she was asking a question. And now Sonia and her mother must be alone with the Wedgwood in the spacious apartment, with only the other to talk to, to look at and to console.

Quite coincidentally, on the girls' third day in Wilno the two queens each suggest that, if anyone has not already done so, the time has surely come to write home.

'Think what a pleasure it will be to write. You'll all have so much to say.' The queen of the day beams. 'But you must do that when you get back to the convent because now you have to devote your energies to... what is it?... Let me see... trigonometry.'

In the refectory at suppertime the Mother Superior unnecessarily claps her large hands. 'After your meal you will all write to your families. You may feel homesick but you, at least, know that you are safe. Your mothers and fathers need to know that too. I will allow an extra hour before bedtime.'

Dear Mama and Dear Sonia.

Marta hunches over the refectory table, twirling her pencil between her fingers. She doesn't know what to say. She would be able to write

29

reams to her father or Gienek, asking questions about the war and their successes. But she doesn't know what to say to her mother and sister. She can't write to her father and Gienek because she doesn't know where they are, and if she writes to them care of her home address the other two will realize letters have been sent, but not to them.

We're all fine here in Wilno, Ania and me and all of us. We came by train overnight and most of the next day, and now we're staying in this convent with a ferocious Mother Superior and going to a local school, which is not bad. Our classmates are quite friendly and the headmistress is as elegant as a mannequin! There's plenty to eat. Ania's grandmother lives not far away – do you remember? And we're going to visit her at the weekend. Apparently she has some sort of farm.

I hope you're both all right and not too lonely. Let me know if you hear from Tata or Gienek.

I kiss you both
Marta

The reply comes almost immediately. The Germans have swept past Poznan, leaving it intact. Marta's mother and Sonia are untouched for the time being. But her father has not been seen since Marta herself last saw him, too busy, given no leave. Now even letters from him have ceased. But Marta's mother has an unfailing optimism, or feigns it, and implies that all must be well. Gienek too has departed, but since there is no bad news nothing can have happened.

Early the following morning, listening to the radio under the tent of her bedclothes in her locked cell, the Mother Superior hears that the town of Sulejow has been burned to the ground; the day after, that a thousand people have been murdered in Bydgoszcz, among them a group of Boy Scouts; two days later, that Krakow has been taken. She keeps the news to herself and trusts that the queen of the day will do the same. What good can come of alarming twenty young girls when they are helpless to do anything about it? She will pray with added urgency, but alone, for many of her nuns are youngsters too.

5

It is a beautiful autumn, and at the weekend Marta and Ania leave the convent to accept the invitation from Mrs Benka, Ania's maternal grandmother, who lives on the farm where she was born, not far from Wilno. They ride the country bus out of town and Ania, window-side, presses her face against the glass wondering when she will recognize some landmark. It is so many years since she was last here. Fields. Trees. Sandy tracks leading off into the fields. It could be anywhere, really.

But suddenly, 'Oh no, look! It's Rupert. We have to get off!' She pushes at Marta, prodding her thighs – oh, do be quick.

Marta dislikes being prodded. 'All right, all right. And who's Rupert anyway?'

The bus driver is laughing at them as they cascade down onto the road and touches his cap, goodbye ladies.

'That's Rupert.'

There, by the edge of the track, stands the strangest, roughest wooden carving Marta has ever seen. It's the figure of a man, no, not just a man, Christ surely, sitting in His crown of thorns on a high narrow seat, His head propped on one hand and a tired, disconsolate expression on His face, as if He's been waiting for a bus for a week now but none has been by. Huge bare toes protrude from beneath His rough robe. He is sheltered from the elements by a makeshift roof of no more than a beam and crossbar. Marta shivers. There is something so forlorn about this sad figure sitting here in an empty countryside.

'Why Rupert?'

But Ania is waving, waving and running. A woman is walking briskly towards them along the track that leads off into the fields. She holds her arms wide and Ania runs into them. The arms fold shut.

Mrs Benka releases Ania and embraces Marta. 'You're very welcome, my dear. I see you've met our Rupintojelis.' She pats the side of Rupert's seat. 'When she was little, Aniuszka couldn't get her tongue round that so she called him Rupert. He's the Man of Sorrows. You see them all over Lithuania.'

'But we're in Poland!'

Mrs Benka laughs. 'Tell that to the Lithuanians!'

Marta points at Rupert. 'I thought it was Jesus.'

'Well, that's the idea now, but it was a pagan thing originally. He doesn't look very happy, does he?'

Mrs Benka is a trim woman in her early sixties, perhaps, as straight-backed as her lithe granddaughter, but her hair is dead white and long enough to be drawn back into a pleat behind her head. She is gaunt, her face bony, all angles and depths. You can see her shoulder-blades through her shirt. And it is a shirt, not a blouse, tucked into the waistband of a dull plain skirt of some rather heavy stuff. She wears laced boots and takes great long strides along the track to her farm. Everything about her suggests a woman who barely sets foot inside. Her skin is tight and brown on her face, dry and leathery on her forearms.

The path leads away from the road at a right angle, with a grassy ridge at the centre where the cart-wheels do not run. There's a low hedge on either side. Beyond the hedges they see beehives and plots where someone grows flowers for cutting. Mrs Benka points to clumps of large, deep-yellow, daisy-like things with black centres. 'Rudbekia,' she barks, briefly. 'And chrysanthemums. But you know chrysanthemums, don't you?' Yes, you know chrysanthemums with their heavy heads of white and russet, yellow and red, bought in the autumn because they keep so well in the vase. 'That one's Poppy.' Mrs Benka points to a tethered light-brown cow which monitors their passing with rotating jaws. 'And that one's Rose. They give us all we need. Along with the chickens.' High-stepping and crooning, kicking back the soil.

Mrs Benka leads them round the house to a shallow porch where an old man is standing, wearing what looks like some sort of leather apron. He has eggs in both hands and is holding them out for Mrs Benka to count. Marta thinks she has never seen anyone so old. He too is bony but his back is humped and he has to look up from beneath his forehead to see where he is going. His eyes are set so deep beneath his eyebrows that they seem to be merely hollows.

'Seven,' he says, and his voice is surprisingly sonorous, as if it were emerging from a different chest. 'Not bad for the time of year. Considering. And I think there's more, only that black one you're so fond of is hiding them again. Cunning, she is, that one. Good afternoon to you, young ladies.' He raises his egg-filled hands. 'Pleasant journey, had you?'

'This is Old Petrkiewicz,' says Mrs Benka. 'He knows this place like no one. Farmed it with my father and told him what to do. Now he tells me what to do.'

'And she takes some telling, hee hee!' cackles Old Petrkiewicz. Treading his shoes off at the door, he steps in to lay the eggs in a bowl on a rough wooden table.

'Since it's such a fine day, I thought the pair of you might make yourselves useful,' Mrs Benka tells them. 'I'll be busy too. I've got onions to string.'

She hands them each a basket with double, heavy-leather straps to go over their shoulders, and sends them apple picking. It's nice to be outside but how odd to be sent out straight away like this, without being offered any tea and cake. It's not that Marta's hungry or anything, it's just that it doesn't seem normal. But as chores go this is no great burden, for the orchard is old, the trees long past their best, and the apples sporadic. Under the branches crusty with lichen the grass has grown long and turned to hay, each stalk heavy with seeds. The girls lie in contentment, scratching, and squinting to see the crickets leap.

'Why do you call her Mrs Benka?'

'I don't know. We just always have. I suppose it's a joke, but I can't remember why.'

Marta objects, 'It seems so formal for a granny,'

'Yes, but she isn't formal, is she?'

'She's not very granny-ish either.'

'That's true. I'm glad she isn't. I'd be sorry for her if she was.'

'Why?'

'Well, it must be awful to be a granny in wartime. You have so many more people to worry about.'

'I haven't got any grannies.'

'I know. You can borrow this one.'

And Ania means it. If ever someone had a granny that you'd want to borrow, Mrs Benka is the one. She doesn't seem like any other woman that Marta has met, and maybe that's why Ania is such a good sort. It goes down the generations.

'Thanks. I will, if she doesn't mind.'

'She won't. She likes awkward people.'

'Ania! You pig!'

'Mm.'

They pick all the apples they can reach and turn over the fallen ones with their toes to see if any of them are free of wasp and worm holes.

'Actually, perhaps we ought to collect all the fallen ones and put them in one basket. Mrs Benka might want to make compote out of them or something. She wouldn't want to waste them, would she? Specially not now.'

Marta imagines Mrs Benka sitting at the table with Old Petrkiewicz at night in the depths of winter, aeroplanes overhead, eating apple compote from her store of jars, musing about the golden autumn.

When there are no apples left she makes to hoist her basket.

'Let's not go back yet,' says Ania. 'It's so lovely here. So quiet. Mrs Benka won't mind. She's got her onions to string. I remember them now, hanging from one of the rafters in an outhouse. My mother always used to bump her head on them and Mrs Benka always said, "Why, darling? I've always hung them here, and you always bump your head."'

Once again they flop spread-eagled in the uncut grass, faces to the sky. This is perfect. Some bird is twittering intermittently and overhead a small aeroplane drones so slowly it seems stationary, held back by a string, and whirring its little engines like a tethered bee. Marta puts up her thumb and the plane disappears behind it. Now you see it, now you don't.

'It's dropping something.'

'A bomb?'

Both girls roll under their tree but push at one another. 'Bombs fall faster than that!'

'Anyway, if it was a bomb the tree wouldn't have been much good.'

They get to their feet and, shielding their eyes, squint up into the sky. Flakes are falling, twisting lazily in the motionless air. They will land not in the orchard but in the next field, so the girls run, racing, not each other but the rest of Poland that may wish to reach the flakes before them. As they run up the hill they see that the plane is trailing the flakes behind it, leaving a trace fluttering down across the countryside. Pieces upon pieces of paper.

'Got one!' Ania has pounced.

'Me too.'

Side by side they look at their pieces of paper, identical, covered in large grey lettering. 'LONG LIVE THE FRIENDSHIP OF THE SOVIET AND POLISH PEOPLES!'

'What about the others?'

'They're all the same. Look.'

'What do they mean?'

'I don't know.' But Marta thinks maybe she does know. Her father has said much about Soviet friendship, and joined those fighting to prevent it before she was born.

Mrs Benka takes a leaflet, reads it, screws it up. 'Since when did anyone announce friendship from the bottom of an aeroplane? If they were our friends, wouldn't we know it without having to be told? And what sort of friendship is it when only one of the friends knows about it? What nonsense. But come along in for something to eat and then you'd best take these back to your Mother Superior.'

It's an odd thing but, once you step through the porch and into the house itself, you might be in the city dwelling of some professor. There are books against all the walls, stacked two layers deep, and more books in piles on the floor. The furniture is dusty, the cushions on the armchairs flattened by time, and indoors Mrs Benka looks like a beady-eyed intellectual of the type that frightens Marta's mother.

Ania stands with a glass of apple juice in one hand and a piece of gingerbread in the other. 'Mrs Benka. Have you still got... you know... my... my things?'

'Your things, darling? What things? Oh, your things! Of course. Did you want your friend to see them?'

Ania squirms a little as if she has overstepped the bounds of decency but doesn't want to retreat. 'Is it all right?'

'Of course it's all right.'

Mrs Benka turns to a corner where books and journals, cushions and folded tablecloths lie in a heap that can't have been disturbed in a long time. She bends over the heap tossing cushions and cloths aside so that a fog of dust flies with them and her fingers turn grey. She shunts books away with a slippered instep until a small lacquered black box appears, stylized red roses on its lid. Hands the box to Ania.

'Look!'

Coiled inside around a hillock of deep green velvet is a necklace of red stones. On the summit of the mound lies a pair of pearl earrings and between them a ring with a stone as clear as glass.

'They're rubies and the ring is a diamond.' Ania's voice has dropped to a whisper as if they were in church. 'Mrs Benka is leaving them to me in her will.'

'You'll get them sooner, as you well know. The day they tell me you're getting married.'

Ania lays down her box and pincers out the necklace, her fingers trembling. She holds the piece up to her neck and displays herself to her grandmother, to her friend. Stretches her neck, twisting it from side to side. 'What do you think?'

'When the day comes they'll be perfect.'

But these are such grown-up jewels. Somehow they make Ania look even smaller and younger than she already does. For Ania's sake Marta nods and smiles. It's not the rubies she envies her but Mrs Benka, who is holding out her hand to retrieve her bequest.

'Put it all away for now because time's getting on. And come back next week, why don't you both. It's nice to have young voices about again.' Mrs Benka kisses Ania on both cheeks, then hugs her hard, folds her arms tight around the small body. 'Such a slender little thing, you are, Aniuszka.' Then she releases her granddaughter and turns to Marta, who has been standing to one side, silent, watchful, wistful. They are of a height and look one another in the eye. 'And you too, my dear.' She embraces Marta, a kiss on each cheek and a hug, but it is a different embrace, woman to woman. And she whispers in Marta's ear, away from Ania's hearing, 'Take care of my granddaughter for me, won't you.'

Gratified by the importance of the request, Marta whispers back, 'I will. I promise.'

After the evening service the Mother Superior says, 'It appears we are about to be visited by the Bolsheviks. As you may be aware, the Soviet Union signed a Non-Aggression Pact with Mr Hitler. But this is the first time I have heard that such a Pact invites its signatories to cross the threshold of another country. Until I say otherwise, you will stay within the convent walls. So no school tomorrow. You can do your lessons in your dormitory and I will send some of the sisters up to help you. Good night, girls. Let's hope these Bolsheviks pass us by.'

But they do not arrive at all. Monday, then Tuesday, then Wednesday. You can tell from the Mother Superior's face, where the two lines between her eyebrows look uncharacteristically uncertain, that she is asking herself how long she should keep the girls locked away. She crosses the square to consult with the Archbishop and on Thursday the girls return to school, where Mrs Zubrowska says, merely, 'Ah!'

6

The air has altered. For one thing, it's chilly morning and evening. Soon the eleven casement windows of the dormitory will be closed, not to be opened again until next spring. One afternoon, as the girls return from school, they hear a banging and a scraping coming from the convent compound. They hear the excited voices of the younger nuns giving one another instructions. They see dust flying in the convent corridors and there are some granules of grit underfoot. It is a strange phenomenon that, even in a place where supervised cleaning is given precedence, dirt lurks, needing only movement to dislodge it. The youngest nuns are moving beds, their own, from the cells where once they lodged into the Guides' dormitory. They are running up and down the stairs carrying folded clothes and bedlinen. They have pushed the girls' beds closer together so that now there is no space for the small bedside cupboards. Now there is space only for a young woman to stand, if she is careful. All the youngest nuns are moving in.

'Why? What's happened?'

'They're moving some men into our cells.'

'Men!'

'What men? Why?'

Sister Irena, overseeing operations, stands in the doorway. She has been asking herself whether there might be a health hazard in this density of sleeping arrangements. She answers without thinking. 'Well, for one, it's Dr Wusztad, the Minister for Education. He's been in hiding since Warsaw fell.'

'Warsaw's fallen?'

Sister Irena claps a hand to her big mouth. Now she fears the Mother Superior more than the thought of German troops overrunning Warsaw. For she knows no one in the distant capital, whereas...

Warsaw has fallen. Marta surveys the map of her country that, like every Pole, she carries in her head. So many towns and cities lie between the western frontier and Warsaw. How many of them have been lost? And, if Warsaw has gone, how soon will Wilno follow?

'Where else?' she asks in the peremptory tones of the military.

Sister Irena stands motionless in the doorway. Says nothing.

'Don't you know?'

Sister Irena tries damage limitation. 'It's difficult to know from here. There's so little information.'

'So how d'you know about Warsaw?'

'Marta, ssh!' Ania is plucking her sleeve. After all, Sister Irena is the Mother Superior's second-in-command. But Marta won't *ssh*.

'Did you read about it? Is it in the newspapers? Is it on the radio?'

'I really can't say.'

Infuriated, as if she were at home with her mother, Marta turns her back and not quite under her breath mimics Sister Irena's tremulous voice, 'I really can't say.'

Ania is well used to defusing situations like this one and quickly asks a question to which, perhaps, there is an answer. 'But why's he coming here? The Minister for Education?'

Sister Irena shrugs. 'Why not? If it's safe for you, it'll be safe for him, I suppose.'

Camouflaged by skirts. Who would seek out a hiding minister in a community of women?

It is easy enough to pretend, and soon to forget the sheltered minister, because they do not see him. Not in the refectory, not on the corridors or in the courtyard. Not even in the chapel. The Mother Superior must have given him a very particular dispensation. She, meanwhile, relinquishes her control of information, since both Sister Irena's gaffe and the arrival of the minister and his family have made that impossible to sustain. Instead, with military economy she gives a daily briefing – at breakfast, to avoid bad news before bedtime – about the latest events of the war, in so far as they can be known. In Marta's eyes the Mother Superior's standing instantly improves.

The week is over and the next passes. Marta and Ania return to Mrs Benka's, where the sun is still high and she is bottling blueberries into the jars Old Petrkiewicz has prepared.

'So what, then? Your Mother Superior closed the gates and opened them again. Well, what else could she do?' Mrs Benka delivers her opinion fiercely as if the girls were about to contradict her. She gives them their baskets again. 'Get out into the sunshine while you can. Winter comes more quickly here than it does in the west.'

They really do not need the baskets, since there is nothing left to gather, but it is understood that they must give the appearance of being about some useful occupation, even though they need not expect to meet anyone who might take note. Off to the orchard once more, each with a large shawl for later on to keep their arms warm. On the way they encounter Father Jerzy, the priest who officiates at the small wooden church just beyond the farm. They dip in brief curtseys.

'Ah, girls! So you're back. Glad to hear it, I must say.'

Like Old Petrkiewicz, Father Jerzy is so wizened he has shrivelled beneath his clothes, and he leans heavily on a pair of sticks.

'Are you busy? On an errand for Mrs Benka?'

'No, Father. We were just going to lie in the sun.'

'Ah.' He sounds wistful.

Marta suspects he was hoping they might say something else. 'Can we do anything for you?'

Father Jerzy straightens up until he is at least taller than Ania. 'Well now. Since you ask so kindly. It's the altar. It needs decorating so badly for the harvest festival, and really there isn't anyone to help, and I'm not as young as I was…'

The priest gives them scissors in the church, and points out the big vases. He shows them the pump and pulls feebly on its handle once or twice, demonstrating both its function and his own inability to draw water. He gives them a sheaf of corn and indicates which of the flowers growing on either side of the path leading to the church they may cut. Then he sits himself down on a small wooden chair by his arched wooden door and prepares to doze.

Marta pumps and Ania trims and arranges. Both wind their shawls over their shoulders because inside the church is chilly and outside the summer has passed. They regret the lost afternoon but there will be others like it. The smell of guttering candles seeps from the boards of the walls. There are rooks outside, raucous over the sleeping priest. The arm of the pump grinds a little as Marta pushes it down and returns to the vertical with a soft squeak, and after a few moments the first gobbet of water belches into the bucket.

There is such stillness in the air, an autumnal sharpness, but her body is warmed by her efforts and the water steps up the sides of the bucket with each pull of the pump. Inside the little church her best friend is arranging flowers and corn-stalks and although Marta cannot see Ania she can picture her, hand hovering over the chrysanthemums heaped in front of her, should it be a red one or a russet one next? She knows that Ania is sucking her top lip in her indecision, she knows that Ania's left foot is slightly pigeon-toed as she stands in contemplation. She feels suddenly almost overcome by a rush of love for her friend, and for this moment, so that when the water tips over the top of the bucket and onto her shoes she waits before she bends to lug the bucket inside.

Father Jerzy's head has lolled back against the sun-warmed wall and his old mouth is open as he snores quietly. He too looks completely content. It's trust, she thinks. That's what it is. The three of us, in this place, on this day.

Ania has come to the door and sees Marta, lopsided with the weight of the bucket, smiling down at Father Jerzy, and she nods.

There are running feet.

'The Russians are coming! The Russians are coming!' A small plump boy, pink-faced with his running and the importance of his message. 'Mrs Benka says to come back. Straight away.'

'Yes, children. Go. Go.' The old priest has levered himself, befuddled, to his feet, talking to them but scanning the horizon. 'Where are they, the Russians? Did you see them?'

The boy points down the track away from the farm.

'I know what.' Ania pulls Marta to follow her. She runs up the stairs of the wooden tower.

'Stop, girls! It's not safe.'

But Father Jerzy's warning peters out as their thudding feet clatter heavenwards. At each turn of the narrow stairway there is a window framing a small snapshot of the countryside. Ten steps and to the north are the yellowed fields where the harvest has been and gone; ten steps and to the west are more fields and treetops whose shimmering leaves are edged with autumn; ten steps and to the south a brushstroke of water cradles the sunlight; ten steps and you can see all the way to Wilno looking one way and maybe all the way to Russia looking the other. But where are those Russians of whom Marta has heard so much, the ferocious Bolsheviks who are said to stop at nothing?

There!

There?

A track runs zigzag between the tiny strip fields, most of them grey-brown where the ridges of the ploughed earth have dried in the sun, just here and there a plot of corn-stalks, or a patch of dusty green. Trailing slowly along the track there comes a slow serpent of moving human forms, winding back to the eastern horizon. But as it approaches Marta thinks the boy must have been mistaken. These people are not marching, they are not the disciplined units of the sort her father commands. Some of them don't even have uniforms! A couple of battered brown trucks bump alongside spattering dust over the shufflers, who plod on without response.

'Oh, Ania.' She laughs suddenly. 'Let's go home and tell Mother Superior the Russians have come.'

But they are late with their news. There is no one who does not already know it by the time they arrive at the convent gates, and the city seems to have drawn a great inward breath, which it is then reluctant to let go again. The few people still on the streets are moving with uncomfortably rapid steps; their faces are closed and their hands grip large bags of potatoes and cabbages. By dusk everyone has gone home, where they will switch on their radios but keep the volume down. And it is only because the city has grown so silent – even the trams know to creep by on tiptoe – that Marta, leaning from the last open window of the dormitory, hears distant voices carried on the breeze. The Bolsheviks are bedding down.

At breakfast the Mother Superior issues her morning orders. The Guides will continue their lives as normal. They will take their daily route to school but must not deviate from it. If they should encounter alien soldiers along the way they will pretend they have seen nothing; if the soldiers attempt to engage them in conversation they will act as if this has not happened. They should be forewarned that Russians are known for disorderly behaviour but all of them, nuns and Guides, should beware of feelings of superiority. Christian charity demands that compassion be extended in their hearts towards those who lack the education and upbringing that they have had, which are the foundation stones of civilization. The Russian state, even before its godless revolution, was an Asiatic one, and its people never had the benefit of the one true Church. This inevitably means that they know no better. Bear that in mind at all times. Dismiss.

Marta and Ania collect their bags and books with eagerness to be on their way, hoping that the streets will be thronged with atheist louts performing unspecified uncivilized acts. They link arms, rather tightly, and set up a brisk and purposeful pace, holding their heads high. Yesterday's second-hand clothes have become *haute couture*. They have the impression that the townspeople, once their hosts but now their compatriots, bestow on them glances of approval for their cultured demeanour.

All in all, though, the journey is a disappointment, for there is not a Soviet soldier in sight. Nor on the way home, even though they slowed their pace almost to a standstill. Nor after dark when it is known that the ill-mannered prowl the streets.

7

The Archbishop's palace has been turned into a billet for a regiment of cadets from out of town, so Girl Guides and cadets take note of each other morning and afternoon. Stefa and Klara, Zosia and Magdalena, arm in arm, pretend not to be looking but giggle into their hands. Kazimierz and Henryk, Riszard and Michal do not have to pretend but lengthen their stride and appreciate the Guides through narrowed eyes. Marta is aware of the cadets not so much for their straight noses and square young shoulders as for the uniforms that remind her of her brother and of her forbidden vocation. She doesn't particularly regret that convention, or, rather, the Mother Superior, will not allow the Guides to be seen conversing with the cadets in a public place.

In the past it has been the Mother Superior's custom to cross the square to the Archbishop's palace to confer with him. No longer. Instead the Archbishop sends messages to her via emissaries who are under instruction to wait by her office until they receive a message in return. For this purpose he employs the cadets, who might as well make themselves useful. The Guides are over the moon and the Soviet soldiers forgotten. Now there is good reason to hurry home to find out which cadet the Archbishop has dispatched today. It is not always the same one, but most often it is tall, black-haired Antoni Kozlowski with the girlish curling eyelashes.

You can tell what a strapping young man he'll be once he has filled out into maturity, even if, for the moment, he is still somewhat gangly. It seems to have taken him no time at all to learn all the girls' names and, although he is entirely proper when he addresses them, each one is convinced, by the width of his smile, that he has hurried over the square for her sake alone. None more so than Ania, who lost her heart to him at first sight. Lying in her narrow bed, crammed up against Marta's, Ania croons her beloved's name.

'Oh, do shut up, Ania. You're like someone out of a soppy romantic story.'

'But he's so lovely, isn't he? You think so too, Marta. I know you do. You can't not.'

'He's all right. Shame about the boring name, though. Half the world's Kozlowski.'

'Well, and so what? It's not your name that makes you special, is it? And what d'you mean "He's all right"? He's a lot more than just all right. He's –'

'I know, I know. He's wonderful, he's gorgeous, you wish he'd get down on his knees to you.'

'Well, as a matter of fact, I wouldn't mind if he did!'

'What? Get married? Are you mad?'

'What's wrong with that? What's wrong with being married?'

'But you're only sixteen. You've got to live. And there's a war to win first, anyway. You can't get married during a war. It's… it's… unpatriotic. No. I don't mean that. It's… trivial. That's it. It's trivial when there are more important things to be done.'

'People can do both. I don't believe they stop getting married in wartime. Some wars go on for years, after all. People didn't stop marrying during the Hundred Years War, did they? There wouldn't have been any new generations if they had, well… of course… But anyway, Marta. You're just against marriage altogether, like you've always said. But you're going to have to get married one day, you know, or you'll end up on your own – because they're never going to let you join the army.'

'You hardly know him. In fact, you don't know him at all.'

'I'll get to know him. Somehow I will. I'll find a way of cornering him, somewhere the Mother Superior never goes.'

'Or her spies.'

'Or her spies.'

But Ania's plan is destined not to be realized because defeated soldiers from the west have been pouring into Wilno, and all over the city women are ransacking their husbands' wardrobes, this time for civilian clothes to offer the humiliated refugees. The trapped military, who know no one, are parcelled out among the city's institutions, and some of the officers are squeezed into the convent. More nuns, the next generation, bring their mattresses into the dormitory. Now it is as if the floor itself has been raised. You leave your shoes outside and step from the doorway directly onto the first mattress and, from there, from mattress to mattress, to the windows.

On their way to school one morning Marta and Ania come face to face with Antoni and another cadet called Wladek, dressed in cassocks. The swathes of black cloth that fall austerely from shoulder to pavement add gravity and grace to the young men's outlines. They meet the incredulous gaze of the two Guides, who have automatically hinged at the knees in the curtsey a cassock demands.

'Glory be to Jesus Christ!' observe all four, and walk quickly on.

'You could have said something then,' hisses Marta.

'No, I couldn't. Not with Wladek there.'

'And me.'

'Yes. And you.'

At the street corner Ania and Marta look back to see Antoni and Wladek doing the same. That night, one of the younger nuns whispers that the cadets are being sent to the Vatican to train as priests. Nobody knows what will happen to the officers.

A further eight nuns arrive in the dormitory with their belongings which, being the property of nuns, are fortunately few. They bring no mattresses because there is no longer any vacant floor space. Nuns double up with nuns. The Guides suddenly feel privileged.

It is mid-October and the days are careering towards a perpetual gloaming. There are the first sightings of Soviet soldiers on the streets. Two or three together one day, then none the following. Then again, a small cluster transfixed in front of a shop window, staring at the customers, who seem to be making purchases inside as if that were an entirely normal thing to do. The soldiers do not speak. They do not accost anyone, but seem to huddle together in an unsoldierly way in the alien city whose script they cannot read – if they can read at all. They are so out of place, homesickness spreading pallor over their broad spotty faces.

Throughout the city they become the subject of dinnertime speculation. Some say they would scarcely be better off in Moscow, which, rumour has it, does not have paved streets or properly constructed dwellings, not to mention shops. There is comfort in this sort of talk but also a profound unease. At the back of the mind lies the suspicion that these gormless youths are not the real Russians, who must be concealed somewhere nearby.

On the day of the first really heavy fall of snow, it turns out that the Soviet Union has signed a friendship treaty with Lithuania. Diplomatic links between Lithuania and Poland are broken off. Wilno is now Vilnius, which, with its surrounding region, has been picked up and handed over to the Lithuanians. Wilno is no more. A different standard flutters from the castle ramparts and street names change so quickly you'd say it was overnight. But it is not only names. Things are done, though you do not see the doer, you do not know how they come about. Wherever Poles have been the managers, Lithuanians are put in their place – back in their place, as the Lithuanians quickly gloat, cheerful too soon – and the Poles are sacked. It happens at the hospitals, at the municipal refuse centre, at the coal-yards and the libraries. Naturally it happens at the radio and the university, and naturally it happens in the schools.

The queen of the day, elegant Mrs Zubrowska, disappears, and in her place on the morning podium is the usurper, elegant Mrs Kaulinskas. She too has glossy hair, and she too bares her teeth in a wide though uneasy smile.

'Children,' she begins, attempting authority but twisting the ends of a silky flowered scarf between her fingers. 'There are times when events around us are such that we are not always in control of those things we would wish to be in control of.'

She puts her hand to the large brooch of carved ivory which pins the crossed arms of the scarf and smiles a smile of appeal. Not a face responds. Not even the Lithuanians, yet, for they have been used to Mrs Zubrowska and grown to like her.

'Sometimes circumstances arise whereby one is forced to… one's choices… one cannot…'

Suddenly she gives up and is looking over their heads to the back of the hall. Her eyebrows twitch. Marta, tall enough to see over heads, twists to glance behind her and concludes there is someone there, in an overcoat. But in this weather people wear coats all over the place. Even sometimes indoors, don't they?

No they don't, say the dormitory nuns, and counsel acceptance and caution.

Marta tosses her head. Caution is what her mother would recommend!

Together that night, while the sharing nuns burrow within the frontiers of their narrow beds for a tunnel to sleep in, Marta murmurs to Ania the outlines of rebellion. They will organize a boycott of the school that will last until Mrs Zubrowska is reinstated.

It is a whispering campaign, and, since lowered voices are by their nature more interesting than raised ones, the message is relayed at speed. By the morning of the second day, half the upper school are assembled in the courtyard outside, demanding Mrs Zubrowska's immediate return. They plant their feet wide and block the gates to the juniors, sending them home, mouths full of tales.

By the morning of the fourth day the parents of the local pupils have all received letters warning them that, if they do not immediately call their daughters off, they will be invited to find alternative employment. The picket line is abruptly reduced to twenty Polish Girl Guides, too small a contingent to block the gates effectively. The juniors skip back to their classes while the rest of the upper school slink past the protesting banners, crestfallen, hangdog, apologetic. The Guides necessarily keep to their posts but in their diminished ranks they feel conspicuous and uncertain. The east wind nips at their ankles and they think of the other pupils and their teachers snug behind the double windows of the upstairs classrooms.

Day five. Marta takes stock and has to concede that there is a problem with morale. The only answer she knows was intended for a different enemy, but who says you cannot fight on two fronts at once, using the same weapons, if need be? She taps her shoe on the cobbles – two, three, four – and the choir takes voice. The first line is hesitant but choral singing always gets louder, given half a chance, and as their conductor cranks up the level with vigorous arm movements the Guides sing lustily, bringing some of the people in the café across the road to their feet in a gesture of collective, but inattentive, patriotism.

On the morning of the sixth day an open lorry pulls into the school gates, forcing the pickets to one side. Soldiers in Lithuanian fatigues jump down and quietly load the astonished Guides up the ramp and into the back. Over the tailgate they see the white faces of their classmates small in the frames of the windows, getting smaller. Then the lorry swings round a corner and the school is out of view.

At the central police station the soldiers hand them over to a station sergeant, who informs them wearily, in a marked Lithuanian accent, that, since the citizens of Vilnius have become exceptionally law-abiding, there is space enough in the cells for each girl to have her own accommodation. They will be released only upon payment of a fine of 150 litas per head, strictly speaking an affordable if irritating sum for the relatively wealthy; out of the question for the convent.

'But…' says Marta, as her cell door is closed behind her.

The cell is whitewashed, the window so high up, the sun so low that she thinks it could almost be night-time. There is a bed in the corner with two blankets neatly folded at its foot. She sits on the bed and wraps the blankets round her shoulders. What will the Mother Superior think? What will she do? Perhaps a telegram will be sent to Poznan asking her mother for the money. What will her mother think? How will she get the money? How long will it take? What if she can't get the money or doesn't receive the telegram? What would her father say if he knew, wherever he is? She would give him an account of what she had done, blow by blow, and he…

Oh, God! Hunched under her Lithuanian blankets Marta feels her cheeks burning with embarrassment, caught in the spotlight of her own thoughts. Her father wouldn't be in the least impressed by her spirit or her bravery. He would tell her that her lack of foresight had led her men into unnecessary captivity all for the sake of a gesture that had achieved nothing. And now here she is, sitting on a lumpy mattress where thieves and murderers have sat before her, on her own, with no way of getting out. Will she end up spending the entire war in this stupid prison, and will everyone outside forget she is here, she and her friends? Her friends!

She taps on the wall, as people are supposed to do; taps harder, bangs; batters the wall with both fists. The walls are thick. No one bangs or taps in reply. People are said to keep their spirits up by whistling but she has never managed to produce anything more than a moist exhalation through the tiny hole of her pursed lips. So she will have to sing again, as by now perhaps the others are doing. But she is getting bored with singing as a means of resistance, not least because it has so far failed to prove itself. However, nothing else remains to her.

She takes a deep breath while wondering how many hours one can sing before collapsing with exhaustion. She looks at her watch – ten past eleven – and, having wasted the first breath, takes a second.

'Cut it out!' Almost immediately a hatch opens in her door to reveal an angry mouth pressed against it. 'That's the most horrible noise I've ever heard, and I've heard some.'

Marta falls silent, affronted. Singing may not be her strong point but it isn't that bad. Then she thinks, if it *is* that bad, it might be her best weapon. She takes another deep breath, with a vengeance.

'Oy! I said –'

But at that moment, in a ragged chorus beginning away to her left, the Guide choir strikes up too, following their drone. Then she realizes that her cell must be the last, and she has been banging hopelessly at an outside wall. So that when suddenly they open her door the prison officer and Mrs Kaulinskas see the tall womanly girl sitting shrouded in blankets on her bed, laughing, with her mouth wide open.

'Are you all here?' Mrs Kaulinskas looks at the list in her hand provided by the station sergeant but cannot yet put faces to the twenty names and has to count them. She has undone her coat in the stuffy room and her scarf is tied at her throat in an ugly knot. 'Then we can be on our way.'

She turns on her heel and the Guides follow her in sullen silence. Where she goes, so must they. Where will it be? Back to school or straight to the convent to be handed over to a tight-lipped Mother Superior, who may not see two and a half hours in the cells as the act of heroic patriotism it might have become, given time. And they have been humiliated: rescued by the Lithuanian while failing to restore the Pole.

At the convent Sister Irena, not the Mother Superior, is waiting.

'Go to the dormitory,' she says. 'And think about what you've done. And, by the way, she had to sell her brooch to get you all out.'

8

Mrs Benka is right. Winter does come sooner in the east. Sooner and deeper. Snow and ice alternate. Sometimes there is no movement from the sky at all, but it bulges lumpily over the ground like an ancient and overloaded basket that may split at any moment. For weeks Marta and Ania are confined to Wilno (they must remind each other to call it Vilnius outside the convent but may cling to the Polish name within it), and there has been no news from Mrs Benka. But, as the February of 1940 wanes, the Mother Superior grants them a weekend's furlough. Perhaps she is hoping to receive a gift of stored countryside wholesomeness from Ania's spirited grandmother.

As usual the girls are the only passengers left on the bus by the time it reaches the stretch of road that will pass the turning to Mrs Benka's farm. Nothing looks the same when everything is white, when sky and horizon are of one colour, when you know that outside the trundling bus there is silence. In the muffled landscape they nearly miss their stop. Even Rupert's outlines are blurred under his covering of snow, and his expression seems gloomier than usual. Each of his huge bare toes has a crystalline cap of ice. They say the blind lose their way on their native streets when it has snowed.

Mrs Benka is unchanged except for a certain bulkiness of outline. Like the girls she is wearing more layers and keeps a hefty scarf over her shoulders even indoors. The stove around which she sits them is insatiable, bellowing for more logs and still more. She brings them tea, then soup, then potatoes and onions, then apple compote and cake. Marta notices how veined her hands are, how knobbled her knuckles, and wonders whether this is new or whether she simply never noticed before.

Pointedly Mrs Benka does not ask them for news of the city – there is little – or for news of their families, because she reckons she knows whatever it is that they know. Better to stick to local events.

'Father Jerzy died, did you know?'

Does that mean the little wooden church is deserted now, boarded up, the smell of candles fading because there is no one to light new ones? Marta can see the door where Father Jerzy set and re-set his chair, trying to find a secure position for it on the uneven ground under the eaves, seeking sunlight. The chair will have been taken inside and the door closed, maybe locked. And inside everything will be growing damp from the untempered cold, and musty. Who officiates at the funeral of the sole priest?

'Poor Father Jerzy,' says Ania.

'He's best off where he is,' says Mrs Benka briskly.

Father Jerzy had come to her in tremulous indignation. Those Russian peasants were hauling the pews out of his church, without a care, so roughly they had knocked one of the doors off its hinges, and they were chopping them up for firewood. When he protested they had laughed at him, and one of them had picked him up and carried him to his chair, dumped him on it and tied him to it so that he would have to watch. But he had closed his eyes. If it hadn't been for Old Petrkiewicz he might have been there all night.

Because the days are still so short Mrs Benka sends Old Petrkiewicz out with a hurricane lamp to see them to their bus. She has packed some eggs and a jar of gherkins for the Mother Superior. They walk in silence towards the main road, matching their steps to the old man's as he puts his feet down in his stolid, inexorable pace. What's a bit of snow to someone who has known this land for longer even than the mistress? Abruptly he stops and raises his lamp to Ania's face.

'I don't know if there's anything you can do about it, miss, but I think you should get your people to take Mrs Benka away from here. It's not the way it should be, a lady on her own when there's a war.

And she doesn't take proper care, you know. Just like her father. He was just the same. Never took proper care of himself, and I can't be everywhere. Not all at the same time.'

'But she's always been here!'

'Maybe so she has. And so have I, longer even than her, in her father's day like I said. And that's why I'm telling you. I've seen a few things come and go but this time it doesn't smell right. So you just go on home to the city and write a letter to your people and tell them Petrkiewicz says so. They'll take my word for it, believe me.'

Ania does believe him but it's not her people who will be the problem. 'Do you think she'd take any notice?'

Old Petrkiewicz rubs the line of his chin with the hurricane lamp and light performs a jagged dance among the branches. He says nothing and seems to be imagining a delegation of Mrs Benka's relatives trying to pull her to urban safety while she grips her doorframe with such grim strength that they will have to rip out the entire structure to lay hold of the woman. Finally he shakes his head.

'Well, I don't. You're right there, miss, I suppose. But I had to ask. I wouldn't be doing my duty if I didn't ask.'

'And anyway, you're here, aren't you?' says Ania. 'She isn't really on her own.'

'I won't always be here, miss.'

Ania suddenly throws her arms round him and cries, 'Well, you must try to be.'

Old Petrkiewicz stands motionless under the onslaught of her embrace. The young always think life goes on for ever.

But, just in case he's right, that evening Ania pens Old Petrkiewicz's concerns in a letter to her mother, which is put in the post the next morning. It will turn out to be only one of countless letters that do not arrive.

The seasons change, Girl Guides have birthdays, soon it will be summer again and with it exam time. Marta has announced that once she has matriculated she will train as a nurse and leave for the front, wherever it happens to be at the time. The Mother Superior is uneasy about this. Since the Guides have been delivered into her care, she should behave towards them with the responsibility of a parent. She cannot believe that Colonel and Mrs Dolniak would wish their daughter to go out into what has become a very wicked world at the age of seventeen. Marta is mature in body, without doubt. Headstrong, certainly. Impulsive, unfortunately – look at that foolish episode with the school boycott! But without experience. She rehearses Marta's objections in her head, *But how am I to get experience without going out into the world?* And there is truth in that but, *in loco parentis*, the Mother Superior remains uneasy.

Then it occurs to her that in fact Marta may well not pass her exams and therefore not matriculate. She has not been attending to her studies with the conscientiousness they demand. And in one area at least she has refused on principle to do any work at all. The curriculum now requires a familiarity with the Lithuanian Constitution. Marta has refused to recognize the authority of Lithuania over her; she has declared that Vilnius is not its capital, that she is living in Wilno, which was Polish when she arrived, and as far as she is concerned it has remained so. So let her stick to her principles and fail. That way, she will have to remain under the Mother Superior's care and tutelage either until the end of the war or until she comes of age, at which point she will cease to be the convent's responsibility. If that makes her cross, well, she will discover she has only herself to blame. The Mother Superior looks forward to reminding her that this too is what is called experience.

But Ania is just as aware that Marta's obduracy may cost her her school-leaving certificate, and she is determined to help. She has turned seventeen as well and knows from the inside that it is an entirely grown-up age to be. If Marta has her heart set on going to the front, then Ania must help her. So she has written in secret to Mrs Benka and explained that Marta is on the point of flunking the Lithuanian Constitution test because she refuses to acknowledge it. Can Mrs Benka help?

She can. She will. She sits Marta down under the apple blossom, having first spread out an old blanket, folded, because you still get damp days, even in late May. She takes Marta's two hands in her own and Marta, sensing the imminence of a homily, prepares to pout.

'Do you want to train to be a nurse?'

'If I have to. If it's the only way to go to the front.'

'Then you have to matriculate.'

'I know.'

'Which means passing the Lithuanian Constitution test.'

'I know.'

'So?'

'If I study it, it means I acknowledge it, and I don't. This is Poland. It was Poland when we arrived, and it's only the Soviet Union that has said it's Lithuania again. It hasn't been Lithuania for ages.'

'Well, I wouldn't put it quite like that. You know the date, Marta, because you keep telling us about your father's part in it. Twenty years isn't exactly what I'd call ages. And you know, from the point of view of some people here, I'm sorry to say that your father's war wasn't the heroic battle for the soul of Poland that people back in Warsaw think it was. It was a land grab that lost them their capital city. No. No.' Marta has drawn a long breath to interrupt. 'I know what you're thinking but stop a minute and listen to me. This isn't what's important now. What's important is that Poland came into being again those twenty years ago because Russia, the Soviet Union, was in chaos. Well, now it's not in chaos. Twenty years have passed and what everybody is thinking now is that this is beginning to feel too much like old times. We were partitioned for all those centuries and now we're partitioned again. Really, the Wilno/Vilnius thing is the least of our problems and I would have thought you'd want to help the war effort in any way you can. And you know what you have to do to do that. You have to pass your exams, otherwise you'll be stuck, sitting there all by yourself in a schoolroom with pupils younger than you and failing your leaving certificate on a matter of principle.

'So never mind what you think, and no, I don't want us to have an argument about it now. Just swallow your opinions and tell the examiners what they want to hear. Then get on with your life. And if learning the Lithuanian Constitution is all you have to do, then learn it, for

56

heaven's sake. You only have to know what it says. No one's asking you to swear allegiance to it.'

Marta's pout remains but seems simply to be sitting on her lips because she hasn't got around to removing it. Encouraged, Mrs Benka presses on.

'Ania says you've been learning about the ancient Greeks and their gods. But I presume no one has asked you if you believe in Zeus and Hera and Aphrodite, have they?'

Marta shakes her head.

'In fact, it's my firm belief that if you are in opposition to something you should make sure you know as much about it as your opponents do rather than turn your back on it.'

Since Marta is beginning to look interested, Mrs Benka prepares to deliver her *coup de grâce*.

'I'm sure your father would think so too.'

Marta can imagine her father nodding agreement, although he wouldn't accept that bit about the land grab. She sighs and shakes off Mrs Benka's talons. Just within her line of vision she sees Ania fishing something out of her bag.

'You didn't! The Constitution. You cow!'

Ania giggles and passes the offending text to Mrs Benka, who opens it out and spreads the pages flat over her knee.

Not many days later the Mother Superior is informed that all the Girl Guides have passed their matriculation.

9

Really, Marta needn't have bothered tussling with the Lithuanian Constitution, and Mrs Benka and Ania might have saved their energies. As the news comes through that faraway France and Belgium, Holland and Norway have fallen to the German conqueror, closer to home there are rumours that the Soviet Union has decided it needs the territories of Estonia, Latvia and Lithuania for military purposes. There is to be an ultimatum. No, there has been an ultimatum and no one is in a position to challenge it.

Vilnius has become a heaving, noisy city, more crowded than it ever imagined possible. Defeated Polish officers exchange unreliable news with diplomats who no longer represent anybody. But week by week there are fewer of these officers, who seem to disappear overnight. If you believe the underground pamphlets that pass from hand to hand, there are dawn raids wherever these men have been billeted and by sun-up there is no trace of them at all. Meanwhile bearded rabbis argue with officials at the post office about the telegrams they have been sending to foreign embassies, to which there have been no replies. And more and more people carrying fewer and fewer belongings arrive from the west unaware that Vilnius, for all its willingness to play host to the incomers, is about to be swallowed in a single gulp down the Soviet gullet.

It is a particularly lovely summer's day. Marta dawdles on her way to the hospital to enjoy the sunshine, turning her face up to it as others are doing, her light print dress easy and loose on her body. The cafés are full, people gossip by the news-stands, a woman in a fashionable pale-blue, tight-waisted dress and high heels leans against the rippled trunk of a lime tree, laughing too much at some comment from a male admirer, while at her feet her small dog defecates with quivering haunches. Marta pauses to watch. Will the woman step into the mess in her elegant shoes, her romantic moment abruptly thwarted? Will the man pull a laundered handkerchief from his pocket to help her wipe those shoes or will he decamp, seen off by the back end of a bug-eyed pooch?

Two small boys with long fishing rods are making their way towards the river. School is out and they have the summer before them. They are carrying knapsacks which their mothers have filled with rolls and cheese, wrapped eggs and slices of ham. Marta turns into Dominican Street and it is as if the city has been transformed from a moving film into a snapshot. The shoppers, the people hurrying to work, everyone on the pavements, all are standing stock still, staring with hands over open mouths at the first of a line of Soviet tanks filling the road. A jovial moon-faced soldier waves from the turret. Under Marta's feet the ground vibrates. By evening the bakeries are empty. A week later they have closed.

But as an interpretation of events this is unjust. The Soviet Union does nothing without popular support, so plebiscites have been organized by the NKVD to allow the People to express their consent for incorporation in the USSR. It's true that the lists of candidates are closed and have anyway been handpicked. It's also true that every citizen is obliged to vote, and that spoiled papers, abstentions and protests will be counted as votes in favour. But the results, when they are announced, are gratifying. A full 92 per cent of the electorate have voted for Lithuania to become a Soviet republic.

The Mother Superior has been informed by the new authorities that she is to carry out regular fire drills. Although she dislikes any interference in the organization of her convent she can see that there is some logic in this – after all, the gentlemen she is now housing all smoke; and the premises are overcrowded.

One a.m. is the hour chosen on the presumption that only if a fire drill is unwelcome and unexpected will it stand up to the test. Everyone knows what they have to do. Some of the nuns are issued with frying pans and heavy spoons which, as the hour chimes, they are to bang vigorously while they bellow warnings from a variety of positions about the convent buildings. Some of the Guides are to run to the roof ready to scatter sand from a battery of waiting covered buckets. In the gentlemen's quarters, they are to stand by their beds fully clothed until given the all-clear. An administrator from the newly constituted neighbourhood committee takes a roll-call to assure himself that no one perished in this rehearsed conflagration.

The Russians have now imposed a curfew too. After dark the streets are so much more silent than they used to be that the unpredictable alarms screeching from the convent unnerve the neighbourhood all the more. Sleep is disrupted month after month. But not only sleep. The authorities choose Christmas Eve to test the effectiveness of the drill, although by now they surely accept that everyone knows what to do in an emergency.

Then one Tuesday the racket doesn't come from the nuns and their frying pans but from a convoy of lorries rumbling along like tanks. It passes under the windows of all the residents of Skupowka Street and halts at the gates of the convent.

Men hammer at the gates. Sister Irena, smoothing her habit, runs to the front gates but does not open them. Behind her the light from the convent is dim; in front of her someone is shining a hefty torch so directly into her face that she can see nothing at all. After a moment the glare of the torch is shifted to one side and when her eyes have recovered she picks out the outlines of seven men. She knows without being able to see that the man with the torch is dressed in a uniform of grey with a red stripe on his hat band; that his feet are comfortable in well-kept boots that someone else has polished.

The officer, Captain Igor Dorushkin, rotates his torch in small circles indicating that Sister Irena is to open the gates. She takes the keys from her belt, unlocks one and opens it, but stands in his path as if her presence alone will hold him off. He pushes past her without actually touching her and flings open the other gate, then steps through, his six ordinary ranks close behind.

Captain Dorushkin now salutes briefly. 'Ask her if she's the head nun,' he instructs one of the soldiers, his interpreter, with feigned ignorance.

Sister Irena puts her hand over her mouth to cover the giggle. 'Mother Superior is expecting you,' she says. 'Please. This way.'

She leads, they follow, all stiff-legged with reluctant courtesy, doing it by the book. The Mother Superior is standing in readiness, gaunt, upright and sterner of face than any commanding officer.

'Dorushkin, Captain Dorushkin,' announces Dorushkin.

The Mother Superior gets straight to business. She points to the clock on the wall and says in perfect Russian, 'This is no time to be paying calls. If you wish to confess I can arrange for Father Ignaz to hear your confessions after breakfast. With so many of you, however, it may take some time, as I imagine there is a great deal you need to tell our Lord. And by the way, anyone who has lived here all their lives, as I have, has grown up having to learn your insatiable country's language.'

Captain Dorushkin responds to her first sentence. 'It is an awkward time of night, I agree, but you will understand that the early hours are when one may expect to find people in. Why else do you suppose that we request your fire drills to be carried out before daylight? Especially since it came to our notice that you have generously given sanctuary to a number of individuals possessed of the wrong objective characteristics. We are here to relieve you of their burdensome presence.'

The Mother Superior shakes her head. 'I am afraid that where objective characteristics are concerned, Captain Dorushkin, only God is able to judge which are wrong, since only God can be objective in His judgement.'

'On the contrary, madame, characteristics can be judged to be objectively wrong if they in any way offend the People.'

'And which People do you have in mind?'

'In the first instance, naturally, the Soviet People, since their consciousness is more elevated. In time, with good fortune and the right education, I dare say even the Lithuanian People –'

'We are Poles.'

'The Polish People, then. It makes no odds. Any of you can be helped to understand which objective characteristics are worthy of admiration and which not.'

'You will understand if I beg to differ.'

The captain inclines his head. Both he and the Mother Superior know, first, that, whatever she attempts to do to protect the inhabitants of the convent, she will fail. Second, he knows something she does not: that, despite the enthusiasm the Lithuanian electorate displayed in the recent plebiscite, regular arrests are needed to strengthen the Soviet state and clear the road for the building of socialism on Marxist-Leninist principles. Fourteen categories of people have been designated as blockages on that road – from followers of Trotsky and anarchists at the top to restaurateurs at the bottom – all to be removed. Although Captain Dorushkin carries the full list in his pocket, he keeps it there. But he has a second list, with names on it. This is the one he pulls out and hands to the Mother Superior as if he is about to send her out to do his shopping.

Without even looking at it, the Mother Superior knows that heading the list will be the names of the Minister for Education and his family, as well as those of all the sixteen officers she has been sheltering. They and the minister, having heard the Russians arrive, will be ready and waiting, eager to stave off awkwardness for anyone else. *Staving off,* thinks the Mother Superior, *is what the future is going to be all about. If we're lucky.*

'This way, then,' she says in the tone of someone bringing a lengthy conversation to a close.

They troop out, the Mother Superior followed by the captain followed by his acolytes followed by the eyes of nuns peeking round banisters with such curiosity that the captain can feel them probing him between the shoulder-blades, and he shivers. His grandmother once said to him that the gaze of a truly holy man can lay bare the wickedness of any man's soul, no matter how carefully concealed. Without a doubt it is only women staring after him, but presumably they are quite holy, and there are rather a lot of them.

The officers, the Minister for Education, his wife and his three children are as prepared as the Mother Superior supposed. Their belongings are packed (have been packed for quite a while, as a matter of fact), their beds stripped and neat. They wear their coats buttoned to the neck.

'As you see.' The Mother Superior steps aside to allow the captain and his men access into the room where their prisoners wait.

'But this won't do at all, I'm afraid,' says the captain. 'Where is the other one?'

'Other one?'

'You have the list.'

She has the list and now looks at it properly for the first time. Many thoughts go through her mind in that instant, too many for her face to disguise.

Only now does Captain Dorushkin withdraw the list of categories from his pocket to tap the relevant clause, reading it aloud to prevent misunderstandings. 'Officers of the former tsarist army, and of other anti-Bolshevik armies of the period 1918 to 1921 and officers and military judges of the contemporary Polish and Lithuanian armies.'

'But,' protests the Mother Superior, 'it says "officers", not the daughters of officers.'

'That, I'm afraid, is splitting hairs. Have you forgotten what your Bible tells you? That the sins of the fathers and so on? And, since Colonel Dolniak is unavailable, his daughter will have to do instead.'

The Mother Superior turns a gaunt and haughty profile, for there is no way out. She is at fault, not before this Soviet buffoon but before herself, for it is her responsibility to protect people who seek sanctuary in her convent, and she has failed.

'Have her called, please.'

So there Marta stands, just inside the door. A soldier steps up to face her. You might think he is about to bow formally and ask the girl to dance.

Captain Dorushkin nods towards her. 'Take her to get her things.'

Her soldier gives her the smallest of prods.

10

Marta leaves the Mother Superior's room with not only the soldier but the captain's interpreter as well. He tags along, anxious to make conversation, eager to show off his Polish. He is somewhat smaller than Marta and trots next to her while she lengthens her stride. She cannot shake him off. Behind them the soldier keeps to an even, unhurried pace, knowing that they will all arrive together in the end. The interpreter plucks at Marta's night-shirt as she runs up the wide stairway. The soldier plods in the rear, one step stolidly after another. Marta looks up and sees, clustered by the dormitory door, all her friends – the Guides and the younger nuns. They crowd towards her in their night-clothes with their hands out and their faces chalky. Their mouths are open and black and silent. Ania leaps out from among them and throws her arms round her best friend, then, turning her back to Marta, stands in a T shape in front of her, her small chest jutting out by way of challenge to the arresting authorities.

The interpreter suddenly pulls a revolver from his waist and waves left–right – and the girls scatter left–right. Ania peels away but crumples in shame. Marta and her escort hesitate, unaccompanied now, on the threshold of the dormitory.

From one wall to the next the dormitory is only bedding, hay mattresses lying end to end with barely the space for a girl's foot in between.

'Which is yours?'

She points.

'Let's go, then.'

Marta takes off the shoes she has only recently put on and lays them side by side at the door, then in her bare night-time feet steps as neatly as she can between two mattresses. The soldier hovers uncertainly, as if going shod into the dormitory is the greatest indelicacy. As if this women's place will be ravished by his boots. He stoops to unlace but the interpreter pulls him up – 'For God's sake!' – and pulls him on. The girl is at the far end of the room in her night-shirt, candlelight behind her, and you can see her rounded shape in silhouette.

'This the one?'

When the girl nods, the soldier crouches and pulls a knife from his belt. He rips the mattress open until dusty hay lies scattered like a theatrical farmyard on the surrounding beds.

The interpreter picks up the bundle of Marta's clothes folded at the foot of her now desecrated mattress. 'Get dressed.'

'Where?'

'Wherever you like.' And he sinks down onto the next mattress and props his head on his hand, making himself comfortable, preparing for a show. The top of his head is bald. 'But get on with it. We can't wait all night.'

'I'll go to the toilets, then.'

She runs with her bundle, hopping from mattress to mattress, but the interpreter is on his feet and bounding in pursuit.

The soldier stands up and peers after them, wondering if he ought to follow. The candle gutters and goes out. He can see the open door faintly illuminated from the hall but he can no longer make out where the mattresses begin and end. So he sits down again, unlaces his boots, ties them together by the laces, drapes them around his neck and, on hands and knees and feeling his way, crawls over the places where all those girls sleep towards the door where all those girls are waiting.

Marta and the interpreter reach the top landing simultaneously. They might have been children racing.

Marta makes for one of the toilets, pushes through the door and bangs it shut behind her; but the interpreter's boot stands in its path.

'You're going to have to leave the door open, you know. Rules. If you get my meaning.'

He is rat-faced, she thinks, and his fingernails are foul. You can tell he can't be a Pole.

'I don't know your rules,' she shouts. 'Our rules are different.'

Stamping on his booted foot with her bare one would be ridiculous. But she will not dress in front of this slimy little weasel. Suddenly she leans forward and screams into his face with all the strength of her powerful lungs, 'Get out! Get out!' – and pushes him with both hands, so violently that the interpreter loses his footing and finds himself sprawled on his bottom outside a locked toilet door.

'Oh no you don't, girlie,' he mutters in Russian, and shakes the door, rattling it as if to tear it from his hinges.

On the other side Marta struggles with her clothes, determined to cover herself with her underwear if that is the least she can manage. And hears a scuffle. The door ceases rattling, and she buttons her blouse. Then, swathed in dignity, she unlocks the door.

The interpreter stands with his back to the opposite wall, his features grotesque with fury. Pinning him in position is the soldier, boots inexplicably hanging round his neck, knife under the interpreter's chin.

'Are you all right, miss? This scum didn't touch you, did he?'

But as Marta does not yet speak any Russian she does not understand his words. His stance, however, is international and she thanks him for it with a curtsey, leaving him goggle-eyed.

For the twenty-two people she has been unable to protect, the Mother Superior has made and served a breakfast so lavish and so fragrant that Captain Dorushkin and his henchmen will be in no doubt as to which is the superior culture. But any breakfast lasts only as long as it is being eaten and, once the last delicacy has disappeared and all that remains are the plates wiped clean with bread, Captain Dorushkin is once again in the ascendant. He looks at his watch and taps it as if it might be faulty, as it frequently is. Checks it against the wall clock in the refectory as if that might be faulty, which it has never been known to be.

Out in the chilly courtyard, frost on the cobbles, all the people who are not being taken away assemble to take leave of and pray for those who are. The tailgates of the open lorries are flapped down and the prisoners loaded, two soldiers cupping hands for the Minister for Education's shoe, then for his wife's, as if preparing to help them mount a pair of thoroughbreds ready for a morning's hunting in the forest. Then away they drive through the night that carries sound, the ones in the lorries looking back at the ones left behind, still and huddled in the courtyard. They can see the figure of the Mother Superior, upright as a flagpole, slightly to one side, and Marta feels a sudden warmth for this unsympathetic woman who supposed that she and the iron gates of her convent could repel all comers.

As they round the corner of the Archbishop's palace, a priest stands, unrecognizable in the dark of the early hours, giving general absolution. *Is he expecting us all to die?*

It seems to be a day for lorries. From all over the city they are converging on the junction at Nowa Wilejka, where, in consequence of a Soviet co-ordinated transport policy, a train is already waiting, its engine glowing with well-stoked coals.

All around it on the pavements citizens are kneeling and keening. Other citizens run alongside the lorries, slowed to a crawl by their numbers, so that the prisoners can shout messages for the runners to deliver. The dawn is filled with a babble of names and addresses. Overnight the great city has become a village where everybody knows everybody else, or imagines they do, or will. It is odd, thinks Marta, that the people on the pavements look more scared than she feels. It is as if the prisoners who are being dispatched to an unknown destination are nevertheless more in control than everyone else; as if being left behind is the greater misfortune, because if you are left behind you are ignorant of whereabouts and well-being. The ones who are sent away may know almost nothing, but they know more.

Fifty to a wagon, the Soviet guard has been told, so fifty it is; the first fifty in the first wagon, the second fifty in the next, and – with all the jostling and shoving, the unfamiliar language, the suspicion that if things go wrong someone is bound to blame him and accept no excuses – any guard could lose count halfway through and no one giving him the time to start all over again. So whose fault is it if number fifty of a particular batch is a woman, and number one of the next turns out to be her three-year-old child? Nobody said anything about making allowances, and all her wailing only holds things up, and you have to bundle her in and crash the double doors together behind her to be able to get on and deal with the next lot. So the child is screaming now, and he wishes to God it weren't, but surely some granny will scoop it up and take care of it once they're all safely inside. It'll hardly die with all those people who'd have that on their conscience, and when they arrive at wherever it is they're going mother and child are bound to be reunited. Nobody wants them split up. What would be the point of that? Mothers and children are meant by God to be together, no matter what the Party says. It's just that, in times like these, that's what happens.

So Marta, who has never been drawn to gurgle at babies, finds herself suddenly with an armful of such shaking desolation that she thinks all the world's sorrows must be concentrated in this toddler, whose sex she cannot guess and whose face runs with snot. She clutches the child for fear that, if she drops it, it might be trampled on, but casts about, as others clamber up behind her, for an unencumbered matron who might relieve her of the responsibility.

The wagons are cattle-trucks adapted for a different purpose, and give the impression of having been well used already. Triple tiers of wooden shelves across the two ends are wide enough for people to sleep on in rows. The two long sides each have double sliding doors on iron runners. The space between the bunks will fill with the people who will have to squat on the floor. But in the middle, under another high sleeping shelf bolted to the ceiling, there is a hole cut in the floor, around which the planks are unpleasantly stained.

People are still being shoved in as if they are livestock and their farmer is late for market. A group tumbling in all together have clothes and faces unlike any Marta has seen before, although she knows immediately what they are because her father described them so clearly. The women, bundled in scarves and coats, don't seem so strange, but it's the men. They are old men, bearded, with long ringlets hanging by their cheeks and wearing identical black hats. There are no young men. In fact, now that she thinks of it, there are no young men of any sort. What can have become of them?

The doors are slammed together and it is too dark to see any more. For a moment everyone but the weeping baby falls silent; then, as the shock of the imposed darkness wears away, just as the darkness itself is diluted by familiarity, names are whispered – 'Zosia, are you here?' 'Jurek, where are you? Jurek?' – whispered as if only the person addressed is supposed to hear. And indeed, so it seems, for after a while some men and women, some children, rearrange themselves. On one side of the wagon, Poles sit with Poles. On the other side, the Jews sit facing them, in silence, and wait.

There is no one here whom Marta knows or expects to know. She lost the Minister for Education and his family in the milling on the platform, so she sits in her corner with the toddler now snivelling on her lap, rocking it and herself backwards and forwards, paced by the frenetic beating of her heart.

She cannot be expected to understand the reasoning that has included, in the round-up, those citizens from the café opposite the school who were prompted so unwisely to their feet when she led the boycotting choir in their patriotic songs. She has no means of knowing that in another wagon sits Mrs Kaulinskas in her knotted flowered silk scarf. Even Mrs Kaulinskas isn't sure which misdemeanour accounts for her arrest – her efforts to placate her new pupils on her first day as headmistress, or the ransoming of those silly Polish Girl Guides. It may of course be the earlier ownership of a carved ivory brooch that turned out to be worth 3,000 litas.

11

The train stands at the junction of Nowa Wilejka for thirty-six hours. Time enough to become introduced, to pass the baby round and watch it snuggle, as you had hoped, on a more practised lap, although not without a pang that it should abandon you so lightly; time enough to bore small holes through the floor of the wagon so that once the train is under way people might post through them tiny furled messages for villagers along the track to find and pass on. Time enough too to realize that there can be no such thing as privacy here.

Every now and then a body shuffles towards the hole in the floor, eyes carefully on the wooden boards because if no one's eyes meet yours then you might, perhaps, be invisible. A piece of cloth hangs down from the edge of the shelf as a flimsy screen, but it doesn't alter the fact that you know why someone is approaching the hole: you can hear them, you can smell them, and Marta is so embarrassed every time that she looks up at the ceiling to avoid the sight, pinching her nose against the stench. She is so embarrassed that she finds she has luckily no need to urinate or defecate any more. She knows, in fact, that she cannot do either of these things, since she has never hoisted her skirt in front of anyone before. But as the first day slides into the second she is brimming with nausea and thinks there is a foul smell coming from her skin. She keeps ducking her head to sniff at a forearm. Her belly is tight and round as a new balloon. Her head swims. Still she does not move but closes her eyes and clenches her teeth.

Someone is tapping her on the knee and she lifts her lids enough to see a long finger, hook hard, going for her knee like a woodpecker. Every peck sends shock-waves through her irritable body.

'Young lady.' His voice is gravelly, part rattle, part whisper. His beard lies like a bib on his chest, twitching with every word. 'Young lady,' he says again because she has not responded. 'Here, take this.'

He is holding out a scrag of dry bread and a glass of something. She looks at the glass and thinks of the germs. Others must have drunk from this glass and where was there to wash it? She wonders how he managed to have a glass at all. She stares at the offering and doesn't move.

An old hag in a wig is nodding at her with emphatic encouragement. 'Go on, dear. Do as Rabbi Lerner says. He knows best.'

The bread is tapping her knee now, so she takes it and the glass, and sits holding them. Now everyone is watching her. Even the baby has left off its snivelling to see what she will do, so there is no escape. She grinds a piece of the bread between her teeth and takes a tiny sip of the liquid, which burns her tongue so that she coughs and gasps and holds the glass away. 'Wha... what is it?' But she knows it must be vodka.

The knuckles push her hand back towards her. And suddenly the voice barks, 'Now! Drink it now, in one!'

She is so taken aback that she tips the stuff down her throat and every centimetre of the way along it sears a path through her body. She thinks she will throw up. The people opposite her are shimmering and merging, they are shouting well done, you see, someone is hugging someone else and she thinks there ought to be a song if she could only remember the words though it doesn't matter, actually nothing does except that she's really bursting for a pee and is on her feet swaying and shaking and hands are holding her to keep her on her feet, passing her along the line to the hole and nothing has ever felt so sweet before as all the stuff runs out I hope not on the floor though who cares anyway screen or no screen her body is becoming itself again.

But thirty-six hours are not enough time to get used to the smell.

71

'Don't fuss, dear. Things only smell bad because you think they do.'

Mrs Bila, four to the left, has taken charge of the baby, a boy it turns out once his hood is peeled off his head, and he's stopped crying enough to say his name is Frantek. Mrs Bila is almost convincing, she is so emphatic. But Marta cannot quite believe her. Mrs Bila isn't going to say that having to go over a hole in the floor isn't dirty, is she? Look at her now telling Frantek not to put his fingers in his mouth because he was briefly off her lap and on the floor. And Mrs Bila just says, don't fuss. But Marta thinks she wasn't fussing, though she is sitting with her hands over her nose, burying her nose between her praying fingers, trying to look as if she's only propping her face in her hands. But at least now she's been once she'll be able to go again.

'Now then,' says Mrs Bila to the baby, with her arms encircling him like a great fat hoop in her thick coat, 'you'll need to stop that crying or Mummy will think we've not been looking after you properly, won't she?'

Marta thinks the mention of Mummy could be a mistake. It will set the boy off again. But Mrs Bila knows what she's doing, and Frantek appears to understand, somehow, that these are difficult times. He nods his little round head up and down so energetically that Mrs Bila laughs at him.

'If you do that your head's going to fall off.'

So Frantek nods harder and harder, Mrs Bila whoops a great pretence of dismay, 'Oh dear, oh dear, look, it's gone, it's gone, all fallen off! Has anyone seen Frantek's head, oh my goodness, what are we going to do? Frantek's head has fallen off. Somebody catch it quick.'

'Here you are, madam.' He must be at least sixty, thin but wiry, and leaning across with his hands held apart, as if they're cradling a ball. 'Is this the one you're after? It came rolling down that fast…'

Mrs Bila takes it and tries it for size. Frantek holds his breath. Some ladies put apprehensive hands to their mouths.

'That's it. Look, everyone, it fits.'

His public clap like mad. Frantek puts his chubby hands to his head, finds it in place and crows. Then he nods it off again.

The old man introduces himself. 'Grabowski.'

In the early hours of the next morning the wheel-tappers begin their shift, moving up and down the train, and all are Poles and Lithuanians because the Soviet invader didn't think to bring his own wheel-tappers along. At each wagon the tappers whisper a single word, 'Omsk.' It isn't enough but it will do. It means the train will be heading due east, destined for sure for Siberia, but at least not for the Arctic north. But Siberia is one of those places which is so large and so distant it's even far from itself.

As Marta sits on her portion of bench, her hips wedged on each side by other hips, she tries to remember what she was taught about the tsars and the people they condemned to Siberia: some for being critical of the autocratic state and some for being common criminals; but she is not a common criminal – or any sort of criminal. She is on this train because she is special, like the Minister for Education. What about Mrs Bila, though? And the old man, Mr Grabowski? They surely are just ordinary. And those tatty Jews? What do they stand for?

'Mrs Bila?' Marta is tentative with this awkward question.

'What?' Mrs Bila is wiping Frantek's snotty nose on his sleeve in preference to her own. 'What's eating you?'

'Why... why were you...?'

'Why was I what? Now come along, Frantek baby. You don't want to be doing that.'

'Arrested. Why did they arrest you?'

Briefly Marta has Mrs Bila's attention, for the length of a pat on the knee. 'I don't know, darling, but look at us. There's this poor little one and his mother, wherever they put her. There's you and me and Mr Grabowski there. There's them,' she nods over at the Jews. 'Look at us all. There's not a young man or a fit one among us. And you know why that is?'

'Because they've all been arrested already?'

73

'That's right. So, now they've run out of men, they're picking up the rest of us.'

'But they can't arrest everybody!'

Mrs Bila shrugs.

There is so little light coming into the wagon it's hard to tell what time of day it is. They've all been rationing their food for fear of it running out altogether. Marta is beginning to feel sick, which means the others must be feeling the same way. Mrs Bila has been giving more or less everything she can find to little Frantek to stop him crying. Good thing he ended up on her lap and not with Marta, who wouldn't have given him quite so much. Perhaps that's how you know, finally, that you have grown up, when you give the food you want so much to someone else, to a child, even though it's not your child.

'Here.' Mrs Bila holds out the baby, at that moment asleep. 'I'm off to visit Mr Lenin.'

Lenin's Corner, they've come to call it, the hole over the tracks where already the steaming mounds have frozen. But at that moment the train jerks and the baby is tumbled into Marta's lap. Anything is better than the waiting, even going to Siberia.

12

Now that they are on the move, they have a guard. He is nineteen, he says, counting off his age on his outstretched fingers. He is grey-eyed and pink-cheeked, and is meant to keep them in order. On her own Mrs Bila could sit on him and he'd never breathe again, and then – well then, there would be one less body in the wagon. Petya, he says, pointing at his chest.

Whenever the train stops at a station large enough to have a water tower, two prisoners are allowed out of each wagon to fetch a steaming bucketful. The first time Petya comes running. He pulls some postcards from his pocket with stamps already printed on them. Only five. Quick, quick, he gesticulates. Mr Grabowski takes one, addresses it, and crams onto it as many of the names in the wagon as he can. He reads them aloud. Within minutes, everyone's name is on a card. Petya grabs them back and jumps off the train again. When it starts moving, and Petya has not returned, Mrs Bila says aloud, for them all, 'Oh that poor boy, I do hope and it must have been his own money, too...' But a few hours later, when they are diverted into a siding to let another train pass, the double doors slide open and there is Petya, clinging to the side of the wagon, his hands blue and stiffened into claws. Mrs Bila sits him on the floor and rubs his hands until he cries.

You could out-walk this train, it goes so slowly, day after day. They pass through villages familiar to the natives of Wilno, now called Vilnius, but which to Marta are only names. Through the slits in the sides of the wagon they see people lining the tracks, waving in slow rhythm to them, and some of the women are crossing themselves. People only cross themselves when times are bad.

Then the train shudders, its wheels squealing, and stops again, and someone comes down the length of the train pulling the doors apart, wagon by wagon. Mr Grabowski gets to his feet, turns his back to the engine and waves at the facing wall, kissing his fingertips, clasping his hands above his head and shaking them the way people do in triumph.

'What on earth are you doing, you silly old thing?' says Mrs Bila, tugging at him to sit down again.

'I'm saying goodbye, madam. If they've opened the doors it means we've crossed the frontier.'

Then they are all on their feet, Frantek in Mrs Bila's arms, facing the blank wall of the wagon, bidding, each of them, a silent farewell to Poland. Most of them have tears on their faces when they sit down again but they do not try to wipe the tears away. They wear them, rather, like jewels of identity.

The air in the wagon is fresh for the first time, but also icy. Marta pulls the blanket the Mother Superior gave her round her ears and eagerly takes the baby on her lap. He is round and warm.

Mr Grabowski leans forward over his knees gazing out hour after hour. Pine trees, silver birch, grass poking through where the snow lies thin, the steely blade of a distant lake. Hour after hour the landscape doesn't change. At night the doors are pulled to. In the morning, more pines, more birch. Mr Grabowski shakes his head. 'Poor Napoleon. If he'd only known, he'd have stayed at home.' But Poland's hopes had been pinned on Napoleon's success in reining in the Russian empire's voracious sprawl, and when he failed there had been nothing but trouble ever since.

It is a single track and the train keeps stopping in the sidings, and then not moving for days on end. Please God, let something happen, even if it's something bad, only not this endless nothingness. This boredom. Even Latin declensions would be better. Marta would commit all the pages of *Pan Tadeusz* to memory if she had the text of the great epic poem to hand. She would...

'Young lady. How is your mind?' Rabbi Lerner, hinged at the hips, is leaning over his thin lap and fixing her with a beady gaze.

Her mind? What does he mean, how is her mind? Sick, does he mean, or what?

'Is it a good one, would you say? Has it a useful memory? Does it like to study new things?'

'Depends on what they are.' The last new thing the rabbi gave her was that glass of vodka, which had been useful, grant you that, but you learn to be cautious.

'I'm not talking about a big memory. Just a quick one. I need another quick memory.'

What *is* he on about? 'I don't know,' she says non-committally.

'Have you ever played bridge? We are three here who can play and we are looking for the fourth. It seemed to me that maybe you might...? What do you say?'

Well, something to do, she supposes. 'I've never played. I don't know what to do.'

'Couldn't be better. I will teach you. There is nothing more suited to learn than the *tabula rasa.*' He rubs his hands in anticipation.

All the rest of that day is filled with bids and no bids, voids and trumps, points and rubbers and suits. It's all very well for the rabbi to insist, as he keeps doing, that you only have to remember what cards have been played in any one deal, for the five minutes it takes. Marta finds herself struggling to remember the rules, never mind the rest. And then her memory can't slough off the clutter of all the cards from the deal before last, and before she knows where she is it's too dark to play any more. All night long, numbers and suits flick behind her closed lids, diamonds are trumps, diamonds are trumps, in rhythm with the train, although she knows the train isn't moving. But then she wakes and the train *is* moving, and the same landscape plods by. So, while Mr Grabowski continues his fixed and mournful monitoring of its passage, Marta keeps her eyes on the cards in her hand, and her mind on her game. Rabbi Lerner partners her because he is her tutor and only occasionally betrays irritation when her covert communications betray the bridge they have built.

But one morning – catastrophe.

'Time for a change,' he announces. 'You know me too well, and I know you too well, which is bad for your development and bad for your game. You must change partners and see if you can fool me when you're playing with someone else.'

'Oh no!' she wails, aghast at her loss. The two women who have made up their foursome have been mere ciphers up to now. She has barely considered them, and now she is to take one of them seriously while the rabbi himself, by a stroke of his decision, is transformed into a foe. 'Can't we carry on as we were?' He shakes his head. 'Just a while longer?' He shakes his head.

'Time for a change,' he says again as if she hadn't spoken, and she clenches her teeth in rage. All right, then. She'll partner one of those women but she won't bother to play her best and they'll all get so bored again he'll have to switch back.

'Who shall it be? Mrs Kaplan or Mrs Taussig?'

Both ladies incline their heads and smile politely. Mrs Kaplan has large square teeth and thick glasses magnifying wet grey eyes. Mrs Taussig has a large purplish mole on her chin. Both women seem to be wearing wigs. Haven't they got hair of their own?

'Well, it wouldn't be right for you to make a choice because think how disappointed and hurt the other one would be, so I will choose for you. Or rather you will choose, but you won't know how. I will think their names in my head over and over again and when you shout "Stop!" the one in my head will be your partner.'

Rabbi Lerner clangs his eyes shut and Marta envisages Mrs Kaplan and Mrs Taussig pushing past one another in his brain, elbows flying, grim-faced. 'Stop!' she shrieks, louder than she meant to, and the rabbi opens his eyes. He reaches for one of her hands and puts it into the hand of Mrs Taussig.

'Mrs Taussig, please meet Miss Dolniak.' He drops their hands and rubs his own together. 'Now then, let us see if you have the wit to beat us.'

Sometimes, when they wake and open the double doors onto the

endless plain, there, standing by the track as if they have been waiting since the beginning of time only for this train to arrive, ancient
men and bent-backed women are holding out heels of bread and
stoppered bottles of milk. The women shout at the soldiers, who have
been trying to wave them away with their bayonets, but the soldiers
are cowed by their grandmothers' generation.

'I should think,' says the rabbi, 'anyone who lives along this line
must have seen prisoners passing by before.'

Now that the doors have opened, you can see the train curving
with the track; you can see it has two engines, one to pull, one to
push. While the rabbi is shuffling the cards, preparing to cut them,
Marta climbs over feet and legs to lean in the opening and look out
both ways. She grips the edge of one of the sliding doors and like an
urchin swings her entire weight beyond the body of the wagon and
out over the rails. Mrs Bila calls to her to be careful but at this speed
even if she fell she'd only get a graze and still be able to clamber back
on. Further up the train someone has just thrown something out, like
a small bundle.

'Oh, look! Something's just been chucked out. I wonder what it is.
We'll catch up with it in a minute. It's just on that bank up ahead. Do
you see it, Mr Grabowski?'

Mr Grabowski cranes his scrawny neck, catches a glimpse of the
thing by the side of the track and yanks Marta back with such sudden
force that her grip on the door is loosened and she tumbles in, losing her
footing. For a snapshot second her arms are flung up, instinctively seeking a saviour, then she falls back to land heavily on the laps of the Jewish
side of the wagon. Rabbi Lerner's cards scatter, Mrs Kaplan's spectacles
are knocked from her nose, there are squeals of shock and hurt.

It is Mrs Bila – safe on the opposite side of the wagon, uninjured,
undisturbed, entertained rather than dismayed, and with sleeping
Frantek on her knees – who asks Mr Grabowski what it was he saw
that made him so rough. With his eyes on Marta who, shaking somewhat, is extricating herself from the dishevelled matron laps, he leans
over to Mrs Bila and whispers. 'Ah, dear God!' she exclaims, and
crosses herself several times.

The information ripples round the wagon shielded behind cupped hands, all the way up the Polish side and back down the Jewish one. When it reaches Rabbi Lerner he drops the cards he had been gathering up and puts his hands over his eyes. Then he levers himself up and teeters to the sliding doors, arriving there as the wagon passes the object by the line. He stares down on it, then turns his back to the pulling engine to keep the bundle in view and begins to chant a wavering tenor lamentation.

Marta is transfixed by the desolation of his voice and by the unexpected melodiousness of it. It is beautiful and horrible. Everyone in the wagon knows something she doesn't, and it has made Rabbi Lerner jettison the game and wail in song instead. Abruptly he stops. He has come to the end of whatever it was and there is complete silence. Only the weighty wheels of the train rumble on as impassively as the turning of the earth.

The rabbi returns to slump in his seat, looking down at his curled palms and shaking his head like a man in permanent dispute with himself. Marta waits, but no one says anything. So she asks, 'What was it?'

'You don't...' begins Mrs Bila, but Rabbi Lerner interrupts harshly.

'A baby,' he says. 'A dead baby. They've thrown out a dead baby.'

'Who has? The soldiers?'

'Maybe. But I don't think so. If a baby dies – and on a train like this one, it could be many babies will die – what should they do? Keep it in the wagon? God help the mother, whoever she is, poor woman.'

Mrs Bila tightens her grip on Frantek, who was woken by the rabbi's chant but stayed quiet. 'Why did you tell her that? She's only a young girl. What's the point of telling her that?' Mrs Bila almost spits her outrage.

'My dear lady. There are many women who have already had children at her age. Miss Dolniak is no longer only a young girl, and no one helps her by hiding from her the terrible things that happen to people, and that people do. In normal times, though God knows there are few enough of those, perhaps you can cherish youth. But now, if she is to survive, she needs to know everything. I beg your pardon if you are offended.'

He bows to her over his hands but Mrs Bila merely glares back stonily and doesn't speak to him directly again.

There is no bridge that day and almost no conversation. Only Mrs Bila chatters desperately away to Frantek, because you have to. And when the bread rations come everyone sits looking down at the portions in their hands, as hungry as ever, but uneasy. Under the circumstances eating doesn't seem to be the right thing to do.

Avoiding Mrs Bila's eyes, Rabbi Lerner puts a piece of bread in his mouth. 'It is my belief,' he pronounces, 'that it is our duty to live. The death of one is not helped by the death of more.' He points at Marta's untouched bread with his bitten piece. 'Go on, Miss Dolniak. Eat. I am not saying you must enjoy it. But you must eat it.'

The trouble is, once she's started, she does enjoy it.

When the train stops in the middle of the steppe by a river one bright morning the wagonloads are allowed to clamber stiffly down in groups of four or five to wash themselves, gingerly, dabbing and rubbing, fearful for their extremities. You can lose toes and fingers in that sort of cold. They think of sluicing their clothes, but Mrs Bila tells whoever will listen to her that it's certain death because the clothes will freeze before they dry. They jump up and down in the sun, those who can, but do not stray from the railway track. The soldiers squat, watching, but have left their bayonets behind. You can see that a man on foot might walk to the end of his lifetime and never arrive at the further rim of the steppe. It would be like walking across the ocean. There are no barriers like space and the risk of being left behind.

Mr Grabowski and the old rabbi have both begun to tremble all over. They're too old for this, mutters Mrs Bila, and too thin. You need to be young like Marta or well covered. She gives herself a slap on her diminished haunches as a huntsman does to his horse. 'You and me,' she says, 'we're all right. But those two?'

She turns, already bending to lift Frantek up into her arms, but he has vanished. 'Oh, Jesus and Mary save us!' The little one is lost, toddled off somewhere and too frightened now to find his way back. She shields her eyes to scan the countryside because the sun is a sharp white disc, searing to the eyes but withholding warmth. Where can the little one have got to?

Then she sees him. Petya has the baby on his shoulders, and is loping with him slowly along the length of the train.

'Hey!' Mrs Bila has the syllable all prepared in her mouth but gulps it back. Further down the track, Frantek is being handed to a young woman in a dark brown coat, who is weeping hysterically and trying to kiss Petya, and Petya is backing away. 'Come on, let's get the old men inside.'

13

Trains come into the station for Rubtsovsk at Junction Square, which is so large it ought to be a parade ground. The railway station lies along one side; its administrative office, small, low and mostly closed, is built of weathered wood. Next to it is Eating Area No. 3, larger than the administrative office and not open as often as it could be. A pair of buffers set high alerts inattentive train drivers that this is indeed the end of the line. To one side is the water tower.

A metalled road leads away from each of the other three sides, linking the station with the vast collectives that surround it, growing sugar beet and cabbages for the Soviet Union, and providing timber. No more than three kilometres away, the roads become tracks. In the spring the tracks, like the paths between the settlements where the workers live, are thigh-high in mud, and the giant freight trucks pull over to wait for the next season. Just as they did at the onset of winter, the drivers clamber down from the altitude of their cabs and wade through the mud to go and get a drink. In other seasons, when the tracks are dry or frozen, the trucks thunder in once a week with their cargo and the drivers smoke together waiting for a train. There are no timetables here because everywhere is too far away and timetables raise unnecessary expectations. A distant whistle implies the arrival of a train. Silence means more waiting. If towards the end of the day no train has arrived, the trucks unload into the square and depart, and the produce rots unless the local citizens decide, in their public-spirited manner, to keep the area clean.

To the north, at a distance of no more than a hundred kilometres, the taiga begins, primeval forest so thick and dark it's said the sun hesitates over it for fear of being absorbed. In the Altai region you'll find broad-leaved trees as well as pines. In the far north, it's only pines. And the gypsum mines. And the asbestos mines.

The windows of Eating Area No. 3 are steamy with the combined breath of the truck drivers who have been there, eating and drinking, since early morning. Eating Area No. 3 is exceptional. You can actually sit down to your bread and soup. When they first built it, they installed the usual high tables for comrades to stand before their bowls, eat and be gone. But in Junction Square, when people are waiting for a train, there is nowhere to be gone to, so they brought in benches and took a saw to the legs of the high tables, which have wobbled ever since.

Rumour has it that a train may well arrive today, and on the basis of that rumour Aleksandr Sergeich of the local NKVD has been told by Captain Nekrasov, his senior officer, to go out into the square and wait for it. It is fourteen degrees below at the last count, and he thinks his toes won't take much more. He knows that he can't in theory blame prisoners for his having to be out here in the cold, but they are said to be foreigners, and if there were no prisoners at all he might be enjoying a drink in the warm. On the other hand he also understands the laws of logic. If a factory is tasked to make scythes, it follows that wheat must be grown to put the scythes to use. The same principle surely dictates that, if trains are built to transport prisoners, prisoners must be found to put in them. Similarly logic dictates that one's superior may wallow in the seniority of his rank. And that's fair enough. Aleksandr Sergeich thinks that if he were Captain Nekrasov, and Captain Nekrasov were him, he would send himself, as it were, out into the freezing air too and do what Captain Nekrasov is doing now. Which is to be seated behind the steamy windows with a glass of tea in one hand and a glass of vodka in the other while the rest of the bottle is wedged upright between his boots on the floor under the table.

Aleksandr Sergeich hears a whistle. He cups a mittened hand behind his earflap to hear it again. He arcs a mittened hand above his eyes the better to make out wisps of smoke. He turns towards the Eating Area and lumbers gingerly over the ice.

Captain Nekrasov is laying out patience for the fourth time. It is the only game he knows that you can play on your own: one of the disadvantages of working for the NKVD is a lack of invitations to join card games in progress. But you always find a seat, even where the place looks crowded out at first sight, and the seats you get tend to improve. You always get the last bottle going, too. He pours himself a glass. It will take at least three-quarters of an hour for the train to draw in after the first sighting – the damn things go so slowly – and there'll be all that business with putting the signal down, which means getting someone out there to do it, and in this weather it freezes solid so they'll have to put a fire to it to thaw it out enough to move.

'It's the train.' Aleksandr Sergeich has icicles in his eyebrows and in his voice. Captain Nekrasov glances at him and goes on laying out his cards. 'The train.' Aleksandr Sergeich tries again. 'It's coming. I heard it. I saw it. It's on its way.'

'Then let's celebrate,' says his superior, and raises the smaller of his two glasses.

The truck drivers begin piling out of the Eating Area to their vehicles. It's no fun watching Captain Nekrasov baiting junior officers and you never know when he'll suddenly swing round and ask for your papers. Especially when he's had a drop and his game hasn't come out three times in a row.

'Your health,' says Aleksandr Sergeich miserably from his posting by the door. From where he stands, if he squints, he can make out the cards laid out on the table and those in Captain Nekrasov's hand. There's a red jack just waiting to go under that queen of clubs, and, if the captain misses it, it won't come round again. He misses it.

'Look!' Marta is leaning out of the wagon as far as she dares, hanging onto the handles but pointing.

This station seems to be built all of wood, with a raised catwalk on a fretwork of stilts to keep the feet out of the mud and the snow. It looks like the American frontier towns of the cowboy films she loves. But instead of gunslingers there is only an unpaved square large enough for an army on parade, with a few battered trucks parked up, and no movement at all. A faint smell of cabbage hangs on the air.

The train's creeping pace stops altogether, but not yet level with the station; it has been held up by something she can't see. A man wrapped to the ears in thick cloth and carrying a burning stick like a medieval torch is climbing a pole by the track up ahead. He is setting fire to something, or trying to. They'll shoot him surely. This must be sabotage. But then he's dropping his flaming torch, which hits the ground and goes out, and the train is jerking forward again.

Somebody is walking along the train hitting each wagon with a stick as he passes it, shouting something. Does this mean they've arrived? She looks at Mr Grabowski, then at Mrs Bila, who stares back at her and swallows. She glances at Rabbi Lerner, who says nothing but tugs at the tangles of his beard. His agitation unnerves her because he may be feeling as she does: that they have been so long on this train that she cannot wait to leave it, but does not want to relinquish its familiarity. If they get off at this unknown place in the middle of she cannot guess where, the close group of people, her wagon people, will be splintered and their closeness will dissipate. What is this empty wooden outpost, so primitive and desolate? How can it be on the same continent as Poznan and Wilno, those civilized cities? But of course – and she shivers – it's not on the same continent.

'Come along, then.'

Rabbi Lerner rubs his thin knees into action and shuffles stiffly towards the double doors. People are clambering down from the wagons ahead and the man with the stick is banging on their wagon again, irritated at their dawdling. There's to be no hanging back on this train. Petya stands on the icy platform and hands down the old women, even offering an arm to Rabbi Lerner and Mr Grabowski. But once the wagon is cleared he creeps up to Marta and stands so close she has the impression he is trying to hide behind her, and she wonders at him. She looks round to watch more and then more people climbing jerkily down from the train, dark little figures with pale blobs for faces, like a drawing of a crowd rather than a real crowd. And there's a slow wave of noise too. As each wagonload of prisoners is told to get out there is a surge of voices but then as they reach the ground they fall silent, only to hear the excited voices from the wagon behind. It's nearly the end of March but it's still so cold.

Facing them, halfway across the expanse of the square, a man stands adjusting his hat, appearing to sway a little as if buffeted by a wind, but the air is perfectly still and their breath hangs in droplets before their lips. Behind him and to one side stands another man, shuffling from foot to foot. The man in the hat nudges him with an elbow.

'Anyone here speak Russian?' he shouts, in Russian, and even those who don't understand at all think his syllables sound slurred.

From further up the train Marta sees a man stepping forward slowly, supported by two women. It is the Minister for Education. Holding him under the elbows the way you do with people leaving their hospital bed for the first time after a long illness, the women guide him across the treachery of the icy ground. Words are exchanged, then the man in the hat begins to speak, but he is too far away, his voice swallowed up by the cold air. He stops speaking and turns to the man next to him, who stumps off to a car parked on the furthest side of the square. Everyone waits in silence. The man returns, carrying a box and a megaphone. He upturns the box and the man in the hat climbs onto it holding the megaphone. He puts the megaphone to his lips and shouts through it. Then he hands the megaphone to the Minister for Education, who translates through it to his audience of fellow prisoners.

'Now hear this, you scum,' calls out the minister in elegant tones, and hands the megaphone back to the man in the hat for the next sentence.

'If you think you have come here for a holiday or a rest-cure, you are mistaken,' the minister translates.

Another pause for another sentence.

'You will all die here, you bloodsuckers, you.'

'That's a good one, that is. Bloodsuckers yourself!' Mrs Bila waves a fist.

Released by her voice, others join in. 'That's right! You tell him!'

But Captain Nekrasov is feeding another sentence to the Minister for Education. 'You have travelled a long way and do you know what for? To lay your bones in Soviet soil. Because we know who you are, we know all about you and what you did.'

The megaphone is passed back and forth.

'You came to our fatherland and tried to strangle our infant revolution when it was still in the cradle.'

Marta sees the Soviet Union, an enormous baby overflowing its giant cradle, rocked by an old nurse in a flowery headscarf. But here comes someone and shoulders her aside. It is Marta's father with his face twisted in fury. He puts his hands round the baby's neck and squeezes and squeezes. The baby's eyes pop. Its tongue protrudes, bright purple. Marta edges closer to Mrs Bila.

'But you failed and our infant prospered. And now here you are again. This time, however, you are here to work...' Captain Nekrasov makes chopping motions with an imaginary axe – 'to look' – he taps his eyes – 'and to learn' – he taps his forehead.

The Minister for Education translates but ignores the mime.

'You can forget your slimy Polish manners.' Captain Nekrasov grabs the Minister for Education's hand and kisses it, clicking his heels. The audience stares. 'You can forget your bows and your curtseys' – one of each, prettily executed. 'And you can say goodbye to your salons and dainty ways.' Captain Nekrasov drinks tea from a delicate cup, extending his little finger. 'No more servants to brush your clothes. No more slaves to work your fields.' He is warming up nicely with the exercise. It isn't so bad out here on the cold square after all. 'Here you will learn how a superior society does things. You will see at first hand why it is that people all over the globe envy us and long to emulate what we have achieved. And when you go home – if you go home, which you won't – you will take with you such tales that your downtrodden masses will listen to you with their poor hungry mouths open, unable to believe that a society such as ours can exist in this terrible world.'

The Minister for Education is tapping Captain Nekrasov on the arm. Pass the megaphone, my man, or I won't remember everything you said. But he did not become Minister for Education for nothing, and his memory serves him well. Once again he puts his energies into his translation, leaving the words to speak for themselves, but at his side Captain Nekrasov feels prompted to repeat his charade, kisses his fingers, dips and bows, sips his tea, brushes lapels and tills the soil.

The prisoners, most of whom have been hauled off their tiny smallholdings, begin to giggle at the thought that they might ever have enjoyed the sort of life the man on the box has claimed for them. But the pantomime is fun. By the time the Minister for Education reaches the final sentence, which he delivers slowly, pausing for maximum effect, he is all but drowned out by captive laughter. A wave of applause – no one knows where it begins – ripples through the crowd. They clap and clap with their hands high above their heads. *That's it!* thinks Marta, and tears of pride for her countrymen fill her throat. A moment ago they were being harangued, but now they're fighting back, everyone together. She throws her applauding hands up towards the leaden sky.

Captain Nekrasov looks at the suddenly rowdy prisoners uncertainly. He beckons Aleksandr Sergeich and from his box bends to mutter into his ear. 'What are they playing at? Why are they laughing?'

Aleksandr Sergeich shrugs. Foreigners. Who can tell?

Captain Nekrasov snatches the megaphone back from the Minister for Education. 'Now listen, you Polish vermin! You can laugh today, but you won't be laughing tomorrow. Tomorrow you'll be wishing you never interfered in the affairs of our great country... What?... What?' The Minister for Education is trying to tell him something. 'What d'you mean they're not all Poles? What are they then?'

The Minister for Education cups his hand round his mouth to preserve the integrity of the moment. 'A fair number of them are Lithuanians. A mistake, perhaps?'

Captain Nekrasov badly wants to retort that Soviet officials don't make mistakes but he decides not to. He squints out at the prisoners. They all look pretty much the same to him, although they are rather far away. No one has prepared him for this and he feels aggrieved. Why do they always dump the tricky problems on him? He has it on good authority that Lithuanians are all basically peasants, but he was told to expect a trainload of Polish aristos. What is he to do if he can't tell the difference?

Obviously, even if some unfortunate peasants have somehow got themselves mixed up in this consignment, he can't take it upon himself to send them back. How would he ever explain that? But at the same time he doesn't want to be responsible for sending the peasants where only aristos are supposed to go. Frankly, he'd prefer not to be responsible for anything, because if you're not responsible for anything you can't in theory be blamed for it. Although that doesn't always seem to work in practice either. But he *is* responsible. He's the only person in a position of authority, here on Junction Square, this morning, on the 22nd day of March in the year 1941, and he's all alone, you might say, on this upturned box, with thousands of prisoners waiting for him to decide who's a Pole and who's a Lithuanian. It's simply not fair. How can he decide?

Then he has an idea that seems to him a stroke of genius. *They* can decide! Then, if anything goes wrong, they can take the blame. He clears his throat and raises the megaphone to his lips. Shouts into it and hands it over to the Minister for Education.

'You will shortly be setting off for your destinations. If you are Poles, you will go either to the *leskhozy*, the logging camps in the forest, or to the asbestos mines. If you are Lithuanians you will go to the sugar beet fields where you will work alongside our own people for the time being. I will give you fifteen minutes to make up your minds whether you are Poles or Lithuanians. All Poles stay where you are and the Lithuanians go over to that side of the square.' Big wave of the arm so that everyone can see.

The Minister for Education, having pronounced his final syllable, restores the megaphone to Captain Nekrasov, who hands it to Aleksandr Sergeich. The Minister for Education bows to Captain Nekrasov as only a Polish aristo can, and supported by his wife returns to the prisoners, where a certain amount of milling about is going on.

90

Mrs Bila is recommending to Mr Grabowski that he swiftly take on Lithuanian nationality. 'Now don't you be a silly old thing,' she cajoles. 'What's the point of killing yourself in those mines or whatever when you can stay nearby and go to the sugar beet fields? Your health won't stand it, you know that.'

'Madam,' says Mr Grabowski, too courteous to remind Mrs Bila that he is probably no older than she is, even though he may be less robust of constitution. 'In Wilno I was a Latin teacher before I retired. Fields of sugar beet are as foreign to me – as alien, I should say – as asbestos mines or any other sort of mines. Whereas in the summer months I, like many of us, spent many happy days in Ponary among the trees. I feel perfectly at home in forests of every type, and I have no intention of being anything other than a Pole. I was born a Pole and I shall die a Pole, with nothing else in between. Perhaps I might suggest that mining and forestry are not occupations usually suggested for the ladies, particularly if they are… um… how shall I put it… mature?'

'Cheek!' mutters Mrs Bila, and says no more.

'What are you going to be?' Marta asks Rabbi Lerner.

'It's a good question,' he says. 'What do you think? Are Jews Poles or Lithuanians?'

Marta, stumped for once, shakes her head.

'Well, there you are. But I think, we'll just stay where we are. Why move about more than you need to? You, of course, know exactly who you are. Yes, of course you do. And your father would be proud of you, hmm?'

Nevertheless a contingent breaks away and crosses the square. Among them are some people who have just rekindled a fondness for the history and myths of Lithuania. It's only a pity that their grasp of the language is a little rusty, but that will improve with time. Marta glares at the departing group with generalized contempt, since, like Captain Nekrasov, she cannot tell just by looking at them who is a Lithuanian and who a Pole.

14

In the square the Poles by conviction draw together, proud of themselves and of one another, sentenced for being Poles by these Asiatic louts who can't distinguish between a Pole and a Lithuanian, between rich and poor; who know no God, whose uniforms are shabby, and who live like animals, with no moral sense.

Uniformed men, invisible or in hiding before, are approaching. Encouraged by their numbers, Captain Nekrasov shakes out his shoulders. Now he is sanguine about striding across the square to where the prisoners wait and the train's rhythmical panting has subsided.

'All right, all right. Well, there's no point in hanging around, is there?'

He turns, and, by a miracle of organization that makes a deep impression on him, a line of tractors rolls from behind some buildings, each pulling a huge flat trailer without sides.

'On they get,' he instructs the men in uniform. 'Tell them to get on. Get them on board.'

The gentle press of people on the move shoves Marta forwards and for the first time she is afraid. Her feet stumble in one direction but her head is twisting about trying to find her companions from the train. Where is Mrs Bila? What has happened to Mr Grabowski and the rabbi and his people? She thinks she sees the top of Mrs Bila's head but for some reason too far behind to be able to reach her, to be able to join her. Mr Grabowski is too short so she can't pick him out. The rabbi has disappeared.

'Mrs Bila!' she bellows. 'Mrs Bila! Where are you?'

Someone has grabbed her by the elbow and she tries to shake the fingers off but the grip is resolute.

A voice in her ear. An amused voice. 'It's all right, my dear, it's only me.'

'Mrs Benka! Oh, Mrs Benka.'

She would like to throw her arms round Ania's grandmother, like to have Mrs Benka's arms round her, but they are shuffling, inexorably on the move.

Mrs Benka tucks her hand firmly into Marta's elbow. 'That's better. Now if we stay like this we won't get separated, don't you think?'

Marta swallows to return her voice to normal. 'What are you doing here?'

'Very much the same as you. Why did they pick you up?'

Marta finds she is not yet ready to answer.

'Because of your father?'

She nods.

'Well.' The hand in her elbow squeezes it. 'Then you have him for company. That's good.'

'And you too?' She's sounding anxious. Careful now.

'Yes, yes.'

'But why you, Mrs Benka?'

'I think, because I am a landowner parasite exploiting and oppressing the masses.'

'What masses?'

'Old Petrkiewicz, for one.'

'But he –'

'I know.'

'Where is he? Is he here too?' Although, if he's the masses, perhaps the Bolsheviks have donated Mrs Benka's farm to him. But then, that would make *him* a landowner.

Mrs Benka brings her other hand round and holds Marta's arm tighter. 'I'm afraid, when he saw them coming, he got a pitchfork and stood with it on the path and shouted at them that they're weren't coming closer while he was alive. I was trying to tell him that it wouldn't do any good, but he wasn't listening.'

'What happened?'

'Well, they didn't stop and he rushed them with his pitchfork and stuck it into one of them. I don't think the man was injured, really. Old Petrkiewicz wasn't strong enough for that any more.'

'Wasn't?'

'The soldier pushed him off and he fell over. He hit his head.'

One by one they are levered up onto the giant trailers to squat, backs against backs, for warmth and support – so many of them that if they do not huddle close, those at the edges may topple off. Forty, fifty, sixty. Marta cannot turn to count. When finally it is accepted that there really is no more space the tractor sets off, dragging its load back the way it has come.

Twice a day they stop to let people relieve themselves by the track-side, men to the left, women and children to the right. In the mornings a few loaves of bread are thrown to each trailer for the people to divide as they see fit; the muffled driver hands up two buckets of water and a single tin cup to pass round. Drink or wash: you decide. Where does the water come from? They must have containers of it on one of the trailers. At night they have to stay where they are, the only warmth each other's bodies. If it snowed they would shelter under the trailers, perhaps, but the sky remains clear. Once again Marta begins to dream of arrival, somewhere where there will be a roof, and enough water. Something more to eat than this. But Mrs Benka says only, 'I hope so, dear.'

Halfway through the third day the trees begin. Within an hour the track is running in a meandering line cut through the forest, and the air is suddenly warmer. Looking up between the branches where tiny dark nodules promise buds in the imaginable future, Marta sees blue sky. A sharp cold blue, but blue none the less. She feels the muscles of her body loosen just a little.

The driver, who for three days has crouched over his wheel under his coat, the earflaps of his hat tied under his chin like an old woman, shows signs of life. He shouts something, without turning his head, and stabs the air ahead. Everyone shifts to be able to see, kneeling, hands on other shoulders. There is a clearing. There are some low wooden buildings like barracks, row upon row of them going back into the trees, whose lowest branches seem to merge with the roofs as if the wooden planks were branches only yesterday. Four small square windows are set in the long sides of each building and a single stovepipe at one end is topped with a vertical, unmoving column of smoke. A few bundled figures stand, hands on hips, to watch the convoy of tractors arrive.

The driver reaches forward and switches off his engine and with a slight shudder the tractor falls still. There has never been a silence like this one. There is no movement in the branches of the trees; there is no birdsong, no breeze, no footsteps; nobody speaks. But there is a smell of woodsmoke from the low buildings, and of cold damp earth. No one wants to be the first to move.

A horseman comes galloping down a track that leads into the forest beyond the buildings and the hooves are like gunshots on the hard ground. They must have been going a fair distance because the horse is sweating. Its rider is wearing boots and a heavy coat with large buttons. He pulls the horse up sharply and it prances from hoof to hoof on the spot. The horseman brings out a short whip from under his coat and waves it once. Then one of the bundled figures breaks away from the others and walks up to the prisoners as slowly as if he has all the time in the world and no one to count it. He limps badly on one side but circles the trailer, keeping to his uneven amble, eyes on the newcomers all the way round, and all the way round they keep their eyes on him. When he has completed his circuit he parks himself between the trailer and the low buildings and plants his feet to form the wide base of a triangle.

Marta finds it all but impossible to look at him. His hair is longish and sparse, lank and grey. He is bearded but round the whiskers his face is blotched with red patches, the skin both shiny and scaly. His unfriendly gaze is mottled, the whites of his eyes thick and yellow. Layers of rags have removed his shape. The topmost layer is some sort of stained reddish-brown coat with a length of twine holding it at the waist. His feet are wound round and round in what seem to be pieces of black cloth that cannot ever have been washed. There he stands, moving his eyes slowly from person to person, as if he is assessing them one by one for some awful future purpose. And one by one, as they feel this fixed glare descend on them, they turn their faces away, like forest animals that have been stared down.

All at once he appears to have satisfied himself. He points to his chest and announces in a voice rattling with phlegm, 'Pavel Kuzmich.' As he turns and leads the way to the door of the nearest building, his left shoulder rises and falls with his limp, while he beckons to them to follow.

Slowly they climb down from the trailer and set off after Pavel Kuzmich. Their legs are cramped and complaining, the older ones groaning, the younger ones feeling like the old. The other bundled figures have still not moved but are also assessing them, sullen-eyed. Trying not to attract attention, Marta keeps glancing at them and thinks that she has never seen such indifference on any human face before. Here they are in the forest, where nothing ever happens, and new people arrive and they couldn't care less.

Pavel Kuzmich has come to a stop at the door of the nearest building and is still beckoning. But as the first of the prisoners reaches him he steps in front of the doorway and blocks it. He puts out a hand and grabs the woman, as most of them are, and pushes her to the side but pulls the next one in. And the next, pushes the fourth aside, pulls in three more. When Marta and Mrs Benka arrive he barely looks up but, shaking his head, prises Marta's arm off Mrs Benka's elbow and separates them.

'No!' shouts Marta. 'No! No!' That's a word anyone can understand, surely.

Mrs Benka makes a grab for her but finds Pavel Kuzmich's arm solid as a tree trunk between them. Marta catches sight of the man on the horse. He is not looking. His head is high, his back is straight and both he and his horse seem to be attending to something on a horizon beyond the dense trees. The tussle going on a few feet from the horse's hooves might not be happening.

'Sorry, granny,' mutters Pavel Kuzmich in Russian and with a hand on her chest shoves Mrs Benka firmly away. She stiffens at the touch but falls back.

Marta finds herself propelled into the group Pavel Kuzmich has already selected. He seems to be counting under his breath with each choice he makes and, reaching a final figure, nods to confirm it. He holds up both grimy hands signalling a pause, then leads his chosen group into the building. Looking at her companions for the first time, Marta sees that they are all very young women and girls.

They are in a long low room of pale, new, unplaned wood, rough splinters in the walls and on the rafters of the steeply pitched roof. Two wide shelves run the length of the walls. The floor is stamped earth and there is a table in the centre, almost as long as the room. Against the end wall a hearth of burning logs is heating a vast pot suspended over it on a triangle of twisted wire fixed to the crossbeam above. The steam is odourless, so it's only water.

Pavel Kuzmich allocates them each a tin mug and a spoon, and as he hands them round he grips each mug and each spoon extra tight in his hands, with a little shake under the nose of the young woman he's giving them to: these are precious; don't you lose them. He points to the cauldron. If they want a drink of hot water, there it is. He points to the shelves, folds his hands together at shoulder height and lays his cheek on them. He takes a girl by the shoulders and turns her to the shelves, pushing her slightly. Go. Choose yourself a space. Mark your territory. She goes, slowly, shyly, aware the others are watching, and lays her bundle on a top shelf halfway down the room. Turns to face inward, seeking the awful man's eyes, fearful he might find something amiss in what she's done. But he merely nods and limps heavily among the other women, touching them one by one on the shoulder to set them on their way. Marta decides to pick a spot before he can put his hands on her. He notices and says to himself: *Aha.*

Then he's gone, out of the door, presumably to see to the next batch. But he returns almost immediately, dangling a couple of spades in each hand. He bangs these together to attract attention and jerks his head towards the outside. They follow him, and in their pairs begin to complain.

97

'He's foul, isn't he?'

'Have you ever seen anyone so sickening?'

'Have you seen his face? Ugh!'

'I hope he doesn't stick so close to us all the time. Jesus and Mary! The stink!'

Behind their building there's a shallow pit surrounded by a high wooden fence of slats with a hole like a small door cut into it. He points to it with a spade, then, passing the spade to the nearest girl, mimics hoisting his tattered clothes, squats and pretends to defecate. Grins. Now he has revealed his teeth too. He points again. More spades are leaning against the wall. Go on then, girls. Get going. Latrines have to be as deep as a house is high.

At least the earth isn't as frozen as it would have been a month ago. But the deeper you dig the harder it is to throw it up. What they need is some buckets and ropes, but those have not been provided. Is this how it is to be, digging the deepest holes you can simply in order to fill them up again? And is Mrs Benka somewhere nearby, digging the latrines for her hut too?

By dusk, Marta knows the names of the young women who have been digging by her side. She knows where they have come from, how they were arrested, how many of their belongings they were allowed to bring. Some of them had an arresting officer who turned his back while they packed. Some of them had an officer who took their stuff for himself, or for his wife, or his girlfriend. Above all she has learned that the others were scooped up for no reason. None of them seems to know why she is here. None of them has a father who tried to strangle the infant revolution while it was still in its cradle. So the fact that, uniquely, she has one who did doesn't seem to carry weight any more.

Her heroism seeps away under the weight of chance. But then it occurs to her that, if she is the only one who is not here on false pretences, she has the most significant role to play as a conscious representative of her country and what it stands for. She will pit Poland's honour against the Soviet Union, and against its grotesque representative, Pavel Kuzmich.

But the handle of her spade jars a blister and Poland's honour recedes. Nobody at home knows she is here. Even Ania in the convent doesn't know she is here, only that she is not there. What if that man in the square was right and she stays here for ever – if she dies here among strangers, leaving her bones in the ground like he said? If these huts were empty and waiting for them, the bundled ones and the man on the horse expecting them, then there must have been other prisoners here before her. And the others must have been prisoners who have all died already and their bones are somewhere in the forest; prisoners who were made to dig their own latrines on their first day too. But how long did they live in this hut and use the latrines? How many days? Or weeks? Or years?

Next to her a girl with fair hair hanging over her face is crying as silently as she can, grimy tears on her cheeks and her nose running. As Marta turns to her, she finds her own nose is wet, and quickly rubs it on her sleeve.

'Come on,' she says, more briskly than she intended. 'We'll be all right. You'll see.'

15

Night comes slowly to the forest, as if the light is being inhaled back into the sky. By dusk all their hands are blistered and they are feeling sick for lack of food. If they only had more to eat, if they had only had more to eat in the last two and a half months, they would be digging better. What's the point of bringing them all here to work, which is what the man in the square at Rubtsovsk said they were to do, if they get so little to eat they can't do any work? But what a ridiculous man, with his box and his megaphone and his bits of play-acting!

The silhouette of Pavel Kuzmich bulks out of the darkness, only his gargoyle of a face illuminated by the hurricane lamp he dangles up by his ear. He swings it. Time to go in. The young latrine-diggers trail back into their hut, some more dishevelled than others. The steam from the blackened cauldron reeks of cabbage and there are two slices of black bread to go with the soup.

A pair who have been working side by side now sit warming their hands on their tin mugs. You can tell by the way they lean against one another that this is an old friendship. One of them is slim with straight dark hair she has tucked behind her ears. She's Basia, and the other one, stocky, snub-nosed and freckled, is Hania. When Hania speaks, her voice rasps like the voices of little urchin boys who shout too much.

'Hey, you two! Come and sit here.' She pats the rough trestle table to indicate the space opposite.

Marta turns. Who is that other person Hania has invited? Behind her, with her head hanging so low that her fair hair falls over her face, is Dorota. Sad Dorota, Marta has dubbed her, already deciding that Dorota is to be her project. The poor girl needs jollying along. She needs encouragement.

'Let's join them,' she says, and leads Dorota to the bench.

The soup stinks. The few bits of cabbage floating in it are slimy. Hania and Basia, Marta and Dorota clutch their mugs for the warmth but do not drink.

'We have to,' says Basia eventually. 'There's no choice.' But having spoken these few words she goes on staring despondently into the steaming liquid.

'Always listen to Basia,' croaks Hania. 'She doesn't say much, but when she does she's always right. Dammit. So here goes.' She takes a swig from her mug. 'Oh, for God's sake. That's vile! Persuade me, Basia. Why is it better to drink this stuff than not?'

'Because we need everything there is.' And she dips a piece of black bread into the liquid and with everyone watching drops the sodden piece into her mouth. Chews it. Swallows it without expression.

Hania peers into her face. 'Don't tell me you liked that.'

But Basia doesn't answer. Just smiles and repeats the procedure.

'See what I mean? So reasonable it drives you mad.' Now Hania dips and swallows.

'Come on, Dorota,' urges Marta. 'Let's say we're doing this for Poland.'

Hania splutters into her mug. 'Well, I hope Poland's grateful.'

'She will be when she finds out.'

'Who's going to tell her?'

'We will. When we get back.'

'Oh, and how are we going to do that?'

'First step, by eating cabbage soup, of course.'

'Second step?'

Marta scowls. 'I'll have worked that out tomorrow. Then I'll let you know. But I'll tell you something. Look at this place.' She draws a circle with her nearly empty mug. 'The wood looks new, doesn't it? And we had to dig the latrines. Doesn't that mean we're the first people here? They built this camp for us Poles because they knew we were coming.'

'Oh, come on!' Hania is laughing. 'How could they know we were coming? I mean, us in particular? I bet they just keep building barracks in the forest and then run around filling them up.'

Basia wipes her last piece of bread round the inside of her mug as if there really were goodness to be had there. Will they be competing, her Hania and this girl Marta, for the first gesture and the last word? She hopes not. If there are battles to be fought here, let the fighting not be among themselves.

'We should sleep,' she says. If she gets up now, so will Hania.

'Yes, mama, no, mama, whatever you say, mama.' Hania pulls a face for everyone to see, but without spite, and follows Basia to their section of shelving.

Marta closes her eyes, her fingers still curled round the handle of her mug, and wishes Ania were there as well. But then realizes that if Ania were indeed there it would mean that she would have to have been arrested too. Mrs Benka wouldn't be in the least bit pleased to see her granddaughter in this camp in the forest over two months' journey from home.

Someone is pulling her shoulder. Marta lifts her head from the table. It's Pavel Kuzmich with his lamp again. He directs its dim beam to the shelf where she left her bundle and she stumbles over to it, climbs up and lies down between the bodies already stretched out. Will he never leave them alone? Where did Dorota go?

In the morning it's not yet fully light when the door is flung open. It crashes back against its holding wall and the entire hut shudders on its frame. Everyone is awake, remembering where they are, hungry, apprehensive. And the ones who did last night's digging are stiff in every muscle.

The cauldron is back to hot water, a murky brownish water that they assume is supposed to be tea, flavoured with cabbage soup. Two slices each of black bread. Marta sits with her new friends. Dorota's father is a bank administrator and she has two little sisters who are only ten and eight. Dorota is as tall as Marta but willowy and long-waisted. She's terribly pale, her skin floury white under the dirt.

Marta looks down at her hands, at her wrists; she prods her calves under the table. She is thinner. Well, of course she is. Hania must have been a podgy thing, then, she's still quite solid. Marta likes Hania's freckled face, though she is a bit pushy. Her parents are both doctors.

'Both of them?'

Hania nods. 'Of course.'

'But who looked after you when you were little?'

'Oh.' Hania shrugs. 'Various people.'

It seems a lot of the time they've let her look after herself. And after school she ran about pretty much as she wanted. Lucky Hania.

But then Hania adds, 'Actually, it's all down to Basia. My parents had this idea that Basia was sensible, you know. Reliable. They thought that if Basia was around I wouldn't get into any scrapes.'

'And did she?' Marta turns to Basia, who smiles and makes a vague movement of her head that might be yes, might be no.

Happening to glance up, Marta sees Pavel Kuzmich leaning against the stove, eating, and watching her. For a second they lock eyes before she turns hers away. The man is truly horrible, though she has noticed that he, too, has only two slices of black bread and a mug of watery tea. He looks exactly the same as yesterday, as if he has slept in his clothes. But they have all slept in their clothes.

Pavel Kuzmich claps his hands and limps down the room, counting a number for each woman as he passes her and taps her shoulder. When he gets to twenty, his arm guillotines a barrier through the air and he yells, *'Brigada pervaya!'* Then he counts out another twenty. *'Brigada vtoraya!'* And again. *'Brigada tret'ia!'* And the last, *'Chetvyortaya!'*

Brigada must mean brigade. Is he dividing them up? He claps his hands again. *'Brigada pervaya so mnoi!'* And limps to the door. No one moves. Back he comes, sighing theatrically. He grabs the first girl, and the second, and tugs them to their feet. Repeats, *'Pervaya brigada so mnoi!'*

They all understand now and follow him out. At the door Hania turns and rolls her eyes at the ones still sitting. But then, as she makes to leave, one of last night's surly bundled figures pushes in past her. He has come to fetch 2nd Brigade.

Outside the air is quite still. There is a line of light lifting between the trees and, abruptly, the shrill trilling of some bird. Marta knows nothing about birds and isn't interested, but Pavel Kuzmich puts a rag-covered hand to his ear and cups it, the forefinger of the other on his lips. They all stop short, distilled in the positions they were in until the bird trills again. Pavel Kuzmich throws his arms wide, which sudden action makes the bird, a black and brown thing, flap away in alarm. '*Vesna!*' he shouts, and clasps his fists above his head in triumph. '*Nastupayet vesna!*' Something has cheered him up.

He is still squinting up into the branches to see where the black and brown songbird went when the ground begins to vibrate. Pavel Kuzmich shakes his head as if clearing nonsense from it and hands each member of 1st Brigade one of last night's latrine spades. He takes one himself and shoulders it, lumbers to the front and shouts at the top of his voice, '*Brigada pervaya, marsh!*'

You can't mistake that, and the twenty young women, ordered into a column, prepare to march, with their spades like rifles on their shoulders.

The vibrations are now audible as horse's hooves, and yesterday's rider gallops up just as the column has got itself into order. He pulls up his mount with such an extravagant tug on the reins that the horse tosses its head and snorts a protest. The rider looks down on them from his great height, then wrenches the horse round, and the two of them leap away to inspect 2nd, 3rd and 4th Brigades.

'*Desiatnik,*' explains Pavel Kuzmich incomprehensibly, and pointing down the track in the opposite direction leads his brigade to their first day's work. The spade lying over his left shoulder rises and falls with the rising and falling of the shoulder, and as he goes he leans heavily on the stick he grips in his right hand to take the weight from his limping right leg.

The sun has risen but between the tree trunks still hangs low enough to catch them directly in the eyes. Theirs is an unhurried tramp over the forest floor because Pavel Kuzmich sets the pace. This is the first time in two months that they have been able to move properly, to stretch their legs, and initially they enjoy it. But within minutes the unused legs begin to tire, even though the ground is flat, and a communal fear grips them. Marta is marching just ahead of Hania and Basia – well, not marching but, like everyone, hauling her feet forwards. They weigh so heavily at the ends of her legs. She hears Hania mumbling, not to her companion but to herself, like someone rehearsing their times tables. Then all at once Hania announces, 'It can't be done.'

'What can't?'

'This. On what they've been giving us to eat. Five hundred grams of bread a day, is it? You can live on that if you're stuck in a train and not moving, but an active body requires a minimum of...'

Hearing what you supposed spoken by someone who probably knows is disheartening. All the girls within earshot find their legs buckling; a minute later the entire column falls back. Pavel Kuzmich must have sensed that his unit is trailing because, without altering his pace, he raps his stick against a tree trunk and barks, *'Vperyod! Marsh!'*

March, march. How can they march?

An hour. Another. They are desperate to sit down; their knees are trembling, their calves and shins are burning, their ankles have stiffened and will not flex any more. Still Pavel Kuzmich heaves himself along as if nothing can stop him, his shoulder rising and falling, rising and falling. Marta glues her eyes to the man in front of her and is revolted. This is the first day of uncountable days to come and this vile and fearful man must know how weak they are. That's why he is so evidently enjoying himself, wielding his bit of power, making them suffer just because he knows he can.

But can he? Marta assumes 1st Brigade are alone on this forest track – God alone knows where the others have gone. Pavel Kuzmich is in charge, it's true, but he's on his own. If they all just sat down now, what could happen? He's not armed. He's got his stick, of course, and his spade, but so have they. Twenty spades against one. And if they all sit down together he won't be able to make them get up, not all on his own. The question is where to sit? The ground is damp where the sun is getting through, thinly snowy where it never reaches. There aren't any cut logs or stumps. But it might be worth it, just to make their point that this walking is too much, that they won't be able to do anything useful if they're completely worn out by the time they arrive. She nudges Dorota, who is tottering with her head down, misery dripping from her nose.

'What say we stop? Just stop and sit down and have a rest?'

Dorota lifts her head and stares at Marta. 'What? You mean just like that?'

'Yes. If we all do, all at the same time, what can he do?'

Dorota doesn't want to provoke something awful. 'Let's ask Hania.'

Marta is about to demur but then thinks better of it. She raises her voice. 'Hey, Hania. I don't know about you but I've had enough of this. I need to sit down. But at this rate Quasimodo over there is going to keep us walking till sunset. What if we just stop and refuse to go any further? Just sit down and don't move?'

'Bad idea.'

'Why?'

'Because, if we sit down, I promise you, with the state our legs are in, we won't be able to get up again.'

'But that doesn't make sense! We'll have to stop at some point.'

Hania doesn't reply.

All the same, without consensus you cannot stage rebellion and Marta drags on, conscious that next to her Dorota is finding it harder going than she is. Distract her somehow. If it were the Girl Guides, of course, they'd sing to keep themselves going. She wonders how many kilometres they have covered; every step they take forward they will have to take back again in the evening. At least they will know the way because there is only one way so long as you stay on the track. But she's supposed to be thinking about how to ginger Dorota up.

'Tell me about your little sisters. What are they like? Are they nice or a nuisance?'

106

Dorota wipes her nose on her cuff and says, 'Well, the big one, Jola, is always…'

But the track has suddenly ended in a huge clearing where trees have been chopped down. Except there are no stumps. It looks as if there never were any trees here, though that's not possible, since the forest is tall and dense all around it. The ground is black, blackened, with patches of sand. And someone has stuck a stake into the ground at either end of hundreds of long rows. Thousands of them.

Pavel Kuzmich lays his stick down, lowers his spade and begins digging a hole by the nearest stick. They stand and watch, and now that they're no longer walking the soles of their feet sting. Slowly, methodically, approaching his hole from each side, Pavel Kuzmich digs deeper, commenting as he goes, '*Vot tak, i vot tak, i vot tak.*' Straightens. Beckons. Come and look and see how it's done. Without enthusiasm, without interest, they inspect his hole. It's neat and round and about twice the depth of the head of his spade. Now you. He shakes his spade at a point about a metre further along. Each of them must dig a hole a metre from the last one, and each has her own row.

Marta glowers at him and thinks how easy it would be for them to rush him and beat him to the ground with their twenty spades. She finds he has met her eyes and thinks he has read in them what she was thinking. His seem to be telling her that out here there is no point because out here there is never any escape.

The soil is light and, if you could only throw enough energy into your spade, it would dig more easily than the heavier stuff behind their hut. But the spade itself is heavy today. All the same it takes no more than a few minutes to dig the first hole, so that's encouraging. A few to dig the second and by the third and fourth, as she gets into the swing of it, gets used to the technique, she's managing a hole every eight spadefuls. With twenty of them going, at this rate they'll be done in no time. She's sweating a little and stands up to rub the moisture from her nose. She looks back at the line she's covered. Looks out into the clearing where the stick markers stretch away in their lines so far away that the furthest are almost invisible. *We're going to be here for ever.* She leans on her spade to flex her back and closes her eyes. When she opens them again, Pavel Kuzmich is standing there with his feet planted into their wide triangular stance.

He points to the spot where he expects the next hole, puts a finger in his mouth, pats his stomach – '*Bez raboty khleba ne budet*' – and taps his forehead with the finger. Do you get my meaning?

Khleb sounds like bread. What is he saying about bread? She glares at him. Irritation is all over his face. He pushes her along and starts digging again himself, then stops and pretends to be chewing something. But then takes his spade and drops it while opening his foul mouth to display its blackened stumps, to show that it is empty. Digs. Chews. Now do you understand? She does, but in a fury that brings such sudden tears to her eyes that she has to dip her head to hide them. How dare he make their pathetic slices of bread dependent on the amount you dig!

Basia is at her elbow. 'Dig more slowly.'

'What?'

'Dig slowly, then you won't get so tired.'

'Tortoise and hare,' advises Hania, coming up on the other side. She taps her nose and points at Basia. 'Told you so. The wise one has spoken.'

Hour after hour Marta scrapes away with her spade, but she is flagging; it takes her longer to dig each hole, and each hole is shallower than the preceding one. Along the lines she sees it's much the same for the others, even for Hania and Basia, no matter how good Basia's advice might be. Dorota is a number of holes behind, her body sagging like a sapling whose support has been removed, and the tears are a torrent on her face. Marta feels a twinge of satisfaction that she is tougher than Dorota, physically more robust, altogether made of sterner stuff. But she must remember that she comes from a different background. Her father is not a bank administrator, after all, and, since he is not, it's up to her take over. So Marta casts her spade noisily aside and tries to run back to Dorota but finds that her legs won't move that quickly.

She loops an arm round Dorota's shoulders and says, 'We're bound to stop for a rest soon. Look!' – pointing to the sky where the sun is as high as it can get at this time of year. 'It must be nearly lunchtime. If we all collapse because we haven't eaten or had a rest, Quasimodo will have to carry us all back. Can you imagine it?'

'No,' sniffs Dorota, but at least she laughs.

Pavel Kuzmich comes lumbering down the lines calling as he goes. '*K stolu, devushki. Obedat' pora.*' He's patting the air with flattened hands, down, down, they can either sit on the damp ground or go on standing, it's up to them, and frankly he doesn't care. He hands out two slices of bread each.

Marta glances round to be sure everyone has their bread before she begins to eat hers. She ought to keep note of everyone's morale. Hania is looking all right, under the circumstances, and Basia almost serene, which is extraordinary. But what about the two young ones, Sophie and Maria? They're together, though Quasimodo has shoved himself between them, poor things. She wonders whether she should rescue them, but that would mean getting up again and she has an enormous urge to conserve her energies for later tasks that may prove more important.

'Oof!' she says, and rubs her legs. Basia nods sympathetically at her. 'You all right, Basia?' Basia nods again. 'If it weren't for old Quasimodo we could pretend we were on a picnic, couldn't we?'

Basia speaks. 'I don't know about him.'

'What do you mean?'

But Basia's quotient of speech has been all used up.

Instinctively, 1st Brigade have formed as tight a circle as they can, sitting so close to one another that you couldn't insert the handle of a spade between them. They do not speak at all but concentrate on their two slices of bread, on the taste in their mouths, on the saliva the chewing brings. But then, too soon, they have finished, and simply sit, their chins tipped down onto their chests, eyes shut, each mind closed to the ones on either side.

It is dark when the twenty members of 1st Brigade drag themselves back into the hut. They have been on their feet for twelve hours except for the brief lunchtime break. They have eaten two slices of bread for breakfast, two at lunch, and now, probably, they will get two more, and some of that soup whose stench is already filling the hut. Not quite half the holes have been dug – which means that tomorrow will be exactly the same as today, but by tomorrow they will be more tired than they were today because of today's work, and tomorrow they will know what to expect. As they slump against the table the other brigades are filing in and it would be good to ask them where they went and what they were doing, but it would take too much effort and, anyway, they can find out another day.

The last time they washed was the morning of their last day on the train. Somewhere there must be water in this place because what is their soup if not made of water? Marta stinks. Next to her Dorota stinks. Everyone stinks but everyone is the same person she was. Or maybe not. Not because they haven't been able to wash but because their lives have changed so much they must have been changed too. She wishes she could wash, but she wishes much more that she could sleep and that, at least, she can. In a minute, as soon as she has finished wiping her last piece of bread round the inside of her mug, she can.

''Night,' she says to her companions on either side, but they are already asleep.

For some reason the picture comes into her mind of Petya running down the train with little Frantek, looking, looking, then handing him into the arms of his hysterical mother. They must be here somewhere too, or somewhere like it. What must it be like to have to look after a little child *and* do all the work, *and* have nothing to eat? So she is lucky, then. God preserve her from having to look after children. Ever.

In the early hours Marta wakes with an idea whirling in her head. When they get to the clearing she will take over Dorota's planting and Dorota can continue hers; that way, with luck, Dorota won't lag behind. The thought of it fills her with energy. As long as she paces herself and doesn't squander her strength, she should be able to keep going and protect Dorota from trouble. The only problem might be Quasimodo. If he cottons on to what she's about, he's bound to do something to thwart her. Behind her closed lids she can see the blotchy skin and the rheumy eyes. She can smell him. She can smell herself too. If she gets up now, before Quasimodo shows up, while it's still dark, she might be able to discover where they get the water from. She might find a bucket.

Slowly Marta eases herself from her space between the other girls and guides herself to the door. She opens it, but only a little way, listens at the opening, opens it some more. All the time she is expecting to be face to face with Pavel Kuzmich, but there is no one there. It is still night-time and a half-moon reflects off the patches of snow. Stiffly, trying not to step on a twig or slip on the ice, she creeps round the other side of the latrines and the hut, and realizes how many more huts stand beyond. This is almost like a village, but constructed on a grid. Planned on paper and built on the snow and the ice in the middle of winter. If there are eighty people in each hut, there must be... but she cannot see how many huts there are. Even if it was light she wouldn't be able to see them all. One of these days, when she has a free half-hour, she will explore the layout and make an estimate of the imprisoned population. Free half-hour! Who is she kidding?

Between two huts she makes out something smaller and lower. A cloud drifts over the half-moon and the landscape is obliterated. What if this is only the first of many clouds and she has to wait here, as good as blind, until dawn? They will come out of their huts and surround her. The bundled ones will close in on her until she cannot breathe and... Stop! Stop this, now. If that happens, she will simply explain that she came out to use the latrines and took a wrong turn in the dark. But she cannot explain. She cannot make her words understood, any more than they can theirs.

The cloud has moved on, and the moon re-illuminates the squat building. Closer to it now, Marta can see it is a well. There is no question it is a well, but nowhere can she make out anything that looks like a bucket. Maybe the water's not too far down. She picks up a stone and, gripping the parapet, drops the stone down. There is no splash at all. The stone has landed on hard ground, has even bounced. So the damned well must be dry.

111

She can taste the disappointment like metal in her mouth. All this careful effort – and nothing. And now she must creep her way back as she crept her way out, let herself into her hut and close the door, climb back onto her bunk and lie herself down as if she had never left it. Please God let there be no more clouds.

Along the way Marta fixes her eyes to the ground, watchful again for anything that might make a noise under her shoes. As she approaches the hut before hers and looks up she thinks there is the outline of someone standing in the doorway, a bulky, ill-defined figure. But it doesn't move. The only thing she can do is pretend it isn't there, that she hasn't seen it.

But for the rest of the night the image flickers behind her eyelids and her sleeping is uneasy.

16

Come the morning and, if anything, Dorota is even more hangdog than she was yesterday because now she knows how far, how long she has to walk, and her blistered palms sizzle with pain wherever they touch the shaft of the spade she carries against her shoulder. Marta plans to jolly her out of it.

'You were going to tell me about your little sisters yesterday, but you couldn't.'

But today Dorota can. She talks and talks about her two little sisters, so different, both so sweet; about her father, so lanky and tall; about her mother, who is so loving. She talks about happy hours baking biscuits and reading fairy-tales to her sisters at their bedtime. Everything she has ever wanted has been left behind in that small family apartment.

The kilometres pass, and still Dorota talks.

'I'll get you back there, I promise,' says Marta emphatically, regretting the chatter she has unloosed. 'You just see if I don't.' And she gives Dorota's hand the warm squeeze of commitment and friendship.

Dorota replies, simply, 'Thank you.' And a moment later, as if she has thought it over, 'I know you will.'

Plan number one has done the trick. The clearing is in sight and the walk doesn't seem to have taken nearly as long as it did yesterday. Now for plan number two. She'll have to wait for Quasimodo to turn his back or get busy with whatever it is he does while they're digging, and then she'll quietly get herself onto Dorota's row before Dorota can start, saying casually, Oh, that one was yours, wasn't it. With luck, Dorota won't even remember.

They have come to a halt, and Marta, who has placed herself at the head of the marching column just behind their limping brigade leader, calls back.

'Everyone all right there?'

To her surprise, someone seems to be giggling and there are a couple of long moans, drawn out for effect.

Basia nods at her and smiles. Hania gives her a smart salute – yessir! – and what looks like an ironic grin.

'*Na rabotu!*' announces Pavel Kuzmich, and hoists his spade. But as Marta guides Dorota to the place where they left off digging yesterday Pavel Kuzmich barges into them, saying, '*Syuda, syuda,*' and propels the pair of them to a new area some rows beyond. What? Marta is in no position to argue, or even to ask why he's moved them. Too bad. She'll just have to arrange the swap after the midday break.

In some ways it comes more easily today. Her arms, her body, even her feet remember how things should be done – the best angle for the spade, the amount of pressure she has to put on it to make it sink into the soil, how much she needs to bend. But her muscles are still complaining about yesterday's work, and the food is so little... so little. She feels sick all the time. She must take it more slowly than before, really pace herself. But, if she doesn't get as many holes dug in the same time as the day before, then how will she be able to make up for Dorota?

It seems warmer than it was, the tiniest bit. Perhaps in these extreme places the weather and the seasons turn more quickly. Everyone knows how the rivers here freeze solid in winter and then in spring how the ice cracks, great plates of it snapping under the insistence of time. Then the land is knee-deep in mud, so that carts, lorries, everything gets stuck. How can people live here, how can they possibly want to live here? But they don't want to, of course. That's why this has always been the place of prisoners, made to do the work needed by the great Russian empire, the great Soviet Union, and which no one, given the choice, would ever do. So every now and then they have to kidnap people who won't be given the choice,

114

pressgang them, make them dig holes, day after day. She wonders whether the other three brigades from her hut are also digging holes somewhere among the trees; whether, in fact, everyone is out digging.

What for? Quasimodo knows – but he would never explain. He gets too much pleasure from pushing people around, and keeping them in the dark. Over to her left Dorota is struggling, about ten holes behind, but not looking too dejected. Hania and Basia seem to be in the section they were all in yesterday. It doesn't make sense what Quasimodo did, shunting her and Dorota away like that.

'Marta!'

'What? What is it?'

'It's Pavel Kuzmich. He's saying it's time for our break.'

'Thank God for that.'

Down they hunker in their circle, facing inwards. Odd how that came about. It wasn't anyone's idea. It just happened yesterday, as if forming a closed circle is what you do when you're tired and hungry – and frightened.

Something makes her look over her shoulder and she sees Pavel Kuzmich get to his feet. That must mean the lunch break is over, so if she's going to make up Dorota's digging she'd better get over to her row before Dorota notices. Off she goes, but midway there he is again! Quasimodo takes her by the elbow and won't let go for all she tries to shake him off, grips her elbow and directs her away from their rows and into another new section. Limps back to the rest of the circle, who are on their feet now and watching warily, grabs hold of Dorota and points towards Marta. Go over there, he's telling her. That's where you dig now. Dorota shrugs. Why should she care where she digs? All she wants is to be allowed to stop.

It looks as though there aren't many rows between them and the edge of the forest, not as many holes to dig as they managed before their break, so by evening, if all goes well, it should be done. Well, that's good, though she's a little disappointed that she won't have needed to help Dorota. But the main thing is that Dorota is all right, that she's not worn out and unable to go on.

And so it turns out. It's not yet evening and all the holes are done.

In all the great clearing, all the holes are done. They stand where they are, 1st Brigade, survey their work and are impressed. They lean on their spades and try to count all those holes, count the rows and multiply. Have they done all that in only two days, they who have never dug holes in the ground before? Now they can start the trudge back to their barracks, and sleep. Whatever tomorrow brings, it will not be digging holes. It can surely not be digging holes.

But as they begin to form into their column, even without commands from Pavel Kuzmich, they see rolling into the clearing from its further end the tractor and trailer that brought them from Rubtsovsk. There is a bulky heap of something on the trailer, something piled high, but the clearing is so large, the tractor so distant, that they cannot tell what it is. Curiosity restores their energy. They break out of their formation and scramble down to the ponderous vehicle and its cargo – a hillock of tiny pine saplings, soft as feathers, inviting caresses.

Marta strokes the silky curling spines and runs her fingers through their gentleness. Something like a sob rises in her throat with compassion for these baby trees, as if she wants to protect them just for their littleness. Now she knows what tomorrow's task will be. She looks down at the pale-green softness she is rubbing between the pads of her fingers, saddened that she already grieves for the future of this young and helpless living thing when it cannot have any notion of its destiny, since it has no notions at all. It will be planted. It will grow. When it is big enough it will produce the cones from which, perhaps, other saplings will emerge, and then they will grow. Tomorrow she will plant it, and the next one and the next, knowing what their fate is to be long, long after she has left this place: the fate of all small things – to grow, and then to be destroyed.

Quasimodo and the tractor driver are hauling the saplings off the trailer by the armful and dumping them on the ground. The women are helping; Hania has climbed right onto the trailer and is up to her thighs in a foam of tender green, pushing the saplings to the edges of the trailer so that the others can bundle them off. And the picture enters Marta's mind of executioners cheerfully preparing their unwary victims for slaughter. Hania, of all people, bending her stocky figure, scooping and pushing, her freckled cheeks flushed and excited as if she were a child again, playing at a new game.

Judging by the length of the shadows, it's not yet time to go home, but the hillock of saplings on the trailer has become a hillock of saplings on the ground. Will Quasimodo expect his brigade to start distributing them, a tree for every hole, one by one, until dusk? How many could they do? You could easily carry four in each hand, but the clearing is enormous. It would have made more sense to unload the saplings in batches at different points so that there might be less tramping back and forth. But it's too much to expect sense from these people.

For some reason Quasimodo is leaving the little trees where they are, no planting charade, no shouted and incomprehensible directions. Instead he has hauled himself onto the emptied trailer, whose surface is gritty with soil and dropped needles. There he sits, cross-legged, grinning horribly out at them, his spade and his stick lying by his side. He bangs the floor of the trailer with the flats of both hands to get their attention, then beckons, flapping with his hands like someone trying to fan himself on a sultry day. Now he is shouting something.

Marta and Hania are the first to move. Then the rest of them, once they have noted that Pavel Kuzmich is nodding vigorously, clamber up behind. The tractor driver is leaning against his huge rear tyre and cackling noiselessly at the slow workers. Most of his teeth are missing too. Marta has never seen him face on before, so he might, after all, not have been their driver

But who would have believed it? They are getting a ride home.

It took around an hour and half to walk to the clearing this morning and it will take almost as long to drive back but who cares? They are resting, dozing, noting the forest through half-closed eyes as it drifts by. This is luxury. All the same, as the sun dips down, and because they are not walking, it is suddenly cold. They edge closer together and tuck their hands into their armpits. Someone is humming quite tunefully, and her voice mingles with the steady growl of the tractor as if this were intended, a growl whose vibrations pulse into their bodies, sound from outside, sound from inside. There is a particular quality to sleep in the open air, a sleep teetering on the rim but never putting out its foot for that final step down. Small dreams flit through Marta's head, and she nods them by. Somewhere her mother is peeling fine paper from a silky garment folded in an expensive box. She unfolds it and unfolds it, and if she goes on like that it will be much too long for anyone to wear. Layers of pale silky stuff trail on the floor and her mother is laughing lightly at it, disconcerted. At the other end of the room her father, in uniform, is collecting the fabric up, winding it over his arm, looping it, but there is too much of it and as it piles up his face is beginning to disappear. There's a girl in the background but she isn't Sonia, she is Basia, her hair behind her ears, eating a gingerbread heart, nibbling round its edges, round and round, just the way Sonia does. Then she pauses, looks up and waves at Marta, smiling, stops smiling and with serious concentration returns to her nibbling. But behind them all are the ghosts of trees, dark and filmy, silently tiptoeing past on secret errands. Something has brought them to a standstill. The trees take root again as if they had never moved and someone is screaming, which Marta thinks is out of place. People shouldn't scream in a forest, since as everyone knows forests are places of silence. But the screaming goes on and now, to accompany it, a heavy object is pounding on the ground, jolting her.

The tractor isn't moving but Quasimodo is on his feet, towering over them, and he is screaming. He's grabbed Basia by the shoulders and he's shaking her; he's gesticulating with his stick in short stabs towards the end of the trailer. Dazed but awake now, Marta is struck by how smooth the stick is, how polished. Thousands and thousands of hands must have stroked it repeatedly for thousands of years for it to have got like that. Now 1st Brigade gape at the excited and angry man, wondering what's got into him as he pushes them roughly, and looks as if he might start laying about him with his stick. What's the matter with him? What on earth does he want now? Why can't he ever just let them be for a while?

'Get off, you idiots!' There's a crack in his voice, an infuriated command but also an appeal. 'For God's sake, just get off!'

Without thinking, they tumble off. The tractor trundles away and as it rounds the bend the soles of their feet pick up a distant vibration. The man on the horse comes flying down the track. He must have passed the tractor. He yanks at the reins and barks something at Quasimodo, who barks a reply. It's only now, hearing the incomprehensible Russian, that they realize he ordered them off the trailer in Polish.

It's not more than half an hour from here to the barracks and 1st Brigade march in silence. Only Dorota has spoken, for all of them, when she said, with her hands in her fair hair, 'Oh God!' They watch Pavel Kuzmich's back, lumbering unevenly in front of them, and each of them remembers what she has said about him in his presence. He must have understood it all. But, if he could speak Polish all along, why did he keep shouting at them in Russian? It must have been obvious to him that they didn't know what he was saying. He's even worse than they thought. He's deliberately fooled them to draw them out, to make them say things they'd never have dared say if they thought he'd understand. And now, for all they know, he's said something to the man on the horse, and there'll be double trouble. The blessed interlude on the trailer was all set up to catch them out.

The smell of the cabbage soup simmering in the cauldron turns Marta's stomach. She is too angry to eat. She will not eat. But her body overrides her person, and when Basia quietly takes her tin mug from her, dips it into the cauldron and hands it to her, she finds herself salivating for the revolting thin liquid out of sheer need. And like everyone else she glances furtively at the chunks of bread in other hands. How do theirs compare with hers? Even so her fury doesn't subside. It pursues her beyond the meal, and she wraps her blanket viciously round her in her place on the shelf, but then twists in it, turns, shifts, her legs uneasy stretched out, uncomfortable the minute she bends them at the knees. She rotates her feet at the ankles, clockwise, anti-clockwise, rotates her wrists, but nothing stills her.

She must lie quiet; she must not keep the girls on either side awake. But their breathing is steady. They were more tired than annoyed, so why is she more annoyed than tired, with her teeth clenched, she discovers, and her heart throbbing so violently in her chest she feels her entire frame pulse in concert with it. She releases her teeth; takes slow breaths. But the teeth have clamped together again. If she doesn't sleep, tomorrow will be impossible. They have taken away her food; they have made her filthy. Don't let them filch her sleep as well. But they have. It's no good. She can't stay in here lying awake all night.

Wasn't it only this morning that she was out there in the frozen air, creeping about in the dark under the intermittent glow from the half-moon? If there was half a moon in the early hours, there ought to be some more or, if less, at least some. She remembers how clammily cold it was and drags her blankets off the shelf, the one they provided and the one the Mother Superior gave her. How did that woman happen to have a stack of blankets packed away in the convent all ready to hand for when the time came? Was she used to soldiers bursting in and arresting people? The person to talk to is Mrs Benka. She must find Mrs Benka. Perhaps those older ones might still be awake.

Outside Marta focuses on the solid blocks of the other huts, willing one of them to have at least a candle in the window, but the darkness is unbroken. She won't find Mrs Benka tonight. Probably she'll have to wait till later in the year when the days are longer – unless Quasimodo makes them work fifteen hours a day until dusk. Why has she come out? It's so stupid always thinking things will be better if only you're somewhere else. All she is now is cold.

But there's a light over there. Not a candle, but the tip of a cigarette that someone is puffing on between their lips. If they were holding it in their fingers it would be moving, up to the mouth and down again, as Gienek's forbidden cigarettes do when he sits by his open summer window with the door closed. This one isn't moving, it's just glowing more strongly, then more faintly, more strongly, more faintly. Like a lighthouse, like a flashlight. Like someone sending a message, in Morse code. But there doesn't seem to be a varying rhythm in the cig-

120

arette's brilliance. Whoever it is is smoking steadily, and rather fast. She is certain it's Quasimodo because he always seems to be wherever she is, so she might as well make use of her sleeplessness and beard him, here and now.

Marta approaches the point of light with deliberate steadiness. It's true she can feel her heart again, but that's normal. Now that she's getting closer she fancies she can make out not one shape, but two, and it brings her up short. Quasimodo she can face, but Quasimodo and reinforcements is another matter. Now there is a second tip of light, growing more intense, and for a moment the two dance side by side as fireflies might in those faraway hot places. The second shape is not as bulky as Quasimodo. They must have spotted her because she has been moving, so she'll have to go on. She feels so exposed, like a mouse cornered by a motionless cat gauging the moment to leap. A mouse might try to run out between the cat's paws to save itself but she's too tired to run. Quasimodo can't run either, but his henchman might.

He's getting up, his cigarette rising with him. It's definitely Quasimodo, more shapeless than ever with a blanket round his shoulders. He's waiting for her. She stops a few feet away and briefly they are like trolls in the forest, turned to stone. Then he gives her an ironic little bow.

'Good evening. Have you come to pay us a visit?'

'I...' Marta's voice cracks. She clears her throat and tries again but her mouth is so dry she cannot speak. Then the other person is getting up and holding out a hand.

'Marta, my dear,' says Mrs Benka warmly. 'I am so, so pleased to see you. Come and join us, why don't you?'

17

'Mrs Benka! How are you, Mrs Benka?'

Marta has her arms round her, Mrs Benka clasps her as tightly, all the while trying to keep her cigarette out of the girl's hair.

'There, there.'

'I thought you said you were her granny.'

Mrs Benka gives Marta a swift, warning squeeze. 'I am.'

'Then why is she calling you Mrs Benka?'

'Everyone always has. It's a family thing.'

'Funny family.'

'Most families are.'

'You're right there, granny.'

'Come along and sit down with us, my dear.' Mrs Benka pats the log where she has been sitting.

Marta is baffled. What is Mrs Benka doing out here with Quasimodo in the icy night, talking to him as if they were old friends? But they can't be on such good terms because Mrs Benka lied to him about being her grandmother, and seems to have warned her not to say anything.

She tucks her blanket under her and perches on the log. 'How are you, Mrs Benka? How have you been doing? Are you all right?'

'Pavel Kuzmich put me in the geriatric ward. Well, that's not quite fair. There are three families as well, you know. Mothers and little children. You should be very grateful to us. We make your delicious soup, among other things. And I have to say I've never seen such a load of half-rotten cabbages in all my life. It's a disgrace. A disgraceful waste!'

How will Quasimodo react to this criticism? But he merely says, 'I told you. They've been sitting at the railway sidings near Rubtsovsk since last year. Of course they're rotten. What do you expect?' He turns to Marta. 'Your granny here has a sharp tongue, and I reckon it runs in the family. I've told her to be more careful what she says and who to.'

'And I've told him I know what I'm doing.'

Marta hopes Mrs Benka does know what she's doing. She's uncomfortable in this conversation. All the things she wants to ask Mrs Benka she can't because of Quasimodo, who is tapping her on the arm.

'Want a cigarette?'

'Oh. I don't smoke. Thank you.'

'You will if you know what's good for you. No one here doesn't smoke and keeps going. It keeps you warm, and you don't feel so hungry if you smoke.'

Marta waits for Mrs Benka to object. As her granny she should, but Mrs Benka doesn't say a word. Of course, she's smoking too, but all the same.

Test it out. 'My best friend Ania smokes,' she announces untruthfully but with complete conviction.

Next to her Mrs Benka's thigh muscle stiffens, but again not a word. Well, that was impressive.

Quasimodo pounces. 'Well then, now's the time for you to start, and join your friend. Go on. Have one. I won't always be so generous, believe me. These are currency. If someone offers you a smoke you don't pass it up. And that's the law. The number one law, and you best learn it.'

He holds out a thin rolled thing, and Mrs Benka passes the stub of her cigarette across and leans close to her, putting her lips close to Marta's ear.

'Don't play games, dear, when you don't know what you're playing with,' she whispers, then straightens up.

Marta puts the thing between her lips, at once fearful and exhilarated.

Quasimodo is offering instructions. 'Hold it still, and, when the tip of this one touches yours, you suck. Got that?'

A moment later she is doubled over, the back of her throat seared by the most horrible sensation. Tonsillitis was never as bad as this, and she'd rather be hungry.

Quasimodo is chuckling, of course, gravel rolling in his throat. 'You didn't suck, you silly girl, you breathed. I didn't say breathe. That part comes later.'

Marta is aggrieved, put upon. They're having a laugh at her expense. She gasps and holds the cigarette out to Quasimodo. Here. He can have it back again if it's so damned precious. Her voice is hoarse again – from smoke, not fear.

'You have it.'

'Oh, no. You're finishing this one. It's the same for everyone, the first one.'

'Then why have a second?' she croaks crossly, but purses her lips round the evil little tube and takes a brief pull at it, trying to shut down the back of her mouth. All this to-do about smoking, and for-bidding it. If her mother had only given her a cigarette and lit it for her, she could have been sure Marta would never want to try another one. Perhaps if she just holds it, it will burn down, and that'll be the end of it. But Quasimodo and Mrs Benka are watching, and expect-ing. She takes another puff and immediately blows out the smoke that's filled her mouth.

'Better,' encourages Quasimodo. 'Now another one, but hold the smoke longer.'

Venom in her eyes, but he can't see that. There is something funny, though, in having a smoking lesson from a prison guard. She draws again and this time counts to three before blowing the smoke out.

'And one more.'

She counts to five. Her mouth tastes like the smell of garbage. Never again.

'And one last time. Look, you're nearly there.'

It's true. The cigarette is short now. If she's not careful she'll singe her fingers. This time some of the smoke gets to the back of her throat again and she splutters it out. A small drift of it comes out of her nose, and she thinks, *Oh*.

At least that's over.

'And now,' says Quasimodo, tucking both hands inside his blanket, 'tell me. What's brought you out tonight? In fact, why do you keep coming out?'

Why do *you*? *You're* the one who's always out.

'Keep coming out?' asks Mrs Benka.

'She was snooping around this morning.'

'I wasn't snooping.'

'What were you doing then, if it wasn't snooping?'

'I was looking for water. To wash in. *I* don't like being dirty.'

'Nobody likes being dirty. And did you find any? Water?'

'I found a well.'

'And?'

'It was dry. I threw a stone in and it bounced. It was dry. What's the point of a dry well?'

'It wasn't dry, it was frozen. It takes longer for spring to reach down to a well. Nobody gets to wash much between the end of the big snows and the start of summer because it means breaking the ice, and the water in our well starts so far down you'd have to hang a donkey over the edge to reach it. You can't just lean over with a stick and smash it up.'

Held by its tail, the terrified donkey paddles its hooves over the chasm.

'What happens in winter?'

'We melt the snow. You can spend half a day shovelling enough of it to get a good bucket's worth.'

'Then where does the water come from for the soup and the tea?'

Quasimodo juts a blanketed elbow towards Mrs Benka. 'That's them and their department.'

'There's a trickle of melting snow coming down from the hills. We go with buckets and we carry what we can.'

Marta considers this. If she really wants to wash that much she could go and get herself a bucketful from that trickle, but it would mean walking through the forest where the moonlight doesn't shine before dawn or after dusk. So she says only, 'I see.'

Quasimodo persists. 'And tonight?'

'I couldn't sleep.'

'Oh ho! Couldn't sleep! You haven't been doing enough work! Tomorrow you can do twice as much as everyone else, then. We'll make a real little Stakhanovite out of you, you'll get an extra spoonful of your granny's lovely soup, and then you'll sleep. You'll sleep all right.'

'What's a Stakhanovite?'

'Why couldn't you sleep, Marta?'

How can she explain her rage and its reasons to Mrs Benka with Quasimodo crouched under his blanket and mocking her? She shakes her head as if to say, it doesn't matter now, no special reason. But Quasimodo has picked up Mrs Benka's question and wants to gnaw on it as well.

'Yes, come on. Spit it out. You must have a reason. Now don't be shy.'

Shy! She's not shy. She just doesn't think it's good manners to say what she really thinks in front of Mrs Benka because, apart from anything else, it might lead to her having to repeat the things 1st Brigade said about Quasimodo, and about him telling the man on the horse.

She directs herself to Mrs Benka. 'How did you know he, Qua... Pavel Kuzmich, could speak Polish?'

'We chatted about this and that, and I found out.'

'But how did you chat?'

'In Russian, of course. We all speak Russian in Wilno, dear, you should know that. It's had its time being under the Russian yoke on and off for long enough.'

'Quasimodo.' He's said it. Oh, God.

'What's that?'

'Quasimodo. It's what they call me, my brigade, behind my back, thanks to your granddaughter.'

'Marta!'

'I...' Help, oh, help. Change the subject. 'But why do you speak Polish, Pavel Kuzmich?'

For a moment he doesn't answer, then he shrugs under his blanket. 'I was married once. To a Polish girl.'

Marta all but exclaims out loud, but checks herself in time. The thought of this awful old man and a Polish girl. She pictures her mother in her father's arms when the couple have supposed themselves alone, her father's lips on her mother's neck. But Quasimodo's mouth with its stumpy black teeth, the smell of his mouth, his scaly skin... Married. In the same bed. Imagine him unwinding those strips of cloth from his feet, peeling off the layers of filthy clothing, and underneath...

Mrs Benka is standing up. She presses Marta's shoulder. 'I'm going to go to inside now, my dear. Early start tomorrow to fetch the water for your tea. I'll let Pavel Kuzmich tell you his story – if he feels inclined to. I hope you'll feel sleepy soon. Good night – and good night, Pavel Kuzmich.'

'Good night, Mrs Benka,' in unison.

'And don't let the little bugs bite! Oh, ho ho.'

18

Now it's just the two of them. Mrs Benka was a protection. Marta rehearses excuses for leaving too, but she can sense Pavel Kuzmich about to speak.

'Your granny told me your father's one of them military men. A professional soldier.'

'Yes.'

'And that's why you're here. They couldn't find him, so they had to make do with you. Because he was top brass in the units that tried to destroy our Revolution. Well, I was on the other side in that war. Not that it was what you'd call my choice. Not in the sense of being a professional. Though of course I went as happy as the next man, to defend the homeland.'

What's he talking about 'to defend the homeland'? It was the other way round, everybody knows that! It was the Poles who were defending! Still, no wonder they took Wilno if the Soviet army was full of old men.

'It's very simple, really, what happened. We were on foot. Your lot were on horseback, of course. But we managed to push the invaders right back into Poland. To begin with at any rate. Then, I don't know what went wrong, you don't when you're on the ground, that's for the commanders to know, or perhaps they don't know either, they only pretend to and it's for history to find out, but something happened and we found ourselves being pushed back again. It was a bad day, that one. You could call it a rout, and suddenly everyone was running, making for home. And somehow I got separated from my unit, and I thought I was left behind, done for. But then I come across this horse. A Polish horse, without a rider, grazing under a tree with its reins trailing. And I think to myself, maybe he's been killed, that rider, or maybe he's simply taking a piss in the woods, I don't know, and I don't wait to ask. I just see that here's a nice Polish horse. So I climb on board. Trouble is, I've never ridden a horse. Where would someone like me ever get to ride a horse? Well, I grab those reins, stick my feet in the stirrups and give that horse such a wallop. And off it goes. Bolts off with me, heading for home like a pack of wolves is after it, not to my home, mind you, but its. Horses always want to go home, they say. What would I know?

'So there I am, galloping in the wrong direction, bellowing at the horse to stop, but it doesn't understand Russian, this Polish horse, and I suppose the strange voice frightens it even more, so the more I shout at it the faster it goes. And me too scared to throw myself off, like the Tartars do. I just cling on for dear life only hoping that I won't fall off and the horse won't put its great foot in a hole and fall over. But it just goes on and on, with its ears back and its neck stretched out like a goose that thinks you're the fox come for the goslings, and all of a sudden we come on this smallholding, and the horse veers round a corner without a word of warning. So, of course, that's when I do fall off, and hit the ground with such a smack that after that I'm out cold.

'When I woke up, I was lying on some cushions with a damp cloth on my forehead and a beautiful girl sitting by my side. It was like a fairy-tale, and I was Ivanushka Durachek – the dim-witted one who always gets the princess because he has a good heart. So I married her. She said that horse had delivered me to her like the postman bringing a present on her name-day. She shouldn't have said that.'

'Why not?'

'I was no present. She died.'

'She died! How did she?'

'In childbirth. It had been five years, and we were thinking there wouldn't be any children. So we thought, well, it's sad, but we've got each other.' Pavel Kuzmich stops abruptly, and in the dark Marta hears him swallow.

'That's so sad.'

'She was only twenty-five, like me.'

Twenty-five! But that makes him… that makes him the same age as her father, and her father isn't an old man at all. Her father is upright and strong, and his skin is clear.

Pavel Kuzmich still hasn't explained, though.

'Why did you keep speaking Russian to us when you could have spoken Polish all along?'

'I don't much care for Poles.'

'But… what d'you mean? You married one!'

'That was different. She was my Ewa.'

'What happened to the baby? Was it born?'

'It was. It was a girl. She'd be about your age now.'

'She *would* be? Does that mean she…'

'Yes. She died too. Not then. Not that same day, but three days later.'

Pavel Kuzmich gets up and walks a few paces away, taking deep breaths. Marta sits very still without speaking, afraid of saying the wrong thing, of interrupting whatever is going on in his head. After a while, his breathing grows lighter, and he returns to the log.

'It was my fault. I didn't know how to look after her, how to feed her without her mother. I didn't know what you do with babies. So I went to Ewa's people but they, her brothers especially, they hated me. Her brothers said Ewa wouldn't have died if it hadn't been for me. They said they'd always known it would turn out badly, and I wasn't good enough for her. That she shouldn't have gone with a Soviet soldier like me who was hardly better than a peasant. They said it wasn't God's will to have Soviet babies on Polish soil, so they turned me away. And the baby died. Starved to death.'

Pavel Kuzmich fumbles under his blanket and pulls out another strip of paper and some more precious tobacco, and, with his head bent to the task he can't see, rolls and rolls. Then he lights up and sucks hard with his head turned away.

But it was their sister's child! What sort of people could they be? She sees the brothers, abreast in an implacable line barring a wide doorway. And there stands Pavel Kuzmich, with his back to her, pleading with them, one arm cradling the swaddled baby, which is mewling feebly with its hunger. How could they look at that and turn him down? Listen to that and turn him down? Sonia and Gienek would have helped him. She would too. Of course she would. It's not believable. He must be making it up, though he doesn't sound as if he's making it up.

'What happened then?'

Pavel Kuzmich has a mouthful of smoke. 'Then?' He exhales slowly through a tiny hole in his lips, almost whistling. 'Then I came home. There wasn't any reason to stay in Poland any more without Ewa, without the baby. So now you know, young Polish missy. That's how I knew I'd made a mistake. Not with my Ewa. Not with her, God save me, but with her people. *Your* people, if you'll accept my meaning. Because, when people have more than the next man, well, you know how they've got it. They'll have stolen it. There isn't any other way. And we know about being poor. That's the good Christian Russian way. You may be poor, but you're not richer than the next man – that's the point, and that's how it's always been. When you're at the bottom of the pit you're never alone because all your family, all your friends, all the village, the whole *oblast*, is down there with you. And I'd rather be there than on the top of the hill with gold plates and silver cups but all alone. That's what I thought. And I *was* all alone. I didn't even have the plates and the cups. So I came back. At least, I thought, I can help my old parents. But that didn't work either.'

'Why not?'

'They arrested me on the border.'

'But what for? What had you done?'

'Well, if I'd told them the truth, can you imagine? I'd have had to say I was kidnapped by a patriotic Polish horse. "A horse?"' Pavel Kuzmich twists his head to one side and puts on a harsh inquisitor's voice. '"How did this horse kidnap you?"' Now he answers meekly. '"Oh... um... I was riding it." "And why were you riding it?" "I thought it would get me home quicker." "And where were your com-

131

rades?" "They were trying to get home too." "Also on Polish horses?" "No, on foot." "Ah! So you chose a bourgeois method of transport to leave your comrades festering…" No, actually, they'd have been more interested in why we were trying to get home in the first place. Getting home isn't in the rulebook unless you're coming back victorious. The least you can do is die properly on the battlefield. But I was just a stupid ignorant Russian peasant, like my brothers-in-law said, and I didn't realize that. So when I said I'd been a prisoner of war I didn't know that there's no such thing in this country. Being captured is as bad as going over. I should have told the truth and let them shoot me for all the good it did me. I haven't been able to see to my parents, in fact I don't even know if they're alive or dead or in a place like this, sent off for the crime of being my parents. Fifteen years and more I've been here. Some of us have been here longer, and some of us have died off. So when they decide to shove in a whole lot of new people there's usually room. Or we have to build new barracks like we did for you. But my fifteen years, that's just for starters. I'm here for life, so they said.'

'You mean you're a prisoner?'

'Of course. Everyone here's a prisoner.'

'But… you're in charge.'

'I'm not in charge.'

'But you are. You're in charge of us. You tell us what to do.'

'No. I tell you what *they* want you to do. I couldn't care less what you do, unless it affects me. Any of you.'

'What about the man on the horse?'

'The *desiatnik*? The foreman? Yes, him too.'

'He's a prisoner?'

'Like I said. No one here's a free man. Well, except the director.'

'But the horse, and he's got a coat!'

'Well, yes. That's his privilege for what he provides. I report to him and he reports to them. Sometimes he tells the truth and sometimes he doesn't, as it suits him.'

'But why has he got a coat and a horse and you haven't? I mean, couldn't you have instead of…'

'Being Quasimodo? He volunteered. He's the eyes and ears.'

'A sneak!'

'A sneak.'

'That's vile. It's... it's... dishonourable!'

'Oh, you Poles and your honour. Listen, young Marta. Honour is a luxury. Did you know that? A luxury. That's what I've come to think. If honour helps you survive, then good for honour. Let's keep it. But if it doesn't – chuck it away. Do you see?'

Pavel Kuzmich throws out buckets of it, one to the left in a great arc of splattering liquid, one to the right, and Marta imagines it landing with a splash, honour running down the walls of the huts and pooling into puddles. He sets his buckets down.

'I don't know why the *desiatnik* is here. I've never asked him because I'd rather keep my distance. But I do know that somewhere he's got a wife and kiddies, and he's stupid enough to believe that one day, if he can only keep going, he'll get out and go home. So he's simply doing what it takes, and who am I to say he shouldn't? Let him go running to them, if he thinks it helps him. Let him check up on us, and gallop up and down counting every little thing to keep them happy. What do I care?'

'But who do you mean by *they*?'

Pavel Kuzmich merely jerks his head, chin first, somewhere over his shoulder. 'Just them. The NKVD. Moscow, if you want. The state. There's them, and then there's everybody else.'

'So... we're on the same side. You and us, I mean. We're together.'

'Oh, well, no. Not necessarily. It all depends on what's happening and who it suits, and what might happen, and who'd get what, and all the rest of it. One day we might be together, but the next we might not.'

'I don't understand.'

'Of course you don't understand. You've only just arrived. You haven't a clue, but you'll find out. You'll learn. And when you do you'll find the first lesson is the same as the last lesson. It's always the answer to the same question. You want to know what the question is? It's "What's best for me?" That's the only question. Don't ever waste your time asking another one because any other one will send you off looking for the wrong answers. What's best for me? That's your question. You keep asking that and, who knows, maybe you'll get out in one piece.'

'But that's so selfish! What about helping one another. Surely it's better if we all help one another!'

'Sometimes it is, and sometimes it isn't. If helping somebody else is best for you, then you go ahead and you help. But if it isn't, you turn your back. Believe me. And sometimes it looks like you're helping someone, but it isn't that at all.'

'What do you mean? I don't understand again. You're not making any sense!'

'All right, all right, don't get yourself upset. Let me try and explain. Remember yesterday? The digging, and your little blonde friend, the wispy one who looks like she's half dead already? I moved you both, didn't I? Well, I did that so that I could make up what she hadn't done in the time.'

'That was nice of you,' says Marta, somewhat sourly, recalling how cheated she'd felt, deprived of her good deed.

'Rubbish,' continues Pavel Kuzmich. 'And the trailer. Why do you think I let you get on the trailer?'

'Because we were tired.'

'Do you think I care if you're tired? Why would I care if you're tired?'

'I don't know.'

'Because, if you're tired, maybe next day you won't be able to do your digging or your planting or whatever. And why do you think I made you get off?'

'Because the *desiatnik* was coming?'

'Exactly.'

'And he would have been angry with us.'

'No, you silly little fool. He would have been angry with *me*. Same as the digging. I did it for me, not for you, so get that into your head. The digging looked like I was helping you, but I wasn't. Not really. Like I said before. I don't care what you do unless it affects me, and some of the things you do *do* affect me. It goes like this. There are work norms for everything. So much has to be done each day, no matter what, or the rations go down, or there aren't any at all. It's what I was trying to tell you all the first day: you don't work – you don't eat. And if you lot don't fulfil your norms, *I* don't get to eat. And, God help me, it seems I still want to do that. Though I don't know why I bother. Maybe we all struggle to survive even when we think we don't want to. Maybe we just can't help it.'

'Why not? Don't you want to get out too, like the *desiatnik* does?'

'I don't think I will any more than I think *he* will. And even he knows he won't really, if he's honest. But maybe he's just the type that keeps on hoping. Some people are like that. But why would we get out? What's in it for them to let us out, or anybody, for that matter? What do they care? And if we all die off, well, that's no problem either. There's always more where we came from. Or where you came from. Room for another whole countryful of people here.' Pavel Kuzmich spreads his arms, then folds them under his blanket again; rearranges the blanket. 'This is a big empty place. Lots of room in it. Lots and lots of room.'

'We'll all go home when the war's over.'

'Listen to her! When the war's over... when the war's over. What are you expecting? That daddy's going to come galloping in, all fat and rosy in his uniform and shiny boots, and run home with you? No, no. Nothing so simple. There were places like this before there was a war, and they'll be here after too. It's just the way it is.' A long chilly minute passes. 'And now you must get in. Look at you. You're shivering. And so am I.'

She is shivering now that he draws her attention to it. Marta fears she may have frozen onto her log and be unable to prise herself off, fears her limbs may have become rigid. But she has one more question.

'Does Mrs Benka know all this? Did you tell her all this?'

'Some of it. She asks different questions from you. She's been around a long time, that lady, and she's seen a lot.' He turns to limp towards his hut, but stops. 'Oh, and listen, you. Remember what I said. Remember that question and never forget it. What's best for me, do you hear?'

'Yes.'

'Promise me you'll always ask that question.'

'Yes, yes.'

But she doesn't want to, since it goes against everything her parents have taught her. It goes against everything she believes.

19

Now Marta is sure as she picks her way back that she will not be able to sleep at all tonight because she has so much to think about. Fat and rosy, he said, scathingly about her father, as if he knew what her father was like. But actually, compared to Pavel Kuzmich, her father *is* fat and rosy, or he was the last time she saw him. One day long ago, when that runaway horse deposited him into the arms of his Polish princess, presumably Pavel Kuzmich was fat and rosy too. Ewa could have been sorry for the Soviet soldier with a bang on his head without wanting to marry him. The compress, the cushions, the comforting hand on his unconscious brow, all the necessary details that Marta might find in one of her mother's borrowed romances, couldn't by themselves have been enough to persuade the surprised nurse to accept his proposal. (Down on his knees with a bunch of wild flowers?) So Pavel Kuzmich must have been a handsome young man. The trouble is, she can't imagine how. She can't substitute blooming young skin for the scales and the blotches; shining eyes for the rheumy eyeballs with their puckered lids; healthy teeth... hair. What colour hair?

That's what's done it to Pavel Kuzmich. Fifteen years and more, he said. She cannot, will not, be here for fifteen years and be changed out of all recognition. And yet it's already happening. She hasn't seen herself, but one thing's changed. Her periods have stopped – thank God. But why?

Marta eases herself onto her shelf, glad of the warmth of the two bodies on either side, glad of the breathing that surrounds her. What's going to happen? And what were the questions that Mrs Benka asked, so different from her own? And then she's asleep.

Only a few minutes later, it seems, she is woken by someone twitching at one of her feet. She crawls into consciousness and recognizes Pavel Kuzmich with a finger to his lips. The same finger beckons her like an articulated claw. Last night. Yes. Of course, last night. Unless it is still night. But somehow she knows it is morning, dark of course, but morning none the less. Clearly he has a secret. Marta sits up and shunts her bottom to the edge of the shelf, paddling herself forward with her hands. Looks at Pavel Kuzmich. What is it? Silent head shaking, ssh, come. Even with his limp he can move without making a sound. All the others sleep on with a sort of determination to remain in their separate other worlds for as long as they can. They have no good reason to let themselves be wakened.

Pavel Kuzmich leads her out and round to the other side of the hut, beyond the latrines. He is pointing. 'There,' he says in a low voice. 'A little present.' In the dark she can just see a small shape on the ground. When she reaches it she finds it is a bucket of water three-quarters full. She looks round, but Pavel Kuzmich has disappeared.

The water is icy but she rubs her face, her neck, her arms, her feet, her calves. Then finally, again and again between her legs and between her buttocks until all the water has gone and her skin is fierce, tingling from the cold, from the joy of it. If only she could wash her clothes as well.

By the time 1st Brigade reach the clearing Marta has related Pavel Kuzmich's story to Dorota, Hania and Basia. Hania says, 'If it's true, it makes you want to spit,' Dorota's eyes have filled with tears for the dead Ewa and the dead baby, and for poor Pavel Kuzmich. Basia says, 'I thought there was something sad about him.' Then they disperse among the others as they walk, until everyone is in the know. Pavel Kuzmich plods on as though nothing's going on behind his back. He leads them to the mound of soft green froth in the corner of the clearing. Turns to face them, and they assume from his expression that he will not be surprised to learn that his history has been circulating.

There is a meeting of eyes, and a brief nod from the brigade leader.

'We piled these saplings up yesterday evening for warmth,' he explains. 'Every growing thing needs warmth, but they'll be all right once they're planted. They'll survive until the ground warms up and then just you watch them grow! Take as many as you can and it's one to a hole. Like this. And make sure you firm them in. Hands and feet, like this.'

He demonstrates as he talks, crouching at a hole, patting, pressing, treading. This is one small tree that is bound to take root. One among so many, all the same. That's a point. These are all pine saplings, but the surrounding forest is mixed.

'Why are we planting trees that are all the same?'

'There was a fire here. You can see that from the ground, can't you, all black and sooty still. You get them coming in off the steppe sometimes, in the summer. All this here, it just burned down to the ground in a day or two last year. There was nothing anyone could do, though they shot the people who'd been working here on the logging.'

They shot them? Dismayed, 1st Brigade stare at Pavel Kuzmich, who is so matter-of-fact as he pats in his baby trees.

'They reckoned it was a dropped cigarette. Then of course it doesn't take a minute for it to be a cigarette dropped on purpose, does it, and sabotage – you see? Anyway, the point is, we're all here to provide the state with timber. And pines, well, you look on them as a crop, not a forest. They're the quickest growers. In they go, one, two. Up they grow, three, four – and bang, wallop, we chop 'em down. Then we plant more. And that's the way it goes.'

Even so, there is pleasure in setting the little trees in place, firming them in, as Pavel Kuzmich instructed. And you look back down the row, and there they sprout, upright, hopeful, their wiry fibrous roots nuzzling into the dark earth for moisture while above ground the fluffy spines reach for the light, drink it in. Yes. They will grow. They will all grow. Why shouldn't they?

But when it's time for the midday break the girls are aching again, in their knees, in their backs. So much crouching, so much bending, getting up, getting down. And there's Pavel Kuzmich saying: Don't sit down yet, don't be in a hurry to sit down. And he's showing them how to pummel themselves down the legs, from the hips to the ankles and back up again, don't leave anything out, not shins, not calves, not knees back and front. And so they begin, and then turn on one another, pummel each other with flat hands and fists, harder and harder, shouting 'Ow!' but laughing, become suddenly children again. And Pavel Kuzmich watches, and nods.

This time, when they sit, their circle is wider and looser, and they see how Pavel Kuzmich, sitting with them now, eats his pieces of black bread as slowly and thoroughly as anyone, sucking each individual crumb from his teeth and swilling his mouth with the sour rye saliva. Then he begins rolling a cigarette from the fragments of coarse tobacco he's pulled from his pocket.

'Slowly does it,' he says, demonstrating his handiwork. 'The slower the better. You've got your baccy, and you've got your bits of newspaper, and here we go.'

'Newspaper?' Marta says eagerly.

'Ho, ho. Last year's. But it could be yesterday's and you still wouldn't know anything. Now watch. You don't want to pack it too tight or you get through too much baccy in one roll. But you don't want it to be too loose either or you don't get a smoke at all. The main thing is, like I said, take it slowly. You remember law number one, eh? Law number two says, if you want a rest, you can't have one. But if you want a smoke, well, everybody knows a man has to have a smoke. Even the *desiatnik* knows that because he needs a smoke too, even his horse for all I know. So, the longer it takes to roll your ciggie, the longer the rest. Get it? Here we are. All done. One puff for me, and one for you. Want it?'

He holds out the cigarette to Marta with a faint wink as the other girls gasp. They didn't know she smoked. She could be shot! Now what?

Then, 'Sure,' she says nonchalantly. 'Thanks.' And lights the rolled thing from his, sucks carefully, counts to seven, blows out. Actually, it's not so bad after all. You might get to like it.

But Hania is leaning forward across the circle from her with a hand stretched out 'Can I have a puff?'

What? Well, of course. Now she'll be on the other side and see what Pavel Kuzmich and Mrs Benka saw last night.

Hania nods thanks, takes the cigarette, inhales deeply on it and blows out slowly, oh so slowly and luxuriantly through her nose. Inhales again and sends out a perfect smoke circle that sits momentarily on the still air like a disembodied and astonished mouth before dispersing into the awed silence. She raises an eyebrow and returns the cigarette to Marta. All eyes follow it.

'Nothing left of it now, is there?' says Marta, and brusquely stubs it out, bending the long stub in half as she does so. Well, it's no surprise that Hania smokes. That's what you get when your parents don't look after you properly, doctors or no, and leave you to run wild. Over to her left Marta hears Pavel Kuzmich snorting with pleasure. But he's leant over and picked up the crushed stub. Nursed it back into shape.

One by one they return to their planting, but Pavel Kuzmich lingers, waiting for Marta, who is rubbing the backs of Dorota's calves. He steps up to her and whispers, 'And how was it with the water this morning?'

'Wonderful.' He receives a smile of gratitude.

'Did you use it all up?'

'Oh yes.'

'Didn't share it? Didn't take it in and share it?' Marta is dumbfounded. 'Good girl, keeping your promises. You see how it works?'

Marta feels heat pumping into her face. She is ashamed, but furious with Pavel Kuzmich all over again for making her so. That bucket wasn't a present after all, but a test, and as far as she's concerned she's failed it. And now look how pleased he is with himself.

'Well, you're wrong. I should have shared it, and next time I will.' If there is a next time.

'What? One bucket between eighty? You'd get a drop each!'

'That would still be better than being greedy with it the way I was.'

'Why?'

'Because... because... It's a question of principle. And it wasn't

141

even survival anyway. So it's worse. If I hadn't had the water I'd still be the same as I am, like all the others. Still be alive, wouldn't I? It's just that it felt good. It made me *feel* better, that's all. It didn't change anything important, it didn't keep me alive or anything.'

'And you don't think surviving happens up here too?' Pavel Kuzmich taps his head. 'If you feel better then you *are* better. It gives you strength.'

Marta wheels away.

20

The season is on the move. There is birdsong every morning before dawn, and fluttering and nest building. The ice on the surface of the deep well has melted and they take it in turns to haul up buckets for washing. Of course the water is freezing; of course there is no soap, but a small sense of dignity is restored. Except for the lice.

Marta thinks that it's not simply the irritation, the little moments of pain, the longer ones of unreachable itching that are so distressing. It's knowing that crawling things are living in the seams of your clothing, procreating in the creases of your body, multiplying there.

Dorota with her fine skin is covered in welts. Something in the lice mandibles has set up a reaction and she cannot keep still. The training in first aid the Girl Guides were given never addressed anything like this. Marta tries to think what her mother would suggest, but her mother would be so horrified at the mention of lice that it would be impossible to get anything helpful from her. Mrs Benka, then, who is shredding cabbages as if she were back at the farm outside Wilno, seated at her trestle table. Her nose wrinkles against her work because half the leaves are brown and slimy.

'Don't look, dear, or you won't touch your soup again. We just have to tell ourselves there's some goodness in these leaves, no matter what condition they're in.'

'Mrs Benka, what do you do about lice?'

'Kill them,' says Mrs Benka firmly, laying down her knife and pincering her fingernails sharply. You can almost hear the insects crack.

'No, but if you've been badly bitten and your skin is all sore. What then?'

'Is your skin bad, dear? Show me.'

'No, it's not me. It's Dorota.'

'Is she the sickly blonde one?'

'Do you know her?'

'No, no. Something Pavel Kuzmich said.'

'What did he say?'

'Oh, nothing special. I forget.'

Marta clenches her teeth. She doesn't like the idea of Pavel Kuzmich and Mrs Benka smoking in the dark and discussing her and her friends. But she has to sort Dorota out first.

'What would you do? What would you put on?'

'Well, my first thought would be calamine. But of course we haven't got... Let me think.'

'Please, Mrs Benka. Ania always said you were a witch. She said you always knew which herbs and things to use when people were ill.'

'Well, yes, but it's a question of what there is here... Oh, of course. Foolish woman that I am. We can try two things, can't we? Let's make her some nettle tea to drink and a poultice of dock leaves. The nettles have got the poison that gives you the rash, but if you drink the tea, it works the other way. Now you be careful, Marta. Grab the leaves through your clothes when you pick them because they're young at the moment. At their best, juicy and vicious. And of course you'll find the dock leaves not far from the nettles.'

At last, Marta can do something for Dorota. There's still just enough light to hunt out the nettles and the dock leaves and to bring her booty back to Mrs Benka, her hands stinging, pink blisters rising, in spite of the precautions.

Mrs Benka gives her a wry glance and passes back one of the dock leaves.

Pressing her dock leaf between her palms, Marta watches. If she can only observe with care, if she can only remember, maybe she too will become the repository of knowledge that people will turn to. Mrs

Benka dips a mug into the cauldron of boiling water in her hut and drops the nettles in. She is aware of Marta's quiet breathing at her shoulder, and recognizes that she has gained an apprentice, at least for this evening.

'Now, dear. Fifteen minutes, and not a moment less. As for these...' She bunches the dock leaves together and tears them, again and again. 'I need something heavy, like a rolling pin, to crush them with. Press out the juices. But of course...'

'What about a stone?'

'Yes, a stone, if it's big enough, and smooth enough.'

But all the stones that Marta can find are small, and sharp. Something heavy. What's heavy? A bucket of water's heavy but too big. A person is heavy. Could the juices of the dock leaves be pressed out by grinding them under her heel, with all her weight on her heel? Mrs Benka considers this. They can try. Marta strips off one foot and Mrs Benka lays the bunched dock leaves on the ground, on the board she uses to shred the cabbage.

'Give me your hands. We don't want you falling over and doing yourself an injury.'

Balanced on her heel, with Mrs Benka holding her by the hands as if they were about to begin a minuet, Marta pivots slowly from side to side.

'Let me look.' Mrs Benka inspects the green mess, scrapes it up, turns it over. 'Again.'

More pivoting.

'That should do it.'

Now the dock leaves are judged to be sloppy enough, and Mrs Benka scrapes them into another mug, while Marta wipes her heel.

Together, in the growing dark, they proceed to Marta's hut, no longer searching out the way because the path is familiar, well trodden, every projecting root, every dip anticipated by the soles of their feet. This is how animals in the wild engrave their meandering tracks across the mountainsides, year after year following the same narrow path. Mrs Benka carries the mug of nettle tea in one hand, the mug of dock leaf slop in the other. Marta would have liked to be the bear-er of one of them but thinks it wouldn't be correct to ask. Mrs Benka hasn't suggested it because she can imagine Marta in such a hurry with her offering that she'd spill it.

Dorota is cheered just by the sight of Mrs Benka, who is beginning to look as all witches should. Strands of her long white hair that have escaped from her bun hang by her face, and her masculine stride heralds comfort to come. Here is someone who knows.

'Drink this up first. All of it. It doesn't taste that bad.'

Medicine is not supposed to taste good, only to do good, so Dorota gulps it down.

'Now this stuff. Ideally, I'd spread it over the swelling and bandage it on. But we can't do that, since you've got bites all over. Like the rest of us. I'll tell you what, dear. I'll leave it with you, and you do your best to put some onto the worst bits, then try to lie still to let it do its work. You can tell us in the morning if it's helped.'

'Thank you, Mrs Benka.' Dorota, like all patients, is reduced to infancy by the omniscience of her doctor.

Marta notes with satisfaction that inclusive 'us' – *You can tell us in the morning*. Briskly Mrs Benka retrieves the emptied mug of nettle tea and waits, with her back turned tactfully, while Dorota reaches into her crevices with fingerfuls of green goo. There is only one mug per person and Mrs Benka cannot go back to her hut without them both.

That night Dorota sleeps more easily, the treatment and the being treated having assuaged her, while the lice have temporarily fled.

It's not spades now but two-handed saws and axes. Pavel Kuzmich has been teaching them how to fell trees. You hack out a wedge shape into the trunk, and then, one at each end of the saw, you cut through the rest. Then you push. The broad-leaved trees always fall away from the line of sawing. But pines are treacherous and may come crashing down in any direction. Marta imagines that this is a sly revenge for the calculation that went into their planting.

None of them knows how to swing an axe. 'Come on, *devushki*,' exhorts Pavel Kuzmich, 'all together now. One! Two! Three!'

The blades glance off the tree trunks, barely chipping the bark, and Pavel Kuzmich wipes tears of laughter from his eyes.

'*Bozhe, bozhe*. This is better than the theatre must be, I tell you. Now look.'

He grabs Marta's axe and gives her tree two almighty thwacks; a neat slice drops to the ground as if someone has merely been cutting cake. Then 1st Brigade try again, harder. But this time they jar their shoulders. Marta drops her axe. This is hopeless. All around her the others pause to see what Pavel Kuzmich will say and in their silence they hear the echo of axes ricochet from deeper in the forest where more accomplished loggers are at work. Pavel Kuzmich is nodding to himself and rubbing his bad leg.

'Well, well,' he says. 'We all have to learn once.'

Now he has instructed them to cut up the felled trees into lengths and lay out the logs in square stacks to a height of a metre and a half. Each evening the *desiatnik* will be coming by to count how many stacks have been set up.

'You lot get on with it,' he says. 'I'm just going to go round and make sure you haven't left any axes and saws lying around under the trees. It'll be on my head if you have.'

It's harder than it looks. For one thing, there are so many small branches and twigs sticking out that they have to chip off to get the lines straight and keep the stacks neat. The piles of brushwood build up to one side and everyone is sweating and exhausted trying to haul the logs into place. It takes so many layers to reach the required height, more than you'd think. Pavel Kuzmich hasn't said how many of these will be expected every day, but they know they will not be meeting the norms. If their rations go down as a result they'll get weaker, their production rate will drop, the rations diminish further. Then they'll die.

'I've got to have a rest,' says Dorota, and drops instantly to the ground just where she's been struggling with a log. Thank God *she* said it. Pavel Kuzmich isn't there to disallow it, so they all squat down. But through her feet Marta senses the approach of the *desiatnik*'s horse.

'Smoke break!' she shouts, and in a moment they are all fiddling with strips of newspaper and shreds of tobacco. The *desiatnik* bounces up and circles them. He looks down on them in automatic disapproval. Their stack of timber is impeccable, but there's only the one. And their brigade leader is missing.

'*Gde Pavel Kuzmich?*' he barks.

Well, they know what that means by now, but there's no obligation to show they understand. Marta looks up at him with contempt and wonders what would happen if she offered his horse a puff on her cigarette, but remembers Mrs Benka's sharp whisper, *Don't play games when you don't know what you're playing with.* Pavel Kuzmich comes limping through the trees with a couple of axes over his shoulder. So he was right. They had left some tools behind.

Seeing the *desiatnik*, Pavel Kuzmich simply nods but doesn't alter his pace. The *desiatnik* waves an arm at the stack of timber and over the area of felled trees; over the furiously smoking brigade. He lets out a stream of invective, while his horse, used to this, just stands there shaking its ears. Then, up, away, and off again. He couldn't just trot away, could he? He has to arrive and depart in the most flamboyant manner he can. But he's hopeless, thinks Marta, her contempt increasing. Put a sabre in his hand and he wouldn't have a clue what to do with it. He needs lessons from the Polish cavalry. They'd show him how to look good on a horse.

'Well, well,' says Pavel Kuzmich, and heaves the axes off his shoulder. He lays them down into the circle of seated smokers and pointedly counts them off. 'One... and two. Hm?' There is no response. 'I turn my back, I leave you to work on your own while I go hunting for the equipment vital to our country's economic development that you lot hid in the forest – sabotage that is – and as soon as I'm gone you all sit down for a smoke break. And that's how the *desiatnik* finds you when he happens to show up. Marta, since you're the military one round here, you should speak up for your troops.'

Fine! She will. 'Actually, we sat down because we were exhausted. This logging thing is too much on a few pieces of bread. And then the *desiatnik* came so we started smoking.'

'Well, you've learned one thing at least. Now it's time to learn some more. Tell me, did he get off his horse? Of course he didn't. The day he gets off his horse they'll be taking him off to bury him. He sleeps up there, I tell you, he shits up there, for all I know, poor beast, but he doesn't get off because, as long as he's up and we're down, the world seems a little bit better. Now. Which of you's ever ridden a horse?'

Silence. They are all city born and bred.

'But, Commander.' He turns to Marta with a grin that makes her jaw clench. 'Surely, with your fine military father... He must have taken you trotting round the parade ground every week with your little sword shining in the sun?'

'My father isn't in the cavalry.'

'Oh. What a pity. But don't tell me you've never ever been...'

'Well, not really riding. I've sat on a horse a couple of times.' When she was about five, someone, not her father, suddenly swung her up without preparation, onto this giant animal, and she had burst into tears.

'Thank God for that. Someone with experience. So you can inform us. What can you see from the back of a horse?'

'What can you see? I don't understand.'

'Can you see over the heads of the people on the ground?'

'Obviously.'

'Can you see up the skirts of the fine ladies?' Marta flushes angrily. 'That's a stupid question, of course. Since you *are* a fine lady you're not interested in what's up your skirt. I'll ask differently. If you're on your horse, and your horse is standing next to a table, can you see the mouse hiding under the table?'

'Of course not!'

'Good. Well, the *desiatnik* on his horse can only see what he can see when he comes to count your stacks. So you've got to give him lots of what he needs and nothing more. What he expects to see is a nice neat structure with straight trimmed logs. But who's to say what's underneath? So. If you don't want to starve to death out here, watch me.'

Pavel Kuzmich grabs a log and drags it a few metres from the brigade's first effort. He lays it down. Lays three more until there's a square of logs on the ground. He repeats that. Then he piles up all the loose crooked branches, twigs and bits of brushwood he can find inside. Finally he heaves a row of logs onto the top. It has taken him less than ten minutes, working on his own. He turns to them, hands spread see-how-it's-done? And bows.

'The *desiatnik*'s job is counting your stacks, not inspecting them, not if he can help it. He just wants it to look right so he can say it's all been done. So. Work as I work, *devushki*, and you'll not only meet your work norms, you'll over-fulfil them.' Then as if it has only now occurred to him, he adds, 'But don't get yourselves too excited about that. If you do too many, they'll set *that* as your norms, and they won't increase the rations, whatever you do. That's the thing about rations. They only ever go down, never up. Never, ever up.'

'But what are these stacks for?'

'For? What are they for, Commander? They're for your firewood, for cooking your soup.'

'You mean... you mean... we've been brought out here to plant saplings that will grow into trees that we have to chop down and burn as our firewood? How does that help the Soviet economy?'

But that night 1st Brigade share their new skill with the others in their hut. In their different sections of the forest all the brigades have been striving, but failing, to meet their norms. If logging is what they are being forced to do, then let them do as little of it as they can get away with.

21

One heavy summer morning Marta wakes up feeling she hasn't slept. Although it's still not long after dawn, the lines of light around the windows are particularly sharp, and the birdsong, which lessened after the birds raised their young and sent them packing, has grown penetrating again. Something is going on outside. The day is even hotter than usual, for she finds her nose and her forehead already sweating. All around her the young women of her hut are bending and straightening, in a ritual of strange movements; their limbs seem to be entwined like grey snakes tangling in a mound, and their morning voices are piercing but also indistinct. Something must have happened to their tongues. She has to pick her way across the floor with enormous care because the girls will not keep still, will not keep their distance, but loom at her, plunging their faces into hers as she passes, then withdrawing them into tiny portraits too reduced to recognize.

She knows she has to get to the latrines, only a few steps away now, but the lie of the land has changed and she has no choice but to walk steeply uphill to reach them, while overnight the ground has become stonier. Sharp-edged flints slice through the soles of her shoes. Still on the path something pushes her violently from behind and she vomits suddenly, retching bile because she has nothing else to bring up. Just as suddenly the urge to vomit passes and she knows that a mug of sweetened tea is all she needs. But there is no tea and nothing to sweeten it with. Someone is carrying a bucket but she can't tell who it is, and she calls out, 'Hello?'

"Morning, Marta,' says the someone, concealing her identity. 'Hey, are you all right?'

'Me? I'm just… I think I need to sit down. It's so hot, isn't it?'

The someone is holding her arm. 'Steady on. You've gone green. Here. Have some water. Splash it on your face.'

She reaches her hands into the bucket but the water is like knives on her skin and she cries out. The bucket tips over but for some reason the water doesn't spill. The latrines are sliding away now, and the hut too. She grips the ground, but it hurts her hands, and she feels the earth moving under her fingers, which are not strong enough to keep her in place. If she lies down, and stretches out on the ground, at least she won't be able to fall. She lies down, but all the length of her body her skin sizzles from the contact. She pushes herself up again and the vomiting returns.

She can see Basia and Dorota with Pavel Kuzmich, coming towards her, the girls one on each side of his limping gait, talking at once. Look. There's Basia, and her mouth is opening and closing. She must be saying something. But Basia never says anything. What's got into Basia? As they come close Pavel Kuzmich's uneven footsteps crash into her ears. He's being so noisy and yet she knows there are times he can move as silently as a cat. Why is everyone so loud today?

'Well, well, Commander,' he is saying. 'I'd never have thought you'd be the first.'

'First what?' she says thickly.

'Malaria. No one spends the summer here without, or not many. But you're the lucky one, aren't you? You've got your granny round the corner. I'll go and get her. You girls, you get her back into the hut.'

But by the time Mrs Benka can be found and hurries, alarmed, to her shelf, Marta no longer knows who she is.

Mrs Benka clambers up to sit beside her with her back against the wall of the hut, her head and shoulders hunched under the eaves of its steeply pitched roof and, with a hand on Marta's steaming forehead, ransacks her mind for all the remedies she knows. Bee stings, nettle rash, headache, stomach cramps, irregular periods: she can deal well enough with those. But malaria isn't in her repertoire.

Is it better for the girl to eat or not to eat? She must drink surely, she is sweating so much. And something ought to be done to bring her fever down. *Salix alba.* That's the one. Willow bark stripped from the tree and boiled up. But there are no willows here that she has seen. That's the trouble. Over all the years you learn; you listen and learn from the ones who know until it has become second nature to reach for the plants that heal – but of course only the plants you have, only the ailments that come your way. And now, when her wisdom is most needed, her cupboard is bare.

This poor child. She looks down at Marta, whose eyes are not closed but staring up at her in bewilderment. And the sweat pours from her. She keeps moving her legs away from each other and pushing her blanket away. She seems to want to strip her clothes off too. Mrs Benka wipes Marta's face, wipes her hot arms, but with each touch of the cloth Marta flinches, all the time restlessly moving. All this from the bite of a mosquito. There are mosquitoes at home too but their poison carries no special threat. She has no fears for herself because mosquitoes have never been much interested in the taste of her, but some of the old ones in her own hut won't survive this, that's certain.

Even Marta isn't what she was when she came visiting with Ania, looking so womanly. But now? The girl has got so thin. Her wrists are knobbly, and the bones of her face have become sharp. She looks so much older, the way people can in illness. Even if she recovers from this, if the starvation rations go on and a winter of this follows, and then another, Marta's youth will be sucked away. For herself, it's another matter, because she has a tough constitution and a hide like dried horsemeat. Besides, she has lived.

Her neck is getting stiff, bent forward by the angle of the roof at her back. Still, it's good that Marta managed to get herself a space on the top shelf where you don't get trodden on. Mrs Benka remembers how she asked Marta to look after Ania for her, and how solemn Marta had looked accepting the charge. She remembers feeling immediately foolish, even guilty for having asked one sixteen-year-old girl to protect another. And yet, of course, this was exactly what Marta wanted. To be asked, and then to carry out the request. To be in charge. But does she have any idea what that means? Mrs Benka herself is not at all sure. Giving orders and being in charge are not the same thing. Being in charge means having responsibility, truly taking it and all its consequences... but, above all, being in charge of oneself. That's the hard one.

In all her life Mrs Benka has never imagined a place like this. Never known there could be such deliberate privation. That people may starve for lack of food she has understood, even if she hasn't experienced it or ever witnessed it. But that people can be *starved* on purpose, and then made to work as if they have been normally fed, out of... out of what? Malice? Ignorance? The urge to power? And to what end? What is being achieved here? Or have places like this simply become ends in themselves?

And look what it does to the rest of us! When it comes down to it, the worse the circumstances, the smaller our horizons. Let me only be safe, let the ones I love only be safe, I haven't the wherewithal to be bothered about any others. If it's the last thing she can usefully do, Mrs Benka tells herself, she will get Marta well again. So do something instead of sitting about pondering what can't be altered. Get some water into the girl, cool her down, whether she likes it or not.

Marta recovers as others fall sick, although, as she predicted, Mrs Benka is not one of them. Rumour has it that Pavel Kuzmich himself has fallen sick.

To Mrs Benka's impotent fury, the *desiatnik* has informed her that, as soon the fever drops, each of her younger patients is to return immediately to her duties in the forest. Just in case she feels inclined to prolong someone's symptoms, he will personally be coming round to check, even if it means getting off his horse, and it's people like her who make trouble and keep his long days so impossibly busy. Should he discover that she is being lax, she will not be allowed to tend anyone else.

So Marta totters out to find 1st Brigade reduced to twelve and without their leader. Word has come from Pavel Kuzmich that they are to carry on as usual while the *desiatnik*, who is obliged to make twice-daily observations now, points out that norms are norms and a depleted workforce is no excuse. They'll just have to work harder while they wait for their comrades to get better. Put their backs into it. Marta knows she is still not well. She hasn't been eating even the meagre rations because she couldn't keep anything down. And presumably some of the remaining twelve may fall ill as well – which will mean that any day now there'll be even fewer of them.

There must be some way round this. Remember Pavel Kuzmich's magic question: what's best for me? But it won't be his, it will be *her* question: what's best for *us*? And what is? Getting more food is best for us, not working so hard is best for us, but how to do that?

Mrs Benka has decided to shred her cabbages outside the young women's hut so that she can keep an eye on Hania and Dorota, on Jola and Agata and Maria – on them all sweating away in there, tossing and vomiting and crying that they see monsters. She disappears and in a while returns, dragging a pile of cabbages bundled behind her in a blanket.

'First Brigade! March!' cries Marta, and, enfeebled as she feels, tucks her own blanket for the midday break as always rolled under her arm. Then she limps off with a hugely rotating shoulder to the head of the shortened column, which duly giggles at her impersonation. But 1st Brigade without Pavel Kuzmich just isn't right. You get used to something, to the point where you don't notice it, and then, when it isn't there, its absence is more than simply an absence. And it's hard to think of Pavel Kuzmich lying there as ill and helpless as she was a couple of weeks ago. Ill and helpless and all alone, probably. *You're the lucky one. You've got your granny.* Mrs Benka would look after him if she could, but Mrs Benka has got her hands full, nursing the sick ones in Marta's hut and shredding the cabbages she dragged over on her blanket. Clever of her to think of that as a way of transporting them when you don't have a basket, dragging them... Yes! Oh, yes!

Pavel Kuzmich said that the *desiatnik* only counts what's been done that day. He doesn't inspect. And now that he's set himself to checking on Mrs Benka, what with all the galloping about he's going to have to do, he might even be negligent about his counting. Can't rely on that, of course, but still. He'll count what he sees, as Pavel Kuzmich says. He won't be asking himself *what* he's seeing. He won't take in exactly *where* he is.

Marta about-faces to the brigade. 'Now listen. This is what we're going to do.'

All morning the twelve of them dismantle the hollow stacks that Pavel Kuzmich taught them to build. Then they drag the logs and the brushwood on their blankets to a new area. No chopping. No sawing. They eat their bread. They stop for their rest break. Taking it slowly, nursing their strength. By evening a new set of stacks is ready to be counted, and they have already selected the site for tomorrow's subterfuge. Marta surveys what they have done with satisfaction. Let him come! Let him count! Everything's in order, Mr Foreman, sir. Your blessed norms have been met. We don't work, we don't eat. Well, is that right? Here's *my* version. You don't feed us, we don't work! They will still get their rations tonight, and tomorrow, and the next day. But, best of all, they are paying back.

That evening when they return to their hut Marta hurries to tell Hania and Dorota how well the brigade did today, how much easier the work will be when the others rejoin them. She is elated because she has smoothed the path for them, and lightened the burden of labour. Hania is sitting up. Dorota is dead.

They have to bury the body immediately because of the heat, so they leave their hut to find a spot in the forest where they can dig a grave. They have determined it is to be done properly, to the correct depth, with steep straight sides. What they are looking for is trees that might remind Dorota's emerging spirit of the Polish countryside, even though she was a city girl. Basia has noticed a clump of birches, slim and pale as Dorota at her best.

The digging is easy. They are many and take turns. And they have become adept. Marta thinks how similar this is to digging the latrines. The end result is much the same. Instantly hot shame wells over her. Where do these unwanted thoughts come from?

Someone has made a rough coffin with unplaned planks like the ones the huts are built of, and while the girls were digging the grave Dorota has been laid in the box with her hands crossed over her chest. Marta is astonished by the numbers quietly gathering, scrawny young women with skeletal young children, more matronly ones with older children, old men but only a very few young ones. Hundreds of people. Where have they been all this time and what were they doing? Have they been in other parts of this vast forest, logging under the directions of their own brigade leaders? One of the young men has a face she knows she's seen before, but somewhere else. Strange how you only recognize people when they are where you expect them to be. But she cannot think where she expects that young man to be, and anyway he's moved on.

When they bring the coffin out Marta is taken aback to see that the bearers are the bundled ones, those other brigade leaders, walking side by side with the box on their shoulders, swaying in synchrony, no danger that they'll let her slip. They must have done this before, so many, many times, and Dorota is only this year's first. All over the forest there must be graves like hers, except nobody knows where. How awful if one day people had to dig and found themselves opening up a hole where there was already a body, decomposing, or just bones.

Mrs Benka looks white and dry, her skin like crumpled paper. She has taken this death harder than anyone. Pavel Kuzmich is walking beside her when he shouldn't have got up. His eyes are too bright. He didn't have to come out. He isn't Dorota's father or her uncle. He isn't even Polish. But then it occurs to Marta that, for all the deaths in the forest, the last time he saw a *Polish* girl's funeral it must have been his Ewa's, when he couldn't help overhearing her brothers' malevolent muttering at his back.

The bearers reach the graveside and lower the box down on a blanket, which they slip out as the coffin touches the ground. You can't be profligate with blankets. For a moment everyone stands motionless until someone suddenly kneels; then everyone kneels, except for the bearers and Pavel Kuzmich, who has gone to stand with them. No one notices the *desiatnik*, who has dismounted among the trees and is holding his horse on a loose rein. The animal drops its head and begins nibbling at a tuft of stringy grass.

There ought to be prayers and choirs, but they have to make do with the gentle hissing of the forest. Then the mourners, crossing themselves, step up to shovel earth into Dorota's tomb, and Marta finds Pavel Kuzmich has shuffled with a trembling gait to stand next to her.

'You shouldn't have come out,' she says, cross mother to disobedient child.

'Poor thing. She didn't look like she'd get through this place, not from the start.'

'All she wanted was to go home.'

'It's all anybody wants.'

'But she had two little sisters!' protests Marta, indignant.

'So?'

Marta pauses. Then, in a mutter, by way of confession, 'I promised her I'd get her home.'

'Oh, promises.' Pavel Kuzmich spits a bitter laugh. 'Never any point making promises.'

Pavel Kuzmich's fever has dropped, so in accordance with the rules he is on duty again.

'Right,' he says to 1st Brigade. 'Where to? You'd best lead the way, Commander, since I don't know where you've been logging these past few days.'

Suddenly embarrassed, Marta heads the brigade to the site of their last deception and immediately Pavel Kuzmich guffaws. 'My, my! You lot have been at it, haven't you? And he bought it, did he, the *desiatnik*? Took the easy way, and why not? But look, children, you can't carry on like this.'

'Why not?' Marta is stung.

'Because it's getting obvious. You can tell a mile off, even from on top of a horse, that this wood's drying out, it's not been cut yesterday. And I can see how you did it. You dragged the stuff through on your blankets, didn't you? See?'

He points back between the trees and it's like a trail, dust and flattened grass that any Girl Guide on her first day could follow. Marta flushes. She should have noticed that herself.

Pavel Kuzmich shrugs in sympathy and spreads his hands. 'Sorry, Commander, but that's the way it goes. Back to work, eh?'

22

It's early October, more than two years since the Girl Guides were hustled away to the sanctuary of the convent in Wilno. Inside their hut, whenever a girl's birthday has come around, the others have surrounded her and waved their mugs of cabbage soup in rhythm as they sang, '*Sto lat, sto lat, niech zyje, zyje nam! Jeszcze raz, jeszcze raz, niech zyje, zyje nam!*' There should be cakes; there should be flowers – and for the summer birthdays, including Marta's eighteenth, sometimes there have been, hunted down and plucked from the forest. But, like all wild flowers torn from their lodgings, they wilted within the day. And the days themselves are dwindling, the nights getting cold again, while the word is that by now you could expect the first snows. It's only a matter of luck that none has fallen. But, while the seasons move in great drifts of time, it's Marta's diarrhoea that, nightly, keeps waking her. Sometimes she can cling to sleep and will her innards to stay quiet, but too often she leaves it late and has to launch herself from her shelf, flailing for a foothold. Then she is treading on feet, on hands, she doesn't know and doesn't care, clenching her buttocks, holding her breath to get to the latrines in time.

It has happened to them all and everyone knows you cannot help it, but it's one humiliation she doesn't want to repeat. Those sharp waves of premonitory sweating and the sudden sloshing behind her anus as if her tired intestines have lost their control, have forgotten what they are supposed to do. And the stink! So direct, so total, so completely hers. And then trying to wash out her ragged knickers in sand and putting them on again damp and gritty while her guts are churning a new alarm.

This time she is all right. By night, in the darkness that she has come to know so well, the stench of the latrines is more bearable. No flies in the dark. Afterwards she leans over the deep well and hauls up some water, hand over hand. Wipes her face. Steps out of her knickers and splashes her buttocks. There's a full moon tonight but in fact she doesn't really need light to find her way around this place any more. For all the years she lived in Poznan she never knew its streets and alleys as intimately as she *feels* the relationship between every hut out here in her transported world, so constrained in the very vastness of its setting.

There is a sound in the distance, like music. Like muffled music. Some sort of instrument and voices together, but the line is broken, the melody bursts and stops abruptly, breaks out again, like something being pumped in gushes of energy.

All at once it's louder. A door has been opened and the noise bursts into the forest night. No regard for the sleepers, Marta thinks sternly, even before wondering who it could be. There's some laughter. Men's voices, but a woman's too.

'C'mon, Kolya! Let's have that one again.' In Russian. A man she doesn't recognize.

A giggle from the woman, and applause. Chords on a guitar and they sing, in harmony, not the unison Poles always rely on, but they are raucous, and Marta can't follow the words at all. Perhaps because they are slurring their words, or it's something too coarse for her to have picked up. Halfway through they break off because they have to laugh, so hard it makes them cough. They're coming towards her in their group, although she can't yet see them. She's still holding her knickers and now won't have time to put them on. She tucks them into the waistband of her skirt like a washcloth and begins to back round the well, putting it between her and the singers. Who are lurching between some huts now, about seven of them, and they are drunk. If she can see them, they can see her. And they do.

161

'Hey, look! See that? Over there? We've got company. Whoozzat? Come out and sing! Come on out, stranger!'

She doesn't know the voice and it's too late to duck down. But she doesn't reply and doesn't move.

'Someone's shy! Don't wanna be shy when you're with friends, isn't that right, Lyuba?'

''Sright. Don' never wanna be shy with friends.' The woman's voice is thick with drink.

'You go on, Lyuba. You go see who 'tis.'

'Na, na. Not me. Might be a bear. Or a spirit. Push me in the well.'

'Push her in the well! Push her in the well! Thass an idea. Let's put Lyuba in the well!'

They cluster round the woman and jostle her, while she hoots high-pitched squeaks.

'No, but tell you what. Someone's gotta tell the well. Someone's gotta bell the well, the cat, see the well, whoozzat at the well, see what I'm saying?'

'Why don' you all shut your faces and leave the big stuff to me? Cowards the lot of you.'

This voice she knows, for all its slurping, and here he comes, Pavel Kuzmich more uneven than ever, straight for her across the trodden earth.

'Bit chilly for a stroll, eh, Commander? Or were you just out for a quick crap?'

Marta backs away. His steaming breath is fetid with his drinking.

'And me? You wanna know about me? Well, I'm pissed. No point being sober out here if you can get pissed, and me and my good mates back there been brewing us up some stuff, and tonight's the night it was ready so we thought we'd have us a little celebration. Brew it up together and drink it down together. Thass communism for you, what we've got here. Best sort there is. Share and share alike. Thass how you pull through.'

'I thought you said it was what's best for me?'

'Did I say that? Well, maybe I did, but that was then. Different things for different times. Mind you, this stuff is poison. Rots the brain away. But who needs a brain? Nobody needs a brain. All you need is a nice bottle and nice people to enjoy it with, isn't it?'

'I don't know.'

"Course you know! But tell you what, Commander. Let's have a dance under the stars. Keep ourselves warm that way. We'll get Kolya to give us a tune. Hey, Kolya! Lady here wants to dance. Give us a tune!'

'I don't want to dance. Pavel Kuzmich, please go away. You're drunk.'

"Course I am! Said I was. Trouble with you is, you're not. So why don' you come and have a quick one with us. Do you the world of good. Little drinkie, then we'll have you dancing. All it takes is a little drinkie and all the world is easier.'

'I don't drink and I don't dance. Leave me alone.'

'Don't drink? There's nobody who doesn't drink, not in the whole wide world. Nobody who knows what's what. But thass your trouble, Commander. You don't know what's what, which is why you need me to show you. Always have. Be dead by now without Pavel Kuzmich, wouldn't she? Well, let him help her one last time.'

Pavel Kuzmich takes a sudden lunging step forwards so that his hot face is pressed against hers. Her back is against the well wall and she is trapped in the circle of his noxious presence.

'Summertime,' he says, and windmills an arm over their surroundings. 'Been an' gone. Now we been havin' autumn. Nice one, is autumn. Not too cold. No mozzies. Trouble is, comes one day, gone the next. An' I tell you something, Commander. It's better'n winter. Winter's cold, oooh!' He clacks his blackened teeth and wraps both arms around himself, hugging a frozen chest. 'But I'll tell you a little secret, juss between you'n me. When winter comes, what d'you think they give you to eat? Come on. Guess! Come on, Commander.'

'I can't.'

'Nothing! Nothing more'n they give you in the summer. How you going to live on that?'

'I don't know.'

'Well, I say nothing. But thass not the whole truth. 'Cos there's some folk get more. Know who that is?'

'No.'

'Well, your luck's in, 'cos I'm here to tell you. It's the pregnant ones and the ones with the babies. And some of us are saying that's not fair, 'cos some of us can't never be pregnant. But Pavel Kuzmich isn't like that. I wouldn't grudge a woman with her baby an extra piece of bread or a bit of fat in her soup, would I? Well, would I?'

'No, you wouldn't.'

'No, I wouldn't. Juss the opposite. So I've been thinking. There's the commander. Lovely girl she is, the commander.' His hands caress the outlines of an upright guitar. 'Feed her up a bit and she'd be juss what a woman should be. Big green eyes.'

'Go away!'

'Go away, she says. Now why would I want to do that? On a lovely night like this and a lovely girl like you. Go away? Not me! Did I tell you what I've been thinking? I've been thinking, there's the commander with her lovely green eyes and no baby. An' that's a shame. Such a big shame. And when winter comes she'll be a cold commander, and getting thinner and thinner. She's already skin an' bone, like a cow you wouldn't keep, but she doesn't have to be. And here's Pavel Kuzmich, all ready and willing to help. What d'you say, Commander?'

Pincers have closed Marta's throat and her heart is struggling. She should scream but there is no sound in her; she should push him away but she seems to have lost the strength to move at all. Pavel Kuzmich lunges for her jacket, but stumbles and grabs out for anything to help him keep his balance. He clutches at a piece of cloth, which comes away in his hands so that he falls heavily, landing slumped at her feet. He turns the cloth over in his hands trying to make out what it might be. Rims it with his fingers. Recognizes what his trophy is and chuckling with pleasure waves it up at her.

'Oooh! You were waiting for me and got yourself all ready. Come on, Commander!' He grips one of her ankles and shakes at it. 'Nice and warm down here, warmer any minute. Lemme show you.'

But he is a collapsed thing, down on the ground, disabled, can't move easily. She has height and youth and, now, authority. She kicks Pavel Kuzmich's forearm with all the power of her other foot, spitting out, 'Don't be disgusting! You're old enough to be my father!'

There is a sudden silence. Pavel Kuzmich's hand still bangles her ankle, but loosely. Her tattered knickers are bunched in his other hand and his head is bent to his chest. Now she can hear his breathing, slow and rasping. She can hear her own, taut and shallow. She puts her hands to her midriff, clasping herself by the ribs as if this might calm her breathing, and feels her palms pushed apart, then drawn together.

Pavel Kuzmich releases her ankle. 'Disgusting,' he mutters, his thick tongue blundering into the syllables. 'Yes. Of course. Thass me. Commander says I'm disgusting. Doesn't like Pavel Kuzmich. Old man. Old enough to be her father. Nasty old man.'

Gingerly, as if they might break, he lays Marta's knickers on the cool night earth and pats them a couple of times, crooning something. Then he rolls stiffly to all fours and, puffing with the effort, groaning, pushes himself to his feet. Backs away from her. Only now she notices the others, clustered close together in a speechless, oddly shaped dark mass. The neck of the silent guitar protrudes at an angle, like the handle of a saucepan, she thinks, inappropriately. Pavel Kuzmich is still murmuring to himself under his breath, treading out a backwards retreat with his head down. A few paces off, a safe distance away, he pauses.

'I only meant...' he says, and his voice has cleared, suddenly sobered up. 'I only meant...' And again stops. Then he snaps round, yanks one of the drunken singers out of the group and shoves the figure stiffly forward, a hand on each of the man's shoulders. 'If you have any sense, have him, then. Your little friend.'

What little friend? What's he on about? Marta doesn't speak or move. She wants to bend and pick up her knickers but dares not. She wants Pavel Kuzmich to take his companions and go away. She wants to crawl back to her top shelf in the hut but the motionless group is blocking her path. Worse. Pavel Kuzmich is propelling the reluctant man towards her, pushing him with his knees in the man's calves, step by step towards her, and the man, so unwilling, looks as if he may topple .

'Your little friend,' repeats Pavel Kuzmich. 'Your travelling companion.' A two-handed shove in the small of the man's back plunges him into Marta, and both cry out, flinging up their arms to ward off impact.

Petya! That was the face she saw lurking in the wake of Dorota's cortège. But what is he doing here instead of plying his trade as prison guard, back and forth on the line from Rubtsovsk?

Inches from each other, but he too cannot look her in the face. He too reeks of Pavel Kuzmich's filthy brew. He's shaking his head violently. '*Nyet. Nyet. Mne eto ne nado. Nikogda nekhotelos'. Prostite menya.*'

He's apologizing, and would rather be anywhere but here. Petya holding back tears as Mrs Bila rubbed his frostbitten hands; Petya loping the length of the stationary train with little Frantek in his arms. They are nose to nose in the dark for a brief embarrassed moment, then simultaneously about-turn and slink away.

Back in her slot on the shelf, Marta massages her icy feet. She hadn't noticed how cold they were until now. But all through the night, puncturing the fretful sleep she was certain would not come, is the memory of Pavel Kuzmich's hand patting the small mound of her discarded knickers as if they were a runaway kitten.

23

Pavel Kuzmich is already outside waiting for 1st Brigade but he has his back to the hut and keeps his back to the girls. He seems to sense when they have assembled, lined themselves up. He doesn't greet them, doesn't nod at them or even acknowledge that they are there. He stumps off along the forest track, eyes to the ground where his feet will tread, as if he must give all his attention to picking out a safe path. With his axe on the shoulder that rises and falls and his polished stick helping him along, his silence is strident.

'What's with him?' asks Hania of anyone who can hear. 'He's in a mood today.'

Marta shrugs.

'P'raps,' continues Hania, 'he's feeling ill again. He shouldn't be out but can't stay in because of the *desiatnik*.'

Marta shrugs again.

But Hania is persisting. 'I mean. Don't you think?'

Marta wants Hania to drop it, leave it alone. She wants to walk, and think, and try to understand what has happened. She's tempted to blurt, *You don't know what he did last night.* She wants everyone to know what a vile, revolting creature he is, but she is too ashamed to describe what happened. How his hand consoled the dropped knickers.

But why does she feel so empty this morning? She didn't do anything wrong, she knows that. In fact, she ought to be proud of herself. She stopped Pavel Kuzmich dead in his slobbering drunkenness – and without screaming. But her knickers. Why didn't she put them on again quickly enough? Pavel Kuzmich can't have been right, can he, that she was... it wouldn't have entered her mind. And she stopped him! She stopped him with words and she kicked him off. She can still see him, slumped in that lumpy, smelly heap, muttering. She can still feel the imprint of his fingers on her ankle.

Think of something else. Think of Dorota. Poor dead Dorota under the ground, or in heaven, or somewhere in between. Pavel Kuzmich must have a horrible headache now. Well, serve him right. May it pound in his head like the hammers of God. She's never going to speak to him again, and obviously he's never going to speak to her.

All of a sudden a wave of such loneliness surges over Marta that her eyes fill and she gasps out a great shuddering sob. Instantly, here is Basia at her side with a hand on her shoulder and her sad, sympathetic face, enquiring, 'What's the matter, Marta? Were you thinking about Dorota?'

But Marta is not a weeper. Will not be. 'Yes. No. I just sneezed.' She sniffs and wipes her nose on her sleeve.

'All right,' says Basia, 'if you say so,' and returns to silence.

How is Marta going to get through the day? Work. That'll be the way. Put all her energy into the logging, even if it means the Soviet state benefits. One day won't hurt. And she'll sit as far away from Pavel Kuzmich during their smoke breaks as she can. Not that he'll come anywhere near her. He wouldn't dare.

And so it turns out. Only Hania and Basia wonder to themselves why Marta is as out of sorts as Pavel Kuzmich. But all the chatter, when there is time for it, is about him. Pavel Kuzmich, meanwhile, takes himself and his tobacco away from the group, squats on a log and smokes with his head hanging between his knees. Marta has positioned herself so that she cannot see him. Instead she looks out into the forest stretching away from her, growing darker and becoming more dense the more distant it is, mile upon mile as she knows, beyond the reach of any eye, beyond her imagination. And for the first time in a long while it occurs to her that she may be here for the rest of her life, as Pavel Kuzmich has been for over fifteen years and expects to be to his death. And the only thing that has been holding that thought back has been her daily banter with him. Now she has lost it. No fault of hers, but she has lost it, and oh, she is so, so sad.

There is only one person she can tell, and that is Mrs Benka, who will give her comfort and sensible words. But that evening Mrs Benka is nowhere to be seen.

Come the morning, 1st Brigade are outside their hut, 2nd, 3rd and 4th Brigades too. But no leaders appear. It's not just Pavel Kuzmich who's gone missing; the bundled ones haven't shown up either. For a few moments, partly out of habit, the young women keep to their ranks. If they break up, who knows, a gleeful *desiatnik* may bear down on them flourishing his whip, or their leaders will turn up without explanation but angry because they, too, are wary of the foreman.

Still nobody. In low voices they begin to ask one another what on earth can be going on. Privately Marta suspects the men are all drunk again and haven't slept it off, but that doesn't answer what they are supposed to do now. Will today be their first holiday?

Ten minutes have passed, fifteen, and still the brigades have held their formations. But this is getting silly, and they want to disperse, although no one wants to risk being the first. Marta thinks, well, I will if no one else will, but is forestalled by Mrs Benka in a hurry, her body leaning forward as if she's struggling against a headwind.

'Into the hut, back into the hut, everyone.' She shoos them in with her arms spread wide so. Old Petrkiewicz and the chickens. 'Sit, sit, sit.'

Down they sit, along the two sides of the table. Mrs Benka has some sheets of paper in her hands and a pencil. Her eyes are bright with exhilaration. She looks down the table at the expectant faces who have picked up her mood. Then she sees that she has left the door open and leaves her place to close it, firmly, but quietly. Returns.

'Now. Young ladies. Fellow Poles.'

They sit taller. This is going to be important.

'I have just found out that, although we didn't know it, Germany has invaded the Soviet Union.'

'Wha…?'

'Way back in June. Think of that. Nearly four months ago, and we didn't know it.'

What does this mean? What will it mean for Poland in the war? Their silence fractures.

Now Mrs Benka bangs the table. 'Hush. Shush! Listen to me! The point is that the Soviet Union and Poland are now apparently on the same side. Do you understand? And! And! I have also found out, although I wasn't supposed to, that there is to be an amnesty of Polish prisoners so that a Polish army can be formed to fight the common enemy – although, if you ask me, how you can give people an amnesty when they haven't done anything wrong… But that's as may be. Think how many people that means! All those men who were arrested last year, even before we were! They'll be freed to fight for their country at last, and, as things stand, we're to be released as well. The NKVD have sent a delegation from the town of Rubtsovsk to find out how many of us there are here. But the director has asked them not to let us know because he says he won't have enough workers for the winter, and they've agreed. But – now listen to this. They can't keep us here, not now that we know. So…'

Mrs Benka lays the sheets of paper on the table, and places the pencil squarely on the top.

'One of you get everyone's names down. I'm going round all the huts and I'm going to get the names of every Polish prisoner by tonight, and tomorrow we'll take the list to the director's office, and they'll have to let us go. Do you understand? Now, who's going to do it?'

Automatically she looks at Marta, but the girl is so taken aback that Mrs Benka passes her over. Basia, the quiet one, is on her feet, hand reaching for the papers, for the pencil. Good girl.

By nightfall Mrs Benka has a thick sheaf of papers and is shaking her head over the numbers. She has brought Marta into her hut, where the old ones are, as excited as the young – some of them, a couple bemused, too weak, too far gone to understand.

'Look at this. I thought I knew how many we were, but this is amazing. Over a thousand! Can you credit it? You can be somewhere, and you can think you've learned about it, and then you discover you know nothing at all. I can see why the director doesn't want to let us go. He'll never find the people to replace us in time, and then he'll get the blame when his production falls.'

'Mrs Benka.'

'Yes, dear?'

'How did you find out?'

Mrs Benka shuffles her sheaf of papers into a neat pile and takes trouble to pat all four sides as if it matters that they be just so. 'Ah,' she says. Then, looking straight at Marta, 'Pavel Kuzmich told me.'

'Pavel Kuzmich!'

'Yes. In fact, he told me a lot more than that.' She continues looking at Marta. Prompts her. 'About the other night.'

What can he have said? He'll have made up something awful.

'He told me what he did, Marta. He was horrified when he sobered up and realized what he'd done.'

Oh. 'But why did he tell you?'

'I think he wanted to confess. And he wanted to apologize, but he was too frightened to talk to you. So he thought, since he thinks I'm your grandmother, he should talk to me. I thought that was very brave of him, as a matter of fact. But perhaps he knew I'd understand.'

'What do you mean, you'd understand?'

'I'm sorry, dear. I didn't put that well. What I meant to say was that I'd understand his motives. That he meant well.'

'What d'you mean he meant well? How could he mean well when he...'

'He was drunk. He wasn't himself. He was really drunk.'

'Well, he shouldn't have been. It's revolting, when people get drunk like that.'

'Oh, yes. In normal circumstances. But are you going to tell me that these are normal circumstances? Being locked away in a place like this for ever? Don't you think that makes everything different?'

'But we're going to be leaving.'

'He isn't.'

Marta stops short and thinks for a moment. 'Did he know about the amnesty then?'

'No. That's the point. He thought you... we... you were going to

171

be here through the winter. It may have been an odd way, sorry, dear, a horrible way of behaving, but I think he truly was concerned about you. And he thought that if you... um... well, you know... got pregnant, you'd get more food, and you'd get through the winter. It's all he meant, I think. Really.'

'Then he should have apologized to me himself. In person.'

'And if you were in his shoes, would you?'

'If I were in his shoes I wouldn't have behaved like that. He was vile. You don't realize.'

'No, I suppose I don't. But perhaps we don't know what it's like to be in his shoes.'

'Why are you defending him? I don't understand why you're defending him. You ought to be on my side.'

'I am, Marta. It's just that his side and yours are the same. And mine.'

'They're not! They're not! They can't be.'

'In the end they are.'

'Why? Because of Germany?'

'No, no. Because of the Soviet state. And because, well, these are particular times.'

'It's not fair!'

'No.'

Marta's jaw is clenched so tight her teeth are hurting. Mrs Benka doesn't have any idea what it was like with Pavel Kuzmich slobbering all over her, pawing at her, his breath steamy and stinking. And the others standing there watching, not doing anything. And how can Pavel Kuzmich be on her side if he's the one who knew about the amnesty enough to tell Mrs Benka? He must really be with the NKVD, no matter what he said to her all that time ago. Let Mrs Benka answer that!

'How did Pavel Kuzmich know about the amnesty, then?'

'Lyuba told him.'

'Lyuba? I don't understand. How did *she* know? And who is she, anyway?'

Mrs Benka sighs. 'How do we know who she is? She's a Russian and

172

she's a prisoner for some reason. But look, Marta. Pavel Kuzmich told you about the winter rations, didn't he? He told you that there were two groups who get better food. Actually, there are four. They give you a bit more if you come down with pneumonia or something like that. That's official. Unofficially, if you're a woman, a young woman, a pretty young woman, and you're prepared to... if you're prepared to please the director from time to time. Do you know what I'm saying, Marta?'

Marta can feel her face is flaming.

'And Lyuba, like Pavel Kuzmich, is here for a long time. I don't know why. And she is doing what she has decided is the best way of keeping herself a bit better fed than she'd be otherwise.'

'I see.'

'Do you? Anyway, it seems that she was on her way to the director's house, and she didn't know that the NKVD delegation had arrived from Rubtsovsk. But she overheard them.'

'And she told Pavel Kuzmich?'

'No. She told a young man she's fond of. He told Pavel Kuzmich.'

'Is his name Petya?'

'Good heavens. Do you know him?'

'He was the guard in our wagon. I didn't know he was a prisoner too until, you know... I thought he was a guard.'

'Yes. Pavel Kuzmich says he was, but he got into trouble. Something to do with postcards.'

He used his own money, Mrs Bila had said. Which was generous of him. What would she say if she knew it had got him locked up? Oh, no! The postcards. If Petya got caught and they never got posted, then no one at home knows where anyone is.

Marta's voice is shaky now. 'Will they let Petya go, do you think? With the amnesty? I mean, if he got into trouble for helping Poles, and they're going to let the Poles go, can't they let him go too?' She's pleading, as if the matter were in Mrs Benka's hands to decide. But Mrs Benka just looks at her and doesn't reply.

Marta has another question. 'I still don't see why Pavel Kuzmich told you about the amnesty. I mean, if the director needs us for his norms and if we're not here, then the people who *are* still here will have to work ten times as hard, won't they? Pavel Kuzmich as well.'

'I expect so.'

'So it doesn't make sense. Him telling you so that we can get away.'

'People don't always do things that make sense. Sometimes they do them out of emotion, and mostly that isn't sense. I think Pavel Kuzmich making it possible for us to leave may have something to do with you.'

'With me? Why?'

'Think about it, dear. And go to bed now. Or leave me alone so that I can go to bed. I need to be up early.'

Marta has a sudden longing to kiss Mrs Benka good night, to receive a kiss in return, but she holds herself back. At the door, her fingers already closed around the handle, she pauses.

'Can I ask you one last thing?'

Mrs Benka bestows on her a resigned smile.

'You remember when you first met Pavel Kuzmich, when you first talked to him? That night when you both made me smoke a cigarette? When you'd gone, so that he could tell me his story, and he told it me, I asked him if he had told you what he told me. And he said you asked different questions from mine. What did you ask him?'

'I asked him what had happened to his leg… his limp, you know.'

'Oh. What *did* happen to his leg?'

'It was when he was felling a pine tree for the first time. It didn't come down the way he expected it to. It fell on him and broke his leg in several places. They never treated him of course, so it healed badly. Good night, dear.'

24

Ambush the NKVD people first thing in the morning – that's the way to do it. They'll be having breakfast with the director, and according to Lyuba he's never at his table before eight o'clock. Lazy bastard!

Mrs Benka is the Pied Piper. At every hut she passes, and she doesn't miss one, people are sucked out of the door into her procession. Even the frail ones, the sick ones. Marta had thought most of the camp had come out for Dorota's funeral, but this crowd is going to be twice the size. They are grimly quiet, their faces set, prepared for confrontation. At their head stalks Mrs Benka, cradling her chubby sheaf of papers. She's so gaunt now she can tie her layers of clothing twice round her and her legs, poking from the hem of her coat, are spindly as a deer's. But her eyes glitter with such determination it seems quite proper she should be in the lead.

The director's house is painted a pretty pink with heart shapes cut into the shutters. It stands away from the camp in a sizeable garden of its own with apple trees and fruit bushes. He must have had some juicy mouthfuls in the summer. Didn't he care that ten minutes down the path all those people labouring for his norms were only getting 500 grams of bread a day? How could he swallow anything and enjoy it knowing that? Marta is flexing her fists. She'd like to put chains round his neck, stuff 500 grams of his mouldy black bread into his mouth and then make him chop down pine trees that crush your legs.

Mrs Benka and her followers swarm into the garden, too many of them to fit in, so the latecomers station themselves round its perimeter fence. The first wave surrounds the house standing ten, fifteen deep, and those that can cluster at the windows peer in.

The director's dining room is divided by a table of polished new wood around which six men have settled themselves comfortably on his sturdy chairs. There is a samovar on the table, a pot of jam, a large loaf of white bread thickly sliced and laid on a blue-and-white cloth in a basket. There's some sausage and a jar of gherkins; a vodka bottle, half empty, and a glass at every man's right hand.

So many faces at all the windows that the morning sunshine is suddenly dimmed. You'd say it was an unpredicted eclipse. The breakfasters, five men from the NKVD and the director, glance up from their plates in surprise at first, then alarm. They look wildly round the room, but they can tell from the windows that there is a mob out there, albeit a silent one, menacing in its very silence.

They've been rumbled. Someone – who? (swift suspicious scowls all round) – has let the cat out of the bag. The director pushes back his chair and outside they hear the scrape of its heavy legs on the floorboards. He takes a decisive angry step towards one window but just as suddenly stops in his tracks. The pressed faces stare at him with neither sound nor expression. His breakfast is utterly spoilt, and it's his favourite meal of the day. All those people outside might want some.

There is a sharp, efficient knocking at his front door – an alert rather than a request to enter, because the door is simultaneously opened from the outside. It is not locked. There has never been the need to lock it before. In marches some bony old female in filthy clothes with a bundle of papers and her nose most unattractively in the air. The space behind her bulges with people. The director opens his outraged mouth to say, *Get those characters out of here*, but fails to complete the first word. Bony female is already talking in one of those strangely contained voices everyone can always hear. She addresses him in only slightly accented Russian.

'Good morning, Director. I'm sorry we've interrupted your breakfast but we won't need to stay long. I have brought you the complete list of all the names of the free Poles that you so kindly requested.'

'I never req– '

'I'm sorry. The list that Comrade Stalin requested, then. I believe your visitors have an interest?'

She flickers appraising eyes over his five guests, opts for the weightiest, and plunks the papers on the table in front of him, having first slipped his plate of bread and sausage to one side.

'I think,' she says to him, 'this is what you came for.'

His mouth is chock full with the gherkin and sausage he crammed into it before her entry but was subsequently too astonished to chew. Now he masticates frantically, then swallows with a mushy gulp. He lays a proprietorial hand on the papers and gets up, clearing his throat of crumbs. Runs his tongue over his teeth. Prepares to make a speech of acceptance on behalf of the Soviet state. That director fellow had better keep quiet, good breakfast or no. But the woman hasn't finished. Suddenly she shoots a hand out to the vodka bottle and pours herself a slug into the nearest glass.

She turns to face them one by one, lifting it aloft a fraction each time. Then she declares, 'To the victory of the Polish and Soviet forces!' – and downs the glass in one.

He'd like to do the same but she's still clutching the glass, and it's his. She understands, and pours a measure for him, then goes round the table tipping out the bottle for all the others. They are all on their feet now, drinking to joint victory.

'That's settled, then,' she says. 'You'll be sending someone with identity papers for us, won't you?'

'Of course, of course,' says the man from the NKVD. 'There'll be a photographer first, and then we'll have the papers done. I'm… er… grateful for these.' He taps the list of names. 'Just what we came for, as I'm sure you know. If you hadn't dropped by we would have had to come looking for you. Most grateful. Very useful. Indeed.'

The director is standing miserably to attention. His erstwhile workforce is massed round his house. In a couple of weeks they'll be gone, but during that time they probably expect him to go on feeding them, which is plainly unreasonable if they're not going to be pulling their weight in the forest. However, now is not the time to be saying so. He nods his head poisonously to Mrs Benka, who turns on her heel. Outside, those damned Poles have struck up some turgid song. They can't sing, Poles. That's for sure. He needs another drink but the call to victory has finished the bottle.

It was easier leading her cohorts to battle than persuading them to disperse once battle has proved unnecessary. Mrs Benka struggles her way out thinking she may stifle in the press of enthusiastic bodies. Everyone wants to pat her shoulder and make congratulatory pronouncements while all she wants is a glass of hot water. She never could stand the taste of vodka.

It takes three weeks for all the photographs to be taken (snapped against the white backdrop of a storehouse wall) and for the identity documents to be prepared and authorized. While they wait, the impatient Poles try to work out a route back west. Between them those who think they can remember attempt to put together a map of the Soviet Union, which they draw at night, and in secret, on some pieces of paper that Mrs Benka was able to hold back. They did consider gluing the papers into a single large one with resin, but after much discussion and argument – they've got all day for that now after all – they decide to number the pages, one being the most easterly regions, up to nine for the areas closest to the Polish frontier.

They are getting jittery. The first snows have fallen, and melted. The second snows might come at any time. And then there is the fear gnawing in the pit of the stomach (which no one wants to talk about) that there might be a change of heart, that the Soviet authorities, for their own reasons, will rescind the identity cards and they will be captive again. No one knows what is happening out there in the world. The Germans invaded in June, on the 22nd at 4.15 in the morning. They know that now, four months late, but only because Lyuba eavesdropped on the NKVD men's low-voiced meeting with the director. The director has a radio. He must have known, but it wasn't in his interests to give any information away. Never before have they felt the lack of information so keenly.

As the days get chillier and shorter, like everyone 1st, 2nd, 3rd and

4th Brigades, now disbanded, spend more and more time in their hut, as close to the stove and the blackened cauldron as they can get. Although it's not yet colder than it was when they arrived, knowing that every hour is sliding into the winter they've heard so much about makes them shivery with apprehension. When spring is scheduled, the vestiges of winter can be borne. And maybe, when they first arrived, they still had a little fat on their bodies, even after the weeks on the train. Now the wind from the Mongolian plain, when it comes hurtling in, will whistle through the hollows of their bodies as if they were no longer human but a set of moaning bamboo pipes.

For the first time they exchange addresses because this is the first time it has seemed worth it. They take it in turns, by way of entertainment, to describe their families and the apartments they lived in, and as she listens with straying attention Marta thinks with wet eyes about Dorota, and her love for her little sisters and their family baking sessions. Dorota never got round to giving her address so how will anyone be able to tell her parents what became of their eldest home-loving daughter?

The day after the photographer left, expectation and premature enthusiasm caused everyone to collect together all their belongings, to make rolls and parcels and packages of them. Be at the ready. Who can risk being left behind if the order comes, and then goes again as quickly? And it's astonishing how variable different people's possessions are. There are some people who seem to have arrived with suitcases of clothes and family treasures. It was all down to the arresting officer how much you were allowed to bring. Others, like Marta, have almost nothing. So her packing is achieved by rolling up her blanket and attaching her tin mug to it with a piece of twine.

As the days pass and nothing arrives from the NKVD headquarters at Rubtsovsk, most of the prepared bundles are unpacked because their contents are needed. But at least by now everyone has become expert. Everyone, young and old, can turn their belongings into luggage in a matter of minutes. No regiment striking camp could be more proficient.

25

One freezing morning they come running, banging on every door, shouting the residents out. Now! Come now! It's today! And already the passing footsteps are no more than their own echo, as hollow on the frosted ground as the blows of an axe ringing alarms through the virgin forest. Within a moment everyone is outside, and there, growling up the track, come the tractors and their huge low-wheeled trailers, to trundle them all back to Junction Station near Rubtsovsk.

Marta elbows herself a path through the growing crowd, searching for Mrs Benka. This time they will travel together.

'Come with me, Mrs Benka. Hania and Basia said they'd wait for me to bring you back so we can all go together.'

'But my dear. I can't go with you just like that. Some of my old ones are so frail.'

Well, in that case… She'll go and find her friends and bring them to Mrs Benka and those frail ones.

Mrs Benka reaches out a hand in restraint. 'Wait a moment, Marta dear. I have something for you. In fact, I have two somethings for you.'

'Give them to me later. I'll just get the others.'

But Mrs Benka has reached for her authority and will not be stopped. 'Slow down, dear. I'll do it now because I can. Stop, Marta. Stop still and pay attention if you will.'

Is there a trace of icy sharpness in her tone? Marta dreads to hear that, and is rooted.

Mrs Benka pulls two small objects from her bag. 'Hold out your hands.'

Marta tucks her rolled blanket under her arm and holds out her hands like a communicant. Mrs Benka places a small, hard, knobbly packet into the open palms.

'What is it?'

'It's some of the jewellery you've seen. Who knows? You may need it.'

'But it's Ania's. It's for Ania's wedding! It's your most precious thing.'

'No *object* can be my most precious thing, Marta. All the same, if you get it back to Ania, so much the better. But believe me, dear, she'd much rather have her best friend home safe and well than any baubles for her wedding day. And if she doesn't then she's not the grand-daughter I thought she was.'

It lay so sweetly on Ania's neck the day she modelled it, empha-sizing the childlike look of her. 'But what about you?'

'I said *some* of the jewellery. Not all of it. I've kept some in case I need it too.'

'You make it sound as if we won't be going together!'

'Don't wail, you silly girl. We will. Or I hope we will. This is just in case, but, if we go on arguing here, we won't be going at all. And now here's something else.' Another package, lighter, wrapped in a piece of friable, yellowed newspaper.

'What is it?' Unwrapping even as she asks.

Inside is a polished wooden spoon, not pine, but some other wood whose swirling grain gleams softly in her hands. She turns it over. The back of the handle has burnt into it in tiny letters, PROPERTY OF THE COMMANDER.

'Where is he? Where's Pavel Kuzmich?'

'I'm afraid I don't know. He gave it to Petya for you, and Petya gave it to me. He said to tell you that a spoon is always important. Everyone always needs a spoon.'

'What d'you mean, you don't know. Why don't you know? Where's Petya?'

'Hush, dear. Listen. Pavel Kuzmich has been arrested.'

'How can he have been arrested? He's already a prisoner, isn't he? What's he been arrested for?'

'Sabotage, Petya said. There'd been some fiddling on the logging. He wasn't clear.'

Oh God, help him! It's all her fault. If she hadn't been so clever moving logs with her blanket... But he was the one who showed them how to cheat on the stacks. He'd made her promise, hadn't he, to keep asking his question. What's best for me? And she had promised, but only to keep him quiet.

'What will happen to him?'

Mrs Benka does not want to be asked this question and busies herself with retying her bag of belongings.

But he's my friend. He's been my good friend. I want Pavel Kuzmich. Who's decided it was sabotage? It must have been the director. He's the only one with the authority, unless it was NKVD people, and they're not here any more. If she goes to the director now and explains that it was all her fault, he'll let Pavel Kuzmich go. He might not want to listen but she'll make him. She'll point out to him how much he needs Pavel Kuzmich now that the Poles are leaving... She'll tell him... she'll tell him...

'Marta! Come *on*!' Hania has grabbed her arm and is tugging her. 'We're going. What on earth are you doing? Come on or we won't get on a trailer together. For God's sake, Marta! What's the matter with you?'

Mrs Benka is pushing her while Hania is pulling her but Marta doesn't want to go on any trailer. She doesn't want to go anywhere. She can feel her feet stumbling away, one after the other, out of her control. All she can see is Pavel Kuzmich with a black cloth wrapped round his eyes, leaning on the wooden stick that it must have taken so long to polish. She sees just his hands, rubbing and smoothing a piece of wood, but it's not his stick. She sees the stick drop suddenly to one side and again Pavel Kuzmich is crumpled on the ground at her feet.

Hurry, Marta, hurry up, don't you see? It's the *desiatnik*. He's so fed up that these people have been given passports while he has to stay on here, horse or no horse, that he's lashing about in frustration. You can see tears, of rage or just tears, and he wants this operation over as quickly as he can manage, get it over with, get them out – and out of his sight. The bundled ones are scurrying about as he bellows at them, getting in everyone's way, flabbergasted by the turn of events. What has to happen out there for the NKVD to swan in and demand *their* release?

Once again, it's nearest to the trailer and up you go. No hanging about to find your friends or relatives, but the mothers have learned their lessons in this all too well, and they latch onto their children with claws as fierce as Hania's, while the children, uncomprehending some of them, hang back tugging and squealing. Paying attention to childish discomfort is a luxury – sorry, children, mama will console you later just as long as you don't get separated. Here, this one's mine, shove him up, haul up behind and if necessary push an elbow in an old neighbour's face, just don't get separated.

Basia has waited. The rest of the brigades have already gone. You can see the rear wheels of their trailer and the shape the bodies make, coalesced into a single silhouette, and you can tell without being able to see that all the faces are pointing forwards. Now the three friends will be together, although Marta notices none of this and doesn't care. She doesn't want to leave. She wants to scour the camp for Pavel Kuzmich and thank him for his polished spoon, and for his kindness. But they're not letting her.

Marta, look! Here's Mrs Benka. That should cheer you up from whatever the matter is. Let's help her get the old ones on. But Marta sits motionless as a sack of cabbages and leaves Hania and Basia to lean over the side and haul up Mrs Benka and her frail charges. One of the bundled ones has clambered into his seat and has started the engine of his tractor, his coat up around his ears just as it was the day they arrived.

The tractor sets off down the track towards Rubtsovsk, locked into its immutable pace. The wheels toil over the forest earth, munching down the kilometres where 1st Brigade used to walk behind Pavel Kuzmich with his axe and stick, his shoulder rising and falling with the limping of that once crushed leg.

26

Junction Square at Rubtsovsk is frozen in time. There are the great lorries parked up waiting for a train to leave – any train. There's the great expanse where Captain Nekrasov addressed the prisoners through the Minister for Education, and told them they would all die on Siberian soil for the crime of being Polish bloodsuckers. The square is as bleak as ever, oversized for its purposes; and the wind from the steppe, still only in rehearsal, plucks at the seams of garments, demanding entry, and finding it.

Not all the Poles who were dispersed through the forests and the mines and the sugar beet collectives are gathering here again. Many have died, mostly in the mines. Of the babies who were born in captivity, very few have survived. The only living Poles who are not now flooding into the square are those who opted to be Lithuanians in order to avoid the hard labour. Since the amnesty is specifically for Poles, the NKVD have concluded that one change of nationality per prisoner is sufficient.

But the circumstances have altered. Now the Poles are not prisoners any more, and Captain Nekrasov, who is peeking at them from behind the murky windows of Eating Area No. 3, is shifting uncomfortably on his buttocks. The war isn't going well. Somehow the word has got round that the Germans are winning it, despite the optimistic messages blaring from the flagpole loudspeakers at every corner. It's generally agreed that these are a pest. You can't turn them down, or off, and the relentless vigour of the massed choirs marching to glory is simply exhausting.

And now, to cap it all, here come the bloodsuckers, so white and skinny it looks as if the blood has been sucked from *them*, but jubilant, waving their damned identity cards, the *udostovereniya lichnosti*, which allow them to travel. In fact, with these documents they are more free than their captors, more free even than Captain Nekrasov, whose position is contingent on circumstances he cannot control and the whims of people he may never meet.

The incoming Poles are still streaming in as slowly as a silt-filled river, but a small group of them – a delegation, it is to be feared – have detached themselves from the crowd and are making their way towards Captain Nekrasov, whom they have spotted behind his window. They really don't look presentable at all, this handful of men and a scrawny, sharp-eyed old hag with her hair dragged back in a dirty white bun. They march into Eating Area No. 3 as if they own it, no preparatory knocking, no discreet coughs, and arrange themselves in front of him. Captain Nekrasov wishes he had not sent Aleksandr Sergeich out for more cigarettes. He could do with reinforcements.

One of the men, who in better times would be a burly type, steps forward. 'When is the next train south due?' he asks without courtesy or preamble, as if time is short when everyone knows that time is endless.

Captain Nekrasov finds himself answering, 'I haven't the faintest idea.' Then amends his answer. 'That's to say, some time today if you believe what people tell you, which I do since I don't have an alternative.'

'Where is it scheduled to go?'

How do you tell these people that nothing is ever scheduled? 'As far as I know it's going to Alma Ata.'

'And is that the train that's waiting out there?'

'You'll have to ask the driver.'

'There isn't one there.'

'Well, if one shows up you can ask him. But that's got to be the train you want because we never have two in a day.'

'Good. In that case, we want to buy the tickets for a whole wagon.'

A whole wagon! That's fifty tickets! 'I am not the stationmaster,' says Captain Nekrasov. 'You buy railway tickets at the station.'

'Not according to the stationmaster. He says you have to give the permission. He says he can't sell this quantity of tickets without a stamp from you on this piece of paper.'

The man lays the paper on the table in front of Captain Nekrasov where it immediately soaks up a small puddle of spilt soup.

Damn the stationmaster for knowing that Captain Nekrasov spends so much time in Eating Area No. 3 that he takes the precaution of carrying his official stamp with him and always places it next to him for official occasions such as this. Except that there never have been any official occasions such as this.

It's all very well for the stationmaster to pass the problem on to him, but to whom is *he* meant to pass it? If he does not stamp this soggy paper and they make a complaint – which, who knows, they may be able to – then he'll be for it. If he does stamp the paper and wasn't supposed to, he'll be for it too. How is he to know if he's supposed to or not? There's no rulebook for this. In principle, if people have got the money, and this man seems confident that he has, then he should be able to buy all the seats in a wagon bound for Alma Ata. All the seats there are, come to that. It's just that, as a notion, a group of civilians getting on a train and going all that way of their own volition seems so unlikely, it's making him nervous.

Suddenly the scrawny hag with the dirty bun lets out a shriek of alarm and points out of the window. 'Oh, my goodness, look at that!'

Everyone cranes to get a glimpse of the horror, at which point the hag grabs Captain Nekrasov's stamp and bangs it firmly down on the paper.

The once burly man picks up the paper and flaps it gently to dry out the soup stain. He smiles in a most friendly manner and says, 'Thank you so much, Captain. We're deeply grateful.'

'I didn't do anything,' protests Captain Nekrasov, simultaneously outraged at the woman's cheek and relieved by the fact that, truly, he didn't do anything.

187

The delegation begins to file out of the door, thoughtlessly letting in the dank air.

'By the way,' says Captain Nekrasov, and the delegation pauses, holding the door open. 'Fifty tickets is a lot. But there's a lot more of you outside than just fifty.'

'Don't worry,' says the man. 'Look. There's another group on their way right now, do you see?'

'Just think of that!' says Mrs Benka, gushing at Marta as if she were a small child. 'All our tickets, all our fifty tickets, were paid for by three of the people. Doesn't that show how lucky we are? How generous people are? How we're all together in this wagon, the fifty of us?'

Yes, yes. Marta nods dumbly but her blank expression doesn't flicker.

Mrs Benka pretends not to notice but leads the way to the stationary and silent train. At least she's taken the precaution of getting them to fill her a bottle of soup. It won't feed many but it looks more substantial than the watery stuff she made in the camp. The train is lifeless and there's no one in sight, but she wouldn't be surprised if somehow it managed to sneak out of the station while people were still negotiating with Captain Nekrasov. Poor fellow. He did look sick, but these are the perils of petty authority.

The fifty ticket holders install themselves, filling all the compartments of an entire wagon. Out in the corridor, opposite the door to the platform, there's a samovar on a table, hot to the touch. As Mrs Benka makes to lift the lid, using the hem of her coat to protect her fingers from a scalding, a voice behind her snaps, 'Leave that alone. Nobody touches that but me.'

Mrs Benka swings round to see an enormous headscarfed woman with her hands on her hips. Her furious grin is a chequerboard of large teeth and black gaps.

'Of course, of course.' Mrs Benka snatches her fingers from the burning lid to acknowledge the samovar keeper's privilege.

'It'll be five kopeks a glass. Don't go thinking you'll get anything for free. Nothing's free.'

Mrs Benka bows and sidles backwards towards the door of her

compartment, while the large woman seats herself at her table, her knees spread wide. Under her coat her calves bulge unhealthily over the tops of her worn boots. Will all those five-kopek payments flow into the coffers of the state or into the deep pocket of this woman's baggy coat? And who would blame her?

She notes that Hania and Basia have settled Marta in a corner seat so that once they are under way the girl can look out of the window. It's a sweet gesture from these young women, who do not know what's the matter with their friend. Who may not know, of course, what has become of Pavel Kuzmich. Should she tell them? Well, maybe not now. Not in Marta's hearing.

Up ahead there are raised voices, and a deep asthmatic sigh from the engine, which draws breath, pants, jerks, shudders and jolts into motion. People are running along beside the train, running across the vast square towards it, waving frantically as if to say: Hold that train, we have tickets. Will they all make it, or does it relieve the tedious existence of a long-distance train driver to ensure, always, that some *bona fide*, ticket-bearing passengers are left behind? Slowly, slowly, the train begins to move. Mrs Benka stands in the corridor gesticulating at the runners, willing them aboard. If they put on a spurt and a leap, they might outrun this ponderous creature in its first minutes. But now the train has gathered speed and it's impossible to tell which people, if any, are standing stranded, steeped in dismay on Junction Square, their bundles at their feet, their useless tickets crumpled in their hands, watching the departing train until they cannot see it at all.

Marta sits with her face turned away from the others, grateful to Hania and Basia that they have made this possible, and makes a pretence of looking out at the passing scenery. But, facing forwards as she is, she can see that the landscape they are slicing through now runs all the way to a distant, flat horizon. Hour after hour over the steppe, featureless as a turgid snow-speckled ocean. The people who live here, if any do, must find their way about using the stars, as sailors used to. Sonia had paid attention when their father talked about the stars, the constellations, the planets, but she never had the patience. Thank God she's in a moving train that knows where it's going rather than out there, blinded by space, where nowhere looks different from anywhere else.

'I'm so glad we're going south,' pipes up Basia, pressing her quiet voice into louder action for Marta's sake. 'It'll be so much warmer there, won't it?'

Yes. While Pavel Kuzmich awaits his execution in the gathering cold.

Hania has rolled a cigarette and holds it out to her but she doesn't respond, so Hania shrugs and lights up for herself. Smoke rings are suspended in the morning light. The others in the compartment have yet to notice anything is amiss in that corner over there by the window as the cigarette passes round.

Mrs Benka reaches into her bag and pulls out her bottle of soup. It's grown cold, of course, but that won't change the nourishment, only the pleasure and, frankly, pleasure isn't… She nods to Hania and Basia opposite. 'Let's have your cups.' They hold them out and sniff the contents, all expectation. 'Marta?' Who shakes her head, ever so slightly. I'm not hungry. Leave me alone.

All at once Mrs Benka loses patience. She hisses into Marta's ear. 'And what good is any of this going to do him? You sitting here moping, paralysed because you feel so guilty. We're not in church, you know, we're trying to stay alive.'

Hania and Basia are straining their ears. What does Mrs Benka mean? Who is she talking about?

'It's what Pavel Kuzmich wanted you to do. He made you that spoon, didn't he? What for? To admire it? Hang it up on the wall like a piece of peasant carving to show your friends? Have you the slightest idea what he'd think if he could see you now, "Commander?" Pouting out of the window and wallowing in your misery. Well, I'm sorry, but you're going to have to snap out of it or you'll let us all down.'

Tears roll down Marta's face and constrict her throat so that, starving as she is, she really doesn't feel hungry. Hania and Basia are staring at her, horrified, and a little frightened. This is not the Marta they know. Something important has happened and they have not been told, so they are offended as well. The others in the compartment have suddenly realized there's a scene going on in the window corner and wish they had been attending to it earlier. Someone among them should have been able to pick up what was being said.

'Now!' orders Mrs Benka, who has already removed Marta's mug from her blanket roll and tipped some cold soup into it. It's thick with congealed fat, but Marta dips Pavel Kuzmich's pristine spoon into the glutinous mass and forces it down like medicine. It *is* medicine. Think of it as medicine. Actually, there isn't much of it, since Mrs Benka has shared it with the entire compartment.

Afterwards Marta rubs at her spoon to restore its sheen. It's too easy to see Pavel Kuzmich's grimy hands polishing it with sand for hours on end, running the pads of his fingers over its surface, probing, enquiring after any roughness there, rubbing again. What was in his mind while he did that? When did he start making it? It must have been after the amnesty was announced and he knew that she would be leaving. But did he already know then that they were going to shoot him? It would have been the *desiatnik*, of course, who ratted on him. One day he decided to inspect the stacks and discovered they were hollow, or he saw that there were whole areas where there weren't any stacks at all because 1st Brigade had been moving them. And, since he had counted them and totted up the norms, he'd be in trouble himself if he didn't report what he'd discovered, because if *he* could discover it so might someone else. Marta can imagine Pavel Kuzmich shrugging and saying, 'Well, there you go. That's how it works. It'd be his head or mine. So he chose mine. I'd have done exactly the same in his position.' Trouble is, Marta doesn't think he would.

27

It's well after nightfall by the time they pull into the station at the capital of the Kazakh Soviet Socialist Republic, Alma Ata, where this train will terminate. But the platform is massed with people who seem not to know this, or who hope that what they have been told might not be true. Hundreds of them have set themselves down, on the offchance, to be as close to a train, any train, as it is possible to be. And here they are sleeping, entire families, propped on one another for support like stooks of corn.

Inside the station, the waiting room is packed even more tightly. An enormous chandelier hangs low from the ceiling but only a few of its bulbs are illuminated. Every bench, every chair is occupied by sleeping bodies, and, where a figure is rocking rhythmically back and forth, if you bend close enough you can make out a low tuneless crooning. Somewhere among the shawls a fractious baby is too hungry to sleep.

Set against one wall is a trestle table covered in heavy red cloth hanging to the ground. The table is piled with periodicals and pamphlets. Posters rise up the wall behind it and Marta recognizes Lenin and Stalin. The other figures must be important ministers in the government or the Party. She lifts a swathe of red cloth and peers underneath. A woman is stretched under the table on her side with a clutch of small children lying at right angles to her in a row, like piglets suckling on a sow. Maybe there is room for another body. She crouches down and creeps under the curtain of cloth. The woman and children do not move. She eases herself onto the floor and pillows her head on her bundle.

It is airless down here and deeply dark. When they arranged themselves so cosily in their wagon at Rubtsovsk, she did not know that other people would also be on the move, from places she has never heard of to other places she has never heard of. She imagined, somehow, that leaving the camp would mean a series of train journeys all the way home, or at least directly all the way to the newly forming Polish army. But no one knows where it is. No one seems to know where the Germans are. All that mattered was going south in flight from the onset of winter. She has papers that say she is allowed to travel but she does not know where she is going or how she will get there. All these other people must have papers too. They will all be trying to get on trains too small and too few to take them, and nobody has any food.

What's tomorrow? What will this release amount to? In the camp there was the black bread and Mrs Benka's thin soups; there was the well that will soon freeze over; there was the trudge along the forest track to work; there were the smoke breaks with Pavel Kuzmich. Marta closes her eyes.

The official hides behind the small window he had hoped to shut and points out in a voice growing first shrill, then hoarse, that there are only the four classes: soft with reservation and soft without; hard with reservation and hard without. The soft with reservation is by definition reserved for senior echelons of the Party, who are the only people allowed to travel this way and who may or may not arrive to take up their seats. The hard with reservation were spoken for yesterday. And it was foreigners then too. In fact, the entire train is bound to be already full. He's prepared to sell as many tickets as anybody is prepared to pay for but he cannot guarantee that anyone will actually get on the train, so won't they please go away and wait, somewhere else.

But the unfortunate fellow is not to know that these awkward passengers, all Poles it turns out, have only been living in his country for a year or two, and, thin as they are, dirty and unkempt as they are, they have yet to learn how to be fully afraid. They may not be the higher echelons of the Party but they have papers to prove that they are free men and women and they intend to exercise that freedom. These may be exceptional times. In which case, they will have to resort to exceptional measures.

When the first train draws in, they storm it. The official slams down his window so that he does not have to witness the soft with reservation filling steadily.

The word is that the train is bound for Chimkent. What's there? Who can say but that it's further west. The engine will be struggling because they've got just the one at the front. No one said to put another at the back. No one said it would be so overloaded. The driver complains there are too many passengers and he doubts they'll make it. Some people, rather a lot in fact, are going to have to get off. Nobody moves.

The driver considers getting down from his engine himself and leaving them all there to sit in the cold, but as he puts a foot onto the platform he sees a phalanx of hideously dirty men blocking his path with their arms folded. They don't look up to much. If he could take them on one by one, he'd send them reeling onto the track, but there's a good twenty of them and doubtless more lurking somewhere behind. He still has height, though, up on the footplate, and he scours the station over their heads for the NKVD. This is one of those times when you'd actually welcome the bastards, but they must have been called away because there isn't a sign of them. And when you think how usually they're strutting about like a bunch of cockerels in a yard! On second thoughts, if he takes it steadily, maybe the train will manage after all. 'All right, all right.' He retreats into his engine, his flat palms giving the air tiny soothing pats – calm down there, comrades; we're on our way.

The land is flat as flat. Again there is nothing to interrupt the yowling of the winds that blow from the east. Although they are in the fug of the closed compartments, three perched on each of the three tiers of bunks on either side and some on the floor, the passengers look out onto the desolation of sheer space and shiver. This is a dismal land that goes on and on without variation. On one side, to the south, there are shadowy mountains, but very distant. The steppe is yellowish green, broken only by small bushes and some scrub. Occasional silvery rivulets wriggle over the dry ground as if searching for something, lose heart and disappear into the earth.

Mrs Benka finds she is shaking her head. There is no sign of humankind out there and yet they say this is the land of the nomads. What can it do to the spirits to be born here, then to spend your days here, knowing it is for ever? Could a man or a woman, transported from this place to less bleak surroundings, really think back to these plains with longing and speak wistfully of home? A terrible malaise drops over her. Cosmic elements have shaped this landscape as a warning from some scoffing deity that hubris will find its nemesis here.

But then, look!

As if by way of rejoinder, there plodding parallel with the railway line goes a line of men in long sheepskin coats down to their ankles, each leading a camel with early-morning frost on its muzzle and pulling a rough two-wheeled cart piled high and covered with skins. Neither men nor camels raise their heads as the train passes but keep to their measured gait, one foot after the other, walking to eternity. And again the steppe is all there is. Now Mrs Benka doesn't know whether the men and their animals testify to human endurance or obduracy. If, that is, they are here by choice. One never knows these days.

Mrs Benka is still troubled by Marta. The talking to she gave her yesterday doesn't seem to have done the trick, harsh as it was. The girl is still gazing only inward, chewing over the past. This sitting and brooding can only make things worse when what she needs is to be doing something. But what? Mrs Benka straightens her back as if sitting more upright will be an aid to productive thought.

Whenever the train approaches a station, no matter how small, she notices that it slows to walking pace although it usually doesn't stop. Perhaps the driver wants to allow them time to admire the bronze busts of Lenin and Stalin, frowning out towards the track from their whitewashed plinths. But occasionally, when they reach one of the larger stations, the train does stop, so that a few daring types may leap off in search of the boiling water that, officially, is all there is to be had.

That's it! Mrs Benka rummages through her bundle, which, like everyone, she keeps on her knees for fear of losing it. Among the jewels intended for Ania's wedding, those she did not give to Marta, are the pearl earrings and the diamond ring. She picks out the earrings and lets them lie for a moment in her palm: two tiny milky globules dropping from silver clasps. She can remember so precisely what it was like on her own wedding day when she fastened them to her earlobes, just as her mother had once fastened them to hers. They are a young woman's ornament, fashioned for soft young ears. It's wicked how the body dries and shrivels while the mind it encases peers out at a changing world and fancies itself unaltered. How pretty they would look on Ania. Well, too bad. They have another role now.

'Marta, my dear,' says Mrs Benka, on the sharp side to jar a path into her attention. 'Next stop, I want you to take these and jump out. See if you can barter them for something to eat.'

She can tell Marta is scanning her mind for a plausible excuse. Instantly Hania stirs, ready to offer to go instead. Mrs Benka places a stilling hand on Hania's knee. Shh! Don't you move, don't you say a word. She adds, 'I'd like to go myself, but I feel a little weak today.' That's the way. Get to her through her sense of duty.

In the compartment, others are sorting through their belongings. Mrs Kwaszniewicz, one of those Mrs Benka had been sure wouldn't survive the camp, is pulling out a bouquet of artificial flowers of the sort people sometimes sew onto the shoulder of a ball-gown. What had possessed her to bring those when she was arrested, or had it been some uncanny foresight? But what value is there in artificial flowers? From one of the bunks someone is handing down a delicate silver cross on a fine chain. Marta herself is fumbling with her bundle for the knobbly packet of rubies.

Mrs Benka leans forward and closes her hand over Marta's. 'No. Not those. Not yet.'

The train is slowing. Will it be another majestic slide past the bronze busts, or a halt? Slower and slower, and eventually the train stops in silence, not by a platform, but in some sort of siding next to the stationary wagons of an empty goods train. Beyond it they can make out the roof of a station building.

'Now run along, dear, and see what you can find. And maybe get some water too. But don't dawdle, will you.'

28

Clutching the water bucket containing other people's treasures, Marta clambers down. The goods train is blocking her route and whichever way she looks it stretches away. She'll have to go underneath. You can, they ride so high from the track, but ducking down she sees little heaps of excrement, one next to another, between the rails. She imagines all those people, bottoms shivering while they squat and strain, male and female, seeking privacy perhaps but coming upon others who had thought to find it too. She picks a way through only to find another goods train and then another between her and the station platform. This must be some sizeable place to have so many lines in the sidings.

Just as she is about to bend under the next set of wagons she notices, standing all on its own, a tawny calf, half grown and shaggy, with a length of twine round its neck. What is it doing here? She edges towards it and holds out her hand. Instinctively the animal shrinks back, bracing itself on its front hooves, then quite suddenly dips its head, raising its blunt nose, and begins sucking hopefully on her fingers with a rasping mouth. It sucks and sucks, then sorrowfully releases her hand and hangs its head again. Marta sniffs her fingers and finds they smell oddly sweet and slightly cloying. Poor calf. When will it feed again, or has it been dragged along so that it may feed others?

'You wanna buy something, miss?'

Marta hasn't heard the woman's approach. A Kazakh woman, broad-faced with eastern eyes, in a bright red overshirt and long flowered green skirt. Her hair is hidden under a tasselled white head-scarf. The two regard one another, Marta hesitant, the woman immo-bile. She can wait for ever. Her weathered face is deeply lined round the eyes, maybe from smiling. She's holding out a rough cloth, sag-ging under the weight of its contents.

'What do you have?'

The woman nods towards her cloth. Flat rounds of baked dough and a clutch of brown eggs looking as if they have only just been filched from beneath their mother's unsuspecting body. Marta reach-es out for one of the eggs. What can they do with these? But the egg is heavy, solid. Hard-boiled.

'And you?' says the woman, clicking her tongue to get her egg back until it has been paid for. 'What have you got?'

Marta fishes in the bucket and displays her currency on her flat-tened palms. The woman wraps a muscled forearm round her cloth of produce to protect it and pincers up the pearls between finger and thumb. She holds them dangling up to the light. Twists them about. Shakes her head and replaces them.

'No value,' she grunts. 'No colour.'

Now the silver cross on its fine chain, which looks poignantly frag-ile draped over her broad hand. She likes it, but can't make up her mind. What will it be worth?

'Let's see *them*.' She nods towards the artificial flowers.

Marta hands them over and the woman beams. She holds the flow-ers against her bosom and squints down to gauge the effect; holds them against the side of her face and raises her eyebrows for Marta's opinion. Marta nods vigorously. Actually, they do look very fine.

The trade is complete, and Marta makes to turn back to the train. But Mrs Benka said to get hot water too and, proud of her bartering, Marta wants to return with everything and earn herself general praise as well. She turns to bid farewell but the woman, leading her mourn-ful calf by its twine collar, is already striding quietly away between the goods wagons and out to the steppe.

Marta tucks the bread and eggs into her coat and slips under the last wagon to reach the platform. She'll have to go into the station for the boiling water but now she understands why her train was diverted into the sidings. This station is teeming with people, all men, horribly gaunt and tattered, looking so ill they might lie down and die where they are any minute.

She creeps quietly among them along the platform, hoping not to be noticed, but as she goes she overhears snatches of Polish. These men: are they supposed to be the new army that a man called General Anders is forming? It's not possible! They can barely stand upright, let alone fight. She is bewildered, uncertain what to do. If they know there's a train out there, standing beyond the goods wagons out of sight, they'll want to get on. Of course they will. And so they should, especially if they *are* the army. But there isn't room.

Marta sidles into the station keeping as close to the walls as she can, peering between the thronging bodies for the cylinder with the hot water. Sees steam on a window and makes for that. Sets her bucket down on the stone floor under the tap, which coughs and drips when she turns it. The cylinder must be empty. She glares at it in disappointment, but these poor men must have used it all up, and quite right. They have to have something! As she bends to pick up the empty bucket, scalding water gushes violently from the tap and with a choked gasp of shock she leaps back. Hard-boiled eggs roll out from her coat-front, their shells cracking and splintering as they hit the floor. She's down on her knees, raking in eggs with great scooping movements of her arms, sweat on her forehead, tears in her throat. The water is no longer cascading into her bucket because someone has turned off the tap.

A pair of feet in crumbling boots straddles the bucket; a bony hand so thin it's almost transparent cradles a retrieved egg whose fall has webbed the shell with a lace of fine fault-lines like the surface of an ancient painting. Inexplicably, as she looks down on it displayed in that starved palm, the egg's serene shape seems to be hinting at some long-forgotten wisdom. Just as quickly the notion vanishes as she thinks that if this person were sensible he would have bolted with his find to gobble it down, in hiding somewhere.

'Thank you,' she mumbles, embarrassed, eyes down, but courtesy requires she look up.

Should she know this face behind its beard, so hollowed, the eyes so sunken, the skin so waxy? But there is something. And he too seems baffled by some memory, quizzing her features one by one for reminders. For a second, as if the effort is exhausting him, he closes his eyes and his lashes lie long and thick on his sharp cheekbones. It can't be! What have they done to him in so little time?

'Antoni?'

The familiar raised eyebrow of amusement as he left the Mother Superior's office with her messages for the Archbishop; the wide smile. 'Miss Dolniak. I wasn't sure, you've ch— But your eyes are the same.'

'I thought you'd gone to the Vatican.'

'That was the plan, in a way, but it was meant to be a ruse. Anyway, it didn't work. They arrested me almost immediately because they said I must be a Polish officer.'

'Why? You're not an officer. Why on earth?'

He scuffs the thin soles of his boots on the ground. 'These. My boots. They were nice boots, then. Apparently only officers have boots. That's what they said.'

'And now?' she says. 'What about now? Are you going to join the army?'

'Well, I will when somebody finds a train.'

The train. 'Oh, no!'

'What is it?'

'My train. I was supposed to be getting food for people on the train, and water. But here I am... It's probably gone without me. Oh, God!'

'There's a train? Really? Where?'

'Out there,' she says, pointing. 'Beyond those goods wagons. I think they diverted it there to hide it... from all of you, I suppose, because it's jam-packed.'

'Well, we must get *you* back on at any rate. Put your food in my hat and let me take the bucket.'

His arm is so emaciated, surely he won't be able even to lift the bucket. But he does, suppressing a slight grunt. His hat is worn and soft. She folds it round the flat breads and the eggs like a bag.

This is a terrible thing to be doing, ducking out of sight of one's forlorn and stranded countrymen who may wait days for transport, who deserve it most, who are the needed ones. But what about Mrs Benka and her frail charges? It's a nice question, but come on, Marta, be honest. You want to get back on that train and be out of here for your own sake!

She slips under one goods train, then the next, then the third, and there is her train still, but it's setting off. It's on the move.

'Help! What shall I do?'

'Run for it.'

'I'll never get on!'

'You'll get on something. That's better than nothing.'

Now he is running ahead of her, awkwardly, gasping, water splashing from the bucket with every step. Why doesn't he just put it down? But buckets are as precious as water. 'Run parallel with the track now!' And he veers to the right, struggling along beside the moving train. Looks briefly back and shouts, in triumph, 'Yes!'

A coal wagon is trundling up towards them with a ladder up its side. 'Make a grab for that.' And he shoves her towards the ladder.

She's still clutching Antoni's hat with her booty wrapped inside so only one hand is free. She launches herself at the ladder with a leap of desperation that she will never be able to repeat and manages to hang onto one of the rungs. Her grabbing arm feels as if it is being torn away as her legs thrash over open space, while she is dragged along. But now one foot has found a purchase, then the other, and she hauls herself up, only now thinking, what about him? And what about my bucket? At the top of the ladder, she tumbles face down onto the coal and lies sprawled for a moment without moving. Every joint of her body is burning from the wrenching she's given them. As her breathing calms, she scrabbles onto all fours and only then realizes that Antoni is clinging to the ladder, panting hoarsely, his head dropped to his chest.

'Antoni! I'm so sorry. Here. Give me your hand.'

The train is picking up speed now. She must help him up before he is so tired he has to let go and fall off. He lifts his head and nods but almost as if he hasn't taken in what she's said. Then she sees he's trying to haul the bucket up. So she flattens herself again for safety, and reaches out for it. He closes her fingers round its handle, but lying down she can't pull it up. There she stays, helplessly, her arm hanging over the edge, dangling the swaying bucket from her aching fingers. Hand over hand he pulls himself onto the coals, then, crouching, he leans out over the track, takes the weight of the bucket and reels it in.

Marta doesn't move but opens and closes her hand, flexing the fingers where the handle of the bucket has turned the joints white. She turns her face to one side to see if Antoni has found a secure position and finds him cross-legged and grinning at her. Laughing at her, actually.

'What's the matter with you?' she asks crossly.

He lifts both palms, entirely blackened from the coal. 'You should see your face.'

'Oh.'

'But we have water, don't we?' He pushes coals aside to make a well to wedge the bucket upright. 'I don't have any sort of cloth. Do you?' She shakes her head. 'We could use my hat.'

She has laid it down and its soft sides fall open to reveal the bread and eggs. They both look at the food.

Marta thinks, I can't offer him other people's rations, but I can give him mine. She takes out an egg and tears one of the breads in half. Holds it out to him. He's shaking his head, no I can't, this isn't mine, and she's shaking the food at him, go on, you have to. So he takes the egg and begins peeling it carefully. Instantly it becomes grimed with coal dust from his fingers but he doesn't notice, or doesn't care. He takes a tiny bite from the top of the egg, cupping his other hand underneath lest any morsel fall, and closes his eyes over the taste. This egg is going to take a long time.

'Have some bread with it. Go on. Please have some bread with it!'

Antoni takes the doughy half-moon from her and alternately nibbles on it and on the egg. It's plain he is struggling not to cram it all into his mouth at once, that he wants to make it last as long as possible. Watching him, Marta thinks she has never imagined that seeing someone else eat could be as pleasurable as eating herself. The train rocks slightly beneath them and the moving air is chilly. The coal is like stones under her buttock bones, but, although she feels all these things, none of it matters.

Antoni finishes the last mouthful and licks his coal-dust fingers, licks his coal-dust lips.

'What about you?'

'Oh, I'm not hungry.'

'You're such a bad liar, Miss Dolniak.'

'Marta.'

'Marta, then. But still a bad liar.' Antoni takes his hat, shakes it vigorously and dips its brim into the now tepid water. 'Face, please.'

She closes her eyes and juts her face forwards him. As he dabs at it she remembers how her mother used to scrub her chin and cheeks when she was little, after every meal, clamping her head still with one hand and rubbing with the soaped flannel in the other. Antoni is so gentle he is almost tentative. It's nice but he'll never get the dirt off like that. What would her mother think if she could see her daughter now, sitting on a wagonload of coal having her face washed by a man she barely knows? What will Mrs Benka say? But how will she get to Mrs Benka again, with the water and the rest of the food and the colourless and therefore valueless pearl earrings? The earrings! Where are they? Her mouth opens in dismay and she's screwing up her eyes with the worry of it. Ania's earrings. Selling them was one thing, but losing them…!

'What's up?' Antoni is about to dip his hat into the water for a second time.

'I had some earrings to barter. They weren't mine and the woman didn't want them. But I've lost them, and they weren't mine, don't you see!'

'You couldn't help it. They'll understand,' he says blandly, as if it's of no consequence, and turns back to the bucket where, as he dips his hat once again, he spots something small gleaming at the bottom under the water.

29

Basia and Hania have scrambled to sit on either side of Mrs Benka, whose pale face has turned grey with worry. How dared she take it upon herself to decide what was best for Marta in her grieving! How dared she shove her out with a few trinkets onto railway lines possibly teeming with NKVD or hostile locals, as if this could be some sort of corrective, as if a few awkward moments of reality would jolt her out of her distress!

Mrs Benka sits hunched in culpability. Everyone's eyes are on her; she knows that, she feels it, and it's no more than she deserves. The poor child, on her own, on an alien station... No one can think of anything useful to say and the silence grows louder, more accusing, as the kilometres rattle by.

Hania and Basia are trying to picture what Marta might be doing at the moment: how she might feel when she realizes her train has left without her; how she will suppose no one made an effort to find her when, in fact, Hania did leap down to try to hunt her out. The trouble was that, just as she took in the number of goods trains parked up between them and the station, the engine exhaled a steamy sigh and she felt bound to scamper back. But maybe, had she not, at least Marta would have had a companion. Two would fend better for themselves than one alone. Mrs Benka's self-recrimination is spreading.

She has the earrings, Mrs Benka keeps intoning to herself. Pearls, good-quality pearls. They should fetch something, to keep her alive for a while, if she trades them well. But of course Marta did not take her blanket or her tin mug or the spoon Pavel Kuzmich laboured over with such care. She has not got the packet of rubies that Mrs Benka gave her for precisely such an unintended separation. All these are still here, a small mound of ownerless belongings on the top bunk, the pathetic remains of the departed whose estate amounted to nothing more.

Perhaps Marta will come upon other Polish travellers – God knows there seem to be enough of them – who will let her join them, who will help her. They could not fail to welcome a young girl on her own, but it will not be the same. Bonds of experience, of memory, of shared jokes – these will have evaporated like high clouds in a summer sky, and Marta will be the outsider hovering at the rim of a closed circle. And all because of blundering and foolish Mrs Benka with her home-spun psychology.

She thinks of the tall, busty girl who towered over Ania on their visits to the farm; thinks of her uncharacteristic wail when Pavel Kuzmich first separated them and sent them to different huts; of her first cigarette out there on that cold night with Pavel Kuzmich; of Pavel Kuzmich himself and his confession, so terrible to hear because of the man's weeping. There is no question that Pavel Kuzmich was fond of Marta, but in what way? As a young woman with whom he foolishly hoped to have some relations? But he knew the picture he presented to the world. He cannot have supposed that Marta could possibly want him. As a daughter, then? He was old enough to have a child of her age.

She stands up suddenly, urgent with the need to be doing something. At least she can look after Marta's possessions in case they hear of her somehow. She reaches up and gathers the blanket with its contents carefully off the top bunk and sits down again, clutching it to her, to lay the bundle in her lap. Slowly, sadly, she unwraps it. The mug, sticky, encrusted like all the mugs for lack of water to wash it. The spoon. That spoon. She runs her fingers over its astonishing smoothness. So much work. So much care. Such devotion. There's the packet of jewels. And... what are these papers? Oh, Jesus and Mary! Marta's ticket and her identity card.

*

'We can't stay up here. It'll get much too cold.'

'I haven't got a ticket. They wouldn't sell us any because they said there wasn't a train.'

'You can come into our compartment.'

'How? What if an inspector comes? They've got NKVD on the trains too, you know.'

'We'll hide you.'

'How?'

'I don't know! But we will. I know we will.'

Now that the earrings have been found, and there is still some water in the bucket, cold by now and murky, but water all the same, and she has not lost her bread and eggs, Marta's confidence has entirely returned.

Antoni smiles at this outburst of certainty. Let's assume she's right. After all, he doesn't want to stay out here on the coal in the dead of night. All night.

'All right, then. Next time the train slows, we'll get down and run to the first compartment we can get into, then walk through the train.'

'What if there's an inspection while we're doing that?'

'The toilets?'

But he wonders how many others without tickets will be crowding into the toilets when the word comes down the corridor that an inspector's on his way. No matter. Deal with that problem when it comes. He clambers to his feet, gingerly, arms out like a scarecrow for balance, and scans the horizon ahead. The train has been running in a straight line for hours. No gradient, no obstacle to prevent it. But he can see the track bending in front of them and, for the first time, a few trees. Perhaps there will be a settlement of some sort there and the train will slow. To be ready they must ease themselves over the side and cling to the ladder.

Looking down, Marta watches the stony ground by the track slip by. Looking up, she sees that Antoni's boots, of a quality to have had him imprisoned, now have almost no soles at all. She hopes the train will slow down soon, because her hands are freezing. When she gets back to their compartment Mrs Benka will rub her icy fingers back to life, and maybe Antoni's too.

The train is whistling, which it did not do when they stopped before. Is that a warning that it's going to go rushing past whatever is ahead? But no, it does seem to be braking.

Antoni is higher up, sees more. 'Jump!'

She falls off rather than jumps and lands, feet then bottom then back. Antoni is a few metres further up the track and lopes back for her, and now they have to run again to reach a compartment, any compartment, and get themselves inside the train before anyone outside it notices. Antoni has thrown himself onto a step and is tugging at a door that seems to be locked, or he hasn't the strength. Someone is looking out, someone's astonished face pressed to the glass. Man or woman? Can't tell. For heaven's sake, won't they help? They will. The door is opening, slowly, because a sudden swing of it might knock Antoni back onto the track. An arm is pulling him and the bucket inside and the door is closing again. She hears him shouting, 'No. It's not just me!', and the door swings open again. She's out of breath, she really is out of breath trying to catch up, but the train is going so slowly now it's almost at a standstill.

'Come on, young lady. Get on with it.' A gruff voice. And the hands that grab her under the arms are so strong she nearly shrieks. Then she's half lying on the floor of the corridor, her legs still protruding, her heart pounding too hard for her to move any more at all. 'Dearie me!' Again the iron fingers dig into her arms and drag her in. She hears the door's metallic clunk as it slams to behind her, and the train shudders to a halt.

'Up, up! Get up!' Brindled whiskers at the level of her face. 'They're coming in, the inspectors.' He's pulling at her and Antoni is pulling at her.

Her head is swimming but she sees the bearded man slip into a compartment. She puts her hand into her pocket for her ticket, but it isn't there. Can she have dropped it in the station or under a goods wagon or while she was buying the food? She can't remember when she had it last. And her identity card. Where in God's name is her identity card?

'Anto…'

But he's on his knees to be down with her at floor level. 'Shh! Put your arms round me!'

'Wha…?'

Her confusion is abruptly suffocated as her face is plunged into the rank cloth of his coat. His arms are tightly wound around her so that she can neither draw back nor breathe, but, as if by some instinct, her own arms creep round his back and hug him to her.

A moment later she feels the toe of somebody's boot prodding her under the thighs. 'All right, all right. Very nice and cosy, pair of lovers, eh?'

A large hand on her shoulder and another on Antoni's make them stare up in alarm at the grey jacket with the little red stripes at the collar.

'No, not at all,' stammers Antoni. 'This is my sister. We haven't seen each other for two years. I thought she'd disappeared.'

The official, who is a family man, looks down into their faces, from one to the other. 'I can see the likeness,' he says, nodding. 'Fair enough, for now. I'll be back when I've been down the train. Be sure you have your papers ready then.'

After all, the train is moving again, so no one's going to be getting off, and there are times when you can afford to be soft-hearted. Pleased with himself, he shoulders a path through the people in the corridors, demanding papers as he goes, nodding, raising his eyebrows, hand out for the next one.

Antoni drops his arms, so Marta lets hers drop too. 'Which way's your compartment, have you any idea?'

'No. Let me look.'

Marta pulls a window open, leans out and peers down the length of the train towards the back in the direction the inspector went. She can still feel Antoni's arms round her the way you can feel the strap of a watch you've just taken off. All the compartments look the same. Maybe it was nearer the engine. She looks to the front.

Mrs Benka stares down at Marta's papers spread in her lap. She has been smoothing them out with the edge of her hand over and over again, mindlessly. The girl will be helpless without these documents. They'll re-arrest her. For sure they will. They'll bundle her onto a transport back to Siberia and it will be on Mrs Benka's conscience for the rest of her life. Marta won't have the resources, hasn't got the fat on her, to survive the coming winter. Silly old woman with your big mouth! You should have let her sit there and mope if that's what she wanted. She'd have got over it in time, and at least she'd be here, and alive.

Hania and Basia, and indeed everyone in the compartment, has understood what it is that is laid out on Mrs Benka's knees. Her thoughts are not far removed from theirs and no one knows what to say.

Mrs Benka's chest heaves with nausea. She's got to move. She folds the papers neatly into four and pockets them, patting the pocket, pressing the pocket. 'I'll be back,' she announces, as if she thinks someone may try to stop her, and clambers cautiously over the feet of the seated passengers, who all look up at her, knowing what's on her mind, fearing what she fears, saying not a word.

The corridor is so full, the people seem to be holding one another up. Perhaps some of them haven't even got their feet on the ground. But if she doesn't get some air she is going to collapse, which would serve her right but cause even more problems.

'Please!' she pleads, swimming her elbows between the bodies. 'Please.'

'Hey, let the old lady through, there. She doesn't look too good.'

'Need some air, dear?'

'There you go. Steady does it. No need to hurry or we'll all fall over.'

They're passing her along the corridor to the door between compartments where the window is open. She really is going to vomit, but as she leans out the blast of cold air makes her gasp and the nausea disperses.

'That's better, isn't it?'

Her head is outside but she nods it anyway, thank you, whoever you are. Long breaths of air, the clean air of the steppe mixed with acrid gusts wafting back from the engine. She turns her face away from its smoke and narrows her eyes, gazing back the way they have come. It's not possible. Can it be?

'Martaaaa!'

30

Important objects are restored to their owners. Mrs Benka takes back
her pearl earrings and with trembling fingers wraps them in the
handkerchief from which they originally came. She does not account
to Marta for the trembling, which will continue for some while yet.
She is delighted to have the earrings back, relieved as a matter of
fact, if a little miffed that they didn't pass muster. For her part Marta
makes loud exclamations over her ticket and identity card as if she
were a young mother and they toddler twins lost and found.
Meanwhile Antoni lurks wanly in the corridor, his face pressed to the
compartment glass, waiting to become the subject of conversation.
Here we go.

Marta is whispering something to Mrs Benka so quietly that everyone else in the compartment has to lean forward to catch what's being
said. Soon all heads turn as one to look at him.

It's a long time since so many women, of such varying ages, have
paid him so much attention. The two young women must be those
friends Marta has told him about, Basia and Hania. One of them, a
snub-nosed freckled person, is staring at him with such unabashed
appraisal that he realizes he is blushing. The other one meets his eyes
but immediately looks down, her own cheeks dusted with pink. The
old woman, Mrs Benka, is already trying to get up, as if she wants to
greet him like a man, extending towards him one of those capable-
looking hands that promises a firm grip with a dry palm. You'd feel a
fool bending to kiss that hand. The other women are wearing the
expressions that in normal circumstances people bestow on newly

christened babies – heads on one side, eyes moist with concern, lips pursed for kisses.

Evidently he is welcome. They are looking terribly sorry for him, so much so that for the first time he begins to feel terribly sorry for himself. It was different when everyone was in the same boat, but now that he is the unique object of strangers' compassion he fears he may burst into tears. In a way he wishes he could, if only to be wrapped in all those motherly bosoms. But he swallows, calling himself to order. Look at them. They haven't been having a party of it either. They're making a space for him where no space existed.

Just as he is about to worm his way into the compartment, the pressure on his body increases as some sort of flurry further up the corridor suggests movement there. The inspector! He dives into the compartment.

'Up!' commands Mrs Benka, leaving her place to give him a foothold and patting the top bunk. 'Get up there and lie against the wall. The others will hide you.'

In a second he's up there, stretched out on his side with his face to the wall. The three women who were already there shift themselves to make room and then sit with their backs to him, legs dangling down, documents held in readiness for the inspector. Antoni feels the warmth of bony buttocks pressed against his own and tries not to imagine how it might be to be lying here like this and everyone with more flesh.

Marta is bolt upright and bright-eyed at ground level, a legal passenger once again. She would rather be up on the topmost bunk screening Antoni, but suddenly remembers how attentively the inspector looked into her face, and then his. That inspector might recognize her. He'll enquire after the whereabouts of her 'brother'. She stuffs her papers into Mrs Benka's hands and drops her head to her chest, pulling her lank hair over her face. Then lets her head slip sideways onto Hania's shoulder and closes her eyes.

A moment later the inspector is at the door. He inhales deeply, inflating his chest, broadening his back. His shoulders are now immense. Incredulity at the depths to which mankind can stoop spreads over his face.

'This compartment is soft with reservation!' he bellows, giving the interlopers the opportunity to recognize their mistake and prepare to decamp.

But they know it's soft with reservation. It's very comfortable, or would be if there were six of them in here and not twenty-one – twenty-two if you count Antoni.

'Soft with reservation...' Perhaps, being foreigners, they need further explanation. '... means it is reserved for people of exceptional objective value. Not for criminal elements, gypsies or other ordinary riffraff.'

All but Marta, who is after all judiciously asleep, gaze at him blandly.

The inspector tugs at the hem of his jacket. This train is teeming with characters who, so he's heard, have just come out of the camps, so they're possibly all convicts. They certainly seem to think they can get away with murder. That's what's so bewildering – that they've been let out to rampage about the countryside causing mayhem wherever they go. Twenty-one of them, he's counted, sitting all over the place with their bundles and what have you, in their filthy clothes. Perched up on the couchettes like so many crows on a wire. And who's going to get the compartment neat and shipshape for the higher echelons after they've gone? Well, not him, praise be. He'll be off shift and well away from here by then. So just check they've got those damned identity cards, and that they've all got a ticket, and get out of here.

'Papers,' he says tersely. And to think he's got to be doing this all day. And tomorrow too, no doubt. And the next day until all this travelling about comes to an end. Top row first. One, two, three. Other side. 'Next. Mm. All right. Next. All right. What about her?'

'I've got her papers,' pipes up Mrs Benka, perhaps a shade too quickly. 'Let her sleep. Please do. She's expecting, you see. Poor thing's been sick all morning and she's only just dropped off.'

So they *do* speak Russian, after all that! As to being pregnant, his

215

wife has had her bad times with morning sickness too. He can remember a whole fortnight when all you heard was retching and groaning from cockcrow to bedtime. He hopes never to have to be near that sort of thing again. He stamps Marta's papers and moves on.

Nobody speaks. Nobody moves. You'd think they're all considerately keeping quiet to let the pregnant girl get her beauty sleep. In fact, now that the inspection has passed without mishap and it has been proved that a secure means of hiding the young man that Marta smuggled in has been discovered, everyone has remembered why it was that she was sent out in the first place. Did she succeed? And, if so, what did she buy and where is it?

Hania is best placed to find out. 'Hey, you.' She jiggles Marta's head off her shoulder. 'We're starving here. What did you get?'

Marta reaches into her coat and fetches out her flat breads and the cobweb-cracked eggs.

Hania holds up a semicircle of bread. 'You've already been nibbling, you greedy thing.'

'Not me.' A whispered hiss, but loud enough. 'Him. Antoni. You should have seen them. Honestly, they're much worse off than us. So I gave him mine.'

'Nonsense, dear.' Mrs Benka is handing round the food. 'We all share. What difference does one extra make?'

Quite a lot, actually, they all think, but keep the thought to themselves. Marta is torn. She is longing to bite into the bread, to taste an egg again. But if she does then her selfless gesture will have been lost, the cost of her generosity borne by others. Too bad. She can ponder on that later. For now, as she accepts a portion of dough and half an egg, these are all that matter.

Mrs Benka is on tiptoe reaching up to the top bunk, tapping Antoni's ankle. 'Young man. The inspector's been and gone. Sit up now and eat something.'

Antoni's head peers down. 'I already did. Miss Dolniak gave me a whole egg out there, and some bread.'

'Then have a little more. You need it.'

'No. Thank you.'

'I can't split half an egg twenty-one ways.'
'Then give it to Miss Dolniak. After all, she's eating for two!'
Mrs Benka laughs. 'Well, we'll call it reward for hard work.'
Marta's joy and humiliation are complete.

31

Antoni isn't shy exactly, not diffident. But after the success of his single quip he barely speaks. You could say he's grown unused to being among women because where he's been there weren't any, but in fact he is silent because he is asleep. Stretched against the wall behind a triumvirate of sentinel hips he is rocked by the unchanging motion of the train and his steady breathing eats up the kilometres. For everyone the tedium of travel grows a little less.

All the women in the compartment, those lithe enough, take turns to scramble up to the couchette to hide him. All of them regard him as their secret, but Marta, keeping a beady eye on the rota of protection, struggles with her equanimity. Surely they ought to acknowledge that Antoni is, in a certain sense, hers. She found him. She brought him. In fact, let's face it, she knew him before anyone else. Though that word, with its biblical connotation, makes her blush.

Mrs Benka watches the expressions scudding over Marta's face and manages not to smile. At least Pavel Kuzmich is no longer uppermost in the girl's mind. But she is mistaken. It is remembering Pavel Kuzmich that has planted a particular notion in Marta's head.

Antoni is her wounded soldier (all right, not exactly wounded and not yet a soldier), and she will look after him. Nurse him back to health. That, indeed, is what all that Girl Guides' training in first aid has turned out to be for. Fate is involved here. Destiny deposited Antoni in his exhausted state by the hot-water cylinder in the station. Destiny prompted Mrs Benka to select Marta to go foraging for provisions on that particular occasion rather than another. When you think of all the hundreds, the thousands of people crossing the end-less map of the Soviet Union, straightforward coincidence cannot account for these two people meeting again the way they did.

There is meaning to every detail, the gushing of the boiling water, the bartered eggs rolling over the floor, even the sad calf sucking her fingers beside the goods wagons – it's like decoding the iconography of a religious painting. Whichever way she relives the event, and she is doing so in real time over and over again, it's obvious that some guiding higher entity, maybe a guardian angel, managed the entire sequence so that she should arrive on the station with her bucket at precisely the same moment as Antoni. Since that is so, by taking care of Antoni she will be making amends to Pavel Kuzmich. It's conse-quently crucial that she, and no one else, should have him under her wing.

Antoni continues to sleep with a sort of deliberate intensity, but there comes a point when, for all his efforts, he can sleep no more. He sits up looking crumpled. His hair is tousled and the outlines of his face seem softer. He has not been aware of the train pulling in at another station, of Hania scurrying out and returning with more of those local flat breads, a minute disc of stale cheese and a capful of raw maize. The bucket of water she brought in is still hot – uncloud-ed by coal dust – and they have saved him some. He sips at it, con-scious of the thickness of his saliva, of the stink in his own mouth. Now that he has become a permanent member of this compartment community he must contribute what he has to the kitty.

Sliding down from his couchette, Antoni finds his legs are buck-ling at the knees from under-use. He catches a glimpse of himself reflected in the darkening window and sees a gaunt face, smaller than he remembers, and bisected by a beaky nose. Perhaps his bulbous beard and his curly hair, long and thick with dirt, are dwarfing his features. Could one of these ladies cut his hair? Has any of them a pair of scissors? Don't be silly.

He reaches into the deep pocket of his coat and pulls out a squat tome, which he hands round for inspection.

'*The Problems of Leninism,*' reads Mrs Benka, fearing the boy has been got at and is about to deliver a harangue. 'Yes, dear. Very interesting.'

'Is it?' he asks, surprised. 'I haven't tried reading it. But it rolls the best cigarettes.' He rips out a page with long-fingered deftness and plunges his hand back into his pocket for his tobacco. 'Better than newspapers, if there are any left. Much cheaper too, and the paper's perfectly flimsy. Smoke, anyone?'

Within minutes the air in the compartment stings the eyes. Antoni never would have believed that even elderly ladies from good families could reveal themselves to be such a band of determined puffers.

The puffers, meanwhile, smile over Antoni through their cigarette smoke. He's quite an addition, isn't he, this young man with his pockets like a magician's top-hat. Look at him now! He's fished up a complete pack of cards. What they wouldn't have given for a pack of cards before. He's shuffling them with absent-minded nonchalance, as if his hands can do this all on their own while his thoughts are elsewhere.

'Shall we...?' he begins.

'Do you play bridge?' Marta leaps in.

'Do *you*?' asks Mrs Benka in surprise. 'You never said.'

'We never had cards, did we?'

Antoni bends his head. 'I'm willing to learn.'

'You play, don't you, Mrs Benka?'

'Of course.'

'So do I,' croaks Mrs Kwaszniewicz, on her last legs maybe, but who says her memory fails her?

'Good,' says Marta, before there are any other offers. 'In that case, I'll partner Antoni. And Mrs Benka, you play with Mrs Kwaszniewicz.'

Mrs Benka confides a quiet snort into her sleeve. Hania and Basia, if they can play, certainly haven't been given the opportunity to say so. They're going to have to sit by and watch. But it's Mrs Benka's experience that bridge is more a pleasure for the participants than for observers and she predicts that, if everything goes to plan, the two girls will lose interest before the first trick is up.

For a moment Marta rests the shuffled cards in her cupped hands before dealing, and closes her eyes. In truth she can't remember all the rules, it's been so long since she sat opposite the rabbi with his explanatory finger stabbing the air. That was on the way out, when they didn't know where they were going or what was awaiting them. Then they were prisoners. Now they have their identity cards. Then they were hungry and crammed into the stinking wooden cattle-wagon. Now they are intruders in soft with reservation, but if anything they are hungrier. None of the people who were with her then is with her now, and she cannot find out what has happened to them.

Anxiety grips her. What if she never finds out? What if she never meets her family again? Change the subject. Change the subject. 'Did everyone who got arrested get amnestied, get identity cards like ours?'

Mrs Benka shrugs. 'I don't think so. I think it was only Poles. The Lithuanians didn't, did they?'

Antoni is nodding like a man who knows. 'It *was* only Poles, to form the army. But then it sort of seemed to be Poles generally.'

'Not the Jews?'

'Well, they're not Poles, are they?'

That's true. But what's the point of keeping the old rabbi locked up? Marta cannot imagine him swinging an axe in the forest or digging in a mine.

'What I *did* hear, though...' Antoni has spotted a fleeting alarm in her face. 'They're letting some of the Russians out, to join the army too. People who weren't sentenced to more than eight years. They need as many as they can get at the moment.'

Marta's spirits lift briefly. Maybe Petya will be released so he can enlist too.

In a drone, not because she is bored but because that is the way all people the world over intone their times tables, Marta dredges up the rules the rabbi taught her. But she does it with an eye on Mrs Benka's face. For sure Mrs Benka will not be able to refrain from wincing, if ever so slightly, should Marta get something wrong. And such is her concentration she doesn't notice the amused and one might say indulgent expression in Antoni's eyes as he attends to his first lesson.

Mrs Benka and Mrs Kwaszniewicz win the first rubber, which isn't

221

a surprise, since Antoni is a beginner. They win the second for the same reason. Mrs Kwaszniewicz is mashing her long yellow teeth with a satisfaction that grates on Marta's nerves. Even Mrs Benka's eyes have a tactless glitter. Clearly the two old women have contrived some silent means of communicating their cards to one another, which suggests cheating, or the possibility that they've been partners before. Marta inspects them for twitches and grimaces but their faces are no more expressive than a dressmaker's dummy.

Antoni senses restlessness in his partner. 'Why are spades top trumps?' he asks in a tone of childlike innocence, as if he really wants to know.

Mrs Kwaszniewicz cackles. 'Because every grave needs a spade to dig it with.'

'Though no one can live without a heart,' says Mrs Benka.

'And diamonds could buy us a lot to eat,' says Antoni hopefully.

'Yes, and you can bash idiots over the head with a club,' caps Marta, vigorously miming the action over a head notionally clamped between her knees. 'I'm tired. Hania, you want to take over?'

She dumps the cards in Hania's lap and clambers over her to hunch in the corner, resting her head against the wall by the window. Antoni taps Basia's shoulder. Take over from me, would you? He eases himself across to sit next to Marta and while the next hand is being dealt leans over to her and whispers, 'Everything passes in the end.'

What? What's he saying? It doesn't seem to mean anything, but she feels a warmth, some sort of consolation in the fact that he has said anything at all.

Unaccountably, Hania and Basia, who have never played bridge before, are beating the two old women hands down.

Marta keeps an eye on the game from beneath grumpily lowered lids. The girls are putting on a tremendous show, there's no way round that. And Basia's memory is fabulous. Well, you'd expect that, somehow. Quiet people are like that. Still waters run deep, so Marta's mother always said, implying that Marta's rapids must by definition be shallow. All that turbulence clattering over the polished stones.

What about Antoni? Is he deep? Still shielded by her eyelids, she swivels her gaze sideways and up and encounters Antoni's eyes squinting down at her, veiled by those lashes. Has he been watching her all this time? She wonders whether her thoughts were distorting her features, giving her away. Wonders what she looks like through Antoni's eyes, or anyone's. Self-conscious now, she feels the heat of Antoni's thigh lying against hers as a distinct pressure. But the compartment is so squashed there's no way of telling if it's deliberate, and she can't even shift over slightly to put it to the test.

'You know,' he's murmuring, slightly inclining his head towards the bridge players. 'Next time we stop I'm going to have to sell the cards.'

'Why?'

'Because I haven't contributed anything. I've only been living off what the rest of you have been selling.'

'I haven't contributed anything either.'

'But you haven't got anything, have you?'

She does. She has the jewels that Mrs Benka pressed on her, but it's understood that their very preciousness, the fact that they were intended for Ania to wear on her wedding day, means that they are currency of last resort. Anyway, they're not hers. She has her spoon with its tiny burnt inscription, PROPERTY OF THE COMMANDER. But who'd barter for a wooden spoon? And surely that inscription is also an instruction, a prohibition. If it's labelled as her property, it's not to be parted with.

She presses her face to the window and begins to notice how what was a continuous surface is fragmenting: gaps between the sleepers, huge slabs of wood lying side by side under the track, laid down from horizon to horizon, slicing through a treeless landscape. They must have been dragged here from some Siberian forest for this railway, for all the railways like this one, by people like Pavel Kuzmich, over years and years. Squat and faceless, bent almost double, each puny figure walks backwards, lugging a heft of wood as big as a coffin, as if it's his coffin. The train is slowing.

'Antoni...!' But he's already up and beginning his scramble to the couchette, reaching for camouflage behind the women on the top shelf.

Slowing. Slowing. The wheels not rolling but grating against the brakes. Hissing. Metal on metal. And they have stopped.

But this is not a real station; there is no platform, just a sort of raised wooden jetty erected in the middle of nowhere without a waiting room or ticket office or hut or shed of any sort behind it.

Their door is yanked open. A man in railway uniform and with a coal-blackened face bulks in the space.

'Out!' he orders. 'Everybody out. This is the end of the line.'

'What do you mean it's the end of the line?' Marta flares. 'How can it be the end of the line? This is the middle of nowhere.'

'It's the end of the line for you. Get along, now. I'm not waiting all day.'

'Excuse me,' says Mrs Benka, with menacing restraint. 'We have tickets to Chimkent and stamped passes that allow us to proceed. We will remain here until we arrive at our destination.'

'Oh no you won't, granny.' He pulls a gun from his pocket and pushes it into her face. 'This is the end of the line for you, I said. Now, who's going to be first?'

32

The train has gone. Silence has fallen over the sixty-odd people, men, women – even some children – who tumbled out onto the wooden jetty for fear of the railwayman's revolver. Whichever way they look the land is an ocean of dusty grey-green scrub whose vastness makes them cluster closer together. In a moment disbelief may turn to panic. Marta rotates slowly on the wooden jetty, 360 degrees of sameness. How will they eat? What will they drink? Nobody will ever find them or even think to search.

'Look!' One of the children, a boy with shoulder-blades like knives, is pointing up towards a rise in the land.

It's some sort of pony, rolling in from the north-west, borne in a ball of swirling dust, galloping at a furious pace, the legs of its rider flapping against its flanks. It doesn't alter its pace as it approaches, a brown pony with black muzzle and matching tail, which it carries high. The horseman is wearing a sheepskin hat and loose, thick, dark trousers, and his eyes are narrowed into matchsticks against the sun and the flying grit. On and on, no slackening, they make directly for the jetty as if they mean to ram it. But at the last minute they slew from the collision – centaur rather than pony and man, they move so as one.

Now they have halted, the pony's sides barely heaving. The rider is a middle-aged man whose face is older than his age, lined and grizzled, never indoors. For all their numbers the Poles shrink into themselves, thinking that being assessed by such a one is how an unprotected rodent must feel caught in the sights of a bird of prey.

'You're them Poles,' announces this man in Russian, pre-empting denial. 'The cons they put out, from the train. We heard about you.' How? There is nobody. 'Word gets around.'

He stands in his stirrups and twists about, the increased height apparently adding significantly to his view of the land. Nothing untoward disturbs his expression and he settles back in the saddle.

'They sent me to fetch you. From Teren Uziuk.'

What's Teren Uziuk?

'*Kolkhoz.* Cotton collective. We need the workers because our young men have been taken off into the army, so you'll have to do.'

They stare at him.

'But we have identity cards,' protests Antoni. 'We're supposed to be travelling to join the Polish army, not working in a cotton collective.'

'Polish army? All these women? Anyway, you're not travelling now, are you? Not any more, identity cards or not. And you know the rules, same in the Kazakh Soviet Socialist Republic as anywhere else. Anyone not working is a parasite and liable to arrest, that's what they always say. So you've got your choices.' He looks at them, then leans forward until his chin drops between his pony's pricked ears.

Choices! thinks Marta. *Choices between what and what?* 'What happens on a cotton collective?'

The centaur shakes his head and laughs. 'Go and ask Comrade Stalin. It was his bright idea, fifteen years ago it must've been. I think he was sitting at his breakfast eating his caviar and wondering what he should turn his hand to next, and he got to thinking about the lands to the south-east, where there were more sheep and cattle than people, and the people were herders, like they'd always been. And he thought to himself, you can't have people doing what they've always done, that's not the Soviet way. So he said, from now on you Kazakhs are going to stop your herding and become cotton farmers instead. I'll tell you how much cotton you have to grow, and then I'll buy it from you, once I've decided the price. It won't be your cotton and it won't be your land, it'll be the People's land, but don't go thinking that means you. Oh, and by the way I want you to give me all your cattle and all your sheep.

'Well, half of us didn't want to give him our cattle and sheep because we knew he'd kill them, so we killed them first, to stop him taking them. The other half scarpered. Went to China, most of them. The third half died in the famine. That's the great advantage of communism – you get three halves. So that's where we are. All stuck in the one place, morning, noon and night, growing cotton that was never meant to grow out here. Animals, yes.' And he gives his pony a slap of recognition on its rump, to which the pony barely reacts. 'Animals you can grow, so long as you keep them moving and let the land rest. But cotton! Don't make me laugh. Anyway, this time of year, it's picking. And that's what we need you lot for. But it's not all bad, you know. Food and drink up there. See? By that tree, on the horizon.' A spine poking into the sky like a pin. 'Make for that.' And already he has kicked his pony into a canter, rocking in a seesaw back the way they have come.

Marta stares after the departed pair until they can no longer be distinguished from the haze on the brim of the world and there is only silence. Was there a man on a pony at all? But what a terrible thing, to be made to be what you are not on some distant leader's whim. That tree looks a long way away, but if the centaur is to be trusted there may be something to eat and drink today.

Someone has spied a truck the size of a matchbox coming from the direction that produced the pony. Its progress seems less direct because it cannot cope with the uneven terrain as the pony did. So it veers between scrub and hollow, trailing a zigzag column of dust that subsides as softly as a bride's veil. Now it's close enough to make out the tinny growl of the engine. Two men both in sheepskin hats, one gripping the wheel, shoulders hunched against the effort of steering a safe path, the other bracing himself with a hand out of the window clamped to a rim on the roof. He's getting a rough ride none the less. This land is better suited to cattle, sturdy, barrel-chested ponies and loose-kneed pad-footed camels.

The truck pulls up by the jetty; the two doors open and the men jump down. They're walking among the motionless crowd, making a selection by pulling on a shoulder, grabbing a forearm. Mrs Kwaszniewicz but not Mrs Benka, some of the other frail ones, and all the smallest children, who immediately set up a wail as they are plucked away from their mothers and dumped on the truck. One man stays on the truck to prevent them from scrambling down again, and the wails become shrill with terror. Marta watches a woman with a small baby being nudged into the truck. She wonders in what conditions this woman gave birth to her baby, how old it is, who its father might be. Were her rations different?

The man up on the truck is gauging his vehicle's capacity. He has a load of screaming toddlers and half a dozen doddering old things, who, let's face it, won't be much use to anyone in the *kolkhoz*. Well, that may be the official view, but in his world you take care of the grandparents, just as they once took care of you. The nursing mother has seated herself with her back to the cabin, and is inserting the baby's face, its lips already rooting like a leech, into her heavy clothing.

He holds up a thick finger. 'One more,' he says, in a voice unexpectedly high for his burliness. 'One of the mothers, to sing songs to this lot and keep them quiet.' The women surge forward but he grabs one at random. 'No more room. Sorry. That's the way it is. The faster you walk, the sooner you'll be with the kiddies. Malik's walking with you. Ah! That's true. I can take one more in the cab. You!' Mrs Benka has made it into the ranks of the incapable. She is simultaneously grateful and offended.

The truck sets off on its return journey, the buzzing of its engine drowned by the squeals of the frightened children and the desperate soprano of the token mother belting out a jolted hiccuping lullaby.

The man called Malik is almost as wide as he is tall. He walks from the hips in short mincing steps but he covers the ground as if he could carry on indefinitely. He could be fifty years old, or eighty, and must have grown up like one of those camel drivers – undismayed by perpetual horizons. So the gap between him and his lagging disciples grows until, seeming to sense it, he stops and looks back, hands on hips, and waits for them to catch up. 'Not much further.'

A trickle of river ahead of them, its banks fringed with mulberry trees planted at regular intervals. Beyond they can see what looks like a compound of huts around which the ground is tamped hard by the passage of generations.

As they get closer, they see that the houses are flat-roofed and extremely low, built of sun-dried bricks fashioned from grass and mud, bound with crumbly mortar. Two small glazed windows are set in the wall of each hut opposite the door, through which anyone but a child going in and out would have to stoop. Piles of dried animal dung are stacked outside and in the last of the evening sun they give off a sweetish, musty, lingering smell. Marta looks about her for the animals, for some sort of stockade, but all she can see are a few short-legged ponies, hobbled, nibbling without pause at the grass. *God, this is primitive*, she thinks. But what else could you use to build a dwelling in this depopulated place but the stuff of the earth? There are no trees to provide logs for a stove, or rafters for a planed roof. But what did they live in before, when they were herders?

At least these houses have a more scattered feel to them, as if people rather than administrators have decided where each one is to be. But there *are* no people – for all that the compound could house a few hundred.

'Where is everyone?' she says to Antoni, who has trekked the whole way in dejected silence.

It's not Antoni but Malik who answers. 'They'll be back. The kiddies are in their school and all the rest are finishing their shifts – same as you'll be tomorrow, cotton picking. But don't expect a welcome party. We're glad to have you, 'cause we need the extra hands, but...' He makes a show of scratching all over his body. '... we don't want your lice and the typhus they bring, so there's not going to be any mixing. No offence, but we want to stay alive. We want our kiddies to stay alive. No offence, I hope.'

Marta and Antoni exchange appraising glances; each takes note of the grime and dishevelment of the other. Marta's skin is crawling, as if the lice, brought centre stage, feel urged to extra activity. If she were the Kazakhs, she thinks she'd keep away too. But typhus! What if she gets that and dies, or Mrs Benka does?... Or Antoni?

As they file into the compound there's a jostling behind Marta. The women whose children were plucked from them are surging to the front, shrill with enquiry. Instantly a choir of childish wailing responds from one of the huts. Like calves, she thinks, who recognize their mother's mooing across a meadow. The women herd into the hut and emerge, each with her tear-streaked toddler in her arms, and the air is filled with the bubbling of subsiding sobs. Mrs Kwaszniewicz and Mrs Benka creep out into the open, both looking exhausted. They'd have insisted on walking with the rest of them if they'd only known.

Malik points out the hut for the men and another for the single women. To Marta's relief the mothers and children are directed somewhere else. Almost on hands and knees she crawls through a doorway to find herself in a space disconcertingly larger inside than it looked from the outside. The earthen floor is covered by thin mattresses of some red fabric decorated with pink and green flowers, but in the centre, directly under a hole in the roof, a shallow concave brick stove set over the embers of a fire gives off a little heat.

Marta lies down on one of the mattresses. The mud walls, grey as dried clay, smell of smoke. Somewhere out there Antoni is lying in a hut like this one and tomorrow he can tell her who his companions have been. Maybe after they've slept the two of them will be able to work out a way of getting everyone back onto a train. Marta feels under her head for her bundle and is reassured by the knobbly feel of the jewels. She closes her eyes, seeing behind them not the steppe and its *kolkhoz* compound but the log fire at Mrs Benka's farmhouse, with Old Petrkiewicz standing in the doorway, his arms piled with chopped firewood.

She does not hear the *kolkhoz* women returning from their work, nor the chirruping of the Kazakh children brought back from school and nursery. She does not wake as the fires are fed in neighbouring huts, nor smell the baking bread. She does not notice the sudden drop in temperature as the sun slinks behind the horizon, and tonight she will not see the vast ballooning black sky with its dense stitching of stars. No matter. Tomorrow night will do just as well.

33

'*Lineyka! Lineyka!*' Someone is shouting, making the rounds, pausing at the door of each hut. At first, in the depths of her sleep, the voice sounds to Marta like a distant street trader and as she wakes she wonders what is this *lineyka* he is selling. She smells smoke hanging in still cold air. Smoke. For cooking. She crawls to the doorway, thrusts her face out into the open and all but knocks over an earthenware jug of milk. To one side is a wide platter with rounds of flat bread.

'They've brought breakfast!' she shouts over her shoulder. 'Breakfast! Do you hear?'

Hands like twitching antennae reach out of blankets. Marta takes a swig from the jug and nearly spits her mouthful into her lap. It's not that it tastes bad, exactly, but her mouth had been expecting something else. This looks like milk, but it's much stronger, and somehow sharp.

'What's up?'

'You try.'

The jug passes round the hut and noses wrinkle at the unfamiliarity. But the breads are hot and the milky stuff has a promising solidity to it. Taste is neither here nor there these days.

Marta is sitting with her back to the doorway and doesn't notice Malik's approaching feet until one of them prods her very lightly on the buttocks. 'What the...?'

'*Lineyka.* I've been calling, but you're such a lot of sleepyheads.'

'What's *lineyka*?'

'It's when you get your work norms, isn't it? Comrade Stalin sends along to say how much cotton he expects, so that's how much we pick. And if we don't make our norms, the collective doesn't make its total. Everyone can understand, no? So come along out and learn how it's done. Did you enjoy your breakfast?'

He has such a pleased expression that Marta, who was on the verge of saying something about the strange milk, thinks better of it. 'Oh, yes! What was the drink?'

'*Kumys*. Mare's milk, because you are honoured guests. Now look.'

Malik has been cradling an armful like a white cloud. He waits for the occupants of the women's hut to get themselves out and gather round, then lets his cradled cloud fall to the ground in a gentle tumble light as cobweb. Into it he plunges a hand and pulls out a piece that dangles pathetically from his fingers as if it has just been shot.

'You,' he suggests, and pulls a reluctant Basia to stand before him. He turns her to face them and she flushes crimson from the sudden attention. Shaking out the winged bird as a magician might, he transforms it into a mere rectangle of cloth with a wide strap at each corner. 'This here is your *fartuk* and this is how you put it on.'

Top two straps tie round the waist. Now, see? Bottom two round the shoulders and the cloth has doubled over into a bag. When you bend, the bag opens. As you stand up straight, it closes against your body. Simple. Now all you have to do is fill it up.

It takes no more than a minute to change the identity. Wear the white *fartuk* and you are a cotton picker; take it off and the state decrees you are a burden on the community, a parasite, just an extra mouth to feed.

'Forty kilos each for you women.' Forty kilos of fluff? It sounds a lot. 'The men'll have to make sixty, so don't complain. It's got to add up or they don't pay us, so then we can't pay you. That's where you go.'

He swivels Basia, aproned in white muslin, hands her a second *fartuk* and gives her a tiny shove to start her off. Where she goes the others follow, round the compound fence, through an opening and out onto the steppe. But the flat lands are abruptly broken here by a block of bushes, waist high.

The Kazakh women have been at work for an hour already. Dabs of colour from an amateur's pallet, a flat blue sky, red blouses white-fronted, dusty grey-green cotton leaves hiding their skirts. A distant brownish haze at the horizon trails towards the end of time. Wearing one *fartuk*, they have laid the second flat on the ground at the end of each row. The women plod down the rows, pulling the white bolls big as fists from the bushes and stuffing them into the apron-bag that dangles from their shoulders. When it's full they empty it into the apron on the ground and set off again. The novice pickers watch for a moment, thinking: that doesn't look so hard.

And it isn't, but for one thing. The forty kilos.

At dusk the Kazakh women set their feet wide on either side of their heaped *fartuks*, bend at the knees and in a single movement hoist the day's work onto their backs to take it to be weighed in the compound. When they pass the Poles, they eye the emaciated newcomers with their pale hair and gawky movements – with their typhus-bearing lice – and transmit nervous smiles. No offence, Malik said, but the message is clear: keep your distance.

Marta cannot have picked half the norm, but she can barely lift it either. As she begins to drag her sorry little load, fearful the prickles of the scrubby ground may snag the muslin apron and tear it, Malik minces by. He takes her *fartuk*, gives it a savage twist and lays it over her shoulders.

'Light as a feather,' he mocks. 'You'll learn. Over there.'

Over there the women are chatting, smoking, nonchalant, while their bundles are weighed. Does he stand here all day, this tall thin man with his sheepskin hat pulled down so low you cannot see his eyes? One by one he drops each knotted *fartuk* onto a hanging scale, grunts, writes and hands it back, and the woman lugs the day's work to a shed like a hangar shielding a snowy mountain.

Marta hangs back. She doesn't want to be the first to have her poor performance noted. But the thin man has her in his sights. Let's be having it: he reaches out with a grin. His dreary day is turning into theatre, with all the lurking wildlife of the steppe for his audience.

'Fifteen!' he hoots in a thin-chested falsetto, holding up the miscreant's pitiful yield as if he is expecting the others to bid for it. 'Our kids do better than that!'

Marta casts about for a retort but cannot find one. But now the man is weighing Basia's load and Hania's, and they have done no better. When the last of the Poles have discharged their aprons, the lanky master of the scales disappears into the hangar, still chuckling.

Marta, Basia and Hania slouch towards their hut, sullen and in silence, but someone is shadowing them, pace for pace. They can hear the extra footsteps. An urgent whisper cuts into their despondency.

'*Devushki*, young ladies!'

It's a woman, beckoning with one hand, the other covering her nose and mouth. Is she protecting herself or hiding? Now that she has their attention she is backing away, beckoning but warding off, leading them to the edge of the compound and the shelter of the far side of the fence. She spreads her *fartuk* down like a tablecloth, patting the ground to encourage them to crouch. Using her curved fingers like rakes she scrabbles in the dirt, scooping stones towards her. Piles them into the *fartuk*.

'Heavier than cotton,' she says. 'A kilo of cotton and a kilo of stones. Just be sure it's all cotton on the top.' Then she straddles the heap and pretends to urinate over it, raising her skirts and whispering, '*Shushushushu*.'

'That's so kind,' whispers Basia, and moves to embrace the woman, who leaps back in alarm. Turns and runs. Tomorrow they will none of them know who she was.

Antoni has seated himself next to Marta and, under the sky they missed last night, tightly wrapped in their coats, they scrape out the bowls of porridge that Mrs Benka has been labouring over all day. Mrs Kwaszniewicz, who is the better cook, wasn't able to help; feeling off-colour, she said. The porridge has a mustiness to it and tastes of nothing much at all. 'They're paying us in grain,' Mrs Benka said, apologizing for the blandness of her cooking, 'which makes sense, I suppose, though God alone knows where it comes from. These poor people! It must be hard if your whole life was made round eating meat, and now there isn't any.'

Now Antoni leans towards Marta. 'What's that spoon?'

'What?'

'Your spoon. You're always rubbing it and cleaning it. Is it some sort of talisman?'

'Not exactly. Well…'

'May I see?'

What's there to see in the dark? She passes it over and Antoni weighs it in his fingers, traces its shape, strokes it. Strokes it with pleasure for its smoothness, more akin to satin than wood. But the smoothness is interrupted on the back of the handle. 'It's got writing on it. What does it say?' He holds it up in a pretence the moonlight will be enough to read by.

Marta gives out an embarrassed little cough but no words.

The writing is too small for the pads of his fingers to distinguish and, besides, she seems to want to keep the message to herself. 'Here.' He holds it out.

'Actually,' she confides on impulse, 'it says "property of the commander".'

Antoni laughs. 'Why? What does that mean?'

She shakes her head. Shrugs.

'Commander. Is that you? Come on, do tell, Marta. Are you the commander?'

She shrugs again. 'Sort of.'

'Sort of!'

It sounds so different in his ironic tone. Is he mocking? But Pavel Kuzmich was mocking too.

'Actually,' she says again. 'There was this man, Pavel Kuzmich. He was our brigade leader. He was awful, I mean he *seemed* awful. Well, we thought so anyway…' On and on she goes now, about how Pavel Kuzmich separated them out into huts then counted out the brigades. How he ordered them about in Russian and they didn't understand. How one day he broke into Polish and how awkward they felt, realizing that he'd been able to understand them all along. She recounts

Pavel Kuzmich's story about the Polish girl he met, how he married her, how she died, how his in-laws turned him and his starving baby away so that he decided to come home, only to be arrested and sentenced to life. How he taught her to smoke and showed them all how to cheat with the wood stacks...

Then her story falters, tails away and there is the silence of the night again. And yet Antoni senses that it is an incomplete silence, temporary, biding its time.

Eventually he prods, 'You were going to say something else.'

No. No, that's it. There isn't any more to say. 'Only. He's the one who made me the spoon.'

Antoni is bewildered. Nothing is clear and tonight nothing will be.

From the furthest point across the compound someone is playing a jangly stringed instrument and a man's voice, high and nasal, chants to it. Every now and then there's a burst of laughter from the Kazakh women. Marta and Antoni strain to hear, instinctively leaning forward in the dark, but they can't make out any words they can understand.

34

By the end of the week the weigh-master is applauding every Polish *fartuk* as his scales sag.

'Now there's a happy man,' says Mrs Benka. 'From his point of view it's all coming out the way it should.'

Antoni stares at the eight-wheeled truck reversing out of the hangar with its mountain of cotton. The driver's teeth are clamped over a drooping cigarette of cheap *makhorka* and he is clasping Malik's hand – which means Malik has to trot to keep up. Then the driver releases Malik and revs out onto the steppeland track, churning it into a dustbowl. One more delivery for Comrade Stalin just as he ordered.

'What on earth can it do to the machinery?' Antoni wonders. 'I haven't the faintest idea how they spin the cotton, but with all those stones... you'd think...'

'Who cares about their machinery?' says Marta. 'What worries me is running out of stones.'

'No, but really. The waste! The waste to the state, which thinks it's got everything under control. The waste of work. The waste of... I don't know... everything... of people. Really. What's being produced here that will turn out to be useful to anyone? And do they know where each load comes from, or what if someone finds out? Mind you, I suppose everyone's doing it. Marta? What's up? What's the matter?' She looks sick. Even under the dust and the muck on her face he can see she looks sick. Mrs Benka has bustled off, without saying why. 'Marta, what is it?'

'Just what you said – about people finding out.'

Marta turns to follow Mrs Benka. Is that it? Isn't she going to say any more to him? She herself seems uncertain. She keeps opening and closing her mouth, flashes a glance at him as if she's wondering if he can be trusted.

'You remember Pavel Kuzmich? I didn't tell you everything, but... well, I think I killed him.'

'You think you what?' Antoni stops dead, so Marta has to as well. 'How did you kill him?'

'Well, not actually killed him. Not directly. We all got ill. We got malaria, and then so did he. While he was too ill to supervise us, some of us were better enough to be forced back to work. But although we were still weak, and there weren't as many of us, we still had to meet the norms. And I had this idea which I thought was brilliant. I thought that, instead of cutting the wood and stacking it, we could just keep moving what we'd already done to new places, and as long as the *desiatnik* counted it we'd get away with it and not have to work so hard.'

'Isn't that more or less what we've been doing here?'

'Well, not really, because we do pick some cotton, after all. We do pick all we can manage to. But what I dreamt up was that we would-n't be cutting any new wood at all. And then they found out, and blamed him. And they shot him for sabotage.'

'You didn't kill him,' says Antoni firmly. 'They did.'

'But I did something that made them.'

'Made them? Made them? Nobody made them anything. It's *their* camps, *their* system, *their*... don't you see? How can you possibly think you made them, and blame yourself? Let me tell you something, Marta.' Now he's gripping her by the wrists. 'We're stuck here in this God-forsaken place when we, I, really should be with the new Polish forces, wherever they are, to get the Germans out of our country – and out of this one, for that matter. But these people won't let me because they're so crass, so unbelievably stupid, that for some reason they can't see that their unspeakable system is harming them as much as the war is. They throw people away in camps and mines, throw them away, they force herders to become farmers in places where

239

nothing will grow – and then set impossible targets, so of course people fiddle. And did you know that the people on this collective aren't
allowed to leave it? Malik told me. You have to have an internal passport to go from one place to another, and they aren't allowed them.
This whole stupid country is just one enormous prison, only the different bits of it are organized a bit differently. A bit. And do you know
what? I think the Soviets are as bad as the Germans.'

Marta flicks her hands out of his grasp. 'That's not true, Antoni.
The people are good. Mostly the people are good. All the Russians
I've come up against have actually been decent enough. Or tried to
be. Most of them.'

'Really? Well, you must have been very lucky, and perhaps you
haven't heard what we heard – that a whole lot of the Polish officers
who got arrested by your beloved Russians have disappeared. Just like
that! Gone. Nothing. Nobody knows where they are. And, while
we're about it, you should have seen what the conditions were like in
the camp where *we* were. There was no fatherly Pavel Kuzmich there,
I promise you – though of course he was a prisoner. No smiling Malik
– though he's not a Russian. All we had were guards and guns and
viciousness. And anyway, look at you, the state you're in! Get a mirror, Marta. Remind yourself what you used to look like. Ask yourself
how you came to be skin and bone and scrawny as… I'm sorry. I'm
sorry. I take it back. It's just that I –'

'Don't apologize, Antoni. I've a pretty good idea what I look like.
But it hasn't been the people that did this to us, it's been the system,
not the individuals, don't you see? And scared individuals.'

'But it's individuals who made the system, and then the second
generation has been moulded by the system the first generation made.
And as to the rest, when people are that scared they'll do whatever it
takes to keep themselves out of trouble. Everyone will denounce his
granny and sell his sister, if he thinks he has to. If he thinks it'll help
– except it never does.'

'Because of the system. You said it! And what are they supposed to
do about that?'

Antoni faces her, features white and pinched, flexing his fists as if he were thinking of throwing a punch. Nose to nose they glare at each other, until suddenly he drops his fists and cups her cheeks. 'All right, Commander. If you say so.'

Now they have to pull out the plants whose only remaining value is to feed the cooking fires. Pull them up by hand, tug and strain on the crackling things that struggle to stay where they are. In this arid land they have plunged prospecting roots deep into the ground and will not yield without a fight.

Marta has her hands, sore and callused, around the main stem of a stripped bush. She has planted her feet wide for stability and her stance reminds her of the childhood story of the farmer who grew a turnip so big he couldn't pull it out. Yanking away on it, he calls out to his wife to come and help. He pulls on the turnip and she pulls on him, then calls the child to come and help, who calls the dog, who calls the cat, who calls the goose. When eventually – but only with the help of the farmyard mouse – the giant root leaps from the vegetable patch with a searing roar of protest, they all fall over landing on top of one another on their bottoms, legs in the air. It made her laugh when she was little, but her mother, who read it to her, insisted there was a moral to the tale. Even the smallest and most insignificant of creatures have a role to play, she said, and their little efforts shouldn't be derided. But listening Marta didn't think her mother could really believe that, since she was so shrilly and amusingly afraid of mice.

Marta pulls and pulls but the cotton bush doesn't budge.

'Need a hand with your turnip?'

She feels Antoni's arms round her waist as he braces his feet to pull. Everybody grows up on the same stories. But there is no pulling, only the gentle pressure of the arms and the weight of his head laid on her shoulder, the warmth of his breath on her neck. Without thinking, Marta lets her body lean into his and, closing her eyes, lets her cheek rest against his face. But his beard is tickly and although she tries to control her giggles her body begins to shake.

Antoni's arms drop. 'What's so funny?'

'Nothing. Sorry.' She rubs her cheek. 'It's your beard. Scratchy as a broom.'

Antoni swipes over his jaw with an imaginary razor. 'There! Gone! Smooth as... as yours. Try again?'

'Like before?'

'Exactly like before.'

They resume their position, Marta facing the cotton bush, Antoni's arms round her. Cheek against cheek. The arms round her waist tighten and she closes her hands over his, twists her face towards his...

'Antoni! Antoni! Oh.' Basia has been running, zigzagging between the bushes. Now she doesn't know where to look, but Antoni has sprung back.

'What's happened? Has something happened?'

'Mrs Benka needs you. It's Mrs Kwaszniewicz. She's had a heart attack. And she's died, Antoni.'

Antoni is sorry for Mrs Kwaszniewicz but puzzled. Why does Mrs Benka need him?

'She says we have to bury her quickly because everyone thinks it was typhus and they won't believe it wasn't. We have to dig a grave.'

How do you make a coffin where there is no wood? People die here too so they should know; they must have spades for the planting season, but the Kazakhs have recoiled from the waiting body and melted away into their fields.

'Don't think too harshly,' counsels Mrs Benka, seeing Marta's frown of condemnation. It could have been typhus, after all. They're only being sensible.'

On their knees, the Poles hollow out a shallow trench with their hands. They lay Mrs Kwaszniewicz in it, wrapped in her lice-ridden blanket, and pile stones over her, the largest and heaviest they can find among the scrub on the steppe. Someone says there may be jackals out here.

It could have been typhus and soon enough it will be. Mrs Kwaszniewicz's single grave calls up others, and a small cemetery radiates out into the open plains like a discarded hand of dominoes.

Two young women and a man all die within a week. Since almost everyone is ill by now it appears to be chance dictating who lives and who does not. The year turns. Funerals punctuate the weeks in the cotton fields while the work of clearing the bushes goes on. As the spring of 1942 approaches, the workers of Teren Uziuk prepare to plant the new season's crop.

35

Antoni has left. It was the centaur that did it, galloping in one morning with rumours of some sort of Polish army-in-the-making back at Lugovoy. Before he went, Antoni had come to seek Marta out, and then stood there, by the door of her hut, fumbling for good words but finding none at all.

'Go!' she'd said. 'Please.'

'I can't bear this. I've been thinking for months about when I could finally enlist, but now the moment's come I –'

'Stop it, Antoni! You're right. It's the whole point. Go. Go on, go! Just go!'

'I can't just go. Who knows? It might be months, or years. It might be... I might...'

They had lurched together as if some invisible person had given each of them a shove, and as Marta's arms went round him her first thought was, *My God, but he's so terribly thin. How will he survive?* – clutching him with all her strength, but having none.

'We're like a couple of stick insects, aren't we?' he'd said, and forced a little laugh. 'Or dry twigs. We'll get splinters off each other if we're not careful.' Then he had hugged her all the tighter. 'But I'll settle for splinters.' He had cradled her jaw and stroked her face, as if memorizing her, feature for feature, with the ball of his thumb; pulled her face closer and laid his forehead against hers. 'You take care, Commander, do you hear?' He had turned, and run out of the door, but was immediately back and kissing her. Then gone again, but stopped once more, stooping in the low doorway. He'd pulled a schoolmaster's admonishing face. 'And don't forget that!' – wagging his finger. 'Because you'll be having to do it all over again when I get back.'

The cotton fields are to be criss-crossed with irrigation channels. The first ploughing has been done. A second is to follow once the planting lines have been drawn. Dreaming of the saddle and the steppe, the ponies will traipse between the shafts of the ploughs and then the harrows. After the harrow, the sowing, then constant hoeing – and in due time the picking once again. They will live off Mrs Benka's grain gruel and the flat breads, drink the brackish water from the shallow, shrinking pools where small frogs paddle in decreasing circles. They will wait for rain. The cemetery will spread its stony mounds further into the plains, and one day will be differentiated from the next only in how much blood there was in the diarrhoea today.

One mid-morning Mrs Benka picks a path between the ditches, hurrying towards them with a bundle in her arms.

'It seems to me,' she says, 'that it would be useful to know what's going on in the world. How our Antoni is getting on. Did he meet the army? Is it truly there? I don't know how you feel, Marta, but maybe you could go and find out. And perhaps Hania and Basia here would go with you because obviously you can't go alone. And you might bring us back some news of the world.' She has locked her unmoving gaze on Marta's eyes. 'It's only a suggestion, of course. But I baked some bread for you to take. On the offchance. And I brought all your papers and so on. A little rummaging in your hut, which I hope you'll excuse.' She's shaking the bundle at Marta. Go before I change my mind.

'Hooray for Mrs Benka!' cries Hania. 'Anything to get away from cotton. I've been saying that, once the war is over and won, I'm only ever going to wear wool – or bark and leaves. You coming, Basia? We don't have to ask Marta, after all. She keeps whingeing on about having to dig irrigation ditches when in fact what she's cut out for is stripping guns. But we all know what she really means by that, don't we?'

'Shut up, Hania.'

By the time they reach the halt it is beginning to grow dark, but far away along the track a soot-black point buzzes like a fly against a window-pane. They have no tickets and nowhere to buy any, so they must keep out of the driver's sight and then, when the train draws level, run like hell. The ground slopes a little on the far side of the track. Perhaps, if they lie down flat on the earth, their dusty clothes in the dusk won't attract the attention. Night descends so quickly it will be completely dark when the time comes, and maybe the driver will be chatting and having a smoke.

In single file they slink across the track and slither to their stomachs, heads down, like Indians in a cowboy film, Marta thinks suddenly, lurking to ambush oncoming settlers. There is something about this train that feels unusual. Its vibrations seem to come from deep within the earth as if the engine is ploughing a way through, gouging out a new path and laying track as it goes. It must be very heavy. And, thank God, it's slow! The engine has passed and cautiously they raise their heads. Flat-bed wagons bearing great black smooth-sided crates. Not carriages, no windows. No people. So it's some sort of goods train. No running board either. Where are they to get on? On their feet now as the great thing lumbers by. There is no ladder to cling to on any of these wagons and in a moment the train will be grinding away from them leaving them standing here like a bunch of thwarted savages, tomahawks drooping, while their intended victims trundle to safety. And, now it's gone, the bisected air is closing together behind it, and their only chance has been snatched away.

'Hey, look!' Hania is suddenly sprinting along the track in pursuit. At the very back of the train is a little low-walled box, open to the sky, like someone's afterthought. Running, leaping, tumbling in, the pounding of their hearts will not quieten too quickly because it's only now they are safely aboard that they realize how frightened they were, which frightens them all over again. But the little open box is made to measure, and they feel gathered in by it, and somehow restored. It's quite comfy in here, really, with your back up against the wall and your knees up by your ears.

We're on the move, thinks Marta; we've got our bread; we've got enough tobacco for a few smokes and this sky has more stars threaded across it than any Polish sky ever had. Well-being and self-congratulation settle on them as she tears off pieces of bread and hands them round. They lean back to munch slowly on their supper as if dry bread were all anyone might want, as if the gentle passage of the stars is being unfurled over their heads solely for their entertainment.

Hania rolls their cigarettes because she does it so well, even in the dark when she can't see what her fingers are doing. They light up and take long happy drags, the tips of their cigarettes pulsing vermilion against the night. Marta breathes deeply, thinking she can actually feel the nicotine seeping contentment through every fibre of her body. There is something so peaceful travelling like this, when there is nothing more one can do but rock with the rocking of the train and let the mind wander. How long will it take to get to the army in Lugovoy? How will Antoni look in his uniform? Will he be surprised to see her? Will he be pleased? Well, of course he'll be pleased, but will he, among all that soldiery, feel able to do anything more than nod with polite recognition?

But the train has stopped. Marta holds her breath, and senses Hania and Basia holding theirs. Footsteps crack into the void like a sudden profanity in church. It's more than one person. In step. Marching in rising volume. Closer. Will they go past? Why would they go past? Where would they be going?

Something metallic raps twice on the side of their box. 'Out!'

Their hearts are pounding again. Marta puts a staying hand on the bent knees of the other two as if to say, don't move; as if to say, maybe they'll go away if we pretend we're not here. But of course they won't go away. They must be able to hear the runaway hearts, smell the fear. Slowly Marta straightens her slumped back and peers over the side. Two men. Soldiers. Carrying guns with bayonets fixed. She stands up. Hania and Basia stand up.

'My God!' exclaims one of the soldiers. 'Girls!' But he gestures sharply with his bayonet all the same.

Down they climb, clutching their bundles tightly against their bodies, palms clammy. One of the soldiers walks in front of them, the other behind, all the length of this endless train that has been brought to a halt on their account on a huge curve of the track. Marta wonders what must be out there in the dark that would cause the track to curve, in a landscape like this one. Will they be shot now or only later? Perhaps not immediately or they'd have done it already.

The soldiers aren't saying a word, not to them, not calling to each other. They're not the ones in charge but they've been sent by the one who is – sitting at a small table bolted to a side wall of the wagon close to the engine, an officer of some sort, middle-aged, like Marta's father. Like all fathers. But he's heavier, not so spruce. And his hair is thin; bags under his eyes as if he hasn't slept in days.

There is time to take note of all this because his amazement at the sight of them has silenced him. He has been expecting a band of armed ruffians. But he collects himself soon enough. In time of war you learn to jettison surprise. He motions them to stand before him, backs to the engine, so that he can study them from under half-closed eyelids, part contempt, part exhaustion.

Eventually he says, 'Of course you know the penalty for sabotage.'

Sabotage? What sabotage? Marta's lips are dry. Her tongue is thickened and heavy. 'We were only sitting there. We weren't doing anything wrong.'

'You were smoking. The driver saw your cigarette tips as we rounded the bend.'

'Isn't it allowed?'

'On a munitions train?'

Marta hears herself gasp like one of Mrs Benka's throttled chickens. She feels sick and in the dim light of the hurricane lamp on the table Hania and Basia's faces are green.

'Don't tell me you didn't know.' For a long time, a long, long time the officer looks from one face to the other and back again, then huffs a sigh of exasperation. 'No. Perhaps you didn't.' He puts his elbows on the table, props his chin in his hands and glares morosely at the grainy tabletop. Fatigue is all over his face. 'Oh, sit down, sit down.'

He closes his eyes and knuckles the squelching eyeballs. Opens the first two fingers of each hand like scissors. Blades away the urge to sleep from the bridge of his nose out to his cheekbones. Everyone watches. The girls sidle towards a narrow bench and sit on it, pressed close, knees tightly together.

'And why were you on this train at all?'

We were looking for work. We got lost. Angels dropped us from the sky. 'We're trying to get to Lugovoy.'

'Why?'

'Because... because there's a Polish division forming there. And our friends have gone there, and we wanted...'

'Poles. Poles.' He seems to be informing himself. Well, it explains the peculiar accent. 'But why on this train? Why not take a normal train?'

'This was the first.'

'Poles,' he mutters again. You'd think everything was explained in that single syllable. 'For God's sake.' He yawns so cavernously that the water oozes from the squeezed corners of his eyes. Then he says, 'You know I've got a daughter about the same age as you three.'

'And my father,' Marta ventures, 'he's an officer too. In Poland.'

'Is he? Is he so? And tell me, young Polish lady. What would he say to you if he were here now?'

Marta looks down. She's been trying not to think about that. He would be so ashamed. Couldn't she tell a munitions train when she saw one? Didn't she think for a moment what a lighted cigarette...? She who always made such a song and dance about wanting to join the military when all she was, was... If she only lets it, her mind will burst with his unspoken and unanswerable recriminations.

'Oh, give them some tea,' says the officer. 'Go on. Give these Polish war heroes some tea. Though, believe me, if the rest of your countrymen out there are anything like you three, then I don't know what sort of army they're going to cobble together. And we're supposed to fight alongside them, are we? Did you know that?' To his soldiers, who didn't. 'Well, God help us in this war, that's all I can say. An officer's daughter.' He's shaking his head. 'What do they teach them?'

249

One of the soldiers prepares to hand out glasses of tea. The engine hisses into the night and the train jerks forward. Scalding tea leaps from the glasses over the soldier's hands and he curses. The girls are effusive in their thanks and take tiny sips of the tea, too hot to swallow, too hot to taste. Wonderful.

'What are you going to do with us?' Basia's voice is a tiny whisper, but the question is brave.

The officer puckers his eyes at her as if he hasn't noticed her before and shakes his head slowly from side to side in a wagging pendulum tipping under its own momentum. 'What do you think I should do?'

'I don't know. We only wanted to get to Lugovoy. We were thinking we'd have to follow the track and walk.'

But he's not listening. 'My daughter,' he says, 'Tanya. The one your age. She's supposed to be getting married next month, you know. She had it worked out in her head last year, before the Germans came. "Wait a while," I said to her. "This is a bad time for a wedding, and your Kolya will be at the front." As it happens, he's already taken a hit and they've sent him behind the lines to convalesce. Send him out again, of course, as soon as we can. As soon as he's been properly patched up. She knows that, of course. But I said to her, "Tanyushka, why the rush? And you with your dreams of looking like a princess at her first ball." But she hasn't got anything special for the occasion. Kolya's in no position to get her anything pretty. And nor am I.'

Now a thought seems to spring to mind and he looks across the table at the three girls in their tidy row. They don't seem very appetising, any of them. And their clothes are in such a terrible state you'd think they'd only just made it out of besieged Leningrad. But you know what they say about Poles. He takes a squint at their wrists. Not a watch among them. Any more. Maybe they haven't got anything after all. And, in the end, what difference is it going to make? He's either got to have them shot and rolled off the train or let them go. Keep them on as far as the halt at Lugovoy and let them go.

Marta has tracked every movement of his eyes. She understands perfectly what he's about, but can he really be implying that without something changing hands he might… She has the necklace in her bundle, for a second time: the jewels she has safeguarded with such proud care for Ania's wedding, whenever that should be – and now she's going to have to trade them, hand them over to this Soviet officer for *his* daughter's wedding in exchange for their lives. But what if he takes the necklace and then shoots them anyway. He wouldn't do that, would he?

The officer is drawing a deep breath, ready to pronounce sentence.

Oh, what the hell, he thinks. Forget it. A bunch of schoolgirls. No harm done, after all.

Offer him the necklace now. Better that than having to plead afterwards.

Marta puts her hand into her blanket roll, squeezes her wooden spoon for luck and then draws her hand out. She gets up from the bench and turns her fist, knuckles down, over the officer's table. Opens the fist and releases its contents into a small collapsed mound of deep colour. Flickering light from the swaying hurricane lamp dances over the cut prisms of the gems. Everyone's gaze is glued to Marta's offering. Even the two soldiers, who have propped their redundant bayonets in a corner, are entranced. They step forward half a pace to be closer. They have never set eyes on anything like this before. Hania and Basia's mouths have fallen open. They had no idea Marta was carrying treasure with her. They had no idea she owned such stuff.

The officer is gazing down, both hands hovering, cupped as if to scoop water from the shimmering surface of a bucket. So now we have it: it turns out these Poles are as well off as everyone has always said. Yet he has an unpleasant feeling that these jewels may be all this girl has; that she's bartering them for her life. It feels like thievery, if he accepts, when she might need them more if she gets herself into another tight spot with someone in authority who isn't the softie he is. But that would mean someone else getting the necklace, someone without a daughter about to get married with nothing special to wear. Besides, if he doesn't accept, she and her friends there will think they can break Soviet law, and the rules of war, with impunity. Go all over the shop smoking on munitions trains and expecting to get away with it. They'll get a rude shock. Better they learn the lesson now.

Marta wonders why he's hesitating. Why doesn't he just take the necklace, pocket it, and tell her she's free to go? Perhaps he's scared his soldiers will tell on him. But who'd they tell that would listen when everybody is bribing their way round the country. Oh, Jesus! Is this what Mrs Benka meant her to do? *Sorry, Ania. I didn't mean to come back without your necklace. Really I didn't.*

The officer's hands drop onto the table and the necklace disappears. 'More tea?' He nods to one of the soldiers to step closer. 'Tell the engine driver we're stopping for a moment at Lugovoy.'

36

What have they been expecting? Polish soldiers of the newly formed army, smartly kitted out, marching, drilling, presenting arms, stripping their weapons? There's none of this. Instead, a crowd of shabby grey-faced men shambling like sleepwalkers. And over there, under the eaves of a single-storey brick building, shrunken figures huddle on the ground sad as chained monkeys. What sort of army is this? The Soviet officer was right. God help us in this war. Even Antoni isn't as wretched as some of these, and like him they're at the age when they ought to be at their best.

Beyond a brick barracks are rows of small brown tents like the ridges of a potato field. We'll start over there. But someone calls out, 'Hallo-o!' It's an officer, hoisted to his tiptoes with his mouth open in a dark O of astonishment, brought face to face with specimens of a species he had thought extinct. He doesn't move but waits, rooted where he is, for them to reach him.

Are they looking for someone?

A friend. Oh dear, how out of place that sounds. A friend who came here a few days ago to sign up. While we... we are nurses thinking to register and...

And who is this friend?... Antoni Kozlowski? Oh dear me, there are Kozlowskis by the dozen, aren't there, and with six thousand people here, and still being processed, you'd be hard put to... Are you nurses fully trained?

'Trained?' says Marta. 'Yes. Well. The compulsory summer thing, you know?'

'Not more than that?'

'I...' She could pretend. She could lie. Anything to get them to take her on. But this is for real.

'Well,' says the officer, interrupting her indecision. 'It's not for me to say yes or no. That's for Major Palucha. But my guess is that we're not likely to find trained personnel out here anyway, so whatever you know it may have to be good enough. I'll get you some paper and you can all write out your applications, and we'll see if we can find your friend.'

Will it be long, the wait? Seated at a mess table in the barracks, each has reconstituted her short life, made a summary of herself on a single sheet of paper. Names. Parents' names. Addresses – which once were. The change of addresses, the change of schools. On the page it looks suddenly so contracted: surely they have done more than this, have more to offer than this. That Major Palucha, in command of this little bit of Poland, won't be much impressed.

Marta read and reread her encapsulated biography before handing it over. She learned French and German. She learned history and maths and every clause of the Lithuanian Constitution. All those exams, all that learning by rote, whole chunks of the epic *Pan Tadeusz*, all those declensions and conjugations. In the end, what was it for? So that she could sit here, at a barracks table that someone has scrubbed clean with a stiff brush, waiting for a reply from Major Palucha, while outside thousands of bedraggled, sunken-eyed young men, looking older than their grandfathers, totter about between the tents dreaming of becoming an army.

She folds her forearms on the table and lays her head on them. Hania and Basia, who were murmuring together a moment ago, have fallen silent. Beyond the open windows there's an occasional distant shout, too indistinct to understand. But it's unnaturally quiet. Six thousand men gathered in one place and it's so quiet.

Footsteps. Boots hurrying on a concrete floor. Marta raises her head. It's another officer, older, with an air of bringing news. Papers snapped between fingers and thumb flap slightly as he moves.

'Which one of you is Marta Dolniak?'

Heat in her cheeks. What's she done to be singled out? He's brandishing the pages in front of him like an accusation. She must have written something ridiculous, but she didn't. She checked. They all checked each other's.

'It's me. I mean, I am.'

'My dear young lady.'

His large hands are heavy on her shoulders, and she thinks he's about to kiss her on both cheeks, but he restrains himself abruptly like an occasional uncle who has only just noticed that his niece is all grown up.

'As soon as I saw your name, and your father's name... I couldn't believe it. I was at your christening, did you know that? Well, of course you didn't, you were only a baby...'

All that effort and he hasn't even read it through. Her name was enough. Her father's name. Just as her father's name got her arrested in the first place. In the awkwardness of the moment she blurts, 'So will you take us on? As nurses?'

'What? Yes, yes. But first things first. Come along, come along, my dear. Welcome to Tenth Division.'

Now he drapes the avuncular arm round her shoulders and guides her out.

'That's nice!' says Hania. 'How's about welcoming us too?'

'I expect he would if he'd been at our christenings. Come on, or we'll lose our way.'

'Our trouble is, we don't have enough captains and colonels in the family.'

Once again a young soldier is detailed to make tea while Major Palucha explains that nothing is as simple as it might have seemed. Apparently 10th Division is not going to put itself together to fight alongside the Soviet army against the joint enemy, after all. It's going to leave.

'Leave? Where to? Why?'

'This is a long story. Are you ready for it?' Major Palucha leans back in his chair, stretches out his long legs and crosses them at the ankle. 'You've heard of General Sikorski, of course.'

Of course. They sit taller. Wladislaw Sikorski, head of the Polish government-in-exile in London. Underground pamphlets about him had circulated in Wilno.

'It all started this last December,' says Major Palucha. 'General Sikorski came over from London to negotiate with Stalin because the amnesty the Soviets had promised wasn't working the way it was supposed to. He took General Anders with him, since, as you know, Anders will be heading the Polish army here, and the pair of them went off to Moscow to complain that there were still thousands of Poles locked in camps and prisons who should have been released. But Stalin gave them the brush-off. Said it couldn't be true. Wouldn't be budged. Pretended to put in all sorts of telephone calls to all sorts of people, but wouldn't be budged.

'Then Anders complained that the condition of most of the men who *were* coming out was so bad they weren't ready to form *any* sort of army – they hadn't the weapons, they hadn't the uniforms, they weren't trained, and worst of all they were starving. And the rations that had been promised weren't arriving either.

'Well, apparently they argued this way and that way, but in the end Stalin and Sikorski signed an agreement that said Poland and the USSR would give each other full military support, with those Polish armed forces on Soviet territory fighting side by side with the Soviet army. But, between you and me, I don't think General Anders thought much of that agreement. It was all very well for Sikorski, who'd been in Paris and London all this time, drumming up support, and maybe thinking that keeping in Stalin's good books would give him a strong hand in negotiating the peace – if we win. When we win. But Anders, you know, he was locked up in the Lubyanka in 'thirty-nine, and he learned a thing or two about the Soviet Union that Sikorski doesn't seem to want to imagine. The final straw comes for Anders when the fellow in charge of Red Army supplies suddenly announces they'll be *cutting* the rations for the Polish army down to twenty-six thousand, while Anders has seventy thousand men to feed – and those are already going short because they're having to share with amnestied civilians, women, children and old folk. People like the three of you, as a matter of fact. The Soviet view is that rations are intended for combatants and not their civilian hangers-on. It's what the British are saying too, as a matter of fact.

'But now there's a new line. They're saying that any military personnel too weak to fight can be evacuated out of the Soviet Union. Easier to get rid of them than feed them. And, since Tenth Division is entirely made up of men too weak to fight, we're leaving, though it's been the devil of a business getting agreement from the authorities for the trains. But it's already begun. Some of our people have already left Lugovoy, just a couple of days ago. And the rest will be pulling out within the week.'

Major Palucha is pleased with the effect his story has had on his old friend's daughter. All agog, hanging on his every word. Nice-looking girl, too, with those green eyes. Get her a couple of months' proper food, a bit of soap and some shampoo, and she'll make some young man very happy to have her... on his arm.

'Um... excuse me.'

It's one of the other two. He hasn't paid them much attention, or any, as a matter of fact. Freckly thing with a cheeky face, and this little dark one with her hair behind her ears and a mousy voice. He turns to her.

'The ones who've already gone,' she says. 'Do you know who they are? Their names?'

'My dear young lady, there were too many for me to know their names, and I hadn't met most of them, personally. But we can find a list. Janusz!' He beckons the tea-serving soldier with an energetic wrist. 'You can find us that list, can't you?'

'You have it, Major. In that drawer.'

'I do?' Major Palucha tugs at an ill-fitting wooden drawer. 'Why, indeed. My young corporal here drew it up and he's an efficient fellow. All nice and alphabetical so you'll be able to find your people, if they're on it. I presume you are looking for someone?'

Marta has directed a fixed gaze at the single window that can't have been washed since it was set in its frame. Out of the corner of her eye she can see Basia's finger stepping methodically down the pages. Now Basia is handing the pages back, thanking Major Palucha.

'Well?' he says, fatherly, and trying not to smile. 'Is he there, your "beau"?'

'Not my beau,' she says. 'But no, he's not there. So he must still be here.'

Hania and Basia are looking at Marta, who is examining her window again, counting the desiccated flies packaged in their corner cobweb. She feels a heavy pressure on the bridge of her nose, an awkward dampness in the nostrils. She coughs first and only then sniffs. Blinks.

Major Palucha clears his throat and claps his hands a couple of times. 'Well, well. But I hadn't quite finished. How about some more tea?' That should give the girl time to set her face in order. And look, here's our splendid Janusz with fresh glasses and a particularly solicitous hand hovering with its offering towards that mousy little one. Wherever way you turn...

'There is one other thing. When there was all that arguing over rations, the government-in-exile, and the British as well, for that matter, both said we shouldn't be worrying about our amnestied civilians for the moment. Fight the war first, they said, and think about the civilians later. That's what finished it for General Anders. The idea of leaving Polish civilians behind on Soviet soil, at Stalin's mercy... He had a pretty good idea what would happen to them. So, when Sikorski sent a telegram telling him to concentrate on his army and not the civilians, Anders ignored it. He's convinced that whoever gets left behind will die. That's when he decided that *everyone* should be evacuated, the strongest along with the weakest – and all the civilians we can manage.

'We've persuaded the authorities, for the moment at least, to let us take the non-combatant members of our families with us.' The three young women look at him politely. How nice for the family members. He notes the incomprehension. 'So I propose, Marta, that you instantly become my niece.' Now they get it. Look at those smiles. 'Now what about you two? Janusz, don't you think it's time you had a little sister? Someone you have to take care of? This one perhaps?' He clasps Basia's forearm warmly. She blushes. Janusz blushes. 'Excellent. Now you, young lady. Miss... er...'

'Hania Janta.'

'Very good, very good. A name with a bounce to it. Hania Janta. I like that. Shall we go out and see if we can't find you a family?'

'But... Uncle. What about our people back in Teren Uziuk? There's about thirty there. All sorts. I mean, some old women, some young ones with kids...'

'Well... We'll just have to accommodate them somehow, won't we? Do you know all their names and their ages? More or less?'

Immediately Marta and Hania glance at Basia. Consequently so does Major Palucha, always quick to size up capabilities.

'Here.' He gives her the three pages with the three biographies that he hasn't read. 'Use the back of these and put down all the names you know. I'm sure we can find men out there who'll be overjoyed to be reunited with their mothers or their wives. Come along, Hania Janta. Let us go and look for some.'

And out they go, Major Palucha and the doctors' daughter. Marta would have liked to accompany them in a search of her own, but will not be so blatant. What is she to do but sit where she is and stare at the grimy window-pane?

Basia makes a show of sucking on the top of her pencil and frowning like a small child who cannot remember how to spell her name. The pencil tastes sour and her mouth floods with saliva. 'There's Mrs Benka,' she says, for something to say. 'How old is she?'

Marta has no idea. She has never asked. Well, you don't, do you? Old, that's all. 'I haven't a clue,' she says. 'I don't know how old my grandmother would have been. I haven't got a granny.'

But in a sense she has. Ania offered her Mrs Benka all that time ago in the orchard, and then Mrs Benka offered herself. The trouble is now, for Mrs Benka to be safe, she has to become someone else's. Only so that it will look right on paper, but Marta feels bereft all the same.

'I don't know. Let's say seventy, shall we?' suggests Basia, and writes it down. 'He did say more or less. Now what about Mrs Bartol and her two boys?'

On and on they go, Basia mentioning names and pretending she can't remember the accompanying ages. All the older women are accounted for and some of the younger ones; then there'll be the few older men, the ones that are still alive. Outside the brightness of the day may be fading but the opaque window gives no clue.

'Oh, Marta!'

What? Marta twists her head to see what it is behind her that has made Basia exclaim. In the doorway. Antoni.

Basia drops her head over her paper, muttering, 'Julek must be five by now. Karol... three? Four? It won't matter that much, will it. Now what about...'

Marta has bounced to her feet. Don't be silly. Sits down again. Gets up. Holds out her hands.

From beneath her eyebrows Basia sees Antoni's fingers lock with Marta's, and Basia drops her chin to her chest once more.

'Basia,' Antoni calls out over Marta's shoulder. 'Did I never tell you that Mrs Benka was my grandmother?'

37

Mrs Benka sits back in her seat on the train the Soviet authorities have put at the Poles' disposal. Since there may not be another, it is as over-crowded as every other train she has travelled on in this benighted country. Opposite her but on the floor, their backs against the shins of the more fortunate, crouch her two adopted grandchildren, asleep. She looks down at them and thinks about destiny, or perhaps Destiny. Is it employing her as a medium to unite this young pair? But given that she will no more trust in destiny (with or without its capital) than in God she has to conclude that it's just one of those things. All the same. Marta's head is leaning on Antoni's shoulder. His head has top-pled onto hers. They are either unaware of this, or content. Content, clearly. Look how tightly their fingers are interlaced, even in their sleep.

Goodness me, they *are* so young. Of course, everyone looks younger when they are asleep and defenceless – except the very old whose crumpled flesh is further aged without the support of wakeful-ness. But when youthful features slacken, unselfconscious for once, they soften into childhood. Look at Marta. Her mother might almost recognize the baby she once sang to, but for the chiselled lines of famine. And Antoni's black hair is still thick and springy, as if it is, in itself, a proclamation of defiance against his circumstances. Even if he were fully fed he'd still be lanky, gawky, too many corners at the knees and elbows, not yet at the mature weight of adult manhood. Under their closed lids with those extraordinary lashes his eyes are blue. Marta's are green. What colour would their children's be? Then

Mrs Benka, catching her musings as they run ahead of her attention, chides herself. All in good time, in these bad times.

But what if she really were Marta's grandmother? Would she be sanguine about this young man's easy intimacy? When Marta first introduced him into their carriage, all those months ago, his presence and his manner had been a tonic. All the women felt it, she no less than the others. But really, what does she know about him? He doesn't exhibit any of the diffidence with women that the son of a good family ought, which suggests more experience than makes her quite happy. Will he lead innocent Marta a dance? Yet all the expectations, the conventions, the right order of things never survive war and turmoil, so why worry? He seems a nice enough boy, a good enough boy. And he appears to have the measure of Marta, which says a lot for him. He mocks her forthright statements and her quick judgements. He even laughs at her, and she seems to like that. Look at what happened when Marta got round, finally, to confessing.

'Mrs Benka. I lost the necklace.'

'You lost it?' Mrs Benka had felt a moment's anger at what sounded like carelessness.

'People lose things, when there's mayhem.' Antoni must have picked up her tone, and jumped in to smooth things over. 'I lose things all the time, even without the mayhem. I had a ring once, and lost that. And it had been my grandfather's. It's not the end of the world, you know.'

'But the necklace wasn't mine to lose, Antoni. It was Mrs Benka's. And I didn't actually lose it. I had to sell it... trade it.'

Mrs Benka had raised her eyebrows.

Marta had itemized the journey to Lugovoy: the munitions train with its little box at the back where the girls had smoked. Their arrest. All of it. And Mrs Benka nodded each event by like acquaintances filing in to dinner, then opened her mouth to comment – but too late. Antoni was giggling. Giggling!

'What's the matter with you?' said Marta, clearly furious. There she'd been, bargaining for her life, and he thought it was funny.

'Your faces… I can just picture them… and you, Commander, waving your fag end around for everyone to see… Very professional.'

Marta had heaved a breath to fuel her retort but Antoni had laid his hand, so briefly, along her cheek and said, 'Hey. It's all right.' Composed his face. Lost the composure. Hiccuped into giggles again. Mrs Benka had been alarmed. But, would you believe it, Marta was chuckling too, and there they were, the two of them, laughing into one another's faces as if they had the compartment all to themselves.

Now the two heads loll forwards onto their chests and then jerk up again, and still they do not wake. Just as well they're sleeping now. When they do wake up, all their present ease will be elbowed away by nausea and the griping pains of hunger. The longer they sleep the better. She only wishes she could join them but it is her misfortune that, the greater her discomfort, the more alert her mind.

All day, and fitfully through the night, Mrs Benka has been tracking their westward progress from one Soviet Socialist Republic to the next. The train crossed the great Amu Darya at dawn, more like a stretch of inland sea than a river. Surely if you were standing on one low bank you would not be able to see across to the other. A great sluggish mud-green expanse seeping in glutinous passage towards the Aral Sea to the north with its floating caravans of vast barges, roped together in ponderous convoy. The river is almost like a border, although in this southerly region it is desert, stones and sand on both sides. But flat, flat, still flat.

As the sun climbs, the heat increases through the windows and eventually even Mrs Benka dozes, numbed by monotony, while ahead of them station loudspeakers interrupt the crackle of martial music with hectic warnings to the local populace to clear the area. A death train is approaching bringing with it cholera, typhus, plague.

At the great Caspian port of Krasnovodsk, that's exactly what they think. Somehow even the driver, who all this long while has kept to his post, seems to have got wind of the danger he's in. The very moment the train creaks to its halt against the buffers he leaps down from his cab and legs it away down the platform, through the deserted wastes of the enormous station building and out into the wide depopulated boulevards.

Slowly Major Palucha rubs his sticky eyes, picking grains of sleep from the corners. He draws his shoulder-blades together and stretches his arms over his head. Gets to his feet and stretches his arms to both sides. All round him men are asking, where are we? Have we arrived? Where have we arrived?

He clambers down to the platform and notes that it is deserted. The engine is hissing quietly, water dripping onto the track. The cab is empty. He climbs back up and makes his way the length of the train, calling people out of the carriages. That is how he discovers that twenty-three of his men have died since they left Lugovoy.

The corpses are laid in line on the platform wrapped in their blankets, and word of them gets round. Which is worse: that twenty-three young men have died here, on the brink of rescue, or that no one is surprised? Major Palucha cannot stop to consider. Somehow they have to be buried. He sends one group to look for water in the station and then sets off into the city, where he comes across a Turkmen policeman, who holds out his hands to ward off the stranger.

No point trying to get close to the man, who is plainly petrified. Major Palucha stops in his tracks and calls out, 'What on earth is going on here? Where is everyone?'

The policeman backs away to a distance he deems beyond contagion. 'It's your people,' he shouts between fingers netting his mouth and nose. 'Bringing plague.'

'Plague?' bellows Major Palucha. 'It's not plague. It's starvation, dammit!' And typhus, he mutters, but under his breath.

It's two days' sailing to Bandar-e Pahlavi on the northern shore of Iran, and the Soviet sailors, whose own rations are inadequate, are so distressed to see the skeletal Poles that they press on them the salted herrings and bread they had been looking forward to themselves. Salted herrings. A taste of home. But Marta has been gripped by stomach cramps and nausea so bad that all she wants is water.

Everyone else, however – Mrs Benka, Antoni, Basia, Hania, Major Palucha and Janusz, Mrs Bartol and her two little boys – everyone falls on the herring and the wedges of black bread, gasping and munching and swallowing. And all the while the ship is sliding out of the harbour, away from the Soviet coast, into an expanse of navy-blue sea no more ruffled than the haze of a mirage.

Marta keeps away from the eating and up on deck leans on the railing, watching the Soviet Union retreat. As they'd filed on board, Major Palucha had reminded everyone that this was the beginning of Easter weekend, which now seems to Marta appropriate. Perhaps this rescue will be a sort of redemption. That's it, she thinks. That's over and done with. I'm never setting foot in a communist state again, I swear.

38

Marta is no sailor. In fact, she's never been at sea before, even if the Caspian isn't supposed to count, since it's an inland sea. But after the crossing they've had she thinks she could survive the storms of the Atlantic. Only a few hours out, there was such a wind whipping at the water that the MS *Odessa* was tossed in every direction at once. You didn't know what to hold onto. And everyone was so ill. So terribly ill. She had thought she would die, but even as she was retching her empty guts into her throat she knew that the others were much, much worse off. They had eaten the salted herring, and there wasn't enough water. And then the bucketing of the ship...

She had recovered before the others, and then she was certain *they* would die. Antoni, Mrs Benka, Basia and Hania, poor Janusz trying to be gallant to Basia... But who can be gallant when he's in that state? Bodies are such tyrants. Now they're all lying face down on the deck, exhausted. And she doesn't know what to do for them. Some nurse she is! Major Palucha is as weak as the rest, which must be deeply humiliating for him, except that his face is so grey he probably isn't even thinking about that at the moment.

She was alone last night under that astonishing moon, flat and biscuity, and pasted so close against the black sky that she felt she could reach out and snap off a piece. The air was velvet soft, the sea entirely calm. You couldn't believe it could pitch and heave into the churning grey mountains that had made everyone so sick. And now, it's neither grey nor blue, as the picture books have it, but emerald green.

She can see right down to the bottom, where it's lightly ribbed sand with small fish, and now a few bigger ones.

The ship seems to be coming in beside a spit of white sand, into a sort of lagoon. On the other side of the spit there's a vast bay, glittering with silver needle-points in the sunlight. Other ships line up behind theirs, streaming back to the horizon, the furthest merely a spot of darkness. The port ahead seems large, but it has an emptied look about it, like a city in the early hours before the trams are running.

A row of figures, toy soldiers at this distance, are propped to attention on the quay. And they *are* soldiers. They must be, they're in such a straight line. Whose are they? She can't yet make out the colour of the uniforms, and anyway she only knows what Polish and Soviet fatigues look like. Set back behind them are some huge white tents. White tents on white sand, and now, with the sun getting higher in the sky, the horizon itself is growing whiter along with the line of the sea. Brownish uniforms. Greeny-brown. Whose are they?

Major Palucha has joined her, leaning over the side. 'What a night,' he says in a voice shaky at the memory. He wipes his mouth inwards from the corners with thumb and forefinger, rubs the pads together, checks them surreptitiously as if he expects to see flecks of last night's vomit there. 'You wouldn't think an inland sea could get up to such tricks.'

'No.'

He glances sideways at her. 'You look remarkably well, under the circumstances.'

'I didn't eat any herring.'

He shudders. 'Sensible girl. We're all wishing we hadn't.'

'Who are those soldiers?'

'Those? Our good friends and allies, the British, who have finally stopped sitting on their hands.'

'I don't understand.'

'No. Well. They didn't do anything to stop Hitler from invading Poland – for all their fine words before it all began. "They bomb you, we'll bomb them," you know? We believed the words, which it turns out was naïve. They weren't ready to fight in 'thirty-nine, so they were stalling for time. Still, when the invasion came they did declare war for our sakes, and then found themselves having to fight pretty much on their own when all their allies were occupied. So, as I said, good friends and allies now.'

'But what are they doing here? I mean, *here*?'

'Securing the supply routes to the Soviet Union. The Russians are our allies too, remember.' He pulls a face. 'Now. For the time being.' But he cheers up. 'And the Americans.'

'The Americans! I thought they didn't want to fight.'

'They didn't. But they were attacked and they had war declared on them. Not just the Japanese, but Germany too. Didn't leave them much choice, did it?'

'Oh, but then we'll win, won't we? Any day now. We're bound to.'

'We have to believe it. But any day now? I wouldn't be so sure. Anyway,' he adds, clapping his hands together, 'I'd best get everyone up and ready. We'll be in port shortly. What a tale you'll have to tell your father, eh, when the time comes!'

Marta nods and stares out at the British troops, who have begun a precise march down towards the quay. Major Palucha must be one of those naturally cautious men, a pessimistic type who always pretends things are going to be worse than he really thinks they are, to protect himself, and maybe others, against disappointment. But for heaven's sake, if the Americans have joined in too, surely...

Twenty-four hours is all they've had, but twenty-four hours is all you need so long as you know what you're doing. And Lieutenant-Colonel James Atkins knows exactly what he's doing, which is why he's here. The equipment is ready. His ranks are ready. Everything is laid out. Now it's just a question of getting things done. All the same, there seems to be some sort of hullabaloo going on up there on board. Instead of filing down to land, there's a knot of people all jostling at the top of the gangway and someone appears to be trying to come down backwards. Senseless.

Nothing else for it. Lieutenant-Colonel Atkins trots smartly up the gangway with a brace of the ranks, in step, close behind. He is unprepared for the fetid stench that envelopes him, even in the open air up here on the high deck, where you'd imagine the breezes from the sea would have been at work. But it feels as if he is stepping into some enclosed space, invisibly domed, its poisonous vapours sealed in. Corpses are laid out at his feet, row upon row, rather neatly as a matter of fact. He has no passenger manifest but at a guess fully one-quarter of the people who boarded the *Odessa* at Krasnovodsk will not be disembarking on their feet on Persia's northern shore. His unflinching eye roams slowly up and down the rows of bodies, then, with all the steadiness of a Pathé news camera, zooms into the faces of the living, who, quite frankly, look barely different from their dead.

He about-faces to the two ranks motionless behind him. 'All right there. Stretchers. As many as we have. And be quick about it.' Swings round again. 'Everybody stand back.'

Almost nobody understands the verbal command but they shuffle to the limits of the deck, obeying the vigorous breaststroke of his arms.

It's taken under twenty-five minutes to clear the area of bodies. Lieutenant-Colonel Atkins has been keeping a time check as his soldiers run relay, nimbly up the gangway, then burdened and therefore gingerly back down. Fortunately the surviving passengers are mostly men – as far as he can tell at a first glance. If there was a preponderance of women, there might be a lot of the wailing and hand-wringing that other peoples sometimes go in for. As it is, there is total silence. Unnerving, but easier to work with. Luckily he alerted the local authorities yesterday, anticipating there might be a few burials to deal with, but they'll just have to find more spaces than he bargained for.

His job, the job at hand, is cleaning up the living, who have begun to creep down the gangway, some of them in a hand-over-hand sideways sidle as if they're finding the incline vertiginous. Legs are buckling and not a few are coming down onto their knees with a *crump* to make the imagination wince. He has ordered his men not to touch anyone unless absolutely necessary, callous as that may seem. And he can see from the faces of some of them that callous is what they think it.

Just at the bottom of the gangway an ancient crone in drifting rags has toppled face down. If it weren't for the young woman standing directly in front of her and blocking her fall, she would have smashed her nose on the quay-stones. The young woman has plopped to her knees and is babbling up at the corridor of soldiers, making no sense and impeding the descent of the rest of the passengers.

'For God's sake, do something!' Marta shouts. 'Can't you see she's exhausted? She can't walk any more.'

Mrs Benka, spread-eagled but fully conscious, notes the warmth of the hot stones under her cheek and wonders at the polished toe of a booted foot a few centimetres from her eye. She listens with interest to Marta's spiralling fury. The girl's hand on her shoulder is rather heavy and she really would prefer her to remove it. Besides, all this bellowing at British soldiery won't come to anything. Since when have the English taken lessons in Polish? But it seems Marta has suddenly thought of this herself, because she is now repeating her demands in French, even – silly girl – a few words in German until she suddenly stops. But of course there's no response to any of that either.

'Hey, Marta!' Now here's Antoni down on one knee. 'Forget about them. Look, I'll take her right arm and you take her left. Put it round your shoulders and when I get to three we'll lift her up. One, two…'

Mrs Benka is alarmed. In between her own bouts of vomiting through the night she saw Antoni in such paroxysms of retching she thought he must turn himself inside out. They'll drop her. They're bound to. However can they not? If she could, she'd lever herself to her feet under her own steam, but she has no steam any more. To that extent, Marta is entirely correct. But, my goodness, what appalling timing!

*

That to-do down there is becoming a hazard. Any minute now

someone is going to blunder into the woman on the ground and trip over her, and then there'll be a real mess. Lieutenant-Colonel Atkins takes the gangway at a run – pushing past the shrinking ditherers – leaps the final few feet and hoists the crone onto and over his shoulder like a fireman using a bundle of old clothes to perform a demonstration rescue to assembled recruits. Actually she weighs barely more than a bundle of old clothes. He strides off in the direction of the tents at speed and, arriving at the first one, slides the bundle from his shoulder and deposits it on the sand. He looks back to the quay and sees, to his satisfaction, that he has unblocked the logjam. Passengers are flowing steadily, if slowly, towards him down the gangway. There's nothing more for him to be doing here. Now all his careful organization can take over. A good mug of hot sweet tea wouldn't go amiss.

Major Palucha has managed to make it to the front, where he finds Marta squatting beside that Mrs Benka, who has managed to sit up. The young man Marta seems to be sweet on is bending over, offering the old lady his hands to help her up, but she looks as if she'd rather stay where she is for the time being. Well, there's no hurry. He'd better find out what's intended. That British officer seems to have disappeared but there are others around. The question will be how to communicate. He closes his eyes to rummage through his memory for something useful in English but inexplicably lights on *This is my uncle Harry*. Maybe they'll have laid on an interpreter.

He steps into the first tent, where a red-headed corporal has been waiting, slumped in boredom on a wooden chair, but now jumps eagerly to his feet. Major Palucha has just enough time to observe that the tent is a sort of corridor, with flaps at both ends, and leading to a second, when the corporal points a jabbing forefinger at him and shakes his head with theatrical emphasis. What's this? No entry? Not allowed? Private? Frowning, Major Palucha backs out again, the corporal matching him step for step. Outside the corporal directs the same forefinger at Mrs Benka and Marta and begins on a vigorous nodding routine. Someone has been explaining the importance of

271

mime in these situations.

'NO... MAN!' he shouts carefully. 'FIRST... WO-... MAN! MAN... LA-... TER!'

'I think he means us,' she says to Mrs Benka. '"Wo-man" is us.'

'I think I gathered that from the pantomime. It would help if they could find someone a little more... linguistically varied, wouldn't it?'

'Will you wait while I go and find all the other women,' says Major Palucha, and tramps back along the waiting queue, beckoning, tapping shoulders as he goes, like an impresario making his selection for the chorus line. And it's like a wave. As the women are filtered out, and the message passes down the line, the men sit down where they are on the white sand. Whatever's about to happen, it's going to take time. A brief warm breeze huffs a breath of resin, fragrant from a giant cedar near the tents, and as one they inhale deeply. Who knows? Maybe good smells begin here.

39

Major Palucha has found a Mrs Dablinska, who used to teach English and expects to do so again. He bustles her to the head of the queue with one hand clipped to her elbow as if she might make a run for it. The red-headed corporal, who had returned to his slump on the wooden chair, is now all efficiency and anxious to get going. Mrs Dablinska, every inch the teacher, steps to the head of her class, restored to selfhood. She rubs her hands together, clearing them, perhaps, of chalk. A podium seems to grow beneath her feet. The corporal has a sizeable box that he holds close to his chest as if it contains a squirm of new-born kittens. He mutters to Mrs Dablinska, who nods and nods, making mental notes.

'The gentleman says we are please to leave our papers and valuables in this box. There are envelopes for each one of us.' And a pen to write their names.

The corporal receives Mrs Dablinska's papers and a small packet from her, and inserts them into a large brown envelope on which he has her write her name in capital letters. He makes a great show of licking the flap and sticking it down, pressing the edge of his hand over it. Then he raises the sealed envelope, holding it aloft by two corners, high enough for everyone to see, and displays it to the right and left with conjuror's solemnity. Marta fully expects the envelope and its contents to disappear before her eyes. The corporal lays the envelope into the box and pats the box. All safe in here. His explanatory mime over, he deals out envelopes. The pen passes from hand to hand; sealed envelopes pile up in the box.

Now he holds open the flaps of the tent to allow the assorted women in. Closes the flaps behind them. The tent is empty but for some sacks neatly folded in a corner. It is warmer in here than outside, despite the shade, because there is no breeze. Mrs Dablinska leans towards the corporal and addresses him in a low voice so that his reply is equally muted, but Mrs Dablinska stiffens and shoots a worried glance over her classroom. The corporal shrugs. Mrs Dablinska turns. She is not happy with her text.

'We have been asked to take off all our clothes.' All? 'It's because of the lice, he says. They want to burn our clothes. They'll give us some more, he says.'

Suddenly they cannot look one another in the eye. Some of them have never undressed completely in anyone's presence before, let alone in front of strangers. And this corporal – he doesn't look as if he's going to leave the tent. He's collecting the folded sacks and distributing them, not enough to go round but one between ten, say. Now he's handed them all out, and he's saying something to Mrs Dablinska.

'He asks you to… hurry up because they have so many people to process.'

Nobody moves. Mrs Dablinska looks at the ground, then at the corporal, who yawns and stretches and shuffles a few steps. Now he's turned his back. She unwinds her shawl and rolls it into a sausage. Posts it into the nearest sack. Mrs Benka grabs Marta's wrist on one side and Basia's on the other and pulls them round so that they are forming the beginnings of a circle. On either side others join in until eventually all the women are facing inward. Nobody speaks. Their breathing is slightly laboured as the layers drop to the ground.

Mrs Dablinska has gained courage. Somewhat shielded, she hopes, by the bodies of everyone else, she goes from one to the next, holding out a sack to be filled. Lays it down. Picks up another. The two empty pouches of her breasts lie against her breastbone like flaccid little balloons awaiting inflation. Her upper arms are narrower than her elbows, her thighs thinner than the bulge of her knees. She appears to have no stomach and no buttocks, which makes the huge

274

pale tuft of her pubic hair grotesque. All this they see and pretend they do not, for they know they might as well be gazing into a mirror.

All naked, they huddle as close as sheep expecting a nip at the ankles. The corporal is already at the further end of the tent holding aside the flap to usher them through. The soft white sand is cool beneath bare feet as, trotting with trepidation, they corral themselves into stage two.

Mrs Dablinska in the lead comes up short. This tent is peopled with soldiers, each standing guard by a wooden chair whose legs have been plunged into the sand. Heads turn to the women and swiftly turn away again. The corporal has somehow made his way in, slinking past flat as paper, and is addressing Mrs Dablinska from the corner of his mouth, and, since he does not look at her as he is speaking, she does not look at him to reply. Her nakedness in the presence of his uniform is by the by so long as eyes do not meet. All the women have thrown one arm across their breasts, the other pressed over their genitals.

'He says they're going to shave us.' Mrs Dablinska takes in a great quavering breath. 'He says to sit down.' Barbers' chairs. Barbers in uniform clacking their clippers.

Marta follows her feet, eyes down. She perches her buttocks on the rim of a chair, feeling as she has never felt before how her naked flesh opens onto the wood. She hunches over the hollow of her stomach, shoulders scooped forward, forearms hugging her midriff as if without them it might plop into her lap. She squeezes her eyes shut.

Scissors first. Hanks of lank hair with their clinging infestation drop onto the sand, to be gathered up later and burned along with the clothes. For a moment she is sorry for the faceless young soldier whose fingers are tangling with the crawling, unwashed mass. Then she is sorry only for herself. Now it's the clippers. A large hand holds her head steady, pushes it forwards till her chin is forced into her throat. The clippers run up the back of her neck and the skin between her shoulder-blades shudders. The hand tips her head to the left. She wonders what it looks like, the furrow in her hair, like the progress of a

275

scythe, perhaps, cutting the grass for hay and all the panicked field creatures scurrying for safety. This is good, she repeats to herself. This is necessary to be rid of the lice. Her hair will grow back in time. The hand tips her head to the right and it seems to her that her head is shrinking like a shrivelled lemon, that the hot gripping fingers will leave indentations like hail marks in the mud all over her balding scalp.

It's done. The clipping has stopped. Marta opens her eyes and explores her stubble with wandering fingers. Someone else's head is wobbling up there on her stalky neck, so in a way she isn't who she thought she was, without her hair. Thank God there are no mirrors, nothing shiny enough to act as mirror, no darkened windows. She gets up. When are they going to get clothes and where from?

She makes to move through the tent but the soldier's hand is on her shoulder, pushing it, turning her to face him. She doesn't want to face him. She doesn't want to see his face lest she remember it. If he has a face he will be a man. Like this he has been a silent hand guiding clippers over her head. So as he turns her she swivels her head to look fixedly down the line of her shoulder at the tent wall, but senses that he has moved, he is no longer standing up, no longer at her level. Where is he?

And then she feels him. His hands are pressing her legs apart and the clippers are probing into her pubic hair, hair that she has never really looked at, snagging in the hair and pulling at the lips of her genitals. Tears stream down her cheeks, inside her nose and into her mouth, bubbling inside her mouth, and she cannot stop them. But through the salted blur she thinks she recognizes Mrs Benka, bullet-headed and rigid, with a soldier kneeling in the sand, nuzzling at her pudenda with his clippers, his face a mask of expressionless distance. Beyond Mrs Benka misty-grey figures are stumbling away, out of this tent and into the next, their arms stretched ahead of them.

Marta leaps away from her soldier with his clippers, his job only part done, and flees, running half blinded after the others. At the entrance of the next tent she blunders into another soldier hugely barring her way. She tries to dodge him but he shoots out an arm unyielding as a tree trunk. A shriek rises in her throat but all at once

276

he's let her go and she finds she's holding something. Instinctively she makes to fling it from her but as her hand clasps the thing more tightly, the better to let it fly, she recognizes what she is holding. A large square cake of soap. Soap!

Two long pipes run the length of the roof pole of the third tent. Water pours down into the sand below, pitted and darkening. The water is tepid but it pours and pours. The women rub themselves, scrub themselves, over their stubbly heads, under their breasts, between their toes, round their heels, between their legs and never mind the soldiers stationed along the walls. The medicinal stink of carbolic stings her eyes but Marta cannot cease her washing, almost flaying herself in the ecstasy of it. But someone is tapping her on the arm. At first she cannot see for the water in her eyes; wipes them with the backs of her hands; looks round. A large hand protruding from a saturated military cuff is beckoning her out. Time's up, miss. You've had your turn. A large paper towel is pressed into her hands. Her cake of soap, much reduced, is taken from her.

As she steps back from the water pipes, wrapping her towel round her, Marta discovers she is breathing so fast she is almost panting. Her frantic scrubbing has taken all that remains of her strength, and she is exhausted. The towel blots the droplets from her tingling skin as she lurches to the exit and her wet feet gather clinging Cinderella slippers of fine white sand.

Underwear, clothes and shoes are piled on spread blankets ranked by size – CHILD, SMALL, MEDIUM, LARGE. Nobody currently is large but Marta is at least tall. She steps into a pair of flapping red-and-white polka-dotted knickers and reaches for the nearest dress. Hundreds of burnished mauve sequins glimmer dully like fish scales on deep-red satin. She can see from its shape that it's meant to hug the body, emphasizing hips and breasts – the hips and breasts that were once the bane of her life. But it hangs so loosely on her that the clattering folds droop with disappointment. She winds the strange fabric one and a half times around her and, clutching it in place, searches out a black patent-leather belt. All the shoes of her size are high-heeled thin-strapped sandals. Who can have donated these garments?

277

Mrs Dablinska, whose shaven head is perfectly round, reads the printed sign propped behind the blankets: A GIFT FROM THE AMERICAN PEOPLE.

40

They regroup on the sand under the enormous cedar tree. Marta's sequinned gown crackles when she moves, but now it has pooled into an umber puddle round her crossed legs. Mrs Benka is wrapped around in deep maroon. Basia's in something with puffed sleeves of pink-and-white checks. Mrs Dablinska picked out a dark-blue tailored suit, which would be appropriate but for the jacket hanging so loosely on her shoulders that the sleeves droop over the backs of her hands. So she resembles what she is: a shrunken woman in someone else's clothes.

Heads without hair are such surprising shapes, and so disconcertingly small. You notice the features more. Noses seem enlarged, eyes magnified. Hania turns out to have a livid magenta birthmark, like part of a map, on the back of her head, which was hidden by her hair. She can't see it of course, and no one will tell her. They have all examined one another shyly, equally and simultaneously blemished simply in being shorn. The only comments they have exchanged have been about soap and running water, about inhabiting clean skin. The smell of carbolic.

The red-headed corporal was waiting for them outside the final tent, and as they emerged he acknowledged them with faint nods, ticking off numbers. Marta wonders why he didn't laugh. He looked them over and didn't even smirk. There's going to be food, he said, when the men arrive.

Marta rasps a hand over the sequins on her knee. It's like caressing a dead fish. For some reason this makes her think of Mrs Benka, who was suddenly so overcome with fatigue that she collapsed at the bottom of the gangway. She's tiny in her swathes of maroon over there, resting her back against the cedar's great grey trunk. Her forearms are so wrinkled and papery, looking somehow... cooked. Her skull is grizzled. She looks so much older without her pleat of white hair. Her eyes are closed. She's not dead, is she? Marta scrambles up with much rustling and Mrs Benka opens her eyes. Pats the bark-flecked sand beside her.

'Mrs Benka. How are you?'

'Hungry.'

'Is that all?'

'All? It's all-consuming... as it were. And you, my dear. Have you recovered yourself?'

Marta would rather she had not asked.

'They were very correct, you know, under the circumstances.'

Marta merely nods.

Mrs Benka changes the subject. 'Look over there. On the hillside above the bay. That plantation laid out in squares.' Blocks of deep green. 'What do you think it is?'

Marta shakes her head. No idea.

'Tea. I think it's tea.'

Tea! You drink tea but you don't think of it growing or, rather, you can't imagine how it grows. How does Mrs Benka always know these things?

'They're coming, some of them.' Mrs Benka nudges Marta's knee.

She has already picked out Antoni by the way the young man swings his shoulders as he walks. But those shoulders seem to have expanded. It must be something to do with the jacket he's wearing, which has swelled his torso to a triangle of slate-grey. The upstanding black hair is gone, of course, but a man with a shaved head is less shocking than a woman. Will he be tactful? She looks from Antoni to Marta and thinks she detects apprehension on the girl's drawn face. Has he recognized her? He has. His smile is huge. Really, he must have extraordinarily good teeth. A neat, strong chin too, now that the beard has been removed.

'You look like the cast of an operetta about to have a picnic,' he says, and slides down to the sand opposite Marta. His long legs in their ridiculously wide trousers make a pair of sharp upturned Vs. 'You should keep your hair like that, you know. It brings out the best in your eyes. And your eyebrows.' He reaches out and grazes one of them with an extended fingertip.

It tickles very slightly, but at the same time Marta is suddenly conscious that the only hair she has left is her eyebrows, and she knows that Antoni knows this too. That the only hair he has is his eyebrows, and he knows she knows it too. She cannot prevent the image coming into her mind of a soldier with clippers on his knees in the sand in front of Antoni, and the blood floods her face for the thought, and for the realization that the image in her mind might be paralleled in his.

Abruptly she pushes his hand away from her face, rolls herself to her feet and plunges away from the cedar's shade. More and more men are padding over the sand from the tents, their newly plucked nakedness covered by American generosity of stripes and checks, in high-waisted trousers and sharp-lapelled jackets. Each man carries a hat furrowed at the crown, but none of the hats matches the suits.

Antoni has got to his feet in dismay, staring after Marta. 'What did I say, Mrs Benka? Did I say something wrong?'

Mrs Benka has a shrewd idea but it's not one she wants to confide. 'Nothing, I think. Best let her be. Leave her alone for a while.' The crowd sitting in the sand is growing by the minute and over their heads she spots the carroty corporal, pink-faced, bustling about with his ranks. 'Look,' she says, wondering if she must be forever dreaming up distractions. 'Here comes our red-headed Jesus with his loaves and fishes.'

And, indeed, the soldiers are approaching the crowd, only their khaki legs visible as they teeter comically behind towers of stacked mess tins.

'Food. At last. I'll go and get her. Help me up.' But meets her already making a return, scuffing a slow path through the sand.

Mrs Benka hooks a little finger through one of the straps of the

281

sandals Marta dangles from her hand and gives a little tug. 'I wonder if the woman who put these in the collection bag thought the person wearing them would have to be walking on sand?'

'Or walking at all?' Marta snorts, and on tiptoe parodies an inelegant wobble, windmilling her arms.

Mrs Benka hurriedly releases the sandal. That's better. 'They're bringing lunch,' she says, 'in boxes. What do you think it will be? What would you like it to be?'

Marta screws up her eyes in concentration. She cannot think what she would like it to be because she cannot remember the tastes she might long for. All she can think of is bread. 'Anything. I don't know. How silly. I don't know. I ought to know and I don't.' How the imagination shrinks. Have they stolen that too?

Having asked the question, Mrs Benka herself has set to wondering and finds the thought of apple fritters lurching into her mind with dominating insistence. She tries to replace them with pork cutlets and potatoes, but the apple fritters will not be budged. Now she fears that whatever it is this British army is providing will come as a disappointment. The apple fritters are in her mouth now. She is salivating for them; can taste them, crisp, tart and sweet all at the same time, as she used to make them for Ania when she was little, and visiting. Ania hooped them over her fingers like oversized rings, then nibbled them off, one by one. It made Old Petrkiewicz shake his head at the tiny girl and her questionable table manners. She laughs out loud.

'What is it? What's so funny?'

'I was thinking about Ania, and how she used to love apple fritters.'

'Oh, I *know*. She still does. Oh, Mrs Benka, I miss her so much. I want to go home. Let me go home.'

Why did she say that? What an idiotic thing to say. What's Mrs Benka supposed to be able to do about it? Against her will she folds herself onto Mrs Benka's shoulder and suddenly weeps there. Stop it! Stop it, you silly cow! Crying all over poor Mrs Benka just when she's about to get real food, when she hasn't shed a tear even when things were so much worse. But here she is, blubbering, and soaking Mrs

Benka's shoulder and making a terrible noise, yet she cannot stop. With all her will, but she cannot.

'Sshh, dear, sshh.'

Mrs Benka clasps Marta's sobbing body, feeling the heave of the girl's rib-cage against her own. Over her shoulder she can see that Antoni, goggle-eyed, is making to run across the sand. Mrs Benka shakes her head faintly and the poor fellow stops in his tracks like an obedient puppy. How she would like to transfer Marta into his embrace, where perhaps she best belongs. But it isn't a young man's comfort that she needs at the moment. It's her mother's. And how much, in all the talking they have done, they do not speak about. Is Marta's mother still alive, after all, under German rule? Her father, wherever he is; her brother and sister? And Mrs Benka's own Krystyna and Ania? You have to assume that all is well, since you cannot know, for to make space for the smallest doubt, to release the reins on the imagination and allow it to trample on those assumptions – and how easily it might do that – would be to remove all the props that keep you going. There are times when the unspoken, the unspeakable, rings in the ears.

41

Real sheets. Real white, laundered sheets tucked tight at the corners on real mattresses in rows on the floor of a huge hall in some sort of institution that the British have taken over. A turbaned Indian in British uniform led them in, spread both hands wide – make your choices, *mesdames* – and backed out, closing the double doors behind him with a barely audible click. Marta cannot remember any anticipation of pleasure as intense as this, where the longing to lie down on this pristine bed is checked only by the desire to delay the moment because the longing itself gives such pleasure.

She jangles out of her spangled dress, lays it at the foot of her mattress, and in her flapping underwear creeps into the delicious bed. The sheets smell of soap and the open air and a hot iron. She stretches out her toes and flattens her shoulders. Wriggles and wriggles into luxury. Hears herself sigh. If she closes her eyes she will be instantly asleep – which will mean that in what will feel like only a moment she will be awake again, required to get up and leave this bed. So she must stay awake as long as possible to be conscious of her pleasure and prolong it.

What a day it's been! First there was that strange food the soldiers brought out to the cedar tree: an orange glutinous mass that Mrs Dablinska found out was beans – apparently baked. 'Truly,' she kept insisting. 'That's what they said.' Then there was that square of pressed dates. The sweetness of them had burst in her mouth and seemed to swell and fill her whole head. She had forgotten about sweetness. She had nibbled and nibbled on her dates and then sucked at her coated teeth to cling onto the taste. Afterwards they had come round with something that they said was coffee, spooned in a brown dust from a tin, hot water poured on top, and again a sweetness, quite different, in a spoonful of thick white gluey stuff, also from a tin. She could have done without their coffee and sucked at spoons of this stuff for ever.

She had thought the food would revive her. She had expected to feel her lost strength flow the length of her in a wave from her toes to her head. But instead her body had been astonished, shocked actually, and she had felt the blood drain from her head until such dizziness came over her that she had had to lie down. And all around her the others were lying around the cedar on the sand, amazement in their eyes. She heard Mrs Benka murmuring, 'We shouldn't have eaten it all at once,' and thought, how could we not eat it all? And then she had passed out.

When she came to it was with the smell of petrol in her nostrils and the sense that this petrol smelled unusual; then the thought that everybody's petrol seems to smell different. She had heard the rhythmic growl of heavy engines ticking over, revving, ticking over, and had levered herself up on one elbow to watch a line of trucks lumber around the bay to park, one behind the other, over by the tents.

She had seen the drivers jump down from their cabs, obviously not British, dark-haired and noisy, joshing each other with gently bunched fists and ruffling each other's hair. Some of them had their arms over each other's shoulders. They had been smoking, and she had thought, yes, that's what I want. A smoke. Without thinking she had got up and walked towards them, on her own, and seen them break out of their laughing group into a line, all staring at her as if she had just plummeted from the moon. Well, she must have looked outlandish, with her mauve sequins and no hair. They had fallen silent, and when she reached them she had realized that they didn't have a language, not even a word in common. And she had been taken aback by their beauty; they had such lustrous eyes, like dark chocolate, such white teeth and burnished muscular arms. Faced by the crowd of them she had felt pasty as beeswax, and starved. So she had been embarrassed, but it was too late to do anything about it, or turn back.

She had stopped a few paces away and tentatively put her fingers to her lips in an empty V, sucking hopefully through them. They had laughed at her mime, one of them shaking out a cigarette for her from a box he pulled from a pocket in his loose trousers, while another lit a match and cradled it upright in his cupped palms. She had leaned over those dark hands to light her cigarette and inhaled so deeply the hot ashy tip had rushed up the cigarette as if she would smoke it out in a single breath. They had stared. But they could have had no idea what joy that inhalation had been. A proper cigarette. Not camp tobacco but something fragrant.

She had bowed her thanks, and they had bowed too, with their right hands over their hearts, so she had copied them, which had made them laugh even more. She must have done something wrong for them to find it so funny, but their reaction annoyed her a little. She had the feeling that her presence was inhibiting them; that she was spoiling their easy friendship; that she had barged in, the uninvited foreigner. So the best thing to do was to edge away, back to her own people, who were sitting up now, sleepy faces all turned towards her. She felt she was being judged by both sides, and found wanting. She had not behaved as you should, though who was to know how you should? But something told her that, had she been a man, the Poles would have admired her willingness to be the first to cross the sand and try to strike up a friendship; had she been a man, the Persians wouldn't have stared so; wouldn't have left off their male camaraderie; wouldn't have laughed at her the way they did. She had felt exposed. She had thought, with fleeting horror, that maybe these men also knew what had gone on in the tents a couple of hours before, and that they were imagining her stubbled nakedness under the inappropriate clothes.

The red-headed corporal was picking his way among the seated Poles, bending, tapping shoulders, pointing out the trucks, and the Poles were getting to their feet and brushing themselves down. They had forgotten her – except, of course, Antoni and Mrs Benka, Hania and Basia. The four of them had made a beeline for her, Basia's Janusz close behind. Hania had said, in her loud voice, 'Hey, you. You couldn't get me one of those too, could you?', puffing on a phantom cigarette, while Basia was smiling, saying nothing, but looking wistful. Mrs Benka had that look on her face, the compressed lips and amused eyes. Antoni was very white. He seemed strained.

They had been lifted bodily into their truck, one man above leaning down and hauling them up, another giving a great shove from below. The tailgate had been closed and away they had gone, their driver racing wheel to wheel with another, the sand spiralling out in plumes behind them. Then steeply up into the mountains by the bay, past terraced rice fields, past the geometric tea plantations and up into thick vegetation above.

If only they had been going slowly, in file. If only they had been stationary, she would have feasted on this landscape. She would have gazed down at this transparent sea to the ribbed white sand on its bed, at the patches of purple in the glittering green. But she thought she had never been nearer death. These lunatic drivers, come to rescue them, were going to kill them by mistake when the Russians, for all their efforts, hadn't managed. It would have been funny if she had not been so frightened. She kept telling herself that the drivers surely knew their road and their trucks, that she must trust them. She wanted to shout out to Mrs Benka that it would all be all right, but the wind in her face made a gagging ball of air in her mouth. And then, as they turned another bend, she caught sight of the carcass of a rusted truck lying on its side, hundreds of yards down in a gully of tangled plants and bouncing water – an old tumble that no one could have survived.

On and on, up and up. But as they plunged through the trees and over the crest she heard herself cry out, one high voice singled out in a sudden chorus of disbelief. The view of the sea was gone. The trees were gone. On this side of the mountain and as far as she could see into the shimmering distance, it was crag after crag of parched brown rock, and the fairy-tale land where sugary dates grow might never have been.

*

287

It was fine as a silver hair deep in a valley, a thread of water, and around it a hazy brushstroke of green. After some minutes she could make out scattered trees, patchy fields and a few flat-roofed, rock-coloured houses. The trucks were slowing down, the race put aside. They pulled up on a stony circle under a gnarled tree grey with dust. The driver leaped down, opened up the tailgate and handed them out, a strong dry palm gripping hers, the other supporting her under the elbow. He motioned to them to follow and led them round the corner to some sort of flat-roofed house with a shaded low-walled platform in front of it. Faded carpets one on top of another were thrown over the floor; weighty cushions covered in carpeting ran round all the walls.

The driver invited them to sit themselves on these cushions, and disappeared through a dark rectangle of doorway that led into the house. She heard his deep voice calling out in the darkness beyond the platform, heard the immediate response, a cry of affable recognition. A moment later he re-emerged, arm in arm with an older man, grey-haired and heavily moustached, who inspected the seated bald Poles with a single sweep of the eyes and disappeared again.

The driver plumped down by the doorway, crossed his legs and lit a cigarette. Nobody spoke. The grey-haired man returned, nonchalantly bearing an enormous tray with glasses of tea. He passed round the platform, dipping his knees slightly before each person so that they might help themselves. The image of a bishop offering communion wine flitted through Marta's mind as she reached for her tea. Two lads were pacing the older man behind him, his sons maybe, no longer little boys but not quite adolescent, their skin so darkened by the sun the creases at their elbows were the colour of charcoal. They carried plates of cakes made with nuts and honey. When Marta glanced up at the child in front of her she caught a look of such pity in his mournful eyes that she tried to smile. The boy murmured something and passed on.

The driver had pulled money from a pocket but the grey-haired man shook his head and seemed to kiss the air while he held one palm up like someone stopping the traffic.

Mrs Benka had gripped her by the wrist. 'These people,' she'd said. 'They are so generous. Who are we to them? They are so generous.'

Again Marta sighs in her bed, pulling the covers round her. Maybe it's a parable. A biblical parable, this country: a land of plenty, of milk and honey on one side of the mountains, infertility and desert on the other, and she may take it as a metaphor. The land itself is neither here nor there. The people are the point, and they will change her fortune. With that thought she allows herself to sleep and with that thought she wakes. But she is clammy with sweat and shaking from head to foot. Her knees have drawn up tight into her chest with stomach pain of a sort she has never known before. Liquid diarrhoea is oozing into the lovely white sheets.

Now she has no thoughts at all as she rocks desperately in her own mess. The cramping subsides long enough for her to think about the sheets and who will wash them. Can she escape before anyone finds out she's the one who has fouled her bed? Then another spasm racks her, and a groan rolls from her mouth on a wave of bitter vomit. The double doors have been flung open, slamming back against the walls on either side. The floor is pulsing to the rhythmic thud of multiple tramping feet. What a waste of soap.

42

She is covered in snails hauling trails of slime up her body. She's been trying to keep them away from her face, pushing at them frantically to keep them from her face, but they don't seem to notice. A big wooden board. That's the thing she needs. She'll have to go and find a big wooden board, but the snails are in the way. She bats at them with both arms but they go on creeping wetly, inexorably towards her face. She wants to scream for help but she has to clamp her mouth shut against the snails, probing for her teeth.

Nothing is certain except that she is floating. She paddles out a hand and ripples her fingers just under the surface. Brings them up to her face. They are dry. So she is floating without water. But there *is* water. She feels it in a cool trickle from the corner of her mouth down her chin and into her neck. The coolness seems pleasant at first but the trickle on her neck irritates her skin like a determined fly crawling steadily down to her shoulder. She brushes it away and hears, 'Ah.' It was like a breath, perhaps her own. Ah. Did she say that? It was whispered, and you cannot recognize a whisper because whispers have no voice. But she might repeat it, and compare. 'Ah.' No. Impossible to tell. Something is moving her head, holding it and moving it, slowly up, then down. She ought to find out because it might be unhealthy. She hauls both hands to her head and encounters a third. She snatches her hands away, thrashing her head to rid it of the extra hand. Something has happened to her. No one has three hands. She is sure she did not have three hands before, so something bad must have happened. She will have to find someone to ask, but then they will see her third hand. Perhaps if she waits it will disappear. Wither and fall off, like a wart. The thing is to time it. Give it a minute. No. A minute won't be enough. Give it five minutes. She starts counting.

It's dark. Or rather dim, as a room might be in the middle of the day with the curtains drawn. But her room doesn't have curtains, since the light never bothered her. Curtains make a room, her mother says. But she likes the line of her window, on the top floor of their block. No one can see in, says her father, so it won't matter. Well, I suppose so, says her mother. It just seems so odd, not wanting curtains. Then Sonia didn't want them either and took hers down, but found she couldn't sleep in the summer with the dawn so early, so she's had to put them up again. This might be Sonia's room then, but it doesn't have that feel. Sit up and have a look. That'll be the way. But she can't sit up. *Don't be so stupid. Just sit up and look.* But she can't sit up.

What's that smell? Long breath. Breathe it in. Harder. It's like... it's like... Jesus, how annoying. It reminds her of something, of some-where... it's just a matter of... Where has she smelled that before? Long, long breath. Walking past, when the door is open. The door has to be open or you wouldn't get the smell. So it has to be summer or the door would be closed to keep in the heat. Then you open the door, and you get the smell. More in winter, come to think of it, because the door's been closed. But there's somewhere else you get it too. At home. Not in her room, not in Sonia's or Gienek's. Not in her parents'... The corridor. The chest in the corridor, when you open it. In among the spare feather beds. You see. You only have to concentrate.

It's enormous, this place. Like a school hall, only the desks are all lying down. In their rows, but lying down. Some sort of game. They're going to have to jump from desk to desk without touching the ground, which might be fun. Ania will be good at that – she's so nimble. And she won't break anything. It's surprising that there was-n't any warning, though. They've never had a game like that before, and now here we go, without a word of warning. She'll have to get her mother to write them a note to say she can't take part. Her feet are far too big to do any jumping.

She is in a tent. In bed in a tent. Where is everybody? Where's Mrs Benka?

Her knees hurt. She rubs them and thinks how cold her fingers are on her hot knees. How bony her knees feel. They must look horrible. Have a look. She opens her eyes and begins to peel back her bedding.

'*Tss, tss, tss.*'

Someone is pushing her gently back. It's a man with very dark eyes, and a stethoscope. She's in bed. She's ill. Why didn't anyone say she was ill?

The man leans down and says something, but she doesn't understand.

She looks into his eyes and shakes her head. Don't understand.

'Do you speak French?' he asks, in French.

Of course she speaks French. Very well, as a matter of fact. *Un enfant doué pour la traduction.* That's what they wrote.

'Are you a doctor?'

'Yes.'

'So… is this a hospital?'

'Well. That would be an exaggeration, but it's the best we can do. I'm told you are a nurse.'

Who told him? 'I… well, not really. Not yet. But it's what I want to do… until the war's over.'

'And then?'

'Tell me when the war's going to be won and I'll work it out.'

He smiles silently. Nods silently. 'You have been very ill, you know, like so many of the others. But you will recover soon enough.'

'Where is this hospital. This place?'

'This? Tehran. South of the city but on the outskirts. The land was marked out to be the air-force school and, who knows, maybe one day they will build it.'

Tehran! How did she get here without knowing? 'How long have I been ill?'

'You have been here a week. How long you were ill before that I don't know. There were too many of you for us to find out or for them to keep records.'

'Where is everybody else?'

He moves round to the end of her bed as if there are important notes there for him to consult, although there is nothing; as if by moving he can dislodge her question.

But she repeats. 'Where are they?'

He shrugs. 'Here, some.'

'And the others?'

'I think you know.'

'Who?'

No answer.

'Who?'

'I'm sorry. I don't have names. We never had names, there were too many of you all being brought together, do you understand? The only thing I can suggest is that when you are able – and you are not yet able, believe me – you will have to see who you can find. They will bring you something to eat, but it will be very small. That's necessary at this stage.'

She is giving him impatient little nods with her chin as if she already knows all this, but she's staring at him with enormous angry green eyes. He wonders if she supposes that all these deaths are his fault. She doesn't look like the sensible sort, who do as they're told. He wouldn't be surprised if she took it into her head to start running round now to find her friends. Well, let her try. She won't get far.

'I'll come and see how you are tomorrow evening.'

'Thank you, Dr…'

'Shirazi.'

'Thank you, Dr Shirazi.'

'Until tomorrow, then.'

Marta lies back. Tehran. She has no idea how far Tehran is from the place with the mattresses and the crisp white sheets, the turbaned

Indian, those wide double doors. The sheets! She peers down into her bed and it is clean. Did she really do something terrible in her bed or was it part of the delirium of being ill? If she really did, somebody will have had to lift her, foul and stinking from those sheets, and wash her down, and carry her here, while all the while she was unconscious, presumably. Better not to know. Never to know who it was. Many of them, he said. So many they don't know the names of who's here and who isn't, that there wasn't time to find out anyone's name. He's over near the door flap, bending over someone else. When he leaves she'll nip across and see who it is.

She can see his mouth opening and closing in conversation with the prone person in that bed. His French is very good. Rather formal, though. But then, so is hers, learned from books and repetitions. What a strange thing that is, when two people have to talk to each other in a language that isn't native to either of them. Could you ever get to know someone that way, both of you never quite expressing what you mean because of this clogging barrier between what you think you want to say and what actually comes out. Suppose she had to speak French all the time, would it change her into a different person?

He's gone. Marta swings her feet one by one out of her bedding and dangles them over the floor. They look like someone else's feet, pallid and flip-flapping in the air on the end of someone else's skeleton legs. She eases herself to the ground and makes off towards that bed. One, two, and she's an astonished heap on the floor, flopped down like a rag doll. It would be funny... but she's stuck.

'Hey, you. What happened?' Someone heaving at her under the arms, up to kneeling.

'Hania!'

'Give me your arm.'

Hania winds Marta's arm over her shoulder and humps her to her feet, swivels her hip to the side of the bed and tips her back in. Panting heavily, but she is strong enough to do it.

'Thanks.' Marta is aware she sounds gruff. She feels gruff for needing rescue, and for Hania being in better shape than she is. 'Weren't you ill too, then?'

'Well, I was. But not as bad as the rest of you.'

'Why not?'

'I didn't eat all that stuff. You know, those beans and the dates, and the cakes. I mean, I did. But not much.'

'Why not?'

'Because I knew that if you've been starving you should only eat in tiny amounts.'

Doctors' daughter. 'Why didn't you tell me?'

Hania laughs. 'Since when can anyone tell you anything? Anyway, it wasn't only that. You had typhoid and I didn't.'

'Typhoid! How did I get that?'

'It was the ship. The water was probably bad and you were one of only about ten people who got to drink any.'

Marta pulls a face. So much for being sensible and not eating the salted herrings. 'What about the others? Mrs Benka and –'

'She's all right. And so's Basia.'

Will Hania not mention Antoni? Will she have to ask?

Hania stands in silence, relishing the moment. Gives in. 'And, in case you're interested, Antoni will recover, although he's pretty bad. Mrs Benka thinks it was when he found you passed out in your bed back there and getting you out that he must have caught it. And then he came down with typhus as well.'

43

They have been in this hospital camp four months now, and in the heat of July it is less cool in the tents than it would be outside in the shade, but outside there is no shade. There are only the lines of tented wards for the Polish refugees, most of them gravely ill, who keep arriving by the truckload in flurries of noise, some having crossed the Caspian from Krasnovodsk, others coming entirely by road, from Ashkhabad on the Soviet side of the Alborz mountains, first to Mashhad and then to Tehran. You can see the mountains beyond the city, vestiges of snow glinting on the highest peaks, even at the height of the hot, dry summer.

Everything is provisional because none of this was expected. The British, who are said to be in control but whom nobody ever sees, apparently got the tents up and handed them over to the Red Cross while the first batch of refugees were still on their way; the Red Cross have garnered a few doctors from the city, almost all Armenians and White Russians, to work the daylight hours on the Red Cross payroll; the night-times, when most people seem to die, are monitored by Iranian doctors whom nobody pays, but none of the doctors has any medication other than aspirin and quinine, caffeine and camphor. As there are only a few trained nurses, most of their nursing staff must be drawn from those Polish women well enough to be on their feet and take responsibility. The women, mothers many of them, already regard themselves as experts in hygiene. This is just as well, since they will not be able to offer much more.

Just inside the entrance to each tent ward is a gas canister with a

Primus stove on which a saucepan is kept permanently on the boil for sterilizing syringes. The woman designated as ward nurse sleeps opposite the Primus stove; a sheet screens her from the double line of beds for the patients who come and go, few of them leaving on their feet. The beds have wooden frames and straw mattresses on bases of roped coconut fibre. Raffia matting on the earthen floor is rolled up and burnt when things get too bad.

The far end of the tent is divided: clean linen, soiled bed-sheets. Behind the tent are the latrines. There is a tent with cauldrons for the laundry; another with cauldrons for cooking, largely rice. Everyone, once she is considered able, is scheduled to take her turn at the catering, in the laundry and on patient care. Poles have devised the rotas.

There is bed space here for 500 people, although many more are brought though the gates, since it is evident that only a percentage will survive long enough to need the beds. Some of the tents have been marked for the serious cases, who are all together in isolation – to protect the others. Makeshift hospitals like this are dotted round the city, some in unfinished buildings, some in schools, and everything seems provisional – except for the perimeter fence, two metres high of barbed wire, that has been erected by the cautious British to keep out the curious and incautious Iranians. If you must have an epidemic on your hands, at least keep it within bounds.

The fence is doing its job. It has held the locals away from the infested foreigners, but it has not entirely deterred them. One morning, when the air was still clear and cool, Marta, Hania and Basia had linked arms to take some exercise along the spiny confines of their hospital camp. From a distance they could see what seemed to be large stones lying at irregular intervals along the line of the fence. But as they got closer they found them to be parcels roughly wrapped in newspaper. Warily the threesome had nudged these parcels under the fence with their toes but then backed away and sat on their heels, scrutinizing their find from a small distance.

'Well,' said Hania. 'Aren't we going to see what's inside?'

'What if they're some sort of booby trap?'

'Oh, Marta. Who would want to hurt us?'

Basia was shaking her head but Marta persisted. 'If not us, then the British. They might have been set for the British.'

'But this wouldn't be the place to get the British, would it? And why would they want to get them either?'

Resolutely Basia began peeling back the layers of newspaper, with Marta and Hania watching, but leaning nervously away none the less. Inside were three eggs, a loaf of bread and a handful of dates. Some family had donated their breakfast to the ailing strangers – and bothered to deliver it. Basia rolled the gift up again and the girls collected as many parcels into their skirts as they could. On their way back to their tent ward they met others making their way out, heading with calm expectation directly for the wire.

Marta's hair has grown into a feathery cap and her upper arms are now as wide as her elbows. She feels well, but also somewhat bewildered. How odd it is to have been released from a prison without bounds into a freedom behind barbed wire. So long as the refugees keep coming, bringing new infestations with them, so long will the hospital and its intimidating fence remain. But, once the need has passed, no one can say what will happen next. The young men who recover will depart to join General Anders and his army – this time, it's been agreed, to fight alongside British rather than Soviet units; but everyone else will once again be at the disposal of forces beyond their control. Marta has no idea where she will be sent, only that it cannot be home to occupied Poland. This doesn't yet trouble her as much as she thought it might, partly because she has no time to brood on it, but above all because her work here is vital: everything she does may save a Polish life.

When she is on the wards she is on her feet most of the day, moving from bed to bed taking temperatures; giving bed baths; pulling soiled sheets from beneath the bodies of men, who turn their faces away in an agony of embarrassment – my body has done this, not me. She is especially sorry for the men who were soldiers before they were arrested, and who had been used to seeing to themselves.

In the evenings she spoons small quantities of boiled rice into the mouths of people who beg her for more, but she is under orders from Dr Shirazi. She sits between the beds of craggy-faced boys and tries to take their minds off the cramping of their stomachs by telling them the stories of every cowboy film she has ever seen. She exaggerates the gory bits and they are well pleased. She listens while an old man who has lost his sight from vitamin deficiency describes the different grasses that grow round the village in the Tatras mountains where he was born and to which he says he will return. Of course you will, she assures him fervently, and neither of them believes it.

At intervals throughout the night she must wake to give injections: into the muscle for quinine; under the skin for camphor and caffeine. Only the women who were nurses before the war are allowed to give intravenous injections, and for that Marta is not alone in being grateful. The Red Cross, it's rumoured, are planning some course of intensive training, and with that in mind they've crated through a supply of white gowns that the nursing staff wear as pinafores over their clothes. But so far the training remains a rumour. If anyone were to ask why, they would reply that no one ever told them over a million Poles had been deported into the Soviet Union, and for sure no one had given any warning that they would arrive in Iran in their hundreds of thousands, and in such a sorry state. Marta, though, is in no hurry. She is popular on the wards and, besides, Antoni is still here.

The men seem to be slower to get well. She remembers thinking – it seems so long ago – when they were outside Wilno at the junction of Nowa Wilejka, waiting for the train to set off to Siberia, how disconcerting it was to be locked up so brusquely among men and women, who had turned out to be as powerless she was. She had supposed, before, that adulthood brought with it autonomy. It had been shocking to discover that wasn't true, and that those older than her had known it all along. And now, mopping at these diminished men, she wonders whether they have been so humiliated by their powerlessness, their enforced passivity, by being done to, by being deprived of action – when surely that is what being manly is all about – that they have lost the ability to fight altogether, even when their adversary is disease. So she makes an extra effort with the men: it will be up to her to make them into warriors again and restore them to the spirit they were all brought up to admire. After all, if she doesn't, what sort of army will General Anders end up with?

But when it comes to Antoni – ah, then, she is torn. He too is slow to recover, having at first been slow to sicken. Initially, Mrs Benka tells her, there was some doubt that he would recover. But Mrs Benka had kept that to herself, hoping that the boy's life would be secured before Marta was well enough to climb out of bed, go in search of him and find out on her own. So it had been. Even so, Marta feels sick with the grief she has been spared.

Now, late every night, after all the doctoring has been done, she perches on the end of his bed and they talk and talk, their voices dropping lower as others drift into sleep. These are the best hours of the day. They are so… comfortable. Antoni, Marta thinks, knows her better than anyone knows her, better even than her father does. She has told him so much, not only about her childhood and her family, but her thoughts as well, what inspires her, what irritates her. And Antoni has listened and laughed, sometimes squeezing her hand. But to her annoyance he clams up when she asks him to tell her about all the things that happened to him after his arrest, about the people he was with.

'I'd understand,' she persists. 'And I've told you everything.'

'But that's not how I am, Marta. I don't find it easy telling people things. And I don't want to. I prefer it this way too. I'd rather listen than talk. Sorry.'

'You make me think you're trying to hide something.'

'Oh, grumble, grumble, Billy-Goat-Gruff.'

'Not so Billy!' And in the dark both smile.

A part of her that she does not recognize wishes she could keep Antoni in this semi-invalid condition, safe, and with her. The Marta she knows, and whom she salutes, is made of sterner stuff. This one commands her to pull her silly self together, will him back into full strength, and pack him off to join General Anders, from where he may never return.

*

Dr Shirazi's shift begins in the early evenings. Like all his colleagues he has offered his services gratis to the Polish refugees, and has to do a day's work before. He's already a tired man when he signs himself into the tent hospital and its stringent quarantine routines. Rumour has it, says Mrs Benka, who scoffs at rumour, that the sheer variety of infectious diseases the Poles have brought with them is beyond these doctors' experience, so they don't mind not being paid. It's an education in itself.

Marta will have none of that. 'They're doing it out of the goodness of their hearts.'

'Oh?' Mrs Benka's thin grey eyebrows arch in a parody of disbelief. 'Goodness of their hearts!'

'Well, you're the one who keeps saying how generous the Iranians are. Don't you remember? When they paid for our tea and cakes coming here? The food they leave us.'

'Different Iranians.'

'What d'you mean?'

'Those people have nothing to gain. And the ones who keep leaving the parcels, we don't know them and they don't know us. They've nothing to gain,' repeats Mrs Benka, as if she's only just thought of the implications of that. 'Not even our thanks. They're anonymous. Now that's true altruism, isn't it?'

'They're not anonymous,' asserts Marta stoutly. 'God knows.'

'God. Yes, of course!'

'And, and,' Marta is triumphant, 'how can a doctor treat someone anonymously? They're bound to know. So you're not being fair. You're setting a standard of altruism that Dr Shirazi and the others couldn't match however hard they try.'

Mrs Benka senses herself trapped. Maybe Marta is right. And yet, and yet. 'Nevertheless, Dr Shirazi is gaining something. Treating us is making him a better doctor. He'll advance. It will be good for his career. Although, to be honest, dear, I think we are learning something as well. Whoever would have thought of feeding people dying of pellagra with raw minced lamb – not us! But it works. And turnip juice for gallstones! Yoghurt for diarrhoea! If ever I get home I shall remember these remedies, except that I trust I'll never need them again. All the same, I insist our being here will turn out to be good for Dr Shirazi's career because it will make him a better doctor. But that doesn't mean it will make him a better *man*.'

'Don't you think he is a good man, then?'

'I couldn't say. Perhaps he is, but then again perhaps he isn't. But it's not the point. Being good and being a doctor don't necessarily go together, don't you see?'

'No, I don't. I think you have to be good to want to be a doctor at all.'

'No, you don't, dear. You probably want to be loved.'

'Loved!'

Dr Shirazi floats before Marta's eyes with his aquiline nose and straight lips. He is so distant, so quietly correct in his manner, even a little stiff. He doesn't give the impression of someone who wants to be loved. He gives the impression of someone who wants to get it right, who doesn't want mistakes on his conscience. Though, of course, all of them who are getting better are grateful to him. Is that what Mrs Benka means by being loved?

So Marta has found herself observing Dr Shirazi and his manner as he stops by each bedside, takes a pulse, asks a question. His hands are dark against the white cuffs, and he bends, straight-backed, to be sure to catch the answers. On one occasion he seems to sense he is being watched and flicks his head towards her before she can look away. At a distance you'd think he has only one eyebrow, like a furry black caterpillar that's paused in its journey across his forehead. He smiles suddenly and she could kick herself for being caught staring. Still, it's a nice smile. It widens his austere face. Softens it. He has invited her to join him on his ward round, since, if she is going to take up the intensive nursing course should it ever take place, she may as well begin her studies straight away. She is flattered that he thinks her capable, that he will share his opinion on his patients in those elegantly muttered asides. Too often he simply shrugs, stifling a red-eyed yawn, and together they roll the body in its sheet.

The day before yesterday he brought with him a couple of cuddly toys that someone must have pressed on him in the world beyond the wire: a fat teddy bear and a flop-eared rabbit with a patched nose. He stood in the middle of the tent hugging the animals like a lost child, turning on his heels to cast about for the right recipients. In the end he made for a pair of cots, side by side along the far wall. One contained a girl, the other a boy, and neither had spoken at all since they were brought in. Dr Shirazi tucked the teddy bear into the girl's lap and wound her arms round it as if he was about to tie a knot in them. Then he leaned over the boy and repeated the procedure. The children's blank faces didn't alter, their vacant eyes didn't flicker, but Marta thought they clutched their toys closer to them. By the time Dr Shirazi was preparing to go home both children were dead.

Marta had looked down at the small body as she gathered the top corners of the girl's sheet, preparing to roll it onto a stretcher that she and Dr Shirazi would have to carry between them to the tent morgue. Tomorrow morning it would disappear in one of the trucks that arrive every day, for these bodies have to be buried immediately.

'Why did you give the toys to these two particularly?'

Dr Shirazi gripped the bottom corners of the sheet. 'Because dying alone is a terrible thing. Their pain was bad enough. But for a child. First to be alone and then to die alone. Is that not the worst desolation?' Looking down he nuzzled at the lifeless toes with his fingertips through the tousled fabric, for a moment bringing to mind Marta's father and his early-morning Sunday efforts to get her out of bed in time for church. Then he said, 'It is always this that makes it so hard. The children.'

Dying alone, and without names. Nobody had known their names, and the children hadn't divulged them. He hadn't said dying was terrible, only dying alone. If you are a doctor you have to get used to people dying, and what has that to do with being loved? The trouble is, she thinks *she* may be getting used to people dying – perhaps because they are not close to her. She is sorry for the little ones who didn't live out their lives. She is moved by the old man, who had clung so determinedly to the images of his village as if his memory were a photograph album he had lugged across the continents. But she feels she is becoming matter-of-fact about what cannot be altered. So she wraps sheets round the bodies that will be buried wherever it is they take them, and, when she can find one, slips in a holy picture; but what goes through her mind is the repeated incantation, let my family only be safe. Let Antoni only be safe. Don't let Mrs Benka die.

Just before he left to go home, Dr Shirazi had complimented her. 'You did very well,' he said.

'I was only doing my job,' she'd responded, gruffly, unschooled in accepting compliments.

'You're not expected to do anything else,' he said. 'After all, I am only doing mine.' There had been a silence, and he had added, 'We can't do more than we can do. And I am sorry that someone like you should have to face these things.'

Then yesterday as he was coming in he had handed her a small heady bouquet of pinkish roses, as if he wanted her to hold them for him while he took off his jacket. It had taken her a moment to realize they were a gift to console her for the deaths of the two children. It was kind of him to try to make her feel better, but there wasn't anywhere to put them until Mrs Benka, breathing them in, had found an empty can with a torn illegible label, and stood them in that.

'Lucky girl,' she said. 'Lucky for all of us. When was the last time we saw roses?'

But the airless heat of the tent is bad for flowers and they are already wilting, unobserved, in their place on the boxy table by Marta's bed.

44

Antoni has decided that he is strong enough to lean on Marta's arm and shuffle out into the velvety darkness where they can sit on the stony earth and look north towards the city and its distant lighted windows. The smell of petrol hangs in the air. Antoni's bare ankles gleam whitely.

'I shall have to start exercising and get these flimsy things back into shape.' He slaps his atrophied thighs. 'What do you think, Commander Nurse Dolniak? How long should it take?'

'I haven't the faintest idea. Mrs Benka will know, or Dr Shirazi.'

'Oh, yes. He'll know all right.'

'What's the matter? Don't you think he will? I'll ask him.'

'Well, you'll have plenty of opportunity to do that.'

'Antoni! What *is* it? What's the matter with you? You sound so... so sour.'

'I heard you got flowers.'

How word does get round. 'Yes. Roses. They smell marvellous. Shall I get them and you can have a sniff.'

'Marta. No. I don't want to sniff Dr Shirazi's roses.'

'Why not? Oh, for heaven's sake. He was only trying to cheer me up.'

'What about?'

She has not told Antoni how many people have been dying, since there is no need for him to know. It could be bad for morale. Optimism is the thing when people are ill, or they may take a turn for the worse.

'I couldn't do what you do,' he says suddenly.

'What?'

'Sitting with people. Telling cowboy stories to children who don't wake up next morning.'

Well, if he knew about the roses... She shrugs. 'It's what nurses are supposed to do, isn't it?'

'Do you talk to them about God?'

Now she's uncomfortable. 'No. If someone comes and sits next to you when you're in your sickbed and then starts prattling on about God, you can only think one thing. And since I'm not a priest I can't give them absolution, so what's the point of making them panic? I'd rather die without knowing I was going to, wouldn't you?'

'If I'd really gone to the Vatican – the way we cadets were supposed to, remember? – I'd have had to be giving them absolution.'

'So you would.'

'But I don't think I could.'

'Why not?'

'Because absolution is about setting people free, isn't it? Freeing them from guilt or from their sins so that they can enter Paradise pure and cleansed.'

'Yes, and what's wrong with that?'

'Well, everything, really. It seems to suggest that, so long as you can get into Paradise, it actually doesn't matter what has happened on earth because now you've got all eternity in bliss, or whatever, and the short time you spent on earth wasn't important. It was just a prelude. A sort of hanging around and waiting for your turn. It makes a nonsense out of life to treat it as only a rehearsal. At any rate, it does to me. I mean, on that basis, what was the purpose of life in the first place? Why not just skip that bit and just all be in Paradise?'

'But isn't that the point? Not everyone can? There has to be some... selection.'

'Why? Because it would get too crowded?'

'Don't be silly, Antoni... it's serious, it's –'

'But it makes no sense. You get selected by the grace of God over which you have no control, or you get selected because your sins are forgiven you through true repentance. How can it be both? Or either, come to that? And the business of forgiveness. Marta. Think about it. A priest has the right – no, he's charged with the duty to forgive people their sins if they are truly sorry. But, when people do awful things to one another, isn't it for those who've been hurt to do the forgiving? How *dare* the Church, any church, decide it has the right to dole out forgiveness on other people's behalf?'

'But it doesn't forgive them on other people's behalf. It forgives them on God's behalf. And anyway here, Antoni, if you had been a priest and you'd been here... these people are the ones who've been hurt. They're the victims, not the culprits.'

'But not free of sin. You're not divested of your sins by being a victim. You're just a sinner who's been horribly treated by worse sinners – and if they repent, well, hooray, off to Paradise with them too.'

'But it's not meant to be for you... for people... to judge that, because it's too large for us, isn't that the point? It's not for us to judge, it's for God.'

'I'm sorry. I don't buy that. It seems too conveniently circular to me. God makes the world. Puts people in it he's created in his image. Lets them run around doing awful things to one another on the grounds that he's given them free will and couldn't possibly interfere, but then says: Oh, and by the way he's the only one to decide who can be forgiven and who not when it comes to eternity. Really, what was the point of creation in the first place if it was all going to be one horror after another? And don't tell me it's all a test of faith because, honestly, Marta, I've begun to wonder. I don't think I believe in any of that any more... or not enough. Or not in the right way.'

'Really?' She is shocked. 'Why not?'

'Isn't it obvious? What God's creatures are capable of doing to each other.'

'But it was the atheist state.'

'Still God's creatures. Given free will to be atheist – and then set about destroying believers. Where's the logic in that?'

'God isn't supposed to be about logic, is He?'

'All right, then. It's an odd way of indicating his existence, or his purpose.'

'But He doesn't have to indicate it. It just is.'

'It just is what?'

'Nothing. It just is.'

'No matter what happens? No matter who dies, or suffers? At whose hands?'

'I suppose so.'

'All-loving, all-knowing!' He's mocking and she flinches. 'I'm sorry. I'm not getting at you, but I can't go along with all that. At least I think I can't. Or let's say I'm not so certain any more.'

'Just as well you didn't go to the Vatican then. Perhaps you should set up with Mrs Benka. She hasn't just begun to wonder. She doesn't believe in God at all.'

'I know. But I'd rather set up with you.'

Such a big black sky. The stars here aren't as many, nor as bright as they were in Teren Uziuk because from somewhere beyond the barbed-wire fence there is a permanent haze of smoke as if from hundreds or thousands of small fires. Its sweetish, heady smell reminds her of the dung fire Mrs Benka cooked over in Teren Uziuk.

What does he mean exactly?

'Set up with me?'

'Afterwards. After the war.'

'But "set up with me?"'

'Oh, don't you see? Wait a minute.' He scrabbles to get to his knees facing her, wobbling somewhat. 'When I come back, Commander Nurse Dolniak, will you marry me?'

He has all the pallor of the bed-ridden and his face is a disc of paper in the night. She has a vision of them side by side in the church in Poznan, Antoni a spectral groom, thin as a pencil with his scrubby black hair unnaturally short, and she in her sequins and sandals, or got up like a nurse on her father's arm. He is in uniform, of course. And her mother looks on, hands clasped under her chin with a look on her face of both astonishment and triumph. *You'll never find a husband if you go about dressed like that.* The endless argument about putting on her white gloves before going out into town. *But I don't want a hus-*

band! You will, Marta. You say that now, but you will. When you meet the
right man, believe me, you will.

And of course she *has* met the right man. Here he is, wobbling on his knees, waiting for the answer which is such a long time coming. Suddenly she remembers Ania, who had so longed for Antoni to go down on his knees for *her*, way back when they were still children, and how Marta had scoffed at the very idea of marriage. But now here she is, the one who wants to be with Antoni, not only with Antoni rather than with anyone else, but with Antoni rather than not. In fact, what she wants is for him to put his arms round her and kiss her and kiss her, and... Yet at the same time panic grips her as if walls are closing in, doors clanging to, bolts drawn across. Just as it did when she was younger, marriage sounds like an ending rather than a beginning. A happy ending, the fairy-tales would have it, but an ending none the less, an entombment piled high with shopping bags and cupboards for the best chinaware. Lists and routines and households. Is it possible to have the husband without the household? Without that window-wiping, curtain-measuring life indoors, seeing to the mending while the children recite their homework?

Can't there be another way of being married? She cannot imagine it. She needs to ask Mrs Benka, but Mrs Benka has been a widow for so long she might not remember. And maybe, because Mr Benka died without warning, so long ago, all she will remember will be those things she regrets having lost. But isn't that the point? If you want to be with that man, then perhaps you have to accept all that domestic wifely stuff as well. Although Ania's mother didn't do that, or at least not in the usual way. When Marta thinks of Ania's mother she doesn't think of pastry and ironing and serving tea, but of an easel and large watercolours draped on the furniture to dry. In Marta's family drawing room Ania's mother was dubbed 'that crazy Krystyna' and 'a bit of a bohemian' — affectionately, it's true, but with a sort of distancing relief. *She* may be a bit of a bohemian, but fortunately we are not. And that's the trouble. Ania's mother's mother is Mrs Benka, who let her daughter grow up to be a bit of a bohemian, which ironically ended up with Ania longing to get married. Whereas Marta cannot but be her own mother's daughter, for all she wrestles with that, for all she struggles not to turn out the same. She can't paint. She doesn't know how to be bohemian.

She has been silent so long that Antoni has sat back on his heels looking rebuffed. Hurt. He thinks she doesn't want him. She does, she does. It's all that other stuff.

Antoni had thought she loved him as much as he loved her. It had not occurred to him she would turn him down. His voice is tight with disappointment. 'I'm sorry. I only meant…'

'No, Antoni. My… my darling. You don't understand. It's not you. It's just that I'm… this sounds so stupid… but I'm afraid.'

'Afraid? You? What of?'

'Of getting married… of *being* married.'

'But why? What's so terrible about being married?'

How do you try to explain to a man what a man cannot possibly understand? When he was single her father was a young officer. Then he got married. He remained an officer, and in time he was promoted. He had a wife, they had an apartment, they had three children but outside the apartment his life was unchanged – and he was outside it most of the time. What was her mother when *she* was still single? Marta is chilled by the realization that she never asked. Her mother was her mother, and her husband's wife, and never once complained that she had lost the person she used to be. But not complaining need not mean there is no complaint. Perhaps the only reason she wielded the threat of spinsterhood over Marta's head, as the penalty for being unladylike, was that spinsterhood was comparatively worse. So bad that it cannot be borne. And indeed, Marta has never met a woman who was not married. Widows, yes, but never one not ever married at all. 'You're going to have to get married one day or you'll end up on your own,' Ania had said. So Antoni is offering to rescue her, throwing a lifeline against remaining alone in a world where no woman remains alone. Being alone is a terrible, terrible thing. But she doesn't want to be rescued, passive princess in the tower: what she wants is Antoni, here, as he is now, his breath and hers mingled, his body so close to hers you wouldn't know whose was whose.

Something hot slicks through her abdomen, and she swallows.

'Marta?'

'Sorry, sorry. I was just thinking. I'm muddled. I'm trying...'

'Please. Marta. Tell me this one thing. Are you turning me down? Are you really turning me down? Because if you are I don't understand. I thought we –'

'No. Oh, Antoni, no!'

'But you're not accepting either?'

'I am, I think. I am accepting you... it's just –'

'The marriage bit? Maybe one day you'll tell me why, but if you like we could live in sin like a pair of gypsies.'

'Don't be silly! You don't mean that.'

'No, I don't. But you know, if that's what it has to be, if that's the only way you'll have me, then I would mean it.'

Living in sin! Long cigarette holders and gypsy clothes. Her parents would refuse to visit. Sonia's face! She's grinning even as she knows they can't do that.

'But if you want you can wait till I come back. If that would help.'

What if he doesn't come back? There'll be thousands of spinsters because of all the men who never come back, living sad and lonely lives with nothing to look forward to. By being single because there's no other way.

'Don't go.'

'I have to.'

'I know. Don't go. Please don't go. You're not well enough and there'll be plenty of people for General Anders to make up his numbers.'

'I have to.'

'I know.'

'And I couldn't live with myself if I didn't.'

'I know.'

'And you couldn't live with yourself if I didn't.'

Couldn't she?

'You couldn't. And what would you say to your father?'

311

She would say, I only wanted what's best for me. And get that awful, unanswerable look.

'What would *I* say to your father? Have a heart, Marta.'

Have a heart, put aside your cavilling and accept the man because you love him and you want him, and because he is back on his knees. In the dark she too kneels up and stares into Antoni's face, which she cannot properly see, as if she has to memorize its details now lest she never get the chance again. She cups both hands on his jaw and runs her thumbs along the line of his cheekbones, rubbing up and down in tiny movements like someone painstakingly polishing and smoothing a roughened surface.

He removes these hands and kisses them one by one on the heel and, still holding them, straightens his arms until hers are pinioned by her sides. She is four years old, her father instructing, keep your arms straight, don't bend your elbows, and with his hands under hers lifts her balanced on those straight arms up, up, higher than his head, and she is proud and terrified, holding her breath.

I want to be loved.

'And I'm not going now. Not right now. As you keep saying, I'm not fit yet. Look!' He keels stiffly to one side like a bottle someone has nudged over with a sudden toe.

'Antoni!'

Marta bends over him in instinctive alarm. Instantly his arms are on her shoulders, and as he rolls onto his back he pulls her down on top of him. A car hoots in the distance. She lies perfectly still but feeling that her quickened heartbeats are shaking her and shaking him, rib-cage to rib-cage. Her body is still bones and corners, a long way from the round breasts and hips that so vexed her, that used to make men turn in the street to look. How she hated that. But now, without the womanly shape, without flowing hair, she is stretched the length of a man's body for the first time, face down, frozen by uncertainty. Really her heartbeats are a problem.

Something is pressing into her abdomen and she shifts slightly before she realizes what it is. Surely he can't! She wriggles to be free.

'Shh. It's all right.'

'Antoni, I don't…'

'It's all right. You're perfectly safe. I couldn't if I wanted to.'

'Why not?'

'Because, as you keep pointing out, I still haven't the strength.'

The strength! What strength is needed? She feels such a child now, clumsy in her ignorance and angry that she doesn't know, that no one has ever told her. She has learned what people with power can do to those without; she has learned how the system works and how to read the shifting expressions on an official's face. She is learning what it takes to live, but above all how little it takes to die. But she doesn't know about the particular strength that is needed, that Antoni hasn't got.

But she wants to know. She *will* know. There is a tingling heat between her legs and she wants to touch it. She wants Antoni to touch it but dares not say so. She lays herself over the hard ridge of him thinking, if she could only rub herself from side to side on that, but she does not move. If he were not still weakened, if he did have the strength… why does it have to be that he doesn't? Thank God he doesn't. She holds her breath. Notices how still he is, like a corpse. *Don't think of corpses.*

Gradually the pressure from his body subsides and he seems to be breathing again. How odd that one small part of a man can behave so separately from the rest of him, can have intentions that he himself apparently cannot fulfil. But if he knows he can't do it, then he must have done it before. Who with? When? Surely not when he was a cadet hiding out at the Archbishop's palace; surely not after he was arrested. So when? She can't ask. She has never found anyone so easy to talk to, but she cannot ask about this. Suddenly she is made shy and all the old ease they had evaporates.

She rolls off and lies by his side on her back looking into the sky. They'll never again be able to be the untroubled friends they were before. Every time she meets him now this thing will be between them when it was so easy before.

Now what? It's absolutely necessary to say something to break this silence. Their previous silences have been companionable or plain fatigue. But this one, she can't just leave it. She can't just mutter, best be getting back, then shake herself down and offer him her arm back to the tents.

It is so late now that the lights of the city are going out and the stars are brighter. She could just sleep out here in the warm night, close her eyes and sleep here where she is, on the ground, why not? There weren't many nights when you could do that back home, when you knew it would be warm enough all night long, without the early-morning chill just before dawn that left you stiff and curled up against the cold. But here... the air is so soft. Next to Antoni, why not? But what will people think – the ones who are always up in the early morning, patrolling the fence for the strangers' gifts? Or the strangers themselves! If they can peek through the fence and see these two shapes snoozing in the open, what will they think? But it doesn't matter what they think. It only matters when it's people you know. Who know you. Mrs Benka. Always up and out before everyone as if she needs to be tracking the world while it's still empty. What would she think if she were to stumble on them? I see, dear, she says, with a sort of amused finality in her tone, and peers over the top of her glasses, all arching eyebrows and question marks. No, you don't see, says Marta, cross at being misunderstood over something so important. You don't see at all.

'What don't I?' mumbles Antoni, who has fallen asleep.

'Nothing. Shh. Sorry. Nothing. Go back to sleep.'

Marta turns on her side to face him and watches his sleeping profile, untroubled, so it seems, by the things that trouble her. She lays her arm over his chest and immediately one of his hands loops up to clasp it.

'Ssh!' she repeats, under her breath.

'Mmm,' he says, and turns on his side away from her, still holding her arm, drawing it over him as if it's a covering. Now she's lying with her face against his back. Yes. She can sleep like this, why not?

But something has penetrated the floating balm of the moments before deep sleep and Antoni is briskly awake. He squeezes her fingers and sits up.

'We mustn't,' he says. 'I'd like nothing better, but we mustn't. Your friend Hania would never let us hear the end of it. Word gets round and where are you? Come on, my love. On your feet. Help an invalid back to his crib.'

In fact, he is helping her up, hands gripping hands. 'But this won't hurt, will it? I can manage this.'

He kisses her as if he's eating her and she finds herself gulping him in. And again there's that pulsing heat, twitching between her legs, as her entire body yawns towards him. But his strength, such as it is, goes into his kisses.

No one was about as they slipped back to the tents, hand in hand. She helped Antoni back into his bed and saw how his legs were trembling, all the muscles shocked by having to bear his weight. He had put his arms round her neck to whisper good night and she thought of a small boy unwilling to let his mother go. There's tomorrow, he said, and was asleep.

She cannot sleep, though. She plays over every syllable again and again. She touches her lips and tries to recreate exactly his pressure. There's tomorrow. Imagine tomorrow.

But she is distracted by a sudden spasm in her abdomen, and then an involuntary gummy trickle into her bed. What the…? She sits up and by the light of the rising sun seeping dimly into the tent she makes out a dark smear on one of her thighs. Pats it with a fingertip and brings it up in front of her face. Sniffs it. The metallic smell of blood. It's been so long she's forgotten about having periods – every one the expectation of a baby that isn't to be. Antoni had thought he was proposing to a woman, probably unaware that at that moment she might not have been fully a woman at all. But now it turns out that she is, sufficiently restored to health to be fertile again. All this time, these months and months she was effectively barren, but tonight, with Antoni… should she read something into this? Is it Antoni who has reminded her woman's body that it *is* a woman's body?

In the back of her mind she hears Mrs Benka's dry chuckle. Not

315

one for signs and omens, Mrs Benka. It'll be the food that did it, dear.

And then it occurs to her. Pavel Kuzmich with his drunken clumsy offer! It wouldn't have helped her in the least, would it? She couldn't have got pregnant if she wasn't having periods.

45

Sleep on it, people say, and you'll feel different in the morning. The resting mind may recognize solutions that the feverish wakeful one passed over. Last night the marrying thing was insurmountable; this morning she is hollow-eyed but triumphant. She will become a doctor, like Hania's mother, who was kept so busy – out of the house *and* for the benefit of society – that she even had to let her daughter run wild. And it didn't do Hania any harm at all. Although, of course, the sensible Basia had been there to keep an eye.

Marta sits up and rubs her palms over her cap of hair. She could run to Antoni now and whisper him her discovery: you won't believe what I thought up in the night. And he, half asleep, will gaze at her through blurred attention and a dozy smile, and maybe mishear or misunderstand. No. Leave it till tonight and meanwhile think about it further, nurture the idea, prepare herself for his searching questions so that she doesn't sound the impulsive creature that everyone always said she was. Take it slowly. Don't rush it. It matters too much.

In the evening Dr Shirazi will arrive, already rubbing his eyes. Destiny invented him for her, conjured him up to be her teacher and guide, and then lead him to the tent where she lay sick so that when she recovered she might become his disciple, and he so thoughtful with his deep dark eyes and quiet smile. She likes the way he truly cares about his patients – no matter what Mrs Benka might cynically presume. She will be the most attentive student nurse he has encountered; she will ask questions and listen to the answers too, write them down, commit them to memory. Once the war is over and she is home again, she will apply to study medicine, and they will be astonished at what she already knows. Airily she will respond to that astonishment by saying that she learned her skills in the field, and that her teacher was a great doctor, a man of quiet and dogged generosity who spoke to her in such elegant, formal French that she sometimes wondered who he really was.

All day Marta carries out her duties both more soberly and with more determination than before. Every bed has become her school, every feeble patient not simply a suffering human being but a breathing textbook whose pages and paragraphs she must cram into her mind. Halfway through the morning they bring in an old man, delirious with fever, his lips cracked and his skin so dry it seems somehow parched from inside.

She is told to give him water, but carefully. She doesn't need to imagine how the water tastes to him, or how desperately he wants more than she is allowed to allow him – she remembers all that. But now she tries to understand what, exactly, the water is providing to his system as it trickles down his scrawny throat. His Adam's apple rolls and bulges under his wattles like a trapped ball as he gasps for each swallow, and when she withdraws the cup he struggles after it, which makes her pat at him as you might a child fighting to wake from a nightmare. His body is wrong to demand and demand more. His body doesn't know what's good for it.

She looks down at the gasping old man and sees his eyes fixed in entreaty on her face, and she cannot meet his eyes. He is not really old. He has been aged. Maybe he was a soldier, and will be one again; maybe an officer wielding authority. But, at the moment, she is the one wielding authority because she has control of the water cup. Which is all that matters to him. Which she can proffer or withhold.

'Please, nurse. I beg you, just a little more.' His voice is as dry as the stubble turned grey in the fields.

'I'll come back within the hour,' she says, knowing that to him the hour will be an eternity.

She turns away clasping the half-empty cup close to her stomach to keep it out of his sight, but senses the twin studs of his eyes

318

boring through her from back to front, latching onto what they are looking for. *What's that heartless girl going to do with the rest of my water? Pour it away?*

She moves about the tent that is her responsibility. Changes sheets. Boils up syringes. Checks temperatures and blood pressure. Checks the time. Returns to the old man to mete out the rest of his water but he hasn't lasted the hour.

Marta stands at the foot of his bed gazing down at him in disbelief while her hopes of a medical career shrivel inside her. His mottled twig hands clutch his sheet as if he's only just won a tussle against someone trying to pull it off him. It seems to her that the tight twists of cloth in his brittle fingers are all that is left of her great plans. Why didn't she let him have all the water he wanted if he was going to go and die on her anyway? At least he'd have enjoyed the drinking while it lasted.

When Dr Shirazi slips into his evening shift he is carrying a bunch of tiger lilies. The roses won't have lasted, that's what his eldest sister warned him. Roses never do well in airless places when it's hot. They're not good keepers. Always better on the bush than in the vase. And, indeed, he notices his first bouquet on the box by Mademoiselle Dolniak's bed near the little gas stove, their stalks thrusting upward, but the heads drooping like sleeping travellers, the petals thinned and already fringed with brown. For a moment he rubs one of the wilted blooms between finger and thumb and sniffs their dusty fragrance. Still cradling his lilies, he takes up the tin can vase and empties it onto the earth outside the door of the tent, throwing the dead flowers to one side. He refills the can and stands the lilies in. Now to find the girl. Who is sitting in a heap of dejection on the ground by the bed of a new patient, already deceased.

She takes in the approach of the trousered legs, the hem of white coat.

What a wan and hopeless face is this, so ringed about the eyes! 'Mademoiselle Dolniak.' Now he needs both hands, so he stands the encumbering vase on the ground at the foot of the bed. 'Allow me to help you up.'

But she sits on, staring up at him with the numbed expression of someone who has finally seen more than she ever wished to see.

'What has happened here?'

She gestures at the occupant of the bed above her head. 'He died.'

Dr Shirazi is baffled. People are dying around them all the time. What is it about this one that is worse? 'Was he a friend? A relative?'

She shakes her head.

'Was he… particularly distressed?'

'He wanted water.'

'Did you not give it to him?'

'I did. But I gave him only half a cup.'

'Well, but that's exactly right.'

'But he wanted more. He wanted more so much.'

'More could have killed him.'

'But if he was going to die anyway why couldn't I have given him more?'

'Because you could not know he would die anyway. Perhaps if you had given him what he wanted his death would be on your conscience. I can assure you that in this case it is not.'

'But that's not all it's about, is it, conscience? It's about easing suffering too, isn't it?'

'Of course. But we're not magicians. People are all different. Circumstances, conditions change. We study, and then apply what we have learned, and learn some more. That is the limit of what we can do, Mademoiselle Dolniak. In the end, we are in God's hands, and it may be He makes decisions that are unfathomable to us. Ultimately it's not our decision, so, if something does not go as you feel it should, you must not blame yourself.'

'Then why bother at all?' mutters Marta, but in Polish, and therefore to herself.

Dr Shirazi frowns at the alien syllables and adds, 'But of course we have to keep on studying. We know more than we did and not as much as we shall. But now, I think, we should put some of that into practice. I don't think you should sit here any more. Go outside and walk about for a while. Come.' He holds out his hands and hauls her

320

up, but doesn't immediately release her hands. He peers into her face. 'I will find someone else to help me with the c–... to assist me.'

He watches her for a moment as she slouches out of the tent towards the dusk. Every line of her body has a downward pull to it, as if she were festooned with weights. It's a body fashioned out of disappointment, apparently over the death of this one old man lying here like a crow fallen on its back, claws in the air.

Mrs Benka has had a long day and the evening is welcome. But why is Marta looking so glum? 'Hallo, my dear. Come and sit with me a while, why don't you? Let's have a cigarette together.'

Marta drops to the ground like a string of onions fallen from its hook. She reaches for the cigarette and sucks at it furiously, pausing between inhalations to glare at its tip, the focus for the inadequacies of the world.

Should she ask or should she wait? Mrs Benka waits.

'You're a doctor,' says Marta savagely, by way of accusation almost.

'Not really, dear. No.'

'But your herbs and potions...'

'Local lore, you know. Palliative rather than life-saving. Why?'

'But the malaria! Most of us got through that.'

'Yes. Luck. It wasn't my doing, I'm afraid. I didn't have anything that could help with that except for cooling people down and whispering encouragement. I think sometimes just being cared for by someone is half the trick, but it really wasn't in my hands, you know.'

'*You're* not going to say we're in God's hands, are you?'

'Well... call it what you like. Why? Who said that?'

'Dr Shirazi.'

'Did he?'

'And if he's right, if in the end we really are in God's hands, then there's no point making all that effort, or any effort. Why not just leave it up to God? But then why am I asking you, of all people, since you don't believe any of it?'

'Just because I don't believe it doesn't mean you shouldn't put the question. But you know, it's a turn of phrase, isn't it? "We're in God's hands." People don't really mean it, I don't think, because if they did truly mean that everything is decided by God then no one would plant apple trees or potatoes or take dancing lessons or cut their hair. They would indeed simply sit back and leave it all to God, don't you think? I doubt if he meant it literally, dear. Lilies of the field and the rest of it, although maybe Muslims don't have the lilies of the field. Nevertheless, I'm sure he was speaking figuratively. There he is, look, so let's ask him.'

'Oh, no. I couldn't.'

'Not? Why not?'

But Marta is shaking her head vigorously. 'I'd be embarrassed. If he meant it figuratively I'd feel such a fool, and if he didn't we might find we'd offended him. And anyway I don't have those sorts of conversations with him. Well, obviously not. I mean, he's the doctor and I'm just a sort of student nurse. And besides, he's so... proper. No. Distant. No. Oh, I don't know. Actually, I don't know what he's like. Whatever he says it's on the same level. Everything he says, you know, it's always complete sentences, and always so formal, like –'

'Shush!'

'Why? Oh!'

Dr Shirazi is walking towards them, shoulders forward, hands in his pockets. A few paces away he stops, opens his mouth to begin one of his sentences, looks from Marta to Mrs Benka and back, drags out a hand from a pocket to mask an apparent yawn, and nods a couple of times.

'Well, well,' he says. 'Good night, madame, mademoiselle. I trust you will both get a good night's rest. Until tomorrow.' He turns to leave – then swings back again. 'Please try not to be too concerned, Mademoiselle Dolniak. We have only so much energy, so we must conserve it, and use it wisely. In the present difficult circumstances, that means we should deploy it on those who are still alive, which is not what I would wish, but it remains so. Good night again, and try not to let yourself become saddened.'

'See what I mean?' says Marta, without conviction, when he seems to be out of earshot.

'Which?' whispers Mrs Benka who fears his hearing may be acute. 'The language or the sentiment?'

Marta doesn't answer. 'I'm going in. I'm tired.' She scrambles up. 'But I'd better check that everyone's all right before I go to bed.'

'And I will come with you.'

As they cross the men's tent they pass by the row where the old man was. The body, of course, has been wrapped and removed. But someone has left a small tribute of flowers at the foot of the empty bed. Mrs Benka recognizes the tin can vase. 'Lilies of the field,' she murmurs uneasily. Marta, though, is stalking purposefully on, head held high. Mrs Benka lingers awhile by the flowers, inhaling their heady lily fragrance. By morning there will be a dusting of deep-orange pollen on the trodden earth floor.

Marta dearly loves Mrs Benka, but she thought for a moment she wouldn't be free of her. How can she go out again with Antoni under the scan of those shrewd eyes? She'd never say anything, of course, but it's not only what Mrs Benka says that matters. Yet now that Antoni's bed is only a couple of rows on, the thought of lying outside again, wrapped around in his arms, which is what she has been waiting for all this time, doesn't seem right. What if he wants to kiss her again? Which he will, surely? She wants him to, she wants to kiss him back, but tonight it would be like a form of blasphemy. She cannot get the image of the parched old man out of her mind. Besides, Dr Shirazi talked about deploying one's energies on the living, but he meant medically. He wouldn't be too pleased if he thought his nursing staff were losing precious sleep by rolling around with his patients under the night sky. Imagine if he came by... And now there is Antoni, pretending to be asleep, unless he really *is* asleep.

She creeps up and bends over him to check, and swoosh! He's done it again. She thinks of a spider. She thinks of an octopus. How many arms has he got!

'Ant—'

'Shh. I know. I know about the old man.'

'How do you know?'

'Basia told me.'

'That beady-eyed Basia. What doesn't she know!'

'You ought to sleep, anyway.'

'So should you.'

'You more.'

'Why me more?'

'Because you're a hard-working woman and I'm lying around in bed all day as it is. But kiss me. No one can see. No one's looking.'

'I bet Basia is.'

'Well then, look under the bed before she escapes.'

So she extricates herself from the tentacle arms to be able to kiss him, but just in a comforting nurse-like way today. Lays a brief lip-shape on his smiling forehead, transfers it to the bridge of his nose, to his left cheekbone, then the right, and the old man drifts into the wings...

46

Antoni is nearly strong enough to do almost anything now. But he keeps his embraces chaste. If only he wouldn't. What harm would it do, since he has to go away? Everyone says that things are different in wartime, the usual conventions brushed from the tablecloth. Everyone always says so. But he's careful of her reputation, which makes her love him all the more, though it infuriates her too. Surely he must feel how ready she is. So ready she thinks she almost knows what to do.

Every night, when they creep like surreptitious children back to their separate tents, her body grumbles at her. There is an ache in the openness between her legs that won't go away, a wetness. And she cannot sleep. One night she flings an exasperated hand to her genitals and presses on the whingeing parts, shut up, why won't you! And finds them hot and swollen, leaping to the pressure of her hand, as if her hand is not hers but Antoni's, not her hand but Antoni himself. Her body swallows her fingers while Antoni has an arm under her shoulders and all his weight on her, and she feels that she herself is disappearing into her own heat, that nothing exists but this surging point like an itch, not an itch, nor quite a pain but a rising intensity that has never been known to the world before. It's rolling over her, engulfing her and she almost cannot bear it, hears a croak and a gasp and under her fingers her genitals are pulsing in spasms out of control. Sweat trickles under her arms, on her forehead; she feels her cheeks are burning.

Oh God, what have I done?

It's not that she's never touched herself before. She has – in defiance of all the prohibitions: it makes you ill; it makes you mad; it's a sin. Everything she's been taught instructed her never to do this, the warnings beginning long before she had any idea what they meant. She only knew that God and her parents expected her to keep her fingers to herself, although, if they caught her at it, she was never certain which of them would be the most distressed. She hadn't kept her fingers to herself, but her curious probings and tweakings never led to anything like this.

For hours she tosses in her bed, tangling her sheet, writhing to escape from herself thinking, *I must wash, I should wash*; thinking, *I shall never do this again*; thinking, *Everyone will know. Just by looking at me, they'll know. How can they not?*

When she wakes for a moment her mind is blank before it remembers, then she scuttles out to the wash tent to scrub away her own heavy fishy scent. She rakes soap through her hair too, and rubs at her face as if she might slough off the old skin to reveal another, undefiled, beneath. But in the tiny flecked mirror dangling from the central tent pole she sees only the purplish rings under her eyes and in them an expression of inconsolable shame.

She cannot face anyone. But they're relying on her. They wouldn't want to have her anywhere near them. But the ones who are the weakest – they're barely conscious, most of them, and they need looking after – they have to be looked after. You can't shilly-shally over them. What else will she have on her conscience if she hasn't the guts to go out and see to them? That'll be the thing to do. Stick with them; spend the working day with them, as her penance. It would serve her right if she caught something from one of them and fell ill all over again, though what good that would do anyone else? Which is exactly the point. She must stop thinking about herself and work off what's she's done.

She ought to eat something before her shift but she's not hungry, and anyway where the food is there are people and she can't face anyone. Maybe she'll find a moment later, when everyone's busy, and sneak off by herself. If she works all day without stopping she'll be able, truthfully, to plead exhaustion and go to bed early. But going to bed, back to bed, where she… How could she? Why couldn't she just have…? Her impatience, her stupid, stupid impatience.

The main thing is not to see Antoni, not let him see her. He knows her so well he'd see in a minute that something has changed and he might want nothing more to do with her. She must work it off: offer to do an extra laundry shift, which no one likes; offer to do all the bed baths; not stop all day. And she doesn't.

During the lunch break Mrs Benka encounters Hania over the samovar and asks if she knows what has come over Marta. She's seems so out of sorts. Yes. Hania's early-morning greeting was rebuffed, Marta muttering incoherently about being especially busy today, although as far as Hania can see today is no different from any other. Well, she's certainly white about the gills, observes Mrs Benka. Do you suppose something has happened? Both minds immediately turn to Antoni. Has there been a falling out? Those two? It seems impossible.

So the two women, the young one and the granny, ferret out tasks for themselves in the relevant men's tent. But Antoni, who is so nearly completely well, isn't to be found, not in the morning, not in the afternoon, and they can't keep prowling round the vicinity of his empty bed without tickling the suspicions of his recovering but still bed-ridden neighbours, toying with their boredom. Where on earth can he have got to?

Come the evening and Marta is even more exhausted than she had planned to be. She hasn't eaten because anxiety blocked her gullet, so her limbs, unsustained, are fluttery. The sheets she boiled have already dried, bright and sun-bleached on the line that stretches the length of two tents. She has tended to the day's newly arrived patients more diligently than they will ever be cared for again. Her face is white and her hands are trembling, but in the invisible depths of her she tells herself that she feels better – so long as she does not think about Antoni. By tomorrow her appearance will no longer betray her, but her demeanour may, her uneasy gestures may. How can she speak to him in an ordinary way ever again, look him directly in the face? Pace

327

for pace he'll follow her around pestering, what's up, what's the matter with you? To which there is no answer that can be spoken.

If only there were a priest here so that she could confess and be purged. Maybe there is one, among the sick, mumbling paternosters in his delirium, but how do you find him? Slip from bedside to bedside, maybe, and ask, or lay your ear to the murmuring lips and eavesdrop. She'll be spotted. Spotted and pointed out. Who seeks out a priest when they haven't got terrible things to confess! Tomorrow's tomorrow. Now she'll slink into her bed, pull the sheet over her head and plummet into sleep.

But as she totters towards the flap of the tent where her bed is, eyed from an anxious distance by her pair of questing friends, her path is blocked by Dr Shirazi, carrying a packet that has been professionally wrapped in flowered paper. One look at her and he clamps it under his arm, lunging towards her. Lines of concern track his forehead.

'Mademoiselle Dolniak!' Out shoots a steadying arm. 'You do not look well. Please be seated.' Doctor's fingers press the pulse. A moment's silence. A shaking head.

'I'm just a little tired. There was a lot of work today and I didn't have time to eat.'

'Not at all?'

'No.'

'That may be the answer then, although... Here. Sugar is needed.' He presses the flowery packet against his thighs ripping off the neat wrapping. Clearly it was meant to be a present for someone.

'No, no. You mustn't. Please don't –'

'Enough.'

The beautiful paper lies torn and discarded at his feet. What a waste. If she had been given that package, Marta thinks, she would have unwrapped it with care, smoothed out the paper until it was ironed flat, to use again. Such lovely paper.

He pulls the top off the box and a dusting of white powder floats out. 'Here.' He holds the box under her nose. There are odd lumps hidden among the powder.

'What is it?'

'It's *gaz*. A confection.'

'What's the white powder. Sugar?'

'Flour. Eat.' He shakes the box at her and flour covers his fingers. 'One, two pieces now. I command it as a medical necessity.'

They'll be furious, the person who was expecting a present and now isn't going to get it. But she wasn't the one who opened the box, and Dr Shirazi is her commanding officer, as it were. The lumps look peculiar in their floury bed, shapeless and heavy, but he wouldn't press anything on her that was unwholesome. Fairy-tale land of dates and honey. She picks out a piece and taps it against the side of the box to dislodge the excess flour. A small cloud rises briefly, then floats down to settle on the toe of Dr Shirazi's shoe.

'Oops.'

He shakes his head impatiently. 'Eat.'

She scrapes tentatively at one edge with her front teeth. 'Mmm!' in surprise. It *is* sweet – though not as sweet as dates or the glutinous tinned milk the British soldiers spooned into their coffee – and chewy. And it's sort of scented. A proper bite now. It has pieces of nut in it. Delicious. She closes her eyes to finish the first piece and immediately wants another. He did say to eat two, but sitting here munching away like a pig at a trough while he's standing in front of her holding out the box, flour all over the place, does seem greedy. She opens her eyes and looks up. He's nodding, go on, smiling. That unexpected smile, which transforms his face. It makes him look so much younger and she wonders how old he is. She takes another piece. Thank you.

'So you like it?'

'It's wonderful.'

'I am glad. It is my favourite. But I can never eat *gaz* without being covered in flour all over the front of my shirt.'

'Why don't you have a piece, then?'

'Ah! But they are yours.' He places the box in her lap.

He can hardly give them to anyone else now, can he? 'In that case, please take some.'

Now both of them are speckled and she senses that she has flour on her nose, which she tries to wipe off with the back of her wrist, but that is floury too. Dr Shirazi is watching her and giggling like a schoolboy. The more she wipes, the more she spreads the flour. 'Aaagh!'

'It is as I said. All over in flour. Allow me.'

Dr Shirazi takes a handkerchief from his pocket and lightly mops her nose clean. Flick, flick. His fingers dance across her cheekbones. He leans forward and blows so suddenly so that she blinks, and the remaining particles scatter. Flour dust, coal dust. Oh, Antoni. Last night, displaced from her mind by Dr Shirazi and his sweets, hurtles back and with it the hot blood of desire and its concomitant shame.

'What is the matter, Mademoiselle Dolniak? Is something wrong?'

'No. I… No. I'm sorry.'

Dr Shirazi backs away, flicking the flour off his clothes with his handkerchief, wiping his hands, wiping his lips. When he looks at her again her face is in her hands. She cannot still, can she, be brooding over the death of that one old man, among the many? He swallows what he had been about to say, turns on his heel and sets off to see to his patients without the assistance of his most assiduous nurse.

'So Antoni has gone,' comments Basia, drying her hands in the wash tent by Marta's side.

'Gone?' Marta is bent low, her hands scooping the water she was splashing from a basin onto her face. She straightens up, and dripping water disappears into the thirsty ground. 'I didn't know he'd gone. Where's he gone to?'

'Oh, I'm sorry.' Basia is abashed. It isn't right that she should know something about Antoni that Marta doesn't. 'It's Colonel Palucha. He came by this morning and asked Antoni if he thought he was well enough to go for an assessment. You know. For the army.' Marta hasn't moved but is staring into the tent wall and Basia scrabbles for words of consolation. 'But it's only for a few days. It's only for the assessment. He'll be coming back first, even if they find him fit. He will be coming back.'

For all she knows Antoni may have been looking for her to tell her so, to say goodbye. But she was in hiding, wasn't she? 'I was very busy today,' Marta mutters, to herself. 'I didn't get to see him today.'

It's only the assessment. He will be coming back. Basia's words roll around in her head like an incantation. Believe quiet Basia, the one who always knows. Let her be right. Let her only be right. He will be coming back. He will be coming back.

She leaves Basia without another word, ignoring her friend, forgetting that she is there at all, and goes out into the night, her hands unconsciously clasped in prayer. Dr Shirazi steps in front of her from the side, as if he's been waiting.

'Mademoiselle Dolniak.'

'Oh. Dr Shirazi.'

'I intended to say. Earlier, but it was… My sisters. I have been speaking about you to my sisters. Telling them how hard you have been working for your compatriots. Too hard, possibly. They have asked me to invite you to be their guest at our holiday house under the mountains. It is cooler than here. The air is very pleasant.' He falls silent, waiting for a response, but there is as yet no response. He goes on. 'It would be only for two days. We understand that you would not wish to be away for long.'

Marta is gazing at him as if she has not understood. But she has understood perfectly well. This is on purpose, she is thinking. This is Destiny. Colonel Palucha has taken Antoni away for a few days, and Dr Shirazi's sisters are inviting me. It was all meant to be so that when we meet again everything can be as it was.

47

'I am very grateful to you,' says Dr Shirazi in a low voice as he escorts Marta out through the gates of Tent City. 'You are my excuse for a short holiday. We have a car waiting.'

It's true. He hasn't missed a single night's work among them. Pah! So much for Mrs Benka's scepticism over his motives. A man who was seeking purely to further his career would take days off when he was tired.

Cupping her elbow, Dr Shirazi guides her towards a dusty black car with a running board and a tubular horn attached to the window-frame. A small grizzled man in a grey collarless jacket and peaked cap is dozing on the running board. His moustache fluffs out in a feathery ripple with each breath. He won't be too pleased to have to wake up.

'Where are we going?'

'Where everyone goes in the heat of the summer. Everyone who can. North, where the air is cooler under the mountains.'

He hands her into the car ahead of him, then settles himself at her side. The driver, mumbled into wakefulness, is plainly embarrassed that he wasn't on his feet and opening doors. He mutters under his breath as he starts the engine and pulls the car round and away from the hospital compound.

Dr Shirazi picks up where he left off. 'Our summer house, as I believe I said. It's what we do, the family. People gather there at the height of summer. Those who can,' he says again, and rests his shoulders against the upholstery. His holiday having begun this early morning, he cannot help himself but close his eyes.

Marta is leaning forward for a view of the passing streets. The sun is still low, the air still pleasant. But soon enough the heat will weigh heavy and all movement will be an effort.

Dr Shirazi's chauffeur clutches the wheel as if he imagines he can keep the car from jolting his passengers, but the stony track is rough and Marta has to clench her buttocks to avoid toppling onto Dr Shirazi. On either side the land is flat and stony, with odd streaks of green in the ground. But within minutes they have turned into a rutted lane so narrow that the sides of the car are only inches from the walls of the tiny mud-brick houses that line it. The car windows are closed, but the air is thick with a penetrating smell of urine and faeces and the engine's hum disappears in a blast of competing voices as shocking as a punch between the eyes. The lane meanders so sharply that Dr Shirazi's chauffeur is now inching the vehicle through a mass of people, who have to retreat to safety into the nearest open doorway. Other twisting lanes lead away from this one – and no doubt from those as well. This place is a maze and they will never get out.

Instinctively Marta shrinks back. Who are all these people? Hooded beggars crouched by the walls are getting to their feet as the car approaches, alerted by the excitement of the crowd, and there are children everywhere, little boys, shouting as they run, dodging between men carrying twin loads in baskets from poles across their shoulders. What is it they've got? She peers into the baskets as the car nudges past – melons, nuts, some green stuff. Small boys teeter with rounds of bread piled high on flat boards they hold at shoulder height, barefoot, pattering urgently. Women shrouded in black lean in the dark rectangles of doorways cut sharply in the mud walls and berate the men with the baskets. The children are ragged, their clothes the same dusty grey-brown as the mud bricks of the buildings growing out of the lane. Some of them are as thin as she has been. Their shoulder-blades throw deep shadows on their backs. Down a turning she sees a group of children splashing in a ditch and the water looks filthy.

Now the car is completely blocked and has to stop. There's some commotion up ahead. Absolutely she has to see, winds down her window and pokes her head out of it a moment before Dr Shirazi, re-alerted, gives an abrupt warning bark, 'Don't!' Too late. She is hanging out of the window. What's happening?

They're trying to heave an enormous box onto the back of a man bent double in readiness, five men, six perhaps... no, more, all gesticulating and yelling instructions. They have raised the box on one edge, now other men have appeared from a doorway to join in at levering up the other, and they are hauling the load up onto the waiting back. He'll surely collapse, won't he, if it's taking so many of them to lift it between them. With each heave they're grunting, '*Yah Khodah! Y'Allah!*', and the man staggers slightly, unbalanced by the great weight, but finds his feet again. More people are making for him as if to join in the heaving and grunting, but all at once the box is in place and he has disappeared beneath it. Just a pair of thin streaked feet in baggy trousers bearing an enormous box away, trotting off round a corner.

Now that he's gone, all attention is on the car and on the fair-skinned, light-haired foreign woman gaping out with round green eyes and astonished mouth. '*Khanoom! Khanoom!*' The children swarm, jumping up and down, thrusting hands up into her face, begging, are they, but giggling too.

'*Tss!*' Dr Shirazi pulls her back in her seat and throws something out of the window. The children scatter and the car sets off again; the driver, apparently cursing, presses irritably along the lane, forcing the pedlars, the women, the clamouring children against the walls. Marta hides back in her seat, her heart thudding as if it is recovering from fear, although she thinks she was not frightened. They swing round another corner and trodden earth gives way to cobbles. The car is rattling now and it's as if they've passed through an invisible gate that has locked behind them, closing off the noise. The mud-walled houses are gone. The crowd has gone, and they are heading uphill along a wide tree-lined boulevard. Smooth tarmac has replaced the cobbles.

'There's water!' Marta exclaims, winding down her window and forgetting Dr Shirazi's weariness and lolling head.

He opens his eyes again. 'Yes. It comes down from the mountains.'

Clattering down deep open ditches on either side of the road between the trees and the shaded pavements.

'It's a wonderful sound. Just the sound. It's like music. For the soul,' she adds, poetically.

'Not just for the soul. Some of them even have to drink it. They wash in it. They wash their clothes in it. Those people you saw. And they get their germs from it, of course. More recently yours.'

'Mine?'

'Those of your compatriots. The camp and the quarantine were a good idea and necessary, of course, but ultimately, if the cholera or typhoid bacteria arrive where there is already poverty, the two will be bound to come together. You could call it a law of nature.'

'So those people... have they been dying too?'

'In large numbers, I'm afraid. Just as your people have.'

'I'm sorry.'

'It's not your fault. No one is blaming you.'

'I understand that, but if it weren't for us they might be all right.'

'Well, until the next infection. The water isn't clean, you know. And if people drink what others have washed in... it is inevitable.'

'But you? You don't have to drink that too?'

'We are more fortunate. Is it not always the case that the poor live at the bottom of the hill, and that clean water begins at the top?'

Is it always the case? She had not thought of water as the indicator of wealth before, but does it have to be so? This isn't the time to begin a discussion with Dr Shirazi, who clearly wants to rest. But look! There are soldiers ambling along in twos and threes, in British uniforms. And Soviet uniforms! She shudders, and once more Dr Shirazi has unshuttered his eyes, understanding the cause of her sharp indrawn breath.

'Are you disturbed by our Soviet occupiers?'

'Our occupiers too. With the Germans. The Russians and the Germans. They've always been our occupiers.'

'But not the British?'

'No, of course not!'

'Why of course?'

'Because they're on our side.'

'Of whose war? No, no.' He can feel the hackles rise. 'Don't worry, Mademoiselle Dolniak. It is simply that for us it has been the Russians and the British who always sought to be *our* occupiers. And now they are. Yet again. The Russians arrived from the north, the British from the south, and it appears we were unable to prevent them'

'Why did they come?'

'The British did not think our king had sufficient animosity towards the German government. So with their new Soviet allies, your old occupiers, they removed him.'

'So that was a good thing, at least.'

'Certainly he had become unpopular, although not for that reason. But the British helped put him there in the first place.'

'Why?'

'It was a time of chaos and they wanted a man who would protect their interests.'

'And did he?'

'Enough, I think. But he also modernized us, you know. Before him, you could not travel anywhere without being attacked by tribes and bandits, and he put an end to that. A strong man. You have to admire a strong man, and we do. Yes, he modernized us.'

Marta does not think the tangled streets, the barefoot children, the mud-walled houses seem very modern. But she is afraid of offending Dr Shirazi, whom really she does not know, and who has invited her to stay with his family. It is an honour. It must be, but she wonders whether he thought her so sickly that she, rather than anyone else, needed convalescence under the mountains where everyone goes. That king, the old one. He can't have been all that strong if Iran was so easily invaded. But then so was Poland, and she had once thought no one could beat the Polish army. But she was just a child back then. What did she know?

'Where is he?'

'Who?'

'The king? The strong one?'

'He? Gone. Abroad. They sent him to Mauritius and gave us

instead his son. Who is young, and they think he will do as he's told.'

'And will he?'

'At the moment he has no choice.' Dr Shirazi gesticulates towards the sauntering occupiers.

If even kings have no choice, thinks Marta, what hope is there for ordinary people in ordinary countries? Are all countries either occupied, or about to be? Britain is not. Not at the moment, and maybe will not be unless it is invaded by Germany. But the Soviet Union? It has been invaded and has not yet managed to drive the invader out. But here, in this country, it is an occupier. So you can be occupied and an occupier all at the same time – but no... The Soviet Union is not occupied because even if the Germans are winning this war, as everyone keeps saying, the government is still Soviet. So that's the difference, then, between invasion and occupation. Is this new king, the one who has no choice, not in charge of his own government? Does he have to do everything the occupiers tell him, and only that?

The boulevard goes on and on, uphill, turns a corner, and she can see ahead of them the sweep of the mountains massively jutting against the sharp blue sky. A rim of bright snow toys with the sun. Imagine walking about in your home town every day with a backdrop like that. Actually, this *is* a modern-looking street, with its solidly imposing buildings which look so new. There are more people out on this wide avenue now, not only soldiers. Men and women walking. Some of the women are wrapped in the black shrouds but some are not. She doesn't know what to make of this. She has been brought up to believe that all the women of the east are hidden beneath veils and kept like chickens behind barred doors by jealous and rapacious husbands.

'Those women,' she says, and then doesn't know quite what to say next. It may be impolite to comment on other people's customs.

'Which?'

'The... the ones in black. Why are they wearing veils?'

'Because they can.'

Because they can? Who would want to dress like that? 'I don't understand.'

337

'The king. The last one. The one the British removed. He forbade the wearing of veils and sent his police out to tear them off any woman who wore one in public. Now he is gone, his police have other matters to attend to. So the veils have returned.'

'But they're not all wearing them.'

'Not everyone wishes to. My sisters do not, as you will see.' Marta is relieved. 'But my mother does.' Oh. 'It is a matter of generation. And is it not often the case that what one regime prescribes, the next forbids? What one proscribes the next imposes?'

'So what is the new king forbidding now, or imposing?'

'Nothing. He has not the power yet, because his country is at the moment simply a military base on the outskirts of the European war. If our occupiers win it and then depart, we shall see. If, that is, they do depart.'

'Why wouldn't they depart once the war is over?'

'Well, perhaps you should ask why they should. Ours is a piece of land that many people seem to find interesting.'

All those brown mountains. Why in heaven's name? She must have raised an eyebrow or pulled a face, because Dr Shirazi is explaining.

'It is *where* we are that interests them, and of course our oil, which since the last few decades, we have learned, no one can be without. Unfortunately when it was discovered, by the British of course, we didn't realize how important it would be. And we didn't have the expertise. But we are getting it. There are those who say we already have it. So the question then is, if we really do have enough people who know how to run the industry, will the British leave our oil to us? I do not think so. There is no one here who thinks so. Look around the world and you will see that wherever the British arrive they take, but they do not leave.'

'You make them sound so bad. But they went to war for us.'

'Out of a love for Poland? Is that what you think?'

'Why not?'

'I think it was out of obligation. They were bound to, by a previous treaty.'

'I know that, but all the same they were fighting for us alone until

338

last year, weren't they, because all those other countries fell. Anyway, the point is they will win it! We will win it!'

'You are very certain.'

'The Americans are helping now. How can we not win!'

'The Americans. Yes.' Dr Shirazi shrugs. 'We do not know much about Americans except that they, at least, do not interfere continually in the affairs of others. Maybe, if they are successful in this war, they will have some influence on their British friends and persuade them to leave us alone. But I doubt it.'

'Why do you doubt it?' cries Marta impatiently.

'Because history tells me that people in a position of strength cannot bear not to wield that strength. And not only are the British strong, but they are a scheming, wily nation. The world's great meddlers, in our experience, and not only ours. They take pleasure in manipulating distant events, sometimes directly, with guns and boats and aeroplanes. But they are also the masters of indirect interference.' He raises both hands and waggles the fingers of a puppeteer. 'They are so cunning they get others to do their work for them. They even persuade people to oppress themselves. Do you think there are enough Britons in the world to keep control of all the countries they govern? Of course not! They make the people do it on their behalf. That is clever and, if we were sensible, we would learn from them and do as they do. But we are not sensible, and anyway we have a long way to go. To catch up. But of course that is of no interest to you.'

'Oh, but it is,' declares Marta stoutly, although in fact he is right: Iran's difficulties with the British, whatever they are, do seem somehow far away, even though here she is, being driven up an Iranian city street, guest of an Iranian doctor who is discussing his country with her in his structured, carefully modulated French.

Dr Shirazi is not fooled. He regards her ironically for a moment and then asks, 'And what do you think will be needed for your traditional occupiers to leave your Poland alone?'

'Well, winning the war, to begin with.'

'Yes. And then?'

And then? 'There will be some treaty to guarantee our borders.'

'Was there not one before? After the last war? And was that treaty obeyed?'

Marta is nonplussed. What can you do except make treaties on the assumption that the nations who sign them will abide by them?

Dr Shirazi is grinning. 'You see, treaties only have meaning for the weak. The strong can ignore them when they are sure that no one can prevent it. So your country was weak, and two stronger ones marched in. And no one prevented it.'

'But it *is* being prevented now. I mean, that's what the war is all about. And, when it's been won, then Germany won't be strong, and won't be able to march in again.'

'And Russia? Who will prevent Russia?'

'The British will. And America. And they'll be able to because they'll be strong, if they've won.'

'Perhaps. But remember that Russia is now on the same side and will expect to be rewarded. However.' He shrugs.

Marta tries to think what Mrs Benka would say to this. She can hear the old woman's voice. *Rewarded! For invading us in the first place, and then defending themselves when it's their turn to be invaded?*

Then it occurs to her. 'You said the British are strong. And that they're bad. But they stuck to their treaty with us, didn't they?' Although, at the back of her mind she hears Colonel Palucha's quiet scoffing: *The British said they would support us but then sat on their hands.*

Dr Shirazi laughs out loud. 'I will have to be more careful arguing with you, Mademoiselle Dolniak. And maybe you are right. Or maybe the British have one sort of regard for people like themselves and another for everyone else. For your sake I hope that they are strong enough. For ours, I hope that we may continue to guard our neutrality.'

'But how can you be neutral? It's… it's not moral.'

'What is not moral? That we felt some affinity with the Germans, who have never tried to take our country over? Whose behaviour to us has been courteous? *They* have never put signs up in our restaurants saying Persians are forbidden to dine there. It has been the British who looked down their noses at us as if we were cockroaches in the rice. If the Germans have always been *your* enemies that does not mean that *we* should take up arms against them when they have done us no harm. And in the meantime we have to keep our eyes open and see who is winning. What is to be gained, after all, in binding one's destiny to those who lose? Believe me, Mademoiselle Dolniak, this is as true of the individual as it is of a nation. A man can only trust his family, but outside his own house he needs to find a protector who is more powerful than he is himself. But he must never forget that this person may cheat him or betray him in the end, which is why it is always essential to be on the winning side.'

'Even if it changes?'

'Of course. That is why we have to be vigilant. Keep our eyes open, and test the wind.'

Marta slumps back in her seat. This doesn't feel right to her. There is something about Dr Shirazi's view of the world that she is sure is deeply flawed, but she can't put her finger on what it is. One thing she knows for certain. If she could only trust her family, and no one else, since she has not got her family with her, she would have been entirely alone. But she has Mrs Benka, she has Hania and Basia. She has Antoni, to whom she intends to entrust the rest of her life. How sad it would be if you couldn't trust anyone outside your family. What about Ania? Dear, sweet Ania, who she longs to be with again almost as much as she longs to be at home with her parents and Gienek and Sonia. He's wrong. Dr Shirazi is wrong, wrong, wrong. You trust your friends as much as your family, but they can't become your friends if you're not prepared to trust them. Which means that at some point you have to decide to put your trust in a comparative stranger, who might then become your friend. That's what she'll tell him, but not now. Later, perhaps, if ever they have another conversation like this one.

She nestles into the corner of the car and closes her eyes, but the driver is leaning out of his window and squeezing his horn at a man on a tiny donkey trotting resolutely up the thoroughfare in the middle of the road. For all the hooting, man and donkey do not waver from their course and the driver has to swing round them. He pokes his head out of the window and brandishes a fist at the donkey's flapping ears. Swivels his head as they overtake and directs a salvo of curses at the trotting obstacle. Behind them the donkey rider's answering volley is swallowed in the roar of the accelerating engine. Then the driver is hooting again as he hurtles into the path of another car rushing down the hill towards them. Marta grips the door in terror and shoots a glance at Dr Shirazi but his eyes are gently closed and his face is serene. At least he seems to trust this crazy driver.

48

The tarmac has given place to another dirt road and the car has stopped in an alley between high blank walls, one of which has a flat black door set into it a little way ahead. The driver is already out of his seat and has opened Dr Shirazi's door for him, and Dr Shirazi is unpacking himself from his seat. The two men are smiling broadly at one another, chuckling at each other's remarks. Now both of them have come round to Marta's side, Dr Shirazi holding her door open, the driver backing away with his hands crossed over his chest as if he's holding his ribs together. He nods and smiles the way people do when words are not available to them. Marta wonders whether this is the end of the road and they must now clamber up into the mountains on foot.

But the driver has retreated to the black door and is pounding on it, bellowing like someone who's been kept waiting. But there is no waiting. Immediately the door swings open and inside, bowing and muttering, a diminutive old man with a swathing cloth wrapped around his head hops from foot to foot in excitement. Phrases flow back and forth. In his own setting, among his own people, Dr Shirazi seems a different man. His voice is deeper but also rises at moments almost to a falsetto as he relates something to the old man, who is clutching his sides in high-pitched cackles. All at once Dr Shirazi returns to French and his gesticulating manner falls from him.

'Mademoiselle Dolniak. This is Hajji Javad, who has been looking after this house for longer than any of us remembers. He is pleased to meet you. He is telling you that you are most welcome. He says that you are like the moon.' Dr Shirazi then makes an aside to Hajji Javad, who laughs even more, but shaking his head, '*Na, agha, na!*'

'What did you say? What is he saying?'

'I said that you will have to eat more to become like the moon.'

Marta wonders why it should be anyone's aim to be like the moon, but Hajji Javad, who has been throwing sharp glances at her, is now backing and beckoning, and finally leads the way up a flight of stone steps. At the top he steps aside. Dr Shirazi, hard on his heels, also steps aside, and Marta climbs – one, two – and gasps.

She has emerged onto a square garden bounded on three sides by long two-storey buildings, the fourth being the wall over the road. In the centre is a rectangular pool laid with tiles of deep blue, and there is a small fountain playing. But the main thing is the shade. Real shade from enormous plane trees whose branches link arms, whose leaves speckle the light on the ground beneath. She becomes aware that Dr Shirazi is examining her expression, and realizes that she is smiling with a sort of unconscious rapture. People have made this place. This is the first man-made place of real beauty that she has seen since Colonel Dorushkin's trucks took them away from the convent.

'I will show you round our garden later, but my sisters are waiting. Please.' The hand under her elbow again, guiding without touching.

Now they are leading the way, Hajji Javad's slippered feet almost silent on the pathway behind them. They pass under a creeper-covered trellis arch, fragrant with something. There are fruit trees, peaches and apricots, against a wall. They step up onto a wide, steeply roofed veranda, closely boarded in old wood, and into the house.

In the dark interior there is silence as if, behind the cracked opening of doors, people are clustered, holding their breath, and Marta senses an atmosphere around her of expectation. Her curiosity is tempered with nerves. She cannot stop swallowing. But what is there to be nervous of? These will be Dr Shirazi's sisters. Just sisters – who don't wear veils. All the same. They are like their garden, the first people to whom she is being presented who have nothing to do with prisons or transports or death. She never was easy with ordinary chatter but now she thinks she has forgotten even how to begin. But

344

maybe, deprived of language by the lack of one they share, they will simply sit and smile brightly at one another, in courteous but equal discomfort.

They have come into a large airy room with tall windows giving onto the veranda. Two women and a girl are standing at the far end, grouped together as if they're waiting for someone with a camera to step forward and add a portrait to the family album. The women's glossy hair has been waved, their faces carefully made up. They look to be in their early twenties, barely older than she is except that they are... glamorous. Marta quells the urge to wipe her hands on her skirt.

One of them, the tallest, smiling a red-and-white welcome, steps forward, places her hands on Marta's shoulders and kisses her expertly on both cheeks. 'Finally,' she says, in French as pure as her brother's, 'we have waited for so long to meet you. I am Leila. This is Farideh' – more hands and kisses – 'and our little one, Massy... Massoumeh. She wants you to know she is ten years old.'

Massy grasps Marta by the wrist and leads her to an armchair right at the end of the room. 'Please, mademoiselle. You must sit here. On this chair. I insist,' she says, plump with importance at having grabbed the role of hostess, but also as if she's expecting Marta to demur.

There must be something special about this chair, although it looks the same as the others, heavily upholstered and ornate, with a highly polished occasional table at its side. The sisters watch with satisfaction as Marta parks her buttocks gingerly on the pristine flowered fabric. Then they sit too, tea-party fashion, on the chairs clustered nearest to hers. Marta looks around to see where Dr Shirazi will put himself but he has disappeared.

He must have left instructions about feeding up the moon because they begin immediately. She's surely been waiting, peering through a keyhole for her cue – an elderly woman with an enormous tray. She is a triangle of white muslin, tented in a veil that drapes her from head to toe like a painting of Our Lady. The tray is so heavy that she has wedged her elbows into the ridge of her waist to help her support it as she begins a slow advance into the room on painful feet. It's her ankles, collapsing inwards. Must be killing her.

Massy jumps up and skips across, babbling warmly at the old woman, who beams her cheeks into deep wrinkles. Her hair is thick and grey, where her veil has slipped back, and parted in the middle. Massy begins to unload the tray onto the small tables. Tall glasses of something pale yellow, plates of tiny cakes, heart shapes, crescents and stars, studded with nuts, glistening with sugar. Small plates, each with a tiny knife on it. An enormous bowl of apricots and peaches – are they from the garden? A smaller one of raisins and dates. Those magical dates. The old woman piles fruit onto a plate, lays a tiny silver knife alongside and places it in front of Marta. Go on, she nods. Eat.

'Please, please,' encourages Leila, and raises her glass of pale-yellow liquid to her lips.

It is the juice of some fragrant fruit. As Marta takes her second long sip she sees, over the rim of her glass, the old woman rearranging her veil over her hair in a gesture so automatic that she can't even be aware she's doing it. What is this drink? Sweet. Tart. Cool.

'You like it, don't you?' observes Leila, setting her glass back on her table. 'I am glad. It is important to us that the first thing you take in our house gives you pleasure. Anyone who is our brother's friend is dear to us as well and we have waited so long to meet you.'

'Yes, and you look almost like his description of you,' declares Massy, and is immediately reproved by both older sisters, who revert to Persian to do it.

Marta blushes at the thought that in her absence Dr Shirazi has been describing her at all. Wonders what he said. How does she look to the outside world now? How does she look at all? Too thin still, apparently, to be like the moon. Do these three sisters look like moons? She mustn't stare. There'll be time enough in the next couple of days to take surreptitious peeks at them.

The old woman is back, with a smaller tray now, and tiny glasses of tea. As Marta looks up to thank the heavy delivering hand, the old woman murmurs something and strokes Marta's cheek. Her speaking voice is low and a little hoarse.

Leila translates. 'Maryam says, "May God's shadow never leave your head, and may He restore you to complete health."'

Marta nods and smiles and blushes even more. 'That's very kind,' she says uneasily. So Dr Shirazi *has* been talking about her.

'Karim tells us that you are a very fine nurse,' says Farideh. Her tailored blue suit looks as if it comes straight from a fashion magazine. She sits with her elegant legs at the awkward angle that modesty requires but is leaning forward to place a smooth hand on Marta's arm. Karim. Is that his name?

Marta takes in the silkiness of the hand on her arm and brusquely tucks away her own, reddened and raw from repeated washing with hospital carbolic soap. 'We are all nurses. All the women become nurses because there are always more and more people coming in who are ill.' But Dr Shirazi said that beyond Tent City there were just as many people infected as inside it, though he didn't mention who was nursing them. 'I am trying to learn from your brother. He is a fine doctor and since I would like to become a doctor too, when I get back to Poland, I am trying to get as much experience as I can.'

'Back to Poland,' echoes Leila, in a distant voice.

'But where *is* Poland, mademoiselle? What is it like?'

Marta stares at Massy. 'I can't...' she begins. Then, 'Do you have an atlas?'

'Oh, yes. Of course.'

'Run and fetch it, Massy.' The two older sisters watch the young one rush off. Their faces are indulgent. This one is our rapscallion, they seem to say. She's taking her time learning how to behave.

Massy bounds back, heavy on her feet, with an enormous tome under her arm, and tries to open it on one of the small tables, but the weight is too much, and the table threatens to tip. 'On the floor,' she says, and sits down with the atlas spread across her lap. She puts on a knowledgeable expression and riffles through the pages, giving each a glance as if Poland might take her by surprise and turn up anywhere.

'Massy!' Leila is shaking her head severely now, though Marta is certain this is for her benefit, what a naughty little sister we have.

'It's all right,' says Marta. 'I like sitting on the floor.'

The carpet spread over the floorboards is like a reverberation of the garden, a rectangle of blue at the centre with fantastical twining green tendrils and points of white and yellow, the eyes of secretive flitting birds. It's soft. Not harsh and worn like the brocade cushions of the teahouse. Marta rocks from buttock to buttock to settle herself next to the little girl and peer into the pages as they flicker by. But the script is Persian. She's going to have to do it by geography alone.

'There!' Finally she points. 'That's Poland. Or it was.'

'And where's your house, mademoiselle?'

'It's... It's... here!'

Somehow she is convinced that her fingernail on the dot that has to be Poznan is also pinpointing Jablonska Street and the heavy apartment buildings where the sticky-leafed lime trees grow. Sonia is at her table, head bent over her homework, absently fiddling with the end of her fat plait. Gienek is sitting at his open window, smoking forbidden cigarettes, which the rest of them can smell on his clothes all day. And there comes her mother, burdened with shopping, pausing in the street to call up to Gienek to come down and give her a hand. Marta tries to insert herself into this domestic scene, but, whichever way she tries, none seems appropriate. She struggles to prise apart an opening in an invisible wall, wedge an arm in the gap to clamber through. But she cannot hold the edges apart long enough to begin. Is even her imagination barring her return? Tears come to her eyes and have started to roll onto her cheeks before she can disguise them, swallow, cough, sneeze – all the things you do.

Farideh is on her knees on the garden carpet, holding out a snowy handkerchief, rubbing away at the soft, still short hair of Marta's bowed head. 'Come, come. Don't cry.' She sits down closer to Marta and gathers her up, rocking her and crooning into her ear. Her schooled French fails her, so she drops into Persian. *'Azizam, chi-e? Chera geriyeh mikonid? Geriyeh nakon. Azizam, khub misheh, hamechi dorost misheh. Azizam. Geriyeh nakon, areh. Azizam.'*

The consoling phrases buzz around Marta's head like a trapped fly and she thinks what a good thing it is she can't understand any of it. If it were in Polish she'd really be blubbing by now. She sniffs and swallows, then sits up sharply in a gesture of recovery.

'I'm sorry. I was remembering.'

'Perhaps you would like to tell us... About your home, how it looks, how it is to live there...'

'Oh, I'm sure you don't want...'

'Please, mademoiselle. Please, plee-ease!'

This child is not being polite. She really does want to know. But where to begin?

'Well...' she says, drawing out the word for time. 'My father is a soldier...'

49

The sisters are married but neither has a child. The information comes from Farideh, in a lowered voice when she offers Marta a choice of bathrooms. Western and eastern: flushing toilet or tiled squat-hole. You vouchsafe the absence of babies in the intimacy of a bathroom, behind the closed door, arms wrapped around the guest's folded towel, clutching it to the barren belly. Marta realizes that Farideh is apologizing on behalf of both sisters that they have, as yet, failed to reproduce, and she doesn't know whether she should murmur some commiseration or an assurance that any day now… or mutter a spell. What she cannot express is her relief that there are, in fact, no babies to be danced on her knee and admired while she has to exclaim how like their mothers they are, or their fathers.

She has been shown the wedding photographs of the would-be fathers, Hushang and Farhad, but she can't remember which name belongs to which man, which man to which sister. She hopes that Farideh and Farhad belong to one another. It would make remembering easier. In their silver-framed pictures both men, in clipped moustaches, were staring over the photographer's shoulder, sternly, to show that they had what it took to undergo this business of picture-taking. By contrast, Farideh and Leila had the easy wide smiles of people accustomed to the lens. Marta sympathizes with the husbands. Even when she tries to look pleasant for a camera she always emerges ferocious. Antoni had made great play of quailing when he took a peek at the portrait glued into the corner of her Soviet identity card. Anyone with a face like that deserved to be locked up in a logging camp, he said. You can tell some people are criminal elements just by looking at them.

This is a large house but, when children eventually arrive, will there be room enough for everyone? She hasn't understood quite who lives here or whether this is simply the retreat for the hot summer months. It is extraordinary how much cooler, how much fresher the air is up here than down the long hill in the city. Mrs Benka had chewed on her lips rather but muttered, 'Hm. Well, you'd better have a good rest then, dear. We all need one.'

Evidently Farideh thinks so too. She leads Marta to a room with a high bed and mottled marble washstand and, twitching at the brocade bedspread, strokes her wrist with an extended little finger. 'Perhaps you would like to sleep for a while,' she suggests. 'Our brother told us you need a time of recuperation.' So it's an order, then.

Marta is not tired but obediently climbs onto the bed and lies back. Sighs slightly. Closes her eyes. Actually, an hour alone, and in rare silence, would be good. It's so hard being polite in a foreign language with people who are also using a language not their own. Farideh retreats and pulls the door to behind her, leaving Marta to wonder whether she might sneak out in a while and explore without a guide. Unfamiliarity and upbringing ought to pin her to the mattress, but they don't. She swings down off the bed just as someone is tapping on her door. Scratching on it, you'd say. She swallows back her '*Entrez*' to open the door a crack. There's a slice of Massy's face, round-eyed, hands cupped over her mouth to contain the giggles. Marta understands whispering is to be the thing.

'What's the matter?'

Massy is only just audible asking the polite question. 'Are you tired?'

'No.'

'Do you want to come out into the garden with me?'

Is this a naughty invitation, or does the child want to go out and needs Marta accompanying her as an excuse? The garden is tempting, and if she has to she can be profuse in her apologies. Outsiders are always so clumsy. They can be each other's excuse. She bends to fasten her shoes but sees that Massy is barefoot. Silently they slip down the corridor towards a rectangle of sharp light.

'This way.' Massy skips ahead, following a flagged path between fleck-barked plane trees so tall they're like a study in perspective. How long can they have been here? Who planted them? Some distant ancestor with the comfort of his descendants in mind, scooping out hole after hole, settling saplings for good purpose. Such kindly forethought. You'd have to assume that the house and its trees would survive. You'd have to assume stability. They sneak past a low building at right angles to the main house. Fragrant cooking smells pour from it and hang in the still air. For all the sweets and cakes they fed her on, Marta's mouth fills with saliva. She glances sideways into the doorway and spots Maryam hunkered down in front of a huge shallow dish, slapping a cloth of dough back and forth between flour-dusty palms and talking non-stop to a figure out of view in the shadows, who grunts periodically in a voice without gender.

Massy has noticed that Marta is enticed, inclined to loiter, and grabs her by the hand. They speed under an arch, and what appeared to be an enclosed garden opens out into a wide orchard with fields beyond, creeping towards the mountains. Slow insects hover and hum. Beneath their feet the remains of last spring's grass crackles in brown fragments. It's been months since it rained and there'll be more to wait till it rains again. Marta's bare soles flinch and she stops dead, rubbing the prickles from them. But Massy runs on, her feet inured to the scratchy ground. Now she's waiting under an ancient tree with rutted trunk and branches akimbo.

She points up. 'Will you help me?'

Her whisper is so low, Marta has to bend to catch the words. Who is there to overhear? Perhaps what Massy wants to do is so forbidden that she's trying to keep it secret even from herself. But all she wants to do is climb a tree, after all. It's obvious what she needs because the lowest branch is out of reach. Marta interlaces her fingers into a stirrup for Massy's foot and hoists her up. For a moment it looks as if the branch is still out of reach but then Massy has her arms around it, slings a leg over it until she's lying face down, panting, and pink with pleasure. Now she's astride, then on her feet and zigzagging up towards the crown with its grey-green latticed canopy. She's done this before, so someone else must have helped her.

Now her diminished face peers down between the branches. 'And you, mademoiselle?' she hisses. 'Aren't you coming up too?'

What is it that has made her identify Marta as a fellow tree-climber? But it's been a long time, not since she was a child herself. Oh, come on! Don't be silly! Marta tucks her skirt into her knickers, leaps for the branch and, hanging by her hands, walks her feet diagonally up the trunk. Old memories guide her. The bark is warm and dry and slightly pitted. Tree climbing was always best done barefoot, and her toes curl and grip. The orchard spreads out below, but looking up she can see the line of silver snow painted along the crest of the mountains. Massy has the right idea. What better perch could there be than this? She lays her cheek against a branch and inhales its scented dust. You could sleep out here, if it weren't for the risk of falling out. You could build a tree house. The spread of the branches is perfect for a tree house. She replaces the small figure of Massy in the upper branches with the small figure of Ania. That's better!

Just above her she hears Massy snuffle a small sentence of dismay.

'What's wrong?'

'It's my mother.'

Swathed like Maryam but the white muslin is embroidered all over with tiny blue dots. Just a foreshortened triangular shape from here, calling for her youngest daughter. She passes under the tree and has not looked up. Then she's gone.

'We'll have to go down.'

Two naughty children mumbling on their lips to keep quiet, they clamber down, always harder than going up. Marta jumps from the lowest branch with regret but thinking she can come back another day. Massy is a little way behind but, surprisingly, when she reaches the lowest branch she dithers at the drop.

'Wait. I'll hold you.' Marta clasps Massy round the legs and takes her weight, and, as Massy slithers down, her skirt rides up round her waist. 'Well, here we are. Down again.'

Marta turns and finds herself face to face with Dr Shirazi's stony-eyed mother. Three things strike her: one, that this veiled woman doesn't look as old as she should; second, that the tiny blue dots on the white muslin are in fact exquisite flowers; third, that she, Marta, has blundered.

Massy is in disgrace and has been packed off to tidy herself up. She had assumed her mother would stay out at the mosque at her prayers until half past one, as she does every Friday. But out of courtesy to her son's guest she made a point of hurrying home instead of staying to chat with her friends – and look how the guest repaid her!

Zahra Khanoom does not speak French. She does not need to speak anything for her opinion to be plain. She eats the chicken and rice and aubergines that Maryam has placed before them in silence while her daughters make frantic conversation. Leila and Farideh seem torn. They think it's funny that Marta was caught dusty and leaf-streaked with Massy in tow, but they are also bemused that a fully grown woman would do such a thing. Disapproval flows across the table from Zahra Khanoom, quelling Marta's appetite. Now that she thinks about it, she is shamefaced about her scramble in the branches in her hosts' garden on her first afternoon. But when she meets Massy's eye she receives a look of such cheeky complicity that, on balance, she thinks she'd rather have the little tomboy as a friend than the laconic mother.

Halfway through their meal Dr Shirazi appears, newly shaved but still bearing the faintly rumpled look of a man only recently woken from deep sleep. Clearly his older sisters are bringing him up to date as he shovels in Maryam's delicious lunch. He glances across the table to Marta, his lips pressed together in a twitching smile.

'Well, well,' he observes dryly. 'I learn a little more about you Poles every day.'

Such as what? wonders Marta, ready to bridle.

As usual Dr Shirazi is answering the unasked question. 'For example, that to please the wilful daughter of their hosts they will engage in all sorts of dangerous activities. *N'est-ce pas?*'

'Oh, but…' begins Massy, all combed and fluffed up by Maryam's firm ministrations.

'I think so, Massy,' insists Dr Shirazi, and that conversation is declared over. But as he turns again to Marta she sees him struggle to keep the frown of disapproval in place. 'You will meet my father shortly. And my brothers-in-law, and my younger brother, Behzad.' He looks at his watch. 'I expect them any minute.'

He leans towards his mother and they exchange remarks. Marta has the impression that Zahra Khanoom is being clipped and dismissive, but how is she to tell? Dr Shirazi appears deferential… it's his mother, after all, but again Marta is certain that in Persian he's not the man he is in French.

A distant door. Voices. Cheerful shouting in various male registers, Hajji Javad's thin tones recurrent as a refrain. A sudden burst of laughter from them all. From the set of Zahra Khanoom's lips and the glint in Massy's eyes, Marta guesses that their morning's transgression has already become anecdote. Dr Shirazi has reached for a toothpick so half his face is invisible behind his hands.

The sisters' husbands look like their pictures and, disconcertingly, like one another. Maybe they're brothers too. Dr Shirazi's father is heavier than his son in that way of late middle age, all the extra weight carried before him, but elegantly dressed in a dark-grey suit. His eyebrows and nose and mouth prophesy how Dr Shirazi will look in time to come, although he seems less solemn as he strides into the room, scanning Marta with shrewd, still laughing eyes. The brother Behzad is a plump young man of Marta's age, with a tiny pouting sac either side of his full mouth. There is something pampered about him, and soft. If you were to prod him in the midriff the flesh might not bounce back.

All around her people are on their feet, all except Zahra Khanoom, sisters embracing husbands, and father, brothers, kissing one another on the cheeks. Lots of noise. The room balloons. Sudden hands proffered in businesslike French handshakes for the guest, and the room deflates.

Maryam is in the door with her piled tray. She knows that the newcomers haven't eaten and the dish of fragrant rice is heaped again. As Dr Shirazi moves round to sit beside her, Marta notices that Zahra Khanoom's face has relaxed with her family round her table. Everyone is talking at once, but not in French. Waves of speech boom against Marta's ears and she feels suddenly weary.

'My brothers-in-law studied in England.' Dr Shirazi leans closer to mutter his explanation. 'And my father, of course, never had the opportunity to study at all.' He waits for the puzzlement to arrive on Marta's face, then adds, 'But he is a modern man.'

Marta wonders what that will mean. 'And your brother?'

'Behzad was supposed to go to France to study this year, but of course with the war that's not possible. So now we are trying to find something for him to do.'

Marta glances at Behzad with surprise. Why isn't he doing his military service like any boy of his age? 'Doesn't he have to do military service?'

Dr Shirazi accords her a crooked smile. 'In theory. But there are ways round that. And he's lucky that we have the means. A generation ago he'd have had to have gone.'

Marta gawps. 'But… but doesn't he want to go?'

'My dear Mademoiselle Dolniak. My father and I haven't been working from morning till night to send Behzad off to be bullied by some uncouth louts from the villages. I told you. In my country we look after our own. If we don't nobody else will.'

And what about the defence of the country?

'What are you two discussing?' calls Leila from across the table.

'Behzad's career,' replies Dr Shirazi. 'Mademoiselle Dolniak thinks all young men should be in the army.'

'Of course she does,' says Farideh. 'Her father is a soldier.'

'Is he?' Dr Shirazi turns in surprise.

Marta squares her shoulders. 'He has been all his life.' Then she adds pointedly, 'He was fighting the Russians in 1920.'

Dr Shirazi begins an ironic salute but seems to think better of it.

'And where is he now?'

'I don't know. How could I know? I don't even know if he's alive.'

There is silence round the table, while Farideh translates this exchange for the benefit of her parents and the husbands. Zahra Khanoom raises her palms in front of her face, slanted upwards as if she's trying to catch raindrops, and rocks minimally, murmuring, in her chair.

'She's praying for him,' whispers Dr Shirazi.

Now Marta meets the eyes of the stern veiled woman and finds them warmer. Zahra Khanoom is nodding slowly at her and Marta is frustrated that she doesn't even know how to indicate gratitude in another culture's gestures. But all the while the image of Antoni marching, drilling, proving he's finally up to it, plays silently like a scratchy film at the back of her mind.

Courtesy wrenches her back to the table and she notices Behzad eyeing her with poorly concealed curiosity. 'And have you found something for your brother to do?'

'Earlier it would have been easy. We would have given him a position in our company, like my brothers-in-law. But now...' Dr Shirazi shrugs. 'Well, times change and one has to adapt.'

'Why? What's happened to your company?'

'It was mainly transport, you know. We had a fleet of lorries. But they have been commandeered, by your British friends. It's one of the reasons why the people are going hungry, that we cannot deliver foodstuffs. The other, of course, is that the British have taken the foodstuffs as well. At least, that's what the people believe.'

'And have they? The British?' Dr Shirazi shrugs again. Marta doesn't believe it. 'So now you don't have a company any more?'

'No, no. We do. We have...other interests. Cinemas.'

'Cinemas!'

'They have become very popular here.'

'Oh, yes! Of course.'

'You are an enthusiast?'

'I used to go... when I was at home. I used to like cowboy films.'

'Really?' Dr Shirazi's forehead is striped with astonishment. 'Not romances?'

'No. My mother always tried to take me to the romances with her, but I didn't like them.'

Dotted round the table, the French-speakers are eavesdropping intently.

'But perhaps you were just a child in those days. And now... you have grown up?' It's just a suggestion.

Marta is on the point of insisting that she'd still prefer the cowboys, when it occurs to her that maybe Dr Shirazi is right. Because of Antoni. So she smiles, and says nothing.

Dr Shirazi continues. 'Behzad' – and he nods towards him – 'might take over running one of the cinemas, for the time being. *N'est-ce pas, mon petit frère?* And then, when all this is over, he can go to France as we planned, and study law.'

'But your company?'

'We are all in the company.' His arms open and sweep everyone in the room into a heap. 'My father, my brothers-in-law, Behzad, myself.'

'But you're a doctor!'

'Yes, of course. But you don't think we could have afforded my studies if it wasn't for the company, do you? And I will tell you something that will surprise you.' He drops his voice, but only for effect. 'The one who really runs it, the one with the real head for figures,' he taps his own, 'is my mother. She may not be able to read and write, but Allah protect the man who tries to cheat her. When it comes to business, even my father leaves the last decision to her. Isn't that so?' And he bursts into Persian, no doubt repeating what he's just said, judging by the nods and smiles and laughter.

But Marta is thinking, *Can't read and write?* Now she wants to inspect Zahra Khanoom all over again, as if the matriarch will look different in the light of this new knowledge. She feels somehow that Dr Shirazi was determined she should know his mother is illiterate. She wants to ask why that can be, in a privileged family like his. She is confused, even a little frightened. The furniture, the dining table, the sisters' fashionable clothes are all so familiar; the confident French that Dr Shirazi and his siblings speak; yet perhaps it's no more than a mask, only for show, and underneath lurks an entirely different world.

50

This time the tapping on Marta's door reveals Farideh. *'Venez, venez!'* she beckons, all gleaming teeth. 'We're going to have a musical evening.'

Reluctantly Marta slithers from her bed and smoothes her tired skirt. Farideh has changed her clothes and is wearing a long flowing dress of some wafting fabric. It's grown too dark to tell the colour. Such wardrobes they must have! Marta blesses her single outfit. Since they appear to know so much about her they must be aware that this is all she has, except for the American dress with sequins, which Dr Shirazi did not alert her to bring. It's best having few clothes. Then there's no anxiety about making the wrong decision and being inappropriately dressed.

But Farideh has other ideas. She has grasped Marta firmly by the hand, as if a looser grip might let her make a getaway, and is directing her into another room, brightly lit, where Leila is waiting with silky stuffs slithering over her folded arms. Farideh's dress turns out to be smoky blue.

'Good,' declares Leila. You'd have thought Farideh had accomplished a major mission.

One by one Leila lays dresses out on a divan, spreading the skirts tenderly, with gentle shakes to dislodge creases. A black one, a red one, midnight blue with white edges, olive green.

Farideh points to the olive green. 'Like your eyes, don't you think?' She holds the dress up the length of Marta's body and in the mirror Marta sees the green of her eyes intensify, reflecting the depth of the silk. 'Let us help you.'

No question about it. No doubt that she wants to change. She wriggles with discomfort. Even now she prefers to dress in privacy, and looks at her body as little as she can. But these sisters are fussing about her, pulling at her buttons and shaking out the garment they're so pleased to lend. Is this what a harem is like, women dressing and undressing one another, all eyes and fingers and assessment? She tells herself this is what they always do, and they are women too. But such glossy ones, so preened and powdered. So scented. She feels uncouth next to them, with their rounded elbows and smooth movements.

Farideh pours the olive-green dress over Marta's head and it trickles down with a faint hiss, weighing nothing. This alarms her. It makes her feel that she might be naked. But its length is exact, tickling her ankles, the slender line swinging from her shoulders. It's too loose but she doesn't care. This is not her idea.

'Perfect,' pronounces Farideh, and Marta cannot disagree. 'And these also, please' –holding out a pair of low-heeled silvery slippers.

Marta slips them on and is gratified that they fit well enough. Just like Cinderella, she's about to say, but remembers that maybe Cinderella has not made an appearance here.

Now Leila is brushing at her hair, which has grown just long enough to take some shape, and to gleam in the light. Farideh proffers a chubby pot. Then fingers out a dollop of goo, which she rubs rhythmically into Marta's carbolic-roughened hands. All this for a concert. What if she doesn't like the music or, worse, still doesn't know when a piece has ended, and applauds in the wrong place? She did that at home once, taken on a grand occasion by her parents, and the auditorium had swivelled its head as one, to glare at the ignorant display. But her hands do feel pleasantly smooth and she finds herself stroking them on the sly.

Pitter-pattering behind the sisters she follows them to the veranda, where Hajji Javad is setting candles at intervals along the perimeter. You have to admire how they walk, floating almost, their heads motionless. Has someone taught them this? The husbands are already there, in dark suits, and Massy, looking older in a long maroon gown that sits well against her skin.

This will be no concert. Behzad, in one corner, is winding away at a gramophone with its white lily trumpet, a pile of records to hand. He selects one and dips the needle to its surface. Out pops a reedy orchestra sawing at a waltz, like the waltzes they played in the hotel in Warsaw where the family once holidayed when she was no older than Massy. The sound fills her nostrils with the memory of coffee and hot milk.

Farideh and Leila are gliding along the wooden floor in their husbands' light embrace, and Marta grabs her throat in horror. She cannot dance. At all. Not at all. And here comes Dr Shirazi, handsome and rested, dressed like a man from one of those romantic films he was so anxious to press on her.

'Ah!' he exclaims, appreciating how she looks in his sister's dress, and reaches for her hand.

'I'm sorry.' Her cheeks are so hot she's glad of the candles' dim light. 'I can't dance. I don't know how.'

At the age when she was supposed to learn, she had seen to it that she trod heavily and consistently on her teacher's feet. Eventually, when he could take no more, he informed her mother that there are some people who simply don't have dance in their souls, and for everyone's sake they are best left alone.

Dr Shirazi is crestfallen. More than that. He cannot believe it. 'Surely, in those elegant halls in Warsaw I have heard so much about from your compatriots... surely there has been dancing there?' He's almost pleading with her, as if the discovery that there was no dancing would destroy a deeply held conviction.

'Oh, yes. Of course. And in Poznan,' she adds stoutly. 'It's not that there's no dancing, it's just that I can't dance.'

If anything Dr Shirazi looks even more disappointed, but for a moment he stands his ground, still feathering the tips of her fingers with the tips of his. Massy rescues him. She bounces up and babbles an excited sentence. Dr Shirazi offers Marta an adult-to-adult shrug but, clearly relieved, takes his little sister in his arms and off they go, *one*-two-three, *one*-two-three. It's evident to Marta, skulking with her back against the wall, that Dr Shirazi is an elegant dancer, and even

Massy knows what she's doing, despite a certain gawkiness at the knees and elbows.

Two shadows approach in a pincer movement, Shirazi *père* and Behzad. She cannot communicate with the one and despises the other's lack of civic duty. She wishes she could bolt. She wishes she hadn't accepted the doctor's invitation. As the shadows take shape and become aware of one another, Behzad defers to his father and returns to the gramophone. The older man bows to Marta, laying his right hand on his heart, briefly touches his mouth and smiles apologetically for the lack of a language in common. He won't have understood her excuses to Dr Shirazi and he won't understand any she makes now. This is going to be awful. Everyone will watch her clumping over the polished shoes.

But as her partner guides her away from her refuge by the wall she realizes that he is almost as uncertain and unpractised as she is. Within a minute he has trodden on her toe and mumbled an apology, then she has bumped into him and grumbled her own. Then he has taken a lunge to one side that propels her into Farideh and husband, who were circling in blissful harmony. Shirazi *père* stops dead, shaking with such laughter that tears stand in his eyes. He wags his head, bowing out of this one, and pats her ruefully on the shoulder. 'Karim-jun!' he calls, but Dr Shirazi has already arrived, little sister dumped in a corner, and Marta is handed from father to son, passed across like a parcel, she thinks, before she can make her escape.

'My father is determined to learn western dancing,' says Dr Shirazi, grasping her waist inexorably. 'But of course it's not usual in my country and he has not had the opportunity of our generation.'

They still haven't moved and Marta thinks if she can only spin out the conversation he might take pity and grant her a reprieve. 'Doesn't he dance with your mother?'

'My mother!' Dr Shirazi coughs a single guffaw. 'She entirely disapproves of men and women dancing together, which is why she is not with us tonight. But of course, if my father wishes us to be able to do it, she would not countermand him. And, as I said, he is a modern man and will not force her to dance against her will. Now, shall we…?'

'Where did you learn?'

'I? In France.'

'And your sisters?'

'I taught them.'

'And their husbands?'

'They learned in England.'

Only two to go, God help her. 'And Massy?'

'Massy, little *sheytoon* that she is, copies everyone. And, before you ask, Behzad is still learning. If you had danced with him the experience would have been no better than with my father. *Alors!*'

She is shackled into this dance and wonders whether her childhood ploy might work on Dr Shirazi, but something tells her he will not be as easily deflected as her poor bruised teacher. 'It's perfectly simple,' he is saying, and she imagines him with his sisters, home from Paris and eager to pass on the latest thing. 'You can walk and you can count. Therefore you can dance.' Nothing to do with soul, then. He's tapping the *one*-two-three on the small of her back with determined fingers. Now he's following the rhythm with his feet and slight bends of his knees, but still not moving from the spot. He nods a commanding *Do what I'm doing*, and she begins, *one*-two-three, dipping her knees on the *one*, this is how they must have taught him, two-three, she's never lacked a sense of rhythm, and, without warning, his right leg pushes her left to take a step back and he's gripping her so that she won't fall, and back goes her leg, they are face to face, bolt upright like a pair of clockwork toys locked together. To the side two-three, then he steps back, which brings her forward two-three, and round, then again. And again. It's quite easy, really.

Dr Shirazi's hand on her waist is lighter now, his hand round hers no longer a fist but a warm dry palm. She realizes she has been holding her breath, so she sighs and releases herself to his guidance, and to the music that is spinning them both around the veranda; closes her eyes, feeling her body being whirled as freely, almost as smoothly as if she were on her winter skates when the cold air and the exhilaration make everyone's cheeks bloom. There is the clasp of his hand on hers, the light pressure of his head against hers, and she could go on and on. But the record stops and Dr Shirazi says, '*Et voilà!*' He is looking down into her face as if to say, that was all right, wasn't it? And she is struck by the depths of his eyes, by the warmth in them, and by their tiny crow's-feet of amusement. In his way he is as glamorous as his sisters, and he might make a good friend – once you got past the reserve.

Dr Shirazi continues to hold her as if he expects the music to start up again but Hajji Javad appears beside them with a tray of tall glasses of juice. Shirazi *père* is applauding her, clapping his hands high above his head and shouting something to his son. 'He says,' translates Dr Shirazi, 'that now you can teach him.'

Marta turns to the older man, shakes her head, and bows with her right hand on her heart. Both men burst out laughing.

'What's the matter?' she asks, offended. 'What have I done?'

'Nothing, nothing. But this…' Dr Shirazi lays his hand over his heart. 'This is what *men* do.'

The night is hot and still. Maryam and Massy have rolled out mattresses on the flat roof of the kitchen for the women to sleep on. The men are all somewhere else. Marta lies in the pyjamas Farideh has lent her, looking up at the sky, the same sky that she has stared at night after night lying beside Antoni in Tent City. But here the air is clear and the stars so dense you couldn't put a hand between them. In one of the trees, a nightingale is burbling a small fantasy. What is it about nightingales that is so sad? Is it the song itself or the fact that they sing alone? All that loveliness – and no one replies. Somewhere, in his training camp, Antoni is under this sky and maybe he has a nightingale too. Perhaps, before he goes away, they will be able to find someone with a gramophone and dance together, as lovers should. Perhaps Dr Shirazi will invite her again and she can suggest that, just for the evening, some of the others might come too. The veranda is large enough for a proper ball.

Farideh stirs on her mattress. 'Are you sure you are comfortable?' she whispers.

'Very comfortable.'

'Did you enjoy the dancing?'

'I did. I didn't think I would, but I did. And thank you for lending me the dress.'

'Please keep it. What's mine is yours. Please keep it.'

'I can't do that!'

'No. Please. You must keep it. You can see it is too small for me now. Marriage has made me larger.' She gives a short, awkward laugh.

'But there will be no occasion to wear it again.'

'Of course there will. You will be here dancing with us again.'

'Well, I should like that... thank you. But tell me. Do you ever invite your neighbours or your friends to come and dance as well?'

'*Mon Dieu. Quelle idée!* Of course not. This way of dancing, it's just for the family. Not to do in public.'

When Marta wakes, although it is only just light, she is alone on the roof. She listens for voices but all she can hear is the faint hiss of a breeze from the mountains passing among the leaves of the plane trees. The mattresses the others slept on are still laid out, to air maybe, or because they didn't want to wake her. Even Massy must have managed to creep away in silence.

Other people's mornings. Other people's rituals, so awkward for the outsider who doesn't know what they are. Is Zahra Khanoom praying somewhere, as people at home might go to early Mass? Have they already had their breakfast, so soon, or is breakfast not a habit? She's hungry. The dancing, and sleeping under the sky... but she can't go in demanding food. There's a heaped tray of fruit on the big table. Perhaps she could take something from that. Or pick a peach or an apricot from a tree. The last time she ate fruit from a tree was at Mrs Benka's, before the Russians came. Everything here is so different from home, and yet they have the Russians in common. And tea. A glass of tea. That's what she needs first. And, to be honest, something solid, and then a smoke. She's dying for a smoke. But there weren't any cigarettes in sight yesterday, though it can't be that Iranians don't smoke. The lorry drivers at Bandar-e Pahlavi lit one cigarette from another.

Perhaps it's a class thing. Working types smoke and people from good families don't. But the Shirazis are wealthy rather than upper class, with the fleet of lorries they once had, and now their cinemas. Dr Shirazi is the first of his family to have the chance to study – that's what he said. And his jovial father. How she'd like to be able talk to him. Zahra Khanoom is another matter. She really seems to come from an alien world, and Marta senses that the doctor's mother resents her, or, if not that exactly, that she disapproves of her for some reason. The tree climbing. It must be to do with that.

Marta rubs her face, smoothes her hair and, barefoot, climbs down the steps along the kitchen-block wall in the borrowed pyjamas. What's mine is yours. Do they mean her to keep these as well? She feels exposed in night-clothes, and carries the sheet that covered her to throw over herself should she spy one of the men. She must be careful not to wear it like Zahra Khanoom's veil, though. They might think she was mimicking and mocking. But there's no sight of the men.

The sisters are in the dining room talking in lowered voices and sipping tea, but Massy gives her a great shout of welcome, and everyone asks her if she slept well, and enough. Everyone tells her that they must have been so noisy they woke her before she was ready to wake. They are all apologizing and over their voices Marta hears Maryam banging pans in the kitchen outhouse. She realizes that no one has breakfasted because they were waiting for her to wake.

Courtesy is terrifying, she thinks, as she scurries off to wash. It would have been easier if they'd only done what they would always do, even if it did wake her, for now she knows that her presence has put everyone out.

She cannot find her old clothes. Instead, on the chair where she left it, there's a light belted flowered dress. She lifts it to her face. The crispness of the fabric tells her it is new and she knows it has been left here specifically for her. Quickly she puts it on before anyone should come in and begin fussing over her as they did last night. The dress fits perfectly. So perfectly that it makes her uncomfortable.

51

The men have gone. All of them. Dr Shirazi too. Well, of course they have. The working week has begun again and it's not for them to be sitting at leisure in their holiday home as women can. But Leila and Farideh are taken aback by the expression on Marta's face, just when she was looking so pretty in the new dress. Her old clothes smelled of poverty and death. But up here under the mountains, now that she is resting, she shouldn't be thinking of poverty and death. And she mustn't be concerned. They gave her things to Maryam, who will return them, washed and pressed, as good as any nurse might wish for. Yet even that piece of news doesn't make her smile.

Massy, being Massy, blurts what they cannot. 'Don't you like us, mademoiselle? Don't you want to be with us?'

Marta looks into the little girl's face and sees there genuine hurt. The moment she had seated herself for breakfast Massy had weaselled onto a chair beside her and kept plying her with food until her sisters sharply told her to stop. *Does* she like being with them? She doesn't dislike it, but she's not at ease. She wouldn't be at ease anywhere among strangers if she couldn't get away. And now she can't. She knows only that they are a long way up the hill from Tent City, and no one out in the streets would be able to help her get there.

Taking Massy's hand in hers, as if the gesture might belie the words, she says, 'But my people... In the hospital. I have work to do there. I should be working.'

'Karim is looking after your people, and there must be many other nurses, surely. And we are so happy to have you with us. Aren't we?'

Massy nods her head hugely and grips Marta's hand. 'They can manage without you for a week.'

'A week!' She hasn't meant to squeak. 'Dr Shirazi invited me for one or two days.'

'But what a poor invitation that would be. Who could be so inhospitable? Besides, it's not possible to look after someone properly in one or two days, and you will not have rested in such a short time.'

How is Marta to explain that she is perfectly rested already, that she didn't need recuperation in the first place – her word against a doctor's, their older brother's. Even his mother addresses him with respect rather than command. If it weren't for that, she's certain Zahra Khanoom would be glad to see the back of her. But my fiancé is there, she wants to say, to which she imagines they will point out that he will be only too happy to know that his bride-to-be is being so well cared for. And she *is* being well cared for. She has eaten more good food since she arrived in this house than she has had in years. She is provided with new clothes, her old ones are being laundered. There is hot water and cool juices, attentive hosts and shade in the garden. No convalescent could hope for more. How could she be so ungrateful!

The sisters are batting blandishments between them.

'Maryam is so pleased that we have a guest. She is baking and cooking, and we'll have a real celebration.'

'She's going to make ice-cream!'

'Yes, she's going to make ice-cream, which takes a lot of time, so she only does it on special occasions. So, you see, you are making Massy very happy.'

'We could call for a horse-drawn *doroshkeh* and go up into the mountains, and walk there. Perhaps you would like to swim. There's a lake where the water is so sweet.'

'Or we could go to the local bazaar, if you like, and buy the fruit and vegetables for Maryam. Then you'll be able to see how they try and cheat us.'

'And we might visit Avenue Lalezar.'

'What's Avenue Lalezar?' asks Marta weakly.

'Oh, it's back down in the city where all the best shops are. And we can sit there and drink coffee together.'

'And when Karim comes to visit us in the middle of the week, and he promised he would, he will be able to tell you how your people are.'

Marta's face brightens and the sisters, gratified, relax in their chairs. If Dr Shirazi comes in the week, then perhaps she can go back to Tent City with him. They have been so kind. They are trying so hard. She will not be rude.

'I would be most happy to do all those things.' For all that she squeezes sincerity into the sentence, it resonates like someone practising her French homework.

'What shall we do first? What shall we do first?' Massy is sitting on her hands to prevent herself from clapping.

The three faces turn to Marta. Guest's choice. Two years ago none of these outings would have excited her, but today they all appear exotic.

'Let's buy vegetables,' she says firmly.

'We'll tell *Maman*!' Triumphant exit.

She will not stay the full week. Antoni will be back from his assessment any day now and may be about to sign up. She cannot be away as he prepares to leave. And it isn't right that this family should be pampering her like a pet dog on a cushion when Mrs Benka, Basia and Hania are sweltering away in Tent City, washing sheets and emptying bedpans. No, she will not stay the full week. When Dr Shirazi comes she will thank them all as fulsomely as she can, return the dress – no, she cannot return the dress. They would be mortified. Fold the dress, then, tuck it under her arm, and retrieve herself with her hospital clothes.

What she wouldn't do for a smoke.

Marta sidles from the room and out into the morning garden, where she comes upon Maryam and Hajji Javad squatting comfortably, backs against the outside wall of the kitchen house, sucking on the nozzles of a pair of hubble-bubbles. Each inhalation gurgles, throaty as a death rattle. The exhaled wisps penetrate Marta's eager nose and she sighs.

'*Khanoom!*' Hajji Javad is on his feet. The foreign visitor needs something. He's all bows and mutterings, hand on heart. She keeps hers rigidly by her side but stretches her face in a desperate, mute smile. Maryam reaches out and raps for attention on Hajji Javad's foot as if it were a door. Delivers him a terse sentence, to which he responds with an exclamation of incredulity.

'*Khanoom. Befar'maeed! Befar'maeed.*' He hooks up the snaking tube of his hubble-bubble and presents it to Marta, captured and clamped between his hands as an offering.

Oh, at last! It's not as powerful as a draw on a cigarette, not the same grab at the back of the throat, but it makes her head swim with pleasure. The pipe bubbles and gurgles as she makes up for lost time. But already they're calling out for her along the garden paths, from different directions. Marta fills her lungs with one last gasp of smoke, holds it in, breathes it out, then Hajji Javad is helping her up as tenderly as he might if she had been an old woman with stiff knees.

'*Khanoom.*' Maryam squints up at her and pats the ground where Marta was sitting, and, with the nozzle of her water pipe clenched between her teeth, gives it a little shake. You come out here for a smoke any time you like. Things are looking up.

Someone has whistled up a *doroshkeh*, already waiting in the lane outside the door. The horse is half asleep but shivering its ears against a phalanx of flies. The cabby adjusts his dusty cap and gathers the reins into his lap with a chirruping of the tongue; the horse hauls up its head and the flies lift away in an irritable cloud. There's not much space in the *doroshkeh*, so they must sit knee to knee. Zahra Khanoom, shrouded in black for this excursion, addresses her daughters in a low voice with what sounds like a string of instructions, but she could be telling them a story for all Marta knows.

Once out of the lane, the horse is threatened into a desultory trot past walls and houses Marta cannot see, but in a matter of minutes they are slowing again. Stopping. If this is it they could have walked. Vegetable stalls, one next to another, run the length of a long wall, each one almost hidden by a press of people, men and women, all talking at once. Zahra Khanoom appears to duck her head and simply barges a path through towards the stall she wants. The others dive after her, staying close, and the crowd flows together again. No one seems to resent their brusque arrival.

The stall-holder greets Zahra Khanoom with familiarity, all the while staring past her at the foreigner with the short light hair and green eyes. Zahra Khanoom calls him to order, pointing to some aubergines and peppers, and behind his stall the man piles vegetables onto a set of scales. Hands them over wrapped in a cone of paper, but Zahra Khanoom picks them out one by one and flings them back, shouting abuse. Her veil clutched closed under her chin, and still berating him, she brandishes her free hand at him while he pretends to flinch. He sighs heavily, shoulders up, shoulders down, and reaches for a second cone, fills it with aubergines and peppers. This time they are accepted. Grudgingly Zahra Khanoom tips the vegetables into a basket she's had tucked under her veil. Now, all of a sudden, she turns to Marta and fixes her with hard eyes. The basket is on the ground at her feet, and she's issuing some demand.

Before she's done Farideh and Leila are engaging their mother with winsome cajoling but Zahra Khanoom is adamant about whatever it is. A portion of the crowd draws near, fallen silent and curious.

'What does she want me to do?'

'She wants you to buy cucumbers.'

Why on earth? 'Why does she want *me* to buy cucumbers?'

The girls look shifty but at her elbow Massy hisses, 'I'll help you.'

Marta glances at Zahra Khanoom and sees the glint of challenge in her expression. Her own glance becomes a glare. All right, then. I'll buy cucumbers if that's what she wants! 'How many does she want?'

'Two kilos.'

'Two kilos, two kilos.' Marta steps up to the stall and points imperiously at a heap of cucumbers behind the vendor, repeatedly jutting out her index fingers. He bends and fills a paper cone with cucumbers from a heap somewhere out of sight at his feet and, with an enormous grin, hands it across. Marta adopts a fierce expression to peer into the cone. Some of the cucumbers are soft, their skins shrivelled like an old woman's forearm.

'What sort of idiot do you think I am?' she screams in Polish. 'Just because you've got more money than anybody needs and a big house up on the hill? Do you think you can treat me like some sort of toy for your children to play with? Well, you can think again.' And she flings the cucumbers back at the bewildered vendor.

Her spluttering sibilants are still hanging in the air as he refills her cone with fresh green fruits that she tips directly into Zahra Khanoom's basket. Then straightens up with her hands on her hips, eyes narrow as a cat's. But Zahra Khanoom is beaming a wide toothy smile so much like Massy's, and again Marta is struck by how youthful this mother of five looks under the cascade of her enveloping veil.

'*Dokhtaram.*' Marta is engulfed by flapping black cloth and the smell of nutmeg as Zahra Khanoom embraces her, a long firm kiss planted on either cheek.

'What did you say to him?' The sisters are entranced. You sense they want to applaud.

'Oh,' says Marta, and flicks her hands dismissively. 'I just said that I wanted good cucumbers, not bad ones.'

52

Come midweek and the evening that Dr Shirazi comes home again, Massy has piled up stories to tell him. The older brother nurses his glass of tea and keeps indulgent silence for the baby of the family, tumbling with words. From time to time he makes an exclamation and raises wry eyebrows at Marta.

'Well,' he says finally. 'I leave you here so that you may rest a little, and my sisters drag you all over the countryside, hiking, swimming and arguing with market traders.'

'It gave me great pleasure,' she says, grateful for the stiffness of the formulation, but actually it had. More pleasure than she cares to admit.

That little lake in the foothills had been every bit as sweet as promised, draping a stole of silken water over her shoulders when she hesitated in the shallows before striking out. Farideh and Leila had left their manicured selves behind on the shore, where Maryam sat guard over their belongings to protect them from wandering goats. In their swimming clothes the two older ones splashed and called out to Massy, sleek and gleaming, and curving somersaults in the depths. They were all children that afternoon, and the husbands would have been amazed. Unless, spirited away from their obligations as dignified married men, they too would dive and roar and punch the dimpled water.

Maryam had brought a pile of towels and as each girl scrambled back to the crackling grass she folded them to her, as she must have done when they were toddlers. Fleetingly Marta had thought that these towels signified yet more laundry for the old woman to pound in her cauldron, but tossed the image aside. Today was her holiday. They crouched in a line by the water's edge, looking down into the faces of their reflections, and gobbled fat peaches. Juice dripped from their chins onto their knees and mixed with the sugar from Maryam's confections. They had slept, and then watched a column of ants in their two-by-twos hauling sails of dry leaves down into a teeming crevice.

That evening, when the men came home to the house – all except Dr Shirazi, on patrol in Tent City – Leila and Farideh were coiffed and painted, entirely restored. The married couples chatted round the table and Marta's eyelids had grown heavy. Her afternoon swim had exhausted her, but she had chosen it. She had actually chosen it! She stretched her shoulders in satisfaction and thought that she might creep down and see if Maryam was still awake. Late as it was she found her, back propped against the wall, dozing over her hubble-bubble. Next to her Zahra Khanoom puffed and sucked, peering quietly out at the mighty columns of her midnight garden. Without a word she passed the nozzle across to Marta.

The following day the sisters had taken her, by *doroshkeh* again, halfway down the long hill to Avenue Lalezar with its coloured awnings and French fashions. They had sipped tiny cups of potent coffee, Massy sitting unusually upright and bright-eyed, so that Marta guessed that this was an exceptional outing for her too. At the back of her mind scrawny children scampered barefoot between mud huts, their shaved heads scarred with ringworm. But, when through the window of the coffee-house she saw a trio of Soviet soldiers gazing in at the women with their cakes and cutlery, she thought, you can't touch me now.

Yes, it's true, it was a pleasure, and an interlude of luxury that revived her. But now that Dr Shirazi is here – the smell of Tent City already an alien reek on his clothes – she grapples with guilt that she should have so enjoyed herself; that she has been so richly fattened up at the urgings of his hospitable family when by his own account there is starvation in this land; that she has allowed her mind to wander.

'I must leave,' she declares. Oh, how crude that sounds. 'Excuse me, but I must go back, to the hospital. I am quite well now, thanks to you, to your family, your mother... But I really...'

'They will be disappointed.' He quells her protestations with a nod that seems to acknowledge her need but is a curt instruction too: then shut up.

And they *are* disappointed. Massy, eyes welling, runs from the room stuffing her hands into her mouth, and when the sisters turn to face her from Dr Shirazi's explanation they look slapped. Now she feels guilt-stricken all over again, but anger follows. She didn't ask to be clothed, force-fed and then caressed like a new kitten, just because they are bored. If they haven't enough to do, let them join her cleaning bedpans in Tent City or, if not there, then among their own kind in the hospital where their brother treats the ditch drinkers from the bottom of the hill. But of course those people are not their own kind at all. They are further removed from Leila and Farideh than they are from the Poles.

But are the sisters to blame? They are up here on holiday, after all, and must people be held to account first for being lucky, and then for growing soft on it? Would they become better human beings by being deliberately starved, as the Poles have been, or by being starved out of general neglect, as the ditch drinkers seem to be? Suffering doesn't make you good, she thinks. It just makes you miserable.

It is dawn, and Marta is standing in the garden armoured again by her old clothes, crisply ironed by Maryam, and ready to leave as soon as Dr Shirazi comes out. She holds her new dress poorly folded over her arm. The sisters have lined up in a glum row before her; their mother, impassive, stands a little way off.

Farideh leans forward and plucks the dress away. 'Why don't you leave that here with us? By what Karim says you won't have an opportunity to wear that in the city. Maryam can wash it for you so that next time you come it will be perfect again.'

Marta thinks there will not be any next time, but it would be churlish to say so. 'Thank you, thank you,' she says. Ever since she made her case for needing to leave she seems to have been thanking people all the time, too much. Maryam has enough work to do without laundering a dress that won't be worn again. It will be too tight for Farideh and Leila, and out of fashion by the time Massy is bigger. And anyway she cannot imagine any of the girls wearing second hand. She wishes Dr Shirazi would hurry up. This leave-taking is so awkward.

And now here he is, neat and shaved and upright, Maryam and Hajji Javad on his heels, each carrying a covered basket. 'In that case,' he says, as if they have been conversing, 'we'll be on our way. After you.'

The sisters lunge for her, arms round her neck, fragrant cheeks pressed against hers. Massy's face is puffy. Zahra Khanoom adjusts her veil. Steps forward to take Marta's hand, and gives her a long, penetrating stare. It's not hostile, not critical, but it makes her quail.

Now Dr Shirazi is growing impatient. 'If we're going, we're going.'

Down the steps to the door in the wall. It seems longer than a few days since she first came up into this great shady garden. The car is waiting, the driver at the ready this time, rubbing his forehead with the peak of his cap. She notices a small round mark on his forehead. Hajji Javad and Maryam are stowing their baskets away in the boot, while Dr Shirazi is urging her into the car. But she wants to say goodbye to them, her smoking companions with whom she has felt so comfortable, even though they could not share a word. Too late. She's bundled in, peering up at the two house servants, who are bending to the window, Hajji Javad's hands crossed over his chest, Maryam holding her cheeks in the V of her palms and shaking her head.

Dr Shirazi has seated himself next to her and the driver turns his key. Goodbye, goodbye, she mouths, and presses her hands flat against the glass.

The streets are busy at this early hour before the heat, and the driver cannot pick up speed for trotting donkeys.

Dr Shirazi reaches down to his feet and draws up a neat rectangular package. 'I have brought you... I thought you...' he mutters to the package, and dumps it in her lap.

Automatically her fingers curl round its edges but she doesn't know what to do. Should she open it straight away? She has no urge to, no great curiosity, although good manners require some. But she's had enough of good manners. It's been nothing but good manners all these past days. How she longs to be back in Tent City with her friends, where she can be herself again. She grasps the package to stop it sliding onto the floor but pointedly doesn't start picking at the wrapping.

In the wide thoroughfare traffic policemen in blue and white stand on small boxes, waving their arms and whistling like clockwork toys. They cross Avenue Lalezar, where the awnings are being wound down, where outside the shops people are pouring buckets of water over the pavements and sweeping the moistened dust into the ditches.

She asks suddenly, 'Who bought my dress?'

'My sisters, naturally.' His tone is cool.

'But how did they know my size?'

'I told them.'

He was her doctor. Of course he knows her dimensions. Intimately. She blushes and turns away.

'Did they treat you well?'

'Of course!'

'And Massy. She was not too much of a nuisance? She is very spoilt.'

'Oh, no. She's just... young.'

'Maybe. But at her age my mother was married.' Marta's eyes widen. She wants to ask how old Zahra Khanoom was when Dr Shirazi was born. But he's going on. 'Yes. She was twelve years old when I was born. Or perhaps thirteen. She is forty-two now. We think.'

Three unasked questions answered. She senses Dr Shirazi squinting at her for a reaction and determines not to give one.

'So why isn't Massy married?' It's unthinkable, Massy married off. Yet at ten years old Zahra Khanoom would have been solemn and silent. Not the family's indulged baby but an adult in her little veil, handed over from one family to the other. And she'd thought that was

378

normal, so then perhaps it was. But she was lucky that Mr Shirazi, newly making his way in the world, turned out to be such a cheery fellow.

'Strictly speaking, it's not allowed now, though to be honest most people do what they want. Most people don't even know the law has changed. But anyway my father is against it.' The modern man.

'But he married your mother when she was a child.'

Dr Shirazi shrugs. Yes. Well. That's how it goes.

'It is a disagreement between them. My mother is afraid that if they leave finding Massy a husband too long she'll never get one.'

'But she's only ten, isn't she?'

Dr Shirazi ignores that. 'And she thinks that if Farideh and Leila had married when they were younger they would not now be having difficulties conceiving.'

But the sisters are barely older than Marta is. Why is he telling her this? 'And what do you think?'

'I? I am a doctor. Of course, I don't think girls should be married when they are still children. It can be very dangerous.'

'It doesn't seem to have been dangerous for your mother.' She is deliberately provoking now.

'Actually it was. There was one miscarriage and two babies born dead. And with the rest of us she was lucky. Anyway, she cannot prevail in her arguments, of course, if my father is against it. But she is old-fashioned. And it's natural, isn't it, that people feel their children should do what they did. They want them to live better than they did, but in essentially the same way. Otherwise they think the world as they know it will come to an end.'

'And what do you think?'

'I think that the world as my mother knows it has already come to an end. But of course, like anyone old, she doesn't like change.'

'But she's not old!' Zahra Khanoom is younger than both Marta's parents.

'In years, perhaps not. Although, if we were poor, then she would be considered an old woman. But I was thinking rather of her outlook on life. She has not had the experiences that I have had, or even

379

her daughters have had. Her view of the world is the same as her mother's and her grandmother's. She does not like things to be different. However...' He pauses and wipes a hand once over his face. 'She is fond of you.'

Marta doesn't know what to make of this. She had hoped not to offend anyone, but fondness didn't come into it.

'And of course, it matters to me very much that she should be, although it's my father's opinion I have to listen to. And he – well, you can tell what he thinks. If he didn't already have a wife, he'd have...'

What is he saying? What is he implying? She feels hollow in the stomach. Jesus, what a fool she is. She doesn't know where to look. There's the package. She can open that and take her time over it. Is he suggesting what she thinks he is? The bow slips off the paper and the paper bounces open. Inside is a box of those flour-covered sweets Dr Shirazi gave her the day he invited her to visit, and laid over the top of it is a bright, white handkerchief. She bursts out laughing with such sudden relief that the driver shoots a look over his shoulder. Equally relieved, Dr Shirazi adds to hers his own rolling, infectious laugh.

But he hasn't given up. 'I'm sure you understand what I am saying, Mademoiselle Dolniak... Marta...' He has twisted in his seat. 'Of course, I'm not pressing you. You will want to discuss... matters... with the old lady, since your parents are not here with you. We understand that. We do understand that.'

He stops altogether. Such an assured doctor, so easy among his family, so suave in his suit on the veranda. But now, gagged by nerves or shyness, he stumbles over the formalities. He isn't intimidating at all any more. Poor Dr Shirazi. Marta stretches out a hand to comfort him, but at the last minute withholds the consolation and her hand hovers foolishly before she lays it back on the box of sweets.

Why is the hospital so far away? She ought to croak some reply, a simple, straightforward thank you for your interest but I'm afraid I really cannot accept because I am promised to another. Strictly speaking it wouldn't be true, since she hasn't yet told Antoni that she's decided to brave the marriage thing after all. Dr Shirazi really is a very handsome man, and a good, kind one. No doubt he's a 'catch'. But he is not Antoni. He doesn't make fun of her as Antoni does – he wouldn't know how; and he doesn't know her as Antoni does; and she doesn't know him as she knows Antoni. She likes him a lot but she doesn't love him. Does he love her? Is it possible? It would be terrible if he loved her. Which is worse: to love unrequited, or to be loved where you cannot return the love?

Her mouth is dry and the polite words don't come.

53

The car swings off the main street and within minutes they are back in the narrow dirt alleyways, nudging into the crowd, and the first thought that comes into her mind is that it smells so bad here. Instantly she is ashamed.

Someone is banging on the window on Dr Shirazi's side and he rolls it down. An old man with terrible broken teeth batters them with speech and Dr Shirazi interjects, '*Bale... bale... bashe, bashe. Miyam.*' He starts getting out of the car. Remembers Marta. 'There is a woman in premature labour. I must go. The driver will take you back.'

But she's a nurse again. 'Shouldn't I come with you?'

For a moment he gazes at her as if he's not sure. 'No. No. I think better not.'

Then he's out in the alleyway, engulfed by people and raised voices. Borne away. The driver squeezes the bulb of his horn in a series of harsh blasts and pushes slowly ahead. So they recognize Dr Shirazi here, which says a lot for him. That old man... maybe he wasn't old. What conditions can that woman be giving birth in, and is she only thirteen years old too?

The driver deposits her just inside the gates of Tent City, wheels the car round and crunches off over the stony ground, back to the twisting lanes where Dr Shirazi plunged into the crowd. Now she stands between the two covered baskets, perplexed by conflicting perceptions. There's a sense of homecoming. The large drab tents, that intimate miasma of illness and death are familiar – she knows moment by moment what will have been going on since she left. But at the same time she feels that her sojourn on the hill has turned her into an outsider, all dressed up to look like a nurse, who is at heart an impostor. The old loneliness wells up in her again, and she thinks, I brought this on myself.

A few people are moving about among the tents as if she isn't there, or as if there is no reason to remark on the fact that she is. Well, what did she expect? A reception committee with flowers? She hasn't looked into the baskets, but for sure they'll be crammed with the cakes and sweets that Maryam must have stayed up half the night to make. The best she can do is take them into her tent, hunt out Mrs Benka and discuss with her how best to distribute their contents.

There's so much she wants to tell Mrs Benka, so much she wants to ask her. Above all, Mrs Benka will know if there's been any news from the army, any news about Antoni. What if it turns out that she missed him by staying away those extra days? If she has, she'll find out where his division has gone, and then she'll just have to follow them. Not the way she once pictured she would, dressed as a soldier for battlefield honours, but simply to find him and tell him yes. So that he doesn't have to go away thinking she doesn't love him enough. She cannot imagine loving him more.

She hurries into the shadows of her tent, where the pan with the syringes is always on the boil, but there's not a nurse in sight, all gone about their duties. She heaves the two baskets onto her bed to keep them from the ants. Sees papers, folded, on her pillow. Her name in strong black letters. Unfamiliar handwriting. She opens them out, glances to the bottom of the last page and reads 'Edyta Benka'. Of course she wouldn't know the writing because Mrs Benka has never had cause to write to her before. So that's her Christian name, is it, after all this time? It doesn't suit her. No name other than Mrs Benka would suit her. But why is she writing at all? This doesn't feel good. Perhaps read it later, at the end of the working day. But suppose something's happened to Antoni and Mrs Benka cannot bring herself to say so face to face.

My dear Marta,

I am so sorry I couldn't see you before all the changes, but there was no warning that things were about to happen. I am sure that had we both known, you might have put off your little holiday until afterwards. No doubt it is asking too much for anyone to hope to be able to make plans during wartime, when the days either seem all the same and endless, or nothing but chaos without a moment to think.

The very morning you left with Dr Shirazi, in that nice car of his that we all so admired as it swept you away, some British officers arrived with a great deal of noise and foot stamping, and announced that the camp had been declared over-crowded and a health hazard, to which Hania remarked that it was by definition a health hazard. They said they were expecting new shiploads of refugees any day, who would be needing the beds, so everyone who wasn't part of the working staff must be moved on. As you can imagine they took one look at me and declared me too old to be of use. I tried to protest but to be honest, my dear, I cannot pretend that I have the strength of you young ones, and I knew that the greatest good I could do for my countrymen was to get out of their way. But I had no idea it would happen so quickly. Then, when Dr Shirazi arrived for his night shift the next evening and told us that you would be staying on with his family for a week or so, I realized that I might not have the chance to say goodbye to you as I wished.

Ever since the day Ania first brought you out to the farm and I sent the pair of you off picking apples, I have thought of you as warmly as if you were my granddaughter too – and a proud grandmother I was. I never imagined how events would bind our lives together, nor how powerfully I would come to love you. I know you are by nature an optimist, so for the time being I will put away my crabby old carping and do all I can to believe that we will meet again in happier times. I cannot give you an address because I only know that we are going to Bombay, although it is probable that some of us may be sent to somewhere in Africa.

When the war is over, if it should be possible, I shall try to go to

Poznan and stay as close to Krystyna as she will have me. I don't suppose that my farm still exists, but even if it did, without Old Petrkiewicz to help me, it would be more than I could manage on my own. I know you and Ania thought me stubborn, but you see, I am not such a foolish old woman after all!

There has been no word yet of Antoni, but when he returns, tell him that I think of him with great warmth too, as if he were my grandson in fact – and not simply for official purposes! I will not burden you with advice about how to conduct your life, as we old ones apparently so often feel bound to do, because, if anything, what the last eighteen months have taught me is that someone else's previous experience cannot be taken as a model in a world that won't stay still.

I think often of Pavel Kuzmich, as I'm sure you do, and I am certain, certain that the poor fellow's miserable life was greatly improved by arguing with you. By the way, I know that the little wooden spoon he made for you has become like a talisman, but in the way the world goes, it's quite possible that something will happen and your spoon will get lost. If that should be so, remember that the thoughts and good wishes Pavel Kuzmich had for you remain – with or without the spoon. You were a survivor before you got it.

You will not be alone, my dear Hania and Basia will be working alongside you and in time – I would say, God willing, but you know me – you will all be reunited with your families. Maybe, when all this nonsense is behind us, we can sit somewhere cosy together, with large glasses of tea and a plate of gingerbread, and continue our discussions on human nature. In the meantime, do whatever you think your father would approve of, but remember that Pavel Kuzmich was also right when he told you to look after yourself. Now, do you see? I've gone ahead and done what I said I wouldn't – peppered this last letter with unsought advice.

My love to you, Marta. Don't change who you are.
Edyta Benka

Marta leans against her bed staring down at all that remains of Mrs

Benka in her hands. She imagines the British officers calling up all the surviving older ones and hoisting them into a truck to take them... where exactly Mrs Benka hasn't said, but it has to be another port, doesn't it, to sail to Bombay. Bombay! It's beyond any picture-book she can remember, but then she'd have said the same of Iran, or Siberia, or the desert steppe.

If only she'd been able to come back that night with Dr Shirazi, she might have persuaded them to leave Mrs Benka in the camp, or she might have decided to go with her. No, she couldn't have done that, without seeing Antoni. Whichever way you turn, you lose people.

But at least Antoni hasn't come and gone as well, though how she is to live without Mrs Benka, bundled away and no forwarding address... She must find Hania and Basia, or that English-speaking Mrs Dablinska, who might have understood more. Unless Mrs Dablinska has been shipped off as well. She was elderly too.

But first she must take Maryam's baskets round all the wards where people are well enough to eat. Children first. Even Massy, who got more sweets than she could eat, brightened when Maryam came in with her piled plates.

Rumour spreads, even among the bed-ridden, and wherever she goes Marta is greeted with wide, expectant smiles. Mmm! Yum! Mouths roll around Maryam's baking. The sweets and biscuits have gone a long way because so many people have departed, and the remaining nurses are on double duty, preparing the wards for the newcomers scheduled to arrive any hour. There hasn't been time to talk to Hania and Basia, but that's for later. Something to look forward to.

Soon enough, though, Dr Shirazi will appear, expecting an answer to the question he didn't actually ask. He will think she's consulted Mrs Benka. He will still be under the impression that Mrs Benka's approval is all his suit requires. She can hear Mrs Benka saying, 'Well, my dear, simply tell him that you don't want to marry him. There is no need to mention Antoni, but there's also no reason why you shouldn't.' That's true, but it doesn't feel so simple. It feels as though one ought to have had experience of these things to be able to carry them off.

She conjures up Dr Shirazi to attempt a rehearsal, but retreats before his silent disappointment. She doesn't want to hurt his feelings, because she had begun to think that in different circumstances she would like to get to know him better, to find out more of the man than the face he wears for the world. But that's not possible now. Now, every word between them would be burdened with significance she didn't intend. So, although she knows it's cowardly, she will keep out of his way, put off her reply until tomorrow. And Dr Shirazi is a man with routines. He always goes from ward to ward in the same order – for their sakes, he once said, the nurses' sakes, because the job is hard enough without people springing surprises. She had been touched by his consideration at the time, but now fizzes with contrition. Not for long, though. There is mayhem outside, and she has to join it.

The gates are standing wide for the trucks, one after another bearing their infested cargo. British soldiers with handkerchiefs tied over their faces are pulling stretchers from the backs of their jeeps and lifting bald children down over the tailgates of the trucks. Children with insect-thin legs and shoulder-blades like chicken wings try to hop about, excited to have arrived. There are too many children for the number of adults. A lot of orphans, then, or they have lost their mothers along the way. And the trucks keep coming. Now the drivers are handing the passengers down, tossing them out almost, little brittle men and women, listless without the children's curiosity. Marta has left her concealing corner. No one will be talking marriage tonight.

She spies Hania and Basia each guiding a wraith to one of the tents. She grabs a brace of children and leads them to the newly made-up cots. Tells them not to stray and goes back for more. Someone holds out a bundle to her, which turns out to be a sleeping toddler, or a baby maybe, so thin it's hard to tell. Has its mother gone missing? She takes the child and lays it in a corner cot, where it lies without moving or crying. She ought to tend to it somehow but there are more people being unloaded, more and yet more. Backwards and forwards, people criss-crossing; here and there a glimpse of a white coat. One of them must be Dr Shirazi, his routine in shards.

The trucks have long gone and the most needy been put to bed. It has been such an influx that some of them, those who can and all the nursing staff, will have to sleep outside, under the stars but on the hard ground. Now there's a lull, time to get a glass of tea and sit for a moment. Mrs Benka was right. It's either the unchanging routine or chaos, and probably that's how things will be until the war is over. Can it go on like this for years? But of course the flow of Polish refugees transferred from the Soviet camps will stop eventually, and Tent City will close. Then she, and Hania and Basia, and all the others, will follow Mrs Benka to Bombay, or to that somewhere in Africa. But to do what, exactly?

Basia is coming towards her clasping a young woman by the arm, like an usherette guiding a late arrival at the theatre. The woman is wearing a flowered scarf wound round her head, to protect the shaven scalp from the sun perhaps – or to disguise her baldness. She leans on Basia's supporting arm and talks and talks, without stopping it seems, so that Basia can only nod, mm, and nod again.

They're not just coming towards her. They're making for her, and now that they're close Marta senses that Basia is a reluctant guide; her face is pinched and unhappy.

'Hello?' Marta scrambles up, and glances at Basia, who averts her gaze, then at the young woman, who looks like all the new arrivals, with her sunken eyes and parchment skin.

'Was there a baby that you took in, Marta? Wrapped in blue?' Basia turns to the young woman. 'That's what you said, isn't it? Yes, wrapped all in blue.'

Was the baby wrapped in blue? She hadn't noticed. 'There were lots of little children, and there was a baby. Is it yours? It's this way, I'll show you. Asleep, I think, but I'll show you.'

'Marta!'

'Hang on a sec, Basia. Let me show her, then I'll be right back.'

388

She replaces Basia's grip on the woman's arm with her own, and pivots her in the direction of the tent with the unaccompanied children. What a relief if one of them – and the youngest at that – can be reunited with its mother. She really would prefer not to have to minister to an inconsolable baby.

'But, Marta!'

'What?' She didn't intend to snap but what's got into Basia? Who flinches. 'Nothing. Nothing.'

Marta shrugs, have it your own way, and resumes shunting the young mother into the tent. Halfway across, the woman catches a glimpse of blue cloth trailing over the end of a mattress and breaks free. By the time Marta reaches her she is cradling her baby with her face pressed into its, snuffling her nose over the baby's nose, gabbling endearments. The baby lies there so still that Marta fears it may have died and that the woman has yet to realize it.

But when she lifts her face, tear-stained and ecstatic, the baby's wide eyes, blue as its shawl, follow her movements, and a papery little paw creeps from its covering.

'Thank you,' the woman whispers. 'They said you'd be the one.'

'Be the one?' Marta drops her voice to match.

'Well, that you'd brought the children in and... and you'd know about Antoni.'

'What about Antoni?'

'Where he is. If he's going to be coming here. That's what they told me, that the regiments might be passing through here before they leave, some of them. But everyone seems to think you'd know best. Do you?'

'But what about Antoni? What Antoni are you talking about?'

'My Antoni. Antoni Kozlowski. My fiancé, and my Staszek's father.'

The baby's eyes are glued to the motion of his mother's chin wobbling up and down as she speaks. Blue eyes and such long lashes. But all babies have blue eyes. And this mother has blue eyes too.

'What' – Marta's voice snags in her throat – 'What do you mean, "fiancé"? Antoni proposed to me! Only a few weeks ago. He proposed to me!'

'You must have misunderstood.' The young woman is looking at Marta with pity. 'You see, when he knew I was going to have a baby he gave me a ring, as a pledge for the future. I can show you.'

She lays her baby back on the mattress, stands up and with her back turned spreads her legs with her knees slightly bent, fishes up between them. Now she about-faces and holds out her left hand. A man's signet ring on the fourth finger glistens with the moisture of her body.

'Sorry. That's where I've had to hide it sometimes. It used to fit me well enough but now, of course, it just falls off.'

'So you've got a ring. So what? That could be any ring!' But even as she speaks – shouts, actually, so that the sleeping children stir and begin to wail, she hears Antoni's voice, consoling her for the loss of the necklace. *I had a ring once. It was my grandfather's but I lost it. It's not the end of the world.* Antoni, who couldn't get enough of listening to her talk about the people she loved but divulged nothing himself. 'This is rubbish. You're making it up for some reason. You must be.'

And Marta storms from the tent, but already thinking, why would she make it up? How would she know of Antoni if she didn't know Antoni? And what was he doing with me, then, playing games? Was that what it all was, just playing games while he was waiting to see if this girl was going to show up with her son? Their son?

Full tilt into Hania and Basia, who know.

'Come away.' Basia's arm snakes round Marta's shoulders while Hania is making a grab for her hand. But Marta pushes Hania aside, tries to shake off Basia's motherly arm, though Basia is adamant and won't let herself be dislodged.

Between them they frog-march her away to the furthest point behind the tents where there is no one. And they don't let go. She isn't crying. She isn't saying anything at all. Somebody has to speak. Hania looks at Basia, Basia at Hania. You go first. I can't. You have to.

'Marta.' Urgently. Together. 'Marta.'

They have her clamped between them and take the weight simultaneously as her control dissolves and she sits heavily. Now they are on the ground, all three, Basia holding Marta's hands and caressing her wrists, Hania thinking, somebody help us, as she peers through the gathering night at the immobilized face.

'I thought he loved me. He said he loved me. Didn't he love me?'

'I thought he did.'

'Hania, then. Didn't you think he did?'

'Yes. Yes, I did. I thought he did.'

'He said he loved me and he didn't. All along. He was only pretending so that I'd... And I don't understand.' Marta is still talking into her lap, where Basia's thumbs haven't stopped rubbing on her wrists. 'He asked me to marry him. That's what I don't see. He asked me to marry him.'

The thumbs fall still. 'And did you accept?'

Marta doesn't reply.

'Didn't you accept, Marta?' This time it's Hania. 'Did you turn him down?'

'Not exactly. I mean. I was going to accept. I was going to tell him today. It's just that...'

'Just that what? He asked you and you didn't say yes, like anyone else would? Why didn't you accept?'

'Being married and all that comes after. I was frightened of the change and —'

'But surely. When you love someone. You know things will change. That's the whole point of marriage, how things change. You know they have to, don't you? So you didn't accept because of that. It's how people end up on their own, you know. For ever. On their own. And he'll have thought...'

But Basia is leaning over to her friend. 'Ssh, Hania. Don't go on about it. What's the point now? Can't you see? It doesn't matter what she said or didn't say. It's not the point, don't you see? Antoni and that woman... He must have known her before, mustn't he? She's got a baby, for goodness' sake. He didn't only meet her now.'

Hania's torso stiffens. Her eyes widen as she stares at Basia. 'But that's right! Of course. You're right.' She clenches her fists to thump her thighs. Her sympathies that a moment ago had foolishly swung towards rejected Antoni have lurched back. 'You're right. Of course. That's it. What a rat! What a complete rat!'

54

Dr Shirazi is too weary to remember how the day began. But near the gates of Tent City he comes upon Marta retching over a ditch. He hauls her out, brushes the back of his fingers across her forehead and pronounces her feverish.

'What is this?' – sounding somehow put out. 'What is going on? What is the matter?'

But Marta shakes her head, no reason, no answer. Then, 'Take me away from here.'

'Now?'

'Just get me away from here.'

'And the old lady. Have you spoken to her?'

'She's gone. She's not here. They've sent her to Bombay with all the other old people.'

'*Ah, mon Dieu!* I am sorry. I am so sorry.' But something about her face has given him pause, because his expression alters. 'Has something else happened? Has someone offended you? Because if he has I will kill him. I swear to you, I will kill him.' He draws himself up, breathing raucously, and stares not so much at her as through her, already challenging the enemy.

She believes him. He would take a knife, she thinks, and run Antoni through if he knew. But she does not want Antoni to be run through with a knife. All she wants is for someone to remove the anguish and the yawning bleakness. She does not answer his question but hunches over her knees.

Now he is making her sip at a glass of sweetened tea; he's telling her that he understands how Mrs Benka was like a mother to her, and that there can be nothing worse than losing one's family. She gulps the tea down as it is, burning hot, because the physical discomfort is comforting. Happening to glance up she catches him dipping his head to look into her face, worried and tender, and trying to smile, like her father pulling faces to jolly her out of her childhood hurts: it'll all be better soon, you'll see. At least there are still some good men in the world, she thinks, honourable, and kind. At least someone is unconditionally on my side.

'Now you must sleep and we will go home in the morning.'

But I want to go now! Though there is no means of leaving in the night and she will not scream and weep in front of anyone. She counts her breaths, four seconds in, four seconds out, four in, four out, as she takes off her pinafore and clothes and creeps into bed. Clutching her wooden spoon, she curls knees to chest under the camouflage of her sheet. Closes her eyes.

But her memory has fished out a coal truck and a young man dipping the rim of his hat into the water bucket to wash the greasy black dust from her eyebrows, from around her mouth. Now here he is leaning against her in the compartment of a ponderous train; wrapping his arms about her as she tugs on a cotton bush. Lying on her, body to body full length.

Was it really only a game all along and she was stupid and naïve, believing that he loved her when in fact all he wanted was a bit of fun while he waited for his fiancée? If by some awful chance she had not discovered in time, she might have found herself tending to this woman of his, feeding her, washing her, measuring out medication. Even bathing that ugly baby.

What would he have said if she'd accepted his proposal? 'Oh, sorry. Just remembered. I can't think how it slipped my mind...'? It doesn't make sense.

In the earliest morning Dr Shirazi comes for her and is distressed to see her haggard and grey, her hair matted, dried saliva at the corners of her mouth. He takes her to wash her face and comb her hair. He picks up her pitiful bundle and turns it about in his hands, looking down at it with compassion, and says, Do you really need this? It's just a memento, she says. Of the past. I'll take it along. One should always remember the past. And he agrees. Yes. Nothing is more important than the past – except, perhaps, the future? Mm?

Any minute now there will be the arrival back at the house on the hill, the awful embarrassing arrival. Everyone will gather and look at her, murmuring, holding back, observing the proprieties. All except Massy, of course, who'll launch herself at Marta, have you come to stay, mademoiselle, have you come for good?

And so it is. Massy is puppy-eyed.

'Yes,' Marta blurts, then immediately repents.

Before Massy can press her, Dr Shirazi shoos his little sister away. All she wants is to sleep. For a week, for a month, for ever.

They are so good, all of them, backing away, melting off into their corners, silently, leaving Farideh to lead her to the room they put her in before and coax her into the bed. Leila has grabbed Massy to hold her back, whispering instructions to her, and Massy is responding in urgent whispers of her own.

Everything passes in the end.

When she wakes, the yellow dress that Dr Shirazi had them buy for her is spread over the chair at the foot of the bed. She stares dully at it and closes her eyes again.

They minister to her for the loss of Mrs Benka as if she were bereaved, until she begins to believe that, yes, there was a death, and is oddly consoled. Maryam comes to sing to her in a deep, slightly hoarse voice, cross-legged on the floor and rocking backwards and forwards from the hips. Leila and Farideh sit vigil either side of her bed, and Massy, who must have been told to keep her voice down, hunkers at its foot, blinking like a fat little owl. Sometimes Marta is aware of Zahra Khanoom's quiet presence in the doorway.

One morning she wakes asking for pen and paper.

'Are you going to write a letter, Mademoiselle Marta?'

'Yes. A letter. I think I will.'

So Massy brings one of her school exercise books, untouched; an envelope, an inkwell and a pen. 'Will it be an important letter? I've never sent one to anyone because all the people I know are where I am.'

Eventually, when Massy has left the room, Marta dips the pen and begins, *Dear Mama and Tata...*, then sits for a long time with the exercise book opened on her knees. The pen shilly-shallies over the lined surface. *The situation I am in is...* No. *I need your advice about...* No. This is ridiculous.

Finally she dips her pen again and writes only, *Where are you?*

Later that morning Hajji Javad bears the letter away to the post, delicately cupping the envelope with its unfathomable writing like a butterfly trapped in his palms. But by this time Marta is covering the pages of the exercise book from margin to margin, calling up every word she exchanged with Antoni, interpreting and reinterpreting every modulation of his voice, every expression of his face. She writes about his first appearance at the convent – the handsome cadet sent as the Archbishop's emissary, ostensibly with messages for the Mother Superior but turning his long-lashed smile equally on all the girls. She writes about how quickly he learned and remembered everyone's name; how casually he seemed to be able to talk to them all; she writes about Ania, weak at the knees whenever he passed, and in retrospect wonders how it was that at the time she did not feel the same herself.

Day after day Marta documents her lost love. She cleaves to the chair in her room and writes; they escort her to sit by the pool in the garden and still she writes; they bring her food, which she eats without noticing it, and writes on. When she gets to the end of her story she starts all over again, for she might have missed or mistaken something. Version one; version two; version three. She reads them over to compare them, and finds they scarcely differ. Whichever way she has tried to relate it, what has emerged is the tale of a naïve and credulous girl who was taken in by a practised young man of the world – because she wanted to be. It is embarrassing. It is humiliating. Hania was right after all. Antoni is a complete rat. But it seems you can love a rat, notwithstanding. So then, there is no escape.

*

There is no reply from Poland, but wartime post is bound to be slow.

The summer of 1942 dwindles into its autumn and in the house on the hill they are getting ready to close up for the rest of the year. In every room the women are packing boxes, rolling away mattresses and draping the furniture with dustsheets, while their men are at work down in the city, all except Behzad, who apparently did not find his *métier* running cinemas but has nothing else to do. He trails disconsolately around the house, getting in everyone's way, then out into the garden, complaining that his life is meaningless, that he's bored, and that everything and everyone conspires against him. He is eighteen years old, he keeps saying, and would be in France, studying law, but for the evil forces that prevent him. If this war doesn't end soon he can't see what his life will amount to.

Down in the garden Marta has been watching Hajji Javad tying back the old growth of the apricots against the wall and clipping out dead wood from among the shrubs. 'Why don't you help them inside, packing?' she suggests. 'Why don't you help Hajji Javad looking after the garden?'

But Behzad kisses the air with contempt at the suggestion. 'I don't do manual work,' he says. 'Can you imagine what people would think, someone like me? I am destined to be a somebody, a professional. Like Karim.'

'But your brother's work. There is a great deal in that that is manual, physical.'

'No. He is a professional, and that is how he is seen. Do you know that a doctor can be a really rich man in this country? He can charge what he likes. That's why everyone wants to be a doctor, if they can.'

'But he doesn't charge, does he? He works for free, to help people.'

Behzad kisses the air again. *Tss.*

'And your family is rich enough already, isn't it? Why does it matter so much to be rich?'

Behzad is taken aback. It makes him realize just how much of a stranger she really is, who understands so little. 'You have to be very rich to stay rich, don't you see? If someone comes, a policeman or someone from the government, and wants to take away your house or your business, there is only one way to stop them.' He pats his pocket. 'Money is power. You have to have more than you need to keep what you need.'

'But, if it's your house, they can't just take…'

Marta's objection tails away, as she recalls Mrs Benka's account of Old Petrkiewicz prodding the requisitioning Soviet troops with his pitchfork. And, according to Dr Shirazi, the family fleet of lorries was expropriated by the British – without compensation. Presumably even the Shirazis haven't enough money to buy the British off. But there's something about Behzad that puts her back up, a sort of narcissism. She's noticed him gazing at himself in every mirror he passes as if he's infatuated with what he sees. Vain and lazy, she thinks. That's what he is. Why do they let him get away with it?

'All right then,' she says sarcastically. 'You could be a teacher. You could go down into the city and teach people to read and write. That's professional.'

'No, you don't understand at all. Teachers have no status. Everybody knows that you only become a teacher when you can't do anything else, and they earn so little they have to have two or three other jobs just to pay for some nasty little room in a bad area.'

'But for now. For something to do. You could go and teach for nothing. While you wait for the war to be over.' He really hasn't even noticed that she was mocking him, has he? Look at him, shaking his head.

But her suggestion has given him an idea and the following morning he announces that in fact he *will* teach, and she's to be his pupil. 'I'll teach you to speak Farsi and perhaps,' he says, hugging his little sister, 'Massy can help us.'

At least he's kind to Massy. The little girl skips about behind her brother and holds onto his hand whenever he lets it dangle. He doesn't brush her away. He even lets her sneak onto his lap to be tickled, after a swift look to make sure Zahra Khanoom isn't on the prowl. Now Behzad is at home it's clear who Massy's secret tree-climbing partner must be. Though it's impossible to imagine his plump frame monkeying through the branches.

398

Brother and little sister begin by pointing at objects, naming them and having Marta repeat after them, syllable by syllable. They think her pronunciation hilarious, which irks her. How would they fare with Polish? She's prepared to bet they'd sound even sillier! But they're not the pupils. One thing, though. Her memory is good, and at mealtimes Massy and Behzad put her through her paces for Zahra Khanoom and the sisters. What's a nose? they ask. What's eyes? What's a fork? What's bread? Zahra Khanoom and the sisters applaud, courteous but impressed as well, and the first time she thanks Maryam for a delicious lunch the old woman spreads her arms and declares she's never heard anyone speak so perfectly.

Encouraged by success, the three of them set to work on polite questions and, after that, polite answers and expressions of gratitude. Marta has not imagined that there could be so many ways of saying thank you and so many occasions when they must all be deployed.

The weekend before the family are due to move back to the city, Dr Shirazi intercepts Marta on her way from her seat by the garden pool to the kitchen house for a smoke with Maryam.

'Are you feeling better?'

'Yes.'

'I meant, better in your... your spirit. Not grieving so much perhaps?'

She shakes her head and waits.

Dr Shirazi is holding a piece of paper that he doesn't seem to know what to do with. In fact, he doesn't seem to know what to do with any part of himself: he takes his weight on one foot and rubs the toe of the other against the standing ankle; he pulls at an earlobe, looks away, looks back, and wades in.

'In this country, you cannot know this, but, when a man wishes to be married, it's usual for members of his family to approach the family of the young woman to... er... raise the issue. It can take a long time, visits backwards and forwards, many people involved, many calculations and so on and so forth. But I think all that sort of thing belongs in the past, as I have told my parents. I have made it clear to them that I don't want to be part of all that haggling and ceremonial.

I think one ought to be more direct in one's relations.' He pauses. 'Don't you?... So' – he casts about as if his relatives might be lurking with ready criticisms just beyond the plane trees – 'I wonder if now you feel able to consider my proposal of marriage. I ask you today because we are returning to the city. And we have to decide where... you will live. Unless you wish to return to Tent City.' He stops again, then laughs once. 'Is this how it's done? If not, then I apologize.'

Antoni, on his knees, Commander Nurse Dolniak...

'I'm afraid I don't know.'

'But your answer?'

I don't know you well enough. I don't love you the way I loved Antoni, we haven't talked the way I used to talk with Antoni. You're not my friend the way he was.

Some friend! He debased everything friendship was meant to be. So easy to be with – easy come, easy go.

Is there another way, a better way? Return to Tent City. She could, she *should*, return to Tent City, where there may still be work to be done, reviving, mind-numbing work. But she cannot face that woman and her baby.

If she were at home, her father would have seen through Antoni, seen him off more like. Or tried to. If she were an Iranian her parents would have made their careful enquiries. Look at Shirazi *père* and Zahra Khanoom. They can't have been in love when she was only a little girl, but now they seem as content as her parents are.

For the second time in her life Marta becomes aware that a man who has put an important question is waiting, perplexed and in silence, for her response. But this time the question is sincere.

'I'm the one who should apologize now,' she says. 'But I just wish I could somehow ask my parents. The trouble is, I wrote to them but I haven't had a reply.'

'*Ah, mon Dieu!*' Dr Shirazi pulls the paper he was toying with earlier out of his pocket and holds it out. It is her letter, unopened, much handled and covered in an overlapping jigsaw of official stamps. 'Sometimes, when letters are returned, it can mean simply that there have been mistakes, at one end or the other. It does not have to mean anything more. But, Marta, if I were your parents, wherever they are, I would wish to believe that my daughter was safe, and not alone. We are not meant to be alone, Marta. We do not flourish on our own.'

55

They hold the wedding at Hotel Firdawsi, where Dr Shirazi has insisted to the flabbergasted proprietor that the wedding spread be laid out on tables, not on an embroidered, pearl-encrusted cloth on the floor. According to the sisters this is a small affair, but these are not the times for a celebration of the size they'd have liked. There ought to have been parties and feasts before, parties and feasts afterwards; visits by their family to hers... but of course that wasn't an option.

Guests have been surging in to inspect the Polish bride, whose foreignness has deprived them of all those parties, impossible to remember their names, impossible to keep smiling at them all. So many of them are relatives, and now they are Marta's too.

Shirazi *père* has had his favourite restaurant do the food. The chef buttocks the double doors open for his sons, springy at the knee, with giant trays balanced at shoulder level, wafting cardamom and cloves, barberries and saffron. He follows behind, a dancing pyramid of platters. He has devised more ways of cooking mutton than there are sheep. Only Massy is more excited than her elderly father. Wriggling to keep still, she will not let go of Marta's arm. Not this time. Not any more. Zahra Khanoom has found a corner from where she can observe – swathed in her white and blue, but edged with gold for the occasion – along with the other women who prefer the veil. Dr Shirazi, Karim (Marta has discovered his full name is Abdol-Karim), keeps repeating how pleased his mother is with the way things have turned out. He cannot stop smiling and whenever he looks at her his eyes are huge, almost brimming. From time to time he strokes her hair as if she were an unexpected kitten rescued from a tree. Receiving the caress, she tells herself, *You can do this, Marta Dolniak. You have to be able to do this.*

They have not sat down for this meal until nearly midnight and Marta's eyes are heavy. An elderly man with stippled jowls and an embroidered cap pushes up from the table to declaim a poem, vowels drawn out, rhymes rolling. It must be particularly fine because from time to time the guests clap their hands and exclaim, 'Bah! Bah!' When he's done, he thwumps back into his chair, twitching bright little rodent nods of pleasure at the applause. Then up leaps another, with a competing poem of his own. Tears sit on the wings of his nose and Marta is surprised to see answering tears appear in Karim's eyes as well. He makes no effort to wipe them away but leans over with glistening cheeks to explain the gist of the poem, about enduring love, and nightingales and the hot lips of the sun kissing the snow of the mountain passes.

One after another the men are on their feet, each with the gift of a poem, and then suddenly Karim has loomed to his, to respond. He leans on the table, bracing his weight on his fingertips, all faces, finally, turned to him, but the long droning syllables make Marta's head flop to her chest. No one minds. No one has noticed. They are not looking at her any more.

The guests don't leave the Hotel Firdawsi until after dawn, and all over the great room related children are sleeping like puppies where exhaustion has dropped them. Older siblings gather them up and drape them over a shoulder, cradling the tiniest, but the children sleep on. From the looks she's getting, from the shrillness of their voices, Marta can tell that the parents are cracking jokes that in some way concern her. These are words she has yet to learn.

Behzad sidles up to her as the hall empties, a crooked smirk playing over his lips. He whispers into her ear, 'Be grateful we're a modern family.'

She is startled. 'Why? What do you mean?'

'No old nanny sitting outside your door.' And he snickers into his palm.

'I don't understand.'

'Ask your husband.'

Husband. Karim is her husband. And here he comes, searching for her to stand by his side and say her goodbyes. Actually, he's looking as drained as she feels, so maybe he's not as used to these late-night parties as the rest of them. His hand lies on her shoulder like a paperweight positioned on a crucial letter. At last everyone is gone except for the sisters and the husbands, Shirazi *père* and Zahra Khanoom, Behzad and Massy. They will all spend the rest of this night, although it is already morning, in the hotel.

Karim leads Marta up the staircase to their room, where small lights are lit on both sides of a wide bed. Marta's lips are dry. She stands just inside the closed door with her arms folded over her chest. Karim is rubbing his eyes and stretching his arms, his back to her, facing towards the curtained window. If he opens the curtains it will be to the dawn. Now he turns back and strides towards her with purpose. He puts his arms around her, and her own arms, still folded, dig awkwardly into his chest.

'Well,' he says. 'So you are my wife.' He releases her and pulls her arms apart. 'Aren't you going to embrace me?'

She titters with nerves. 'Of course.' But doesn't move. 'Behzad said something about an old woman outside the door. What did he mean?'

'It's not important.'

'He said I should ask you, and I would like to know.'

'I told you. It's not important.'

She won't let go. 'He said I should be grateful that yours is a modern family. What did he mean?'

Dr Shirazi throws up his hands and sits suddenly on the end of the bed. 'There is a custom according to which an old woman will sit outside the bridal chamber waiting for the marriage to be consummated. She then inspects the bed-sheets. If there is no blood the girl will be sent in disgrace back to her family, who will of course be

404

dishonoured – along with the rest of her family, when the news gets out. Is that an adequate answer to your question?'

Marta swallows. She cannot look him in the face.

'It is, of course, also a protection for the girl.'

'How?' Her voice is barely audible.

'Because, in very traditional families, that might be the first time a husband has seen the face of his bride. If she turns out to be very ugly he may try to get rid of her by pretending that she is not a virgin. But you have no need to worry on either score. You are not ugly. On the contrary. And I know you are a virgin. And anyway, as Behzad correctly said, we are a modern family. We do not do that.'

He looks at her as if he is expecting to be congratulated, but when no congratulations are forthcoming he stands up again. His hands hover at her neck by the clasp of her necklace, but then he drops them. 'Perhaps you would prefer to get ready in private?' Without waiting for her reply he steps out into the corridor and closes the door behind him with a quiet click.

Marta creeps to the door and listens but there is no sound, no departing footsteps. He's simply waiting, looking at his watch, drumming his fingers against his thigh. She reaches behind her head and undoes the necklace of turquoise set in gold – a wedding gift from Shirazi *père*. She lays it on the dressing table. Tiny buttons run down the back of her dress and this morning Massy and Farideh had done them up for her. 'Only women can do these buttons,' Farideh said, 'just like only women or children can knot carpets. Men's fingers are too large and clumsy.' Some she can reach, at the top and at the bottom, but at the centre of her back her fingers cannot grip the slippery little things well enough, and the buttonholes have been sewn to be tight. Leila and Farideh had taken her to have the dress measured up and made at Dr Shirazi's expense. Five fittings – the dressmaker fluting with excitement at the commission.

Her arms are getting tired. She droops them by her sides to rest them, then gives the buttons one more try, but it's no good. Oh, for heaven's sake! You only wear a wedding dress once. She grabs the two halves of the back of her dress and rips them apart as hard as she can.

Buttons roll like small pearls over the floor, under the dressing table and under the bed. With the dress slipping down over her shoulders she's on her knees gathering up the evidence, like a peasant gleaning grains of wheat from a neighbour's field. Sixteen little white witnesses. She pokes them into the toe of one shoe, drops the silky dress over a chair. Turns her back to the dressing table and its mirror and steps out of her stockings, knickers and brassière, drops them on the dress, picks them up and hides them under the dress. She would like to turn off the lights.

They've given her a white satin night-gown – hand-sewn as well, copied by the seamstress from a pre-war French magazine. She slides it over her head and feels a little safer. She lays herself down, close to one side of the bed; since this is an expensive hotel the sheets are clean. Now that she's lying between them she wonders what she should do next. Ought she to call out, 'I'm ready'? But she doesn't think she can ever be ready. She could cough. A small croak escapes her, and Karim opens the door.

Her pale bare arms pinion the covers tightly over her body and she doesn't know where to look, whether to watch as her husband takes off his clothes, which he does, layer by layer, matter-of-fact. The closed door of her parents' bedroom looms massively in her mind. Her father's clothes would be carefully folded, military style. Karim is letting his fall where he stands. She closes her eyes. She's a nurse, for God's sake, she has given bed baths to male patients these last three months without a second thought, so why can't she look at the healthy, well-made body of the man she has just married?

Her mouth is dry and her lips are dry. She wants to moisten them but doesn't want him to notice that she needs to. She turns her head to the side but her cheek rolls into his dry palm, which directs her face back towards him. His dry lips are on hers, his breath is steady – she can hear him breathing through his nose like the surf on the sea. His body is heavy and hot, although hers feels chilled. One of her arms has somehow got itself painfully trapped at the elbow by his knee and she tries to wriggle it free but he doesn't seem to notice that she's uncomfortable. He has shunted the sheet aside with paddling motions of his feet and is pulling up her night-gown, which she tries to push down again with her free hand. He laughs slightly, 'I know, I know,' but releasing her elbow suddenly shifts that knee down between hers. He's kissing her neck with small dry nibbles and she thinks of the twitching nose of a rabbit. He's lying between her legs and his naked penis is pressing hard against her.

He brings a hand down and puts his fingers up between her legs. 'Oh,' he mutters in disappointment, 'so dry!' He raises himself to one elbow and looks down into her face and she quickly closes her eyes again. 'Oh well,' he sighs, and begins prying and pulling at the lips of her genitals. He is pushing fingers into her, really into her, then pressing and kneading at a point near the front of the opening and her face flushes hot with embarrassment. How can people do this and then look at one another next morning as if everything was ordinary? She feels a trickle and pulls in her sphincter muscles, aghast that she must have urinated, but at the same time she feels his fingers sliding with slippery ease and there it is, that hot, building itch that she had felt when she... because it was Antoni... that mustn't ever stop, and she pushes herself towards it, but his fingers have gone and he is in her with a lunge and she squawks at the sharpness of it and wants to get away. But there is no getting away from this piston body, and she feels splayed and flattened. Then pinpoints of the tantalizing itch come and go, and she thinks, *How do I hold onto that, how do I reach that again?* Antoni would... if it were Antoni... Antoni's mouth... She tries to shift herself under the moving weight to find the place, that one place, but there's a sudden gasp and everything stops. She feels her uneven breathing, his uneven breathing. Something inside her pulses and twitches. Karim is murmuring in Farsi but she can't follow.

As his breath returns to normal he raises himself on his elbows, dips his face to nuzzle her neck, and pulls out of her. She winces. It hurts and she feels mucky. Karim is sitting up and has swung his feet out of the bed to sit sideways. He looks down her and pats her thigh through the ropy tangle of sheet. 'Don't worry, *mon amour.*' He bends down to her and whispers, doctor encouraging patient, 'It will be easier tomorrow. I guarantee.' Then he laughs gently and draws the sheet aside. 'And look! That old woman would be satisfied, if she were here.'

But later in the day, when the sun is high and the family prepares to leave the Firdawsi, Karim announces that of course he will not be joining them until next weekend. He is going back to work. Only Marta is surprised. Dumbfounded, actually. Isn't it usual for the newly married to celebrate their union and spend a short while somewhere alone? Apparently not.

The party separates into its two halves. All the women are made comfortable in the car that Karim has ordered to take them home. Boxes and bags of clothes are handed in and piled so high on their laps that you cannot see their faces. Finally Behzad wedges himself in beside his new sister-in-law, hauls Massy onto his knees, and they are ready to depart. The quartet of husbands sets off in the opposite direction in the usual way.

In the city, the Shirazis own an entire block on Bahar Street, where, for the time being, Marta and Karim will continue to live, sharing an apartment with his parents, and Behzad and Massy. Maryam has a room off the hall. Farideh and Hushang live on the floor below, Leila and Farhad on the floor above.

From now on everything Marta does will be within the invisible ring that protects her without question while turning suspicious eyes on everyone else. She will shop with Shirazis in the bazaar, or go with them to the private stalls in the public baths, to be steamed and massaged and wrapped in towels. With them she will make visits to the houses of relatives and acquaintances of long standing, who will make visits in return. Families will strive to outdo each other's hospitality, which will put flesh on her; in every house she will be sized up and priced, and will learn to do the same to others. Like the sisters she will anticipate her husband's return in the evenings, although she will not necessarily spend those evenings with him. It's not an order, not a law, simply the way things are. Whatever. Marta is too tired to care. She trundles about in the bosom of her new family, and although in the depths of her mind half-formed questions squirm uneasily beneath the level of her awareness they never reach clarity because there is no clarity except betrayal and loneliness. Never would she have believed that, even as a body heals, its spirit can sink without rescue into the quicksand.

56

Dr Shirazi is baffled by his wife. Of course she was not the sweet and biddable young woman of the sort he grew up expecting to marry, not gentle like Farideh or contained like Leila, but spirited – or so he thought – with an astonishing array of smiles and scowls. It's what first drew him to her. But after the old lady went to India her face lost its vitality and settled into a sort of passivity that he associates not with serenity but with melancholy. Even the wedding didn't really cheer her up, and they had all agreed it was a fine party. Look how everyone had danced – although she had not. That had surprised his guests. A western woman who doesn't want to dance! Well, he'd said, feeling shifty, she didn't have time to learn before her country was invaded. It had seemed to satisfy them while it saddened him. You dance for joy.

What had disconcerted him the most was that she hadn't wanted any of her friends from Tent City at the wedding. They were the nearest she had to family. She had lived with some of them in that Soviet camp for a long time. But no. No one from Tent City. She'd been more than simply resolute about that. Her voice had risen, and if he hadn't thought it out of character he'd have said he picked up an edge of hysteria there.

It couldn't be, could it, that she was *ashamed* to be marrying a Persian rather than a Pole, and she would lose face in front of her Polish friends? It made no sense. His is a good family so well connected that between them he and his father can get just about anything done the way they want it – except with the British, that is. But

God willing they'll be gone in time. So what has she to be ashamed of? She's not married into some ignorant superstitious peasant family who've never been beyond their village. Her husband is western-educated, studied in France, which is more than she has done. Or her father either, for that matter. So what has she to be ashamed of?

Still, if it wasn't shame that made her keep her friends away from the wedding, what could it have been? Or perhaps it's a Polish custom. She wouldn't have kept her parents away, would she? She couldn't have done that. And he's sorry. Really he is sorry that her parents cannot be here, that she doesn't know where they are. That she doesn't know even if they are alive. She doesn't talk about that. The one time he tried to mention it, with sympathy, she'd brushed the sympathy aside and said, 'There is no question. They are all right.' But she cannot know that. She can only hope. And she knows that his mother prays for their safety.

All the same, if he could only restore that sudden smile to her face! What would it take? Can it be that she is disappointed in him?

It is Friday afternoon. Zahra Khanoom has returned from the mosque, and the whole family, somnolent from lunch, are resting in the room she favours – no furniture but a soft carpet, and flat cushions set along all four walls. Maryam appears in the doorway and catches Dr Shirazi's eye, bringing him to his feet. Something's going on, and by the play of his lips they see that he is pleased with himself.

'Come with me,' he says to Marta. 'I have brought you a surprise.'

'A surprise? What is it?'

'A surprise described is not a surprise, is it? Come along.'

The sisters would like to go too, but their brother's manner has made it clear this is not their surprise and they will have to wait to find out later. What can it be? Karim isn't given to unexpected gestures, he's so deliberate. Not like their father, who can't stop himself trying to give people surprises all the time, who is always bringing presents.

Marta tags behind her husband as he hurries from room to room, dancing a path between the overstuffed chairs and trinket-laden tables. He is so uncharacteristically eager to show off what he's brought that she is curious. Perhaps it has something to do with the apartment he says he has taken for the two of them, in another block just around the corner. He's charging down the corridor towards the main room, the one that Shirazi *père* likes to entertain in. Whatever it is is in there. At the door he stands to one side and bows her through. *Voilà!*

Two figures are seated on the pale satin-covered sofa under the window, but blocked from proper view by Maryam, bending to wield her first tray of fruit juices and sweets.

'Marta Khanoom!' Maryam, hearing her footsteps, turns on her heel, her empty tray swinging round with her as if it's fixed to her chest like a shelf. 'Your friends are here.'

Marta notes Maryam's satisfaction to be the one to announce the happy news. And she registers Hania and Basia, side by side, obediently grasping their glasses of juice. They look workmanlike. Dowdy, actually, is the word that comes unbidden to her mind. Colourless, impoverished. It shakes her. What has come over her that this should be her first reaction? The two young women are riveted. Is this sleek stranger who she ought to be? They stand up and brush themselves down.

Sensing something is amiss, Maryam scuttles out, bundling her veil more tightly around her to ward off the bad feeling.

The doorway is empty. Karim must have made himself scarce so that Marta can be alone for her reunion.

I'm so glad to see you. Say it, come on, say it! And so she is – but the words don't come, stifled by embarrassment for the circumstances, for her secret wedding, for her prolonged silence. Her absence. No excuses will do without the truth, and they may scoff even at that.

'Maryam's already brought you stuff out. Good.' God Almighty, how false, how patronizing that sounds. Shut up if you can't think of anything better! 'Please, sit down again. I mean, make yourselves comfortable. Look, I'm going to sit down.'

Why is she burbling like this? They're staring at her appalled, as well they might. She hears the tones of her mother preparing to offer

412

cake to the new military wives. They don't sit. They stand rock still, watching her face redden.

Hania breaks it. 'Marta, what have you done?'

'Hania!' Basia only murmurs her reproof. Her black hair has grown long enough for her to tuck it behind her ears.

Hania has no time for hostess small talk or beating about the bush. 'Have you married Dr Shirazi? Have you really gone and married Dr Shirazi?' She makes it sound like a crime or a sin to be confessed, owned up to, apologized for.

'Yes.' Why shouldn't she have married Dr Shirazi... Karim? She can marry whom she likes.

'Congratulations,' says Basia, forcing out the nicety. 'Are you happy?'

'Is he a good husband?'

'Yes, of course.' She said that in too much of a rush. But it's true. He *is* a good husband.

'And you live here?' By way of accusation.

'Yes.'

'With servants? Like that old woman?'

'Maryam's not...' Yes she is.

'Hania, stop it.'

Hania shakes Basia's cautioning hand off her arm. 'Why should I stop it? I thought we were friends. She could at least have told us instead of disappearing like that without a word. And no word afterwards. Can you imagine what it was like? Looking for you? Wondering what had happened to you. And only finding out afterwards when Dr Shirazi came by to tell us.'

'Came by to tell you?'

'Oh, yes. But you'll know that he doesn't work in Tent City any more.' Doesn't he? 'But that's not the point. What about Antoni? Didn't you think about poor Antoni?'

'Hania. Shh.'

'Don't shush me, Basia! She has to –'

'Poor Antoni? What the hell do you mean, "poor Antoni"?'

'Hania, what's the point? It's too late now.'

413

'No, Basia, it's not. It's never too late for people to know the truth. Can't you imagine the state the poor fellow was in when he came back from training to find you'd run off with someone else?'

'You just shut up, Hania! Have you forgotten? You can't have forgotten, can you? Antoni left me. He'd already got himself engaged to someone else, remember? He had a baby, for Christ's sake! *He* left *me*. Not the other way round. And it so happened that Dr Shirazi had already asked me to marry him, so I said I would. And I did. Jesus and Mary! What's wrong with that?'

Hania and Basia have exchanged a glance. Basia is holding her head in her hands. Hania's mouth is open. They are both looking as shocked as they should be, and about time too.

'You never said Dr Shirazi had asked you to marry him.'

'I don't have to tell everyone everything, do I? As it happens? Blow by blow?'

'But Marta.' Basia is almost inaudible. 'That girl Antoni was engaged to. It was a mistake. It wasn't our Antoni... your Antoni. It was another one. Another Antoni altogether. We found out only the next morning when he arrived, and that girl came running out to meet him and then just stood there because he wasn't the man she was waiting for. So of course we tried to find you, but you'd gone. How was anyone to know where you were? Antoni was hunting for you everywhere, but then his regiment came and he had to leave. It was awful.'

It is awful. Marta has gone grey. She's moaning and looks as if she might faint.

'Jesus and Mary, we've got to do something. Basia, go and get Dr Shirazi, and I'll stay with her. Hello! Hello, there! Help us, someone. Hush, Marta, hush. It's all right. It's all going to be all right.'

The raised voices coming from the main room have propelled Maryam down the corridor at a run, despite her fallen arches. In Zahra Khanoom's room they have heard the commotion too, such a strange, sibilant spluttering language, Polish. They pick out Marta's voice, shrill, almost screaming. Something isn't right. A moment ago Leila was peeling an orange for Massy but her skilful fingers have locked over the fruit. Zahra Khanoom has raised her head like a mountain goat that has spotted a jackal. Behzad is getting up because a young lady with dark hair tucked behind her ears in a strange style is running and calling in French, 'Please!', out of breath, 'Doctor, please!'

Karim gallops ahead, his family chasing behind. He bounds into the sitting room and barks, 'What's going on?', his tone an accusation, and makes a leap to catch Marta before she hits the ground, legs folded in a pair of limp ribbons.

Hania and Basia take in the two glossy young women pushing in after him, followed by a little girl, and the old servant woman in the veil. At her shoulder is another woman, also swathed, and a podgy young man. They all talk at once, at each other, over each other. Dr Shirazi is on his knees beside Marta, who has disappeared behind all these people shoving in and crowding round her.

Massy (in Farsi): '*Maman*, what's happened to Auntie Marta?'

Zahra Khanoom (in Farsi): 'Ssh, Massy. Karim will see to it. Karim-jun, she isn't dying, is she? May God save her!'

Maryam (in Farsi): 'Ooh, ooh, Zahra Khanoom! If something happens to Marta Khanoom, may the heavens open and strike me down. Look at her, she looks as if she has seen Death walking over her mother's grave. Give her water and then something sweet. Something sweet, and water.'

Basia (in Polish): 'I told you not to say anything, Hania. Now look what's happened.'

Hania (in Polish): 'She'll be all right, you'll see. And anyway it's not my fault. I'm not the one who –'

Basia (in Polish): 'Hania! Stop it!'

Behzad (in Farsi): 'Karim. What's the matter with her? Let's carry her to bed. We can easily do it between us.'

Dr Shirazi (in Farsi): 'Be quiet, can't you, all of you? Marta' (in French), 'Can you hear me? Can you hear me? Have you any pain? What's the matter with you?'

Marta can hear everyone. What's more, of the ten people here, she's the only one who can more or less understand everything that's

415

being said. She pushes herself up onto her forearms, papery white, and blue round the eyes, wiping her mouth with the back of her hand.

'I'm all right,' she says, but shakily. 'Don't fuss, Karim. I'm quite all right. I'm pregnant, that's all.'

'You're pregnant?' he whispers. 'Of course you are! That explains it!' (In Farsi at the top of his voice) 'She's pregnant! *Maman*, you're going to have a grandson!'

From below, their faces are oddly foreshortened, all chins and nostrils. They have their mouths open, emitting whoops and squeals, swooping now to kiss her. Hands on her head, ruffling her hair and smoothing it, patting her for being such a clever girl. Hands all over her, lifting her like a corpse. Maryam, with her veil pulled low, has cupped her palms to heaven in gratitude. They're taking her to her room. They're laying her down. Over their shoulders Marta catches a glimpse of Hania and Basia, jostled to the back by the door. They don't belong here any more. Their faces are so small.

The baby should have been Antoni's but isn't. She should have let him make love to her as soon as he was well and then it would have been his child that she could have carried and nurtured till he came back again, like that other Antoni's fiancée. But he's gone, confused and desperate, thinking she didn't care for him after all, thinking… and now he's not to be reached, since no one knows exactly where the Anders Army has been sent.

Why did Hania and Basia have to tell her? It would have been better not to know. No. That's wrong. She had to know. She always has to know. But she doesn't want a baby. Not this one.

Actually, she probably isn't pregnant; she only suspects she might be, so perhaps she can run away. She isn't really married either. Not before God, because there was no priest, so she doesn't have to… But this baby. Maybe she'll miscarry. She could help Maryam beating the carpets – though of course they won't let her beat carpets, will they, because this will be the first Shirazi of the next generation that they've all been waiting for, ever since the sisters married.

416

But how can she! It's a sin thinking like this, what with Farideh and Leila putting on their biggest smiles when they must be feeling so envious. Maryam with tears in her eyes saying, 'I saw it the day she came. It was written on her forehead that she would bear you sons, Karim Agha. As tall and mighty as Mount Damavand.'

Karim had beamed at Maryam and let her kiss his hands. He'd looked so bewildered, though, for all his joy, because really he ought to have known. They were all looking at him thinking it. Her husband, *and* a doctor, but he didn't know. Yet what he said to his mother was something else. 'Would you believe it! I picked up a starveling and she turns out to be the fertile one.' Then he'd laughed and said, 'Perhaps we shouldn't let Leila and Farideh eat so much. Make their lives a bit harder. After all, look how they breed down in the slums.' That was cruel of him. On two counts. He must have thought Marta wouldn't overhear, or he'd forgotten how much she understood.

But Antoni! Poor frantic Antoni. Sorry, sorry. Sorry for him, sorry for me. When they find out where the Anders Army has gone maybe they'll let her know and she can write to him. But what should she say? *Wait for me!* She can't say that. She's married and she's having a baby. Can it really be real when you can't feel anything?

'Is it better now?' Karim is in the doorway with his fingers round a tall glass. Usually it would be Maryam bringing drinks but today is special. He wants to sit with his wife and think about the coming of his son. 'It's best to rest to begin with, when one can. For the first few weeks, just to make sure.'

Come clean while they're alone. 'I might be mistaken.'

'I don't think so.' Can his medical eye see something the mirror hides? Or it's wishful thinking overriding his judgement.

'I haven't been sick or anything.'

'That's not compulsory. Don't worry.'

'But… I might just be late. You never know.'

'How late?'

'Eleven days.' He's right, of course. Ever since her periods began again she's been as regular as clockwork. That first one, in her bed in

417

the staff tent, after she and Antoni… after he said he didn't have the strength. What a fool she's been! The one thing in her gift, the one thing that's happened to her that depended on a decision that was all hers to make – and she ruined it. From the moment the Germans came across the border until Tent City, every moment of her life was in somebody else's hands until Antoni asked her to marry him. All she had to say was yes. Just that. One little word said straight away and it would all have been different. And she hadn't, running scared from the spectre of domesticity. And what has she got instead? Even more domesticity, but with the wrong man – a good man, a fine man, but not the right one. Why had she rushed off like that? Why hadn't she waited to find out more? And, above all, why had she accepted Karim's proposal? So she was afraid of being alone when her letter to her parents was returned, but anyone with character can face being alone, surely. And anyway she wouldn't have been alone. Mrs Benka had written: You won't be alone because you have Hania and Basia. But she had plunged off, as she always does! What sort of escape is this, and expecting the wrong man's baby? Waiting to swell and swell, and then have the wrong man's baby.

Will it be terrible?

'Karim. That woman. The one in the city, in the lanes. Was she all right?'

'What woman?'

He is mystified. He had thought she was dozing, and her question breaks into his own reverie. What is she talking about? She mustn't let her herself get in a state because a baby in the womb hears every-thing and feels everything – or at least that's what Maryam and his mother will have him believe, which makes him laugh.

'The woman in the slums,' she repeats. 'We were in the car and a man came asking for you. You said it was a woman in labour. Don't you remember?'

'Oh, yes. Yes. She survived. The baby didn't, though. It came too early.'

'That's awful.'

'Not really. Not for them. They had so many children already. I don't think it was so awful for them, and anyway the baby would have been a girl. The woman's husband accepted that it was God's will and he didn't look so unhappy to me. But you mustn't worry, Marta. You don't live like that woman and we won't let anything like that happen to you.'

'And now. Is that woman better now?'

'How should I know? I haven't seen her. Why should I have seen her?'

'In the slums. When you're treating people there. Doesn't anyone say?'

'I don't go there any more, or to Tent City. I haven't been there in weeks. I'm working in a different hospital now, and it's a good thing I am. I learned a lot of course, but you don't go into medicine to spend your life among the poverty-stricken. I have to make my reputation and I shall – so that my new small family, you and our son – will be as proud of me as my old big one is. And now you should sleep, so that our baby may grow in peace.'

He places the glass from which she has not drunk by her side and slips away. But she does not sleep. She cannot sleep. You and me and our son, three blobs welded at fixed points onto a ring that cannot be removed. No matter how fast the ring spins the three blobs are locked onto their separate places.

A terrible lassitude drops over her, compressing her throat, like the lid of a coffin closed over her face. All that effort, all that determination to get through. What was it for? You could fight when there was something, someone to battle against. You could get used to squatting over Lenin's Corner and living on reeking cabbage soup and 500 grams of bread; you could learn to chop at trees and pick cotton; you could get over malaria and typhoid because all of it was outside your real being, and you were doing it with others. Everyone had stomach cramps or frozen extremities. Everyone's joints cracked with cold as the muscles weakened. There had been something to prove in dealing with all those things because you had in mind another future, when external forces would let you be and you would finally make your own life. But the future has been and gone and all there is is this – to be coped with all alone. She can feel the energy seeping away and her limbs are so heavy she cannot move them. She used up all the strength God gave her to get this far, and now there's none left. There's nothing left at all.

57

Fine high ceilings and large square interconnecting rooms in this new apartment. Karim has chosen well, nothing stinted. The sisters, bossed by Massy, have had the place done up in soothing greens and blues. They've taken on a girl, Shirin, all of fifteen, who stood on the threshold looking either shy or surly – it was hard to tell – and speaking in monosyllables of dialect. Maryam had pinned her against the wall with an unforgiving eye and battered her with questions. In the end she'd pronounced, as if the girl were deaf or absent, that she wasn't much but could be taught. 'I know her grandmother, so one step wrong and she goes right back.' But, once the baby comes, Maryam is to move in. The family are agreed that you don't take chances with a first one and since Marta comes from such a small family it's no wonder she's ignorant.

Marta leans back in a large chair nibbling biscuits and watching the accretion of her future in upholstery. The main carpet is almost a replica of the big one in the house on the hill – a tangled garden writhing with fantastical creatures at each corner, fountain playing in the centre. It's like a distillation of all the cultivation that has ever been, and a purchase that Karim made a point of making himself. He had them come in and unroll one carpet after another until, finally, this one. Was it like a talisman for him: that the best of his childhood in the summer home be repeated here? In the long winter days she will lie on it with her child – if Maryam considers that appropriate – and trace the vines and sprouting tendrils back to their source.

Chairs in the French style have been ordered and Leila and Farideh harry the cabinet-maker daily. If they don't, apparently he'll spend his time on someone else's job. In the kitchen Shirin is dropping pans and lids under Maryam's scolding. Everything is well in hand and there is nothing to be done but clear the bowls of their sweets and biscuits.

News drifts through. They've closed Tent City because the last of the surviving refugees have been trucked and shipped out – India, East Africa, America. Soviet forces have finally prevailed over their German counterparts in Stalingrad after six months of carnage, the battle-lines lurching one way then the other. But Marta has not the will to listen to the news broadcasts as she would have done before. The grasping little leech of a body dives and somersaults inside hers, growing inexorably, feeding on her, oblivious to the dullness of her dread. She cannot keep her mind on anything these days. Sometimes she thinks she no longer has one at all. She sleeps a lot. She sleeps more than she needs, while beyond the windows Tehran's icy winter has settled over the streets.

The sisters are always on hand, forsaking their apartments for Marta's, but take rejection with grace. Like everyone they're quick to think up excuses on her behalf. After lunch Behzad reads aloud from a book of folk-tales at a deliberately measured pace, as if it's a lesson in dictation. But as often as not she has dozed off before the donkey driver has been rewarded for his good deed or the young lovers have been reunited. And yet the sonorous words insinuate themselves into her unconscious and when she wakes and finds Behzad's chair empty she thinks she may have learned something all the same.

She'd do anything for a smoke but Karim has forbidden it. Unusual in not being a smoker himself – trust her to find herself with the only non-smoking Iranian in the land – he has now determined that in his house no one else shall be. Even Zahra Khanoom, on her daily visits, has to suck a surreptitious pipe with Maryam behind the closed doors of the kitchen, where he never goes. There was a time when Marta would have ignored the prohibition, but somehow she doesn't have it in her now. The larger her belly the smaller she feels herself becoming, eaten up from within.

Is everything proceeding as it should? Dr Shirazi is not sure. When it came to furnishing their bedroom Marta pleaded the discomforts of pregnancy – phantom discomforts, since he suspects his wife's health has never been better, and twin beds were carried in by a pair of porters who did not bother to hide their astonishment. Now she lies, an engorged caterpillar, encased in layers of winter bedding. There's no reason for it, no medical reason at all, and his father is alarmed. He has never slept apart from Zahra Khanoom, no matter how far gone she was.

When he first set eyes on Marta he pronounced himself smitten. And now whenever he passes by the block he will drop in on his daughter-in-law, hoping to engage in the simple conversations that she has mastered. But his face drops because hers appears so glum. It sends him creeping away to stand in the window, gazing down onto the street, absently telling his prayer beads. 'What's the matter with our little one?' he asks his son. 'Can't you make her happy? Don't you know how to make a woman happy?'

Karim had thought he did. He had thought he would. But to be honest, when he's lying beside her, when he's lying in her, he senses that although her body is there she has taken her mind, her own self, and slyly transported it away.

He asks her what's wrong. Don't I satisfy you? But all she says is, nothing is wrong. Nothing at all.

'Are my sisters not good to you? Behzad. Is it Behzad? I know he can be annoying but he's still young.'

She thinks of Behzad as a spoiled boy, despite the hours he spends trying to entertain her. And of course he is spoiled, although not as much as Massy, little *sheytoon* that she is. It's all his father's doing. 'Let the baby of the family be a baby a bit longer,' he always pleads when Zahra Khanoom tries to suggest it's time she grew up. And Behzad too. 'He's only a boy. We'll find something for him to do that he likes. Why should any son of mine have to go out and make his money at something he doesn't like when I have worked so hard to get somewhere in this world? What did I work for if my sons have to demean themselves the way I had to? No. My sons will be somebody or I wasted my time.' His father's refrain is Behzad's protection – and Behzad knows it.

But Dr Shirazi thinks they're both right. You don't get anywhere if people see you doing lowly work. You lose respect, and what is life without that? If it hadn't been for the war, Behzad would indeed have been in France right now, and would have come back to step into an influential government post, if he wanted it. Marta doesn't understand how things work in the world, so she's impatient with Behzad. Impatient that he doesn't want to do military service. Just because her father is a soldier she thinks soldiering is a good career. But unless you're the general it's no career for a young man with aspirations, and military service is a fool's game. Still, when he asks her whether it's Behzad making her unhappy she says no, she's not unhappy, and shakes her head. Nothing is wrong. 'Is it the food?' No, she loves the food. 'Are you lonely without your friends?' She shakes her head. Nothing is wrong at all.

His mother said, I told you so. 'What did you expect, Karim-jun? Bringing in an outsider like that because she was different, because you thought it would be exciting? It's all because you went off to Paris. People said it was the best thing, the place to be to learn new things. But I was always against that. What's to learn in someone else's country that you can't learn at home? People belong at home, and if you'd stayed at home you'd have accepted a nice girl from a good family just like everyone else does. How is she supposed to fit in with us? She can never fit in with us. Everything she knows, everything she has ever learned, belongs somewhere else. Can you imagine what would have happened to me if I hadn't been married to your father but to some stranger in another country? In that Poland, whatever it's like? How would I have lived with a family like hers whose ways are so different? God doesn't mean us to be separated from our own. She will expect to have what she cannot have, and what she gets may be what she does not want. And then you hope to make her happy! How can you make her happy, Karim-jun, when she's like a fish that you've caught in a bucket and tipped out into the wrong pond? You should have left her alone to swim in her own.'

All that was before the baby. Now Zahra Khanoom's convictions have been swept away like a ball of newspaper bouncing down a roadside ditch. It's as if she'd never spoken, because his wife will be delivered of the first grandchild. His son's birth will root her in his country – in his family – as nothing else could. Her status, of course, has never been in question. She is his wife. But status alone is like armour. It assures the respect of others, but it doesn't keep out the cold that sidles into the soul. He fears the shard of ice that has somehow penetrated Marta's soul, and that that is what is swelling in there, monstrous, and freezing her inch by inch from the inside. Maybe it was always there and he'd simply been as foolish as his mother's blunt accusation implied.

Nothing will be more important to him than the birth of his son, but in the darkest night, as he lies in his bed listening to Marta's stertorous breathing over there in hers, he dreads it too.

58

Dr Shirazi's son is delivered without fuss and in the best possible conditions at the Hospital Razi on the last day of August 1943. He has green eyes and a great deal of soft brown hair. His mother stares at him as if his arrival has caught her off guard. When she glances into his face, she catches unexpected glimpses of her own. They call him Davood. Dr Shirazi suggests that his wife might like to give their baby a Polish name as well. She's seen to hesitate momentarily before announcing that she has chosen Marek, which, she explains, is her father's name. Davood Marek Shirazi. She rolls it around her mouth. It tastes odd. It sounds odd. Which is fitting.

Three days after his birth, Maryam shuffles up to the new mother's bedside with gifts: a saucer on which lie three ripe dates. 'Here you are, Khanoom,' she says. 'You must eat these before sundown so that your next child may be a boy as well.' There's a tiny Koran in a golden box to protect her beauty against smallpox, and a cowrie shell that Maryam immediately sews to the hem of Davood's little shirt.

'Why are you doing that?'

Maryam bends close. 'There are many jealous people around,' she murmurs directly into the maternal ear. 'Envious of a young woman with such a healthy boy.' She spits to one side for good luck. 'If people, women, try to touch him or tell you how beautiful he is, don't let them and don't believe them. They come with the evil eye, Khanoom, and you must beware. But this will protect him and send the evil right back into the eye of the one who sent it, and crack it open then and there. You'll see.'

Within weeks Davood is known to his multiple parents simply as Kookooleh, little one, a nickname conferred on him by his doting Uncle Behzad. Interestingly, also within weeks, both his married aunts conceive. Maryam tells everyone who will listen that Kookooleh has brought God's magic into the world with him – for why else would Farideh Khanoom and Leila Khanoom, who had waited so long for the blessing of children, have become pregnant only with his birth?

Kookooleh is a very pleasant baby, and almost never cries – but then he is not given the opportunity, since he is never without a lap to sit in. His grandmother can't have had enough children to satisfy her urges, she's so quick to cuddle him to her the minute she's through the door. The two mothers-to-be, with their tight round bellies, crowd in behind her, bury their scented faces in his soft milky one and inhale him deeply, breathing in the future. His Auntie Massy, now displaced from her position as baby of the family, settles him astride one jutted hip and sways sensuously between the chairs, humming. She has entirely given up climbing trees.

As the autumn of 1943 advances, Kookooleh spends many of his waking hours on his back on the carpet. He listens to the noises coming from the kitchen and squints at his fingers as they flit past his nose. Then he falls asleep. When he wakes he is presented to his mother's copious breasts until he can eat no more, after which Nanny Maryam's assistant-in-training, Shirin, changes his nappy and dandles him, crooning in a monotone and gazing into his surprising eyes. Marta watches, thinking that probably she ought to be doing what Shirin is doing. But her body, and her mind, do not reach out to this baby that she never wanted. She cannot understand how he got here. All she knows is that his existence has entombed her. Mothers are supposed to love their sons from the moment they first see them but she feels nothing. Nothing at all, except that the future is so long.

Kookooleh's grandmother Zahra Khanoom retrieves him from Shirin and displays him to the leaves and flowers woven into the great carpet where she kneels, draping him over her shoulder; once he has sicked up a mouthful of sour milk onto the muslin he dozes there. Meanwhile, his Uncle Behzad hovers nearby, waiting for his turn. This is when Zahra Khanoom decides that Behzad really must be found proper male employment outside the household, otherwise she fears for his future.

'He's turning into a woman,' she complains to her husband. 'He'll never get a wife that way. What man will give his daughter to another woman? He'd never live it down!'

Very occasionally Zahra Khanoom puts her foot down, and when she does she gets her way. So Behzad is packed off, back to the management of the same cinema that he found so distasteful over a year ago, and no amount of whining helps him this time. His father, always previously his champion, has now become besotted with his grandson instead, and it's fortunate that Behzad is not the resentful type.

Mohammed Shirazi has taught his daughter-in-law to address him as *Pedar-jun* – father dear – although in her mind he remains, and will remain, Shirazi *père*. He cannot take his eyes off the baby. The big green eyes and tiny penis are more precious than all the Shah's jewels put together. Everything has been worthwhile. His firstborn, his eldest son, has produced a firstborn and an eldest son. Others are bound to follow.

But it's not to be. When first Farideh, and then Leila, are hurried to the Hospital Razi, both return with daughters. Beautiful, doe-eyed, huggable and adored. But daughters none the less. Maryam plies their mothers with dates. Meanwhile, fertile as she evidently is, months pass and more months, but Marta the boy-maker shows no sign of conceiving again. Eventually Mohammed the affable father plucks up courage to broach the matter with Karim his unapproachable son.

'Kookooleh didn't mess her up, did he, inside?'

'Why, *Baba*?'

'Well. It's over a year now. Over a year and a half.'

Karim draws into himself with that distant stillness that sometimes makes his father flinch. 'She was breastfeeding,' he says curtly, closing the subject.

How is he to admit that since Kookooleh's birth Marta has refused him entry? No. That is not strictly true. She hasn't refused but there is no mistaking her disinclination. He does not know why. She claims not to know why. Although he has every right, he will not force himself on her because he would get no pleasure from it. He wants his lovemaking to be mutual but she is no more welcoming than a lump of marble. If he didn't know better he would think an exceptionally difficult birth was the cause – but the birth was not difficult. Not at all, as births go. It makes him wonder what can have poisoned her mind against his body, while hers, restored to itself and voluptuous again, attracts him more than ever. Has he ever hurt her with clumsy eagerness? He is as certain as he can be that he has not. Has he offended her in some way? He must assume so, but cannot think how, or when. What he wants above all else is to climb into her bed beside her and have arms open to him, her face turn to him, her lips to widen in the smile that long ago, in Tent City, sometimes stretched from ear to ear. None of these things happens except in the occasional fantasies that flutter down to taunt him when he is off guard. If it were just a matter of satisfying a craving, well, he can get his relief from a prostitute. Which is, in fact, what he has been doing. To be honest, he began visiting this woman – who swears to him that he is her only customer – some months before his son was born. She is a widow, she says, and puts a light in her window to make him turn his head when he passes her house every day on his way into the Hospital Razi.

When Karim tightens his lips and locks up his face, when he measures out his words like dried beans, everyone knows to back off. This is not for fear of him exactly but out of a sort of resignation. Pestering him gets you nowhere. Yet that doesn't mean the subject is dropped. In the privacy of the kitchen Maryam and Zahra Khanoom discuss the remedies they may have to resort to – the drinks, the poultices, the prayers and charms. It will all have to be done in secret, as Maryam points out. After all, look at the fuss Karim Agha made when he discovered that she'd packed ashes in the baby's nappy when he had his first earache. 'What's the matter with you all?' he'd demanded, his cheeks taut with annoyance. 'When the child is ill I will treat him with proper medicine. And you can put your witches' brews away.' Of course Maryam had squared up to him. 'Is that so, Agha?' she'd said. 'And who treated your earaches when you were a baby, eh? There were no doctors trained in France then, were there?' Karim Agha had thrown up his hands and stormed out, but he hadn't been able to answer her.

'What cold people these Poles are,' mutters Zahra Khanoom. 'Perhaps it's the food they grow up on, or they don't see enough of the sun. How can a mother bear not to be cuddling her own baby boy!'

Kookoolch passes along the line of waiting embraces, but not one of them is his mother's. Maybe in the wet green country that she comes from everything is upside down, and it's not your family that nurtures a little boy but strangers. Perhaps that's why they all so long to be soldiers.

The sisters are no less baffled. They have spare kisses aplenty for their nephew, if his mother hasn't, but it's her face that perturbs them and the way she moves. She might be made of pewter for the life that's in her. So heavy. Everything is so heavy. Her face is dull, her gestures wooden. She smiles like a machine. What happened to the young woman who made a scandal climbing trees on her very first day, and who gave that crook at the vegetable stall such an effective dressing down? Now their sister-in-law, once so exotic, has about as much spark in her as a sheep's tail. If he didn't look so much like her you'd say Kookooleh wasn't her child at all.

One morning, behind the door and behind her hand, Shirin whispers to Maryam, 'Karim Agha and Marta Khanoom. They don't... they don't get close.'

She nearly gets a smack for that. 'What are you saying, you ignorant girl?'

But Shirin stands her ground. 'Who cleans their room? Who does the laundry? I'm telling you, they're no better than wooden puppets. Or a horse and a mule.'

So the evil spirits did get to Marta Khanoom, in spite of everything, thinks Maryam, and they've made Karim Agha turn away from her. But all she says is, 'Well, don't you breathe a word about that, do you hear. Because if you do you'll be back with your father before you've even had time to wash your feet.'

The months pass, the days are got through, and Kookooleh takes his first steps, staggering bandy-legged between the outstretched arms of his grandmother and Shirin. His first sentence, 'Donkey man give Kookoo apple,' runs through the household again and again. But when they come to tell her Marta merely nods, murmuring dutifully, 'How clever.'

Truly Shirin is a jewel. Even Maryam acknowledges it, and in the summer months, in the garden of the house on the hill, Kookooleh and his two little girl cousins play at Shirin's knees so happily that their mothers need never be concerned. When autumn comes, and with it the return to the city, Farideh and Leila bring their daughters to Karim's apartment so that the arrangement may continue. Besides, the sisters are both pregnant again and hopes are high once more. Everyone has only one fear – that Shirin herself may marry and then perhaps leave.

'That's a nonsense.' Zahra Khanoom dismisses it. 'Maryam told me. Shirin's father won't let her marry as long as she has work here. She's off his hands, and earns more with us than any husband who'd take her in will ever give her. And if she doesn't marry he won't have to cough up for a dowry.'

'Marta didn't bring a dowry,' Farideh remarks. No rugs, no brocades, no glassware or china. No jewels.

'No, she didn't, but it's not the same. We're not village people, and you know *Baba*.' But there the hint of criticism of her daughter-in-law ends because a dowry really wouldn't have been possible in Marta's case and anyway the second round of babies is, unaccountably, daughters once again.

59

While the Shirazis were procreating, the Europeans, along with their proxies and allies, have been fighting. Those occasional evenings that Dr Shirazi spends at home he immediately changes out of the elegance of his French suit and back into the comfort of his Persian pyjamas, and while he is doing it he tunes in to the nightly news. Until a year or so ago it was Germany's broadcasts that everyone listened to. But then, bit by bit, you began to get the impression that things were not going Germany's way – there was something desperate in the insistent listing of victories – so it became the trend to switch to the new radio station coming out of London. Although Dr Shirazi is not to know it, it is the tinny snatches of these wireless broadcasts that, gradually, have begun to perforate his wife's sheath of depression.

Back in the summer of 1944, when Kookooleh was not quite a year old, she leant her ear against the door and learned of the armada of American and British ships that had crossed that faraway English Channel to prevail on the northern coast of France – an operation planned, she was astonished to learn, right here in Tehran the previous November.

Two months later she heard that in distant Warsaw her countrymen had risen against the German occupier. Although, apparently, Soviet forces were not far off, there was no word of movement from them to help the Poles. No word either of bombing raids in support from the British, nor from the well-armed Americans. No word about the Anders Army either.

Most recently she caught a reference, which she wasn't sure she understood, of something that had happened over a year and half before, something about a grave having been found in the Katyn forest with the bodies of thousands of Polish officers in it, all shot in the back of the head. Who had done this? It didn't seem to be clear. The Russians were saying the Germans did it. The Germans were claiming it was the Russians. Everyone had known about it since the bodies were discovered – everyone except her, because at the time Davood, heavy in her belly and nearly ripe, had somehow stolen away her mind and distracted it from what was really important. They could have told her. Karim could have told her. But no one had said a thing. Someone has massacred the cream of the Polish army, but these Shirazis haven't thought it worth the mention.

For the first time in two years her temper begins to rise, and who knows what the outcome might be if anger were not the first of the emotions to return?

Through the door from the corridor leading to the kitchen she can see her son toddling about on sturdy legs and getting under the feet of his nursemaid. Shirin is trying to prepare the evening meal but has to keep reaching to remove kitchen implements from the child's questing grasp – implements that are useful in her hands, but lethal in his. How patient she is, how unflappable. She seems to be talking to Davood all the while as she chops (and reaches), stirs (and reaches), and lifts and moves steaming pans. The muscles in her neck are ribbed from the weight. Neither the young servant nor her charge notices that they are being observed – or they don't care, and Marta feels excluded, as though by an invisible pane of glass. But, when Shirin lifts the lid and its covering cloth from the great pan of rice, the invisible glass shatters and Marta inhales a fragrance that sets her mind racing.

The first thing she thinks – and wonders at – is how hungry she is. It's not that she hasn't been eating. Clearly she has; arguably rather too much, but it has been done mechanically, without pleasure. But now, here she is, salivating at the smell of rice layered with broad beans and dill. They have been feeding her on rice every day yet the action of Shirin's hand on the wooden spoon, turning over the con-

tents of this particular saucepan at this particular moment, has prodded an old memory to life.

She is running barefoot through the garden of the family's summer house, following Massy, who keeps turning to be sure her new
friend hasn't deserted her, her eyes merry with naughtiness and a finger on her lips. As they run they pass the kitchen outhouse, where
Maryam squats on the earth floor, cooking and talking non-stop to...
it must have been Hajji Javad. That very first day, nearly three years
ago. How did she come to be here, now, the mother of that little boy,
married to Karim, ingested by his family?

Slowly Marta retreats into her bedroom and sits on the edge of her
bed. She must piece this together, from the beginning, coolly, not as
she did before in the frenzy of her misery. She must go back to the
day Karim, then still Dr Shirazi, cradled her delirious head in his
palm to trickle the medically approved quantity of water into her
mouth. She closes her eyes the better to remember. A bouquet of pink
roses. Another of tiger lilies. The first box of floury *gaz* that at the
time she had thought was a present for someone else, so beautifully
wrapped.

But it was a prelude, wasn't it, that first gift, to his invitation –
although, now she thinks of it, he'd made out that it was the sisters
who wanted her to come and stay. All that business about recuperation too, and then Karim sneaking back to the city in the early morning, which meant she had to stay longer with his family. They'd been
playing with her, manipulating her; perhaps even Massy was party to
it. Perhaps Massy had inveigled her into the garden and up the tree
at their behest. No. That, at least, was genuine. Massy really had got
into trouble. But the point was, they had all had an ulterior motive.
They were part of Karim's convoluted courting. I can't ask you to
marry me unless my family approves. Marry me, marry my family.

The yellow dress! Bought in advance like a snare for an indigent
refugee, who is to be abducted, fed and fattened up so that she can
produce an heir. All their sweetness. The sisters. Their gentle sympathy that made her cry, which she hates doing, hates to be seen doing
– it was all a ploy, to turn her into the family milch cow, because it

was thought they were barren! But how did they know, how did Karim know, that rice and sweets and raisins would make her fertile again?

Well, they may have succeeded thus far, but she will not play along any more. She may be the wife of a Persian doctor but to her core she is the daughter of a Polish professional soldier. She will dress in the fashions from Avenue Lalezar and have her hair styled just as the sisters do; and she will paint her nails and her lips as everyone expects; but it is to be camouflage, so that she may prepare the ground for her own, private, counter-campaign to leave the boudoir behind.

But she has some catching up to do.

Dr Shirazi is heartened by Marta's recovery and by the determination that has set such a sparkle in her eyes. He is amused and gratified to see her struggle with the curlicues of an alphabet that he knows, from reverse experience, must be unfathomable. He is forever stooping to collect scattered sheets of paper covered in clumsy scrawls. As he gazes down at the spidery sentences, 'Hassan brushes his teeth' and 'Hamid will build a tower of stone', he thinks how reduced we are, how diminished, when we are at the boundary of someone else's culture. It makes him recall a moment in Tent City, when they were still working side by side, how Marta had boasted that at home in Poland she was known for her eloquence in her native tongue. There is no one here for her to show it off to, poor thing. In Paris, all those many years ago, when he was a lonely and probably over-serious student, he was prepared to walk kilometres across the city to the café where the few other young Persians gathered, just for the consoling wash and lilt of a few vowel sounds. He determines to hunt out his French–Persian dictionary, heavy as a brick, with the pages so well thumbed they are pliable and greyed.

Word gets round that Marta has crawled from her cocoon and, when the Shirazis gather for their late-night weekend supper one Thursday, Behzad presents her with a selection of books designed for young children who are on the cusp of learning to read and write.

'They're for Kookooleh really,' he jokes. 'But you can use them first.'

It was lightly said, but Marta starts back, taken by surprise. Of course Davood will be needing them, since he is a Persian child who will go to school here, grow up here, a Shirazi among the Shirazis. It's just that somehow she hadn't thought of that, of its finality. What had she thought? she wonders.

'You've frightened her, Behzad-jun, with your schoolbooks.' Zahra Khanoom has noted Marta's alarm and is laughing. There is much laughter this evening, about nothing in particular. Everything's going to be all right, after all.

Week by week, with Karim's old dictionary on her lap, Marta spends hours stationed by the wireless; further hours poring laboriously over a pile of newspapers, decoding them. They inform her that Stalin, Roosevelt and Churchill have had another of their meetings, and this time they have been talking about the future of her country, and of its neighbour, Czechoslovakia, and of Hungary beyond. There are to be new borders; the German minorities are to be expelled; free elections will be held. With her finger on the paragraph – you lose your place so easily with this writing – Marta lifts her eyes from the page and wonders who will be there to ensure that those elections are free. She turns the paper over to check the date: 5 February 1945. But that's months ago!

She lays the paper aside and pulls out another. April. Have those elections happened yet? She can see nothing written about them. What she reads is that the Americans have a brand-new President. Will he care about what happens in Warsaw? Will the British? Now that their war is over, they seem to have lost interest, and all they want to do is go home. If only she could go home too. So much has been happening there, and maybe there will be much more. It feels terribly wrong to be away – although, stupid cow, she can't change anything, or prevent anything. And anyway how can she go home? The Russians are still there, by all accounts, overseeing the elections. But, if the war is over, at least she can try to write again. So she writes urgently, demanding news; descriptively – *I am married, I have a son*; lying through her teeth: *I am well and happy.*

There is no reply. Nor, this time, is her letter returned. But there must still be chaos everywhere and letters go astray in chaos. She writes again and prepares to wait, instructing herself to learn patience. These things take time. They will perforce take a great deal of time.

The long summers meander by in the house on the hill. Kookooleh and his girl cousins grow taller, and more shrill. While Marta and the sisters swim in the lake and take rambling walks among the trees of the foothills, Maryam and Shirin wash and pound and bake.

Whenever he can find an excuse, Behzad escapes from the cinema in the city so that he can come home to play with the children. He lets them ride on his back; he helps them build tents out of Maryam's newly washed sheets; he runs around on all fours pretending to be a mountain goat, or a wolf. He is unusually fair between the five children, although no one doubts that it's Kookooleh he loves the most. All the children are always asking when their Uncle Behzad is going to come. They worship him; everyone else worries. Maryam and Shirin are beginning to have their own opinions, but out of loyalty won't air them.

60

Dr Shirazi has come to regret that he ever dug that dictionary out. All he'd hoped was that Marta would be more comfortable if she could chatter away with the women among the family's acquaintances. Perhaps find prettier turns of phrase than the ones she had taken to using: after Behzad was banished from the nursery, it was the twang of Shirin's village dialect that he heard, kitchen Farsi mingled with the immovable and comical Polish vowels. But she's armed herself with a new vocabulary picked up from the newspaper and the wireless. She doesn't need this sort of language, he expostulates. Leila and Farideh don't need it, and don't need to listen to it either. In fact, between the two of them he'd rather stay as they were and stick to French. And, by the way, when they have company he'd rather she didn't talk at all.

It's becoming an issue of contention.

The Shirazi business has picked up again, and this entails lavish dinners to be given in his home for a variety of interested parties. Most of the *bazaaris* who are his guests have managed, over time, to swallow their surprise that the woman who should have overseen the cooking is also sitting among them, and doing the eating as well. But they cannot fathom why Karim Agha allows her to pronounce on national politics when this becomes the subject of conversation – as of course it must. Three years ago, when the British left (if you're stupid enough to believe they really have), she crowed about it! You'd have thought she was almost taunting Karim Agha, who didn't pack her off to her own quarters but simply nodded his head and kept repeating, well, well, we'll see how it goes. When the Russians left, she said it was because the Americans had made them, when everyone knew it was Prime Minister Qavam and the clever deals he'd done, promising them oil concessions that he knew they'd never get.

She is without question a striking and voluptuous woman – not one of them leaves without a *frisson* of fantasy, and her vivacity suggests a lively partner in the marriage bed, which they imagine with envy. But that is where the vivacity, and the voice, ought to remain. And it's the voice that's the problem: not the accent, but the tone. Sharp. Clear. Definite. There.

The first time has become the story everyone knows. According to Fereydoon Hamadi and his sons, they had only just arrived at the house and were putting on their slippers when they caught snatches of a news bulletin on the wireless coming from the main room. Karim Agha had gone ahead and turned the thing off, which had caused his wife to say something to him in French. Then before he had time to introduce them she had expressed astonishment that the authorities had failed to prosecute the Devotees of Islam, who had shot dead that pamphleteer Ahmad Kasravi.

'He was in court,' she declared in her foreigner's accent. 'There must have been police there to see it.'

One of Fereydoon's sons had had to explain to her that the only trouble with the Devotees had been that they hadn't shot the unbeliever sooner. Kasravi's grandfather was one of the respected mullahs; he'd built a mosque. And what did the grandson do? He went about telling people that everything the mullahs had ever taught was wrong and all that mattered now was the new European science. Forget God, he said. Forget the Prophet, peace be upon him and his people. Forget the Imam Hussein. If Kasravi didn't believe, he should have kept his voice down, but he had to make a noise about it. So he was in court charged with slandering Islam, and quite right because that was what he'd done.

'So what?' she'd said in her loud voice, making a noise of her own. 'Murder is murder, wherever it takes place. There must have been hundreds of people there who saw the whole thing.'

So Fereydoon's boy then had to explain that if you're going to prosecute someone you need witnesses who'll say what they saw. Obviously no one in the court was looking at the time.

'Don't be ridiculous,' she'd said.

They all heard it, even though it was under her breath, and Karim Agha went quite white and completely silent. He was so angry he had to calm things down by asking her to find out if the cook had finished preparing the particular dish he had asked for, and then explained – while she was out of hearing – that she had not been long in the country and had a great deal to learn. Her opinions were of course the opinions of ignorance.

More recently she'd taken to weighing into a conversation about Dr Mossadegh. Best man for the country, she said, since he was a nationalist. He'd give Iran some backbone, she lectured them, which it needed, since the Shah was clearly such a weakling, spending all his time drinking whisky and playing tennis with the American ambassador. At least where the outside world was concerned. The trouble with the Shah, she told them all, was that he was too eager to kowtow to London, whereas anyone could see Dr Mossadegh had the right idea. Iranian oil revenues should come to Iran. Not just a royalty but the revenues themselves. It was wonderful, she said, to see a man prepared to say what he thought, for a change, even if it made some people nervous.

Everyone had agreed with that. But you didn't want to hear it coming from the mouth of a woman. Especially not a foreign one. Zahra Khanoom, the real brains behind the Shirazi family business, she didn't sit at table and parade her views before all and sundry, did she? It made you wonder whether Karim Agha was losing control. It made you wonder whether this lippy wife of his was going to broadcast her opinions outside these four walls and, no doubt, tell the whole world who had been at the dinner table to hear them. Then what?

Perhaps if Dr Shirazi's wife were as vivacious in bed as the *bazaaris* suppose, he might find her liveliness outside it easier to bear. But even the most even-tempered, the most rational of men may eventually lose patience. After the latest of her interventions – why have they let that idiot Hakimi become Prime Minister again when it's obvious he has nothing to say for himself? – Dr Shirazi can take it no longer. He makes his complaint in French.

'Marta, why do you keep doing this? Don't you see you are making a laughing-stock out of me? I let you join my guests for dinner, which I can assure you no other man would let his wife do. Isn't that enough?'

'So I have to sit there and listen to their rubbish, grinning like somebody's china doll up on a shelf? What's the point?'

'You don't have to. You can do as other wives do and eat with my sisters. I thought you would find it interesting.'

'It's hardly interesting if you're not supposed to say anything. And I see your sisters every day.'

'Aren't they good enough for you?'

'It's not a question of being good enough or not good enough. It's just that what I want is male conversation.'

'Male conversation? What is male conversation?'

'You know. About the world, the economy, politics.'

'Marta! I beg you. Where do you think we are? And anyway what do you know about politics?'

'As much as anyone else. I listen to the wireless. I read the newspapers. I look around me. I think about what I see.'

'Do you go to the mosque?'

'Of course not.'

'Because that's where my dinner guests get their politics.'

'That doesn't make it the only possible source, and anyway I don't just want to listen to them. I want to be able to argue with them. I have my own experience of the world. Don't forget that, Karim.'

'You'll never let me.'

'Anyway, why did you say the mosque is "where my dinner guests get their politics"?' She mimics his pompous tone, laying on pomposity. 'You don't go to the mosque all that often, do you? If at all. So presumably your opinions aren't the same as theirs. I've never heard you talking about wanting to make the pilgrimage like them. As far as I can see you don't do any of the things they think you should, not to mention doing the things you shouldn't. And look at you now, with a glass of whisky in your hand. Do they know what you drink when they're not here to see it?'

'What I drink is my business, and my opinions and beliefs are beside the point. Like anyone else I believe this country is better off with a strong leader so long as he doesn't tax me unduly. And, that apart, politics don't interest me. I am a businessman. I have business to do. I'm not interested in the Shah or people who disagree with him, I'm not interested in religious fanatics like the Devotees of Islam, or the people who make fun of them the way Kasravi did before they put a bullet in his head – and he ought to have had enough sense to know that would happen. I'm not interested in how many prime ministers this country has contrived to put in place in the four years since the war ended – or what they stood for. I'm just interested in my family's company and my work, and, if other people want to get excited, they can. But not in my house. Not even Dr Mossadegh, no matter how wonderful he may be. Just not in my house, Marta, because politics and business don't mix.'

'Except when you get a message suggesting that for the good of your business you'd better support this man or that man. And then you do, don't you?' She's scoffing, as if she thought it was a matter of principle. Or choice.

'Maybe. But that's being realistic. That's to do with knowing what to say and who to say it to. It has nothing to do with what my opinions are. Opinions don't come into it. In fact they had better not come into it, and your opinions least of all. Don't you see that your pronouncements, made so confidently in front of these men, make them uneasy? They think that if tomorrow you go round laying down the law about our country's domestic affairs, and it gets out that they are associated with me but you've been criticizing this, that and the next thing, you'll jeopardize their businesses as well as mine. And frankly, Marta, I'd like you to leave my business alone, since it's what interests me.'

'I thought you were a doctor.'

'One can be more than one thing. But we were not talking about me and my opinions. We were talking about you and yours, and my guests don't want to have to hear them because, quite apart from anything else, they don't think women have the right sort of brains for these sorts of discussions.'

'And what do you think?'

He smiles. Her blood boils.

'You didn't think so once.'

'And when was that?'

'When you kidnapped me the first time.'

'Kidnapped! What are you talking about, Marta? Are you out of your mind?'

'All right. I'll put it differently. On my first visit to your summer home. In the car as we were driving, on the –'

'What is this kidnapped? Where did you get this idea of kidnapped? My memory tells me that it was more like a rescue. There you were, don't you remember? Vomiting in a ditch, and you said –'

'I meant the first time.'

'The first time?'

'Yes. The first time, when you invited me to stay for a couple of days but then went back to town leaving me behind. You knew I wouldn't be able to get back to Tent City on my own, that I'd be stuck.'

'Stuck! Stuck? I don't understand you, Marta. I don't understand people like you. We offer you hospitality and you say it's kidnap. What are you going to say next, that we laced your food with drugs? Or that I raped you on our wedding night?'

'Forget I said it. It was just a word.'

'But you did say it. And now you want to take it back because it gets you in difficulties. So you prove my point.'

'Because I said kidnapped?'

'It was revealing. And you said my guests talk rubbish, but then you want to be part of the conversation. It makes no sense. And can you imagine what would happen to my reputation if people knew I sat at home of an evening talking politics with my wife? I have to do

443

enough of that during the day, and, besides, you ought to have other topics to occupy you, as my sisters do.'

'But they don't interest me. Children and households – and how their husbands are in bed.'

He looks up sharply. 'Well, of course you wouldn't have much to say on that subject, would you? You're hardly in a position to know.'

'I'm sorry, Karim. It's just that I –'

'No, no, no. We won't go into that any more. I'm not accusing you of anything so you don't need to try and mount a defence. But I think you should understand, Marta, that in this country men seek their companionship, their conversation, with other men, as women do with women. I don't know how it is in Poland but that is how things are here, how they have always been and as far as I can see how they will remain, no matter how much noise you make.'

'Just because something's always been a certain way doesn't mean they have to stay that way. Nothing would ever change if that's your attitude.'

'Most things don't change.'

'Not by themselves they don't. But there's nothing to stop people changing them.'

'*Tss.*' He kisses the air – don't be absurd – just as Behzad always does. Just as everyone does. Of all the gestures of this country it's the one that drives her mad. All the time, *tss, tss, tss*. Can't be done! What gave you that idea? Don't be ridiculous!

'So why did you go to Paris to study medicine? Why not just stay here, sit on the hill and watch your compatriots dying of infectious diseases and losing their premature babies?' Of course, now that he's stopped treating the ditch drinkers, that *is* what he's doing.

He regards her with such frankly undisguised patience that her blood boils again. How can he be so patronizing? But she tries another tack.

'Mrs Benka once said people become doctors because they want to be loved.'

'Loved? Is that what you Poles think? No. Being loved is something different.'

444

Both are silent. Both let their eyes wander among the knotted tendrils of Karim's great green carpet.

'Karim...' He looks up. 'Do you love me? Have you ever?'

He sighs, a man who does not want to be asked this question. 'There was a time when I thought I did. When I thought you might even come to love me. As my mother came to love my father. They came to love each other over the years.' He pauses for a response, but there isn't one. 'But that time has passed – which is normal.'

'I don't think it's normal.'

'Then for God's sake why have you been making it so difficult?' She's never heard him raise his voice before. Never heard his voice crack. 'First you disappear into some sort of private hole, for months, for years. And you won't even look at your son. Then suddenly you come out and decide to run the world. And you still don't look at your son. You don't want to touch me and you don't want to touch your son. What are you, Marta? Have you no heart? No feelings at all?'

There is a brief silence, then she hears herself telling the calm and entirely factual lie, 'I don't know.' Then, 'You should have told me.'

'What?'

'That all you really wanted was a mother for your child, not a friend, or a... I don't know, a...'

'I told you. Men are my friends. With women it's something else. And why should I think to alert you to what for me is usual?'

'But it wasn't usual for me.'

'You had been in our house. You had seen how we do things. You saw how my sisters live with their husbands. If you thought you couldn't make your home here you shouldn't have agreed to marry me. It's a bit late to start complaining now.'

'But I didn't see how you do things. It was the summer. People were on holiday. I didn't know that it was always going to be exactly the same, but just in another house. And that's the whole point. I don't have enough to do, Karim. Davood is with Shirin all the time. She cleans the house. Now there's Ahmad to do the cooking. I don't have enough to do.'

'Do you want to clean the house?'

'Not particularly. But that's not the point.'

'Do you want to do the cooking?'

'I don't know how, though I would learn. But –'

'Do you want to look after your son? Well, don't you? So you see, you should be pleased you don't have to. I don't understand you, Marta. You can go out with Farideh and Leila any day you like. You can take a *doroshkeh* wherever you want. You can go to Avenue Lalezar every day if you want and buy new clothes every day if you want. No one is stopping you from doing anything you want. But somehow it's not good enough. Nothing is good enough.'

'I didn't say anything wasn't good enough. I said I was bored. I don't want to sit on a cushion all day eating sweets and looking at fashions in French magazines.'

'You should be glad you can. It's a sign of privilege for a woman to be bored. I work all day to make enough money so that you don't have to clean and cook and chase after my son. This country is full of people who are so poor they haven't got the time to be bored. Have you thought of that? Have you thought what the women in the slums would give to be in your shoes?'

It can only be a few days after this exchange that Dr Shirazi, drinking tea in the centre of town, gets to hear that there has been some commotion at the bottom of the hill concerning his wife. What? What is it? He gulps at his glass, scalding his tongue. Curses with his hand over his mouth. What has happened to her? It's not what's happened to her, Agha. It's what she's got herself into. His informant, a scabby, weaselly character, is torn between telling the tale with all the embellishments, possible and impossible, and holding out for some money. The tea-house is all ears and tongues. Dr Shirazi decides to get the gist of the story somewhere else.

On the pavement he grabs the grinning fellow by the ears, then hauls him into a passing *doroshkeh* In the enclosed space Dr Shirazi puts a handkerchief over his nose. It's been so long since he had dealings with people from down there. 'Do you know what I'm going to do to you if you lie to me?' His face is dark with menace and the power to carry it through.

'Please, Agha-ye Doktor. As God is my witness, I only speak the truth. Would I risk offending a man like you? I swear on my children's lives... on the Prophet –'

'Stop swearing and tell me what's happened.'

'The lady had to be rescued from a crowd in the south, only a matter of hours, minutes ago. Yes, Agha-ye Doktor, she was alone. No, Agha-ye Doktor, why would I make it up. I swear on... She said she had come to replace you, Agha, no, no, I'm not laughing, Agha. She said she was going to be a nurse, like a hospital nurse for the people. Said she'd do for them what you used to do, Agha-ye Doktor.'

'What nonsense is this?'

'No nonsense, Agha. She had things... you know... with her, things for listening to your heart... you know, things... and a bag and bottles. Somebody has to do it, she kept saying. Somebody has to.'

'So what happened?'

'There was a lot of people, Agha. Such a crowd a dog wouldn't know its own master. And they stole the bag. They said if it was really a doctor's bag it would have opium in it. Did it, Agha-ye Doktor? So then she started shouting, "Give it back, give it back." And everyone was laughing, and then they started a fight over the bag, and the lady sort of fell down in the middle of it. Got a bit of a knock, Agha. They didn't mean to. It just happened. What with everyone pushing and –'

'What do you mean, she got a bit of a knock, you miserable dregs from the gutter? Where is she?'

'In the hospital now, Agha.'

'Which hospital?'

'Your hospital, Agha-ye Doktor.'

Dr Shirazi bellows the address at the *doroshkeh* driver, who, drinking in every word, has already slapped the reins against his horse's neck to change direction. Dr Shirazi leans back in his corner and glowers at the messenger, but without seeing him. If his story is true then he'll get ten rials. If it isn't he'll get a beating he'll never forget.

He won't walk again. Or talk. Never tell another scabrous lie to anyone ever again.

But when the *doroshkeh* pulls up at the Hospital Razi, it's evident the scurvy creature wasn't lying – or at least not this time. Ali Golgan, the administrator, is out on the steps looking anxious. And this is a man who never leaves his office.

'Karim-jun!' Only a quick embrace. 'Come round the back entrance.'

Dr Shirazi throws some coins at the driver, and holds out ten rials to the messenger.

'Oh, Agha. I have six hungry children. Seven, as a matter of fact. How can I put food in their mouths on this?'

Dr Shirazi pulls out another coin. 'Here. Let this be it. But if I hear that you've so much as breathed a word of this to anyone I will come to your house and personally flay you. Do you understand? Your life won't be worth living. You'll be begging me to kill you. Do you understand?'

'Please, Agha. On the life of the Prophet, I won't tell a soul. May my life and my children's lives be damned for ever, I won't.'

The administrator has Dr Shirazi by the arm and hustles him to the rear entrance, where few people have reason to pass by. The messenger looks scornfully down at the coins in his palm and spits. Whoever wants to buy silence ought to pay the proper rate for it, and you shouldn't threaten people if you can't carry out your threats. That doctor hasn't a clue where in the south of the city to find the messenger's house. But everyone knows where the doctor and that loose wife of his live.

61

Marta is in disgrace. Even as he was handing them over Dr Shirazi knew that his twenty rials would not guarantee her anonymity. There were too many other people who would have needed to be silenced: the men who had made off with the bag; the men who had been involved in fighting for it; the bystanders who had egged them on; the *doroshkeh* driver; everyone's wives and children – and finally all the staff of the hospital. Not least Ali Golgan the administrator, a blabber-mouth of the first order, who had only hustled Dr Shirazi round to the back entrance in order to heighten the drama.

It's not that anyone questions Dr Shirazi's professional skills. He's one of the best doctors around. Nor do the slum-dwellers of the lanes in the south resent him for turning his back on them in favour of wealthier clients – in his shoes they'd have done the same. What everyone is so relishing is that this taciturn, austere figure, who never raises his voice but wears his western suits as if their tailoring alone gives him dignity, who shaves so closely every day he doesn't even have normal stubble, has been made to look a fool by a woman – his own wife – whom, apparently, he can't control. Is it any wonder that she has been grounded?

'You are not to go down to the south ever again. Is that understood?' He is so angry you can barely see his lips.

Marta hangs her head. More than anything it was Maryam, plastering her cuts and bruises with some ashy balm of her own devising, who had made her realize the shame she had brought on the entire household. Maryam did not say a word. Not one. Zahra Khanoom has suspended visits, Farideh and Leila are keeping their daughters at home and, because Shirin has retreated to the kitchen, bewildered Davood has no one to play with. Even Shirazi *père* has not stopped by all week. She does not object to being confined to barracks. It's no more than she deserves, and anyway she is still so black and blue from the scuffle that skulking indoors is only sensible. All the same she wonders how long her isolation is to go on.

'Will you play hide and seek with me, *Maman*?' Davood jumps on her.

'Ow!'

She didn't know their apartment had this many places for a child to hide and repeatedly fails to find him. But you can only play hide and seek for so long. Next she has to tell him stories – the plots of cowboy films – and he is entranced.

'Now you tell me one.' Her head aches.

He is lying on his tummy on the carpet, sucking a segment of orange. 'All right,' he says, surprised, and begins in the manner of all Persian fairy-tales. 'There was one, there wasn't one. Except for God there was no one…'

His story is about a bird that gets lost in a dense forest and cannot find her way home to her nest, so she has to ask for help from all the creatures of the wild. Each of them, anxious to please, gives her directions that send her plunging deeper into the tangled plants of the unknown where dangers lurk.

As she listens to her small son chasing after his imagination, Marta realizes that she does not know him. Throughout his six years he has lived his life more intensely with Shirin and his cousins than with her. How odd it is to watch him now, feature for feature stamped in her image, but restrained in demeanour – withheld, like his father. His eyes are so green they might be coloured glass, but his tongue is entirely Persian. Well, of course it is. Farsi is what people will call his 'mother' tongue, never mind that it's not his mother's.

The story runs into the ground. Too many twists and turns, and he can't think how to end it. Mortified, his face flushes. He had hoped to impress her. How well she recognizes that expression, how well she knows what it's like to be on the inside of it.

'That was a very good story,' she says quickly. 'How did you make it up?'

'I didn't make it up. It's all written down here, isn't it?' And he thumps the carpet.

'So it is. Let's see if we can find the end.'

Wincing from her bruises, Marta gets down on her knees, and with Davood crouched low beside her they trace the lost bird's journey through the undergrowth back to the corner at the opposite diagonal. Finally, with a lot of ungainly flapping, they restore her to her nest. All three are triumphant.

'Sing me a song!'

Sing? She has never sung to him, it was always Maryam or Shirin who did that, and anyway she can't sing. She doesn't know any songs. But at the back of her mind a solid-soled shoe taps the choir to order: two, three, four...

'Forward we go to serve you,
Oh Fatherland whom we adore
The young and the old will guard you
From traitors at the door.'

Davood laughs out loud. 'That was funny, *Maman*. Say it again. What does it mean? Can I say it?'

Line by line she goes through the song and line by line he repeats the syllables that don't mean a thing to him. But he has a child's lack of inhibition and his accent isn't bad. Really, she thinks, I should teach him Polish. I should have taught him from the moment he was born. But the moment he was born she had withdrawn everything but her breasts from him, and it hadn't seemed to matter since there were so many others to do the loving.

She puts her finger onto the end of his nose. 'Nose,' she declares in Polish.

He repeats in Polish, 'Nose.'

'Mouth.'

'Mouth.'

'Mummy.'

'Mummy.'

'Davood.'

'Davood. But that's the same!'

'Of course it's the same. It's your name. It's who you are. That wouldn't change, would it?'

'Tell me more Polish words.'

'Bird.'

'Bird.'

'Tree.'

'Tree.'

'Carpet.'

'Carpet.'

'Very good, darling.'

'Very good, darling... What does that mean?'

'It means, very good, darling.'

They hear a noise and together look up towards it. Zahra Khanoom stands framed in the doorway with a piece of dark-blue cloth draped over her hands and held out before her like an offering. It *is* an offering.

'Granny! Granny's come!' Davood bounds over the lost bird's journey and throws his arms round his grandmother's waist. She bends to kiss the top of his head.

'Here, daughter-in-law. I have brought you this.'

The blue cloth is a large square scarf. Zahra Khanoom folds it diagonally, flips it over Marta's head and round her neck, arranging it so that much of her face is concealed. She turns her towards the ornate mirror Karim had made to order. Two veiled women, one tall, one small, gaze out like a passing artist's fancy. Not a bruise or a scratch in sight. And out there no one will peer curiously to see what the woman in blue is trying to conceal because the scarf itself will deflect the enquiry. They will barely notice her at all.

'I'll ask Shirin for some tea.'

'Let's make our tea without her.' Zahra Khanoom pushes past her to the kitchen and orders Shirin out to buy fruit.

Shirin looks pointedly at the fruit piled in its large Bohemian cut-glass bowl but unhooks her basket from its place on the wall none the less. A single pomegranate will do, so long as the buying of it is slow. What she wouldn't give to be able to stay behind and listen to the reckoning. 'Kookooleh,' she calls. 'Come on. We're going to the market.'

For a second Marta thinks that the friendship she has just struck up with her son may be too fragile to survive this separation. Look at him, scampering after Shirin without looking back because tagging onto her skirts is where he expects to be. What he has known all his life. What's in a name? *Maman.* Just a name. Just a sound, and meaningless unless it is invested with meaning. They had a nice time together today but for all she knows she's no more to him than one pleasant auntie among all the others but who happens to be called *Maman.* Why don't you stay here with us, Davood? But Zahra Khanoom means business and Marta is in no position to be difficult.

The door closes and the little boy's high-pitched chatter fades as the two of them take the stairs down to the street. While he was in the room he was a sort of protection, but she's on her own now.

'Good.' Zahra Khanoom beckons Marta into the kitchen, points to the floor for her to sit down, bangs the ashes out of the samovar and rekindles it, boils water for tea. You'd think this was her kitchen. Now she's pulling out the hubble-bubble from behind the box where they keep it hidden in case Karim one day pokes his head in to look. 'Smoke?'

They sit cross-legged and pass the nozzle back and forth, Zahra Khanoom inhaling deeply as if she hasn't had a lungful in weeks. But that's all an act. Shirazi *père* has never objected to anyone smoking, although he wouldn't want to see his daughters with cigarettes out on the street. Fair enough. Marta wouldn't smoke out on the street either.

'I am sorry for you, daughter-in-law,' says Zahra Khanoom at last. 'You are not happy in our family, I can see that. And I told Karim that he made a mistake…'

She told Karim?

'… People should stay where they belong. You cannot mix oil and water, and God did not make people so that they should be all mixed together. Without our own families, without our own people, we are like branches torn off a tree, and what he did wasn't fair. He wasn't thinking. But what you did was not fair either. You should never go anywhere in Karim's name if he has not given you permission, or you injure us all.'

'I'm sorry.'

'You think you understand our country because you live here, but you understand nothing. You think you can meddle in how our people live with your ways, but all that happens is that you bring dishonour on us, and nobody is helped. It's not your business to try and interfere with how God decided to make the world. If He has made one man tall and strong and another small and weak, then that's up to Him. If He has made one woman beautiful, as you are, and another plain like our Shirin, then who are we to say He shouldn't? You're lucky and Shirin is not, and you should at least thank Him for it. And if He has made some people poor and others rich then that is how it is. Nothing happens that is not God's will, and if He does not will it nothing happens. Nothing. All that has come out of this is that those people are laughing at you – you and your little doctor's bag. We've had enough of foreign experts running around the country telling us how we should run our schools or our hospitals or our government, even. But nothing is worse than a foreign woman, who has married into one of our families, thinking she can do the same thing. All those people wanted was the opium, but you were too stupid to see that, and somebody down there has made some good money selling it, while Karim's name has been made a joke. You should be thankful they didn't murder you.'

'I'm sorry.'

'No, you're not. And I know you are not because your mouth is saying one thing but your face is telling me another. You are thinking, if God did not intend people to be mixed together how did He allow you to be married to Karim. I don't know the answer to that except, if it had been meant to be, you would not be so unhappy, and

454

my son would not be so unhappy.'

Marta sits flipping her empty glass between her palms. Does she dare or does she not? Oh, come on. Might as well. 'And are you happy, Zahra Khanoom?'

Her mother-in-law blinks. So surprised to be asked a question when she's still not finished with her reproaches that she answers. 'I have my children, and all of them, God be praised, are healthy. My husband is a kind and honourable man, and since he married me I have never been without anything that I need or want. So I am as happy as anyone can expect to be. Happier than I thought I would be. But tell me, Marta-jun...' She leans forward. 'What did *you* expect?'

Marta is cornered. Hemmed in without a reply. She does not know what she expected. It's what Karim said. You saw how we do things. If you thought you couldn't make your home here you shouldn't have agreed to marry me. But she hadn't thought she couldn't make her home here. She hadn't thought that far. She feels like a thieving child caught red-handed by an angry teacher bearing questions, so she stares with a child's helpless insolence at her interrogator and behind the folds of the large blue scarf her bruises glow.

Zahra Khanoom sits and waits, can wait for ever, watching her daughter-in-law plucking irritably at the edges of the cloth. 'I have an address for you,' she says suddenly. 'Tomorrow, take a *doroshkeh* and go to the crossing of Avenue Lalezar and Sepah Street. On the corner there's a pastry shop. Go inside and buy yourself some cakes.'

That's the trouble with these people, thinks Marta. Whenever someone's in difficulties they stuff sweets in your mouth.

62

Next morning, early, Marta in the blue scarf goes looking for her son. The *doroshkeh* is already waiting outside, and it seems to her that if she is to obey Zahra Khanoom she might as well take Davood with her. Perhaps they can retrieve some of that companionable feeling they had yesterday.

Davood's eyes are round with disbelief as he leans against Shirin. His mother has never actually sought him out before. Whatever can she want? He looks up at Shirin, who, equally perplexed, taps him lightly on the bottom and gives him a small shove of encouragement.

'Go along,' she grunts – a mite curmudgeonly, for this little prince is really hers. 'And see you behave yourself properly, you little devil.'

He clambers up into the *doroshkeh* and seats himself opposite his mother, who pats the seat beside her, a broad, bright smile stretching her lips.

'Come and sit next to me, darling.'

Reluctantly he slides across. Awkwardness sits between them like a lump of cold rice, and Marta wonders whether this is not perhaps a terrible mistake. Why has she inveigled him to accompany her when he'd probably rather have stayed behind with Shirin and his cousins?

'Where are we going?'

'Well, I don't really know.'

'You don't know?' A grown-up who doesn't know! 'Who does know?'

'Maybe the horse.'

'The horse. Shall we ask him?'

'All right. You ask him.'

'I can't. I don't speak horse language.'

'I don't either.'

'Oh.' Now he's disappointed. But he lights on an idea. 'That thing you were saying yesterday. You were telling me. Maybe the horse will understand that.'

'But I was speaking Polish and this is a Persian horse, Davood. He won't understand Polish.'

'Try! Please try. Maybe he's a specially clever horse.'

'All right.' Marta addresses the horse's bony hindquarters, with Davood leaning forward intently, keeping watch for reaction. 'Horsy, horsy,' she chants in Polish, 'where are you taking us?'

'What did you say to him?'

'I said, "Horsy, horsy, where are you taking us?"'

'Say it again.'

'Horsy, horsy…'

Davood copies her, word perfect, tone perfect.

The horse flicks a threadbare tail. Nothing.

'Horsy, horsy, where are you taking us?'

The horse shakes its head and snuffles dust from its nostrils. Davood is delighted. 'He speaks it! He speaks it! What did he say?'

'He said, "Down the hill to buy a cake."'

'That was a lot to say. Are you sure?'

'I think so.'

'What cake will it be?'

'I don't know.'

'Ask the horse again.'

'Horsy, horsy, what kind of cake?' But the horse has come to the end of its repertoire. 'I don't think he wants to say. He wants it to be a secret. A surprise.'

The *doroshkeh* has stopped. Is this it? A small shop front like its neighbours, set back on the wide pavement with a few small round tables arranged outside against the window under an awning, aping the French way. Marta adjusts the folds of her scarf. There are no customers yet, inside or out, because people are still about more serious business. A skinny adolescent girl with a cloth in her hand comes out to wipe the tables and as the door swings to behind her the scent of vanilla and milk floats into Marta's nostrils, igniting them with memory. She stands with Davood's hand clamped in hers, motionless on the pavement, but she has tipped her head like a hunter's dog to sniff and sniff the sweet waft of air. Davood goggles at his mother and sniffs fruitily in imitation.

'Let's go in.'

They push through the door into the empty shop. Creamy layered sponge cakes sprinkled with icing sugar and poppy seeds stand plump under glass domes on a wide counter.

'There's nobody here!'

Davood's disappointed wail pierces the back wall and propels a dumpy woman in through a small door. She is dressed in a white coat like a doctor, but she's knotted her white scarf behind her head. A blonde fringe frizzes on her forehead over rosy cheeks. An altogether pink-and-white woman.

'Good morning,' she says, and Davood jumps. Her accent is just like his mother's.

Marta's face is hidden under the pleats of blue, but surface scratches never changed a voice.

'Good morning!' she shouts in Polish, excitement getting the better of manners.

'Good morning,' says the shop lady again, also in Polish and to Davood, who, well primed, politely repeats the noise back. 'Which cake would you like, little one?'

He repeats that too and looks up at his mother's swathed face. 'What does that mean, Mummy?'

'The lady was asking you which cake you want.'

'Doesn't your little boy speak Polish?'

'No. Not yet.'

'I see.' The woman nods, but incredulous. What sort of Pole is this who has not given her child the language? 'I suppose *he* was against it, was he?' Her fingers stray demonstratively towards her white headscarf – tied for hygiene only, while her gaze fixes on Marta's generous blue folds.

'Oh, no, no. Karim isn't like that. They're a modern family. It's just that…' Marta unwinds her scarf to reveal her face. The bruises are green and yellow today. The scratches nicely scabbed over.

'Jesus and Mary, you poor dear!' The woman's hands fly to cover a small but satisfied shriek of vindicated dismay. 'Did he do that?' She leans forwards and lowers her voice. 'We've mostly married Christians, you know.' Straightens up again, still shaking her head over the extent of the newcomer's injuries. 'Come into the back and we can sit down and have a nice cup of coffee together. Then you can tell me all about it. Oh, I am bad! My name is Danuta Petrossian.'

'Marta Shirazi.' They shake hands formally, each registering the significance of the other's married name. 'And this is my son, Davood.' Mrs Petrossian pats him on the head.

Davood stands between the two women watching their mouths open and close. He had not thought other people would know how to make his mother's noises too. The round lady in white is pushing him ahead of her to the door at the back of the shop. Is she taking him away?

'*Maman!*'

'Yes, yes, Davood. She's coming.'

'You don't understand, this was an accident. All my fault, as a matter of fact.'

'They always say that. You don't have to pretend with me.'

'No, really.' Marta is laughing at the misunderstanding, but already irritated by this pushy female who thinks she knows it all. Still, a nice cup of coffee, a piece of Polish patisserie, and the taste of the language in her mouth. It really isn't the same, talking to oneself.

There's a tiny sitting room off a short corridor behind the shop, a previous life and another time reconstructed. The fleshy upholstery, the tasselled velvet tablecloth, the clusters of tiny framed photographs – it would all sit better in some cramped apartment in Lodz or Lublin or Krakow. In here you needn't believe that donkeys loaded to invisibility are trotting by outside. Marta sinks to the hips into an armchair and draws nervous Davood between her knees.

'Now, let me see, let me see.' Mrs Petrossian rummages through her room, opening drawers, lifting boxes. 'What can we find to keep a young man happy? Ah! Animals. Does he like animals?'

She lifts the lid off a shallow wooden box lined with baize. Tiny carved and painted animals lie head to toe inside, a giraffe, a zebra, an elephant – a veritable jungle carved from weightless balsa-wood. Davood and his mother stare. He has never seen anything like this. She has, but so long ago. Davood's fingers hover over the figures. Is he allowed to touch? The shop lady picks the creatures out one by one and sets them on a low polished table. Dull reflections drop from their feet.

'Davood, be careful! Don't break anything.'

'He'll be careful, won't you?'

Davood nods importantly. It's so funny, these two women, who both don't sound right when they speak. He balances a lion with curly mane on the palm of his hand and raises it to the level of his eyes. The lion's tawny eyes peer past him.

'Now then, you stay right where you are and I'll get us some coffee and a piece of cake.'

Marta leans back in her armchair, breathing in the aroma of brewing coffee. All she needs to know is Danuta Petrossian's home town, her maiden name and how she came to meet her Christian Armenian husband. Everything in between she already knows without asking. This woman is a complete stranger, but she knows so much about her none the less. It binds them, and it will go on binding them, even though in other circumstances, back home, they wouldn't have given one another a thought.

'Here we are. I've made a cup of chocolate for Davood. Will he like that? Do you like chocolate, Davood?'

'I don't know.' He dabs a fingertip experimentally into the hot brown liquid and licks it. Dabs and licks. Dabs and licks.

'Here, darling. Use this spoon until it cools down.'

Danuta Petrossian, née Kalinowska, hails from Katowice, where her father was a grocer. Her parents were arrested with her but did

460

not survive. She kept the box of animals throughout, all the way from Katowice, dreading that she might have to sell them, but it hadn't turned out that way. She met Krikor Petrossian, who is in import–export, outside one of his warehouses when he was supervising the loading of a truck. Import–export is the business to be in. You can get anything. Chocolate, for example, even during the war. They have two small sons, one older, one younger than Davood, both under the eye of her mother-in-law during the working day. The patisserie shop is her best method of keeping homesickness at bay, but it has gone down well with Tehran society. The trouble is, it hasn't done much for her figure – and she slaps her haunches with rueful deprecation. She is planning a trip home.

Home?

His mother sits up so suddenly that one of the wooden animals falls on its side. Davood gazes alarmed at the shop lady, to see if she's going to be angry.

Just as soon as her visa comes through. Her younger brother – just married – has been in touch.

In touch? How?

The wireless. Hasn't she been listening to Cairo? They've got an international station broadcasting the names of missing persons. You only have to write to them and they'll read out who you're looking for. It gets repeated on Polish radio. It's so simple. Danuta cannot think how it is that Marta hasn't done this yet. You didn't know about Radio Cairo? Look, this is the wavelength and the address…

Marta licks sponge cream from her fingers and drains her coffee. She can't wait to leave, although it will be crudely ungrateful to seem be in such a rush. But Danuta is all bustling sympathy and understanding, and hurries her to the door lest she miss Radio Cairo's final broadcast.

It's when Marta starts winding Zahra Khanoom's blue cloth round her face again before stepping outside that Danuta recalls a tip she needs to pass on. 'You do know, don't you, that you won't be allowed to travel unless your husband gives his permission. In writing.'

*

Davood sits in the *doroshkeh* with his fists clenched. He didn't mean to take them but his mother was in such a flurry, hustling him out onto the street all without warning, that he didn't have a chance to put them back. And now the shop lady will have discovered that a baby monkey and a small stripy thing are missing from their green baize nest.

Marta cradles the multi-layered airy confection of cream and apricot jam that Danuta slipped into a box as a parting gift. They had stood in the shop doorway, wedged nose to nose, pretending to argue, Marta trying to pay for the cake and Danuta insisting she should not. It's a present, she said. Because I'm so glad we've met, and if your husband's family like it, well, you can come back and next time I'll let you pay. But she is bound to go back. For the company and the language that is like your own skin, no ill-fitting sleeves or awkward buttons. Danuta's Polish friends have been gathering there of an afternoon for as long as… oh, Danuta can't remember. So many of them, apparently, stayed on, and married. All to Christians. How can she not have known?

'Davood? What are you holding so tightly there?'

She sounds sharp. Her voice is sort of high and shrill. He opens his palms. For a moment she stares blankly at the contents of his hands. Then she notices that the tip of the baby monkey's tail has been snapped off and lies there like a pathetic comma. Danuta managed to keep her childhood jungle collection safe all the way to Siberia and back, but one indulged six-year-old boy has ruined it in a single clumsy moment. She sees herself standing in the shop with the mangled little wooden creature wrapped in a handkerchief, trying to find the words to explain. Apology won't do – not after all this. She is so ashamed that it should be her son that did it, she turns contorted features on him and he shrinks into the corner of the *doroshkeh* with his wrists crossed up over his face. As if he expects her to hit him. Has anyone ever hit him? They can't have. She pulls herself together, though her hands tremble on the cake-box.

Later that afternoon, Davood creeps up to his mother and lays the striped thing and the baby monkey on her knee. Its tail is whole again. 'Shirin glued it,' he whispers experimentally. 'She said you can see it's been broken before.'

63

The letter to Radio Cairo has been sent, composed in Danuta Petrossian's replica sitting room, the return address given – *Would that be all right? Oh, but you have to!* – as Danuta's. Now every morning's waking brings with it a simmering anticipation, a sense of well-being such as Marta cannot remember having for so long. She will renew her campaign of action but the strategy is to be altered: subtle manoeuvre and patience will achieve what impulse and frenzy could not. She cannot wait to be up, and out. Today! Something is bound to happen today.

She declares a new routine – and Shirin can pull all the faces she wants behind the kitchen door. If Davood's afternoons are Persian and for the cousins, his mornings will be Polish and spent with Danuta's two little boys. It is her mission (and Danuta's) to retrieve him for at least a part of his heritage, and to that end the elder Mrs Petrossian has been persuaded to cede her grandsons for the first half of each day. Marta has discovered an enthusiasm for beating eggs and sifting flour so long as Davood is drenched in the language of those other grandparents, the ones who live in a faraway fairy-tale country of nesting storks and dewy meadows.

Zahra Khanoom is not best pleased. This is not what she had in mind. All she intended, she hisses urgently, was that Marta herself should be happier. Nothing is to be gained by sowing confusion in the mind of a small child. No one can be two things at the same time. It is like expecting a donkey to think of itself as a goat. And if the donkey *were* to think of itself as a goat and then starting behaving like one, well, all the order of the world would be turned on its head, and no one would know where he belonged. A child is the citizen of his father's country, not his mother's; he takes his father's religion, not his mother's; his father's language, not his mother's...

'Of course,' retorts Marta, with disconcerting cheeriness. 'I'm not intending to baptize him or change him. I'm just acquainting him with another part of himself. I'm sure he'll cope.'

Unexpectedly stymied, Zahra Khanoom turns to her son to wield his authority. But Karim merely observes that, since Kookooleh will be starting school in a very few months' time, Marta has left it all rather late. At least now she isn't complaining that she hasn't got enough to do. At least now she has a pleasant expression on her face, and isn't that worth something?

As for Davood, he is having it both ways: boys with toy soldiers in the mornings, his devoted girl cousins after lunch. And every evening his grandmother pulls him down to sit with her on the garden carpet so that she can tell him stories. She's done it before, but never so much. She holds his hands in hers the whole time and wants him to keep looking at her face, into her eyes. If his gaze drifts away, she gives his hands a little shake to bring it back again. He'd like to sing her the new songs he's been learning. But he doesn't.

The weeks pass. Oh, how the weeks pass, until one morning they arrive to find Danuta Petrossian, all agog in her hygienic white, waiting out on the pavement under the awning. She's got a pale-grey envelope between finger and thumb, and as they get down from the *doroshkeh* she lifts it to her ear and jangles it as if she's listening for the rattle of something inside. Her plump cheeks have swallowed her eyes.

'Guess what I've got here for you. Just you guess!' As if there could be any doubt.

A swift exchange follows. The letter is snatched into Marta's hands; Davood delivered into Danuta's.

'Come along, little one. The boys have been complaining that you're late. What shall we play today?' Danuta hustles him out to her sitting room so that his mother can be alone.

The postmark is Poznan; the handwriting her mother's; the grey envelope so flimsy she's afraid of ripping the letter if she isn't careful. But her fingers have become sausages, all delicacy lost. She feels her heart jolting her body and her mouth is dry. She puts the letter down on one of the little round tables and tries to calm herself with slow breathing. This won't do. She must take herself in hand.

Danuta has stuck her head back through the door to monitor progress and sees there has been none. Marta is white and tremulous: quite incapable.

'Here. Let me.' Danuta picks out a slender knife from a drawer and slices the letter open. Beats another retreat.

> 43, Koltuna 16–18
> Poznan
> 14 October 1949

My darling Marta,

At last! You cannot imagine how we cried and hugged each other when we heard on the radio that you were looking for us, though what a surprise to discover that you really do live in Persia! How exotic that must be – all those harems and what have you! We knew that you were alive because your friend Ania's granny, Mrs Benka, told us so. (She was in Bombay – did you know that? But she came to live with her daughter Krystyna when the war was over.) But we didn't know where to find you. It's so hard writing this because my hand keeps shaking with excitement. It's only five minutes ago that we switched off the radio. Just imagine if we hadn't been at home and listening! What then? Sometimes I think God keeps a very special eye over our family.

As you can see, we have moved from Jablonska Street because, of course, that place was far too large for a family like ours. We are very lucky. We have been allocated a really cosy apartment with three rooms. Your father and I sleep in one; Sonia in another; and Gienek and his wife – yes! he's married – in the third. His wife is called Halina, and she is a good, dutiful girl who will make a good mother too. At the moment she works at the bakery. (Did I tell you that Ania has married

466

as well?) When you come home you can share with Sonia, although she says that she hopes you will be an easier sister to get on with than you used to be. But I tell her that of course you will! I know it because we have all lived through so much. We are all here. None of us was killed, thank God, and we should be grateful for that – as we are.

But my darling, Tata was a prisoner of war in Munich and so thin and tired when he finally came home that I was really worried for him. But don't you start fretting, Marta. He is quite recovered, although he's not as strong as he was. (But time passes and no one is as strong as they were.) So now he looks after the house and Sonia and I both work in a local kindergarten. The little ones there are all so sweet, with their songs and dances. It makes me nostalgic for the days when you were all small. I feel you would love them too, even though I know you don't care as much for children as most young women do. I used to think that if you only had a child of your own you might feel differently, but of course first you would have to find the man of your heart, as I did. And now you have! You are married! That brings me such joy too!

Marta, my darling. Now that we have found each other again, please come home. We cannot wait to see you. We are already making plans for what we'll do together day by day, and there is so much we have to tell you and you to tell us. Mrs Benka has told us a little but I must say I find her rather sharp and dry. There is something mannish about her, don't you think, and she smokes all the time. She says that the two of you got on so well, but then you can be quite sharp too. She will be delighted to learn where you are, and so will Ania when I tell her mother tomorrow. You won't believe it, but Krystyna hasn't changed at all. She still spends every free moment painting her flower pictures. Write soon and let us know when you are coming. After all these years, I can't bear to wait another week without hearing from you. Everyone sends you hugs and kisses. And you mustn't be concerned. Things in Poland are really as good as they could be!

Write soon, my darling.

All my love

Mama

467

Underneath, in her father's hand, a single sentence:

Your mother is wrong – I have never been better. But she is right – we are counting the days.

Marta reads the letter through again and then, for some reason, sniffs it before folding it back into its envelope. It has a fusty metallic smell about it that disappoints her. In fact there's a lot in it to make her uneasy. It's all very well her mother telling her not to fret about her father, but how can you read that he was a prisoner and not fret? How can you picture him weakened and not fret, no matter what he says either? What does it mean to have been a prisoner of war in Germany? And this house move. What can that be about? Jablonska Street wasn't so very large, and the address at the top of the letter means nothing. Koltuna. Where's that? If they've moved, no wonder her letters didn't get through. But it's the last sentence that leaves her queasy: things in Poland are really as good as they could be. It's not the sort of comment her mother would ever make, and it reads oddly. As if it was added as an afterthought – on the expectation that someone other than Marta would be reading it.

She looks up, wondering, to see Danuta silent in the door-frame.

'Good news?'

'Yes, generally. Do you think they tamper with letters?'

'Of course. Look.' Danuta takes the envelope and prises up the flap she cut through so neatly before. 'Look at that. There's more glue on that flap than it ever had when they made it.'

Is it true as Danuta said? Can Karim really keep her here simply by withholding his signature? All the way home she rehearses: 'Karim,' – said nonchalantly – 'I've managed to get in touch with my parents. I was thinking I should go home for a while. What do you say?' Karim will look up slowly from his plate, weighing his power of refusal. She has not been the wife he hoped for but though he is disappointed he masks it, mostly. A man who considers tantrums irrational in the modern age.

But what if his frustration finally breaks free and he bangs a fist on the table. 'No! Never! You are my wife; you belong to me; you will do as I say!' Actually, she cannot imagine it. He would never say that. But he might think it. And refuse to sign. She will not wheedle. She will not demean herself. 'Please, Karim. Plee-ease.' The image of a winsome little girl pleading to manipulate Daddy turns her stomach. Anyway, he'll see through her, lips pressed together in contempt. 'Well, well. So sweet and malleable all of a sudden. *Tss!*'

Marta plays hostess with brittle vivacity all afternoon, twirling her forefinger through the waves of her hair. On their way out, Farideh and Leila remark on her brightness today. She laughs and kisses them, and thinks how gentle they are, how kind. They have never been anything but kind, yet here she is fizzing with energy, all at the prospect of leaving them. Not very nice of her, is it, but they who set such store by family will understand, when she tells them, how much she craves this visit home.

When they have gone she looks down into the dark street, the two elegant women turning a little matronly, the four tiny girls hopping about in their neat white socks and patent shoes. Soon enough they too will become matrons, shuttling themselves and their children between family houses, eating ice-creams and sharing confidences in the public baths.

Davood is cross-legged on the garden carpet humming one of Danuta's nursery rhymes. Danuta says he has such a good ear, but Marta can't tell. For sure, if it's so, he didn't get it from her, and she cannot remember ever hearing Karim sing. Behzad, though. He has that tender tenor.

The front door opens and Davood immediately falls silent. Runs to his father. Who bends to kiss him on the top of the head.

To Marta: 'You're looking bright-eyed this evening. Has something happened?'

'I've heard from my parents.'

'You've heard from... Well, but that's excellent. Excellent, Marta. Are they all right? How did they know where to find you? Sit down and tell me.'

It is so genuine, his pleasure for her, that she is overcome by honesty. Danuta Petrossian's planned visit home – though she's still waiting for a visa; the letter to Radio Cairo; the response. She even tells him about her unease over some of her mother's wording.

'You'll have to go and find out,' he suggests, matter-of-fact, as if it's merely a question of popping in on the sisters round the corner. 'See what is really going on. Perhaps it's nothing. Although it does seem strange, this house move of theirs.'

'You have no objection?'

'Objection? Why would I object?'

'Danuta told me that I cannot travel without your permission.'

'And does your friend, with all her information, presume to know how I will react? And do you, with all yours, believe her? In the name of God, Marta, surely you know better than that by now! It may be the law, but I don't have to avail myself of it.'

She is abashed. Murmurs apology and then says, 'I'll tell Davood we're going to visit his grandparents.'

'No. Kookooleh stays here.'

'What?'

'He stays here. He has no business going to Poland when even you don't know what's really going on there. All sorts of things could go wrong and I am not having my son tangled up in it.'

My son! My son indeed. 'What could go wrong?'

'Marta, I don't know. But he is six years old. It's not his world for you to drag him there to…'

'I would like my parents to meet their only grandchild.'

'And I'm sure one day they will. But not this time. It's not the right time. It may not even be safe.'

'But safe enough for me?'

'That's your decision.'

'Do you think I would take "your son" if I thought anything could happen to him?'

'You're not taking him anywhere so there's no point arguing about it.'

'But –'

'No point. He stays with me.'

'You just –'

'He stays with me.'

'I might simply take him.'

'You can try. But you'll be stopped at the border. Ours, not yours.'

64

Dr Shirazi is driving. He grips the wheel to weave between donkeys, *doroshkeha*, cars, pedestrians, transport trucks – some of them his own. Irritated, he sucks his tongue, wishing his compatriots would respect the rules of the road as, rumour has it, people do in England. But here everyone is hell-bent on lurching in abrupt loops from one gap in the road to the next, to be sure of getting there first. It is a mark, he has concluded, of a backward society. When modernity comes it will be in the shape of a Highway Code obeyed. And if the English are going to be the model, well, we'll follow the rules behind the wheel – but treat the rest of the world as our private highway. In the meantime, however, to arrive at all he must do as others do. He accelerates.

From time to time he glances at his wife, who sits in the back, resplendent in a fur coat, her soft light-brown hair newly permed, the bow of her mouth carefully crimson. He cannot remember when he last saw her so animated. Even her skin seems alive with expectation. And all because she is leaving. A pang of desolation plucks at him like a sudden jangle from the strings of a *santoor*. Kookooleh is nestled against her arm, his cheek plunged so deep into the dark-brown fur it's impossible to see his expression. On his other side Zahra Khanoom grips her *chador* over her mouth, biding her time.

His mother looks as if she can't wait for her daughter-in-law to get on that plane and take off, but he knows it's not so simple. Zahra Khanoom is fond of Marta, in an exasperated sort of way – and has been truly sorry for her. Behzad became weepy when he got the news, so that Massy has had to console him like a small child, prom-

472

ising him that Marta isn't going away for ever, only visiting and so on and so on. But who has consoled the real small child? Kookooleh hasn't cried or whined to be taken along. Maybe he overheard his parents: not this trip, not this time. Which implies a next time. But Dr Shirazi knows that those who weep are not the only ones in pain. Yet any pain he once had is only memory now.

When he looks at Marta he's another one who can't wait for her to get on that plane. He barely remembers what it was that drew him to her, back in Tent City. She seemed so exhilarating then, in her difference. A fresh spirit. But now he thinks of it as just noise and irritation. She makes him uncomfortable. So then maybe his mother was right. He would have done better to leave Marta among her countrymen and let them find him a wife who wouldn't always have been questioning the way the world is. And yet, and yet. Hasn't he been questioning it himself? She may not acknowledge it but he is as concerned about his country's poverty, its backwardness, as she is. That's why he hoped that some of the ideas from the west could be imported. Clean buildings and hygiene. Just some of the ideas, though. Not all of them. Over there, they put their faith in systems, not in people. The rule of law is so abstract. He's seen it, admired it and was repelled by it, all at the same time. Codes and paperwork to run a country instead of custom and relying on the word of people you know...

Not many people are travelling and porters swarm to the cars. The brawniest trio brandish weightlifters' arms to cut a path to the rich men's tips. They each grab a pair of suitcases, bulging and roped, and run with them, bellowing with success, into the small terminal. The noise, the gust of cold air and the economic standing of the send-off party draw the attention.

Marta clutches her vanity case close to her. She has never flown before and this will be a long trip. Iran Air to Zurich. Czech Airlines to Warsaw. Polish train to Poznan. Maryam had come rushing in the early morning, her face icy in the cold, to hold a copy of the Quran over Marta's head. 'Be in God's care and protection, Marta Khanoom. May He bring you home safe.' Then she had wrapped arms like bat's wings round her and rocked with her, sobbing loudly as if Marta were the corpse of a child lost in a disaster. Marta can still feel the imprint of Maryam's hugging, still sense the weight of the Holy Book above her head. But at the same time the milling Shirazis, for all their raised voices, are already swirling away into a distance that no longer has to do with her.

Dr Shirazi rubs his face and checks his watch. It'll all be easier when she's called through to her flight. It's the hanging round he can't stomach. He looks at his wife in all her loveliness and thinks, what a waste. Their son is yanking at one of her furry cuffs. Saying something to her. She crouches down, and the heavy hem of her coat buckles on the terminal floor, transforming the coat into a glossy brown cave. Davood burrows in and disappears.

Then she's on her feet again, scanning the hall, and spies her husband leaning against a pillar. Leads Davood by the hand and transfers the boy's soft fingers into his. The Tannoy booms and crackles. Propelled by a flurry of waving and weeping, Marta spreads her arms to include them all – and runs.

The plane climbs, banks and turns due west into a sky as sharp and blue as the tiles of Isfahan, while below there are only the mud-brown rocky ranges where nothing grows. She presses her face to the window. In time they will pass over the fertile shores of the Caspian, whose mountains trap the rain. Her life's journey is playing backwards.

Flags. Big ones drooping from tall poles, small ones dripping from strings stretched the length of the terminal roof. Everywhere she looks, the white and red Polish flag with its eagle on the white stripe welcomes her home – although something doesn't look right. Travelling across the time zones, she has almost lost track of the date, but these flags remind her. Armistice Day: the eleventh of the eleventh. The end of the war for some but the proclamation of independence for Poland, a beginning that still had to be fought for. Her father in uniform; all of them in their best; the excitement in the air. She must have been about four years old when Armistice Day decided her on a military career and her parents had let her play soldiers for a full twelve months (shushing Gienek's jeers) before trying to disabuse her.

She pauses at the top of the gangway steps leading down from the aeroplane to the puddled tarmac. If it weren't for the other passengers wanting to disembark behind her, she would just stand here and drink it in. They might have laid it on for her – the words EXIT and ENTRANCE, the smell of the petrol, the mousy-haired men hauling baggage from the hold, the low clouds. If only she had a voice she would burst into song. But her high heels threaten to skitter on the gangway steps slippery with rain, and she reaches nervously for the rail.

'Perhaps I can help madame down?'

A man's voice at her shoulder in courteous Polish, so mellifluous after the evil-tempered indifference of the Czech Airlines crew. She spots breeches and riding boots beneath an enormous greatcoat and his kid gloves are beautifully stitched. She accepts the supporting grip above her elbow and does not turn to look at the man's face until she is safely on the ground. He is bearded and bespectacled. A young Trotsky comes to mind. In fact, with his hat and gloves, there is something old-fashioned about him, as if he belongs to a previous generation. It's fitting, given the Armistice Day bunting.

Cautiously Marta removes her arm from the fingers that seem reluctant to let it go. 'Thank you,' she says. 'You made me feel a great deal more secure. I think I might have slipped otherwise.'

'You are most welcome.' He bows. 'It was a pleasure.'

'I'm so glad to have come home on Armistice Day.' She gestures towards the flags draped along the terminal building. 'It seems... appropriate.'

Laughter lines crinkle his eyes. 'You must have been away for a very long time, madame. The flags aren't out for Armistice Day. We're celebrating the October Revolution.'

Now she recognizes what was amiss with the flags. The eagle has lost its crown. Blown away in a political typhoon. She tries to formulate some apposite comment but Trotsky's double has begun again.

'Unfortunately I have an appointment, or I should have liked to ask you where you've been travelling all this time. But as you see…'

A black saloon car is parked on the tarmac, apparently waiting for him. A chauffeur in a cap is holding the door open. Trotsky hesitates momentarily, and she guesses he's weighing up whether to offer her a ride. But the uncertainty passes; he touches the rim of his hat, ducks into the car and is borne away.

At passport control a middle-aged official leafs through her passport with a look of dejection. Dealing with foreigners makes him uneasy.

'The visa's there. Next page… no, you're turning them the wrong way.'

'Oh! You're a Pole!' He peers at her through the glass of his cubicle, then scrabbles through the pages to find the visa. 'Shi-ra-zi,' he murmurs uncertainly, tapping his thumb on her photograph with each syllable but eyeing the sheen of her coat. He picks up the stamp and holds it hovering over the visa, but, deciding to take a chance, lays it down again. 'It's not in order, you know,' he says stiffly. And closing her passport, unstamped, slides it back to her. 'There's…' He leans close to the glass and whispers, '… a page missing.'

A page missing? What's he talking about? She stares down at her passport, the first she has ever had, and wonders what page can possibly be missing. In puzzlement she glances up and meets his gaze. He narrows his eyes, nods slightly and rubs his own threadbare sleeve, looking the while at the fur of hers. Suddenly she understands what he wants, and disappointment makes her rash.

'You should be ashamed of yourself,' she hisses, but loudly enough for the people queuing behind the line painted on the floor to overhear. 'A representative of the Polish state trying to extract a bribe. How could you!'

The queue wobbles with alarm, and the passport official's neck seems to disappear into his collar. Then he recovers himself and musters a voice.

'I said your passport is not in order, madame. Your signature hasn't been written clearly enough. Do you see?'

He opens the passport at random and bangs a page. But there is such terror in his face that Marta regrets drawing attention to him, despicable little worm that he is. She pretends to sign again, he slams the stamp down, and she clicks away down the corridor in search of her six suitcases. She would never have believed that her compatriots could stoop to behaviour she associates with the east. Now it occurs to her that perhaps the contents of her suitcases might be in jeopardy. For all she knows, one of them may already have gone missing.

But there they are, standing side by side; good leather; quality stuff. She has combed her hair and applied her lipstick. Her colour is high from residual annoyance and as she strides towards her luggage her coat swings from her shoulders with inhibiting authority. Passengers, airport staff, minor officials all regard her from a safe distance, trying to gauge the seniority of her husband, while some paces behind a diffident porter trundles with his trolley, hoping to be noticed.

Hearing someone breathing heavily nearby, Marta glances round. A porter, an old man, is leaning on the handles of his trolley, saying not a word. Thank heavens for that. Someone to help her. But he's so old, and a Pole! She finds herself embarrassed, watching him upending her overstuffed cases and hauling them onto the trolley. She hadn't been embarrassed by the scrum of porters desperate for custom in Tehran. Why is this different? She looks at the old man, who is wheezing now, struggling, and wonders why he is humping suitcases at his age, and what he did before. She would like to ask him who he is and who were his people, but even a traveller just come home can't accost a stranger so intrusively. There is something about him that reminds her of Maryam: two ancients near the end of their days whose lives have not been their own to direct but who aren't complaining. Looking at the porter's expression, contorted with effort at the weight he is heaving, she thinks she perceives her country's entire history engraved in the lines of his face.

She has a bundle of Swiss francs in her handbag and a brick of dollar bills that Karim gave her. She begins to peel off some notes but then wonders whether she ought to get some zlotys first. What will a

477

porter be able to do with foreign currency? She doesn't know. She has come home and she doesn't know. And, as a matter of fact, what does she know about this old man? For all she knows, he may simply be a sly, nimble-fingered fellow who will pocket her tip and spend it on drink before going home to take out his misfortunes on his wife. Rubbish!

Effusively she begins thanking him as he leans his body into the trolley to get it moving. She would step up and help him but fears he might be offended. His dignity matters more than his discomfort.

'You'll be needing to change money,' he gasps.

Marta follows him to the cashier's window, where a woman slumped behind the glass is smoking her boredom away. Her gingerish hair looks as if she's slept on it. She lays her cigarette in a heaped ashtray as she begins filling out one docket after another. She has taken the wad of notes Marta pushed through, and counts them out more noisily than she needs. The old porter's eyes are popping.

Marta turns away from the cashier and under the shield of her coat thumbs out a tip that she knows is excessive. She sees him about to protest; sees him check himself. He shoves the money into a pocket and leans into the trolley again.

'Taxi, is it, madame?'

There's a short queue, and while they are waiting she wants to strike up a conversation with him but cannot think how to begin. All the opening remarks that come to mind seem vapid. So how is the country? I hear Warsaw was completely flattened. Do you have family? They stand in silence. Eventually when a taxi arrives it becomes clear that she has too much luggage and she'll need a second. Behind her in the queue she hears muttered comments about people who swan about with more belongings than they can fit into a single cab. People with glossy fur coats and silk stockings. A second taxi draws up and the driver, young and fit, swings her cases in. As she is about to get in, the old porter touches her arm.

'Excuse me, madame. But you'd best have this.' It's a scrap of paper, and written on it in pencil is the second car's number. 'Good stuff like yours. You never can tell these days, and people aren't what they used to be. But you should be all right.' He nods towards the taxi piled with cases. 'He saw me take it down.'

65

Soft with reservation. Moscow's terminology has percolated to Poland's railways, has it? But at least this time no one will be hiding in the luggage racks. She is first into the compartment and rejoices to find she has the window seat facing forwards, even though dusk will shortly swallow the view. The guard had tried to quibble about her suitcases. Their size. Their number. 'You should have arranged to send them on ahead,' he grumbled. 'Like everyone does. What have you got in here anyway?' But with 50 zlotys tucked under his uniform he has arranged the cases end to end along the corridor, and promised to keep an eye on them. Who knows? There may be more forthcoming when they get to Poznan.

The compartment is stuffy and chilled at the same time. Marta wraps her coat more closely round her and sinks into her corner. Who will they be, her fellow passengers? A lieutenant in uniform stows his bag on the rack, sits himself down opposite Marta, crosses his legs at the ankle and immediately falls asleep. A pale elderly man in brown with a brown hat. A tiny woman clutching a holdall like a doctor's bag. Another man, younger, fair-haired and also pale. Actually, everyone is pale, but then who wouldn't be in this northern zone as winter approaches. They peer at their tickets and at the numbered seats, nod with the old courtesies at the already settled, but looking no one in the eye, and immediately pull out, each, a newspaper. The silence in the compartment is unnerving. What has come over the usually chatty Poles? Or is it that she has grown so used to the ceaseless noise of the east that ordinary European manners seem taciturn?

But this newspaper reading has become a joke. Outside it really is dark and inside they have yet to switch on the lights. Those people can't possibly see a word, but still they don't lower their papers, and so far no one has turned a page. The compartment door slides open again and a man puts his head in, backs out and shouts to the guard about the lack of light. A moment later a pale plastic lily-shaped lamp flickers on over each seat. The man returns, and all eyes flick to take note of the personage with influence.

'Well, who would have believed it! I am in luck. May I sit there?' It's Trotsky from the airport, filling the doorway in his greatcoat and boots, and pointing to the seat next to hers. In some cases reservation is beside the point. The conductor hovers in the corridor chewing on a knuckle. Trotsky bids everyone good day but receives no answer. Undismayed, he lowers himself beside Marta and thrusts his legs out across the compartment. The man directly opposite scuttles his own out of the way.

With the train under way, Trotsky pulls off his kid gloves, finger by finger – like a woman, Marta thinks – and folds them, pernickety, into a pocket. His hands are long and bony. 'Well then,' he begins with satisfaction. 'Five hours to Poznan so we've plenty of time. You can tell me all about yourself. For example, your name.'

He has twisted in his seat to face her and she thinks he has the look of a disappointed scholar about him, like a man permanently on the brink of a discovery that he knows will elude him. Is there something to be gained by withholding her name?

'Marta Shirazi.'

'Shirazi.' He repeats it a couple of times, under his breath. 'And what sort of name is that?'

'Iranian!' A slight shiver in the newspapers reveals that he is not the only one to be interested. 'But you're a Pole, aren't you?'

'Of course.'

'And married to an Iranian? And is that where you have just come from? But how on earth did you get to be there?'

Marta offers him a wide smile. 'Like all Poles,' she says. 'Via the USSR.'

'You don't know how fortunate you were, to be evacuated during the war.'

'Evacuated! Is that what they call it these days?'

Under the small window table the military boot of the snoring lieutenant flops heavily onto her instep.

Trotsky is nodding to himself. 'Ah, of course. You were attached to the Anders Army, was it?'

'You know about that, then?'

'Mm-hmm.'

'Well, I was a nurse.'

'And then?'

'I married.'

'And are you still a nurse? Have you come home to do nursing?'

'I've come to see my family.'

'You've left it rather late, haven't you? The war's been over for five years.'

'I didn't know where they were. They didn't know where I was. Is this an interrogation of some sort?'

The lieutenant's boot lands on her instep again. She shifts her feet away.

Trotsky chuckles. 'Goodness me, no. I'm just passing the time of day. Train journeys are so suited to conversation, don't you think? But tell me, apart from the nursing, have you no other qualifications?'

'I can type. I speak some languages.'

'Such as?'

'French.'

'Oh, French! Oh, really?' he says in French. 'Anything else?'

'Some Russian.'

'Ah, now there's a beautiful language. So... so soft. So honeyed. Such a vehicle for literature.' His eyes, wide and grey, are fixed on hers.

She glares back. 'I wouldn't know. That's not the sort of Russian I learned.'

'What a shame. I *am* surprised to hear that.'

'Are you? I don't see why. After all, they don't speak the language of literature in the camps, do they?'

The lieutenant's boot has found her feet again, and she winces.

'Is something the matter? You seem to be in pain.'

'Just a touch of cramp. All this sitting in one place.' She wriggles her buttocks and rubs her thighs. 'The long flights. You know.'

'I understand. But tell me. Have you been keeping up with developments in your native land? Did you know, for example, that we've been having some remarkable successes catching spies? French ones, as it happens. So anyone with a French passport has been invited to leave. Just as well you don't have a French passport, isn't it?'

Is he asking her what passport she has? He must know she can't possibly have a new Polish one. Perhaps he thinks he's made a witticism that requires an acknowledging titter. So she produces it. But he's eager with information.

'And then there's the new agreement between Poland and Germany. Have you heard about that?'

'I'm sorry. The press in Tehran seems to have missed it.'

He clicks his teeth. 'We've signed a Treaty of Friendship with the German Democratic Republic.'

'With East Germany? Have we? Why have we? After all that's happened, I can't see how we can possibly sign any treaty with any Germans.'

'But you don't understand, Madame Shirazi. Maybe you've been out of Europe too long. There are Germans and there are Germans, if you get my meaning. Good ones and bad ones. We are, at the very least, discriminating. Good ones and bad ones. Never forget that.'

'Oh, I see. All the bad ones went west and the good ones came east. Is that how it is?'

'That is exactly how it is.'

'No Nazis left in the east? No old Nazis at all?'

'None. They have all been packed off to where they belong, one way and another.'

'I can't believe a Jew would want to be friends with any sort of German.'

The silence in the compartment is suddenly tangible except for a particularly juicy snore from the sleeping lieutenant, who jumps as if in agitated nightmare. One of his legs jerks so violently its boot lurches into her knee. Trotsky is smiling fixedly. But Marta, realizing she has gone too far, now cannot stop.

'You *are* a Jew, aren't you?'

'That is an obsolete view of these things, Madame Shirazi. I have one identity, the only one that's relevant and the only one I need. I am a communist.'

He gets up and brushes down his coat as if he's been careless with a sandwich; stretches his arms the breadth of the compartment, and strides out into the corridor and down in the direction of the toilet.

'Are you completely mad?' The lieutenant is pop-eyed. All the newspapers have been lowered. 'Didn't you feel me kicking you?'

'Of course I did. But what's the problem?'

'Jews this and Jews that. Don't you know what he is? He's the Chief of Security Services, in charge of every damned thing and every damned person in the region.'

'Well, he's not in charge of me.'

'Because of your foreign passport? I wouldn't be so sure of yourself, and anyway what about your family? *They're* Polish citizens, aren't they? You open your mouth once too often and it won't be just you in the shit. Begging your pardon.'

All the other passengers, strangers to one another before, coalesce into a united front now. She should have been more careful. 'I only meant we ought to be proud that a Jew can get into a senior position now,' she offers lamely.

'Proud!' The tiny woman with the doctor's bag, which she has been holding all this while on her knees like a pet dog, is bolt upright, eyes a-glitter and her mouth shaping itself up for the next word. But before she can start Trotsky is at the door, sliding it back.

Nothing has changed. The lieutenant in the corner is still in the land of dreams; those slow readers are still deep in their newspapers and that svelte Madame Shirazi is looking with concentration out of the window at the passing landscape rendered invisible by the dark. All she can possibly see is her own reflection – and his. He smiles and raises an eyebrow. Aha! So she *is* looking.

66

Poznan is muffled to the neck in fog. It has clipped the sibilance from the engine's final hiss and muzzled the voices of the station staff. Everyone is getting off here, and the lieutenant leaps gallantly down to the platform to receive Marta's suitcases from the pale young man and Trotsky. But once the baggage has been offloaded her fellow passengers are anxious to be away as quickly as they can.

At her elbow Trotsky is buttoning his greatcoat and pulling on his gloves. 'Are they meeting you?' he asks. 'I have a car. It would be no trouble to take you round.'

Marta thinks of her father and his reaction. 'Oh, no. Thank you. I'll take a cab.'

'Are you sure? Then let me find it for you.'

Before she can prevent him – if she could prevent him – he has plunged into the murk, calling 'Hello there!' and snapping his fingers ineffectually, encumbered by gloves and fog.

Were it not for the cases she would sneak off, except that she does not know where Koltuna is. Somewhere on the outskirts, according to the woman with the doctor's bag. On the outskirts. Living near the centre, Marta never had reason to go to the outskirts.

Trotsky looms, trailing a smaller figure, cabby without a choice, who may have been hoping to sit the weather out.

'There's only this fellow here,' says Trotsky. 'But we'll need him anyway. He can take some of the cases. Isn't it lucky that we can't all have the possessions you do, or no one would ever get around at all.'

It crosses Marta's mind to retort that what she has brought is no more than basic items for her family that the system he is so committed to is, by all accounts, unable to provide. Now is not the time. At least on this occasion there's no need to write down any number-plates.

All the same, Trotsky instructs the cabby to drive ahead so that they can keep an eye on him – or perhaps, Marta thinks, because neither Trotsky nor his chauffeur knows their way about on the grubbier side of town.

'Good,' says Trotsky, comfortable and expansive in the wide back seat of his car, poised to resume. But then he seems uncertain how to continue and sits in silence.

His chauffeur is hunched over the wheel, eyes locked on the tail lights of the taxi, only just visible ahead. Marta tucks her hands into her sleeves and closes her eyes. Minutes away. It can be only a few minutes before she sees them all again. If only she could see out, she might be able to guess where they are, but she cannot even distinguish the outlines of the buildings by the roadside.

The taxi turns off the main road and Trotsky's car swings after it. Turns again, then off the road entirely, and stops.

'Well, then,' observes Trotsky, but doesn't open his door. Is he waiting for his chauffeur to do it for him, sitting there motionless?

You don't expect cars pulling up here in Koltuna. Most definitely not in the early hours. Most people won't have heard them, but Colonel Marek Dolniak, veteran of three wars – now retired, has, before his time, joined the generation of those who don't sleep. As often as not he eases himself out of his bed and tiptoes to the tiny kitchen in order not to disturb the rest of his family. Sometimes he passes his daughter-in-law Halina, newly pregnant and on her way to vomit in the bathroom. Wanly they greet each other wordlessly, each with sympathy for the other's predicament, although hers will pass. At least they're treating her well in the bakery where she works. The nation needs babies. Veterans, of course, are another matter, but maybe that's always been so.

He wasn't mistaken. Two cars are parked in the courtyard three floors below, their engines running and their headlights on, vaguely illuminating the dustbins that huddle up to the north side. This fog is a menace, thick and slimy with lignite. It catches you in the chest. Patting his own absent-mindedly, Colonel Dolniak presses his forehead against the cold window-pane and gazes down. They're not getting out, whoever they are. Oh, yes. A door is opening.

'Is this it?' Marta begins a tussle with the handle but the chauffeur is already there. Whoever this woman is, clearly she matters in some way, although something doesn't match. That hairdo. The coat. The elegant shoes. In a place like this?

The two cars have come to a halt in a courtyard walled on three sides by tall tenements. A doleful street lamp sprouts from a puddle of dim light.

'Get those bags out.'

Trotsky's command is peremptory and the taxi driver, made surly, has to suppress the mutters that instantly well up in him: *They're bloody heavy, Mr Chief of Security, Comrade Sir. You're supposed to be the great communist but you're not lifting a finger, are you, flapping at the heels of the bourgeoisie.*

When the two drivers have hauled all the baggage out, the fog seems to lift a little, and the car doors snap to like gunshots.

'What's the number?' Trotsky is waving the torch his chauffeur has passed him.

Colonel Dolniak can see a woman in a swirling coat and two men... three men. One of those cars is a cab, but the other is official. What is this? Police? Do they have women policemen in this country now? But they're unloading suitcases... one, two... three. More. Four. Five. Six huge things. A point of light dances about. The official-looking chap and the woman are poring over a piece of paper with a torch, and now the torch is flickering from one stairwell entrance to the next. The beam suddenly leaps in triumph under the window where Colonel Dolniak stands and he starts back from the glass. But the torch has been switched off.

All the men, even the official-looking one, are dragging suitcases across the courtyard to the entrance. His entrance. Across the courtyard he spots the shadows of other insomniacs, as vigilant and wondering as he is. In the apartments above and below, for sure there will be someone at the kitchen window. But now he tiptoes to the door that opens onto the concrete landing. He hears the thud of the heavy front door three floors down; hears the feet on the steps echo in the stairwell; the luggage bearers are swearing with the weight of the suitcases and their breathing is ragged. If they're lucky they'll only have one floor to go. It's what he's listening for. It's what everyone is listening for. When the footsteps fail to reach his door, or pass it, he'll creep back to bed, and tomorrow they can exchange views about it all, he and his neighbours. But the footsteps don't pass.

The cabby can't wait to be out of here. When he's hauled up the last of the cases he grabs the notes the woman in fur thrusts at him and gallops down that spooky stairwell as fast as he can. It's not that he isn't curious – what are they doing in Koltuna, the Party boss and the glossy woman? He'd give his eye-teeth to know – but not if it means having to hang around.

'Wait for me in the car,' whispers Trotsky on the landing, conscious of the hour. His chauffeur grunts and begins to plod down. Once he's turned the corner, Trotsky stands for a moment gently banging his gloved fists together, although it really isn't that cold. 'You know,' he strikes up, 'it occurs to me that a woman like you with languages, who's seen a bit of the world, who has... style. It occurs to me. I'm in need of a social secretary. Is that a position you think would appeal to you?'

Marta is grateful for the dark. It's all she can do not to giggle. She hasn't been in the country twenty-four hours and they offer her a job. 'It would be an honour,' she says carefully. 'But the problem is, you see, that I'm only here for three weeks. But thank you so much for asking. And for escorting me. I probably wouldn't have got here so easily if it hadn't been for you.'

'Twice grateful, then,' he says lightly and fishes in an inside pocket. 'Let me give you my card. In case you change your mind.'

She takes the card, wondering if she should shake him by the hand. But, shuffling a little like a man unused to polite farewells, Trotsky deposits a small cough into a bunched glove and begins backing towards the stairs.

'Well,' he says. '*Au revoir.*' Starts towards his descent, then pauses with a foot overhanging the top step. 'By the way. Don't forget you have to register with the police within three days.'

'Why do I have to do that?'

'All foreigners do.'

'I'm not a f–'

'Oh yes, you are, Madame Shi-ra-zi. A foreigner to the new Poland in every sense of the word.'

Outside the door, alone now but for her sentinel luggage, Marta stands with her hand out about to knock but holding back. She doesn't want to wake them. What might it do to them, a knock in the early hours? On the other hand she can't wait out here in the chill. Well, she can, but…

Inside the door, her father has kept count of how many sets of footsteps have departed. Someone is left. Someone is the other side of this frail wooden barrier, breathing, biding their time. He puts his ear against it, aware that his thin legs in their thin pyjamas are trembly.

If she knocks ever so gently, it won't sound officious. If anyone's awake they'll hear it. Two tentative taps and the door flies open.

Just for a second – although later he will remember it as having seemed like minutes – Colonel Dolniak was flummoxed. A young woman dressed in fur, with fingers cupped against the wood at eye level. She was staring at him. He took in a coiffed head, a glint of light on the teeth, from the eyes. Who was this woman coming in the early hours…

'Tata?'

It must have woken the entire block, that drawn-out whoop of joy. No credit to a soldier. And of course the rest of them came running, piled out of bed thinking he'd been attacked or taken a bad turn. Sonia in her night-time plaits and her cheeks pillow-creased; Gienek, tousled and handsome, with his fists at the ready just in case, his Halina clutched about in her night-gown at a safe distance behind; and Jola, his wife, sleep-bleary but courageously wielding her old hairbrush in front of her like a weapon.

How they all gawped. How *he* must have been gawping when Marta stepped through the doorway into the light, the expensive coat swinging from her shoulders, her hair so softly waved, her skin... glowing, lightly rouged, lips red. He had always known that one day she would be a beauty, though she'd scowled when he said so, but he'd never imagined...

They fell on her neck, queuing up for it, all of them weeping, himself included, and Gienek. She smelled so sweet, for all the travelling. She'd slung her coat off in her old way and dropped it without looking across a chair, but it had slid onto the floor like the animal it had once been. When she wasn't looking he had picked the thing up, noting its weight, and slipped a hanger inside. She was so elegant in her tailored suit and silk stockings, her calves such a fine shape. Fathers shouldn't notice these things, but they do. Her hands were manicured. Polished pointed nails.

He saw her glance round the apartment, sharp as ever, taking in, in that one glance, the state of affairs. But Jola, embarrassed in front of her older daughter at their reduced circumstances, began fussing over the bed, dragging the bedding off and tugging at the mechanism to turn it back into its daytime sofa. 'It's all right, Mama,' Marta kept saying, but Jola wouldn't be stopped. Eventually, realizing that Jola needed to be doing all this because she was overcome, he had touched Marta's arm and put his finger to his lips. Their eyes had met, as in the old days, and it went straight to his heart. Meanwhile poor Jola rushed about boiling up the water for tea, wailing that she hadn't anything in the cupboard, she'd have

490

made a cake if she'd known. 'I've got cake, Mama. You wait and see.'

They had all forgotten about the cases stacked outside the door. Between them he and Gienek had manoeuvred them in, and that was when he noticed something small and white on the floor. He picked it up. It was a business card. Egon Mandel, Chief of Security Services, Poznan Region. He had decided not to mention it then, but tucked it behind the photograph of Marta as a little girl on the bookshelf. How had she come to know this man? It made him uncomfortable.

Marta had torn open her cases one by one, yanking the ropes off, looking for something, no more methodical than she ever was, rummaging and flinging stuff about. It was all in the fourth case: bags of pistachios, raisins, dried apricots and apple rings; boxes of chewy sweetmeats in flour, which covered them all until they looked like a family of bakers sitting at tea. A box of tiny pastries, each with a nut on its summit. The goodness from the east. They had feasted on the exotic delicacies, eating and eating, partly, he thought, to cover the fact that they didn't really know what to say. How was your journey? What a lovely coat you have. How is your husband? Marta had not touched a thing but smoked one cigarette after another. Jola winced when the first one came out but he had put a silencing hand on her knee. He could guess why his daughter smoked, and her upbringing had had nothing to do with it.

The fog has thinned, revealing a dejected morning. All Novembers have been like this, Colonel Dolniak informs himself, although it is tempting, sometimes, to claim parallels between the weather and the state of the national soul. He inspects his family's faces. They are grey with lack of sleep, thumbprint bruises under the eyes. All except Marta, who really must be exhausted from travelling without a break. But she is glittery and unduly upright, and she has smoked so much that her hands are shaking. He thinks he understands. She has come home – but it is not home. She has at last returned to the bosom of her family – but she is a bird of paradise dropped from the heavens to be exclaimed over. This is going to take a long time and he feels he is failing his daughter. He ought – ought he not? – to be able to give her guidance. Tell her how to begin her tale. But the trouble is he has been back for four years himself and his own story has yet to be told.

He sighs and rubs the backs of his hands on his sandpaper jaw. No matter how much we know and are known, there are times when loneliness is greatest among those you love the most. He hopes Jola will never find out that every now and then, when he's trawling the shops for bread and potatoes, he makes a detour to a small, smoke-filled restaurant where one or two of the old soldiers who were prisoners of war with him in Germany sometimes sit, shoulders touching, cuddling their tea glasses to occupy their hands. Mostly no one speaks, and it is a relief. If his wife ever knew how much more at ease he can feel at those moments than he does at home she would be devastated. It is not her fault. It is simply the way things are.

Later, when Marta has slept, perhaps, and the others are at work (a daughter and sister returned will be no pretext for staying away), he will give her permission to escape the concern and curiosity he won't be able to wipe from his face, and send her out to visit that crazy Krystyna's mother, Mrs Benka.

67

Two trams and a bus take her back to the quarter where she grew up. Marta looks out of the windows into the thin light, conscious that others are looking at her, so she fakes nonchalance. Is it only her clothes that mark her out, the bulky parcel she's carrying in its exotic wrapping paper, or something else? Trotsky said she was a foreigner in every sense of the word. According to her papers, maybe, but otherwise she's less of a foreigner than he is!

Ten years. She was a schoolgirl and now she's a married woman, a mother with a hint of high society about her – at least as far as these people are concerned. These people! As if she were not of them, and among them.

The city itself seems down-at-heel, the pedestrians (all walking on the pavements) keeping their expressions to themselves. Maybe it was like that before, though she doesn't think so. What strikes her is how little damaged it is. Not like Warsaw, from the small impression she had got from her taxi ride to the station. Warsaw had appeared to be a building site, except that it wasn't clear whether it was construction or demolition in progress. Over his shoulder and throaty with cigarette smoke, the cabby had told her they were making bricks for the new buildings out of the pulverized dust of the old. When the Russians finally decided to move their troops in, he said, there wasn't a soul left alive in the city. They'd let the Nazis do their dirty work for them. And the cabby spat. Marta had repeated that to her father, who had nodded but wondered at the taxi driver's rashness. She could have reported him. The Germans hadn't wanted to destroy Poznan, because they'd always considered it a German city, and theirs. You don't flatten what's yours.

She couldn't say to him that in his way *he* looked flattened. Inch for inch, no doubt, he would still hit the tiny pencil mark on the wall that they had drawn, putting a book on the top of his head. She had demanded it, when she was... oh, four? five, maybe?... so that she would know what height she was aiming to grow to. They hadn't had the heart yet to tell her that little girls grow into women, and women, mostly, aren't as tall as men. Of course, that pencil mark isn't on any wall of theirs, but in the hallway at Jablonska Street.

'Didn't they honour you at all?' she asked him. 'Haven't they shown the slightest gratitude for what you've done for Poland?'

'Oh, indeed they did. They gave me a pension.'

'Well, I hope it's a good one.'

'I'll show you,' he whispered. 'Wait here.' He had crept to the kitchen in his worn slippers and crept back, finger to his lips. 'Close your eyes and hold your hands out.'

Like a trusting child she had screwed her eyes tight shut, feeling them fiery with fatigue. Something light had dropped into each palm. 'Can I look now?'

'Go on.'

She had looked. A small heap of tea lay in each palm. 'What?' Her temper was rising.

'That's it. That's my pension. Or, rather, that's what it buys. But we shouldn't complain. After all, we voted them in, don't you know? We had elections and they won them, hands down. The communists. But they were disappointed because they only got eighty per cent of the vote. And really, when you think of all the trouble they went to, it's true they ought to have done even better.'

They'd vetted the lists of candidates in advance, he said, and had people struck off the register in their thousands. In their hundreds of thousands, just to be sure. Then they marched people from the factories to the polls and, when they got there, told them how to vote.

'It was perfectly simple. This is a democracy and in a democracy you have a choice. Vote for us or lose your job. But I don't understand why they needed to go to all that trouble when they were the ones doing the counting. What does it matter how people have voted if you're in charge of the counting?'

Now Marta is furious all over again. Two pots of tea and eviction from their apartment! Those people don't deserve to be in charge. She's inclined to go straight home again and rummage for Trotsky's card so that she can storm into his office and tell him so. Well, and so she will, in time – when she remembers where she put the card.

Ten years. Yes, these are her streets, where she once took a bet that she could hop on one leg all the way to school, and then on the other all the way back. She had never made it, but her right leg was definitely the stronger. The shops are all still here, although the proprietors' names have been painted out. Food shop, butcher, baker, tailoring. Perhaps the previous owners are still inside, doing exactly what they used to but as employees of the state. Or perhaps they're dead. Poland lost more of her people in proportion to the population than any other country, her father said. And it had all happened while she was somewhere else.

This is her stop. Ania's mother's house is on the next corner. It will be strange to meet Ania's mother now, woman to woman. Mrs Dorosz and Mrs Shirazi. And Ania is a Mrs now, too. It doesn't seem real. There are times when she feels she's play-acting at being a married woman, and this is going to be one of them. And Mrs Benka. Does Mrs Benka know she got married to Karim?

On the corner she dithers a moment. Then on impulse, instead of turning left for Ania's place, she strides straight ahead to the building where, by rights, her family should still be housed. Up the stairs – thump, thump – to the second floor and her old front door. She puts her parcel at her feet and bangs with policeman fists on the door with all the force of her outrage, and her colour is high. A dim yellow line along the bottom of the door tells her they are at home. Dim-witted or slow-moving. She bunches her fists for a second try but hears shuffling footsteps and someone fiddling with the lock. It's always been tricky, that lock. You have to pull it towards you while you're twisting the handle, ease it open with a touch subtle as a safebreaker's. Clearly the interloper is a ham-fisted incompetent.

'Yes?' Some woman with one of those voices paid to be officious. She's got the door open only a crack: enough to display a thick ankle and a heavy brown shoe. Not enough to see down the hallway.

'Could you let me in?'

'Certainly not.'

The door begins to close but Marta leans into it. 'Well, could you tell me who lives here?'

'Second Deputy Kubinski.'

'Who's he?'

'If you don't know that you shouldn't be here.' Now the woman is pushing the door from the other side.

'How many children has he got?' Marta bellows into the diminishing space, but with weight on her side the woman is winning. 'I need to know! It's very important!'

The door closes and the lock is clicked back into place. Marta sticks her tongue out as far as it will go, then turns towards the street. Behind her she hears Second Deputy Kubinski's housekeeper grunt, 'None.'

Marta tucks her parcel under her arm. She'll tell her mother that they were thrown out on false pretences. It has nothing to do with the size of the apartment and the number of people. But she realizes she will not say anything at all because doubtless her mother already knows this and will be thrown into a panic if she learns that Marta has been making a nuisance of herself at a newly designated official residence. Everything in Poland is as good as it can be.

Down on the street she resists the urge to look back up to the windows.

Mrs Benka *has* shrunk. The upright spine has collapsed into itself and Marta is shocked to find they no longer stand eye to eye. Fearing her distress will reveal itself, she havers on the threshold, letting her eyes wander, so she does not notice that Mrs Benka almost recoils.

But Mrs Benka is the one with the courage. 'Well, my dear. Look at you!' Then she puts her wiry arms around the young woman and it turns out she again, incredibly, smells of an apple loft.

'Last time I saw you,' mumbles Mrs Benka into Marta's furry shoulder, 'you were...'

She trails off as both take a moment to recall Dr Shirazi's chauffeur-driven car and the still waxen-faced nurse swept away for a convalescent weekend.

Embarrassed at herself, Mrs Benka pats Marta briskly on both upper arms. 'I'll make us some tea. You know your way about here, don't you?'

She does. Oh, she does. She could swear that that picture of sunflowers lying over the back of the sofa was here last time she came. That August. In her Girl Guides' uniform. 'Come on, Ania, get a move on. Everyone's waiting.' The Guides in the truck outside, exhilarated by the prospect of giving encouragement to the peasants in the frontier lands. Not frontier lands any more. The whole country has been shifted west and what was Germany has become Poland – just as, to the east, what was Poland has become the Soviet Union. Mrs Benka has had to move west or take Soviet citizenship. Can you imagine? But the sunflower picture is damp, draped to dry in the usual way. What is Mrs Dorosz doing painting sunflowers in November? It must have been to cheer herself up with the memory of summer as the year sinks into its gloomiest season.

Marta lifts the painting gingerly lest the colours run and spreads it on the floor to one side. Then stands looking down at it.

Mrs Benka, with a tray of tea and biscuits, joins her. 'Not much good, are they?'

It's not Marta's place to seem to be critical of something Mrs Benka's daughter has done. But the picture makes her uncomfortable. Mrs Dorosz, for all she's something of a bohemian, and Ania, for all she's Marta's best friend, in this apartment have inserted themselves between Marta and Mrs Benka.

Mrs Benka sets the tray down on the table in front of the sofa. 'Come along, dear. Don't mope.' So she senses it too. 'Let's have a cigarette together, shall we?'

'I brought you some.'

'Did you? From Persia?' She turns the carton over and over, opens it and shakes a couple out. Lights Marta's, then her own. A long drag with closed eyes. 'One taste and it all comes back. You couldn't put it into words.'

'And I brought these.' One whole suitcase was stuffed with boxes of sweetmeats and dried fruit. But for Mrs Benka Marta has included a packet of pressed dates.

Mrs Benka examines all the boxes, exclaiming over them with requisite delight, but when she comes to the dates she laughs. 'I shall be a little nervous of these,' she says, tapping them. 'I have the feeling – one bite and it'll be that diarrhoea all over again.'

'Yes.' Marta stretches her legs out, leans back against the sofa and looks up to the ceiling. This is better. 'You know,' she says, 'before I came here I went to our old place. I wanted to know why my parents were kicked out. There was some Soviet-style old hag there who wouldn't even open the door. Second Deputy Kubinski's place now, apparently. The whole apartment – just for him and Cerberus.'

'That was foolhardy. You shouldn't have gone.'

'I know.'

'But maybe there won't be any repercussions. That woman didn't know who you were, did she? Small fry. I doubt if they'll want to follow it up. Anyway, I'm glad you did it.'

'Glad? Why?'

'Because otherwise I might have thought that the girl I once knew and loved had disappeared under all this…' Mrs Benka rotates an age-mottled hand in Marta's direction. '… all this *bourgeois*' (leaning on the word) 'get-up.'

Marta is abashed. She feels she may somehow have let herself down. But she shrugs. 'It's a way of fitting in.'

'Fitting in? I never had the impression that was one of your priorities.'

'It isn't really a matter of choice. I mean. Look at everyone here. They all look the same.'

'But they wish they didn't. No, no. It's all right, dear. I understand perfectly. And tell me. Are you happy?'

'I have a son. Did you know? Davood.'

'Yes, I had heard. But you haven't answered my question.'

'It's peculiar. He looks just like me.'

'Good for him!' Mrs Benka squints sideways at Marta sipping her tea and decides not to press the question again. 'Did you know that Basia and Janusz got married before the army moved out? I must say I was relieved. That young man's mooning over her was getting irritating.'

'I'd love to see her again.'

'Not much chance of that, I'm afraid. He went to England after the war and she joined him from Bombay. I've got their address, somewhere in London. Some small hotel they run. But you know... England.' Mrs Benka grimaces. You might as well mention the moon. 'And Hania. She went to America, to become a doctor.' Now it's Mars. 'But, as I say, I've got their addresses, so maybe you could write to them one of these days.'

'Yes.' She can't picture Hania doctoring away in America, or Basia and Janusz ministering to their guests in an English hotel. All the old connections are being stripped away. There *is* only Mrs Benka now, and she looks so frail. Actually, she looks morose. 'What's wrong, Mrs Benka?'

Mrs Benka knits her fingers. The skin slides on the backs of her hands, loose and papery. She gets up, without difficulty though, and skirts the low table to stand by the window with her back to the room. Some expression she doesn't want Marta to see. She taps sharply on the window-pane, which gives a brief shudder.

'It's this.'

'Poznan?'

'No. Well, not Poznan itself. But the life to be lived here. Or, rather, not lived. I'm very grateful to Krystyna for taking me in...'

'Of course she would! She loves –'

Mrs Benka about-faces. 'Be quiet, dear, and let me finish. She's done it with grace, and all the welcome any ageing mother could wish for. But that's not the point. There's nothing for me to do here.

I may not have been doing very much on the farm – I'd let it go terribly, I know that – but it kept us busy, me and Old Petrkiewicz. But here. I don't have a role. What's a little old lady like me to do? And I have turned into a little old lady. Quite overnight. No, I have, dear, so don't pull your silly faces. And it's something I was determined not to do. I'd almost rather…'

'What?'

'There is something about taking up the challenge to survive when all the odds are against you. Do you remember that sloppy poultice we made for poor Dorota and her infestation of lice? We were so hungry then, bitten to bits, ill all the time. All I could think about was *not* being there. And then in Tent City. All those dying children and stinking, typhus-ridden bodies. I dreamt of comfort and not being on my feet all day long, but at the same time I was alive. Do you understand me, Marta? I was alive because there was a reason to be, and it was a struggle. Whereas here…You know, this country, now. It's like – I don't know how to put this – but it's as if the entire nation has fallen into an interminable depression. It's not despair. It's not anger. It's grey and heavy and fills the mouth so that words are muffled and nothing is clear. We are lucky here, Krystyna and I. She has what she had before, at least, and so long as she doesn't do anything foolish or say anything out of turn they'll leave her alone. It's true there's nothing to be had any more that's remotely as exciting as what you've brought us, but nobody is starving. And, when you get to my age, the things I might once have hankered for are beside the point. The state does everything and simultaneously prevents everything. Do you know, I sometimes feel that I can't even *meddle* the way I always used to think old people did when they'd got beyond anything else, because the state's even taken that over! They do all the meddling anyone could want. I sit here all day and drink tea and potter about. I stand in queues for bread and, if I'm very lucky, sausage, and that's about it. Somehow it's not how I expected to end my days.'

Marta is thinking of her father. 'But Ania's married, isn't she? When she has a baby, they'll need you to –'

'Hmm. Babies. I was never my best with babies.'

Dear Mrs Benka. But she's looking agitated, turning from the clock on the wall. 'Do you need to go out or something? Queue for something? I'll go with you.'

'I? No. Why?'

'You keep looking at the clock.'

'It must be habit. Watching the minutes pass. So slo-owly!' But Mrs Benka's tone rings a false note. Something's wrong.

'I brought her a belated wedding present.'

'Did you, dear? That's nice of you.'

Nice of her? Ania is her best friend! 'It's nothing special. Just a tablecloth. You know, one of those Persian ones, Paisley patterns like fat commas in red and black on a beige-y background. With tiny tassels.'

Mrs Benka nods abstractedly. 'Look, dear. I don't know what time Ania will be back. Why don't you go round and visit other friends for a while and come back later. In the evening, perhaps. Or tomorrow when she has the day off.'

'Mrs Benka. What is the matter? Don't you want me to stay? Am I boring you?'

'Boring me, dear? Never. You never could. I just thought…'

'Well, then. Sit down again.' Marta pats the sofa, Benka-fashion. 'And tell me all about Ania's wedding. Did she wear the earrings? Was she furious about the necklace? What's her husband like? I asked my mother but she said she'd never met him.'

'Oh, Marta.'

Someone's key is in the door.

'Maybe that's her now. I can't wait.'

Marta scrambles up and runs her fingers through her hair. Will Ania recognize her in her 'bourgeois get-up'? Will that best friendship have survived? For the first time she's nervous.

68

Antoni stands just inside the front door, still in his outdoor shoes, knapsack knobbly with the potatoes and carrots he has chanced upon. His look of triumph at today's small victory hangs for a moment on his face before fading to blankness. He does not know what to do or what to say so he turns and flees with the vegetables clutched to his chest. They hear his footsteps hurtling unevenly down.

In that moment Marta grasps what has happened here. All those years she had convinced herself the old ache was fading, and she was wrong. She makes to move after him but Mrs Benka has grabbed her by the elbow.

'No! Wait!'

'Why didn't you tell me?' Marta is shaking.

'I didn't know how to.'

'How could you? How could you let me sit here and babble on at you, and you didn't say a thing. Did you think I'd go away again, go back to Tehran and never find out? Mrs Benka. What have you done?'

Mrs Benka could weep for the sorrow of it. As a matter of fact she often has, though she trusts that no one knows it. But she will not stand accused, and goes sharply on the defensive.

'What have I done? What have *I* done? My dear girl! If you had-n't been so hasty in your judgements, none of this need have hap-pened. Can you have any idea of the state the poor boy was in? He went off to war convinced that you had tired of him and taken up with Dr Shirazi instead, and from what I've been told he was so miserable that he took all manner of unnecessary risks. Lunatic, they called him. Suicidal. Of course it earned him a row of medals and commendations, but things being as they are those have done him no good at all.' Marta is staring at her. 'What was I supposed to do? He hunted me out when he came home. He went to the trouble of hunting me out because he thought I was some sort of link with you. And you can't imagine how disappointed he was when he found out that I didn't know where you lived, only that you were in Tehran and married. But Antoni couldn't let it go. He'd be round here whenever he could and when we were alone together all he wanted to do was talk about you, as if talking about you would conjure you up there and then. And Ania, my poor little Ania, who apparently fell for him all that time ago when you were all in Wilno and she was still a girl, she couldn't keep her eyes off him. We didn't tell her about the two of you. Maybe we should have, but we didn't.' Marta is still staring, her mouth half open. 'Marta? Are you listening to me? The thing is, dear, he loves her now. Do you understand? You haven't been with Antoni for seven years and he loves Ania now.'

'Are you saying she doesn't know?'

'Yes.'

'I don't believe you.'

'Why shouldn't you believe me? I made sure she didn't know. Think about it, dear. If Ania were ever to learn that her husband had been in love with you, and it was only a terrible misunderstanding that prevented the two of you getting married, she would feel insecure for ever. And, as I said, he does love her now. You have to believe that. He really does.'

Marta swings away. Why did she come back to Poland? It would have been better to have stayed in Tehran in ignorance.

'And Antoni? What about him? Does he know why I got married to Karim?'

'Well, dear... in so far as any of us understands that.' She fixes Marta with a stare, and Marta looks away. 'He wanted to write to you, but of course we didn't have an address. I was against it, I have to say. I thought you'd find it too hard to bear when there was nothing you could do.'

'Does he know I have a son?'

'He found out when we did, of course. From your parents. When they finally got a letter from you. I was terribly afraid he would say something, but he managed not to. And Ania and Krystyna were so busy exclaiming over the news that they didn't notice anything was the matter.'

Marta's heartbeats are pounding behind her eyes. Her nose is swollen. None of this has been worth it. Nothing is worth anything. She grabs her coat.

'Where are you going?'

'Home.'

'But what about Ania?'

'You don't think I can see Ania, do you, after this? Don't tell her I came, if you're so good at keeping secrets from her.'

'Don't be silly. How can I not tell her? She still thinks of you as her best friend.'

'Well, she may. And she was. But just at the moment that's not how I feel. For God's sake, Mrs Benka, do you really expect me to stay here and smile at her as if everything was fine?'

'As a matter of fact I do, because Ania is bound to know you were here, if not from me then eventually from your parents, who will be most surprised to discover that the two of you, inseparable before, didn't meet this time round. So then she'll wonder why, and everything I've done to protect her knowing about you and Antoni will have been wasted. And, whether you like it or not, you're going to have to pull yourself together, Mrs Shirazi, because none of this mess is Ania's fault. Maybe it's not yours either, come to that, since we can none of us help being who we are. But don't imagine running away from the situation will make you feel any better, because it won't.'

'And don't you keep telling me what to do. I'm not your granddaughter. And I never was. So you go on looking after your real one and leave me to look after myself, since obviously no one else can!'

Then Marta yanks up her coat from the back of the sofa and slings it round her, struggling with the sleeves as she rushes to the door. But there is to be no escape.

Ania is on the landing, rosy-cheeked from the cold, kicking off her shoes just like a little girl. She looks up at the apparition in fur and squeals, 'Marta!' Just like a little girl, she leaps for her friend, arms round her neck, kissing her frantically. Her cheeks are icy but her breath is hot. Marta's arms have swung automatically round her, but over Ania's shoulder Marta sees first the top of Antoni's head where he hangs back on the stairs, now his face.

'Oh, Marta! At last everything's perfect. It only needed you to come home for everything to be perfect. Look!' Ania's eyes are bright with tears. 'Look. It's Antoni. You remember Antoni, don't you? From the Archbishop's palace? You remember how we all loved him?'

No longer than a photographer's flash, the look that Antoni exchanges with Marta.

'I used to lie in bed dreaming of him but d'you know what I thought?' Ania stands on tiptoe to reach Marta's unwilling ear, and cups her hands round her mouth. 'I thought it was you he was interested in and it made me so jealous. But how could I be annoyed with *you*?'

Ania has grabbed her friend by the hand. Reaches for her loitering husband with the other.

'Mrs Benka!' she shouts, not to know that Mrs Benka is huddled in the kitchen uncharacteristically clutching her temples. 'Mrs Benka, isn't this wonderful? Marta, you're not going yet. You can't when we've only just come home. Take off your coat.' She pulls at it, and Marta is reminded of Massy in the early days. 'What a lovely coat, though. Look, darling. Look at Marta's coat! It's so soft.' Ania hugs the coat and strokes it, all appreciation, no envy. 'I'll hang it up. You don't know Marta' – turning to Antoni – 'but, unless she's changed, she'd just dump it on the floor or something. Wouldn't you?'

Marta stretches a wan smile, keenly watched by Mrs Benka from her kitchen eyrie.

Ania's joy is complete. Now she needs her mother to come home too and all the people she loves the most will be gathered in one room. It has never happened before. How should she take note of the awful stillness in the others when her own vivacity is enough for four?

'Oh, what's all this?'

The boxes of Persian goodies lie open on the low table, the dried fruits, the nuts… A scattering of flour and icing sugar dusts the table top like the dry snow of deepest winter blown through a window, and Ania dabbles her fingertips. Sucks them.

'You're better than St Nicholas, you are, bringing gifts. I've missed you so much!' Once again her arms are wrapped around her friend. 'I can't tell you. When you'd gone, when they took you away…' And now Marta's tears are not out of place. In fact, everyone can weep with impunity, each for their own reasons, which is how Krystyna Dorosz finds them when she comes home.

Here is her daughter, pink and happy as a doll, tears glistening on her cheeks and icing sugar rimming her lips; here is her mother, propped against the kitchen sink, disconcertingly grey in the face and her eyes awash; here is Antoni, deathly pale under his black hair, those girl's eyelashes of his beaded; and here is… Is this elegant young woman Marta the hoyden? Can it be?

'Marta! Come, let me look at you.' Krystyna, who, it so happens, came upon the same source of potatoes and carrots as Antoni, sets down her own bulging bag and, taking Marta by the shoulders, turns her to the light. 'You're a picture. Truly, you're a picture. Isn't she, Mama? A dab of colour in our monochrome city. If only I knew how, I'd paint a portrait of you now and hang it up to remind us. But I never could do people. Give me a kiss and welcome home. We've missed you so much.' Now Krystyna is overcome as well and has to wipe her eyes.

Mrs Benka turns to making tea all over again… good, good, get more cups, some need washing, thank heavens, and those others could do with a rub from the dishcloth.

Antoni is at her elbow, his purchases and his mother-in-law's dangling from both hands. Silently he begins unloading root vegetables into the box under the sink, potatoes on the left, carrots on the right. Mrs Benka will be making a lot of soup. It's her speciality, soup. Under the cover of Krystyna's exclamations next door he looks up at Mrs Benka in mute desperation but finds no comfort there. *What am I to do?*

From the doorway he watches Ania unwrap Marta's belated wedding present, then he watches them all admire it, talking at once. Extraordinary how exactly it fits the table! What lovely things those Persians do make. Hasn't she brought pictures of her husband and her son? Oh, she has! Let's see, then. Hey! That's a good-looking man, isn't it, Ania, though he looks rather stern. Is he? And this is Davood... is that right? Davood. Oh, but Marta! What a little sweetie. He's just like you. And are his eyes green too? Look, Antoni! Look at Marta's little Davood. Now, there's a child to make you want one of your own, don't you think?

But Antoni suddenly needs the toilet, where he will linger until he judges those pictures have been put away. Would it have been any easier if he had been prepared, if there had been some warning? Probably not. But he might have made arrangements to be out of town.

Ania is banging on the door. One of the women must need to pee. 'Antoni? Are you all right? Marta's getting ready to go because her people will be expecting her back. I said you'd see her home or part of the way at least. She said no, no, there's no need, which is just like her. She always says she can manage everything on her own. But you don't mind going with her, do you? I wouldn't want her to have to walk through Koltuna in the dark alone.'

So Antoni unlocks the door and emerges as if he's just been washing his hands. What is he supposed to say? What is he supposed to do? If Ania is the one sending him out on this mission he can't refuse without a powerfully good reason, and none comes to mind. The Fates, he thinks, if they exist, are interfering here and he only hopes they know what they're doing, because he doesn't. He hasn't said a word to Marta, nor yet has she to him.

69

The stairway goes down and turns, down and turns. Marta sets off ahead and at each landing the swaying light bulb picks out a point of lustre in her hair, on her coat. Antoni notes these and is numb. They set off in silence for the bus stop, huffing twin clouds of steam. Soon enough they will notice that they are walking in rhythm.

Antoni has grown into his height. The youthful lankiness has filled out and his face is older. Not lined, but older. It couldn't be better. Marta remembers her own starved body with the deep hollows above the collarbones, and the swollen knees and elbows – the body whose person he fell in love with, invisible now. At the corner she says, and her voice is sudden as a bark in the night, 'That's where we used to live, down there.'

'I know.'

'It's got some Party bigwig in it. Just him and a housekeeper.'

'Second Deputy Kubinski. Yes, I know that too.'

Did he go and knock on the door to find out as well? Bodies may change, but voices do not. Each is thinking, as they walk, that no one ever talked together as much as they have. More than anything it is the other's voice that churns the stomach.

'Careful!' Antoni fancies he has seen a patch of fallen leaves, rain-sodden to make a person slip. He grasps Marta's arm to steer her and steady her but, when the obstacle is negotiated, leaves his grasp in place. His arm is tucked tight into hers; left–right, left–right, rocking slightly from side to side like a unit on the march in their two-by-twos.

If we had married, this is what I'd be doing: taking an early-evening walk out in the mist with my husband. It is so easy, so fitting, his stride and hers, made to match. Meant to. But, if meant to, why not? She catches the thought and lays into it; sharp slaps on both cheeks. Love becomes banal in cramped quarters on a diet of carrots and potatoes, November twelve months a year. Love dwindles. Not with this man. Rubbish! Love dwindles. Everywhere. Full stop... But her parents' has not.

'Look. Here's my bus. I'm fine from here.'

But Antoni is handing her up and getting on as well. Ania did say. But there's no need. There's every need.

The bus is full and they are absorbed into the swaying mass of standing passengers whose breath has fugged up the windows. Marta squeezes through to rub away a smeary patch on the glass for her forehead. Heads turn. Antoni watches them. How little it takes for people to consider you an outsider. But how many of them were born here, in this town, as she was? Her arrival has crashed a crater into the future. How could he ever have supposed it would not? She was bound to visit her family at some point. Which point would have been better than this one? Safer than this one?

She has blinkered her eyes with her hands to exclude the light from the bus, so that she can see where she needs to get off for her connection; or perhaps behind those shielding hands she is simply resting her forehead on the cold glass with her eyes closed.

It's that time of day. The bus is still gathering more passengers than are getting off and in the press of people Marta's beautifully styled hair is growing tousled. She's grown unused to travelling this way.

Antoni elbows close enough to reach out and tweak her sleeve. She'll need to start for the door. 'Next one's ours.'

The sudden cold of the pavement catches them both by the throat. The tram connection is round the corner. Now Antoni has no excuse for taking her arm and has to walk with his hands in his pockets, which hunches his shoulders. They join the line at the stop, and a slow queue forms behind them. Such ordinary things, queues. He ducks his chin into his collar and begins. 'How have you been?'

She shrugs, to seem nonchalant. Mutters. 'Mrs Benka says you know it all.'

'I don't know a thing, Marta. Has it worked out, you and Dr Shirazi? And your little boy?'

'What do you want me to say?'

'I want you to tell me the truth.'

'What for, Antoni? What difference will it make?'

'At least I'd know. If you were happy, then perhaps I could be.'

'But you are, aren't you? Mrs Benka said you love Ania.'

'I do. But... And you and Dr Shirazi?... Not any more?... Not ever? But then why?'

Marta examines the top of the tram stop; looks down at the tips of her shoes stained with rain. 'I don't know,' she says. 'I think I was afraid.'

'Afraid!' He's too loud. The queue shifts closer. Antoni steps on a pace, pulling Marta with him. 'I don't get you,' he hisses. 'You didn't accept me because you were afraid of being married, you said. But you did accept him because you were afraid of what? Of *not* being married? What are you saying, for heaven's sake? Look, I know about the young woman with the baby, because I met her. But what I don't understand is how you could have thought I would do that, how you could have thought I could behave like that. Didn't you know me by then? No, really! Look at me, Marta. Didn't you?'

'I did. I should have. Oh, Antoni. I'd come back just that morning, but on the way Karim... Dr Shirazi had proposed to me – in a way. But I didn't want to marry him, I wanted to marry you – I'd always wanted to marry you – and I was rushing about hoping to find you so that I could say so. But then all the new refugees came in, and it was chaotic of course. And at the end of the day, when I was so tired, Basia brought me this woman and her baby, and she said it was your baby. Staszek, she said. He had very blue eyes. And she showed me a ring. And... Even Hania and Basia thought she was your...' But, seven years on, this sounds like a child in the playground casting about to lay blame. Listing the events has not evoked the shock of

510

that moment, and its anguish. 'I only wanted to be with you.'

Antoni spins on his heels and blinks up into the sky. 'What a mess. God, what a mess!' Spins back. 'But why marry Dr Shirazi if you didn't love him?'

'I thought you'd gone. Mrs Benka had gone. I couldn't find my family. I was afraid of being alone, I expect. I don't know, Antoni. I've never been alone and I don't think I know how to be.'

'Oh, Marta!' He reaches for her and never mind the waiting people shuffling from foot to foot on the pavement behind them.

This is a hug. A real hug that brings her home. Antoni slips his arms inside her coat and everything is as it should be. She has truly come home, the past is neither here nor there and the future is irrelevant. Nothing but now.

Her eyes are closed, but as Antoni's arms tighten around her she opens them and sees a man standing to one side of the queue and regarding her with interest. Something about him makes her queasy. Get rid of him. Shut him out. She closes her eyes again. Done.

What am I to do? thinks Antoni. *God help me, what am I to do?* Like Mrs Benka he doesn't believe in the heavens, or Destiny or any of that, but just at this moment he is ready to accept the notion of providential malevolence. Mrs Benka pretended to be Marta's grandmother, then his: now, in a sense, she really is his. When he had confessed his lack of faith to Marta, she had joked, well, you'd better set up with Mrs Benka. To which he had replied, I'd rather set up with you. And look at him now. Under the same roof as Mrs Benka. He is very fond of Mrs Benka. He has come to love her granddaughter. But it's not the same. Now that he knows it, knows it as much as he has ever known anything, what in God's name is he to do without leaving a trail of disaster?

And Marta. What is she to do? She has a child. Krystyna was right. Such an appealing little boy that Antoni can understand the urge to have a child. But he wants his child with Marta, and not with his sweet and trusting wife. Poor Ania, who sent him out into the murk to see her best friend safely home, can have no idea what she has unleashed. He has no right. He should shrug his arms away, kiss

Marta's married woman's hand, and back away. Make excuses she will understand and back off. But he leaves his arms where they are and, groaning to himself (just a few minutes more, give me just a few minutes more), holds her all the tighter.

A tram trundles up, heralded by its bell. Some of the passengers seated near the window glance down at the couple in a clinch and smile to themselves. Occasionally you catch sight of something that makes you feel better. If those two don't get a move on they'll miss this one. But it looks as if they've decided to do that anyway.

The tram draws heavily away, leaving behind only the embracing pair and a man standing a little way off, his hat tipped over his eyes as a screen from the November drizzle.

Why are they whispering, like children sneaking home from a forbidden expedition? It's not late, only dark. They are climbing the three flights to the Dolniaks' new quarters, fingers linked in a secret interlacing down by their sides as if those dropped hands are invisible, even to themselves. Fine grit scrapes underfoot, and the noise is magnified by the tube of the stairwell. There is no reason why Antoni should not be introduced to her family. On the contrary, they will appreciate his gallantry in seeing her home on such a dank night.

The door opens onto a burst of light and expectant faces. Quickly Marta steps in and quickly makes her introductions. All smile warmly at Antoni, except for Halina, who is fighting her nausea and wondering miserably why morning sickness is not confined to the morning. Sonia considers the tall young man with his thick black hair and wonders how that lucky Ania landed this one. Gienek shakes hands, soldier to soldier, but without particular interest. Marta's mother gives him her hand, tells him how pleased they all are to meet Ania's husband at last, and bids him sit. Marta's father pretends to clear a space on the sofa for their guest and decides he will not, later, comment to his wife about the expression he has noticed on their daughter's face because he cannot say what, exactly, has alarmed him. But at this moment he finds her just a little too lively, a little too effusive in her embraces – and she will not meet his eyes. As he knows his daughter, something is up.

Within the hour, after Antoni has got to his feet with thanks, hand-pumpings and hand-kissings, Colonel Dolniak is certain that these two – so upright and uneasy on the sofa, who flinched visibly when their upper arms happened to touch – know each other too well for his peace of mind. He is sure he overheard Antoni whisper at the door, as Marta followed him out to the landing, 'Sleep well, Commander.' To which she answered with a sharp, 'Ssh!' and a slight, rumbling giggle.

Quietly he pushes the door to, not to close it but to place this small scene beyond it. He will clear the cake plates and the teacups and keep his observations to himself. Marta is a grown woman. A married woman with a child. He doesn't yet know how she came to wed an oriental, but she did it. In some ceremony or other she has given her word which, even if it was not in the presence of a priest, must have the force of a promise – and he brought her up to understand the importance of promises. But he is troubled by the current he thinks he detected between these two, trying so unconvincingly to play at being strangers only recently introduced.

Methodically he piles the plates together, shaking crumbs from one to the next. He stacks the cups. He lays the teaspoons in a nesting bundle on the plates. He carries them into the tiny kitchen, then returns for the cups and saucers. He is preoccupied.

Marta leans her back against the door and watches her father going about these domestic duties so unsuited to a military man. To any man. She remembers how he emerged from her bedroom in Jablonska Street the day before the hated great-aunt's visit carrying her dirty bedding and the broom. He did not feel then that his dignity was compromised by sweeping under her bed, and he appears not to think it is now by having to keep house while his wife goes out to work. She can think of no one in the world as dignified as her father, and she can think of no way of telling him so. His hands look more slender than they should. Antoni was starved, but he is a young man, and young men regain their strength. Her father has been desiccated by his imprisonment, and perhaps the time doesn't remain

513

to plump him up. A flood of love for him comes over her that she will not be able to articulate – a powerful, almost painful love, but one that is permitted.

She moves to gather up the small, embroidered linen tablecloth that her mother laid out for their guest, to shake it out over the kitchen sink. In the narrow doorway she is unavoidably face to face with her father and sees the worry in his eyes. He sees that she sees and lays an open palm briefly against the side of her head.

'My elegant lady.' He has a stab at a sardonic though affectionate chuckle, but even to him it sounds theatrical. He thinks, *If she has not learned now, she never will. I must trust her.*

She thinks, *I can't let him down. But I'm not doing anything wrong.*

70

Mrs Dolniak has been husbanding the Persian delicacies. Word has got round that her elder daughter has made it home, and the Koltuna apartment is becoming a place of pilgrimage. For each batch of visitors she lays out a few of the foreign pastries she has kept fresh in an old tin box, along with a sprinkling of raisins, pistachios, dried apricots and those strangely beguiling chewy sweets covered in flour.

People she has known since she was a child now dart shy glances at Marta as they file into the cramped apartment: a foreign husband – a Muslim! – and a foreign passport have given her celebrity. They sip their tea and nibble on the exotic fare, and then Marta is prevailed upon to talk about faraway places. It's harder than she expected. In the relating, some things turn out not suited to an audience. She can describe the convent in Wilno, she can describe her arrest and the transport to Rubtsovsk; she can recreate the wooden barracks with their unfinished latrines, the cold, the rations, the logging, the malarial mosquitoes and Dorota's funeral. But she cannot talk about Pavel Kuzmich – so she misses him out. She tugs at the cotton bush in Teren Uziuk while Basia brings news of Mrs Kwaszniewicz's heart attack, but Antoni has to be wiped from the scene.

Now Karim takes the stage in Tent City, in the form of a cool hand on the brow of her delirium, and the guests understand that the husband has made his entrance. They wriggle slightly with anticipation as, against her better judgement, Marta delivers a version of the Shirazis that gives her public what they have come to hear: Zahra Khanoom and Maryam have become religious zealots, swathed in piety. Their faces are permanently concealed behind the veils they hold in their teeth; Shirazi *père*, all bristled cheeks and slippers, parades comically through her narration like a clod-hopping, ill-educated peasant stumbled into polite society; the sisters twitter; soft Behzad sports the pout of an indulged brat. Karim's apartment and the house on the hill are converted into palaces, while beyond the fastened gates the massed ditch drinkers beg among the donkey droppings.

Around the table the guests are lapping it up. Marta notes it and is ashamed. How could she be so disloyal! And yet she goes on. And on. But once the evening is over and she climbs into bed beside Sonia she grinds her teeth on her knuckles swearing that next time she will tell the truth. In her silent soul she apologizes to the Shirazis for the lies and the exaggerations, and, when she closes her eyes, there lodged behind them is her son, stroking a tiny wooden monkey with a kink in its tail. When she goes back she'll make it up to him. They'll play all sorts of games; she'll take him for walks in the foothills of the mountains where the streams run so clear; she'll read him fairy-tales and buy him a box of toy soldiers. When she goes back.

Colonel Dolniak spends these evenings perched unnoticed in the background on a stool, watching every expression and listening to his daughter telling fibs. He says nothing but he wonders. If this is what those people are like, why did she marry into them? Her husband remains a shadowy figure, floating in his doctor's attire between the sickbeds. Did she fall for him because he was such a handsome fellow in that swarthy way, or because patients always revere the physician that cures them? Women especially. A young and inexperienced woman is easily overawed by her doctor – just as she may be by her professor, or by anyone with a little power. A uniform – any uniform, as he has noticed – has that effect. Power, or its accoutrements, is magnetic.

And why does she say so little about Davood, whose solemn photograph is passed from hand to hand until it begins to crease? They hear that he is a reserved child, in the mould of his father. They hear, to their astonishment, that he does not really speak Polish. But that is all they hear. And something about her has changed. When she was a girl she could be difficult. Obstinate. But now she is... brittle. Colonel Dolniak grows convinced there is both more to Marta's stories than she is telling, and less.

Yesterday, when he was dusting, he noticed something jutting from one of Marta's stacked suitcases. No doubt he ought to have kept his curious fingers in check, but he gave the object a gentle tug and found himself grasping the handle of a polished wooden spoon, clearly hand-made – made with love, was his immediate thought. Its silky surface invited caresses and as he stroked it he detected tiny indentations under his thumb. Minuscule letters were engraved there, too small to be read without spectacles. So he put down his duster and began the usual hunt, rummaging through the apartment's freighted surfaces – all those objects of memory squirrelled out of Jablonska Street, and decanted here in half the space, too chock-a-block to be seen but... and here's the point... still owned. That, at any rate, was his wife's view. His, now that dusting is his domain, is different. For one thing, all that paraphernalia is forever swallowing his spectacles. Once they were safely on his nose, and he had for the umpteenth time resolved to attach them to a string, he had examined the spoon again. PROPERTY OF THE COMMANDER.

Colonel Dolniak had removed his spectacles and laid them again on the shelf. He stood staring into the middle distance with unseeing concentration. Young Ania's husband, Antoni. Didn't he whisper, that first evening, something like, 'Sleep well, Commander'? So this spoon is a gift from him. But why a spoon? Why 'Commander'? And where, in fact, does Marta disappear to in the early afternoon of every day? He tells himself she is chatting away to her bosom pal, that rather dry old bird, Mrs Benka. But a nodule of unease niggles in the pit of his stomach. He had secrets from his parents when he was a child because for a child secrets are all the autonomy there is. But you grow out of that. Now, the only healthy secrets are the ones you keep from the state.

*

517

Arches. Alleyways. The railway station. The bus station. The echoing entrance hall of the public library. These are all within walking distance of the watch repair shop where Antoni works, and for half an hour every day they meander up and down, or lean against one another in the shadows of anonymous seclusion. Once Antoni said, pre-emptively, 'I cannot hurt Ania.' To which, stung, Marta snapped back, 'And I have a son.' She cannot hurt Ania either. When other people pass by, the two of them pretend to be enthralled by the mother of pearl in a roadside spill of oil, or by a pair of pigeons who have mistaken an unusually mild day for incipient spring and begun to strut and dip and coo. How is one to go on living as if nothing has happened?

'My visa expires on Wednesday week.'

'Can't you extend it?'

'Can one?'

Of course she must extend it, though her conscience twitches. So that, when her mother, who has been miserably counting the days, observes in a tear-streaked voice that there are only eight of them left before Marta has to go, her heart leaps. She has been given permission.

She pens a letter to Karim. There's so much more she has to say to her parents. When will she be in a position to see them again? He will understand, won't he, for who appreciates the importance of family more than he does? She's applying to stay on. She sends her warmest greetings to everyone, above all to Davood, and draws a childlike smiling face at the bottom of the letter.

Now Marta returns to the building where, some ten days ago, she first went to register with the police. A young policeman languorous with authority had turned the empty pages of her passport one by one. Marta, seated opposite, unworried, unhurried, looked at his bitten fingernails and pink scrubbed fingers. Some sort of schoolkid, she thought, with an official's stamp for his latest toy. Couldn't they do better than this? Eventually, when he came to the end, he tapped the passport accusingly and said, 'This is a foreign passport.'

'Well, yes. That's why I'm here.'

'But you are a Pole.' He seemed to be implying treachery.

'Of course,' she retorted. 'It takes more than a passport to alter that.'

He had appeared put out, not so much by her answer as by her lack of anxiety. But, truth to tell, how could she muster anxiety when she knew everything was in order? She had waited, watching the hand with the rubber stamp linger above the document, and thought how odd it was that across the world people in positions of authority seemed to have more in common with one another than they did with their compatriots: lateral connections ignoring frontiers – rulers who understood one another; generals appreciating their counterparts' valour; policemen sharing contempt for the ordinary lives in their petty control. This smooth-cheeked official had nothing to fear in stamping her passport – there was the visa that a previous official had concluded might be granted; there was her photograph, properly endorsed. It wasn't fear that made him delay, but regret. The instant his stamp hit the paper his moment would be over. Marta had decided for once to be patient, since patience would cost her nothing, and nothing would be gained by making unnecessary enemies.

Now, as she approaches the closed double doors of police headquarters – Nazi headquarters, they've told her, during the war – she wonders whether it will be the same juvenile at the desk. It'll make his day to have her come petitioning for special favours. That's how he'll see it. That's how he'll categorize it. And on this occasion she has no idea if he's right because no one has been able to tell her whether applying for an extension of stay is feasible. No one knows anyone who has tried.

Yesterday's mild spell has given way to a chilly wind from the north, and Marta is again wearing her fur coat, so the young policeman recognizes her at a distance and simply points to the chair and holds out his hand. This time she is flustered and has trouble concealing it. She fishes for her passport in her bag, trying to retrieve some of the bravado she rehearsed on the way here.

'I've come to extend my visa,' she begins, matter-of-fact, like picking up a prescription from the pharmacy. If he can't hear the tremulous breath then his antennae are dull.

He hears. And smiles the smallest of smiles. 'A visa can only be granted to an applicant outside the country,' he announces happily. 'I advise you to return... home, to Persia, and reapply from there.'

Suddenly Marta is convinced that he's making it up. If no one she knows has ever heard of anyone trying to extend a visa, because there are so few foreign visitors anyway, then probably this beardless child has never come across the regulations either. *I don't believe you*, she thinks, but throttles the remark.

'Are you certain?' You couldn't be more courteous in tone, but she has caused immediate offence.

The policeman, whose hand was still extended for the passport, now bangs it flat and angry on the desk. 'Of course I'm certain. It's the rules.'

She has another try. 'It's just that. You know. It doesn't seem logical that someone who's already in a country should have to leave the country in order to be in it again. If you see what I mean.'

'What's logic got to do with it? It's the rules. I didn't make them up but they must be there for a reason.' He's on his feet now, looking down at her, which forces her to look up. She will not. Her chair grates as she pushes it roughly back. He is barely taller than she is, and no more steely-eyed. But no amount of glaring will provide the leave to remain that she wants so badly. Both know it.

'Madame Shirazi! Here we are again!'

The policeman spins round to face the figure standing in an opened door behind him. Trotsky beams in genuine pleasure and bears down on his subordinate.

'I'll deal with that. Come this way.'

Trotsky's arm is lightly on her back, ushering her into an inner office. A swift glance behind her assures her of the young policeman's frustration.

71

Trotsky closes the door behind her. His greatcoat hangs massively from its hanger, the sleeves spread as if there were still arms inside. Without it he is slighter than she imagined. This inner office is snug and she shrugs off her own coat, into Trotsky's waiting hands. Burdened, he casts about for another hanger but cannot see one. Carefully – tenderly, is it? – he lays the coat over a chair under the window. Heavily framed portraits of Stalin in his large moustache, and First Secretary Bierut in his small one, jut slightly from the wall, but the light from the window blanks their expressions.

'Please. Do have a seat. Please, please.' He's the boss. He can afford to be polite. Expansive, even. 'It's cold today, isn't it? I'm sure you'd like some tea.'

He goes to a further door, and speaks his order through it. Is this place a succession of offices, one leading to the next like a hall of mirrors? They sit each side of his desk – a large, somewhat scratched affair, with papers piled impressively at either end. Before the tea arrives he's not going to say anything, but he lights a cigarette, apologizes, offers her the pack, lights hers. He pushes a crowded ashtray towards her, thinks better of it, pulls it back, empties it into a bin somewhere down by his feet, and sets it on the desktop midway between them. Marta inhales deeply.

An elderly policeman in a crumpled uniform enters with a tray. How is it possible that the new regime has somehow managed to provide its functionaries with official garb that already looks so worn? There are two cups of tea on the tray, two tinny spoons and a bowl of pale-grey sugar lumps. Trotsky drops three into his cup, one after the other, watching the splashes and the subsequent slow dissolving of the crystals. He stirs his tea with an absent-minded rotation of his wrist, then lays the spoon on the desk. A small stain spreads from it. Now they are alone again.

'You've left it very late, Madame Shirazi. I warned you, didn't I, that you should register within three days.'

'And so I did. I didn't come here to register.' Damn. What is his name? She should have hunted through the apartment to find his card, but how was she to know she'd run into the Chief of Security Services at police headquarters?

'What, then?'

'I was hoping to extend my visa.'

'Aha! So it turns out the three weeks weren't enough. You could have become my social secretary after all!'

Marta pretends she hasn't heard that. 'But your... the policeman out there says it can't be done.'

'Does he so? He's in a junior position, so I doubt if he knows.'

'He seemed very certain.'

'He's probably afraid of getting it wrong. Better safe than sorry. You know the sort of thing.' Trotsky nods at her, two conspirators together who know about the world.

'Maybe if your government wasn't so heavy-handed people like him wouldn't need to be afraid.'

'Heavy-handed? Do you think so?' He seems genuinely surprised. 'We may be a little... stern sometimes, but that's inevitable when you're at war.'

'But the war's over. It's been over for years.'

'Not that war. I'm talking about now, and the Fascist Underground.'

'What fascist underground?'

The tension in Trotsky's face relaxes into a comfortable and patronizing smile. 'You haven't been here, Madame Shirazi. You're not to know.'

'Well, tell me then.'

'I don't think it's something you want to hear about.'

'If it's to do with my country, I most certainly do.'

'Your country? *Your* country? With that?' He points at the passport clutched in her palm.

'But I'm bound to have a foreign passport if I've married a foreigner and live abroad, aren't I? Is that considered a crime these days?'

'You don't seem in a great hurry to get back to your husband. Wanting to extend your visa.'

'I haven't seen my family for ten years!'

'But it's not your family you seem to want to spend time with, is it?'

Marta stares at him. So there *was* someone in the shadows when she's been with Antoni. 'Have you been having me followed?'

'Not you, no. Him. Your… friend.'

'Why? What on earth do you think he's done? He repairs watches, for God's sake. What's wrong with watches?'

'Watches!' Trotsky spits the word contemptuously to one side. 'It's because if they could, he and other counter-revolutionary elements like him, they'd undermine the people's government and try to topple it. If they could. So it only makes sense to keep an eye on them. And therefore all the people they associate with.'

'Like me, for example.'

'Well, that's unfortunate. It wasn't expressly asked for. Perhaps you should seek out better company.'

There *is* no better company than Antoni. But counter-revolutionary? 'What do you have to do to be a counter-revolutionary?'

'Plot the downfall of the government in cahoots with imperialist forces.' He makes it sound like an axiom.

'What imperialist forces? I don't know what you're talking about.'

'The British. The French. I told you about the French spies. But that was just a beginning. We have to be vigilant, especially in this initial period, which you don't appear to understand.'

'I still don't get it. What makes you think Anto–… my f–… those people… have anything to do with the British?'

'He's a returnee from the Anders Army, isn't he? They were all in the pocket of the British and the French. Look where they chose as their theatre of war. Iraq. Palestine. Both British mandates. Look where General Sikorski held his little government-in-exile. Britain. France. Don't you see?'

'But the army was fighting the Nazis for Poland.'

'Not for this Poland, they weren't.'

'They were fighting for a free Poland.'

'No. They were fighting for the old one. The one we have now is really a free Poland – for the first time. Free for everyone so long as they don't set out to sabotage it. Free for all Poles, unless that is, you don't consider me a Pole?'

'Well, I –'

'No, no.' He puts up a silencing palm. 'You have a point. Or at least there are an awful lot of people who think like you. You can be a Pole and a communist. You can be a Pole and a Christian. But you can't be a Pole and a Jew. That's why, when *we* were the underground, we knew it was worth going to prison – for our convictions. For years, as it turned out. So you see, I have earned this.' He taps the official desk.

'What prison?' Marta is dismissive. She has never heard such rubbish. 'Where? When?'

'Oh, a good Polish prison, I can assure you, before the war.'

'People didn't get sent to prison for no reason. What did you do?'

'I was caught on a train with a sackful of pamphlets.'

'And?'

'And nothing.'

'People didn't go to prison for carrying pamphlets. Your lot might send them now, but they didn't then. It was different then.'

'I'm sure that's what you think, Madame Shirazi. But probably the people you knew, your family and so on, weren't involved in challenging the established order because they were doing very comfortably indeed in it, so they had nothing to fear. And if they had nothing to fear they wouldn't make it their business to find out what happened to those who had. People only know about their own experience, and then they think that's all there is. If you've never been in trouble with the authorities you assume that anyone who does get into trouble must have deserved it. It's normal but a false analysis all the same. People have small horizons. Even my father, who kept telling me I should do as he did and keep my beliefs for the coming of the Messiah. Whereas I believed in the coming of the International. And my father never spoke to me again.'

'What about now? Does he speak to you now, since you got this elevated position?'

'My father is dead, as you might have guessed. Like most of Poland's Jews.'

Marta is embarrassed but perhaps not quite enough. 'You make it sound as if only Jews died. And anyway you survived.'

'Yes. I survived. By going east.'

'So you must have been one of those who rushed out to welcome the Soviet armies and throw flowers over them.'

'We were safer with them. We all look for safety, don't we?'

'But they were in a pact with Germany! And Germany was your greatest threat. How could you want to be part of that?'

'Stalin wasn't – and isn't – an anti-Semite. I'm sure of that. He couldn't be. But at that time he must have had good reason for the alliances he made or he wouldn't have made them. And he wasn't alone in his decisions. That's the whole point. The leadership is the expression of the collective movement, and the collective movement wouldn't make the wrong decisions.'

'Oh, wouldn't it? Well, your collective movement arrested me, when I was only seventeen. What was I supposed to have done – a schoolgirl, at the age of seventeen – that was so dangerous? And then I was made to do hard labour on starvation rations. And I –'

'As a matter of fact, so was I.'

'What d'you mean? You'd joined them. I never joined them.'

Trotsky interlaces his fingers, turns his hands away and stretches his arms until the elbow joints crack. 'Even the best systems can make mistakes in the chaos of war. Sometimes correct principles, in the chaos of war, get turned against the wrong people. On the higher plane the principles are right, but people muddy them. And, by the way, those starvation rations of yours, that's what everyone in the

Soviet Union was on. That's what I saw. But they shared, those ordinary Russians. They may have been unsophisticated but they shared. They had nothing but they shared it. That's communism for you!'

'So the whole country starves and you're telling me this is what you want for Poland? There's never been starvation here, and you're imposing on us the system that made them starve.'

'That was the war, not the system. But remember what Lenin said?'

Marta hasn't a clue what Lenin said.

'Lenin kept saying that Russia was a backward country so it would be harder to bring it into the next historical stage. Well, he was right. It *was* a backward country. It still is. But we're different. Poland isn't backward and our base material is of a better sort, so...' He leans forward and whispers with emphasis. '*We can do it better!* We can do it better, and we will. We will always be indebted to the Soviet Union for driving Germany out and for being the leader of the anti-fascist struggle. We would have been nowhere without it and its power. The civilized world would have been lost but for that and we must never forget it. But in terms of the development of society, morally, economically, ethically – we, Poland, will be the model that everyone will look to! You'll see.'

Trotsky's face is so close she can see the pores of his skin. Why is he making speeches at her?

'But Poles don't want to be a model,' she protests. 'We just want to be... you know... Poles. In charge of our own affairs, for once. You're just making...' And she stops.

'I'm just making what?'

'People like you in these jobs, you're just making... you're just making...'

'People like me meaning Jews? Why can't you say it? You managed once before, after all.'

'All right. Jews like you in these jobs: you're just making everyone even more anti-Jewish than they were before.'

'I don't think they can be more anti-Jewish than they were before, Madame Shirazi. And frankly, that attitude only makes us more determined. It proves our point – the few of us that are left.

We've got to have a system where it can't happen again. By whatever means.'

'By whatever means. Like following me and my friends around.'

'I told you. The Anders Army people are part of the Fascist Underground.'

'But this is nonsense. They were people who were in Soviet camps and prisons, who got amnestied so that they could form an army to fight fascism. How can they possibly be part of a fascist underground? They were just as much against the Nazis as you were!'

'No. Not just as much.'

'Of course they were. You can't know anything about the Anders Army. You're simply repeating what someone's told you!' She's said too much. She's said it too rudely. Don't play games, Mrs Benka said, when you don't understand. But she does understand, and this man is getting on her nerves, spouting like a Soviet pamphlet.

'Oh, but I do know about the Anders Army. I made it my business to know, because I tried to join it.'

'You what?'

'But they wouldn't have me. They took one look at my application and said, "Egon Mandel. Is that your name? You needn't bother." So don't tell me their motives and mine were the same.'

Is it true, what he says? And if it is does it mean his motives were simply some sort of revenge? Is that what all this has been about? But she says feebly, 'You could have changed your name.'

'But, Madame Shirazi, when we met on the train it wasn't my name that made you draw the conclusions you did. Was it? And, unlike some of my comrades, I didn't want to have to pretend to be something I am not.'

Time to change the subject. Marta looks at the wall clock and finds it is gone midday. If she doesn't get a move on she'll be late for Antoni, waiting and wondering on the library steps.

'Well. Anyway. The thing is, can you stamp my passport?'

'I couldn't tell you.'

'But you're the...'

He's laughing at her incredulity. 'I don't make policy, and it's as I

527

said. We only know about what we have come across. I've never needed to know about extending people's visas. Leave your passport with me and I'll see what I can do.'

Reluctantly she pulls the passport out and slides it slowly across the desk towards Trotsky's waiting palm. His fingers fold over it, momentarily trapping hers before she snatches them away.

He looks at the wall clock too. 'And now you'd better be on your way, or you'll be late for your rendezvous!'

He lifts her coat from its chair and holds it out for her with an old-world gallantry that she thinks unsuited to his professed convictions. At least now she knows his name. Egon Mandel. Oh, forget it. Let him be Trotsky.

72

While Marta is making her way west across town to police headquarters, Colonel Dolniak throws down his dishcloth and buttons on his coat. He cannot contain himself any more. He must find out what is going on between his daughter and little Ania Dorosz's husband, and then put a stop to it, or he may never forgive himself. He gets no further than the dismal ground-floor vestibule of his block, where the residents' pigeon-holes are ranged. There he comes upon Mrs Benka examining these with spectacles on her nose.

'Mrs Benka!' he exclaims. 'What are you doing here?'

'Looking for you, Colonel. Lucky we coincided. I've been in one accursed block after another trying to find which is your apartment. And now here you are to help. Providential, some would say.'

'More than you imagine, since I was setting out to find you.'

'Ah.'

They regard one another in complete but gloomy understanding.

'Would you care to come up? They're all out, of course.'

Following him up the stairs, Mrs Benka thinks how fortunate it is that they are so clearly of like mind. He is no more anxious than she is to sort this business out amidst the hand-wringing of anguished family members. She thinks too how sad it is to see this military man in only late middle age so physically reduced by whatever it is he experienced as a German prisoner of war. She has heard from Marta, relating it in a gabble of outrage, what a paltry pension he receives from the ungrateful state. Never mind the enforced relocation. She has never been to Jablonska Street herself, but she can easily imagine the muted comfort of the Dolniaks' living before the outbreak of war.

'Here we are.' Colonel Dolniak opens his front door without apology and Mrs Benka admires him for that. Really, he is quite remarkable in his lack of bitterness, and she can see why Marta so reveres him. Here is a man who will not be defined by his circumstances.

He brings tea and a small plate of Persian delicacies. 'I expect you had a surfeit of these over there, but I thought a taste might be a reminder.'

'Actually, no. Marta was once given a box of these sweets and shared them round the ward, but otherwise no. She's the one who's had the surfeit, lucky girl.'

Mrs Benka gives a rueful snort, which Colonel Dolniak instantly decodes. His elder daughter does not, at the moment, think of herself as lucky.

'Tell me,' he says, brushing flour from his shirt front, 'how long has Marta really known Antoni? I'm asking because, you see, I happened to find a wooden spoon with an inscription on it. Something I heard him say made me think he must have given it to her.'

Oh dear. How much has Marta not recounted? It's one thing for Mrs Benka to conspire with Colonel Dolniak to forestall what looks likely to end in catastrophe all round, but another to divulge what Marta might wish to keep secret. Somewhat frantically Mrs Benka scrabbles for a version of the truth that will do well enough. 'No,' she begins slowly. 'The spoon wasn't from Antoni. It was a parting gift from a man called Pavel Kuzmich, who turned out to be a fatherly sort...'

Two hours have passed. They have eaten the soup and dumplings that Colonel Dolniak heated up, and now Mrs Benka is helping him wash the dishes so that no one will be able to tell there has been a daytime visit. Subterfuge is a pity but they are agreed that Mrs Dolniak should know as little as possible. It would break her heart, the colonel has said, to think that her daughter might demolish any woman's marriage – let alone her best friend's – even if it wasn't her intention to do so. It would also break her heart to think how Marta must be suffering from this awful mistake. In fact, it is breaking *his*– for all that the mistake is largely of Marta's own making. And that poor little boy. What is to become of him with his mother fixated on a man who is not his father?

Colonel Dolniak thinks his heart has never felt so heavy. He is a man used to clarity in what is the right thing to do, and then taking action in defence of it. But this situation leaves him helpless and wading through brambles of emotion. It's not his field. But he knows that if this were someone else's story, recounted to him by an acquaintance, he would consider the circumstances only briefly before offering a brisk judgement. Well, it's obvious! The young woman should go straight back to her husband and child and put all that old stuff behind her. Surely she knows her duty. But it isn't someone else's story. For ten years he hasn't seen his beloved daughter, and now he has to lose her all over again. And he can't even bring her comfort.

Colonel Dolniak hears his own sad sigh as if it came from another chest. Mrs Benka is looking at him with more sympathy than he can bear. He didn't realize until today just how close the old woman and his daughter must have been, and he thinks he owes Mrs Benka a great deal. How well would Marta have managed without her? Even his Marta, his 'commander'! It must be so hard for Mrs Benka too, torn between her natural love for her granddaughter and the love that time and shared experience seem to have brewed in her for Marta. He's only sorry he hasn't had more to do with her since she came home to live at that crazy Krystyna's. She'd have been good company, if only his wife didn't find her so intimidating.

It's getting late. Mrs Benka has taken a decision and is determined to see it through, but if she doesn't get a move on she may have second thoughts. She's holding out her hand and Colonel Dolniak grasps it rather than kissing it. They nod at one another and she clatters off, the echoing stairwell holding her retreating presence. Colonel Dolniak stands a while in his open doorway. God speed.

It's half past two as Antoni emerges from the watch repair workshop into the late November rain. He turns up his collar, pulls down his hat and strides out for the library, glad that today they have arranged to meet indoors. As the end of every working day approaches, he feels his heartbeats quicken and the bubble of disquiet swell in the pit of his belly. He isn't sure how much of it is exhilaration because he is about to be with Marta again for their fleeting half-hour alone, and how much is guilt. All he knows is that, as long as she is in this city, a day passing without her is a day not lived. But at the same time he anticipates the return home and Ania's sweet welcome, unsuspecting, chattering and chiding in equal measure, as they all compare what they have managed to buy. Until recently he has been able to hold her in his head just as he holds her in his arms. His mother-in-law is fond and easy-going, making it a pleasure to live under her roof where it might have been irksome. He is so lucky. But if he could only turn back the clock he would.

Someone has been calling his name and he hasn't heard it, hasn't allowed himself to hear it, as a sleeper incorporates sounds from the real world into his dreaming in order not to wake.

'Antoni! For goodness' sake!'

'Mrs Benka!'

But he's not surprised. He has been expecting this. All these days Mrs Benka hasn't said a word, while her very silence has out-shouted his conscience.

But I haven't done anything wrong, that conscience protests.

Have you not? he imagines her replying. *If your mind and your heart are engaged with someone else, does it matter where you put your penis? You're treating Ania as if she were a prostitute.*

No! he retorts, but his tone is clammy. *No, I'm not. How could you say that? I love Ania. I love her as well! It's perfectly possible to love two people at the same time, isn't it?*

Tell that to Ania, comes the dry response. *And then tell it to Marta too, while you're about it.*

No. He's not in the least surprised to see Mrs Benka, only that it's taken her so long. He turns back.

Over by the corner the man they've set on his tail, usually so bored but perked up of late, about-turns as well.

'We're going home,' says Mrs Benka tucking her hand into Antoni's elbow, and gripping it — old ladies totter and may need support. But by the way she marches him off one might be reminded more of a roving schoolteacher finally fingering the truant boy.

Antoni is in no position to demur, but Marta must already be on her way to the library. If he is not there, what will she think?

And what does she? She thinks she's late. All that hectoring from Trotsky has made her miss him. Damn! She wants to tell him about Trotsky and his failed application to the Anders Army. She wants to ask him if there were any Jews among them, just in case Trotsky has been making it up. She wants to find out if he knows he's being followed all the time. She just wants to be with him on her own. Now she'll have to wait until tomorrow. But she can still go to the Doroszes' as usual. They've grown used to finding her already there when they get in. And she's grown used to the pattern of their homecoming. It won't take long. Driving rain always makes you walk faster.

'This has got to stop.' Bluff and baleful as never before, Mrs Benka has got the pair of them side by side in front of her, sullen, defiant, trapped.

'But —' begins Marta.

'No. I'm sorry, dear, but it won't do.'

'We're not doing anything wrong.'

'Only for lack of opportunity.'

'That's not fair!'

'Isn't it?'

'I wouldn't because it wouldn't be right.'

'Then tell me this. Why the skulking about every afternoon if you're not trying to hide something? And if you're trying to hide something then you must think it's wrong.'

'What skulking?'

'Marta. Dear. There's a clock on the wall. And I am not stupid. And soon enough what I can see others will too. Do you want that to happen?'

Marta mutters no into her chin. Defiance is draining away. Next to her Antoni looks pinched about the nostrils. Mrs Benka is not merely making them squirm, she is tearing them apart, and hates herself for it. These poor children.

She ploughs on. 'You must pack your bags and go home on the next aeroplane you can get. It's got to end at some point, Marta, and whichever day you leave it will be hard, but you must go before Ania finds out. Why make her miserable as well?'

Marta is motionless. Obviously she has thought all this already. Obviously she has talked about all this with Antoni already.

'Believe me, dear. I will miss you almost as much as Antoni will, but you simply cannot stay any longer.'

'But I've just applied to extend my visa.'

'Then you must go and unapply. Tell them you've changed your mind. Tell them there's a crisis at home. I'm sure you'll be able to make something up.'

'Antoni.' Help me. Marta has turned to face him, sees the reddening of his eyes, the lips mumbled together to still the wobbling chin.

As he reaches out with his hands, the front door opens for mother and daughter, who have coincided on the landing, calling out, 'Hello! We're home! It's such a foul day out there. Did you get caught in it too? Oh. Is something the matter? Has something happened?'

Look! Antoni has his hands on Marta's shoulders. Marta is wide-eyed. Mrs Benka has a finger upraised like Lenin haranguing the masses. All three are pale as death. Their faces swivel in consternation towards the door.

'It's... I've had news from home. My mother-in-law, Zahra Khanoom. She's ill. I'm going to have to go back.'

'Oh, Marta!'

Ania drops her string bag and Marta notices – and is astonished that she notices – that it contains a shrivelled cabbage and five onions. Ania is embracing her, her own eyes already brimming with concern and loss.

'But I feel I've hardly seen you. Why did this have to happen now?' A tight hug, a small hand stroking Marta's cheek. 'Tell you what. You go home if you have to, and when she's well again you can come back. You'll get another visa, I'm sure. She will, won't she? Your parents here and everyone. Maybe in the summer when it's nice. You could bring your Davood this time, and we could all go somewhere together. Walking in Zakopane, unless you still hate walking as much as you used to. But wouldn't it be wonderful if we could only go back to Mrs Benka's farm, if Old Petrkiewicz was still there and we could show Mama and Antoni all the places where we were? If Wilno was still ours. Oh, damn all this! Why can't the world just let people live in peace? It's all anyone ever wants, isn't it, just to live with the people they want to and not do anyone any harm.' She leans her head against husband Antoni's arm. 'Get on with our lives. It's all anyone ever wants.'

Ania hugs Marta. Then Mrs Benka hugs Marta, and awards her a pair of smart congratulations on her hidden back. Krystyna hugs Ania, then Antoni. Ania hugs Antoni. Antoni hugs Marta and does not know how to let her go.

73

Marta runs from the Doroszes' building, in shoes not suited to running, until she knows she is out of sight, and not once does she look back. All the way home she rehearses how she will tell her family that she has to leave. Can she claim to have had a telegram – but then to have mislaid it lest anyone, her mother in particular, demand to see it, and wail? As she approaches Koltuna, she realizes she has passed from tram to bus and along the pavements like an automaton. If her body can carry her so reliably into the future, then her mind must learn to do the same. Think forward. Only forward. She may never see… Think only forward. But the future is a blanket knitted from lead. They're all at home already. Even before she opens the door she can hear the voices inside, talking together in some sort of agitation.

'Marta, darling. We've been waiting so long. They've brought a telegram and we didn't want to open it. But a telegram, darling! What can it be?'

This is uncanny! Marta rips the thing open. It's in French: 'Come home as soon as you can. Behzad.' Behzad! Why should he, of all people, summon her home? Could it be that something has happened to Karim or Davood? If they're ill or injured, surely he'd have said.

'I've got to go back. Look.' She holds it out and it is passed from one to another and examined. The silence of dread sits on them all. Isn't it true that the worst news is only ever given in person?

She's aware of them, a softly breathing group, watching her through the door packing her suitcases, strapping up the empty ones. Tomorrow she'll have to go to police headquarters and reclaim her passport from Trotsky. She thinks someone up there is leaning over the lid of the world and grinning. This is to be her punishment for having told a lie about Zahra Khanoom. No. It's just a punishment. Mrs Benka was right, of course. If she only could, she would have made love to Antoni, and it makes no difference that there was nowhere they could go. They both knew what they wanted, and in their knowing it Ania was betrayed. Poor Ania. But why poor Ania? She's got Antoni all to herself now, hasn't she, for the rest of their lives. Or perhaps she hasn't. Perhaps this visit has ruined everything, leaving Ania with only Antoni's physical presence but not the person – like the husk of a grain of rye without its kernel. So then nobody has anything. The only difference is that Ania doesn't know it, and, if Antoni is the man that Marta thinks him, then maybe Ania never will.

Time will pass and they'll have children, and when those children are old enough they'll scramble up to sit one on either side of Ania, leafing through her photograph album. 'Who's that, Mummy?' they'll say, pointing to a picture of the two best friends in their Girl Guide uniforms squinting into the sun. 'Well, that's me,' she'll say. 'Long ago. And that girl used to be my best friend Marta. She lives far away now but maybe one day she'll come back for a visit. I can't understand why she hasn't, all this time. She's got a little boy of her own, you know – well, actually, he can't be that little any more. Wouldn't it be lovely if we could all meet again?' But the two children aren't really interested in Mummy's friends from long ago and they've slithered off the sofa to go and play.

The bored young policeman is on his feet so quickly that his chair crashes to the floor.

'I won't be a moment, madame.' A tap on the door. Head round the door. 'Comrade Mandel will see you now, madame.'

'How very pleasant to see you again, Madame Shirazi. And so soon.'

'Yes. But unfortunately I have to go home. They've summoned me.'

'Summoned?'

Well. She has a telegram, hasn't she. She holds it out for Trotsky to see. Look, I have no secrets from the Chief of Security Services.

'Behzad.' He mispronounces it. 'Your husband?'

'His younger brother. I was hoping you might still have my passport. That you hadn't sent it off or…'

Comrade Mandel would not have needed to send it anywhere. He had intended to keep it in his drawer for a while longer before stamping it on the very day the current visa expired. She would have been grateful, and much flows from gratitude. So this morning, when he got up, he'd been suffused with a sense of well-being, but now it's gone, in a single wash of profound disappointment. He has an urge to kick something. Or someone. Like that pimply adolescent in the outer office. But he smiles sadly instead.

'It's here.'

It occurs to him to stamp a surreptitious extension into her passport anyway, so that she should realize the reach of his authority. You can't explain (and mostly people don't want to know) how sweet it is, after all these long, long years, to be the doer rather than the done-to, to be – for the first time – in charge of one's own destiny, never mind of the destiny of others. But she's leaving. And in such an agitated state that the only one to be impressed would be he himself, and surely he's beyond that by now.

He takes the passport from his drawer and lays it front of her on the desk. Marta grabs it and stuffs it into her bag. 'Thank you,' she says. 'I'm relieved. I was afraid it might have been somewhere between here and Warsaw and I'd have been held up. So I'm glad.'

Trotsky walks round his desk to accompany her to the door. 'My car is outside,' he suggests. 'I could see you home to collect your luggage and then take you on to the station.'

'Thank you. But I will manage.'

'I would like to.'

'No. Thank you.' She turns to the door, and turns back. 'You said, "We will do it better." How is it doing it better if all the reward a man gets when he's fought for his country, and been imprisoned for his country, is a pension worth less than a week's worth of tea? When he

538

and his family are kicked out of their apartment because, they're told, they don't need so much space, only to have a Party bigwig and his housekeeper take their place? How is that doing it better? And how is it doing it better when people have to work all day and then stand in stupid queues for hours, and all they get in the end is one measly cabbage and a few pathetic onions?'

'The question of supply,' says Trotsky stiffly, 'is under review. Our peasants aren't yet co-operating fully with national targets, but in time I'm sure they will. It's still early days, don't forget, and the economy has to recover from the war.'

'It doesn't take five years to grow a bag of vegetables. There was never a problem before. You went to the baker's for bread, then the butcher's for meat, then the greengrocer's for vegetables. Then you went home. Now all you've got inside the butcher's shop is the butcher. But he hasn't got any meat. How did you manage that?'

'You are looking at things from the pre-war perspective of the bourgeoisie, Madame Shirazi. Your class always had the money to buy what they wanted. Most people didn't, but you weren't aware of that because it didn't affect you.'

'So now nobody can buy what they want. And what about the other thing?'

Comrade Mandel wishes she hadn't raised the other thing because, in fact, he agrees with her. It pains him that a senior Party official should pull rank to get himself more square metres of housing than the size of his household warrants. People like that subvert the revolutionary principle, as he himself complained not so very long ago in a meeting behind closed doors. Everyone knew that he meant Second Deputy Kubinski, who immediately responded that the undue fanaticism of the purist should be left to the Robespierres of this world, nodding the while in Comrade Mandel's direction. If only the Party had been more discriminating in whom it admitted to its ranks – and then elevated. If only Kubinski hadn't lighted upon the house of an old soldier – especially this one. If only that old soldier's daughter...

'And one more thing.' Marta has tired of waiting for an answer, and Trotsky's protracted silence makes her think there isn't going to be one. 'I've been living in a backward country for the past seven years. Such a backward country that your precious Lenin would despair. And it's not just that some people are very well off – yes, I know, like my husband's family, which means me too – and others are in the ditch. Literally in the ditch. It's not just who's rich and who's poor. It's who's got power and who hasn't. I would never have believed that people could cringe so much to anyone with a higher position than theirs, smarm all over them just to get on or keep out of trouble, but then go and kick the next one down in the teeth. You can't believe anything anyone says because they're constantly trying to work out what it is you want to hear so they can say it to you – if you're high enough to matter, that is. And God help you if you're not. So you can't trust anyone except your own family. And d'you want to know why that is? I think it's because they're all afraid. All down the line. Everyone's afraid. That's what it was like when I was in the Soviet Union as well, except that in the camp where I was I met a man who had sunk so low his life couldn't get any worse. *He* was decent. The only one, but he was decent. And now I come home and I discover that Poland has become exactly the same. Exactly the same. And you call that "doing it better"! Every petty official thinks he's Stalin – until Stalin shows up. Like your baby policeman out there, throwing his weight about but quaking when he thinks you might be round the corner. And now I ought to be going. I hope I haven't offended you.'

'Why?' says Trotsky sourly. 'Do you think I'll take it out on your family?'

Marta's hands fly to her big mouth. 'I didn't mean… it's just that I'm upset because of the telegram. You must understand, I –'

'I think you have said quite enough, Madame Shirazi. Honesty is an excellent quality – even yours, but it's best in small doses. I remember saying something to the effect that you don't belong here any more, and I was right, so it's probably a good thing all round that you've got to leave, don't you agree?' He reaches for the door handle. 'That was most interesting. Goodbye and have a safe journey.'

She's gone. A good thing all round, just as he said. But his mood is even worse than before and he's tempted to go into the vestibule and bawl out that policeman. Except that to do it would prove her right. But, if he doesn't, it would mean he thinks she was. Goddammit.

74

The flight is interminable, much longer than it felt on the way out, hobbled by a headwind. The plane bucks and rattles. Day and night are sluggish. Marta has feigned sleep to deflect conversation from a garrulous neighbour announcing himself as an oil man who loves his job but shrinks from flying. Three times he tries this overture before closing his eyes. Soon he's snoring his hours away.

There cannot have been a death. For all their glum faces her parents agreed with her on this. Nor could anyone be gravely ill in such terse anonymity. Curiosity and trepidation churn in her bowels.

Use the time and invent a story for Davood. Nothing is left but him. If she has to recast herself now, if this is to be the beginning of a new life that has to leave the old one behind, then Davood is the key. Everything will be for him. Everything will be through him. She only hopes that one day, if he ever finds out, he'll be grateful. Immediately she takes the thought back. Why should a child be grateful that his mother devotes herself to him? That's what mothers are supposed to do and if she only looked around she'd see it happening on all sides. It's what her mother did. It's what everyone expects. In time maybe she'll even become good at it.

So. A story for Davood. A really good one with lots of people in it and an exciting plot. But she's no good at stories. So then, which can she remember that might be plundered, and how do they begin? Once upon a time, a long, long time ago, when all the hills were covered in forests and the rivers boiled with fish… Antoni will be emerging from his workshop around now, into the chill, pushing down on the crown of his hat in that unconscious gesture that makes her smile... Forget it... Boiled with fish of all colours. There were purple ones and red ones and green stripy ones, all sorts of fish you don't see nowadays. The fish all belonged to a great king because he owned the rivers just as he owned the hills and the trees. One spring day the King woke up to the sound of birdsong and said to himself... That last hug. She can still feel it, how his arms tightened round her, like but not like their furtive daily embraces, because of the others looking on – Krystyna and Ania, and Mrs Benka watching out for anything unbrotherly. It felt as if he was saying, I cannot let you go. If I let you go I shall never see you again... The King said to himself... What would a king say to himself on a spring morning? What's going to make this spring morning different from all the other ones the King has woken to? He's... he's... I know, he's getting old and thinks that since he'll die soon he'd better decide how to divide up his kingdom between his three sons.

What will happen when Shirazi *père* dies? Will Zahra Khanoom inherit everything? Can she? Or must it bypass her and go to the children, or only to the sons? The King, already feeling weakness falling on him, called his Keeper of the Bedchamber to assemble the princes before nightfall. So off went the Keeper of the Bedchamber, but with a heavy heart because he didn't think any of the King's three sons deserved the crown. First he knocked on the door of the oldest prince, whose name was... Wladek the Mighty. Yes. Wladek the Mighty was a nasty piece of work. When he heard the Keeper of the Bedchamber knocking, he roared out, 'Who's that? Go away! I'm busy!' But the Keeper of the Bedchamber knew that Wladek the Mighty only ever sat about all day eating enormous plates of kebab and rice and aubergine. He was so fat and heavy that his poor horse sagged in the middle whenever he climbed onto it.

The horse had a groom called... Misha, who was tall and handsome, with thick black hair and blue eyes. He was gentle and funny, and all the horses loved him. They nibbled at his face with their velvety lips. *What did you think would happen?* Antoni said. *Did you think I could leave Ania and you could leave Davood and that we'd run away togeth-*

543

er with only the clothes we were wearing, to start a new life? *Did you really ever think that?* he said. *No,* she said, the more miserable for his apparent censure. *Well,* I *did,* he said. *That's just the trouble.*

Misha overheard the Keeper of the Bedchamber trying to explain that the King wanted his three sons summoned to the bedside that evening. 'I'm going to be busy this evening,' bellowed Wladek. 'I'm going to a party. Tell the old man I'll see him some time tomorrow.' So the Keeper of the Bedchamber went in search of the second prince, Bohuslav. But Bohuslav was playing ball in the garden, throwing it up until it hit the clouds, and then catching it again. But when the Keeper of the Bedchamber called his name he lost concentration and dropped the ball. It made him furious. 'You disturbed me,' he shouted, 'and I'd nearly got to a hundred.' The Keeper of the Bedchamber passed on the King's message, but Boguslaw only said, 'I may come and I may not. It all depends on whether I make my hundred.' Finally the Keeper of the Bedchamber went down to the rose arbour, where the King's youngest and most favoured son lay on the ground sleeping in the scent of a thousand pink petals. It was hard, the ground between the tents. Stony. But even though she'd known that Antoni would have to go war, and might not come back, she had been so happy with her head on his arm. She'd gone to sleep with that happiness and woken up with it, exhilarated. Another day. Another evening to come. What is to be done with all the days and evenings to come? She should have stayed in Tehran. Better never to have known. Or not to have known yet, although which time would have been easier? And Antoni. What is he thinking now? Has he gone back to his old life as if she had never barged in? At least he loves Ania. At least she did the honourable thing. He has Ania, unharmed. And she has Davood, who mustn't be harmed. That's what she's there for, to see Davood never comes to harm.

The Keeper of the Bedchamber, for all he tried, couldn't wake the youngest prince, who was dreaming such a beautiful dream that he was smiling in his sleep. I'll return later, thought the Keeper of the Bedchamber. For who knows when his young Highness will dream such a beautiful dream again. He tiptoed away. At the doors of the castle he met Misha the groom, who said to him:

'Ladies and gentlemen. Please fasten your seatbelts for the descent into Mehrabad airport. We will be landing in approximately fifteen minutes.'

Marta stands alone in the arrivals hall surrounded by her baggage. There is no cavalcade of cars to meet her. There is no one at all. Other passengers have been met, clasped to the chest and embraced, or they have walked purposefully by themselves out to the taxis. The oil man, refreshed after his long sleep, barely nods as he strides by, brushing away porters. He carries a single efficient suitcase. The hall has cleared, and Marta is conspicuous, stationary, puzzled. Then she realizes. They don't know that she has arrived because in her turmoil she forgot to send a wire.

'Khanoom?' Wistful porters dance from foot to foot.

She nods, go ahead – and follows them out to a taxi. Her cases can all be crammed together this time, since most of them are empty. The cabby winds down his window to smoke out of it and the winter air rushes into her face. She pulls the large collar of her coat up around her cheeks, turns her face into the fur and catches a scent in it that is Antoni. She presses the fur over her nostrils and gulps at it, here, and again here, and along the rim of the collar, but it's gone.

The lights are on in the living room that gives over the street side of the building, so someone's in. Maybe the cousins are visiting and the door will open onto their familiar shrieks and squeaks, and no one will notice that she is back, so that for a moment she can stand unobserved, the stranger returned, watching the household in its everyday doings, which continues in its ways whether or not the mistress is there. But, when she lets herself in, the air in the apartment is still. There are no voices in the living room, despite the lights.

The door to the kitchen opens, and Shirin comes out with a bucket in her hands. She stops and peers down the corridor as if she cannot believe what she sees.

'Hello, Shirin. Well, I'm home.'

Shirin drops the bucket and, pulling her scarf over her face, bolts back into the kitchen.

'Shirin? Shirin! What's the matter?' Marta follows the maid and finds her hunched on the floor, rocking backwards and forwards, and moaning. 'Shirin! Whatever is it? What's happened?'

Shirin clutches the scarf and shakes her head violently. It can't be told, whatever it is, or for sure not by her.

'Where's Karim Agha? Where's Kookooleh?'

But Shirin will not or cannot answer.

Marta sets off at a run round the apartment, flinging doors open onto uninhabited rooms, but they have the smell of rooms that people might only recently have vacated, as if the particles in the air are only now settling into stillness after the disturbance of breathing, moving bodies. Not so Davood's room. It is not that it's empty — rather it feels as if it has been emptied, even though his furniture and all his childish things are still here. The space bulges with absence. The orderliness of it is not its everyday orderliness but something more final, like when, with the passing of winter, the quilts are folded away into the big chest and the lid closed on the season. Winter's coffin.

Now Marta stands frozen to the place, still grasping the door handle, picturing Shirin rocking on the kitchen floor with her head covered. You can be so wrong. Behzad didn't say in the telegram because he couldn't bring himself to. Shirin can't speak. Dares not. Did Davood become ill so suddenly and so grievously that even his father couldn't make him well? Or was it an accident? But what sort of accident? Davood is no daredevil. If he's told, don't touch that, it's hot, he doesn't touch it; if he's told, don't go there, it's dangerous, he stays. But why Behzad? Why was it left to Behzad? Zahra Khanoom will know and will have to tell her.

They're staring at her in the street and she has a fleeting vision of herself as they might see her: a tousled expensive woman with noisy gasping breath tearing frantically along the pavement.

The parents' house is less than a hundred metres away but by the time she reaches it her face is blotched by panic. She hammers on the door and leans against it, pushing viciously. Inside, shuffling footsteps. Maryam. Who screams, and like Shirin pulls her veil over her face and turns to the wall.

'What is it? Maryam! Tell me!'

Maryam wails. There are words in there but incomprehensible.

'Tell me! What's happened? Tell me now!' She's shrieking like a madwoman.

The women are coming down, Leila, Farideh, Massy – Zahra Khanoom heavy-footed behind them. It must be some crazed beggar making a scene at the door. But when they see Marta they stop dead on the stairs and shrink back. They look scared too. Frightened of her, or of what they know. The faces of the little cousins are pale blurred blobs pressed to the bars of the banister.

'Marta! You're back!' Such astonishment from Farideh. They weren't expecting her. 'We thought you were staying longer. That's what you wrote.'

'Where's Davood?'

Zahra Khanoom pushes past her daughters to take charge. 'Come in and sit down.'

'Where's Davood?'

'Shh, shh. Wait for Karim. He'll explain when he comes.'

'I won't wait for Karim. You tell me, Zahra Khanoom. You know, so you tell me!'

'You must calm down and –'

'How can I calm down? Where is my son? Is he dead?'

'No, of course he's not dead. Why would God let him die? Oh, you poor girl. Of course, I understand what you must have thought. But don't worry, he's not dead. He should be very well.'

He's not dead. Marta crumples onto the bottom step and they swarm to her, lifting her, patting her, bearing her up the stairs between them. The cousins scatter. No one can see it but she has wet herself. He should be very well. What does it mean, he *should* be well?

Zahra Khanoom has taken Leila aside and whispered something to her. It's made Leila pull a doubtful face, but her mother is adamant so she reaches for her coat. Slings it on and hurries out, buttoning it as she goes. Now Zahra Khanoom is raising Marta to her feet.

'You've been travelling, Marta-jun. Why don't you have a bath? Maryam will help you, while we wait for Karim.'

She is so tired. Maryam slides the coat from her shoulders and leads her to the bathroom, mumbling, 'There, there. Everyone needs a nice bath after such a long journey, don't they, Marta Khanoom. You'll feel so much better in a little while, and I'll bring you some tea and rub your feet and then you can climb into my bed and sleep there all night long with me. Nothing to worry about any more. No need to be alone any more. There, there. Come along. Here we are.'

Marta gives herself up to Maryam, who is rolling away her clothes, item by item. There is no one in the whole world like Maryam who can make everything better. The old woman is massaging her shoulders in the water, rubbing soap over her back. She might, if she let go, just fall asleep here in the bathroom.

'Maryam. Can't you tell me? Where has Davood gone?'

'As God is my witness, Marta Khanoom, it's not my business to say. We have to wait for Karim Agha.' The massaging hands falter in their firm rhythm. 'Ah, but it's a bad business. I'm sorry, Khanoom.'

The men are home. You feel it in the air when the men are home. Marta, wrapped in towels, would rush out to beard her husband just as she is, but Maryam restrains her.

'Do things as they should be done, Khanoom,' she says, and holds out some clothes that Marta knows to be Leila's.

Marta lets herself be dressed like a child who hasn't mastered buttons. She finds she keeps taking deep breaths but they snag in her throat.

The Shirazis are in heads-together conference at one end of the room and they leap apart as she comes in. Everyone is here – except Karim. Shirazi *père* waddles over, his arms wide.

'My daughter,' he says. 'Our rose is home again but pretending to be Leila.'

He laughs aloud and kisses her on both cheeks. The roughness of his bristly jowls and the scent of rosewater bring her back to herself. Such a sweet man, this modern patriarch. She lets him hug her and rests for a moment against his bulk. If only everything were as simple as this.

The husbands have positioned themselves in the furthest corner, staying out of trouble, you might say. But it's Behzad she wants to talk to, leaning over the back of an armchair, his prayer beads swinging gently under the playing of his fingers. She truly did him a disservice when telling her tales of the exotic orient. He has long since lost that petulant softness and the overfed adolescent's soft belly.

She turns towards him, her mouth opening to ask, 'Where…?', but Behzad has dropped his gaze and is shaking his head in minute warning. They don't know he sent for her! He doesn't want them to know!

'Where's Karim? Isn't he coming?'

'He's coming,' says Leila. 'He was busy but he's coming.'

75

He is coming, but at his leisure. Sauntering. Imperturbable. His wife, they tell him on the street, has just blown in through the door with the winds of hell behind her. Well, well.

Everyone watches him.

'And was it a success, your little trip?'

'Where's Davood?'

'And your mother and father? Healthy, I hope? And pleased to see you after all this time?'

'Stop it, Karim. Where's Davood?'

'Davood is being educated.'

'What do you mean, "being educated"? Who by? Where?'

'Where the schools are the best in the world, because I will have nothing but the best for my son. He's learning to rule the world. In England.'

Now everyone watches her. She hasn't heard him, or hasn't understood him, or doesn't believe him. It's disconcerting how still she is. 'England!' she mutters, finally.

'You should be pleased. Your British friends. Or perhaps you've fallen out with them since they let the USSR have your country when Stalin called in the debt.'

'How did he get there?'

'By aeroplane, of course.'

'But who with?'

'He went in the care of the airline and he was collected in London by a business associate of ours, who took him to his school.'

'Alone? You sent him alone?'

'Of course. He has gone to learn to be independent.'

'How dare you!'

'*Tss!*'

'How could you? He doesn't speak English.'

'That's why he's gone. So that he can learn.'

'But he's so young! How could you? Don't you have any feeling? And sending him like that when I wasn't here. Behind my back when I wasn't here.'

'When your letter came it was clear to me that you had decided to stay on. For good, as far as anyone could tell. The whole world cannot wait for you, Marta. And how was I to know that you would change your mind and come back early?'

'But... you can only have got my letter a day or so ago.'

He doesn't respond to this.

'You waited for me to leave so that you could send him away.'

Silence.

'That's why you gave your permission for me to go, isn't it? So that I wouldn't be here while you did your dirty work. So that I wouldn't be able to stop you.'

Karim's small laugh is uneasy (she's right), but unworried. 'You could not have stopped me no matter how much noise you might have made. But I agree. It was simpler this way.'

Marta stares at his family, from one averted face to the next. Zahra Khanoom and Shirazi *père*, of course, won't have understood this exchange, not word for word, but they've got the general drift. Zahra Khanoom has taken refuge behind her impassive look. Shirazi *père* is trembling with emotion, sorry for her, for his son, for his grandson, for himself, for everyone. The sisters want all this to stop. They hate it when Karim's mouth is so tight and white, when his voice drops. Even their parents shuffle their feet when he gets like this. And Behzad? Behzad is keeping his head down.

'Well then,' she says lightly. 'It's a good thing I haven't unpacked. Tomorrow I'll get a ticket and fly over there and get him back.'

She waits for Karim to forbid it, but he smiles – mouth not eyes.

'As you wish,' he says. 'But you may not find it as easy as you think.'

But Karim is wrong and it's perfectly easy. There is a flight. There are seats on that flight. He let her have the address of the school without making difficulties. Farhad booked her a room in a hotel in the centre of London. Behzad will drive her to the airport. No cavalcade, this time, to see her off, but when she comes back they'll all be there to welcome her, even if Karim isn't among them. It's as plain as it can be that they are all behind her in this mission to rescue her son. In a way it seems fitting that this has happened, because having to retrieve Davood, rather than simply coming home to him, will mark her new beginning. You cherish what you have to fight for more than what is given you on a plate.

'Thank you,' she whispers to Behzad. 'For letting me know.'

Hands gripping the steering wheel, he shakes his head. Don't mention it. Or, it's a sorry business. Or, I wish I hadn't.

They drive for a while in silence until Behzad opens his mouth to speak. Takes a breath. Changes his mind.

'What is it?'

Again, the head shake.

'There is something,' she persists.

Silence.

'You should tell me. You can't not tell me now.'

'I'm sorry, Marta. It's nothing to do with me.'

'What's nothing to do with you? You wired me to come home. Was that to do with you?'

'I made a mistake. I shouldn't have done that.' Pause. 'You see… Karim… *Yah Khodah!*… There is a woman.'

'A woman?'

'Don't you understand?' Behzad addresses the windscreen furiously and his profile is grim.

Oh yes, she understands. Karim has been having some sort of affair while her back was turned. Indignation flares, then sputters. How can she be self-righteous when she so nearly… but for Mrs Benka she would have... But she didn't. That's the point, and that's the difference. Whereas Karim...

'How long?' But even as she leaves the question unfinished she knows she is asking too much of a younger brother. First things first. Rescue Davood. Tackle Karim later. 'Well, thank you, anyway.'

'But Marta-jun. That woman is none of my business. I called you back because of Kookooleh. What is our household without Kookooleh?' He takes his eyes off the road to look at her and she sees them flowing with tears. 'Maybe one day I shall have a son of my own. I don't know. But never, *never* will I love him more than I love our Kookooleh. Bring him home to us, Marta-jun.'

There are eighteen of them, nine in a row with their heads to the wall, and opposite them nine more with their heads to the other wall. He is one of them but he is awake, while they are sleeping. Or he thinks they are sleeping. He can hear their breathing and sometimes a small snuffle, a yelped whimper. If he reaches his hand out he can touch the edge of the next bed. The gap between is exactly as wide as the little cupboards that separate the beds. Some of the cupboards have got pictures on them of mothers and fathers and little sisters. Some of them have got pictures of dogs. He has understood that at home these children's families keep dogs. Inside the houses. Not guard dogs, but dogs sitting by your chair waiting to eat the food you might drop. The pictures show the dogs inside the houses, with people cuddling them, arms round the heavy furry bodies. Even the dogs are smiling for the photograph.

He is confused. You can see the people cuddling the dogs but they are not cuddling each other. Don't they care that angels can't visit with dogs in the house? In the daytime, when everyone is awake, and tall rooms and corridors echo with all the feet, no one touches. And the way they're all lying now makes him think of Danuta Khanoom's box of wooden animals. Each one has its own nest in the box, separated from the next one. In the summer when it gets hot, will they all lie on mattresses on the roof under the stars jumbled together, or will they still keep that space between them? And the way they walk –

their arms straight down by their sides like pieces of wood growing from their shoulders – they hold them like that to be sure that no one's hand accidentally brushes against anyone else. He's seen it. If one boy's arm bumps into another's he pulls it away as if he burned himself, or did something everybody knows is bad.

When they're sleeping he can pretend they are the same as him, and that what makes him happy would make them happy too: like snuggling under the great quilt in winter with your feet by the charcoal brazier and dozing against the background of adult chatter; like spitting melon seeds across the garden pool with Shirin, or making a tent out of washed sheets pulled from Maryam's line with his cousins; like sucking on an apricot until all that's left is the tart stone with its fragments of taste. But in the morning when it gets light and the boys all wake up he'll remember that they are nothing like him at all. They don't want to know him and he doesn't want to know them. They'll sit up and start calling out to each other and he won't understand. He'll do what they do. He'll copy them exactly and do what they do. *Baba* told him that was the way to learn and what he didn't understand today he would understand tomorrow. But there has been a week of tomorrows and he hasn't understood yet.

And it's so cold. Outside it's not as cold as it gets at home, but inside it feels colder. The wind from outside is coming through the windows, and he can feel his cheeks and nose like pieces of icy earth poking out of his bedding. In the morning he'll have to wear those short grey trousers again and tie that purple-and-grey-striped thing round his neck. He wants to ask what it's for but he hasn't the words. He hasn't any words. He thinks maybe he'll forget how to speak altogether, and when at last they let him go home he'll be as dumb as the legless man without a tongue that his granny gives money to at the gates of the shrine.

'Can't Shirin come with me?' he'd pleaded.

'No, Kookooleh. You're nearly a man now, so the time has come for you to live with men.'

'But why can't I live with men here at home?'

'Because you're luckier than other boys. When you come home

you'll be able to do all sorts of things other boys can't. You'll be important.'

'Can't I be important at home?'

'You will be, when you come back.'

'As important as the Shah?'

'Nearly. But only so long as you do everything you're told.'

If being in this place is going to make him important, then it's going to make all these boys important as well, only why does learning to be important have to be so lonely? All he knows is that in the morning, when the grey light comes through the window and the big bell rings, he will have to get out of this warm bed and run to wash in the cold water; he'll have to do his shu-shu and caca before he can follow the other boys down the stairs into the hall with the long tables where everyone lines up. But he can't do a caca in the morning. He needs to do one now.

He clenches his fists and presses his lips together. Tightens all his muscles and pulls in his bottom. Maybe the caca will go away. But it isn't going away. He can feel it coming down and it needs to come out. Slowly, keeping everything clenched, he climbs out of bed and tries to find the door, counting the beds off with his fingers as he passes them. When he gets to the other end of the room he paddles his hand along the wall until they meet the outline of the door. And here it is. Now he has to find the handle. It's round and very large. He grasps it in both hands and tries to turn it but it won't turn. It seems to slip in his hands but it won't turn. Maybe the door is locked, or is just too heavy for him. He's not going to be able to open it.

There isn't much time left. He'll have to go as far away as he can from the door and find a corner without a bed in it. Is there a corner without a bed? He can't remember what the room looks like in daylight. He's crawling on hands and knees feeling his way. Now he must be right under the window opposite the door because a chilly breeze is moving his hair. There's a bed, and its cupboard. But there on the other side of the cupboard there seems to be a space. A really tiny little space. Davood crawls into it, squashing himself between the side of the cupboard and the wall with the window. When they find out in the morning he will keep his eyes closed and pretend that he doesn't understand. How will they know that it's his caca and not anyone else's? He squats down and hopes he doesn't make any noise.

76

Marta hunches at the window of her taxi, passing through the seat of the mighty empire that still controls so much of the world. But she might as well be in Poland. The streets beyond the glass are washed in grey, the trees are grey – the very air seems grey, wrapped in smoke.

The cabby keeps glancing at her in his mirror, eyes flickering between her reflection and the way ahead. He leans back and says something nasally over his shoulder, then, realizing she hasn't understood, mumbles to himself with a sour expression. The road leading into London is wide and empty, and tall houses joined together line it. Now the buildings have become larger, institutions they must be, a university perhaps, or huge hotels. There are more people walking about, and peering out at them she is shocked.

They are pinch-faced and grim, all of them. How is it possible that this proud and victorious people can look so down at heel, be dressed so badly, so lacking in style, as if they find virtue in the tawdry. What a terrible letdown they are. Somehow she had expected erect figures with proud shoulders – some sense of celebration. Coloured flags. Their striped one blazoned against the sky from giant flagpoles. But there isn't a single one. Don't they like flags?

Every now and then there are jagged gaps between the buildings, empty spaces where the bombs over London must have fallen. But in this part of the city, at least, most of it is standing, so unlike Warsaw, where nothing was left at all.

She will stay the night at the Hotel Russell before setting out again to fetch back Davood. He doesn't know she's riding to the rescue, poor little thing. He must think he's been abandoned for ever, if he can understand what that means. Fury against Karim rises in her like bile and her jaw aches. How will he be able to face his son when they come home again? But she can imagine the reunion too easily – her own searing triumph bouncing off Karim's unruffled calm. Like trying to deflect a tank by throwing gravel at it. Davood runs to clasp Shirin round the waist, the cousins arrive with their mothers close behind, and the apartment is full of noise again, as it should be. But Karim isn't in the least discomfited. He'll behave as if they've returned from nothing more than a visit to the bazaar. Her temper will rise, while he will look on with that slight and infuriating smile. *Tss!*

Outside the hotel, a porter in livery steps forward to open her door, hand her out and shoulder her case. It's a large one and he's taken aback because it swings too easily in his grasp. He hasn't expected it to be so light. His opinion of her changes. You don't come to an establishment like this one without money, and people with money carry suitcases that weigh. How is he to know that hers is almost empty by design because the plan is to go to the famous Harrods and stock up? Smart little suits for Davood are in her mind as well as new outfits for herself. But, judging by what she has seen on the streets, that may be a vain hope. Can it really be that Avenue Lalezar has more to offer than London?

For a moment on the pavement she thinks she can almost taste the resentment in the people passing by. They are staring at her just as her countrymen did; sizing her up, pricing her, but not in the competitive way of the Persians. She wouldn't be surprised if one of them were to reach out and pinch her, part experiment, part spite. Without thinking she draws her cuffs down over her manicured hands, then, seeing what she has done, deliberately thrusts her fingers out again, the bright varnish flaunting points of vermilion. Two women at a bus stop, brown coats, washed-out headscarves, thick ankles, bend their heads together but with their eyes on her. You can always tell when people are talking about you. Well, let them.

*

The windows of her room look over a small park behind a fence with plane trees as tall as the trees in the garden at home. A man in a long coat is holding a squat black dog on a lead and looking the other way as the dog deposits its steaming heap in the middle of a path. The last time she saw anyone with a pet dog was in Wilno. She has never seen any in Tehran, and no one in Poland can afford to feed them any more. She wonders what has happened to all the Polish dogs. Have they been liquidated by order of the government, or just left to starve? The man and the dog move on.

A dull wind is rattling the branches of the trees and although she is inside, behind a closed window, she feels the chill. The sooner she can go to bed the better. Sleep will make tomorrow come more quickly. She hangs up her one skirt, one jacket and two blouses. The sheets on the bed are so cold they might almost be damp. Halfway through the night she gets up and lays her coat over the bed. That's what she needed. The extra weight.

In the morning she puts her coat on over her night-dress, pockets the room key heavy as a hammer, and goes in search of a bathroom. The corridor, dimly lit every few metres, is long, stretching away with closed doors on either side, and there's not a sound. Maybe all the rooms are empty. The floor is carpeted in maroon, but in its centre a path of beige where the pile has been worn away traces the line that shivering guests must have traipsed along ever since the hotel was first built. If this is meant to be a good hotel, what can the others be like? The air is thick, smelling of old soup.

A woman with a scrubbed face emerges from a door at the end, a grey towel drooped over her arm. They pass in the corridor without speaking but Marta senses the woman has paused to look back at her. When she goes into the bathroom she gasps at the cold. There is a small window looking out over pipes leading down the back of the hotel into a deep courtyard, and it's open. She tries to close it but it's jammed. Sitting on the lavatory, she notices a line painted in the bath, a hand's width from its base. She leans over the bath and wedges in the plug where the enamel under the taps is stained green and yellow. One tap produces only a tepid trickle. It must be the wrong one. She tries the other, but it gushes an icy cascade. If it weren't for her mission she'd postpone her bath. She steps into the water ankle deep; these people must be a hardy lot if this is what they call luxury.

In her bedroom she pauses in front of the mirror on the dressing table, her lipstick in her hand. Those people, the teachers in the school where she will find her son, if there are women among them, will they be made up? Her face in the mirror pulls a face at the one regarding it and she lays down the lipstick to brush her hair instead. It bounces glossily under the bristles. She's glad she had it done properly before flying out because even though he's only a little boy it's important that she should look her best for Davood. Too bad about those English teachers. She takes up the lipstick again and leans toward the glass.

Her fur coat slung over her shoulders, patent-leather handbag tucked in an armpit, she follows the smell of something savoury to the dining room on the ground floor. Most of the tables are unoccupied, chairs tucked in, places laid. But here and there people are sitting at their breakfasts, and whispering. One couple, man and woman, are not speaking at all. Two men in hats, businessmen she supposes, have to lean across their tablecloth to hear one another. You'd keep your voice low like this in church, or if you were ashamed of what you were saying. Or fearful. Are these people also afraid of being overheard and reported on? What can they be afraid of? Everyone looks up as she comes in, then immediately down, and again there is no mistaking it: astonishment quickly replaced by disapproval.

A waitress, all in black with a tiny white apron edged in ugly scallops, approaches her and says something. Leads her between the silent, appraising guests over to a laid table in a far corner behind a pillar – for privacy, or to spare the sensibility of the others. Marta slings her coat over one chair and seats herself at another. Again the waitress is speaking. Marta looks up at her, baffled.

'Do you speak French?' she asks, in French.

The waitress hisses impatiently and repeats what she said before. This time Marta makes out words that could be tea and coffee.

'Tea? Tea.'

'Scrambled eggs, madam?'

Nothing in this sentence relates to any words that she knows, except madam. She nods.

'Toast, madam?'

She nods, wondering what all this will produce.

Now she waits in silence behind her pillar, listening to the susurrations of the breakfasters beyond. Depression sinks over her. The sooner she can collect Davood and be out of this lugubrious city the better. She had thought to linger a week, see the sights: Buckingham Palace, the Houses of Parliament, Trafalgar Square. But these famous symbols will only make her heart all the heavier. Monuments to self-confidence built by a whey-faced people who have mislaid an earlier exuberance. Of course the country was crushed by war, but that ended nearly five years ago and no foreign power has supplanted their government or their king. They ought to look at least a bit more pleased with the outcome than they do. Karim has made a huge mistake if he thinks these are the ones to teach Davood how to run the world. They don't look capable. Unless, hidden away behind tall curtained windows, those others, the real ones, are plotting and planning together and talking without moving their lips. It's what her brother-in-law Farhad noticed above all, he said, when he was a student here. How the English talk without moving their lips. That proved everything, according to Shirazi *père*. So then they had all played at being the English, trying to talk without moving their lips. No one had been able to understand a thing the others were trying to say.

The waitress has arrived at her shoulder bearing a round tray, which she sets down on the table. Two small china pots, a third even smaller one, a little bowl with sugar crystals, a plate with a yellowish mound in the middle, a plate with two pieces of browned dried bread, a tiny china dish of butter, perhaps, and one of jam. A cup and saucer.

Marta peers into the pots. The smallest has milk. One of the larger ones has only hot water in it. She pours from the other and a thick dark tea fills her cup. Hurriedly she adds water and takes a sip. It is bitter, as if the tea was made long ago and has been standing. She pokes a fork into the yellowish mound and thinks of Basia and

Janusz, who have been living here for the last five years. Do they serve breakfasts like this to the guests at their hotel? She wishes she'd thought to stay with them. Mrs Benka told her that Basia was in India with her when Janusz, stationed in England, had suggested that she join him and that they make their lives, henceforth, in London. What a shock it must have been for Basia, in faraway Bombay, accepting her husband's decision, only to discover her mistake when it was too late. So we all make mistakes. Tonight, or tomorrow, she will take Davood and go to find them at the address that Mrs Benka gave her. And then leave. Never mind the sights. Never mind Harrods.

Davood's school is not in London. She will have to take a train, but Farhad has told her that London has many large railway stations from which the lines of the world's great railway builders radiate all over their small island. He could not advise her which station to go to. She pulls the paper with the school's address from her bag and takes it to the hotel reception. This morning's receptionist is a man who is at the moment examining the hotel's register line by line, looking for someone. She produces a cough of the useful sort, and he looks up, resting his finger in place on the register.

'Madam?'

In French, 'Do you speak French?'

'A little.' His accent is terrible.

'Can you tell me which is the station I should go from to reach this place?'

He takes the paper and scrutinizes the handwritten address. 'It's to the east,' he announces. 'You'll have to go from Liverpool Street. Liverpool Street. That's the name of the station. Liv-er-pool Street.'

'And is that far?'

'They'll get you a taxi.' He makes to beckon up the bellboy poised for action by the revolving doors but the telephone is ringing. 'Excuse me a moment.' And turns a half-circle away to mutter into the receiver without moving his lips. Now he's covering the mouthpiece of the receiver. 'Are you Madame Shirazi?'

Now what? She nods.

'Well, this call is for you. It's your embassy.'

'The embassy? But why?'

He shrugs. The receiver passes from his hand to hers, and now she turns away, half-body as shield. The receptionist makes a show of dipping his head back to his register but his finger doesn't stray from the line where it has come to rest.

'Hello?'

An Iranian voice. 'Khanoom-e Shirazi? Good morning. I am ringing on behalf of His Excellency Ambassador Hamideh-Noori. I am instructed to request that you visit the embassy as soon as possible.'

'Has something happened?'

'I am not able to say, Khanoom. His Excellency prefers to inform you himself.'

'But I'm supposed to be leaving London this morning and I will be away all day. I think.'

The man from the embassy simply repeats, 'I am only told to advise you, Khanoom. As soon as possible.'

A nod from the receptionist and the waiting bellboy wades through the revolving door to flag down a cab.

77

For all his efforts to be genial, Ambassador Hamideh-Noori cannot disguise his embarrassment. He holds open his door for her, and she passes through from the lobby into a small piece of the pampered Persia she has known, reassembled within the walls of an English red-brick mansion. The room is deeply carpeted, the ashtrays crystal, the brass light fittings hanging heavily from the ceiling. They would shed a sombre light if the windows were not so tall. There are filigree holders for the glasses of tea (translucent as amber and flavoured with cardamom), and the portraits of the Shah and his consort smirk side by side on the wall, glowing with roseate health. Disconcertingly familiar, this dab of colour in a land that has apparently dispensed with it.

The ambassador is making much of her, fussing with her coat, ordering up cakes. He's a large man with sloping shoulders but expansive gestures. Wide. Sitting in a wide chair. A man destined to be at ease, but not at this moment. Finally, when he can't put off the task any longer, he heaves himself to his feet and crosses his silent carpet to an inlaid cabinet. He is opening a drawer and pulling out a piece of paper, and now stands staring down at it, shaking his head in disbelief as if he needs to convince himself a second time that he is not mistaken. Then, shaking his head again, he reaches out his arm (she notices how white his shirt cuffs are, how bright the gold cuff-links), but reluctant to let go of the piece of paper he grips it until the very last minute.

It is a telegram, addressed to her, care of the embassy. Inside it says only: 'I divorce you I divorce you I divorce you.'

What?

'I am so sorry, Khanoom. I am' – he spreads his hands – 'ashamed.'

She sits with the telegram in her lap and no thoughts pass through her mind. She sees herself, a straight-backed recipient of a stranger's formal hospitality, her legs folded slightly to one side, the silk stockings on the calves lying smoothly against each other. Her high-heeled shoes gleam, cleaned overnight by the staff at the Hotel Russell. They have ironed her travel-crushed blouse. It seems to her in her silence that the blouse still smells of the iron with that flat odour of hot pastry. She adjusts herself in her chair, and the telegram begins to slide from her lap, so she traps it with a lurch of her fingers. The paper is flimsy. How do they do it? she wonders. How does the sending of telegrams work? The words originate in one place but the paper on which they arrive belongs to another. So this telegram that is pinned on the slope of her lap is made of English paper, but bearing the sentiments of an Iranian husband, expressed in French. Three times.

'But how can he?' she says at last. 'Like this. Is it legal?'

'Oh, certainly. He only has to make this statement in the presence of a mullah and it's done.'

Ambassador Hamideh-Noori is leaning forward, watching her anxiously, evidently afraid there might be a scene. Diplomatic incidents could be easier to deal with than scenes. But his visitor merely tamps her lips together, in and out, as if she has just applied lipstick and wants to spread its effect.

'Please, Khanoom,' he says. 'Please don't suppose that this is usual. In my experience in this position, this is the first occasion on which I have had to…' But he falters, realizing perhaps that his disclaimer will be scant consolation.

Marta sees how his glance flits over her. She notes the lines round his eyes, the lines at the corners of his lips that display his thoughts. Why? he must be thinking. Why is this woman's husband divesting himself of her? What can she have done to deserve it? If my wife looked like this woman I wouldn't let her go so easily, unless… And his expression toys with what that *unless* might mean. Is this woman a shrew? Has she brought dishonour on her husband's family? Is she frigid, or barren? Marta flinches at these unspoken questions. How should they be answered? She is not barren. Her son – her *son* – is here, in the school where her husband has placed him. As to the rest… But it's not so simple, she wants to tell Hamideh-Noori. She feels a need to justify herself under those speculative eyes. The thing is… But what is the thing?

The ambassador sits forward in his chair and his soft belly humps like an upturned basin. 'Do you think that your husband may wish to take a second wife?' His question is spoken so softly he may suppose he was merely rehearsing it in his mind. 'Of course, the law does not in theory allow it at present, but people still… And he might have thought –'

'He's too modern for that.' Her interruption is curt, bitter. Cynical.

Ambassador Hamideh-Noori winces and ducks his head into his shoulders. 'Khanoom. Truly. This is not easy for me. I wish it were otherwise. But I will do everything that I can with the British authorities for your sake.'

'With the British authorities? What have they to do with this?'

'So that you may remain, Khanoom. Do you not see?'

Yes. She sees. Now she understands what else this telegram is telling her – that there is to be no return to Tehran. There cannot be. But does that mean she must stay here, in this country about which she knows so little? Does she really have to stay here and begin all over again? She could go home, to Poznan – no, she couldn't.

The ambassador has been talking at her and she hasn't been listening. 'There is one thing,' he suggests hopefully, trying to look enthusiastic. 'One thing you might be grateful for. Dr Shirazi is not removing your son. Not for the moment. He is leaving you your son and the boy is only six years old, isn't he? In those circumstances, strictly speaking, he could have removed your son as well.'

'But he hasn't left me my son. He's put him in an English boarding school.' To learn to rule the world.

Ambassador Hamideh-Noori chuckles with approval. 'Well, that's very fashionable, of course. All the best families are doing it.' He muses up at one of the light fittings. 'With an education like that the boy might become an economist or an engineer, and get a good government post. Anything becomes possible.' His eyes return to her. 'So in that case, Khanoom, Dr Shirazi will have his son back once the schooling is finished.'

Over her dead body! If Karim thinks he can play games with her, or mould her son to suit him, he can think again. She'll pull Davood out of that school and send him...

'But.' She stares at Hamideh-Noori. 'I haven't any money.' Not money to live on. Won't Karim give her money to live on?

Ambassador Hamideh-Noori is looking at her with his face stretched in anguish. Look how sympathetic he is, but he isn't telling her that Karim will have to give her money. Support her. And who should make him, since he waited for her to leave the country before he dispatched her marching orders. No wonder he was so calm.

Did Behzad know this was going to happen when he drove her to the airport? Had he been trying to warn her by mentioning Karim's woman? No, because he expected her to come back with Kookooleh. But perhaps the others knew. Even Shirazi *père*. And they hadn't said. Not one of them. Not a word. At any rate, they would know now. Surely they wouldn't think what Karim was doing was right, would they? Or perhaps whatever Karim did was right in their eyes. Because he was theirs – and she wasn't. She had been. But now she wasn't any more. All this stuff about being a modern family, but, when it came to it, Karim had reached for the old traditions to dispense with his wife. The only modern thing about that had been using a telegram as his messenger. Didn't have the courage to do it face to face.

'What am I to do?' As if Hamideh-Noori could help. But there is no one else to ask.

'Is there nobody of... yours here in London?'

'Of mine?'

'Khanoom. I know... I know that you are a foreigner. That you arc by origin Polish – in fact this will help you with the British authorities. They have made it possible for your people, who fought alongside them, to remain in this country. And, you know, when people find themselves in a strange place they seek out their own, which is natural. We all want to be with our own, with people who understand us. Is there no one here that you could go to, no... church perhaps? No relatives? People seek out their own, Khanoom. It's normal.' He's trying so hard but he has done what is required and now he would dearly like to convey her along to the next receiving station.

Marta crushes the telegram into her handbag and stands up. If she cannot, for the moment, think what her first step should be, she will not sit on here, seeming woebegone and helpless. She has dealt with worse. Although never before alone. But she is not alone. Out there in that school, Davood is waiting, innocent and unaware. The world he thought was his has gone: the cousins, Shirin and Maryam, the Petrossian boys, the house on the hill, Zahra Khanoom and her stories. Instead he has his mother, whom he barely knows, who must be his only support and his truest friend, but who doesn't know how to be either. Has she the courage, the mettle for this? And is this, finally, what courage amounts to?

Ambassador Hamideh-Noori sees his visitor shudder slightly and thinks she must be cold. He takes her coat and settles it over her shoulders, mournfully smoothing its fur. He wishes her well. He will do what he can, but what he can will be strictly administrative. Even that, she reminds herself, is more than some people get.

The embassy door has been quietly closed behind her. She stands on the top step of the porch clutching her bag. If this city is to be her home, she had better find out what has to be done to survive in it. What she has learnt before surely she can learn again. Yet another language, yet another way of being. Hamideh-Noori is right. There must be a Polish community somewhere who can teach her what to do and how to behave. It's just a question of finding them. All those men who flew with the British but with Poland in their hearts and then landed to discover that the Poland they had been fighting for no longer existed. They stayed. Did they marry English girls or was there an adequate pool of migrant Poles to choose from? She imagines them in some hall, all dressed up, dancing the steps she took such pains never to master.

But of course! Basia and Janusz. She will go to Basia and Janusz, whose small hotel is surely cheaper than the Hotel Russell. They will advise her. Put her on the right road. Explain to her the ways of this country. They'll know. They've been here all of five years. Or, better still, maybe they'll be able to give her a job. Not cooking, of course. She doesn't know how. But she could sweep and clean, couldn't she? Clean the bedrooms. Strip off the old sheets and lay on the new ones. Sweep under the beds.

The address, along with Hania's address in America, is on a piece of paper in Mrs Benka's large black handwriting tucked in a side pocket of her bag.

78

She can see the house directly across the road from the window where she sits. If it weren't for the sign hanging outside on a post under a tree, Bridge Hotel, you might think it an ordinary house like those on either side. A shallow bedraggled garden leads to a stuccoed porch. To its right a tall window juts from the front with three panes of glass, one looking straight out, the others angled to the sides. But what lies beyond is hidden behind the net curtain hanging from a line midway up the window. The neighbouring houses are exactly the same. One has a brown door. Another a blue one. Basia and Janusz's Bridge Hotel has a blue front door as well, recently painted. No doubt Janusz, a soldier and a Pole, is handy with the brush.

Marta has counted the windows on the four floors of their hotel and tried to deduce from them how many guest rooms there are. But she has yet to move. For the past three-quarters of an hour, she has been sitting here at a table by the window of this – what is it? not a restaurant, not a coffee-house – where people are eating those beans the British soldiers produced in Bandar-e Pahlavi, and drinking tea.

Really, this cannot be a culture where people understand about tea. The cup she has in front of her is as bitter, as carelessly made, as it was at breakfast-time in the Hotel Russell. And they have no sense of how things should be. A line runs from the rim of her cup all the way down to its base, an old crack, black with grime. How can anyone serve up to people in crockery like this and not be ashamed? She cannot sit here any longer. She must get up. Cross the road. Knock on that door.

It has been raining for most of the day, but now it has cleared and the quilt of low cloud is ripping into fragments under a powerful westerly wind. Through the window she sees the rampaging of the sky. The raindrops that spotted the glass are now driving across its surface into lines of water, thick and greasy with dirt. They can't have washed the windows in a long time. Don't they have any pride, these people who run the world? No self-respect? She picks up the cup with its blackened crack and flourishes it at the waitress, who has arrived at her elbow to be paid.

'Not good!' she announces, tapping the cup. She taps the grimy window too and wrinkles her nose. 'Not good!' She takes her hand-kerchief from her bag and mimes industrious scrubbing.

The waitress snatches up the money and the cup. 'We've had a war on, you know. Leastways, we have here, even if they haven't where you come from – wherever that is!' She storms to the back of the café. 'Bloody foreigners,' she snaps to the remaining clientele after the woman in the glossy coat has shrugged at her tirade, opened the door and stepped out. 'Always damned complaining.'

The knocker is in the shape of a lion's head snoozing against the new blue paint. Each time Marta lifts it and lets it fall, the house shudders. Somewhere inside a door opens. A woman's voice calls out. Basia's voice, summoning her husband. It won't be Basia coming to the door, then. And it isn't.

Janusz is tousled in his civvies. Major Palucha's corporal has been fixing something with the stubby screwdriver he's got tucked into his palm like a soldier's illicit cigarette.

'Good morrnink.' He wasn't expecting a putative guest just before lunchtime. The ones that haven't booked usually show up in the evening.

'Hello, Janusz,' she replies in Polish.

'Do you know me? Oh, Jesus and Mary. Basia! Basia, quick!'

Basia must think her husband has hurt himself because she bursts out of a door at the back of the house, her hair behind her ears and a ready alarm all over her face. Her dark hair is lank and she looks thinner than she should. Older. Tired. Perhaps she's working too hard. Perhaps the hotel business has turned out to be tougher than they expected.

'Marta?'

'Basia.'

'Good God!'

Basia and Janusz are looking at each other and do not speak. This is extremely awkward for them. It's what they're thinking. It must be what they're thinking, and Marta should go out and let them talk it over alone. But if she goes out and that door closes behind her she is certain it will not open again. So she sits and smokes the cigarette that Janusz lit for her while they try and converse with looks alone. Did Basia raise her eyebrows? Did Janusz shrug ever so slightly? Marta rests her chin on the heel of the hand that holds the cigarette and through the rising smoke gazes out of the back window. The house has a long, thin, walled garden and a washing line stretched between the back of the house and a tree at the further end. Sheets flap furiously on the line, rain-sodden before but cracking like flags now. Any minute this wind may snatch the pegs away and the sheets will go flying. Marta stubs out her cigarette and launches herself through the back door.

They watch her, side by side at the table, and do not move. The thin heels of her shoes are sinking into the softened lawn and their billowing laundry assaults her. She is stuffing the pegs into her pockets and pulling at the sheets. The laundry problem is only one of the many they haven't solved because hotel guests mostly don't want to look down from their rooms onto a loaded washing line. A hotel garden ought to be a thing to please the eye, although in December...

It's what anyone would do, isn't it? A stranger in a strange place, you find out where there are others of your kind, and you make a bee-line for them. Either one of them, stranded, would have done the same.

'She should never have married that man.'

572

'But I told you what happened, Janusz. And she did marry him. That's the reality.'

'But why do we have to pick up the pieces?'

'Look at her. How can we not? And somehow I feel responsible.'

'Because at first you believed in that fiancée as well? We've been through this so many times, my darling. You were told something and it turned out to be a mistake. But she was the one who rushed off to marry Dr Shirazi. You didn't tell her to do that, did you? Besides, we're not a charity. We could go under so easily at this stage.'

'It won't be charity, and Poles have to help Poles. And she's my friend, darling. My old friend. I know what she's like. She's far too proud to be a scrounger. It's not how she was brought up. And she wants to work. She said.'

'What about the boy?'

Yes. What about the boy?

'And what can she do? Realistically, what can she do?'

She is festooned, sheets wound round her neck and draped over her arms. If she tries to pull down any more they'll end up on the ground and need to be washed all over again.

Janusz makes for the back door.

Basia has hold of two corners and Marta, grasping the opposite pair, backs out of the kitchen into the corridor so that the sheet can be stretched taut and then folded. I'll iron them dry, she announced. But do you remember how little time it took in the sun when they were out on the line in Tent City?

She's dropped that coat of hers over the back of a chair to wield the iron and doesn't seem to have noticed how her elegant shoes have collected galoshes of mud, greying as it dries.

The kitchen fills with steam and the heavy smell of cotton cooking. Her forehead and the wings of her nose glisten with perspiration as she swings her arm, across and across the fabric, heaving it, folding it with undiminishable energy. Look how expertly she does it. *These* sheets, at least, will be crisp and warm when she's finished with them.

The only sound in the kitchen is the slap of the iron on sizzling cotton, Marta's breathing made raucous by exertion, and beyond, out there in the long thin garden, the irritable gasps and coughs of the wind gusting in from the Atlantic. Basia and Janusz lean on their table, elbow to elbow, and watch, stilled by the industry on display.

The room is low because it's under the eaves so you'd have to roll out of bed to be sure of not hitting your head. Basia is embarrassed to reveal that this is the space they had earmarked for a chambermaid – but now the chambermaid is going to be someone she knows. Someone who...

But Marta, plunked down on the narrow mattress, gushes over the cosiness. All you can see from the windows, when you're sitting down here, is the tips of the trees outside, and in spring and summer it'll be leaves. Which is delightful. The wardrobe is small, it's true, but then she has only the clothes currently hanging in the Hotel Russell, where she will go presently, pay up and check out.

Actually, though she hasn't ever thought about this before, there's something appealing, something fitting about living in a hotel – even a small one, because people come and go, but nobody stays. She will watch them and wonder about where they have come from, why they are here and where they will be going next, and she will know what, perhaps, they do not: that you should never assume you can call any place home. That it is a luxury to suppose you will grow up and live out your life in the place where you were born. Or married. Or found your love. So Basia should please stop twisting her handkerchief about in that miserable way. This is just perfect. Simply perfect. Except for the people outside: so glum; so grey.

Basia shrugs. 'They're tired,' she says. 'And they've run out of money. The whole country has run out of money. I agree they don't look very good... we don't look very good' – she laughs – 'but we're healthy. They saw to it that everyone had enough to eat, even if it didn't taste very good, and it still doesn't. But nobody starved, or had to eat crows or rats. You have to admire that.'

When Basia has returned to her kitchen four floors down, Marta sits up on her bed with her back against the wall and her knees hugged into her chest. *Nobody starved. You have to admire that.* If Basia's right, and there was a system here that ensured everyone got enough to eat no matter what, then that was good, although there must have been a black market. She cannot imagine there was no black market. Not like Iran, where a lot of people didn't get enough because if your family couldn't look after you no one else would, or Poland, where the system was supposed to be for the people but couldn't manage it. If Basia's right...

Think what luck it is for her that Basia and Janusz live here. She might have found herself in London knowing no one at all, and what would have become of her then? She had thought she was all alone, but she is not. Poles look after Poles. They won't be sorry they've let her stay. She'll be the best chambermaid they could wish for – she was always good at cleaning. Well, she'll learn to be, that's the point. You learn to be. But it's more than that. It's not just a question of learning to do the things – it'll be doing them without feeling aggrieved. So the time of luxury is behind her. Well, and so what? Think of it as an episode which is now over. She wasn't born into luxury anyway, and managed without anything in the forest beyond Rubtsovsk, just like everyone else. Which means she can again. If her father can accept what can't be altered, then so can she. Stamina, he always said. That's what matters. And knowing how to improvise. That's how our country has always turned defeat into victory. Not just improvise, though. Improvise and think, Marta. Stop and think.

And, when Christmas comes, maybe Janusz and Basia might find a little bed to put next to hers for Davood and she'll give him carp and potato salad. And take him to Mass. He will become her son. So much so that, when his father whistles for him to go back, the boy will square up and refuse. She will remind him who he is and where he came from. She will teach him Polish and tell him stories about his grandfather in Poznan, who fought in three wars and is the best man there is anywhere in the world. One of them. And when he is older maybe she will take him to visit that grandfather – if Trotsky and the comrades let her in. Then Davood can play with her niece or nephew or whoever the baby Halina is carrying turns out to be. Think how important it will make him feel, to be idolized again by a younger child. She'll show him to Mrs Benka and…

Or perhaps it would be better to turn her back on the past and let it be. Begin from scratch tomorrow, become the new person the new place expects, all over again. In the end, does it make so much difference? Ultimately, everyone wants the same things: security, friends, love – and some excitement. Maybe she is young enough to find those things again. Davood can learn to be an Englishman, and believe in whatever it is they believe in. He will grow up looking like one, speaking like one, and forget how things once were. Will that bring him joy? She has no idea. You have to be alive to know joy, and she is alive. He is alive. She is twenty-seven, he'll be seven next year, and both of them are alive, which will have to be good enough for now. If London is where she has come to rest, then so be it. And, if mothering is to be her life from now on, well, she'd better get on with it. How do you know what you might not manage if you don't give it a try?

One thing is for sure. Whatever happens, Davood will have to learn to put up with it, just as she has. And because he is young he will: he'll slip into whichever clothes are required of him, and probably teach her along the way. And he'll pull up his head and stare this unpredictable world straight in the face. After all, isn't that what every good Polish soldier should do?

Postscript

The Officer's Daughter is not a biography or a memoir, but a fiction based on the experiences of a close friend. Much of her story is not in this book, and a great deal of this book, including most of the characters, was never part of her story. I apologize for any unintended errors but I have deliberately diverged from the truth where it suited me to do so. In the logging camp in Siberian Kazakhstan, the *desiatnik* was very unlikely to have been riding round on a horse: probably only the director would have had that privilege. On the cotton collective, the cotton pickers' *fartuk* is an anachronism: as I understand it, this particular apron didn't arrive on the scene until the late 1950s or early 1960s. I have conflated the tent hospital camp in the grounds of the as yet incomplete Air Force School outside Tehran with a number of other such hospitals, and the real Air Force School was located, I think, to the city's north-west, and not the south, where I have chosen to put it.

With the knowledge granted by hindsight, readers may feel some statements made by my characters are either naïve or simply false: Dr Shirazi in 1942 considers the United States to be a country that, unlike Britain, doesn't meddle in the affairs of others; he was not to know that eleven years later the CIA (and, of course, Britain) would topple the democratically elected Prime Minister of Iran, Mohammed Mossadegh. Egon Mandel (whom Marta calls Trotsky) believes that Stalin could not be an anti-Semite, although the infamous Doctors' Plot was already under way. Similarly, 'Trotsky' is convinced that the Anders Army was so anti-Semitic that it would not allow him to join.

In fact, there were many Jews in the Anders Army, not least Menachem Begin, but memoirs of the period suggest that some commanders refused to accept Jews in their units. 'Trotsky' argues that people tend to extrapolate only from their own experience, but then does the same himself, and Marta cannot know that he is wrong – although she has her suspicions. These examples apart, I am sure that experts of various sorts will find enough howlers to complain about – just as I have a tendency to do, given the chance.

Acknowledgements

I would like to thank Amir Amirani, David Edmonds, Firdaus Kanga, David Malcolm, Anne Theroux and Monica Wilson, who read all or some of the manuscript, for their suggestions and encouraging noises. Thanks, of course, to Isobel Dixon of Blake Friedmann, who always lets me know what's going on the minute something is, and to Portobello Books for taking me on. Above all, thanks to Linden Stafford, beady-eyed and implacable editor, whose criticisms are always to the point, and whose sole purpose is to wrest from the authors she works with the best final versions they can manage.

For news about current and forthcoming titles
from Portobello Books and for a sense of purpose
visit the website **www.portobellobooks.com**

encouraging voices,
supporting writers,
challenging readers

Portobello
BOOKS